*She wore nothing but a long cotton night-*gown. Her hair tumbled down her back and her blue eyes were wide with fright.

"I thought you had gone!"

"Jenny!" he said, and took a step toward her.

She retreated, crossing her arms across her breasts. She had never seemed so beautiful to him, nor so desirable, as in her present disheveled state.

He took another step toward her. She fell back, but he caught her wrists and pulled her to him. She tried to resist. He bent over her and tried to kiss her, but she swung her face away from him and her soft black hair swept over his face. Then she was very still, no longer struggling.

Suddenly, wildly, she came to life. Both her hands were on his shoulders, pushing him away. Her eyes were a furious blue blaze of hatred and her teeth were clenched.

"Murderer!" she shouted. "Murderer!"

Fawcett Books
by Taylor Caldwell:

THE ARM AND THE DARKNESS
THE FINAL HOUR
MAGGIE—HER MARRIAGE
GRANDMOTHER AND THE PRIESTS
THE LATE CLARA BEAME
A PILLAR OF IRON
WICKED ANGEL
NO ONE HEARS BUT HIM
DIALOGUES WITH THE DEVIL
TESTIMONY OF TWO MEN
GREAT LION OF GOD
ON GROWING UP TOUGH
CAPTAINS AND THE KINGS
TO LOOK AND PASS
GLORY AND THE LIGHTNING
THE ROMANCE OF ATLANTIS

TAYLOR CALDWELL

TESTIMONY OF TWO MEN

A FAWCETT CREST BOOK
Fawcett Publications, Inc., Greenwich, Conn.

TESTIMONY OF TWO MEN

THIS BOOK CONTAINS THE COMPLETE TEXT OF THE
ORIGINAL HARDCOVER EDITION.

A Fawcett Crest Book reprinted by arrangement with
Doubleday and Company, Inc.

ISBN: 0-449-23212-3

Printed in the United States of America

10 9 8 7 6 5 4 3 2 1

Dedicated with respect and admiration to the
memories of those men, who, like Jonathan Ferrier,
suffered so much and fought so hard
to bring us modern medicine's blessings.

It is also written in your law that the testimony of two men is true.

JOHN 8:17

FOREWORD

I first heard this story of "Jonathan Ferrier" when I was a little girl, and I heard it from our family physician.

The history of medicine has its martyrs as well as the history of religion. Though many know the Saints who died for them, by name, few know the names of the physicians who lived and fought for them, and who were as dedicated to humanity as the Saints themselves.

Few know the names of the men who brought asepsis to modern hospitals, and immunology, yet millions of us now living would not be alive now except for those men. Millions of diabetics are following healthy and productive lives because of insulin—but how many know the name of the man who saved them? Children are now in school who would have died except for the men who formulated vaccines for diphtheria and smallpox and poliomyelitis, but how many remember them?

Scores of these heroes suffered ignominy, exile, ridicule and dishonor to save us. Some were driven mad and to suicide. Yet, they persisted.

Among them was the man, always unknown to me, but whom I have named "Jonathan Ferrier" in this book. If he seems somewhat excessive and bellicose, he was fighting for the lives of all of us who were born, as I was born, in the twentieth century. He was one of thousands, unwept, unhonored and unsung, and remembered, perhaps, only by God.

TAYLOR CALDWELL

TESTIMONY OF TWO MEN

X

CHAPTER ONE

When young Robert Sylvester Morgan had occasion to write his mother, he always made what he wryly called "a first draft." This was done on foolscap paper (he had been taught thrift) and then recopied on a better grade, where he could use his elegant Spencerian—which he loathed—in a way to please his mother, and in words and phrases which would not startle her.

"June 8th, 1901
Hambledon, Pennsylvania
Quaker Hotel

"Dear Mama:"
(He paused. Why in hell wouldn't she let him call her Mother? "Mama," at his age, for God's sake!)

"You will be happy to know that matters have culminated successfully since I arrived here a week ago. Hambledon is a beautiful town of about twenty-five thousand people, not to be compared with Philadelphia, of course, but adequate and lively." (After a moment's thought he crossed out the last word and substituted "up-to-date.") "It is situated on the river, quite broad near at hand, almost a bay, and studded, here and there, with pretty islands. Very picturesque.

"The people are pleasant and friendly and very civil." (His mother's pet word.) "There is considerable industry, but it is located near the fringes of the town, so that the air is clear and fresh, an excellent thing for your arthritis and asthma.

Though on the water, the atmosphere seems dry. There appears to be little poverty and the working class is energetic." (His mother would approve of that!) "The better sections of the town are charming, with broad streets, fine old lawns, magnificent trees—elms, birches, oaks, pine, spruces—and houses which would be considered impressive even in Philadelphia. I have already selected four for your choice and approval, and will take you about to them when you arrive next week. Any of them would delight you." (Would they? Nothing delighted his mother very much. Perhaps he was being uncharitable, or even irritable. He had never felt this way toward his mother before. He paused to wonder, then shook his head, baffled.)

"Behind the town rises a whole ridge of mountains, inspiring at dawn." (He had seen the dawn only once this week and then inadvertently, but his mother liked the mention of dawns.) "The very best people live on the lower reaches of the mountains in splendid residences. As for hospitals, the most important things to me at this time, there is one great one, called the Friends', though it is not exactly Quakerish." (His mother detested Quakers.) "It is partly town-supported. The other hospital is private and select and very expensive. To be on the staff is something to be coveted."

Now came the difficult part of the letter, and he gnawed the end of his pen and contemplated the mountains he so admired through the polished window of his neat little room. He finally continued:

"Hambledon's hospitals serve not only the town but the villages and the farms outside, of course, and have the best of reputations. In fact, the hospitals here would be admired even in Philadelphia or Boston or New York. Very modern." (He frowned at the last word; his mother could not bear anything "modern." But he let it remain.) "I confess I was agreeably surprised. I have met a number of physicians and surgeons here, all enlightened men except for a few, and all gentlemen with distinguished reputations. Three are regularly called into consultation in Philadelphia, Pittsburgh and even New York, for they are specialists in their field. One of them" (he winced) "is Dr. Jonathan Ferrier, though you may find that hard to believe. But I have read his lectures and his articles in the organ of the American Medical Association, and I can assure you that he is greatly esteemed."

He wrote faster now: "It is my belief, based on constant association with Dr. Ferrier, that he has been a much-maligned man, and that he was truly innocent of his wife's death. I need not recall to you that he was forced to demand a change of venue from Hambledon to Philadelphia in order to get a fair trial. But the Philadelphia newspapers were hardly more just than the newspapers in Hambledon. However, as you know, he was acquitted. He has had his license to practice restored, and his place on the staffs of both hospitals. But he is very embittered. He has talked little with me on the matter but quite enough to arouse my own indignation, for have you not always taught me to weigh all things in a proper measure, and objectively?" (A nice touch, there. Please the old girl. I'm becoming a diplomat, he thought.) "I can't blame him for his resolute decision not to practice in Hambledon any longer. He was once the most popular surgeon in the town, and his family is well-bred, established, wealthy and highly respected. Old settlers." (His mother loved "old settlers.") "But you will remember all this was aired in the newspapers. I have met his mother, a great lady though somewhat of an invalid. Mrs. Ferrier is very anxious to meet you and make you welcome." (A rich lie, but certain to elate his mother.)

"Dr. Ferrier is not certain of his future plans at this time, though he mentioned going abroad for some time. I imagine he will finally settle in New York. He had helped to build up both the hospitals, using his own money lavishly, and was very devoted to The Poor." (His mother approved of "the poor," provided they never crossed her path except to furnish her with competent servants.) "He feels that never again can he feel any friendliness for the people of the community, considering their hostility toward him after his young wife's death, their conviction of his guilt prior to his trial in Philadelphia and during it, and what he calls their 'disappointment' when he was acquitted. He was shabbily treated." (Robert underlined this. His mother, herself, though never having met Dr. Ferrier, had detested him upon reading the newspaper accounts and had been "disappointed," herself, upon the acquittal. She was still certain he was guilty.)

"Now the town feels very righteous when it accuses him of 'deserting' his own people. Some are beginning to remember his devotion to them, the free wards he built, and the excellent nursing schools he insisted on establishing in the hospitals. They cannot understand, they claim, why he wishes to leave them! Is that not a commentary on human nature? I sometimes thought, when I was a child, that you were slightly rigorous concerning human nature, but now I know you were correct." (That ought to soften her!)

"There are still currents here." (He stared at these words, pursing up his lips. Then he crossed them out. His mother couldn't endure "currents" of any kind. She considered them impertinent and ill-bred and not to be countenanced at all. Gentlefolk never had "currents" in their lives. All was serenity —if they were gentlefolk.) He substituted: "Dr. Ferrier's colleagues have tried to persuade him not to leave, but he is adamant. His mother is neutral on the subject. But his decision is very fortunate for me. We have come to an agreeably mutual decision on the price of his practice, etc. His offices, very large, very handsome, are near his house, where he lives with his mother, and are marvelously well-appointed. He had a telephone extension from his offices to his residence so that he could be called in an emergency and respond without delay. He now refuses all petitions except from old patients who stood by him during his unfortunate trouble.

"One of the houses I have in mind for us is near those offices, so it will be most convenient for me when I set up practice here. Dr. Ferrier has already introduced me to the most influential doctors and other citizens, and at the cost of modesty I must admit that they appeared to approve of me and my credentials, though this will be my first practice. They were impressed that I interned at Johns Hopkins. They had many searching talks with me! I feel certain that I said and did nothing to arouse doubt in them.

"The rent Dr. Ferrier has asked of me for the offices is most reasonable. I am sure you will be pleased. All in all, I feel extraordinarily lucky in obtaining this practice, though you would have preferred that I practice in Philadelphia. But when you see Hambledon, and breathe its delightful fresh air, and meet the ladies of the town, and understand my good fortune, you will feel reconciled. A young doctor in Philadelphia, in his first practice, has a miserable time—as I have discovered. Jealousy on the part of established doctors is not unknown in Philadelphia; they are very proud of their prerogatives. I did not meet with this attitude in Hambledon. They welcomed me, though they remain stiff with Dr. Ferrier because of his decision to leave them. Their position seems to be, 'We have forgiven you. Why can't you forgive us?' I find that very unreasonable. Do you not think so?" (Of course, she wouldn't think so. She would consider it very magnanimous on the part of the other physicians and surgeons to "forgive" Dr. Ferrier for a crime he had not committed, and she would also consider his rejection of them as "unpardonable." What's wrong with me lately? young Dr. Morgan asked of himself. I never had these thoughts of my mother before I came here; I was always the dutiful son, saying, "Yes, Mama, you are quite right, Mama," when I knew damn well, in my heart, that the old girl was not only a prig but somewhat stupid, too, and pretentious.)

"I have already rented a fine rig with two spirited black horses." (He crossed out the "spirited" and replaced it with a less disturbing word.) "Dr. Ferrier rarely uses any vehicles around the town since his acquittal. He rides horseback and has a wonderful stable of his own."

The young man considered. Then he deleted these remarks about Dr. Ferrier. His mother would be outraged at such a lack of "gentility." "Mama," he said aloud, "you are an ass." His own remark shocked him for a moment, then he grinned and straightened his young shoulders under the excellent broadcloth of his suit. After all, it was time for the old girl to remember that he was no longer a child and no longer dependent upon her.

He removed the big gold watch, which had belonged to his doctor father before his death, looked at it, saw that it was almost ten o'clock and that Dr. Ferrier was calling for him soon. He replaced the watch in his vest pocket and straightened the heavy gold watch chain over his paunchless front. He concluded his letter with a flurry of affectionate remarks, then set out to recopy the edited paragraphs. Upon conclusion, it seemed to him a very priggish letter, itself, but just what his mother would expect. The unexpected, to her, was outrageous. Nothing unexpected occurred to the well-bred, certainly nothing disheveled. Such as life, thought the young man, feeling exhilarated by his new objectivity. How he'd like to lure her into an obstetrical ward! Or a VD one, for instance, not that she'd ever heard of venereal disease and the surprising numbers of the "gentry" who turned up there regularly! She had never heard of a D&C, he was sure. Ladies did not have uteruses. Their children "emerged" gracefully from undefined regions.

Robert had taken up, again, smoking "the filthy weed," as his mother called it, since coming to Hambledon. So he lit a cigarette and relaxed, smiling thoughtfully through the window. It was a gorgeous June day, and the town was scented with its own roses and lilies and warm lawns, and the hearty odors of manure and the adjacent water and chimney smoke. Sun poured down the green and purple mountains in an avalanche of sparkling light, and there was a feeling of vivacity in the air which was not present in plodding Philadelphia. He could see the river from where he sat in his hotel room on the fifth floor. It ran with color, violet and green and shimmering blue, curving and broadening about the town. He saw the ferryboat bustling across the water to the other side, and heard its tooting. He saw other busy river traffic. And there was that island fancifully called "Heart's Ease." Yes, it was heart-shaped, and the largest island in the broad river, but only a woman could think of such a sickening name. It lay quite deeply in the water, and Robert could see the tops of its many crowding trees and a glimpse of the gray granite walls that hedged it in almost completely.

Dr. Ferrier's brother, Harald, and the latter's daughter, lived there all alone except for three servants. This was all young Robert knew of the island, except that Harald's dead wife's first husband had bought the island and had built what was called the "castle" on it, because, on his honeymoon, he had become enamored of the river and the island. He had never lived there himself. But his widow had lived there prior to her marriage to Harald and then for the two short years she had survived after that marriage. Dr. Ferrier had told Robert that much but no more. He appeared reticent on the subject. He had mentioned that his brother had inherited a great fortune from his wife, or at least the huge income on it, for his lifetime so long as he lived on the island. The daughter had inherited only one hundred dollars a month pocket money. However, if Harald should tire of the arrangement and leave the island permanently, he would receive only fifty thousand dollars and the money, in trust, would revert to the daughter. Jennifer? Jenny? Something like that. If Harald married again, he would receive only twenty-five thousand dollars as a "wedding gift" from his dead wife.

Mrs. Ferrier's first husband had owned a tremendous steel mill in Pittsburgh and oil wells in Titusville. Income from both continued to bloat the trust. Very, very nice. There had been no envy in Dr. Ferrier's voice when he had given these facts to Robert. But his dark face had become sardonic and closed, and Robert's curiosity, always very lively, was much stimulated. "Your much older brother?" he had asked with pardonable avidity.

"No," said Jonathan Ferrier, and had appeared amused.

"My younger brother. I'm thirty-five. Harald's thirty-three."

"The child must be just a baby," Robert had suggested.

Dr. Ferrier had seemed even more amused. He had changed the subject. No, he was not envious of all that money. He was a rich man, himself, inherited as well as earned money. His mother had been a Farmington of Philadelphia, and everyone knew that the Farmingtons were immensely wealthy. It was rumored that the Ferriers had come from France, or Belgium, over two hundred years ago and had always lived in this vicinity. Dr. Ferrier owned three rich farms nearby, which he rented out.

"Never deprecate money," Dr. Ferrier had told Robert. "Poverty is no crime, but the populace doesn't really believe that. You can be a saint with all the heroic virtues, but if you have no money, you'll be despised. What does the Bible say? 'A rich man's wealth is his strong city.' The old boys knew what they were talking about!"

It was "the strong city" of Dr. Ferrier's wealth, the newspapers had more than hinted, which had procured his acquittal, for he had been able to "buy" the very best lawyers in Philadelphia, a city noted for its lawyers.

Robert, in his hotel room, and waiting to be called by Dr. Ferrier for another tour of the town, thought about the accusations and the trial, which had occupied the first pages in the Philadelphia papers for months. Dr. Ferrier had been charged with performing a botched abortion on his young wife, Mavis, which had resulted in her death two days later. That had happened nearly a year ago. The defense had had to struggle for weeks to obtain an unprejudiced jury. Dr. Ferrier had testified in his own defense. He had not been in Hambledon at the time of the alleged abortion but in Pittsburgh, and he had witnesses. He had not even known that his wife was pregnant. She had never told him. No, he had not the slightest suspicion of the criminal.

"We had been married over three years," he had testified calmly. "There were no children. My wife did not want any. She had always had a delicate constitution." He had hesitated here. "Yes, I wanted children— No, I can't even hazard a guess at the name of the abortionist. My wife died of septicemia, of course, as a result of the abortion. I am a surgeon. If I had performed the abortion myself, it wouldn't have been botched, I assure you!"

The jury hadn't liked that remark. It had sounded heartless to them. In fact, they had not liked Dr. Ferrier himself, with his tall thin arrogance, his tight dark face, his sharp "foreign" cheekbones, his polished black eyes, his air of disgust and impatience with all that was in that crowded courtroom, including the judge and the jury. He had shown no evidence of grief for his young wife, no sign of pity or regret. He had listened intently to the testimony of fellow physicians and sometimes his impatience leaped out upon his shut face. Septicemia, resulting from a bungled operation with lacerations. "I am a surgeon," he had repeated. "There would have been no bungling." His manner had been contemptuous.

And then he had appeared to be about to say something else, in his bitter impatience. However, he merely clenched his mouth tighter.

The witnesses called for the defense had been distinguished doctors and surgeons themselves. They not only testified that Dr. Ferrier, indeed, could not have performed such a gross operation. He was, in fact, operating in Pittsburgh on the crucial days, under their very admiring eyes. Brain tumors. He had used the Broca method. He had been in Pittsburgh not only those days but the day before and two days afterward, to be certain that his patients were out of danger. Five days in all. Dr. Ferrier had not appeared to be listening to those testifying in his defense. He had sat "like a stone," said one newspaper, "staring blackly into space," occasionally passing his lean hand over his thick dark hair. It was as if he had removed himself spiritually from that place into a solitude that could not be entered by anyone else, a solitude that was gloomy and soundless.

He had been acquitted. The jury, reluctantly, had had to believe the witnesses for the defense. There was no way around it. Still, the opinion remained that had Dr. Ferrier not been a rich man, a very rich man, he would have been found guilty.

There were even some vile rumors—which did not appear in court—that Dr. Ferrier had deliberately "bungled" the operation so that his young wife, only twenty-four, would die. So he remained, in many eyes, a double murderer: The murderer of a young woman and his own unborn child, three months an embryo. Among the many so fiercely convinced was his wife's paternal uncle, Dr. Martin Eaton, a much respected surgeon in Hambledon. This was strange to friends, for Dr. Eaton had, before Mavis' death, been deeply fond of Dr. Ferrier and had regarded him as a son, with pride and admiration. Mavis had been brought up from childhood by

Dr. Eaton and his wife, Flora, after her parents' death. They had finally adopted her, for they had no children of their own.

Dr. Eaton, a tall stout man of sixty, had sat grimly in the courtroom all through those days and had stared fixedly at Dr. Ferrier, and with open hatred. When the jury had returned with their sullen verdict of "Not Guilty," Dr. Eaton had stood up and had desperately shouted, "No, no!" Then he had turned, staggered a little, and then, recovering himself, had left the courtroom. He had returned to Hambledon that night and had suffered a stroke, from which he was still recovering. Hambledon sympathized with him with real compassion.

Yes, thought Robert Morgan, again glancing at his father's watch, there were surely "currents" still in Hambledon. No wonder Dr. Ferrier wished to leave. Someone knocked on the door. Dr. Ferrier was waiting below for Dr. Morgan.

To Robert's surprise Dr. Ferrier was not on horseback as usual but in a handsome phaeton drawn by two of his wonderful black horses, wild-looking beasts with white noses and untamed eyes. Racehorses? Robert thought with nervousness. Surely not. He and his mother did not move in horsy circles in Philadelphia and his one acquaintance with "the evils of racing," as his mother called it, was when he had recklessly accompanied some classmates to a track, where he had unaccountably won one hundred and twenty dollars on a bet of twelve. (He could not remember the name of the horse now, and he was doubtful if he had known it then. But someone had once told him his lucky number was five and so he had bet his money on a horse with that number, though the colors of the jockey were two he nauseously hated, pinkish gray and liverish purple, they reminding him of the anonymous guts in the autopsy rooms. It had not been what was generally known as "a fiery steed." In fact, its languor at the post had been obvious to everyone, except himself, and he had evoked roaring laughter at his choice. But ridicule always made Robert stubborn, so he had placed his bet and had won. It had been a happy June day, he remembered, a day like this, all sun and warmth and with an undercurrent of excitement.) He smiled at Dr. Ferrier's horses, then turned his face on the older man with sincere pleasure.

He'll do, thought Dr. Ferrier, though he's still naïve and he's a plodder. At any rate he's honest and competent, which is more than I can say for a lot of hacks in frock coats and striped trousers whom I know. A Mama's boy. I can make short work of that—I hope.

He said, "Robert. I thought I'd call for you in my mother's phaeton." He smiled bleakly at the younger man, who was only twenty-six and whose stocky build made him appear smaller than his nearly six feet of height. Robert had sandy-red hair, thick and glossy, a round and boyish face pinkly colored, good wide blue eyes, a short and obstinate nose, a gentle mouth, a dimpled chin. He also had a small mustache, the color of his hair, and big shoulders. His hands, too, were big and square, and so were his feet in their black and polished boots. The day was hot; he wore thick black broadcloth and what Jonathan Ferrier usually described as a hard black inverted chamber pot, though it was only a New York derby. His collar, of course, was high and stiff, which gave his florid color an unfortunate enhancement, and his tie was black and fastened firmly with a pearl tiepin.

To Robert's surprise the usually austere and correct Dr. Ferrier was dressed as if for golfing, or for hunting or lawn bowling, in that his coat was a thin woolen plaid, his trousers light gray flannel, his shoes low. Even worse, he wore no collar and no hat. Yet his native air of hard elegance had not diminished for all this informal wardrobe. "Get in," he said in his usual quick and abrupt manner.

(Robert's mother had sternly told him all his life that no lady or gentleman ever appeared on a public street, walking or riding, without a hat and without gloves.)

"And take that obscene pot off your head," said Jonathan Ferrier, as Robert cautiously settled himself on the seat with his host. "A day like this! It must be nearly ninety."

The horses set out in what to Robert was a somewhat hasty trot. He removed his hat and held it on his knees. The warm wind rushed through his hair and lifted it pleasantly. "The horses," said Robert, trying to keep trepidation out of his nice young voice. "Racers?"

"Hardly. But I do have racers, as I told you before. I'm going to run two of them in the fall, at Belmont. Expect one of them to win. A stallion, three years old. Argentine stock. Should run the legs off most of the dog meat we have here. I bought his sire myself, in Buenos Aires."

Robert had been born in Philadelphia. He knew Boston well, and New York. He had interned at Johns Hopkins. But never had he met a man so insouciant as Jon Ferrier, who had apparently visited all the great capitals of the world and who had been born in little Hambledon. Robert had expected that he could kindly condescend to the "natives" of this town, and perhaps even to the famous Dr. Ferrier; he had been warned by his mother to be "gracious." Robert felt like a fool today. In fact, he had been feeling a fool for the past five days. He ought to have remembered that Dr. Ferrier had been graduated from Harvard Medical School and had studied at Heidelberg and the Sorbonne, and that he was one of the small handful of surgeons who operated on the brain, which only yesterday was considered one of "the forbidden chambers." Such a man would, of course, think it nothing at all to import a horse from Argentina for his own stables.

"I thought we'd forget the operating rooms and the hospitals today," said Jonathan. He laughed briefly. "Two diploma-mill hacks in frock coats who have never heard of Pasteur and Liston. But full of dignity and presence. They are slicing and sawing and grinding away at a great rate this morning, and if any of their patients survive, I'll be surprised. Only good luck and excellent constitutions kept their other patients alive after the general bloody slaughter."

"Why do the hospitals keep them, then, Doctor?"

"How many times do I have to tell you to call me Jon? After all, I'm not old enough to be your father. Why do they keep the hacks? Well, one of them is the Governor's cousin, and the other is Chief-of-Staff of the medical board at St. Hilda's, our very fashionable private little hospital. Oil-well rich, on his wife's side; he bought his way in." He chuckled with a dry and cynical sound. "In fact, he is operating on his wife's sister; ovarian tumor. I diagnosed it as probably carcinoma before—" He paused. "But affable Dr. Hedler thought, and thinks, my diagnosis ridiculous. He's possibly just finding it out, or one of the interns is diffidently informing him, or even one of the nurses! He'd never know by himself."

Robert was horrified. "And you say nothing—Jon?"

Jonathan gave him a brief hard stare. "Why should I? Oh, a year or so ago I'd have kicked up a stink. But not now. Why should I? She chose Dr. Hedler. He's very impressive, and ladies love that, and he speaks with the authority of the ignorant. Presence. It's true I'm still on the staff, and the Board, but I've learned recently when to keep my mouth shut. I recommend that to you, too, young Robert. At least for a few years. I had a bad time, myself, when I was first practicing and tried to introduce asepsis into the operating rooms, and white trousers and jackets for the surgeons, and lots of hand washing and rubber gloves. If it hadn't been for my family's name—and money—they'd have thrown me out. My mother had promised a wing at St. Hilda's. The hacks still wear their frock coats and striped trousers and wipe their scalpels in a lordly fashion on their sleeves, or the nurses' backsides, or whatever is handy. With a flourish. And they come, many of them, right from the dissection rooms. One's an obstetrician. He's delivering a baby this morning." He laughed again. "The lady will be very lucky, indeed, not to die of puerperal fever."

"And there's nothing you will—I mean, nothing you can do?"

"No. Would they listen to me, some of them, these days? No. I've heard it said that few would trust me to treat their dogs."

"Impossible!" Robert's pink face flushed with indignation. Dr. Ferrier was amused.

"You haven't the remotest idea, have you, about people, my boy? You'll find out, unfortunately. Look at you. A doctor who can blush. Remarkable. Here's another thought for you: What a surgeon or general practitioner does, or does not, do is only part of the story of a patient's survival. At least fifty percent of his good luck is due to himself and his faith in his physician. Didn't they teach you that in the great Johns Hopkins?"

"Well, yes."

"But you don't believe it?"

Robert was uncomfortable. "Of course I believe it. But still a hack, with all the confidence in the world, and his patient's confidence in him, can literally commit murder in the operating room, or even in the ward."

"True. But those are the overt cases. I had a patient one time with a mere wen on his neck, and he died of shock, the result of his fear beforehand. A minor operation at that. He didn't have any confidence in me. That was a few weeks ago, after—"

After the trial, thought Robert.

"So," said Jonathan Ferrier, "that sort of thing convinced me to get out of here."

"You haven't forgotten, though, that you'll stay and make the rounds with me, and be on hand in the operating rooms?"

"I gave you my promise, didn't I?" said Jonathan with impatience.

The granite cobblestones shone as if polished in the sun. They were rolling down the wide green streets of the better part of the town, with large pleasant houses standing far back on warm and glistening lawns blowing with glittering trees. Here and there the lawns were splashed with brilliant flower beds, and here and there tethered horses drank at concrete watering troughs. Robert could hear the lazy slapping of screen doors in the distance and the hissing of hoses as they watered the grass, and an occasional hammering. The sun splintered hotly on his face and hands; the tires on the phaeton's wheels, rubber and thick, moved over the cobbles smoothly and the vehicle rocked just perceptibly. In the distance, Robert could see the mountains taking on a soft purplish cast, setting into relief the red roofs of rich houses, or the white walls. A lovely, prosperous town, this Hambledon. Robert already felt comfortable in it, and he also felt an eager affection for all who lived here whom he did not yet know.

Jonathan said, "I hope you'll like it here. I had ten applications, you know, for my practice. I interviewed them all. You were the last."

Robert colored with shy pleasure, and Jonathan again gave indication of his unaccountable amusement. "I'm glad you selected me," said Robert, wondering how it was that he was always amusing the older man, and why he was amused at all.

"You were the best," said Jonathan. "At least, you seemed the most harmless. Don't be annoyed. It's very important to be harmless, if you are a physician. Didn't old Hippocrates say that? Yes. In fact, the greatest compliment you can say of us is that we didn't hurt anyone, even if we didn't help. I know an old fart who is very competent with the scalpel—ingenious at times, inspired—but they have to give the patient ether before they get a look at him. A gargoyle, with a temper to match. He could kill with a look, and I suppose he already has. He's harmful. He's usually called in desperate cases, after the first surgeon is about to give up. Really miraculous. But harmful."

Robert had been told at Johns Hopkins that it was not necessary for physicians to "indulge in levity" even among themselves, when it came to patients. Apparently Dr. Ferrier had not been taught that. Sometimes he intimidated poor Robert, who greatly admired him but still did not know if he liked him. He had a harsh and bitter way of speaking and was often contemptuous. At first Robert had thought this all the result of the tragic trial, but others, in a whisper, had assured him that Jonathan had always been this way. "Of course, it is accentuated now, but he was usually a cynical devil." Robert was not certain that it was good for a physician to be cynical in the least, and too objective. He had a very tender heart.

"Don't be too anxious to embrace this damn town," said Jonathan, as they rolled rapidly through the streets. "We have a lot of new-rich here; oil people. The kind of precious vulgarians who refer to their houses as 'homes.' Upstarts. Modesty is something they don't appreciate or value. They think it is a self-awareness of inferiority, and then they stamp on you. We have a few authentic families but not very many. Just an American town, just any town. Mostly populated by fools. Do you suffer fools gladly, Robert? Good. You ought to be very popular here. I never could. That's where the Church and I differ. Violently."

Robert could connect Jonathan Ferrier with many things but not with any church. He was constantly discovering startling things about the other man, some of them disconcerting.

"You—belong to a church, Jon?"

Jonathan turned his head slightly and gave Robert his unpleasant stark grin. "In a way. Why, does that surprise you? The Ferriers had a hard fence to climb over two hundred years ago, when they came to Pennsylvania. They were—are —what you people call Papists. Nominally I'm a Catholic. But I haven't been to Mass for years. You see, once I was as downy-headed as you, Bob. My fellowman soon disillusioned me. I was seventeen then. You are nearly ten years older than that. How in hell can you be so innocent?"

"I'm not that innocent," said Robert with dignity, and Jonathan was highly amused again and chuckled that dry chuckle of his.

"You surely had some of the nurses, and perhaps some of the trollops of the town, didn't you?"

Robert's too-ready color flushed his face once more. He thought of his mother. He was certain she believed him virginal. He remembered the quick and awkward episodes of the past few years, and it embarrassed him now to recall that he had always closed his eyes so that he would not see the women's faces. He could feel Dr. Ferrier watching him, but he stared obdurately at the thin sunburned hands that held the reins so surely.

"I once had an intern from a Methodist medical school,"

said Jonathan with happy remembrance, "who could never bring himself to utter the word 'vagina.' He preferred to call it 'the private parts.' There's nothing," said Jonathan, "less private, in a hospital or an operating room, than those delicately mentioned 'parts.' "

"One has to remember that—er—women have their reticences," said the unfortunate Robert.

"Do they now?" said Jonathan, raising one of his thick black brows. "If there is anything less reticent, or modest, than a woman, I've yet to meet it. A woman in heat can make the most uncouth man seem like a choirboy."

"I suppose you've had a lot of experience," said Robert.

"Good! You aren't all custard, are you, Bob? That's one thing I wanted to be sure of; I was a little afraid, sometimes, that you were too gentle for the bloody arenas we call hospitals."

"I was considered very competent at Johns Hopkins," said Robert in a stiff tone. "Hardly a custard. Besides, my father was a surgeon, too, and before I even studied medicine, I watched many of his operations."

"And didn't faint once, I suppose. Never mind. I'm joshing you. I really like you, Bob, and I'm notable for not liking people. You must cultivate a sense of humor. Never mind. Do you know where we're going today? To watch birds."

"Watch birds!"

"It's too nice a day to watch people. You should watch people only during murky weather, or storms, or when rivers rise, or houses burn. Very revealing. You see them at their worst, naked. Yes, I did mean birds." He indicated, with an inclination of his head, the strap across his chest that held a binocular case. "You never watched birds?"

Birds, to Robert, were somewhat lovable vertebrates who sang in the spring and had feathers. He could not tell one from another, except for the robins and the cardinals. His mother spoke of "their dear little nests," and had once told him, when he was a child, that birds had been created expressly by the anthropomorphic Almighty for the delight of humanity. To Mrs. Morgan they had no being of their own, no joy in life of their own, no celebration in living, no identity. It was obvious to her that they had eggs, but Robert doubted if she knew that they had a sex life also, which produced the eggs and the new, vital creatures. She had evidently believed that they begot as flowers beget, via pollen. Robert, remembering, decided that his mother was a trifle hard "to take." Was she one of the fools of whom Dr. Ferrier had spoken? Possibly. Probably. Robert felt new irritation and did not know its source. Always he had been the solicitous and tender only son, the only child, devoted to his mother. This now seemed puerile to him, and embarrassing. He thought of his father, and suddenly it came to him that his paternal parent had had a lot to endure, and there was no wonder that there had been no other child of that sterile marriage.

She's vulgar, too, thought Robert. She calls our house "the home."

"What're you scowling about?" asked Jonathan. "If you don't want to watch birds, we won't."

"Did I say that?" Robert felt a thrill at the new vexation in his voice. He was rarely vexed at people; he was too kind. "I was thinking of something else. Yes, I'd like to watch your birds. But why?"

"Why watch birds? Some of them are still going north, even now. You can see some fine and unusual specimens, if you know where to look. Why birds? I don't know exactly; I always did, even when I was a kid. The old man was a great bird-watcher. He almost genuflected at the name of Audubon. We gave a park to the city; at least my great-grandfather did, on the outskirts. A bird sanctuary. Birds are restful. They never have their little schemes. They're all bird. Unlike people, who are rarely human in the best meaning of the term. It's the same with other nonhuman animals. They are what they are—honest in their being. Solid in their being. But you never know what a man is."

He's right, thought Robert, struck disagreeably by this truth.

"I have six dogs and eight cats," said Jonathan. "One dog in town. The rest on my farms. Each one a distinct individual but honestly itself. You'll never see a dog pretending to be better than he is; you'll never find a cat without self-respect. Even cattle are faithful to their nature. But coming down to that, man is faithful to his nature, too, almost always. Almost always he is a fool, a liar, a hypocrite, a coward, a pretender, a covert murderer, a thief, a traitor. Name any vice he doesn't have. That's his nature. It's only when he pretends to virtue that he steps out of focus and out of character."

Robert had always liked his fellowman. He was naturally gregarious and trusting. His new irritability made him say, "You know, Doctor, that sounds very sophomoric."

To his surprise Jonathan burst out laughing, the first genuine laughter from him which Robert had heard. "What makes you think," said Jonathan, "that sophomores are invariably softheaded and wrong? Some of the brightest people I've ever met were kids in preparatory schools. They see things whole and they see them truly. Later, adults corrupt and blind them and tell them a pack of winsome lies, and dull their perceptions. Seventeen ends the age of innocence, unfortunately. Come on, now, hasn't anyone ever betrayed you, or lied about you, or done some mischief to you, Bob?"

"Yes, of course. But what does that matter? I keep my own hands clean."

"Cheers," said Jonathan.

Robert was becoming too warm in his heavy clothing. He unfastened his tie and then his collar. He took off his coat. I'm a prig; he's right, he thought. He rolled up the white sleeves of his shirt. The sun was very hot; the soft shadow of trees and the dark caves they made of the streets were very refreshing. The houses were now more scattered and there were many empty lots, dusty and high with early June grass. The scent of stone and vegetation filled the quiet and shining air. There was a great deal to be said in favor of small cities and villages, Robert thought. At least they smelled—honestly. He saw that they were approaching the river and that Jonathan had turned the phaeton toward the River Road. He caught glimpses, between the houses and the trees, of that island which some fool of a woman had named "Heart's Ease." In fact, he saw the red-tiled roof of the "castle" clearly, brilliant in the sun, the walls hidden by trees, and the granite enclosures. The water resembled shot silk, blue and full of bright purple shadows.

"You remind me of Omar Khayyam," said Jonathan.

"Sophomoric again," said Robert. "What's wrong with the old tentmaker? If his truths seem worn and obvious, it is because they are truths. What's a truism? It's a coin that has had a lot of handling, but it's a genuine coin, and it wouldn't have been handled so much if it hadn't had verity."

"I bet you read him at least once a month."

This happened to be true, itself, and it annoyed Robert.

"I do, too," said Jonathan. "Do you want to know my favorite verse?:

> " 'The moving finger writes, and having writ
>   Moves on. Nor all your piety or wit

Can lure it back to cancel half a line,
Nor all your tears wash out a word of it!' "

Robert was startled, first because that verse seemed out of
character in Jonathan and because it was also his own favorite. It had always been unbearably poignant to him and warn-
ingly tragic.

Then he saw that Dr. Ferrier was laughing at him again,
and now they were not only on the River Road, but across
the water the island seemed only yards away.

CHAPTER TWO

Hambledon had not despoiled its river frontage as yet
with factories and disreputable warehouses and shacks. When
Robert remarked on this with pleasure, Jonathan said disagreeably, "Just wait. We Ferriers and our friends have
stopped it so far. But we are already being accused of being
'unprogressive' and 'standing in the way of The Future.' The
Future, apparently, will be complete ugliness, and utilitarian,
if the 'progressives' have their way. Let's enjoy the beautiful,
vanishing America while we can. It's on the way out to make
way for the proletarian cult of drabness."

Robert nodded. "Or Karl Marx's cult of 'for use.' How he
hated the farmer! He once looked at a map of Germany,
showing the cities and then the broad countryside, and he
complained of all that 'waste land.' Why, he asked, weren't
the cities spread out over the countryside, so 'the masses'
could have little plots of land all their own. When it was
brought to his attention that the land was needed to cultivate
crops to feed people, he waved it away as irrelevant."

"So, you learned something else besides how to perform autopsies and needless operations," said Jonathan. "Now, why are you scowling? Never mind. Old Marx was a plagiarist. He got all his ideas from the French Revolution of 1795 and the murderous Jacobins, who probably got their ideas from the Roman traitor Catilina over two thousand years ago. The idea of utilitarianism only and the rule of the undisciplined mobs is an ancient idea that goes back to the sons of Cain. Liberty's a very fragile flower, indeed, and we'd best enjoy it here in America before it's stamped out. You don't think it will be? Young Bob, you're awfully naïve."

"Oh, that's ridiculous," said Robert, with the confidence of youth. "No one listens to Teddy Roosevelt and his 'progressive' ideas."

Jonathan grunted. "This is a new century. Yes, I know, it's only an artificial man-made marking of time. But I've noticed something very odd: New centuries do indeed mark themselves off from the past ones. I don't believe in astrology, of course. But some madman in Chicago sent me 'the planetary aspects of the 1900s.' Don't recall his name. Anyway, he said this century would be known as 'The Prelude to Armageddon,' or 'The Century of Tyrants and Disaster.' Maybe. Maybe. Let's move into this grove of birches. And look for birds," and he grinned at Robert.

The grove of old birches was aromatic with sweet and pungent scents of earth and leaf and fecund ground. The warm sunlight did not penetrate here. The air was as cool as a fragrant cellar. There were large stands of wildflowers and mushrooms, and everywhere sounded the voice of the river and the colloquy of busy birds. Robert, the city man, was exhilarated. He breathed deeply and listened. Jonathan held his binoculars to his eyes and swung them about, searching the tops of trees and the sunlit branches. "There!" he said. "If that's not a delayed grackle, then I never saw one!" He held out the binoculars to Robert, who put them to his eyes and directed them at an indicated branch.

He saw a large bird with a peculiar aquamarine beak and a quantity of brilliant feathers. But the binoculars were focused on a great wild eye, staring, mysterious, reflecting remembered forests and hidden wildernesses and the knowledge of ancient ages. Never had Robert seen such an eye before, which held secrets unknown to man, large, dilated, still, as if listening. He was fascinated and a little awed and, strangely, a trifle frightened, as man is always frightened by the inexplicable. He said to Jonathan, but as though speaking to himself, "What we don't know!"

"A born bird-watcher," said Jonathan. "I never knew a bird-watcher who was smug. Or a zoologist who thought man was the crowning glory of creation. Or an astronomer who believed man was 'little lesser than the angels.'" Jonathan snorted. "The Old Testament boys were cryptic. They never explained what angels they were referring to. Perhaps the ones who followed Satan down into the pit."

Robert stared at him curiously. "You don't have a high opinion of your fellowman, do you?"

"The lowest opinion possible," said Jonathan with promptness. "After all, I literally know him inside and out. If you want to retain your good opinion of mankind, never get too close to it. Squat in your ivory tower and read poetry or spin dreams. Never get out into the streets or mingle with people. Or, God help us, talk to them."

Robert was strangely oppressed. The sound of the river and the cries of the birds became too imminent to him, and now they had an ominous note.

"Birds," said Jonathan, "don't like people. Neither do trees. Very perspicacious of them, isn't it? We are seeing our last of our edible chestnuts though there's a great flurry among chemists and such to find a cure for their present disease, which is killing them. One by one other species of trees will begin to die, as they died in China, when the press of populations moved too closely to them. That's why China is so barren now. It won't be too long before America begins to lose her trees, too, one species after another. No, they don't like people, the old ones."

"You sound like a Druid," said Robert, the sense of oppression growing.

"There may be something to it," and Jonathan was authentically grave. "Remember, we were pagans before we were Christians, and we had a knowledge of the earth then. So did the ancient Jews." He smiled mockingly at Robert. "So, you know about Druids, too? I am beginning to have a respect for you, young Bob."

"Do you think I'm illiterate?" said Robert, with considerable new anger. "Even if my father was a physician, he was a literate man and had a big library!"

"A vanishing race," said Jonathan. "The physician of the future will be a specialist, and what he'll know of the nature of the body and the mind will be strictly circumscribed. Turn those binoculars on that damned island. It's very interesting."

Robert obeyed, though automatically. He was too disturbed by his thoughts. Then he focused the binoculars.

The glasses brought the island so close that Robert felt he could reach out and touch it. It was larger than it appeared to the naked eye. It was truly heart-shaped, the widest and indented part rising out of the blue water like the prow of a ship, the pointed end seeming almost level with the river. He could see the granite enclosure clearly, and the white walls of the "castle," and the crowding masses of trees and the brilliance of flowers beyond them on lawns. The red roof of the building flashed scarlet in the sun.

A figure was climbing up the widest point, and Robert caught a glimpse of blue. The figure appeared young and lithe, climbing with ease and vigor. It moved in and out through copses of trees, rising steadily. Then it reached the highest point, just behind the granite enclosure. Suddenly it was completely revealed. A tall young girl stood there, staring directly across at the grove of birches, and her face, whitely luminous, glowed in the sunlight like marble.

It was a beautiful face, exquisitely boned and delicately formed and strong. A great mass of curling black hair swung about it and fell to the shoulders and below, held back by a red ribbon. The clear, polished brow shone in the light, and the large crimson mouth. The nose was faintly aquiline. Robert noted this, but what demanded his acute attention were her eyes. They were intensely blue and large and dense with black lashes and arched with very dark brows like the gleaming wings of a bird. So extraordinary was the blue of the eyes that the sparkle of them seemed to fill her face, making it blaze.

They were full of passionate and unequivocal hatred, directed at the grove of trees. The hatred struck at Robert and made him drop the glasses precipitately.

"She sees us spying on her!" he exclaimed.

"Nonsense," said Jonathan, taking the glasses and putting them to his eyes. "That island is almost a mile out in the water. She can't see that far." He chuckled as he studied the girl. "Yes, she's staring at this grove, but she doesn't see us. She can't." He gave the glasses back to Robert. "Pretty wench, isn't she?"

Robert hesitated. He looked through the glasses again. The girl was still looking toward the grove. She was leaning on the granite wall, tensely. She was not only tall. She had a lovely figure, curved and graceful and slender. Her blue dress was simple and open at the throat, and the sleeves came halfway down her arms. She wore a coarse brown apron over her dress, like a servant or a girl who worked in the barns.

"I still think she sees us," said Robert with uneasiness. "She's looking straight at me. And she doesn't like it at all."

"A mile, almost, away," repeated Jonathan. "I know. I swam it several times, there and back. The current's very fast. No, she can't see us. She's just hating everybody, as usual."

"Who is she, Doctor?"

"My niece. Technically."

Robert turned to him and stared. "What did you say? Your niece? How could that be? The girl is twenty, or older. And your brother is younger than you!"

Jonathan was silent a moment. The fretted shadow of the birches trembled over his face, and it was bleak and hard. He finally said, "Technically, I said. My brother, Harald, married her mother, a Mrs. Peter Heger. From Pittsburgh and Titusville. She was twelve years older than my brother. And that's her daughter by her first husband. Jennifer. Or Jenny, as she's usually called."

"She's living there? With your brother? All alone?" Robert blushed at his own words.

Jonathan grinned, and Robert again wondered whether he liked or disliked the older man. It was such an unpleasant grimace. Jonathan said, "Ambiguous? Well. That's a nice word for it. The people in Hambledon don't think it's nice at all. However, there're servants there, too, three of them. And Jenny, apparently, doesn't give a damn what people say. Her father bought the island and built that silly house there, called the 'castle,' in a fit of honeymoon preposterousness. He left all his fortune to his wife, who wasn't what you'd call very intelligent to begin with. You can never tell what an infatuated woman will do with money, and Myrtle—foolish name, isn't it?—was infatuated with my brother. He's a natural roamer, and an artist, and didn't have a cent in the world when he caught Myrtle's attention."

Jonathan paused. "My father knew what he was doing. He divided his money between my mother and me and left artistic Harald only a small lifetime income, not enough for his exquisite tastes. He's a very bad artist but thinks he's a genius, as all bad artists think themselves. He's elegant and 'sensitive.' New Cubist, I think. I don't know much about art. I only know Harald's stinks. He never sold a painting in his life, but he's been all over the world. I suppose Myrtle was a Godsend to him. Anyway, he married her and they lived very happily for several years together until she died. She had mitral stenosis and, later, an infarction. I was her physician."

Robert had listened to all this intently. Jonathan's voice, resonant and not too pleasing at the best of times, had become grating and unpleasant, as if he were controlling deep laughter.

"Why doesn't the girl leave?" asked Robert. "It—it mustn't be nice for her."

"What? On one hundred dollars a month, after she'd been brought up like a princess? Jenny's a shrewd piece. And that island was her home for years until Harald firmly took up residence on it. It was her father's. He died when she was quite young."

"I don't suppose they like each other, your brother and—the girl?"

Jonathan laughed again. "There's a rumor they like each other only too well! In the town they call her 'Lilith.'"

Robert knew his Bible. He said, "Lilith? Wasn't there a legend that she was Adam's first wife, or something? 'Now Lilith was a demon.'" He flushed again, his too-ready color. "I shouldn't have said that."

"You aren't offending me," said Jonathan with enjoyment. "I despise both of them, sweet Jenny and Harald. Not that I listen to gossip, which is plenty in the town. In a way, I suppose it's all right, their living in the 'castle.' It should have been left to Jenny, anyway. The servants are there. Still—"

Robert felt an obnoxious taste in his mouth, and disgust. He put the glasses to his eyes once more. The girl was still directing her hatred at the grove of trees. Then, as Robert watched, she bent her head and descended back the way she had come and disappeared. He saw the white flash of her neck through the trees.

"I still think she saw us," he said.

"No. Impossible. She was just hating Hambledon in general. She doesn't go into the town very often. When she does, she often calls on my mother, technically her grandmother. They are great friends. But she leaves at once if I appear. I don't think she likes me."

I wonder how many do? thought Robert, and was embarrassed.

"How about visiting the hermits?" asked Jonathan. "They'll

be your patients, you know. You might as well know them."
His dark thin face was gleeful with a mirth that Robert could
not understand, except that it had a flavor of malice.

"Oh," said Robert. "Perhaps not today." He was again
very uneasy.

"Why not today?" Jonathan was suddenly very brisk.
"They have three rowboats. One is always on this bank.
Come on. Why are you rooted there?"

Robert did not know. He simply felt a reluctance to make
the acquaintance of the ambiguous couple on the island. But
Jonathan took his arm and firmly led him out of the grove.
"I go over there at least twice a week, just for the fun of it,"
he said. "There isn't much fun in my life recently. Don't be
stubborn."

Carrying his thick coat on his arm, Robert followed Jonathan. For some reason he set his hard black hat firmly on his
head. They reached the bank of the river and saw that a row-
boat with oars was pulled up on the thick grass. "Perhaps
your brother isn't at home," said Robert hopefully.

"Now, where would he go? In Hambledon? How are you
at rowing?"

But Jonathan took off his jacket and lifted the oars, after
the two young men had pushed the boat down into the water.
"You can row back," said Jonathan. "It's wonderful exercise,
and doctors need it. They get too fat in their pompousness."

Robert settled down in the boat as Jonathan strongly thrust
the oars into the shining blue water. He had a new suspicion
that Jonathan had intended this visit from the first, and his
uneasiness grew. He told himself that he was not accustomed
to "this kind" of people. All his life had been surrounded by
people on whom one could depend, of whom one was sure.
Good solid people, kind people, helpful, friendly people. Decorous, churchgoing people who always voted Republican
and suspected "Papists" and Jews and "foreigners." People
who made Sunday calls and left cards and never swore or
acted indiscreetly. People to whom adultery was only a word,
and sin something persistently to be avoided. Women who
were modest and not ambiguous, and never showed their ankles or uttered a naughty word; men who wore frock coats
on Sundays and carried canes and talked in modulated
voices. I am certainly a long way from Philadelphia! thought
young Robert Morgan.

He looked at the bareheaded Jonathan Ferrier. Jonathan
was as strange to him as a resident of Tangiers or Constanti-

nople. He had a "foreign" look, lean, hard, dark, hidden. He was also a "Papist," by his own admission, or at least had been so. Of course, his mother had been a Farmington and was a great lady. Robert dwelt heavily on that fact to conceal his feeling of estrangement and his sensation that he had, in some way, found himself in an alien country where the old signs were written in hieroglyphics and not to be deciphered. Yet, Hambledon was only a small city. It was just that the Ferriers were "different." French, or Belgian? One never knew what "that sort" would do next. They were unpredictable, and Jonathan Ferrier was more unpredictable than most. Sinister? Robert thought of that as the hot sun glared in his eyes and the water threw back brilliant ripples of light. Probably sinister. Was it possible that he was really guilty of his wife's and child's murder after all? No, no. Of course not. A swell of water made the boat rock, and Robert clutched the sides quickly.

"Not seasick, I hope," said Jonathan.

"No. But shouldn't we have called first to see if we'd be welcome?"

"They don't have a telephone. Myrtle could never stand telephones. She wanted the island to be very rustic." Jonathan grinned, and his white teeth flashed at Robert. "If there is an emergency, they have a light, a lantern, to be lit on top of their stupid 'castle.' I know. That's the way they'd call me for Myrtle. Or one of the servants would row over and roust me out of bed. Or look for me in the hospitals. Don't worry. Jenny and Harald are used to me rowing over regularly."

"It must be lonely for them." Robert tried to talk over his anxious thoughts.

"No. Not really. Harald's an artist. Remember? He likes his solitude. He says. And—Jenny's there."

"A young girl. Doesn't she have friends in Hambledon?"

"A few. But she's surly by nature and isn't very popular. She's been much worse since her mother died. Did I mention that she detests me? As for my brother, we're not exactly devoted. Here, take the oars and try them out."

The current was unexpectedly swift and the boat was pitching as well as rocking. The two men exchanged places cautiously, and even then Robert almost lost his balance. But Jonathan moved as easily and as lithely as a young boy and was settled before Robert even took up the oars. The sun was indeed very hot, and the current hard against the oars, so that Robert had to pull strenuously. He began to sweat. He glanced over his shoulder. The island seemed a long way off, the water bursting in little sprays against the prow of the steep bank.

"You honestly swam this?" asked Robert.

"It's easy. I'm a good swimmer. But Harald can't swim a stroke. That's the delicate artist for you!"

Robert began to feel his fair skin burn, and his nose. Sweat sprang out at the roots of his reddish-yellow hair, and under his chin and between his shoulders. Jonathan was not watching him. He was watching the island and the closed tight look was on his face again, and he appeared to have forgotten Robert entirely.

"They have no gas and no electricity," said Jonathan in an absent voice. "Myrtle didn't want to spoil the rusticity. I told you she was a fool. So, they have oil lamps and a barge delivers coal in the winter for that stupid pile of rock, and they burn nice apple logs, very expensive, in the fireplaces. And once a week the servants bring in loads of groceries in the boats. If they didn't get high wages, they wouldn't work there, I can tell you. It must cost a fortune for all that pretentiousness."

The water lapped at the boat and the sun glittered on the water and Robert became hotter every moment. Jonathan looked at him critically. "You're making better time than I do," he said. "Swing around a little to the narrow tip of the island. There's an opening in the enclosure there, and a path."

Again Robert looked over his shoulder. The island's wide indented prow was looming above him, he was glad to see. He could smell the flowering earth and the trees and hear the silence above the voice of the river. He dexterously turned the boat as directed.

"Here we are," said Jonathan, and stood up, crossed the seat where Robert sat and reached out. He caught a rope dangling from a pile and tied up the boat swiftly. "All right; we're anchored. You'll have to jump a couple of feet, though." Before Robert could even stand in the swaying boat, Jonathan had leaped onto the bank, which was steeper than the younger man had expected, and had much more of an incline. He jumped; his foot slipped on the damp brown earth, and he would have fallen back into the water had not Jonathan caught his arm.

"Steady, there," said Jonathan. "And here's the path. What? Putting on your coat? What for?"

The girl was standing on the climbing path. She looked down at them with an ugly expression on her beautiful face.

"What do you want?" she demanded. Her voice was lovely in spite of her brutal words and the blaze of blue in her eyes.

CHAPTER THREE

Robert was acutely embarrassed. He looked angrily at Jonathan. But Jonathan was smiling up at the girl, and a more unpleasant smile Robert had never seen before.

"Why, Jenny," he said in a coaxing voice, "didn't you expect me, as usual? Jenny, dear, this is Dr. Robert Morgan, who is taking up my practice. Bob, Jenny Heger, my niece. Miss Jenny Heger."

The girl glared down at them in silence, her hands on her hips. She did not acknowledge the introduction, beyond giving Robert a contemptuous glance. Then she swung about and left them, climbing rapidly like a deer, her long full skirts unfurling out behind her like a sail caught by the wind. Then she was gone. Robert replaced his hat. He was angrier than ever. "I don't think we're welcome," he said.

"Oh, Jenny never welcomes anyone. Don't let it bother you. She probably rushed off to inform the cook that she has company for lunch."

"Lunch? I—I don't think I want to stay."

"But you must meet Harald, the genius with the paintbrushes!" Jonathan seemed ingenuously surprised. However, Robert was mistrusting him more and more. "Harald loves guests. He especially loves me. Come on. You have a tendency to grow roots wherever you stand. Don't mind Jenny, the rustic plow girl. Badly brought up. That fool of a mother.

If Jenny ever smiled, like a normal woman, the world would crack or the Apocalypse come down. Watch where you're walking. This path is very steep and perpetually wet. And full of roots. I nearly killed myself, walking up it, when I got the dramatic light signal from the roof one night."

I don't like him at all, thought Robert with misery. He mocks everybody. He mocks everything. He mocks me, too. Robert began to climb. The shadow of many thick rare trees and shrubs crowded along the path, and it was much cooler and the scent of earth was dank and musky in the shade. Jonathan climbed as easily as if the high path were a city pavement. He pointed out the trees and the shrubs. "Old Pete was very lavish. He imported many of these vegetables. There's even a cactus garden near the house; they take in the cacti for the winter. Monstrous things but interesting. Those oil wells! There're even palms in pots, near what they call the tropical garden. Nothing's been spared. Hundreds of thousands. Enough to build a new wing at the Friends' Hospital for tubercular children." His back was to Robert, and his voice had changed, become thin and vicious. "Not that I think a man shouldn't enjoy his money. I'm not that much of a mousy prig. But he ought to have left something for the hospitals. And the kids. But not a cent."

Robert paused on the path to wipe his sweating face. He was again confused and uncertain. Jonathan continued to climb. He said, "Myrtle promised me that wing. All big serious eyes and trembling voice. She never did, of course. In fact, I had trouble getting her to contribute one hundred dollars a year to the hospitals. 'Dear Pete' had always counseled thrift, and Myrtle was thriftier than a razor, in spite of her general idiocy. Came by it honestly, Pennsylvania Dutch, not the rugged Amish, though. She'd put her hand on my arm and look at me sentimentally, and sigh, and mysteriously promise a fortune. Very coy. But nothing in her will. I should have known." Jonathan looked back and was surprised to see Robert standing on the path. "What's the matter? Are you flabby at your age?"

"No." Robert was more bewildered than ever. "Do—do the hospitals mean that much to you, Doctor?"

The shade was very deep where Jonathan stood high on the path. He was silent, but Robert could feel the bitter penetration of his dark eyes. Then he said, "Once they did. But not now." He climbed more quickly. Robert followed. Jonathan said, "Why so formal? Didn't I tell you to call me by my Christian name?" But he did not look back. He seemed caught up in a gloomy aura all his own. His tall thin figure appeared to glide on the path, like a shadow itself. The path curved, and momentarily he was out of sight. Robert climbed, sunken in uneasy and contradictory thoughts. Now there was a sharp coolness between his shoulder blades. He shivered.

He suddenly arrived into broad sunlight, clean and bright, and the dank scent was gone and the heavy odor of wet moss and slimy earth. He could not understand it, but he felt overpoweringly grateful. All was good again, fair again, filled with simple kindliness and freshness, purged of anything nightmarishly murky or hidden or wicked, here in the sun of affirmation and purity. Yes, man was good, man was uncomplicated, man was the son of God!

He stood on level green grass, filled with warmth and ease. For a moment he did not see Jonathan Ferrier standing, waiting, at a little distance ahead of him on the lawns. Jonathan stared back at him curiously, and then after a moment he was sad. Poor devil. Poor, trusting boy. All was sweetness and light to him, was it? Nothing was complex, elaborated, devious, evil, distressing, embroidered, treacherous, cruel, infamous—no, not to Robert Sylvester Morgan, barely out of the womb. Poor devil, thought Jonathan Ferrier again. I must help him. He must see reality before he is too old to take it with equanimity, and then go on. He called back to Robert, "Here!"

Robert started; then, seeing the other man, he smiled and waved like a boy. "Just stopped for a breather," he said. He looked about him with pleasure. He saw the miniature castle at a distance on its lawns, with minute battlements and rounded towers and slit windows, and he was delighted at the white granite perfection, and not embarrassed as Jonathan was whenever he saw it. A little schloss, thought Robert. He saw a greenhouse, its glass windows sparkling in the sun, and small buildings that housed tools. He saw massed trees and formal small gardens and hedge and red-bricked walks and little lily ponds and an old roofed well. There were spruces, too, and flowering shrubs, all fragrant in the water-clean air, all vivid with color. The river gracefully flowed about the island, lovingly enclosing it. Freshness came from little grottoes and winding paths, and white wooden arches bursting with climbing scarlet roses or blue morning glories. Nothing could be more charming, more appropriate, than all this, and it was no longer mawkish to Robert, not even the pretentious little castle. All it needed, he thought, was a still moat and a draw-bridge. He listened to the riotous voices of the birds, and to the river, and the tootling of the busy ferryboat. How Euro-pean in raw America! The farther bank was high and green, and beyond it stood the grape-colored mountains, and it might all have been the Rhine Valley—which he, Robert, had never visited in his life but of which he had heard. He smiled hugely and, seeing that smile, Jonathan frowned, then shrugged. He was somewhat disappointed in young Bob. If a man could not see preciousness at once and grin at it, then there was not much hope for him. "Come on," he called.

Enchanted, Robert walked slowly toward Jonathan, turning his head from side to side to catch fresh wonders and beau-ties. He was not envious. He thought it all marvelous. Now he reached Jonathan, and in silence they approached the cas-tle. The walk that led to it was slabs of white marble; three broad marble steps fanned to the bronze doors, and on each side crouched white stone lions, life-size. "What do you think of it?" asked Jonathan.

"Beautiful," said Robert. Jonathan gave up. "A vulgar man's dream," he said. "At least, his dream of a dream." But Robert did not hear this ill-tempered remark.

The bronze doors opened before they could reach them, and a tall young man in a crimson velvet morning jacket walked easily down the marble steps to await them. Robert saw him in that clarified light of noon, long-headed, casual, smiling. He had a florid handsomeness, unusual in one so slight and young, and bright, ruddy hair, and excellent fea-tures, well-cut and candid. He came to them eagerly, as if they were the most welcome of guests, and expected, holding out his hands. Now Robert could see his large eyes, bril-liantly hazel and shining with good temper, and his gay and attractive smile, which revealed glowing white teeth. His whole air was frank and boyish and pleased.

"Jon!" he exclaimed. "Jenny just told me. And"—he turned to Robert with that look of deep candor and open ex-pectation. His voice was a lighter version of Jonathan's.

"My replacement," said Jonathan. "Robert Morgan. Young Bob."

"Good! I've heard of Dr. Morgan. How do you like our town?"

"I like it. I like it very much," said Robert with a fervency that made Jonathan smile wryly. He shook hands with Harald Ferrier. This brother was not "foreign," nor odd, nor secret. He was as transparent as the very sunlight and as warm. He made a stranger feel as if he were an old friend about to be strongly embraced. He made a man feel accepted and secure and at ease and more than ordinarily welcome.

"I'm glad," Harald said. "I'm very glad. Bully, as Teddy Roosevelt would say. Well, come in, come in. You're both staying for lunch, aren't you?"

Though his voice resembled Jonathan's, it lacked Jonathan's resonance and deep quality, its undertone of hard grittiness. Robert, lulled by all this goodwill, this tremendous kindliness and affability, hesitated. "Well, I—" he said, and looked at Jonathan.

"We came for lunch," said Jonathan. "Don't I usually?"

"Except when you come for dinner," said Harald, laughing. He winked without reason at Robert, as if drawing him into a delicious conspiracy against his brother. "We get a little bored here without visitors. I'm a gregarious fella; I love company. It seems such an effort for friends to row across that water. Effete."

Robert murmured something. What nastiness had he been thinking of Harald Ferrier only a few minutes ago? He could not remember. But he was ashamed. There was such joyousness about Harald, such simplicity and humor.

They entered a square hall, all black and white marble squares, with four suits of armor arranged along the walnut walls. A dark wooden staircase with medieval overtones rose from the hall to a landing with a great stained-glass window. The hall smelled of the ages, a faint but pleasurable mustiness, and Robert saw hanging banners in various colors, hinting of family standards.

"For God's sake, let's go out on the terrace, away from this fakery," said Jonathan.

Harald laughed without offense. "Everything is fake to Jon," he said to Robert. "But old Pete brought this entire hall from Germany, so what is fake about it? Nothing! And the whole castle is furnished in authentic furniture, brought from all over Europe. Sheraton. Chippendale. Spanish. And there's a lot of Duncan Phyfe, too. Well, let's go on the terrace." He had taken Robert's arm in total friendliness. "Don't listen to Jon. He tries to sour life for everybody."

"Not for everybody," said Jonathan. "But I'd love to make it a little sour for you."

"Dear old Jon," said Harald without resentment. "This

door, please, Dr. Morgan." He opened a large carved oaken door and a blaze of sunlight struck into the hall. Beyond it was a terrace of smooth gray stones and tubbed exotic flowers, all surrounded by little spruces. The white granite wall of the castle threw a sharp blue shadow on it all, and there was fine garden furniture waiting, rustic swings, rockers covered with chintz pillows, sofas in red and blue and yellow. Rattan tables held flowering jars and bowls. The lawns moved smoothly away from the terrace, down to the granite enclosure. The river lay beyond, azure and twinkling, and the farther shore and the mountains gave their own peace and tranquillity to the scene. Somewhere, unseen, a fountain tinkled, and there was a scent of wet stone and luxurious grass blowing over the terrace in a wind as pure as crystal.

Robert put on his coat, after a blush of shame that he had forgotten it, and sat down. Jonathan sat near him negligently, his thin legs crossed, his profile to Robert as if he had forgotten him. Harald was superbly gracious. He smiled at Robert amiably. "A drink before lunch?" he suggested. His eyes were warm and affectionate, as if he had known Robert for many years and considered him a dear friend.

"Whiskey and soda, as usual, for me," said Jonathan, still staring absently at the river. Robert considered. His mother did not believe in strong liquor and he had known, even in college and at medical school and at Johns Hopkins, only beer and wine and sherry. He doubted, in this atmosphere, that any of them would be the proper thing. "Sherry," said Jonathan, as if reading his mind. Robert hated himself for the heat in his face. "No," he said. "Thanks, just the same. I think I'd like whiskey, too."

"Good," said Harald. He struck a bell on the table near his elbow. The sound was abrupt in that peaceful stillness. A moment later an elderly man in a white jacket came to the door. "Three whiskies and soda, Albert," said Harald, in his kind voice. "Please."

The old man smiled at him like a father. "Surely, Mr. Ferrier," he said. "At once."

"And would you mind, Albert, asking Miss Heger to join us here? You could bring the sherry for her, too."

"Whiskey," said Jonathan, still not turning his head.

"Oh, come now, Jon! Don't be disagreeable. Jenny doesn't drink whiskey! She's a lady."

Jonathan yawned. "She usually drinks whiskey, too. Don't put on for Bob."

Harald still smiled. But his eyes looked pained and Robert was sorry for him. Harald nodded to Albert. "Four whiskies, then." He hesitated. "You'll be giving Dr. Morgan a bad impression of us here, Jon."

"He'll get worse, in the town." Jonathan spoke indifferently. He looked now at Robert. "My mother drinks whiskey and likes it. And why not? Such stupidity, thinking women are better, or worse, than men."

Robert did not know what to say. He wished that Jonathan were less intolerable. But Harald was saying with enthusiasm, "Hambledon is a splendid town, really! You'll enjoy it, Doctor. Nothing like Philadelphia, of course, but nicer in many ways—"

"Why, then, are you always scheming with lawyers to leave it?" asked Jonathan.

Harald immediately became serious. He leaned earnestly toward his brother. "Now, Jon. You know that's not true. Isn't Hambledon my home? Didn't I always return to it when—"

"Papa's money began to run out, or he refused you any more."

Harald laughed lightly. "Oh, come on, Jon! This is Dr. Morgan's first visit here and—"

"We mustn't give him a bad impression. Yes, I know. But do you expect he'll never hear about us in the town? There're hundreds of old biddies of both sexes who'll be only too anxious to tell him all about the Ferriers. Better if he hears it at firsthand."

"You make us sound disreputable, or something."

"And that's what we are."

Harald was silent. He continued to smile, however. The door opened and Jenny came out upon the terrace. She had removed her brown apron, but her blue cotton dress was stained here and there, carelessly, with earth, as if she had come fresh from the garden. Her expression was sullen and remote. She did not look at any of the men, and did not acknowledge them when they rose and greeted her. She moved quickly, with the awkwardness of a colt, to a distant chair, sat down, turned her face away, and folded her large white hands in her lap.

Robert looked at her profile furtively. Close at hand as she was, she appeared almost incredibly beautiful, her brow and fine nose and white chin thrown into relief by the vivid water, her black hair tumbling in the manner of a schoolgirl about her long pale neck and rigid shoulders, and then dropping down her straight back. She had a remarkably sweet breast, high and firm; her waist was very small; her hips swelled under her dress with grace and smoothness. Robert thought that never had he seen a girl so extraordinarily lovely. He saw the glint of fierce blue between her black lashes, intent, as aware as an animal's, and as unmoved, but watchful and full of enmity.

"I've ordered whiskey and soda for you, Jenny," said Harald in a very gentle voice, almost pleading. "I'm glad you can join us."

She gave no indication that she had heard him. Her sullen expression did not change. Why, she hates him! thought Robert. Then he had another thought: No, it was Jonathan whom she hated. She had seen him, and Robert, in the grove of trees after all. In that unpolluted air a good eye could detect anybody across even a mile of water. Robert became uncomfortable. As he stared at the girl like a boy he felt his nape tingle and the backs of his broad pink hands. His eye dropped to her bare throat; light lay in its hollow like a tiny pool of quivering water. The tingling increased in his flesh, and he did not know what it was. His eyes dropped even farther to her breast and could not turn away. He did not know that Jonathan was watching him with amusement. He was now staring at Jenny's round white arms, bare from the strong elbows.

Albert returned with a silver tray, a bottle of soda water, and a bottle of whiskey. The men began to watch him prepare the drinks, as if he fascinated them. The silent girl apparently was disturbing their peace of mind, though she did not even look at them. Albert took a glass to her and she accepted it in silence, not turning her head.

"Cheers," said Harald, nodding amiably at Robert. "And good health to you, Doctor, and may you be with us a very long time."

"Thank you," said Robert. He paused. "And please call me Bob." He smiled like a shy youth. "No one does in Philadelphia. I'd like to start it in Hambledon."

"Don't encourage it with patients," said Jonathan. "If you insist on getting very friendly with them, which is not the best thing in the world, let them call you Robert—after a long time of probation."

"You mustn't listen to Jon," said Harald, with indulgence. "He's very formal, for all he doesn't wear the conventional frock coat and striped trousers." He became serious. "Everybody will miss him here. But—under the circumstances—I think it is wise to leave—"

Jonathan took a long drink at his glass. "And you'll like it better, too."

"Now, Jon. Why should I?"

Jonathan held the glass halfway to his lips and looked at his brother. But he said nothing. Harald was at ease again. However, Robert, who was usually not aware of what his mother called "currents," felt that something dark and inimical had moved onto the terrace and now stood between the brothers. Jonathan's stare at Harald was cold. Harald seemed not to notice it. He was sipping at his glass contentedly. Robert was drinking also. He had tasted whiskey but once before in his life, as a child, when he had a bellyache and his father had mixed a concoction of honey, whiskey and hot water for him. He hadn't liked the whiskey. He did not like it today. His ears were beginning to ring a little, though the sensation was quite agreeable. He was still vaguely disturbed at the sudden tension that had lurched into the atmosphere. Then he saw that Jenny was looking at him with the lack of interest of a statue. Her eyes stared into his, clouded and aloof, much more blue than the river and much more still. Only the small trembling light in the hollow of her throat was alive.

Yet Robert knew that she was studying him with hard thoroughness. He suddenly wanted her to like him, to know him as harmless. He swallowed, made himself speak through a tight throat. "Do you like gardening, Miss Heger?"

It was as if she either had not heard him or had no intention of replying to him. Then she shrugged and said in a dull tone, "I just work in my father's rose gardens. He planted them himself. But he never lived to see them flower." Her face did not change, nor the indifference in her voice.

"Sad," said Jonathan. Robert's full mouth tightened. Did he have to mock everything so meanly, even a girl's natural grief for her dead father?

Jenny still looked only at Robert. "Sad," she repeated. "He never even saw the house completed. He never lived a single day here." She spoke without emotion. But the light in the hollow of her throat quickened.

Harald said, "Jenny was only a little girl when her father died. They were very fond of each other. Then Myrtle, Jenny's mother, and Jenny, came to live here. It's a happy place."

"A very happy place," said Jonathan. "Felicity. Charm. Sweetness. Enchantment." He put his glass down with a thump. "And sentimental."

"Don't be insulting, Jon," said Harald, with mildness. "We like it, Jenny and I. It was old Pete's dream. It's unfortunate for him that he didn't live—"

"But fortunate for you," said Jonathan.

Robert wished, all at once, that he had not accepted the invitation. His discomfort was acute. Then he saw that Jenny, for the first time, had turned her face to Jon. It had changed. Hatred was there, more fierce and relentless than ever, but something else was there too, which was secret and violent. Was it despair? Robert had never been famous for his imagination. He had always accepted things at their face value, never looking beneath the obvious for any ulterior meaning. It had never occurred to him so to look. But now he was fascinated by the girl's expression. She had become even paler than before, as if in great pain. Her fingers were clenched on her glass, and the tips had whitened with pressure.

Jonathan was indolently studying the water again, as if forgetting everyone on the terrace. Harald said to Robert, "You mustn't mind his nasty remarks, Bob. He's always making them. There's nothing personal in them, I assure you."

"Always personal," said Jonathan. "Come off it, Harald. I'm a gentleman. I never insult anyone except intentionally."

Swine, thought Harald, still determinedly smiling. He was all serenity and indulgence. He said, "How's Mother today?"

"Do you care? However, she's as well as possible."

Jenny regarded her glass intently. "Hasn't she improved? It's been a month since I last saw her. I thought she didn't look well."

"Heart," said Harald with sympathy to Robert. "Not very serious, but disabling sometimes. That was the trouble with Myrtle, too. She had to take digitalis regularly."

"I'm sorry," said Robert, with a feeling of helplessness.

Jonathan replied to Jenny. "She isn't very well. She's had a lot to bear."

"Let's forget morbid things," said Harald, rising. "I hear the lunch bell. Jenny?"

The girl rose swiftly, her head high and stiff, and swept by them into the house. "Bob?" said Harald, and Robert followed her. She was already disappearing through a wide door which had opened into the hall, and there was startling sunlight in its dimness.

The dining room was very large, with a high peaked roof of timbers. The walls were covered with rich rose damask, and the same rose color hung at tall thin windows, which had a view of the river. Here the furniture was definitely old, and Spanish, dark and heavy, the chairs carved, the seats cushioned in deep red velvet. An Aubusson rug of obvious authenticity lay on the floor in tones of buff and soft blue. The long refectory table had been set with a delicate lace cloth, crystal and gleaming silver. A huge fireplace, rough and of white granite, stood at a farther wall, with copper utensils on the flagged hearth. It was a cold and forbidding room for all its taste and luxury. Jenny was already seated, remote and silent again, not lifting her eyes.

Harald sat genially at the head of the table, and Jenny at the foot where her mother had sat. Robert sat at Harald's right hand, Jonathan opposite. "This room," said Jonathan, "would make an excellent mortuary."

"Oh, come on," said Harald. "You've said that a hundred times. Do you think Jenny likes to hear what you think of her father's house?"

Jonathan yawned. He looked at the immense buffet, dark with age, and surmounted by wrought-iron candlesticks. "Still a mortuary," he said. "Why the hell don't you turn this damned place over to the town as a museum?"

"It's Jenny's home. She might object." Harald was lightly amused.

He doesn't like this place, either! thought Robert, astonished.

"Jenny," said Jonathan, "would you object?"

She did not answer. "Now, Jenny," said Harald, "be nice and answer your dear Uncle Jon."

The girl still did not answer. Again Robert wished he had not come. The strange hostility had followed them here.

"Do answer your dear Uncle Jon," said Jonathan.

The girl jumped to her feet. There were tears in her eyes. "I'll have a tray. In my room," she said, and before the men could rise, she had run out.

"See what you've done. Again," said Harald, but without animosity. He smiled apologetically at Robert. "I don't know what's the matter with those two. Jon is always annoying poor Jenny, and baiting her, and she can't stand him. You'd think they'd control themselves, wouldn't you? Especially seeing we have you as a guest."

"Stop being the perfect host," said Jonathan, not in the least disturbed by Jenny's wild rush from the dining room.

Swine, thought Harald again. He can't behave for a minute. I hope to God he gets out soon. He said with serenity to Robert, "I see we have mock turtle soup today, and a nice fresh fish. I hope you enjoy it. Wine?"

The food was wonderfully seasoned and served. Robert usually had a healthy appetite, and he had been hungry. He was no longer hungry; he had the strongest urge to leave this place, and the company of brothers who so evidently hated each other. He was shocked. He had never seen fraternal hatred before; he had not really thought it existed. He did not wonder what had caused it. It was enough for him that it existed, and he was deeply shaken. It was against nature!

"You aren't eating," said Jonathan, and for the first time Robert heard genuine kindness in that deep voice.

Robert looked at him, and was startled and shaken again. It was as if Jonathan were pitying him! Robert was suddenly and confusedly angry.

CHAPTER FOUR

Harald pleasantly insisted on showing Robert part of the house after a lunch which had seemed disastrous to him. "And don't forget your studio," Jonathan suggested. "The studio, by all means." Harald was not perturbed. "What a joker," he said, with the utmost amiability. He took Robert's arm.

The vast drawing room was in the tower wing, and it had been made oval accordingly. The ceiling was beamed in mahogany, the stone floor covered with Oriental rugs like dimmed jewels, the walls lined in deep green silk damask in a fleur-de-lys pattern, the casement windows hung with tapestry draperies. Here was another big fireplace of whitish granite, but larger, the background bricks heavily coated with soot. In this heavy grandeur the French furniture appeared frivolous: small gilt chairs, little gilt and velvet settees, round marble tables with gilt legs, sofas in bright blue damask and satin, crystal-and-gold lamps, pedestals holding Dresden china figurines of shepherds and shepherdesses in pastel colors, old paintings of eighteenth-century wigged gentlemen and pre-French Revolution ladies with white hair and bared bosoms, ornate and massive mirrors, the frames in intricate gilt design, little buhl cabinets filled with *objets d'art,* and footstools in tapestry and velvet. Apparently some designer had wished to lighten the weight of the room, but even Robert, who knew nothing of balance and proportion and suitability, felt the furniture made the room absurd. He could not explain why. He looked at the windows and again saw the blue of the water, the opposite shore and the purpling mountains.

"Silly, isn't it?" asked Jonathan. Harald only smiled. Robert said, "It is a very nice room." Jonathan chuckled. Robert again had the impression that both brothers were laughing together this time, and this made him feel uneasy.

"Now, what would you have on this island instead?" Harald asked his brother with good humor.

"I've told you before. A sturdy large farmhouse of fieldstone, or, at the most pretentious, a Georgian house. Poor old Pete and his delusions of grandeur! A peasant dreaming of a palace."

"There's nothing wrong with dreams," said Harald. "How can a man live without a dream of something greater than himself?"

"You manage fine. You always did," said Jonathan.

"You're so subtle," replied Harald. "I don't think you yourself know what you're saying most of the time."

There was the breakfast room, round and cheerful, with Amish furniture in birch and maple, which Robert liked at once, and the morning room, as Harald called it with a curious wide-eyed expression, all dark oak and bright chintz, and the library, thin, narrow, long and gloomy, lined with books which obviously no one ever read, and whose leather covers had been chosen only for their color value. The leather furniture in black, dark blue and crimson was ponderous and forbidding, and there was a dank and leathery smell here, as of disuse. Great dull portraits were hung on what wall space remained, bearded Victorian gentlemen and prim ladies. "Old Pete's illustrious ancestors," said Jonathan.

"Don't gibe," said Harald. "If Pete invented ancestors, it did them no harm, nor him, either. He wouldn't be the first in America."

Robert was very weary not only of the castle, which did not seem to him to be as charming as at first, but of the wrangling brothers. There was an undertone in their objective insults which vaguely alarmed him, for though the overtone was light, the one below was vicious. Harald, at least, was tolerant and had a sense of humor, Robert thought. It was Jonathan who was the most offensive, determined to be insulting and even crude. It's strange, thought Robert, I never considered him to be deliberately obnoxious and uncouth and cruel before. That poor girl! If he does, indeed, despise her as he admitted to me, ordinary good manners should have kept him from baiting her.

"Now the studio!" said Jonathan, in a voice ringing with false enthusiasm. "The heart of the castle, the real reason for its being!"

"Oh, shut up," said Harald, smiling broadly. "Bob wouldn't be interested in my daubs." But Robert, who was liking him more and more in contrast to Jonathan, whom he was liking less and less, said, "I don't know much about art—".

"But you know what you like," said Jonathan with a straight face. Robert flushed. Harald took his arm again, as if in amused consolation. "I tell you again, Bob, you mustn't listen to him. Just a rough, unpolished diamond, our dear Jon. Do you really want to see my studio? It's on the second floor with a good north light."

He led the way up the dark and uncarpeted oaken staircase with its somber window of stained glass. Here the dankness of the air appeared concentrated and Robert was conscious of an odd feeling of oppression again. The narrow hall above was lined with heavy oaken doors, carved and cold, and the floor was covered with a narrow Oriental runner. Harald opened one door on a chill and sunless northern light, and they entered a large and bare room, the wooden walls stacked with canvases, the curtainless big window looking out on a river which appeared too cool, too broad, and empty. Some of the paintings were already hung on the walls; one large canvas was on an easel. The room smelled of paint and turpentine and wood and dust, and brackish water.

Robert saw at once that not a single unfinished or finished painting was like anything he had remotely seen before, for none contained anything recognizable. There were whirling whorls of violent color, splashes of red with magenta and blue, black lines in geometric designs, twisting spirals in opposed hues, flat lengths of color that led to no conclusions. He was bewildered.

"Look at this," said Jonathan, drawing his attention to the wildest hung canvas of them all. Robert dubiously approached. There was something like a scarlet sun burning in the very center, but the rays and crooked lines and whirls were violet, green, purple, pink, blue, black, yellow, and every shade in between. On the left-hand upper corner there was a splotch of enameled white dotted with staring black.

"Magnificent, isn't it?" asked Jonathan, with an air of tremendous admiration.

"I'm not familiar with art in this form," said Robert, trying to find some meaning in this furious and incoherent mass. "Just New York Metropolitan, I'm afraid."

"You're provincial," said Jonathan. "Now, I'll tell you what this is. It's Harald's impression of the war, in which he wasn't engaged, he being in Paris at the time, while I was sweltering away in those damned Cuban jungles and getting malaria."

"It does look like a jungle," said Robert, who had never seen a jungle.

"It isn't a jungle," said Harald without annoyance. "Jon's at it again. It's my impression of American towns."

Surely he was joking, thought Robert. Then he saw that Harald wasn't joking at all.

"My impression of undercurrents," said Harald, "which imply vehemence and vindictiveness, bursts of witless energy, a stagnant sun which rises and falls on nothing, really, half-concealed animosities and prejudices, dirty little sins, avidity without an object—in short, almost any small American city."

"You do," said Jonathan, tilting his head as if to study the canvas more critically, "give an impression of stench. Don't you think so, Bob?"

"I thought you liked Hambledon," said poor Robert to Harald.

"Oh, I do, I really do. But that doesn't prevent me from seeing it clear and seeing it whole."

"Oh," said Robert. Jonathan burst out laughing.

"I won a prize for this in New York," said Harald without animosity. "I was offered five hundred dollars for it, but I like it too much to part with it." He pointed to a red ribbon at the foot of the canvas. "I'm proud of it." He smiled in Jonathan's direction. "Of course, provincials don't understand, but this is the coming art-form. You'll see."

"I shouldn't wonder," said Jonathan. "This surely will be the age of the uneducated and mentally illiterate, and artists without art, and men who never learned the discipline of art, or even how to draw. It'll be the age when the color-blind will be doing most of the painting."

"Art must shock, not soothe," said Harald, still good-tempered. "We've passed the age of complacency. And unthinking engagements in directionless activity."

Robert was now convinced that the antagonism between the brothers lay in the fact that Jonathan had served in the recent war but that Harald had deftly evaded it. He himself had wished to serve with Teddy Roosevelt's Rough Riders, but his mother had hysterically objected and his teachers had earnestly assured him that his profession was even more important than patriotism.

"The Republican Party," said Harald, leading the way down the dark staircase, "is too radical for me, too expansionist. I am working on an impression of it. I prefer the Democratic, which is conservative and which despises imperialism."

"But you also love William Jennings Bryan," said Jonathan.

"A man of color. An artist, every inch of him."

Robert did not care for Mr. Bryan. At the bottom of the staircase he said with apology, "All our friends in Philadelphia are Republicans. They seem like sober citizens to me, Harald."

"Sorry, dear boy. They are full of what they call dynamic enthusiasm, which is only exploitation. Look what they did after the Civil War: Indiscreetly set loose a horde of ex-slaves on the population. Radicals. Vulgarians. People without conservative standards, lacking an awareness of the historical imperative."

"He hasn't the slightest damned idea of what he's talking about," said Jonathan. "He doesn't even know who first talked about the 'historical imperative.' Karl Marx said it, in *Das Kapital*. But Marx, as Harald doesn't seem to know, was the worst conservative of them all, and a true hater of what he called 'the masses.' City people! As Socrates said, the most malign enemies of the people are born and bred in the cities. True. The farther you get away from the earth, the more dangerous you become."

"You'd say that, being a farmer," said Harald, in a tone of understanding affection.

They went out into the hot sunshine, and Robert felt relieved. He feared complexities and smothered hostilities, and he had no idea of what the brothers meant.

He had come here, from Philadelphia and Johns Hopkins, believing that he would encounter, in Hambledon, the utmost simplicity, the heart of uninvolved America. But the conversation he had heard between these brothers had alarmed him. Small towns were not, as he thought, simple places filled with good hearts and uncomplex emotions, and bright with honest goodwill. His mother had said condescendingly, "There may be advantages in Hambledon. Fresh air, fresh places, plainness, homeliness. Natural, guileless. You can be a Great Influence, my darling in bringing urban values—in controlled measure—to the unaffected natives." What an ass his mother was! to be sure.

Harald offered to conduct his guests down to the river and the boat, but Jonathan said, "What? In those patent-leather shoes of yours? Don't soil them, pray."

So Harald said his good-byes at the door of the castle, waved his hand with fondness at Robert, and went inside.

"Amiable rascal, isn't he?" asked Jonathan, as he and Robert strolled down the brick path between the lawns.

"I think he's very kind," said Robert with some stiffness.

"He is, he is. That he is," said Jonathan. " 'Smile and smile, and be a villain.' "

Robert had encountered no one who was less a villain than Harald, so he said nothing in reply to this malicious remark. They came upon Jenny, who had put on her brown apron again. She was busy cultivating a rose bed, her rough blue dress hanging over her upturned heels. Jonathan strolled on, but Robert hesitatingly remained behind. The girl ignored his presence. Her hands were brown with warm earth, her knees sunken in soil.

"The roses are very beautiful," said Robert. She turned her head slightly, a trowel in her hand. "Thank you," she said sullenly. Her white forehead was wet with sweat, and her full lips were very red. Her loose hair was in a rich tangle down her back.

"I've enjoyed visiting you," Robert went on. Now she frankly stared at him.

"Why?"

"Well. Everything is so charming." She seemed to muse on his red-gold mustache.

"Is it?" she asked with abruptness, and went back to her cultivating.

Jonathan impatiently whistled to him and Robert started. He had been staring at Jenny's beautiful young body and feeling that tingling again. "Coming," he called. Then he saw that Jenny's hands had stopped their vigorous movement and that she was gazing at Jonathan with that look of despair, or something else, that Robert had noticed before. Disturbed again, Robert went on and joined Jonathan.

Something was very strange here, he concluded. He did not like it.

They rowed in silence across the river. Robert was conscious all the time of Jonathan's harsh study of him. Finally Robert said, "I knew we wouldn't be welcome." He was resentful.

"Of course we were welcome. Harald loves company. He loves everybody. He says so himself."

"There's nothing wrong with liking people," said Robert, pulling strongly on the oars.

"I never did." .

"Then, how could you become a physician and a surgeon?"

Jonathan laughed. "I can still feel pity. Sometimes." He stood up in the rocking boat. "Here. Let me take the oars for the last length."

When they reached the shore, Jonathan released his horses, which he had tethered near a tiny bubbling spring in the grove of birches.

"Why don't you join my mother and me for tea, Bob?"

The sun was already dropping to the west, and the heat was intense. The river was now pure bright gold.

"Thank you, but no," said Robert. "I—I have a lot of things to do. Before I joined you today, I had a telegram from my mother. She is coming here four days earlier. I—I have arrangements to make. She wants a suite in the hotel."

Jonathan's black brows drew down over his dark eyes. He

shrugged. "Very well. Another day. My mother likes you, Bob."

Do you? thought Robert. He got in the phaeton with Jonathan and they drove off briskly.

Jenny Heger continued to cultivate her father's roses after the guests had left. But now there were tears on her cheeks, which she childishly wiped away with the back of her hands, leaving smudges on her skin.

After a while she felt strong hands on her shoulders, and then fingers moving softly through the hot tangle of her black hair. She did not lift her head. She said, "I warned you not to touch me. One of these days you'll make me kill you."

"Sweet Jenny," said Harald. "You're like a young, unbroken colt."

"Take your hands away from me!"

Harald stood up, sighing. "I love you, Jenny. I want to marry you. What's so offensive about that?"

"I will really kill you," said Jenny. She sat back on her heels and regarded him with hatred, her blue eyes one savage blaze.

"I will surely kill you," she repeated. She looked at him with all the power of her strong young body and spirit, and after a moment he strolled off.

CHAPTER FIVE

The warm June weather had suddenly disappeared. Now the sky was gray and misty and the air chill and damp. The mountains were lost in the white fog and moisture dripped from trees and shrubbery and eaves, though it was not raining.

Jonathan Ferrier and his mother, Marjorie Ferrier, sat in the breakfast room of their sturdy red brick house with the white shutters and doors and trimmings of brass, brightly shined. The casement windows were shut tightly, the blue draperies partly drawn, the gas chandelier lit in this early morning, and a brisk little fire rustling on the white brick hearth. It was pleasant here and fragrant with potpourri and wax and coffee and burning wood, the room octagonal in shape, the walls palely painted, the furniture of light mahogany.

Marjorie Ferrier, fifty-five years old, was tall and slender, having retained her girlhood figure and grace. She wore a well-fitting shirtwaist of white lawn and lace, the high neck boned, and a slim, long black skirt of soft silk. Her tall pompadour was black, with ribbons of gray through it, and there were small pearls at her ears. In appearance, she greatly resembled her son, Jonathan, for her complexion was dark, her face thin and planed, her mouth austere, her nose sharp and somewhat long, her black brows straight. But her eyes were brilliantly hazel, and large, like her son, Harald's, with thick short lashes. It was from his mother, the former Miss Farmington, that Jonathan had inherited his "foreign" look, and not from his father, who was of French descent. Harald resembled his father, who had been more Anglo-Saxon in appearance than his truly Anglo-Saxon wife.

Mrs. Ferrier was a handsome woman, elegant and restrained, and only the faint pallor about her lips suggested that she was not in the best of health. She never spoke of illness or disability, for she was a lady. She rarely descended to the personal, for she was a woman of reticences. Neither of her sons knew her well at all, and Jonathan the least. It was her nature to preserve her privacy even from her children, and though she had never punished them herself, she had, in their childhood, only to give them a stern glance to quell them. In many ways they feared her. They did not know that she loved them dearly.

It was one of her aphorisms that a man was truly the head of the household. Since her husband's death Jonathan had become that head. Gentlemen frequently read their newspapers or periodicals at the breakfast table, so she was not offended that Jonathan was reading. She was content to fill his coffee cup from her polished silver coffeepot, to touch the bell under her chair with her foot to summon fresh hot toast.

"Hah!" exclaimed Jonathan. "Here's our nice fat Mr. Taft calling the Filipinos 'our little brown brothers!' That should make them happy, considering they have proud Spanish blood in them!" He chuckled. "And here's a parody of that, by an anonymous American soldier: 'He may be a brother of Big Bill Taft—but he ain't no brother of mine!' What nauseating condescensions politicians can spout!"

"There do seem to be a lot of troubles going on," said Marjorie Ferrier in a mild tone. "Well, the Boer War is over, at any rate."

"Remember what *Life* said about that war? 'A small boy with diamonds is no match for a large burglar with experience.' "

"I never cared for the Boers," said Marjorie, refilling Jonathan's cup.

"No, I suppose you didn't. You are one of the few admirers of the resounding British Empire."

"Oh, Jon, come! The British Empire is the balance wheel in the world. Don't you remember that cartoon in that London newspaper, the *Times,* I think, last year, of Russia and the United States jointly seizing a globe of the world, with Britain reduced to a tiny figurine beneath it? Oh, dear, I hope not! Not so long as Britain is strong, at any rate." Her voice had Jonathan's deep timbre, but was lighter and gentler.

Jonathan put down his newspaper and then looked at it gloomily. "There was an earlier cartoon; I saw a reproduction of it. First published in the *New York Herald,* I think, 1857. Thomas Nast? Wonderful cartoonist. He depicted, then, forty-four years ago, that old bearded Ivan and America would one day be struggling to divide the world between them."

"Absurd," said Marjorie. She rang for more hot toast. "Why should America have imperialistic ambitions? Absurd. And that barbarous Russia, with her Czars, has enough trouble subduing her own people and keeping them from revolt. She is a very mysterious Oriental nation, isn't she? Why in the world should America ever come into contact with her, except perhaps in trade, and we do very little of that? There's no point of real contact between our country and Russia."

"You never can tell about the future," said Jonathan. His mother laughed a little.

"We are a big nation," said Marjorie, "and we haven't even begun to develop it. We still have Territories which are not yet States. It will take centuries, really, to fill America from coast to coast. We have quite enough to do without any foreign ambitions or any alliances with anyone!"

"You never can tell," repeated Jonathan. "What makes you think we won't have 'ambitions,' say in twenty-five or fifty years? If we don't, we'll be unique in the history of the world, and of mankind."

"We are unique," said Marjorie in a tranquil tone. "We had no ambitions, not even in the last war. We'll be giving Cuba her freedom soon."

Jonathan thoughtfully sipped at his fresh coffee. "Unique," he repeated. He shook his head. "No, we're not. We began as ancient Rome began. We'll probably end as she did, too, in a bloody despotism, with dictators, and perhaps Caesars, finally."

"How morbid you are this morning," said Marjorie. "But, then, you were always a solemn little boy, too." She smiled at him fondly, a smile he did not see.

"There's one thing you can always be certain of," said Jonathan, "that it's very unwise not to underestimate the goodwill of mankind. We haven't honestly taken one step forward to true manhood in five thousand years. We're the same old murdering bas—" He stopped. But Marjorie only smiled.

"Not America," she said. "The Spanish-American War wasn't really a war in the full sense. We've been at peace since 1865, over thirty-five years. We'll never have the wars Europeans have, thank God."

"Don't be too sure. We'll begin to feel our oats. It's human nature."

"But, we have two large oceans protecting and isolating us, and again, thank God."

"Oceans can shrink. The Greeks and the Egyptians found that out, and so did Egypt and Palestine, when Rome began to stretch her muscles and look around for new worlds to conquer and exploit."

Marjorie gave him the jam pot. "Jon, dear, you really are morbid. You haven't any faith in your own country. Did I tell you that Jenny is having tea with me today?"

"Dear, sweet Jenny," said Jonathan, and made an ugly grimace.

"Now, Jon. I do hope Harald will bring her. It's such a nasty day, and it's a long row across the river."

"Darling Harald," said Jonathan. "How's the scandal running in the town lately?"

Marjorie was distressed. "Isn't it horrible? Such evil-minded people."

"You can't blame them, when it comes to our Harald."

"Jon, I do wish you'd stop your everlasting sneering at your brother."

He looked at her sharply. "I forgot. He was always your pet, wasn't he?"

No, thought Marjorie, with deep sadness. She said, "Harald doesn't have a very strong character. I thought, when he married, he'd choose a firm-minded girl, who would direct him and guide him. But he married Myrtle."

"For her money."

"Poor Myrtle. We mustn't vilify the dead."

"Oh, certainly not. I wasn't vilifying Mrytle, Mother. I was vilifying Harald, if that's possible. A 'firm-minded girl'? Like Jenny, for instance."

His mother looked at him strangely. It seemed incredible to her that Jonathan was so blind, he who was always astute and perceptive. "Jenny," she said, in her gentlest voice, "is a wonderful girl. I love her dearly. You are so harsh about her. You are quite wrong, and so is the town."

"I know. An untouched lily. Never mind." He stood up.

"Where are you going this unpleasant morning, dear?"

"To try to badger that old—I mean, old Louis Hedler into accepting Bob Morgan on the staff of St. Hilda's." He paused. "I couldn't induce you to part with twenty-five thousand dollars, could I, to match my own twenty-five thousand dollars, for a new nurses' wing?"

Marjorie raised her black brows. "That's a large bribe," she remarked. "For a young man you hardly know."

"But you'll remember that you were considering that—a year ago." He looked at her, and they both remembered indeed that Marjorie and he were going to give that to the expensive private hospital—until the trial.

"Yes," said Marjorie.

"You'll let me mention that, then? They really need that wing, you know."

Marjorie sighed. She played with the handle of the cup. Then she said, "Nothing, I suppose, will change your mind, Jonathan?"

"Nothing."

She said, "I want you to know this, dear. If you want me, I'll go with you everywhere you go."

"And leave sweet Jenny and darling Harald? Mother!"

The pallor about her mouth increased. It was utterly beyond her training to reach out her hand impulsively, take her son's, draw him to her and kiss him, and let him know how dear he was to her. So she remained silent. After a moment or two she said, "Very well. I will keep the promise I made. But is it necessary?"

"Yes. That's why I brought the matter up. Old Hedler's too close to Martin Eaton. Even if Eaton is still recovering from his stroke and just learning to walk again."

He'll never forget, thought Marjorie, and never forgive. He was always a relentless little boy. She said, "How cruel of them. Jonathan, does Dr. Morgan deserve the effort you are making in his behalf?"

"I think so. I hope so. By the way, his mother's arriving today. He never told me much about her, but I gather she's a —well—let me put it this way: a vulgar, pretentious, arch sort of woman. Yet his father was a gentleman. I hope to be able to rescue Bob from her, eventually, and get him married off to the firm-minded character you were referring to. A lady, however. On the other hand, maybe he needs a soft girl to bring out his latent virility."

He bent stiffly and kissed his mother's forehead, and she gave him a cool kiss on the cheek. She watched him go. There was a pain in her which did not rise from her heart. She thought of Mavis Eaton, Jonathan's dead young wife, and her pale mouth parted in fresh suffering. She had never like Mavis, the vital, zesty, tantalizing, Laughing Girl. Pretty blond Mavis, so gleeful of voice, so alive and vivid, so stupid and cuddling and cruel! How Jonathan had adored her. How strange it was for Jonathan, who was so perceptive, not to have known all about Mavis at once, even when she was a child. But men were peculiar when it came to women. The dullest woman could deceive the most intelligent man. Marjorie had subtly expressed her disapproval to Jonathan a thousand times before the wedding but had aroused only his anger and indignation. She had attended the wedding, calm, serene, smiling, while she had cried inwardly and with foreboding. She had accepted Mavis into her house, after the honeymoon, and had behaved toward the girl with kindness and affection. It had been no use at all.

Marjorie shuddered. She pressed her hands hard over her eyes, leaned her elbows on the table and dropped her face into her hands. She dared not say a word. One word would bring disaster, and it must never be spoken.

"Well, now," said Dr. Hedler, "the diploma-mill hack," as Jonathan called him. "That's a magnificent offer, my boy, really magnificent! So good of you and charming Marjorie. But she was always generous. I knew her in Philadelphia, you know, and her family."

"Yes, I know. Nearly everyone knew my mother 'in Philadelphia,' to hear them tell it," said Jonathan. He could not help it; he said, "I'm sorry about your sister-in-law, by the way."

The soft, fat, elderly face across from him changed, and the bulging brown eyes pointed in a hard fashion at Jonathan. But Dr. Hedler sighed and said, "Yes. Too bad. But there was no way of finding out that she had cancer before the operation. We could only sew her up and lie to her."

Jonathan had been regretting his remark, a brutal one, but now he knew that he was, in fact, applying a little blackmail, and that he was dangerous to Dr. Hedler. Good. For Dr. Hedler knew that Jonathan had made the diagnosis of possible carcinoma over a year ago and been ignored, and among the more urbanely ridiculing had been Dr. Hedler himself. Dr. Hedler might be Chief-of-Staff at St. Hilda's, but everyone was aware of his "medical" background, especially the younger physicians, and everyone, even his enemies, knew that Dr. Ferrier was a famous surgeon and diagnostician, and that his diagnosis had been verified in the operating room. Yes, I'm a dangerous type, thought Jonathan, with pleasure.

They were sitting in the dignified but luxurious Chief-of-Staff's office, all paneled wood, heavy crimson velvet draperies, burning fire in a black marble fireplace, rich Brussels rug, and handsome pictures and excellent dark mahogany furniture. It had begun to rain, a warm murmurous rain mysteriously full of promise. It ran down the tall windows in silvery rivulets.

"I have a feeling about cancer," said Jonathan, very grave. "About six people out of ten thousand die of it, in one form or another. That's comparatively few, compared with the other killers, such as diarrhea and tuberculosis. And pneumonia and influenza and diphtheria. These are our present murderers, while cancer is rare in comparison. It won't always be that way. Twenty years ago one person in ten thousand died of it. In forty or fifty years? As we conquer one disease another takes its place. Balance of nature. But cancer is the foulest disease of all."

"It will always be rare," said Dr. Hedler, with the indulgence of the experienced toward the more youthful and inexperienced. "And it only affects the very old in most cases, though Georgia isn't old, I admit. However, she isn't very young either. Do you know that she's only the tenth case I have seen in all my long years of practice?"

I wouldn't doubt it for a moment, thought Jon without charity. But he only nodded his head.

"I've heard of only one case of leukemia," said Dr. Hedler.

"I've had about eight," said Jonathan. "I think that form of cancer is increasing, too."

Dr. Hedler smiled and shook his head. "I doubt it. Well. Let us look again at young Dr. Morgan's credentials. Um." He put on his pince-nez. "Interned at Johns Hopkins. That's very nice." He sighed with a sound of soft suet moving. "I did take it up before with Martin Eaton, you know."

"And he turned down his thumb."

Dr. Hedler was pained. "Jon, he's a very reasonable man, and he did found St. Hilda's, and it's his pride and joy. Gave a quarter of a million dollars—a huge sum! I showed him Dr. Morgan's credentials. He, er, said the staff is filled."

"Closed staff. Curse of hospitals," said Jonathan with contempt. "We need all the physicians and surgeons we can get for Hambledon and the surrounding territory. Keep the newcomers out and off the staff, and we won't be able to meet the demand. And the hospitals we have will deteriorate."

"We have to protect the income of the staff, Jon."

"Protect the staff's income. Let the public be damned. Who said that? Was it old J. P. Morgan, or one of the Vanderbilts? It doesn't matter. The public deserves better treatment from its doctors and its hospitals. What're we here for, anyway?"

"We can't let the new young doctors enthusiastically fill up all our beds! They love that. Gives them a reputation. What of the people who really need beds?"

"We can always intrude our own judgment if a boy gets too ambitious," said Jonathan. "Now, old Martin. He's acting out of spite, and you know it, Louis. I know the other members of the staff will go along with you, if you say so and give Bob Morgan your approval. Old Martin's been domineering you for years; we all know that. Show your independence."

Dr. Hedler turned dark red, but he controlled his fury. "One of these days, my boy, your tongue will hang you." He stopped abruptly. But Jonathan only grinned.

"It almost did once," he said. "We're getting off the subject. Hambledon's growing; so is the whole territory around here. Industry moving in. The medical population has to grow, too, to keep up. Keep denying young doctors a place on the hospital staffs and they'll have to go somewhere else, and Hambledon's the loser. We're lucky to have a fellow like Bob Morgan applying. Let's get some fresh air in this town."

He waited. Dr. Hedler did not speak. "Come on, Louis," said Jonathan, with impatience. "Old Martin will never be able to practice again, and you know it. If you go over his head, and you have the right to, as Chief-of-Staff, there'll be some indignant growling, and then it will be forgotten. Besides, I'm leaving, as you know damned well. Who are you privately considering to replace me?"

Before he could stop himself, Dr. Hedler said, "Martin has someone in mind. He will finish his internship in December."

"What hospital?"

But Dr. Hedler merely shook his head. He looked again at the credentials. Jon said, "Fifty thousand dollars. Where are you going to get that much so soon? Off the street?"

Dr. Hedler silently stared down at the credentials. "Look here," said Jonathan, "take Bob Morgan. Or I'll stay here on the staff and where will Martin's precious protégé be then? I'll tell you something: If I stay, old Martin's going to blow out another cerebral artery. Not that that wouldn't be a good idea in the long run, or maybe even the short run. You'll be doing him a real favor, Louis, if you take my choice."

"When you put it that way— Yes, I can see what you mean. Give me another opportunity to talk with him, Jon. And, as you said, fifty thousand dollars is a lot of money, and we need the nurses' wing practically at once." Dr. Hedler became genial. "Let me thank you, Jon. And Marjorie."

So, it's all right, thought Jon. Blackmail, bribe, a chance for revenge. Who can resist all these? Not old Louis!

"No, no, no flowers," said Robert Morgan to the hotel manager who had just brought in a mighty vase of highly scented field roses, as red as blood and furious with life. "My mother is sensitive to all flowers. But thank you, anyway." He looked longingly at the roses. They reminded him of Jenny Heger. He added, "I'd like them in my own room, though." He would never see roses again without thinking of Jenny. The very thought of her was poignant to him.

He was in the best suite the modest hotel could offer. His mother would be pleased. It had a large sitting and dressing room, all clean, fresh, if undistinguished furniture, brown velvet draperies, red Turkey rug, polished windows. He peeped into the bedroom and saw the big brass bed with its brown velvet counterpane and bolster, its good decorated china and sturdy commode, its thick towels and fine linen hand-towels. Not splendid but more than adequate.

"We'll be happy to welcome Mrs. Morgan, Doctor," said the hotel manager. "Tell her, in my name, that the hotel services are hers to command!"

And she'll certainly command them, thought Robert, and was at once ashamed.

"You haven't found a suitable house yet, Doctor?"

"Not yet. But I have four in mind, and when my mother comes, we'll choose among them."

"We'll be sorry to lose you, Doctor." The door closed after the manager. Robert returned to his own room. It seemed uncommonly small and bare to him, in the dull dusk of the rainy day. He looked at his watch. His mother would arrive at the station in one hour. He must look for a hack at once; they had a way of being invisible when it rained. He put on his hat—and his gloves—and ran lightly to the elevator. He had remembered to put his white silk handkerchief in his breast pocket and to wear the infernal frock coat and striped trousers which his mother felt to be the only uniform for a doctor. He even took his cane with him. He looked at himself in the elevator mirror as he went creakingly down. He had trimmed his mustache very closely this morning. This would definitely displease dear Mama, who would have preferred him with a full red beard. Proper beard for a doctor.

Only an hour ago Jonathan Ferrier had had him called to the hotel telephone to tell him that he was practically certain that he, Bob Morgan, would be named to the staff of St. Hilda's. And, very soon, to the staff of the Friends' Hospital. "A matter of a few days," said Jonathan. "I thought you should know."

"It's very kind of you," said Robert.

You don't know how damned and expensively kind it was! thought Jonathan, a little annoyed that the young doctor should take it all so casually. He said, "You're very lucky."

Robert was puzzled. He said, "Well, I was always told I was born under a lucky star! Hello?" But Jonathan had hung up the receiver. Robert stared at the telephone. These small towns! Central was always disconnecting people. He did not think of that call as he went down the elevator. It had never occurred to him that he would not be accepted on the staff of the hospitals. It did not occur to him now. Had Jonathan had another but unsaid reason to call him? What? Robert had found himself thinking of Jenny Heger again. It was odd that she came into his mind so regularly and that he could see her beautiful face so clearly, and her amazing blue eyes, and the way she moved, and her tumble of black and curling hair. It was unpardonable of Jon Ferrier to bait her so cruelly and despise her so openly. Robert forgot all the gossip he had heard in Hambledon about Jenny and Harald Ferrier. He could only resent Jonathan.

Jonathan spent the dingy cool afternoon in his offices, in the long preparation for his departure from Hambledon forever.

His mother had built the premises for him as a gift when he had set up practice ten years ago. Like the house where he had been born, and his father and grandfather before him, it was built of red brick with white and brass trimmings, a single-story structure nearly three acres from the house, with a dark slate roof. It was not that Marjorie overly disliked the thought of her son having his offices in the large house where they lived, for now there were but two in the family, with two servants, and there were many rooms which could have been utilized. But she knew that Jonathan was a "private" person like herself, resenting propinquity which they both considered vulgar and not dignified and a little nonhuman. "The precious thing which distinguishes man from the lower animals," she would say, "is his love for privacy, for aloneness, his liking for occasional solitude away from his bellowing fellows. It is bestial to huddle, to peer into each other's pots, to mind another's business, to interfere 'lovingly' in his life." She had also thought, with distaste and revulsion, of the invasion of her house by troops of patients, even if it were in a separate wing. So, to Jonathan's gratification, she had built this suite of offices which faced the blank wall of the distant house. There was also a white picket fence between, with a gate that was usually locked. The grounds were beautifully landscaped, however, with softly rolling lawns and shrubs and flower beds and old trees. But many of the older doctors were astonished, for it was still the custom to have one's offices attached to one's residence. Only the poorer, and younger, doctors were establishing offices in public buildings and even over shops. When they would become more affluent, they would buy houses and have their offices there.

Jonathan's offices consisted of a small but well-appointed pharmacy, where he concocted his own remedies and improved on those already available, a comfortable waiting room, a consultation room finely paneled and furnished and with a gas log fire, a small office for his bookkeeper-typist (the spinster and "advanced" daughter of a minister), a file room, and two examination rooms, also heated by gas. Marjorie had had electricity installed, though she disliked it for her own house, considering it too stark. There was a telephone directly connected with the house, and a public one.

The walls of Jonathan's consultation room were mostly lined with his medical books and with cabinets for medical journals. It was a handsome room, warm and large and quiet. Here he had spent the eight happiest years of his life. Here he sat today, at his great walnut desk, another gift of his mother, going through the drawers and slowly emptying them. All at once, he was tremendously depressed. He got up and strolled through the suite, restlessly. The minister's daughter was no longer there; he had discharged her several months ago, for he now rarely practiced and accepted few patients. Everything was silent except for the dripping of the rain and gusts of late spring winds, and the small hiss of the gas fires. The suite already felt deserted and abandoned. Jon paused in the waiting room, which his mother had furnished pleasantly with Mission and rattan furniture and a bright overhead electric chandelier of tasteful proportions. His patients would not gather here any longer; they would be young Bob's patients very shortly. He went into the room where his bookkeeper had sat; the typewriter was covered, the little desk and chair empty. The lady would return, she had promised, under "the new doctor." He slowly entered the pharmacy and saw his jars and bottles and boxes of pills and powders and liquid, all bright and shining under the light, and also waiting. Then he went into the examination rooms, so well-equipped with modern tables and white chairs and cabinets full of his precious instruments for minor operations and inspections.

At last he stood in the short hall with the doors and the silence about him. He stood there a long time, thinking. He still had to go over the files of his patients, with special notations for young Bob. The files of people's lives, with all their ailments and their histories, their fears and their impending condemnations to death! He went into the file room and stared at the rank of green steel files, discreetly locked so that no one had access to them except himself. A man's life was his own.

Was it? In less than a few months his, Jonathan's, was no longer his own. It belonged to no one at all, even himself. He was already an exile. Very shortly, this beloved place would be rented by another and he would be forgotten. He would be—where? He shrugged. He did not know. His mother was not aware that he had been considering never practicing again but going abroad to live in quiet and solitude, perhaps in Cornwall, perhaps in Chartres, perhaps in serried and lonely Spain, perhaps in Berlin. There was no place for him in the world he had known; he was not only exiled, but he was self-exiled. He had never had an enormous affection for his fellowman, for he felt that overt affection was an insult to others and a condescension. He did not believe in "warmth," which was something you extended only to a beloved dog or cat, or, in private, to a wife or a husband or a dear child. But he had compassion for all that lived, especially infants, young mothers and the fearful old. Pain and suffering had been abhorrent to him. He found nothing "noble" in agony, nothing to be offered up for the sake of others, nothing in the way of "reparation," as the clergy said. (On this, too, he had parted company with the Church.) To him pain was an insult to humanity; it should not be countenanced; it was a waste of time, which could be employed in the stern business of being a man. True, pain was inseparable from living, but it should be pain and striving of the spirit, as man struggled toward manhood. Physical pain reduced man to an animal, and Jonathan had fought such pain with grim intensity and disgust, and had usually conquered it. Older doctors had sometimes sneered at him as the "pill-roller." They had considered a certain amount of pain as "salubrious," or a promoter of "humility," though they were careful not to permit a great deal in their own lives or in the lives of members of the family. They distrusted even the new Aspirin, and were annoyed that it could be bought without prescription. But Jon gave it out in full boxes, for a pittance. "What's heroic about a toothache or the pains of rheumatism?" he would say. "Those hypocrites! They don't mind swallowing morphine at the slightest ache they have themselves!" He knew that many physicians were already addicted, and he was outraged that they were permitted in operating rooms. He was working with the

American Medical Association on the dangers of drug addiction, though many of his colleagues still angrily insisted that morphine was "harmless."

A young priest had said to him, "Pain is God's punishment on our fallen race, since the sin of our First Parents."

"And you don't believe in a whiff of ether or chloroform for a woman in childbirth, to relieve her insufferable pangs? Did you ever see a difficult birth, Father? Or a breach presentation? Now, honestly, would you advise operations without anesthetics?"

"Well, no, Jon. Of course I wouldn't. Do you think I'm a Fundamentalist screecher? But woman was condemned to suffer in labor—"

"Maybe ordinary labor. I don't believe in much interference then, except during the last ten minutes or so; it could be dangerous to both mother and child. If you carry your thought on logically, doctors would be outlawed, as they were for the first few hundred years of Christianity, or regarded with contempt as mere vets, and sacrilegious, in the Middle Ages. Even in Britain to this day a doctor is a mere 'Mister.' When Our Lord cured the suffering, He did say, 'Your sins are forgiven you.' But that was in a different context and for a different reason. Surely you know that? We don't believe, any longer, that his 'sin' is the cause of a child being born crippled or blind or defective or diseased. Or cancer a 'judgment' on the anguished, many of them good people who had rarely sinned in their lives. Remember how, in medieval times, a man or even a child who became sick was regarded as a criminal, suffering the condemnation of a supposedly merciful God? Sometimes he was stoned to death. Yes! You know that, Father. What an offense to God that must have been!"

"Yes, Jon, I know. But your ferocious war on pain—which is exemplary—does seem a personal battle to you, a personal insult—"

"That's because I believe in the dignity of man."

He no longer believed in it. He no longer cared what happened to his fellows, because of what they had inflicted on him, because of the derision and hatred even those he had so tirelessly helped had heaped on him. If it had all come from only a few who had not known him at all, even by reputation, he could have forgiven. But it had come from his friends and his own patients, who had eagerly desired—yes, they had *desired!*—to believe the very worst of him. Many still so desired; many were still disappointed.

I was puerile, he thought, staring at the files with rage and bitterness. I expected that some men at least were human. I expected that some had a sense of justice. I actually believed in friendship! What an utter, stupid, disgusting fool I was! No man has a friend. We hate each other instinctively; we love to destroy each other. What other explanation is there for wars, for all the obscene injustice we administer to each other, in full and radiant malice? Nothing delights a man more than causing pain to his brother. Even a rat has better instincts toward his kind.

When he caught himself in occasional acts of kindness, even now, he despised himself. He had vowed, months ago, that never would he lift a hand to help another again. He thought of young Dr. Morgan. Now, why in hell had he bribed and blackmailed to get him appointed to the staffs of those hospitals? Jonathan struck the files angrily with the palm of his hand, in revulsion against himself. He thought of the pain recorded there, and the hopeless hope and despair, and he said aloud, "Good." He had cut his palm a little on the steel and he looked at the drops of blood with anger.

The young priest had said, "You must not desert humanity, Jon."

He had replied, "But humanity first deserted me. I don't care about their pain any longer, Father."

"That is a sin against God. He made you a physician."

"That's why I'm resigning!" He had grinned. But he was resigning because he had lost his compassion—he hoped.

"If man's sinfulness affected all priests that way, Jon, after listening in Confessionals, there would be no clergy."

"I am no priest, Father."

"All physicians, the real ones, are priests, Jon. Once only priests were physicians. You remember that?"

But Jon had not replied. He had left one of the few men who had believed in him.

He was thinking of this now. He felt anger against young Father McNulty, to whom life was very simple. Father McNulty "loved" people. Oh, for God's sake! What was there to "love"? Suddenly he thought of Jenny Heger, the trollop. He turned and went into his office again and sat down at his desk. Aimlessly, he began to clear out the drawers.

He found the small framed photograph of his dead young wife, Mavis. He set it on his desk and stared at the lovely face, framed in its masses of fair hair, at the full soft neck, the full smiling lips, the small but merry eyes, the gentle, sloping shoulders. Eagerness for life shone from the low wide brow, the dimpled chin, the delicate shadow under it. Mavis. Beautiful, laughing Mavis, with the womanly breast, the tiny waist, the swelling hips, the rounded arms and thighs! He took the photograph carefully from the frame and tore it to bits and threw the fragments into his wastebasket. After a moment, he dropped the frame into it, also.

"I'm glad you're dead, Mavis," he said. "I often wanted to kill you."

The house telephone suddenly rang on his desk, and he started, for it had broken the intense and terrible silence. He lifted the receiver.

"Jon?" said his mother. "Wouldn't you like to have a cup of tea with Jenny and me?"

"No, dear."

"I know you're there, brooding. It isn't good for you, Jon."

"It's very good."

"Please come."

"Not while she's there."

Marjorie sighed. "It's getting dusk. Won't you drive Jenny to the bank?"

"No, Mother. I never do. What's the matter with Jim?"

"Nothing. But I don't like you brooding."

"I'm not brooding. I don't brood. I'm just clearing things out."

Marjorie sighed again. "Very well, Jon. But do come home soon. Jenny is about to leave."

"Give her my love." He slammed the receiver back on the telephone. He sat staring at nothing for a long time, while the twilight deepened. A man's whole life. The best years of his life. It had come to nothing at all. It had been destroyed in a single moment, and the years were as if they had never existed. He looked into the dark hollow place which must absorb the rest of his life. He opened another drawer and took a bottle of whiskey from it, and a glass, and began to drink.

Mrs. James Morgan looked about the suite so anxiously prepared for her by her son. "It really isn't very elegant," she said in a discontented voice.

"Mama, it's the very best this town can offer. I know."

She leaned on her two canes and gazed with deeper discontent at everything.

"It's not what I'm accustomed to, in the home."

She turned to Robert. "Tomorrow," she said, "if I am a little better, we must look at the four homes you mentioned, my dear."

He could not help himself. He said, "You mean the houses, Mama."

She frowned. For some reason he was not now intimidated at her frowns. "Homes, dear Robert."

"Mama. A house in which one lives becomes a home to those who live there. But other people's houses are not 'homes.' You don't refer to other people's houses as 'homes,' only houses." He took a deep breath. "To call other people's houses 'homes' is a vulgarism."

"Indeed! Did you learn that silliness in this little town, which wouldn't fit in a corner of Philadelphia?"

"I'm learning a lot of things I never knew before—Mother. And Hambledon may be small, but it is alive."

"I don't think I'm going to like it. Why do you call me 'Mother?' "

"Because you are my mother, and I'm no longer a child."

She stared at him indomitably, but he stared back at her, smiling. "Indeed," she said again. But she was frightened. Was she about to lose her son, as she had lost her husband? The thought was incredible and alarming. But he had become very strange and seemed taller and very male. This was revolting. "I feel faint," she said. Robert helped her to a chair. "I could do with a glass of fresh water," she added. Robert brought her water. He was smiling again. "I am not well," she complained. "All this dampness—"

"Would you like an Aspirin tablet?"

"Robert! I never take drugs! I bear my arthritis like a Christian."

"Pain that can be alleviated should be. It's not valiant to suffer unnecessary pain."

"How you have changed, Robert! In these few short days! I hope that horrible man, Dr. Ferrier, don't corrupt you."

" 'Doesn't' is the word, Mother. 'Don't' is plural, not singular."

"Are you correcting my English now, Robert?" She was very agitated.

"Mother, you are among strangers in Hambledon. In Philadelphia you had friends who overlooked your errors. Forgive me, but it is true."

"My father was an intellectual minister! He didn't believe

that ladies should be overburdened with learning, but he taught me himself."

He didn't teach you much, then, thought the incalcitrant Robert. Then he gentled. "Mother, I'm only trying to help."

"You are impertinent, Robert. You are ungrateful. First, you decline to practice in Philadelphia, where we have old, devoted friends. Then you decide on this miserable little country place and come under the influence of a frightful man —I know it!—who don't, I mean doesn't, have any reputation among respectable people. You bring me here, in this damp town, with my arthritis, and insist on me leaving all my friends—"

"Mother, you needn't stay here if you don't like it. You can always live in Philadelphia."

"Leave you stay here alone? Alone! Among corruptions? You must think I'm an unnatural mother! Robert, how could you have possibly believed that?"

Robert was silent. She said, "Besides, I've already rented our home, for a very good rental. You are all I've got, Robert."

"You have all my aunts in Philadelphia, and my cousins."

"My only child! Thrown to the heathen."

I must be patient, thought Robert. She said, "That murderer! And to think my only child has been influenced by him! It's criminal. He should be driven from the country."

Robert sighed. "He was acquitted, Mother."

"We've come to a pretty pass, in this nation, when criminals can be loosed on the public again to continue their crimes." She put her handkerchief to her dry eyes. "I only know this, Robert: He will never enter the home so long as I am alive."

"I don't think he'll come without an invitation. Mother, wouldn't you like to lie down before dinner?"

She was tempted not because she was really in pain but because bed had always been her retreat and her revenge against her family. But Robert was "strange," and her fright quickened. She must know more of this mystery in order to defend herself. She said, "I am too stimulated by that dreadful journey, and all the soot and the noise. It was my first experience in traveling. I didn't like it. Those vulgar people!"

"It was only four hours, Mother, and you traveled Pullman."

"Four hours of sheer misery, Robert! You don't know what it means to be a delicate female."

Thank God, thought Robert. "Well, it's over now. We can make plans. The house nearest the offices is smaller than the others I looked at, but it's very comfortable. Four nice bedrooms, with a good view. And servants are cheaper than in Philadelphia. There's a nice garden and really pleasant lawns. The price is very reasonable, too. I think you'll like it."

"Only four bedrooms? One for you, Robert, one for me, the other two for servants. Where shall our guests sleep?"

"We can build another bedroom onto the house. There is a lot of land."

"Expensive! What do they want for the home?"

"Only ten thousand dollars."

"Exorbitant! In this little country place!"

"It's in the best section. By the way, Mrs. Ferrier has asked you to tea tomorrow, if you feel well enough." He added, "She is considered the first lady in Hambledon, Mother."

"I shouldn't dream— You said, 'the first lady'? How could that be, with her son a murderer?"

"Mother, the judge and the jury decided he wasn't a murderer! Please remember that. If you call him a murderer here, you can be sued for libel. Well, I must decline the invitation, then?"

"Oh, how my poor head aches! You confuse me, Robert. Decline? Did I say so? How you confuse me!"

"Suppose you think of it tomorrow? You'll know better then how you feel."

"Sleeping in that bed, there." Her thin high voice was full of self-pity. "How can we be sure it don't have vermin—"

"Mother, it's very clean, I assure you. The word is 'doesn't,' not 'don't.' "

He looked down at her. She was a gaunt woman and almost as tall as himself. She had obstinately worn her widow's black weeds over all these years, "as was proper." She was sixty years old, for she had been long a spinster before she had married James Morgan, an impoverished young physician eight years her junior. He had, frankly, married her for her money. Her father had indeed been a minister, but he had inherited a considerable fortune from a bachelor uncle, a scoundrel who had, however, admired the clergy and had hoped that his nephew would redeem him from a possible hell. "It ain't that I believe in hell," he had said to his lawyers. "But you never can tell, can you? Better hedge my bets." Jane Morgan had, in the course of events, inherited her father's money, she being a spinster and her two brothers affluent in their own industrious right. Her father had never expected that "poor Jane" would ever marry, with her long severe face, her cold gray eyes, her wide thin mouth and her dim brown hair. And, worst of all, her stupidity and rigid character. So he had mercifully provided for her future, not dreaming that a young Dr. James Morgan, fresh out of medical school, would ever see her and decide to marry her, long after his own death.

The dim brown hair was thin and white now, and Jane Morgan stubbornly covered it with a cotton and lace cap, as in the days of her Victorian youth. Ladies who did not wear caps in their "homes" were really not ladies. Her long nose had become sharper and whiter and thinner over the years, and beaked down over her grim mouth, which was surrounded by deep lines. Everything about her was rigorous and uncompromising. She had been thirty-four when Robert had been born and had been firmly fixed in her pattern of living and convictions. Sex had been a most horrendous experience for her, and she had been never recovered from the "shame" and indignity of her son's birth. Yet, in the silently feverish and unpliant ways of spinsters she had violently adored her young husband and had almost devoured him.

He had, thought young Robert now, in sympathy, consoled himself somewhat with a gay young widow in Philadelphia and a number of other ladies of happy character, all of them encountered in his examination rooms. In his boyhood Robert had been horrified at this "betrayal" of his mother by that "nastiness" and "unspeakable affront" to her wifehood. Now he congratulated his father and understood, and that, he thought as he looked down on his mother now, was reprehensible of him. He smiled. He doubted that even his minister-grandfather would have condemned poor young James.

Robert said, "I've ordered a nice little dinner for us here in the suite, Mother. Your favorites: chicken broth, lean lamb chops, creamed potatoes, a little buttered turnip, a salad, and some tarts and fruit and cheese. Shall I ring for it now?"

"I don't believe I can take anything, Robert, but a little cinnamon toast and lemon hot tea."

Only a month ago he would have cajoled and persuaded her. But now he said, "Very well. I'll cancel the order and give your own, and I'll go down to the dining room and have my dinner for myself. It would be wrong of me to nauseate you by having my big dinner upstairs."

"Let you eat alone in a public dining room? Robert!"

"I've been eating there almost every night, Mother, and I haven't been seduced yet." Unfortunately, he added to himself.

"Robert! What shameless talk is this? No, I will sacrifice my natural revulsion. Order the dinner, Robert."

"Only one order? For myself?"

She looked up at him sharply. She didn't like that easy tone, that indifferent tone, from a son ordinarily most solicitous. "I will sacrifice myself," she repeated. Robert, smiling under his red-gold mustache, rang for the double dinner. He then excused himself to wash in his own room. He hummed when he went down the corridor. Poor old girl. She was a terrible bore and prig, and, yes, vulgar.

The moment she was certain that her son had left, Mrs. Morgan briskly put aside her canes and moved smartly to the windows to look down on the town. The sidewalks were gleaming with moisture in the dusk. Umbrellas moved in a solid phalanx below, and the gaslights were lit, surrounded by auras of dull and streaming yellow in the rain. But the lamps were scattered, and it was very quiet. Horrid little town. Her Robert would soon tire of it, and then they'd return to civilization, in Philadelphia. Well, she'd see. She'd have tea with that woman tomorrow and let her know that Mrs. Morgan was condescending to her, she the mother of a murderer.

"I really cannot force myself to eat anything," she complained to Robert when the table was laid in her suite and the savory food set before her.

"Oh, that's too bad," said Robert, taking up his soup spoon with enthusiasm. "This is very tasty. Do try a sip."

She ate a very hearty dinner, even more than Robert, and complained and sighed and murmured dolorously all through it. As a thrifty woman she deftly tucked two buttered rolls into her handkerchief for later nibbling. After all, she told herself, she slept badly. And waste was sinful. It had been paid for. It didn't do to encourage gorging in servants, who were allowed leftovers. "Two dollars for this dinner, Robert? Do they think you are a millionaire?"

CHAPTER SIX

"An odious woman, really," said Marjorie Ferrier to her son two days later. "So affected. She spent most of tea-time preening and condescending and bragging genteelly and talking in what she doubtlessly considered a very 'refined' way. How could such a nice gentlemanly boy like young Robert have such a mother?"

"And how could such a nice mother like you have such odious sons?" Jonathan asked her. "It's all inheritance from distant ancestors."

"My sons are not odious," said Marjorie. "Here, dear, do try this English marmalade. You aren't eating very well these days. What a wonderful morning! It's bright and warm again. I think I'll work in the rose garden. Where are you going now, Jon?"

"Taking young Galahad on the rounds, as usual. I want to be sure—"

"Of what, dear?"

"It doesn't matter. Nothing matters any longer."

But everything always mattered too much for you, my son, thought Marjorie with a sigh, as her son gave her a brief kiss and left. She clenched her slight hands on her knees and closed her fine hazel eyes. Would there never be an answer to her prayers? How could she live alone here, in this big house, without Jon? All her dreams had come to nothing. There were no grandchildren, there was no happy laughter anywhere. There was no gay coming here any longer, as once there was, when Mavis was alive and Jon was busy. Jon? She thought about it. When had he stopped smiling that quick dark smile of his? A year after he had married Mavis? Two years? Three? He had stopped within six months.

Oh, God, thought Marjorie, if only Mavis had never been born! If only Jon had never seen her! If only she had died at birth! But life, it seemed, was tragically made up of "if onlys."

She knew it was best for Jonathan to leave Hambledon and never return, but her opinion was not based on his nor those who knew him. There were times when she felt she could not wait for him to go—for every day was a day of danger and impending terror, and pretense.

"This is a fine new rig you have," said Jonathan to Robert Morgan. "Good horse, too. When did you buy it?"

"Yesterday." Robert gave him a sunny smile. "Like it? I do, too. I heard the horse had been sired by one of your own. My mother was upset."

"Why?"

"The expense. She thought I should hire a buggy for a while, instead of buying one. I don't think she's joyful over this town. Besides, Mother is very—well, I suppose you'd call it financially discreet. I told you, you'll remember, that my father didn't have much money of his own; he did a lot of charity work; too much, according to Mother. What we have belongs to Mother. Of course, I'm her only heir, but sometimes it makes things difficult."

"Well, widows have to be providential," said Jonathan.

"I'm hardly a profligate son," said Robert. "I worked in drugstores when I wasn't in school, and mother told all her friends that she didn't consider it very 'nice' but that I was an independent boy and I had *insisted*. The truth is, Mama was always very near with the cash; thought if I didn't have any, I'd not get entangled with females, or something. I had to have more than the two dollars a week she gave me when I was in college—so I worked. Waited on tables and such. A lot of the fellows looked down on me for that, though their parents didn't have half the money Mama has. Dear Mama."

"Where'd you get the money from to buy this outfit, then?"

Robert laughed and proudly held the reins. "I charged it to my mother. She'll get the bill soon. The funny thing about it is that she never asked me how I bought it, acting on the principle that if she did not ask, there'd be no bill and no unpleasantness."

"You'll soon have plenty of money of your own, once

you're established here," said Jonathan. "I've shown you my rates; don't come down on them. They're a little higher than average, but then you're an authentic doctor and not a quack. There's something else I've wanted to talk to you about. When I was a kid, most doctors had only the most elementary medical educations, having merely studied under physicians and gone the rounds with them for two or three years, and reading their medical books. They did a lot of God-awful damage, of course, but a lot of them did a lot of good. They developed, or were born with, a 'smell.' They could smell out illnesses on merely entering a room and could make a prompt and accurate diagnosis on the spot. A sort of sixth sense. Every real doctor has that, even in these days of 'scientific diagnosis,' but it's not held in good repute any longer. The more we begin to rely strictly on laboratory findings, the more dull hacks—though out of good medical schools—we'll find ourselves afflicted with, and any man with well-off parents can aspire to be a physician, whether he's fit for it or not. Just for the prestige. Potential carpenters and blacksmiths in operating rooms.

"Don't take the corners too fast with this horse. I had his dam, too, and she had a way of cutting around. Well. I'm not against full laboratory procedures; I do a lot of it, myself. Stops the guesswork. But we can have too much of it; I've seen some tragic errors when doctors go by the laboratory and not by common sense and careful, personal diagnoses. Of course the hacks couldn't practice medicine any other way if we didn't have laboratories these days, so perhaps many lives are saved. But nothing beats an eye, an ear, and a sense of smell, that sixth sense I've been telling you about."

"And you're afraid I might not have it?"

"We'll see. Beginning today. Even if you don't, and are careful, and lean heavily on the laboratories, you can't do much harm. Now, when I was a boy, we knew a physician in a tall silk hat, stock, chains, and the usual frock coat and striped trousers and spats and a gold-headed cane. Almost illiterate. Big bearded bastard with a voice like an organ chord. He'd 'studied medicine' under another just like himself. Impressive old fart. And yet, I've never met a more acute diagnostician and never a man, even a modern physician, who could cure faster.

"I used to have what they called a 'chest' in those days. I stank up every classroom with the bag of camphor my mother hung about my neck, and I reeked with asafetida, too. That's what really made me a good boxer. I had to be. Then there was goose grease, steeping feet in hot water and big doses of castor oil. I was supposed to sweat it out. Well, one winter my chest was worse than usual, and our family doctor had influenza, and we called in Dr. Bogus. He walked into the bedroom where I was coughing my lungs out, sniffed around the room, said 'Ah,' came to the bed, looked up my nose and down my throat, and said, 'Where's the cat?'

"Now, we always had cats in the house, two or three at least. Love the beasts; still do. My mother was surprised, but I hauled under the bed and brought up my favorite pussy. 'There's the villain, or villainess,' said Dr. Bogus, and picked up pussy and gently threw her out of the room. It seems I was sensitive to cats, but no one had ever suggested it before. I have them still, on the farms, but not in the house. And I still get a 'chest' if I go into a house where a pussy is in residence. Everybody laughed at Dr. Bogus, but he was right, you see. And everybody who laughed still called him in emergencies when real doctors were baffled. He had a nose."

"We can diagnose sensitiveness to animals, or whatever, without having a nose now."

"True. What are they beginning to call it now? Allergies. They're still mysterious. Why does one man drop dead if he takes an egg and another can have half a dozen of them for breakfast and feel 'fine,' as Teddy Roosevelt calls it. Sickening word. No one knows exactly why some proteins can kill some people and not affect others. Allergens, they call them these days. But why? We still don't know. Dr. Bogus didn't know either; he'd never heard of allergies to the day he died. But he knew they existed, just as Aristotle knew the nature of an atom even though he'd never known any scientific instruments. And today our scientists are talking about 'the atom' as if no one had ever proposed the theory before or written down a hypothesis. Dr. Bogus, I bet, could outdo any of your teachers at Johns Hopkins when it came to a diagnosis, even if he could rarely pronounce the name of the disease correctly and didn't know Latin from Sanskrit. He could lay his ear for a second to a man's chest and look into his eyes and come up with the exact thing that ailed his heart. And his weird concoctions, witch-doctor stuff, really, which he whipped up in his dirty little pharmacy, had almost magic qualities, though I doubt he knew what the hell most of the ingredients honestly were, or how or why they worked."

"My father told me about men like that," said Robert with doubt. "Me, I'm the real laboratory diagnostician."

But Jonathan did not laugh. He said, "That's not enough. I expect more from you than that. That's why I picked you over the others."

"Thanks," said Robert.

"The others," said Jonathan, "were strictly scientific chaps. That's not enough. We're going to St. Hilda's first. There're a couple of cases or so, that I want you to diagnose."

"By my sixth sense?"

"By your sixth sense. You strike me as a real doctor; I don't want to be disappointed. Take Leonardo da Vinci. He designed submarines and was laughed at for centuries. But now we not only know, because of him, that they are possible, but we are beginning to design them, too. He designed flying-machines, and now we have men working on such things, and, frankly, I'm afraid of them. The faster we get into communication with our fellows, the faster we'll learn to hate them. The sentimental used to carol that the telephone, by making instant communication possible, would clear up all misunderstandings and foster a spirit of brotherly love. Instead of that it has become an instrument of invasion; anyone can invade your house if you have a telephone, and most of the time it's a lot of nonsense. And a lot of the time you resent the caller and start to hate his guts. Science is going to make the new world a pretty threatening place."

"Antiprogress, I see."

"Don't laugh so smugly, boy. The more weapons you give a man, the more dangerous he becomes, and science is just on the threshold of supplying mankind with really big weapons. Most of them impersonal. When men fought hand-to-hand in battle, it gave them some respect for life, even if they killed in the name of whatever. But a rifle and a cannon—they are only instruments of destruction and you never see the man you murdered, so how can you respect his manhood? Watch that corner. It's pretty busy."

The streets simmered with the warm June sun and the lawns danced with the shadows of the great old trees. Children were racing to school, swinging their books on straps, little boys in knickerbockers, little girls in bright summer cottons and with ribbons in their hair. Small towns, thought Robert, masterfully handling the reins, have a lot to commend them. There's a certain close quality about them, a sense of nearness. He said, "I don't think that isolating one-self is the best way to get along with others."

"But it's a lot safer," said Jonathan. "Besides, who wants their affection? That's cheap and common, as my mother would call it. Give me respect anytime. An island is better than an anthill. One of these days we'll run out of islands, of any kind, and you'll see the heartiest massacres of whole populations. If you live long enough, and pray you don't. Man just can't stand too much of his fellowman."

"You're making me melancholy."

"Melancholy was highly esteemed by the Greeks. Don't underestimate it. Did you ever see a fool who was depressed, really depressed? No. Melancholy, and all the other mental ills, seem the prerogative of the intelligent. You've got to know the world to conclude you can't stand it."

Robert hesitated. "May I ask you a personal question? Thanks. Were you such a misanthrope before your—your—trouble?"

"You mean before I was on trial for killing my wife and child? Well, don't use euphemisms. Yes, I think I was always a misanthrope to some extent. If you aren't one yet, I advise you to cultivate misanthropy. Then nobody will catch you flat-footed, no one will cheat you, no one will stick a knife in your back. You'll always be looking for such things and you'll never be disappointed. But you'll be forewarned, and that's a blessed thing."

School bells were ringing, and churches were chiming nine o'clock; distant dogs barked lazily. A water wagon was roaming slowly along the streets, wetting down the gutters and making little black rivers among the cobblestones. A scent of moistened dust rose in the air pleasantly, and from somewhere came the passionately sweet scent of a linden tree. And always, over it all, the fragrance of garden roses, hot with life under the sun. So peaceful, thought Robert.

"The thing we have to learn, all of us now, is that peace is on the way out as a condition of existence," said Jonathan. "How do I know? I get the London *Times*. Parliament is expressing its 'distress' that Germany is crowding the British out of what they call their 'traditional markets.' "

"So?"

"Now, what the hell did men ever fight for, in all the history of the world, except for markets and new territories? And a right to exploit? Or money? All the high-sounding things don't mean a damn. Our own Civil War, as Lincoln himself explained it, was not to free slaves but to preserve the Union, and he wanted to preserve the Union because he knew that two weak divided countries where once there was one strong one would be an invitation to European adventurers. Why our own Revolution? The old boys considered themselves 'loyal subjects of His Majesty,' almost to the last. They just rightfully resented having their money—their money, you will observe—being taken away from them in taxes for the old country's benefit. There can be no freedom without private property, and money is private property, and that's what we fought for—the right to our property, which meant our liberty. That's why I say now that I was never so alarmed before as when hearing the British Parliament express itself, in its gentlemanly way, as being 'distressed' over bustling Germany's vigorous invasion of British foreign markets. I'm scared to death."

Robert could not imagine Jonathan Ferrier being "scared to death" over anything. He remembered the accounts in the newspapers of Jonathan's disdain of both judge and jury, his black impatience, his gloomy contempt. Yet, his life had been in the hands of those men; he had not feared them at all.

"Here we are. 'Jewel-like St. Hilda's,' as some lady once called it."

They had arrived at the somewhat elaborate wrought-iron gates of the small hospital. Beyond were wide gravel drives and handsome lawns and elms and neat flower beds and benches for convalescents. The hospital itself was of shining white brick with red chimneys and blue-shuttered windows and even curtains against the glass of the expensive private rooms. It resembled some great English mansion and not a hospital at all. Some nurses in white were guiding patients over the grass or wheeling them in chairs, and everything sparkled freshly and someone was cutting grass and the fragrance was delicious on the warm air.

"Well, it looks as a hospital should look, and not a barracks," said Robert. A man came running, as they drove up to the white steps, and caught the horse's bridle. The two doctors jumped to the ground and they entered the hospital through doors opened wide to the fresh breeze and the odor of growing things. It was cool and light inside, the inlaid linoleum polished on every one of its yellow squares, and the hall was lined with comfortable chairs and tables. A nurse at a desk looked up, saw Jonathan; her face closed. She said, "Good morning, Dr. Ferrier. And Dr. Morgan."

The hospital was four stories high and very hushed; the corridors, in spite of Jonathan's protest, richly carpeted. After all, he was told, the patients who could afford St. Hilda's had delicate sensibilities and they could not endure clacking noise. "And the hell with being sanitary," Jonathan had told Robert. "It's a wonder they didn't carpet the operating rooms, too, and the water closets. A lot of the more costly rooms do have rugs in them; there're still a lot of pompous quacks who don't believe in germs, or, if forced to look at them through microscopes, murmur that they're 'interesting little creatures.'"

The very few patients whom he had recently accepted— and who had believed in him in the blackest of times—were on the second floor. So the two young men walked up the wide white-painted stairs, which wound up to the top in a graceful spiral. The hospital hummed with a soft busyness; nurses passed them or approached them; doctors with bags stopped to gossip to each other. Jonathan ignored them all, even those who tentatively greeted him. Robert was embarrassed. He knew a few of the doctors now and when they spoke to him pleasantly, glancing furtively at the silent Jonathan, he replied with a little too much effusiveness. His bag felt hot in his hand.

Jonathan swung open a broad door into a big and comfortable room full of sun. His manner changed at once. "Well, how are we this morning, Martha?"

A little girl, not more than ten, was listlessly lying on heaped pillows, her fair hair streaming about her shoulders. Robert had not seen her before. Jonathan took up her chart from the white dresser, glanced over it swiftly, frowned. "This is Martha Best," he said to Robert. "The daughter of one of my closest friends, Howard Best, a lawyer. In fact, I'm her godfather. Aren't I, Martha?" His face had become gentle for all its darkness, and he went to the child and bent and kissed her cheek. She caught his hand, her blue eyes fixed anxiously on him.

"I can go home soon, can't I, Uncle Jon?"

"I hope so," he said. "Aren't you going to speak to Dr. Morgan?"

The child eyed him shyly but did not speak. When he said, "Hello, Martha," she bent her head and the golden hair fell like a curtain over her cheeks.

"Now, Martha, Dr. Morgan is going to help me with you,"

said Jonathan. "He looks like a big red bear, doesn't he, but he doesn't bite little girls. Honestly."

The child giggled convulsively and peeped up at Robert. Jonathan gave him the chart. "Acute anemia. Intractable fever of 102°. History of severe infection of throat, now reduced. Present slight infection of lungs and nose. Joint pains. Transient bleeding from mouth, bowels, kidneys and nose. Slight liver enlargement. Spleen perceptibly enlarged. Lymph nodes discernible. Pallor. Lassitude. Diagnosis of admitting physician, Dr. Louis Hedler: Rheumatic fever with few signs of heart involvement. Family physician's diagnosis:" There was, as yet, no diagnosis recorded from Dr. Jonathan Ferrier.

Robert laid down the chart. He looked searchingly at the little girl, at her ghostly color, at the lack of pinkness in her lips, at the bluish hollows under her eyes. He thought of something. It sickened him. He had never seen a case—

Jonathan was watching him sharply. "Martha has been slightly sick, so her parents told me yesterday, when I sent her here for four weeks. A little cold, they said. Then two days ago she became really sick, and they called me. She came in last night. Well?"

Robert went slowly to the little girl, who was now staring at him inquisitively. He took her hand; it was chill and faintly tremulous. She let him examine her throat. He took out his stethoscope and listened to her heart. It was a little more rapid than in health, but there were no overt heart sounds. Her tongue was very pale, but her gums were congested. A holy medal, of gold, and on a thin gold chain, hung about her neck, and on the bed table beside her was a rosary. Robert gently dropped her hand; he stared at the silver crucifix on the rosary. He was silent.

"Well?" said Jonathan. His voice was curiously muffled.

"You've taken blood? There doesn't seem to be any reference to a blood test on the chart. I—I'd like to see if there are any blast forms—and the leukocyte count."

Jonathan sighed. "Am I very sick?" said the little girl with anxiety. "Uncle Louis said I had rheumatism. Am I going to be a cripple?"

"Uncle Louis," Jonathan began, "is an old—" He stopped. "Of course, you aren't going to be a cripple, Martha. In fact, when this fever goes down a little, you can get out of bed. And a little later, you can go home." He added, "You can go home."

A cheerful nurse came in, all rosy dimples and bounce,

with a white cap on her high black pompadour. "Good morning, Doctors!" she sang. "We are doing very well this morning! We had a lovely little breakfast, too, and enjoyed it! Didn't we, Martha?"

"Yes, ma'am," the child said with politeness.

"And such a pretty nightgown!" said the happy nurse, admiring the white silk, embroidered garment Martha wore. "Such a nice sleep in it."

"Bob," said Jonathan, "this is one of Martha's private nurses, Mrs. Chapman. Mrs. Chapman, Dr. Morgan, my replacement."

"How nice," said the pleasant woman vaguely.

"Bring me a glass slide from the laboratory," said Jonathan. "And quickly, please."

He sat down on the side of the bed and regarded the child with real tenderness. "Martha, I'm going to prick your ear and take a little blood from you. It won't hurt much; just a little. You aren't going to make a fuss, are you?"

The child immediately looked frightened. Jonathan took one of her hands and held it warmly. "I don't like to bleed, Uncle Jon," she said. "It makes me sick to look at it."

"I won't let you see it, then. You just keep your eyes closed, and when I tell you to open them, you won't see any blood at all. How's Tommie?" he asked, referring to her infant brother.

"He has a cold, too," said Martha. "Not very bad, though, like mine. His knees aren't swollen either." She smiled affectionately. "He's better than all my dolls."

"Of course he is. Your mother will be in soon, Martha, when Tommie is settled. By that time we'll know exactly what's wrong with you—and when you can go home."

"And I don't have rheumatism?"

Jonathan looked at Robert, and the child looked at him. "No," said Robert. "You don't have rheumatism, Martha." He tried to hold Jonathan's eyes, but they shifted away from him. There was a sudden hard silence in the room.

"What do I have, then?" asked Martha with the curiosity of childhood, and the importance.

"We have to look—at things—first," said Robert, and felt sick.

"You mean, it isn't bad at all?" she said in her chirping voice. She was a little disappointed.

"Be cheerful and optimistic at all times before the patient," Robert had been sternly taught. "Never indicate by tone or manner that the patient is gravely ill or in a terminal condition." He thought it nonsense but had not so expressed himself to his teachers.

How did one say to a child, "Darling, you are going to die"?

Please, God, he said in himself, let me be mistaken. After all, I've never seen a single case before. I could be wrong. Let me be wrong. He gazed at the child and saw her beauty and the sweetness of her eyes. He turned away and walked slowly to the window and looked outside and saw nothing. It was wrong for the young and lovely to die! They had a celebration to make to life. Life was not a joyous thing in itself—he knew that, for he was a doctor and had seen too much pain and death and had heard too many desolate cries. But it was like spring, in its infrequent periods, and a child had a right to spring. He heard the door open and shut and the bright voice of Mrs. Chapman, bringing the slide.

"Now, Martha," Jonathan was saying. "Just close your eyes. You'll feel a little prick. Tell me, how is school?"

"I don't like it, Uncle— Oh!" she cried.

"There. Just two seconds. Keep those eyes closed. Good girl! Mrs. Chapman, take it to the laboratory and set it up. We'll join you in a few minutes. Martha! It's all over. You can open your eyes now. It didn't really hurt, did it?"

She gave a small dry sob, then smiled. Robert turned at the window; the sun made a halo of the child's silken hair. "No, it really didn't hurt. Much. Uncle Jon, Father McNulty called the hospital and he's coming to see me today. Isn't that nice?"

"Wonderful," said Jonathan. "Fine." Robert saw his face and turned away again. "And now," said Jonathan, "we'll leave you for a few moments to count all the nice red things in that blood I took from you."

He rose and the two doctors left the room. Jonathan closed the door slowly and heavily. He said, "Well, Doctor, what is your on-the-spot diagnosis?"

Robert could not remember when he had last felt so wretched and sad. "I hope I'm wrong," he said. "After all, I know—it—only from textbooks. I never saw a case."

"Of what?"

Robert hesitated. "Acute leukemia. Extremely rare."

Jonathan was silent. His head was bent.

"Tell me I'm wrong," Robert pleaded. "That's a beautiful little girl—"

"Let's look at the slide," said Jonathan, and they went to the laboratories, not speaking as they walked through the long corridors. In that same silence they soon returned to Martha's room. They heard her giggling as they opened the door. Dr. Louis Hedler was sitting near the bed in a comfortable chintz wing chair, and he had apparently told the child some agreeable joke. He turned his head when he saw the younger doctors, and nodded pleasantly and held out his soft fat hand. He more than ever resembled an amiable toad, and his head and face were completely bare of hair and his nose was snub and broad.

"Morning, Jon," he said. "Morning, Dr. Morgan. Hear you are joining us on the staff. Fine. Hope you'll be happy with us." He shook Robert's hand vigorously. "Now, what's this I hear? You took blood from Martha, with a big knife, she says. Why?" He was still smiling happily, but the huge brown eyes were hard and penetrating.

"Just for fun," said Jonathan. "We like to hurt little girls, Louis."

"I did write down that I thought Martha had anemia as well as, ahem, rheumatism. What did your precious slides show?"

"Anemia."

"Obvious, obvious! At her age. Very common. Nothing to be alarmed about. It's those joint pains that worry me. And a suspicion about her heart——"

"Never discuss a patient's condition in his presence," Robert had been taught. But Dr. Hedler, Jonathan had said, was a "diploma-mill" doctor. Robert had never been taught that a patient was hardly sentient and was always totally ignorant.

"Uncle Jon said I wasn't very sick," said the child, with new anxiety at the mention of her heart.

"Of course you're not sick!" cried Dr. Hedler, with immense joviality. "I—or rather, Jon here will prescribe an iron tonic for you and you'll soon be as right as rain! I promise you." He stood up and patted the child's cheek, but she was looking at Jonathan for confirmation.

"Don't worry, Martha," he said. "There isn't anything wrong with your heart." Dr. Hedler frowned. "Louis," said Jonathan, "I've a case down the hall I'd like to discuss with you."

"One of yours? Don't tell me, Jon, that you give a fig for my opinion!"

"There's always a first time," said the younger doctor. "Coming, Bob? Martha, I'll come in again before I leave."

Jon carefully shut the door behind him, and the three doctors stood alone in the carpeted corridor. "Well?" said Dr. Hedler, with impatience. "Where is your patient?"

"You've just seen her, Louis. And we just came from the laboratories, remember."

"Yes, yes, so you said! You and your highfalutin slides and tests! Anemia, that's what you said, isn't it?"

"To Martha, yes. To you, no." He turned to Robert. "Dr. Morgan guessed it at first examination; it was only confirmed by the blood test. Bob, tell Louis what we found."

"Acute leukemia," said Robert.

Dr. Hedler's mouth fell open with an audible sound. His eyes popped. He swung to Jonathan. "Why, you're crazy! Jonathan, you don't believe what a young fella just out of the ranks of interns says, do you?"

"I do. I believed it last night, before the blood test."

"Crazy, crazy! Never heard anything so preposterous in my life! It's insane. Why, that disease is so rare that hardly any of us see a case for ourselves in a whole lifetime! As rare as an angel in hell!"

"It depends on the kind of angel," said Jonathan. "Louis, stop gulping. The child has acute leukemia. I'd tell you exactly what we saw in the smear, but they'd be only words to you. You must take our word for it."

"You arrogant young pup, with your scientific ideas!" Dr. Hedler was scarlet with rage. "Do you know what you're doing? You're condemning that beautiful little girl to death!"

"Not I," said Jonathan. "God did."

"Blasphemous, too." Dr. Hedler was sweating, though the corridor was cool. He regarded Jonathan with hatred. "No, I won't take your word for it! The child has rheumatic fever—"

"You're not her physician, Louis. I am."

Dr. Hedler breathed heavily. He was incredulous. "Are you going to tell her parents this—this enormity, this guess of yours?"

"It isn't a guess, Louis. I've seen eight cases over the past ten years. It's becoming more common. Twenty years ago only one doctor in a thousand ever saw a case; thirty years ago only one doctor in five thousand saw one. But the Greeks had a name for it: the White Sickness. Remember Hippocrates? He diagnosed it."

"I forbid you to tell her parents, Beth and Howard, this terrible thing! If it were possibly true, it would be bad enough. But a mere guess—"

"Not a guess. Louis, she isn't your patient. You can't forbid me to tell the truth to my patient's parents, even if you are Chief-of-Staff. And I'm going to tell them today. They must be prepared. The child has only a little while to live, at the best. And there's no treatment, Louis."

"Cancer of the blood! That's what you mean, isn't it? Cancer, at her age!"

"One child in twenty thousand now has cancer in some form, Louis. Don't you read the medical journals?"

Dr. Hedler seemed about to strike him. "The child has rheumatism, rheumatic fever! I've seen hundreds of cases. I was never wrong once. And I'll tell Howard and Beth that you are a fool, and not to believe you. Leukemia! Bah!" He slapped his hand against the wall and waddled off, trembling with fury.

"Hambledon's crowning medical glory," said Jonathan. "Smiling old Louis."

"Couldn't we have a medical consultation?" Robert asked with misery. "Someone from Johns Hopkins?"

Jonathan regarded him narrowly. "Don't you trust your own diagnosis? And mine?"

"I never saw a case," said Robert, "before this."

"I told you, I've seen eight. Not in this hospital, though, and not in the other hospital in town. In Pittsburgh. In New York. In Boston. In Philadelphia. Martha's case is classic. Well?"

Robert studied his large pink hands. "There's no cure; there's no treatment. There are remissions—"

"Not for long. And not always. Do you want to lie to her parents, Bob?"

"No. No, of course not. You don't mean it, do you, that I must tell her parents?"

"No. I didn't." Jonathan smiled with bleak pity at him. "But I'd like you to be present. Break you in.

"And now for my other cases. I'm leaving them to you, Bob, with my compliments."

CHAPTER SEVEN

"'*The quality of mercy is not strained,*' except that God never heard that particular saying," said Jonathan, pushing open another door which led into a handsome suite of rooms consisting of a private bathroom, sitting room and bedroom, all cheerfully and expensively furnished and open to sun and wind and perfumed by many flowers. Jonathan put his hand on Robert's arm and said to him in a low voice, "This is a very interesting case. Old Jonas Witherby, eighty years old, old settler, old money, old mansion, good old bonds and stocks and fine old land. I want your opinion."

They went together through the sitting room to the bedroom where, in a Morris rocker, sat an old man with the most beautiful and tranquil face Robert had ever seen among elderly people. He was small and daintily made, with tiny hands and feet and a noble head richly flowing with white and rippling hair. He had the eyes of a young child, clear and blue and steadfast, a snub nose, a sweetly smiling mouth and pink ears. He sat by the window looking at the sunshine and smiling musingly, and when he turned his long head, Robert felt warmth and peace rising in him and something very close to affection.

"Ah, dear Jonathan," said Mr. Witherby, holding out one hand to the older doctor and winking. "I never see you without pleasure. How are you this glorious day?"

"Just terrible, Jonas," said Jonathan. "Everything's just as bad as it can be. By the way, this is my replacement, Dr. Robert Morgan."

The old man clung to Jonathan's hand and smiled merrily

at Robert, then became sad. "How do you do, Doctor? You all seem to get younger all the time. Replacement for Jonathan, eh? You must truly persuade him to change his mind. What will Hambledon do without him?"

"Just jog along as meanly as ever," said Jonathan. He sat down in another chair, crossed his long legs and put his hands in his pockets and studied Mr. Witherby with an ambiguous expression. "Never mind. We won't repeat the old arguments for Bob's benefit. As he will replace me, I am turning you over to him. With your permission, of course."

"Certainly, certainly, dear boy!" Mr. Witherby smiled more radiantly than before and considered Robert with great interest. "Anyone you recommend—"

Jonathan stood up in his dark blue suit and gave the appearance, all at once, of extreme emaciation. He took Mr. Witherby's chart, frowned at it, laid it down. "Still weak, I see. Still eating like that proverbial bird; I know birds; they eat all the time, all through the damned day. But your nurses note down, 'ate breakfast like a bird.' Silly old hags. How did you sleep?"

Mr. Witherby sighed. "Please sit down, Dr. Morgan. You will find that chair very comfortable; I like to look at young faces. Well, Jonathan, you know at my age one doesn't sleep very well at all. I think, lying awake all night."

"And you have plenty to think about." Jonathan, still standing near the bowered dresser, looked at Robert. "Old Jonas here was a widower. Two sons, one fifty-three, one fifty-one. Both married, both deserted by their wives. Bill is in a private madhouse, Donald is a chronic alcoholic. DTs, most of the time. In a private sanitarium which dries him out, then looses him again. No daughters. No grandchildren. Wife," said Jonathan in the bald tone of a clinician, "committed suicide. Very sad, wouldn't you say?"

Robert was disturbed at this impersonal recital, which seemed cruel. He bent his head with apology to Mr. Witherby as if in some way he were guilty of Jonathan. But Mr. Witherby's fine old face took on a sad melancholy and dejection and he folded his hands with resignation on his knees. "It was always said that I had everything, from birth, but in reality, in my old age, I have nothing."

Jonathan snapped a pink rosebud from a vase and fixed it in his buttonhole. He was detached, as if no one were in this room but himself. He said, "Languid, listless, tired, enfeebled, anorexia, vague but disabling pains, sometimes severe headaches, though no hypertension, tachycardia frequently, some indications of mucous colitis, occasional rales in the lungs. Otherwise, no overt signs of disease. Well, Bob? Want to examine the specimen?"

Robert silently opened his bag and removed his stethoscope and various other instruments. No doubt, he thought, the sorrowful old man was suffering some psychosomatic ailments due to his unfortunate relatives and his disappointment in them. His examination was thorough. Mr. Witherby flaccidly submitted to everything as if nothing meant anything any longer to him. Finally Robert put away his instruments and looked long and earnestly at the old gentleman, his kind young eyes full of pity.

"No overt signs of disease," he repeated.

Jonathan moved restlessly. He was not a man to fidget, but now it appeared to Robert that he was fidgeting. He went to the window, stared out, yawned. "When's Priscilla due to arrive today?" he asked.

"Prissy?" Mr. Witherby smiled his enchanting smile. "In an hour or two, I think." Jonathan looked over his shoulder at Robert. "Priscilla, or Prissy, is old Jonas' second wife. Thirty years old, or a little older. A luscious piece."

Mr. Witherby laughed in delight. "That she is, my boy, that she is!"

Robert stared. This made Jonathan chuckle. "A rare old bugger, this Jonas," he said to Robert, making a rude sound. Robert flushed. Mr. Witherby laughed again. "You mustn't listen to our dear Jonathan," he said, putting his little hand on Jonathan's blue alpaca sleeve. "He loves to shock. You must really see Prissy. The Florodora Sextette are witches in comparison. There's only one girl prettier in all Pennsylvania—" and now he smiled slyly at Jonathan—"and that's Jennifer Heger, whom Jonathan loves to call his niece."

Well, thought Robert, I suppose you can't blame the old gentleman. He has to have some happiness in his life. Jonathan said, "Priscilla was the town's most expensive doxy. I assume you know what a doxy is, Bob?"

"Now, now, Jonathan," said Mr. Witherby, not in the least offended. In fact, he laughed again. "Didn't David, in his old age, have a plump young maiden to sleep with him to warm his old bones?"

"But Prissy hasn't been a maiden since she was sixteen, if not younger. But a fastidious little bitch, always. Never slept with anyone for less than fifty dollars; mostly more," said Jonathan. "Look at Bob. He's blushing again."

Robert stared at him helplessly. "Well," said Jonathan, with considerable impatience. "Where's that nose of yours? Smell anything?"

"What a blackguard you are," said Mr. Witherby fondly, and watching Robert with renewed interest. "Here I am, an old man of as many afflictions as Job, and Jonathan can do nothing but tease me. I came in here after a collapse—"

"Something odd about that collapse," said Jonathan, as if meditating. "At first I thought you were trying to show Prissy that you still had it and almost dropped dead trying. Then I decided that Prissy had fed you a little something so she could slip out for some clean air. Come on, Jonas, what was it?"

"Oh, dear," said Mr. Witherby. "You are very disturbing and uncouth, Jonathan. You will give Dr. Morgan some very peculiar ideas about me." His ancient yet angelic face beamed on the younger doctor. "I've known Jonathan since he was born and he was always like this. Very startling 'and unpredictable and forever trying to shock others with the rudest language. But I know him! A kinder heart never beat, a more gentle soul—"

"Shut up," said Jonathan. "Don't be such a sanctimonious scoundrel, Jonas." He looked at Robert sharply and frowned. "Well? Where's that nose?"

What in God's name does he want me to say? asked Robert with that new anger of his. He's been insulting this gentle old man steadily, and his young wife—Robert lifted his head with a jerk. There were those middle-aged sons, one mad, one a drunkard; there had been a wife, who had taken her life. Robert turned his eyes on Mr. Witherby and studied him with more concentration. Then indeed he did smell something and he said to himself, The stench of evil.

He was horrified at the thought. Mr. Witherby, as he had done with Jonathan, put his hand on Robert's arm and the muscles in that arm involuntarily stiffened. "Do I smell badly?" asked Mr. Witherby, in a sweet and coaxing tone. "I was just bathed and powdered like a baby!"

Still clutching Robert's arm, he said to Jonathan, "You've almost persuaded me to contribute to that tuberculosis ward for indigent children, dear boy, at the Friends'. A little more of your refreshing conversation and I'll give you my check. And won't stop payment on it!" He laughed joyously.

I must have been mistaken, thought Robert, and stood very still. It was my imagination, and Jonathan's prompting, that made me smell corruption.

"If you do give me that check," said Jonathan, "it'll be the first decent thing you ever did in your life. You might even get a reprieve and go to purgatory rather than to hell. But you don't believe in either, do you?"

"Jonathan! I'm a Christian! Ask the Reverend Mr. Wilson— Oh, Jonathan, you are teasing me again."

Now they both looked at Robert. Robert said, "You have —you have, Mr. Witherby, some of the usual signs of advanced age—"

The old man actually paled and now he no longer smiled. "Don't say that to him!" Jonathan exclaimed. "If there's one thing he hates it is the mere suggestion of mortality. Haven't you noticed that, in the wicked? Call them any names you wish, murderers, liars, thieves, perjurers, traitors, sadists, and they'll forgive you. But remind them that they are about to shuffle off and you've made an enemy for life. And an enemy like old Jonas here is a very formidable thing. He has ways of reaching out, even from his bed, to strangle people."

Robert heard himself saying, "But, Mr. Witherby, you are remarkably well-preserved, and with care should live—should live—a considerable time longer."

Mr. Witherby's color returned. "I intend to do that, Doctor. Indeed. My parents lived far into their nineties. I love life, Doctor. I find it endlessly amusing, endlessly fascinating. I always have. You mustn't listen to Jonathan, who could find thousands of flaws in a saint. I never had any need to injure anyone, for I inherited all my money and have increased it. I've been unfortunate in my family. My poor first wife came of unstable forebears; I was warned. My poor sons inherited her predisposition. But there, I mustn't burden you with my troubles. Jonathan, when can I leave here?"

"Today. When Prissy comes. That should brighten up her life when you tell her! But, if I were you, I'd buy a mongrel and feed him off your plate before you eat, after this."

"Oh, Jonathan! You mustn't say such crude things." He giggled like a boy. "Prissy knows my will. I have an autopsy ordered."

Robert did not know if he was serious. He was bewildered again; yet he retreated a step from the old man.

"Good," said Jonathan. "Though if I perform the autopsy and even find cyanide, I'll say 'from natural causes.' After all,

Prissy's had to stand you for three years. She deserves some consideration. Bob?"

"I'd like to talk with you a moment outside," said Robert.

"Why, why?" cried Mr. Witherby, staring from one to the other. "Are you trying to hide something from me? Is there something really wrong?" He was nakedly terrified.

"I only wish there were," said Jonathan. "Sad to say, there isn't, though it's still a mystery to me why you collapsed. I think I'll warn Prissy not to be too hasty in the future." He bowed derisively to the old man and followed Robert out of the room. They stood in the corridor. Robert said to him angrily, "I don't know what all this is about!"

"And you didn't smell anything?"

Robert pressed his lips hard together. "It may be I am suggestible. I thought I—" He stopped.

"You smelled a stench?"

Robert moved his head with fresh anger. Jonathan said, "You were quite right, and I'm pleased with you. Dee-lighted, as Teddy Roosevelt would say. That is the most contemptible and vicious monster you probably ever met in your life, and I doubt you'll ever meet another as bad. He drove his wife to her death with his sweet malignance and malice, and he drove one son into madness and the other to the bottle. And I'm willing to bet everything I have that never once in their lives did he ever raise his voice to them or threaten them or speak roughly to them. I bet he never did anything violent in his whole existence, nor inspired open fear. Yet, he really frightened his wife to death and so scared his sons that they ran away from him in the only ways they could. You see, soft and gentle characters are particularly susceptible to the presence of evil. But I'm tough. I know all about him."

Robert looked involuntarily at the closed door. "You don't believe in demonic possession, do you?" asked Jonathan. "Well, I do. There may be many things I don't believe, but I believe in a personal Satan, and old Witherby's one of his best friends. Jonas never swore, to anyone's knowledge; the parsons love him. Children adore him, and so much for that business of 'children always know.' That mass of flowers in there wasn't sent by hypocrites but by people who really admire the old bastard. But I never go in there without making the sign against the evil eye," and he smiled and held out his right hand, extended two fingers and thrust them downward. "My Catholic training. I had a superstitious nurse, too, when I was a kid."

He began to walk down the corridor and Robert had to follow him. Jonathan pushed his hands in his pockets again and bent his dark head. "It was something in you that made you smell something, and if a doctor can't smell evil, then he isn't a doctor in the true sense. There were some houses old Dr. Bogus wouldn't enter for a handful of gold twenty-dollar pieces, and I know why. He was afraid."

"Of what?" Robert was feeling more confidence and was ashamed of himself.

"Of corruption. He told me, when he was a very old man, that you can catch an illness from a diseased soul just as you can catch it from a diseased body. And it's true. He also said it was a killing disease, and it is. Stay away from corrupt people, and they're more numerous than you think."

"Superstition," said Robert. "A mentally ill person—"

"Do you think old Jonas is mentally ill?"

"Well. No. I don't think so. But you never can tell. An alienist, perhaps— I've been reading some of Freud's work—"

Jonathan laughed. "Freud? That incestuous pervert? Yes, he did commit incest, you know. Quite freely and with enjoyment. He projected his own perversions on the whole of humanity. Of course, he did light up, with his own hellish light, some pretty filthy corners and attics and cellars in other people, because he was familiar with those places in his own soul, too. But he was at a loss in the company of good people; actually lost. He couldn't accept virtue. He thought it hypocrisy, lies or hysteria. You'd better look more closely at him."

"The field of mental illness," Robert began, in a somewhat pompous tone.

"Oh, we'll explore it all right! But there is something to the ancient snake pits, you know. They did cure people; shock, they say. Perhaps. I think they just scared, literally, the hell out of them. A rough way of exorcism."

He grinned at Robert. Then someone exclaimed, "Oh, there you are, Jon!" Robert turned and saw three young people approaching with smiles and outstretched hands. One, he saw, was a plump young priest with a kind and boyish face. One was a pretty woman, fashionably dressed in a soft gray silk suit with a lace jabot at her throat and a severe sailor hat of straw on her pile of blond hair. The third was evidently her husband, a loose-jointed young fellow with a bush of auburn curls and large light eyes. For some reason Robert felt a sense of reprieve, or freshness, as if he had just emerged into light from some dank and malodorous cave. He saw open faces, candid and honest, and a vivid youthfulness and sincerity and an actual childlike pleasure.

"How are you, Father McNulty?" said Jonathan, shaking hands briefly with the priest. "Beth, dear. Howard." He indicated Robert. "My replacement, Dr. Morgan. Fresh as a daisy, isn't he, and I guarantee that he's just as innocent, too."

Robert, newly annoyed, shook hands. "Beth and Howard Best," said Jonathan. "Martha's parents."

Robert was frightened. He looked from one smiling face to the other and he wanted to run away. But Jonathan had firmly gripped his arm. "Let's go to the waiting room down the corridor," said Jonathan. "I've just seen Martha. I want to tell you about her."

They all went with him, chattering serenely, and Robert thought of the dying child who was waiting for them. Beth prattled, "I've been worrying so about Martha, and Howard says I'm ridiculous. I am, aren't I, Jon? When can we take her home?" She smiled back at Robert shyly. "I hope you'll like Hambledon, Doctor. Such a nice town and we're right up-to-date; I heard you were from Philadelphia. We'll make you welcome, you'll see! But do try to make dear Jon stay, won't you? We simply can't let him go! We love him so much!"

This dumbfounded Robert. The priest slowed down to walk beside him and he was looking at Robert with curiosity. "From Philadelphia, eh? I was a curate there. Not for long, thank God, and I mean that, Doctor." He laughed. His laughter was rich and friendly. "The old Father was a Tartar. But fledgling priests have to expect that. Soften us up, take the pomposity out of us, strip us down to the shivering hide, then throw us out naked and full of gratitude to anyone agreeable enough to pick us up and dust us off and take us home."

His mother was right, thought Robert. The Papist clergy were full of levity. Then he was embarrassed at his thought. Father McNulty was hardly older than himself. How did one address a priest? He couldn't say "Father." What did the Bible say about that? "Call no one your father except Him Who is in Heaven," or something like that. Robert was confused. He said, "Well, sir, I suppose every profession has its drawbacks," and felt like a fool. The young priest only smiled with the utmost friendliness. He had a face like an apple,

with a double chin and light smooth hair and a dimple in his
right cheek; his eyes were warm gold.

The waiting room was empty and full of sun and comfortable modern furniture, and Beth sat down and took off
her gloves and kept her eyes affectionately on Jonathan, who
sat down very close to her. "Well!" she exclaimed. "Isn't it a
lovely day! Howard, you absolutely must not light that smelly
pipe! Not in a hospital. We just ran into Father McNulty,"
she said to Jonathan. "He was coming to see Martha, too.
Isn't that nice?" Her pretty face was artless and flushed with
sun and fair as a rose.

"My pipe doesn't smell," said Howard Best. He patted his
wife's shoulder. "It's better than those coffin nails Jonathan
smokes and warns everybody not to put in their own mouths.
Well, Jon, when can we take our girl home?"

"Just as soon as her fever goes down," said Jonathan. He
was rubbing the thick gold chain that spanned his middle. He
looked at the priest. "I'm glad you're here," he said.

Howard Best slowly took the unlit pipe from his mouth.
"What? Is there anything wrong—with Martha?"

Beth had stopped smiling. Her pretty color disappeared.
"Martha? Martha?"

In the mysterious way of the clergy Father McNulty understood. He saw Jonathan's grave face, the wide cheekbones,
which were now stark, the evasive eyes. He said to Mrs. Best,
"Now, Beth. Let's hear what Jonathan has to say."

"There's nothing wrong with my girl?" asked Howard Best
in a changed voice. "Why, old Louis Hedler said it was anemia—"

"Martha!" cried Beth, in the ancient tones of a frightened
mother, and the priest reached out and took her hand and
held it firmly.

Robert stood at a distance and again wanted to run and
knew he must stay, even though no one noticed him now.

"In a way," said Jonathan in a gentle voice, "it is, indeed,
anemia. I took a blood test this morning. I don't know why it
wasn't done before."

"So?" said Howard. "It's anemia. That's not very serious, is
it?"

"Oh, no, it can't be serious!" said Beth in a voice like a
prayer. "Not our sweet little girl!"

"It is best to be euphemious with a patient or his relatives,"
Robert had been taught. "One must Inspire Hope." Perhaps,
he thought, wretchedly. He himself had seen practically mori-

bund patients suddenly brighten and almost miraculously recover; he had seen deathbeds quicken into life. He had seen dying men open their eyes and live. But there had never been a case of acute leukemia—that most rare, that almost unknown and mysterious disease—that had recovered. The White Sickness of the Greeks, the silent ghost that struck a mortal blow and never repented.

It was a lie, and a cruel one, to give hope where there was no hope.

Jonathan said, looking into Beth's widened eyes, "Martha has acute leukemia, Beth."

The parents visibly relaxed. They had never heard of the disease. Nor had the priest, it was evident. Now they were hopefully puzzled. "What's that?" asked Howard. "One of your new diseases, which your microscopes just discovered?"

"No. It's very old. But very rare." Jonathan hesitated. "And there's no cure."

One of Beth's hands flew to her mouth. "You mean," she whispered, "like consumption?"

"Beth, dear," said Jonathan, "we can cure tuberculosis now. Sometimes. I wish to God it was only that. Acute leukemia—it can't be cured."

"Do you mean she'll have it all her life, like the effects of infantile paralysis?" asked Howard, sitting down with new stiffness as if he were afraid he would break. "How do we deal with it? Special tonics? Seaside? Mountains?" He paused. "What the hell is it, anyway?" and his voice rose.

The priest held Beth's struggling and desperate hand tighter. Jonathan said, "I'd rather have it myself, I swear to God, than to tell you this, Howard. You see, there's nothing anyone can do. We call it, roughly speaking, cancer of the blood-making organs."

"Cancer!" screamed Beth, and now she frantically pulled away from the priest and jumped to her feet. Her face was terrible. "I don't believe it. I don't believe it! Children don't get cancer! It's just old people! Martha doesn't have cancer! I won't believe it—it's wrong, it's cruel, of you, Jon! Cruel, cruel, cruel, to say such a thing!"

"But true," he said almost inaudibly. Howard stood up and caught his trembling wife to him and she hid her face on his shoulder and shook her head over and over in utter denial, and groaned, "God, God, God."

"I never heard of leuk—what do you call it?" said Howard, holding his wife tightly. "Blood? Cancer? Tumor? Why, Martha has no tumors—it—"

He looked helplessly at the priest, and his young face was ghastly. "It must be a mistake," he said. "Cancer! Martha! It's unheard of, in children."

"No, it isn't," said Jonathan, and he stood up also and moved nearer the agonized young couple. "Doctors just don't speak of it, that's all. You see, it is getting much more common now. I've seen eight other cases like Martha's, Howard. Just eight. And they all—"

"Died," said Howard and there was no expression in his voice.

"Died," said Jonathan.

Howard held his wife even more tightly. He looked at Jonathan as one who looks at an executioner, with instinctive hatred and despair.

"How long?" he whispered.

"I don't know, Howard. I honestly don't know. Perhaps a few days, perhaps a few weeks or months. But not more than a year, not more than a year, and only that if she has a temporary remission."

"I don't believe you!" Howard exclaimed. "Old Louis Hedler would've told us! He said it was just anemia! He saw her last night! He'd know if it was—if it was—"

"Howard," said the priest, and put his hand on the young man's shoulder. But Howard gave him a blind, impersonal glare and shook off that hand. He was panting. Beth had become stiff and still in his arms, and cringing.

"I'll call decent doctors, doctors with experience in this thing, doctors who *know!*" Howard shouted. "Not young quacks, not a man who—"

"Howard!" said the priest with authority.

"I don't care!" shouted the frenzied Howard. "He's lying! I don't know why, but he's lying! He wants to—I don't believe him! We'll take Martha away—to Philadelphia, to competent —one of those clinics—He lies!" He was out of breath. "He's a rotten—"

"Howard!" said the priest, but again Howard shook him off. He pressed his cheek against his wife's. "Don't cry, darling, don't cry. It's all lies. Martha's all right. She mustn't see you like this. We'll take Martha home today. We'll take her to—" Now his eyes swelled with tears of agony and he looked at Jonathan with the utmost ferocity and loathing.

"How you could say such a thing! To a mother and a father!"

"I wish to God it was I," said Jonathan. "I'd give my life, Howard. But it's true. You mustn't hope. It's too true. You must prepare yourselves."

"Oh, no," said Beth, with her lips against her husband's neck. "It's not true. Not Martha. It's just an infection—a bad cold. Martha was never sick a day in her life."

Jonathan sighed. For the first time he saw Robert. Then he said to the priest, "Father, you mustn't let them hope. There's no hope. Just help them, that's all, if you can."

Howard almost screamed, "He's a murderer, and everybody knows it! That's why he said that—! He wants other people to die, too! He probably makes them die! He—" He strangled. "I'll kill him," he gasped. "I'll surely kill him!"

The priest said to Jonathan, "Don't mind, Jon. He doesn't know what he's saying, in his pain. Don't mind. You don't, do you?"

"Yes, I do," said Jonathan. "I mind like hell. Did you expect me not to?"

"Poor Jon," said the priest.

The big pretty room, shining with windows and sun, suddenly appeared horrible to Robert. He heard distant laughter in the corridor and, outside, the crunching of wheels over gravel and the sound of lawn mowers and the call of birds. So beautiful and peaceful, so full of life: He could not bear it. A child was dying, and no one cared out there, and no one knew, and when she was dead, it would all go on.

"There's nothing?" the priest was saying.

"Nothing," said Jonathan, and he walked slowly from the room and Robert followed him. Outside in the corridor Jonathan leaned against the wall as if exhausted, and he said in a venomous voice, "Christ." In the waiting room Howard was incoherently shouting and the priest's voice was low but persistent, and there was no sound from Beth at all.

Robert said, "I can see now, why you must go away. It's bad enough, having to tell them, but this." He stopped eloquently.

"Christ," said Jonathan again, as if he had not heard. He lifted himself away from the wall and walked away. After a moment Robert followed. "We love him so much," Beth had said. Robert wanted to hit something with all his strength.

Jonathan said, "That little kid." He seemed to be speaking

only to himself. "And old Witherby. There's no sense to it, no sense to anything."

In moments Jonathan's bitter face had smoothed itself and he was opening another door and saying, "Hello, Mrs. Winters. How are we today?"

An elderly woman, very thin and with scanty white hair, was sitting high on pillows in a room that seemed oddly barren and deserted to Robert—who was still shaken—even if it was filled with sunlight and there were flowers on the dresser. It was as if no one was really here at all and had never been here and the old woman was merely a shadow. And a shadow did she appear, with her pallor and her cyanosed lips and pale strained eyes. But she smiled happily at Jonathan and when he took her dry hand, she pulled him down to her and kissed his cheek like a mother. "My dear boy," she said. Her voice was low and whispering, and there was a faint pulsing in her throat. But her eyes were shrewd and intelligent. "What's the matter, dear?" she asked. "Has something hurt you?"

"Nothing more than usual," he said. "Now, don't you worry about me. How did you sleep last night?" He took up her chart and studied it closely.

"Wonderful," she said. She looked with mild but polite curiosity at Robert. She had a fine worn face, aristocratic and controlled, and her nightgown was of embroidered batiste. Jonathan continued to study the chart. "This is young Dr. Morgan, Mrs. Winters. My replacement. Robert, this is Elizabeth Winters, my favorite patient, and a saint."

"He talks nonsense," said Mrs. Winters, holding out her hand to Robert. He took the slight old hand; it was very cold, though the room was hot. "We're not going to let him go, are we, Dr. Morgan?"

Heart failure, thought Robert. The old lady had an indomitable appearance, he saw now, and a strong spirit. There was a small bottle of digitalis on her bedside table. It was very strange, but the room did feel empty, as if she were already dead. What had she said? "We're not going to let him go, are we?" Jonathan put down the chart and came to the bedside again.

"Breathing better?" he asked.

"Much better, thanks to you, Jon. I'm sure I feel better than you do."

"I haven't the slightest doubt. You couldn't feel worse."

It was an effort for her to laugh, but she did. However, she studied Jon. "If you leave me, I'll die on somebody's hands." After a moment she added, "I hope so. Jon, why do you insist on keeping this old body alive? I keep fighting you." She paused to get her breath. "You're just perverse."

"Of course I am. I like to see people keeping on living. Besides, we don't have many good people in the world, and when we lose one, we're that much poorer. That's why I want you to live."

"For what?" Now her voice had become a whisper again. Her exhausted eyes looked up at him with unaffected simplicity.

"For me. Let's say that." He nodded at Robert, who opened his bag. "Dr. Morgan is going to examine you, Mrs. Winters, so he'll know, too, how to keep a good soul alive as long as possible."

"He's so young," she said, and with affection. Her breathing was more difficult. Robert examined her with his stethoscope and knew almost at once that she was dying. She had tachycardia and arrhythmias, slurred heart sounds, sudden galloping rhythms, and her lungs were full of rales, sibilant and scattered. Acute left heart failure; it would not be long before her right heart failed also. Robert looked at the digitalis thoughtfully. "Well," said Jonathan, "why do you suppose I prescribed that? Be frank. Mrs. Winters is an intelligent woman and you can't frighten her."

"You gave it because of rapid auricular fibrillation," said Robert, after hesitation. ("Never discuss a patient in his presence, even with another physician," he had been taught.)

"Correct," said Jonathan.

"Sedatives? Diuretics?" said Robert.

"Yes. Opiates. And mercury compounds. Anything else you'd like to suggest, Doctor?"

Robert again hesitated. He thought, I'd like to give her hope. "No," he said.

Jonathan smiled. He looked at the flowers. "Thank you for them, Jon," said Mrs. Winters. She coughed, and put her handkerchief to her mouth, and wheezed for breath. But after the spasm she said, "I know. There wasn't any card. But who would send them except you, dear?"

"Lots of people. The nurses love you."

She was so spent that she only moved her head in faintly smiling denial on her pillows. Again Jon bent and kissed her cheek. "Keep alive," he said. "I need you." He added, "My mother is coming in to see you this afternoon."

"Sweet Marjorie," said Mrs. Winters, and closed her eyes. Jonathan left the room and Robert followed him. They stood near the door in silence for a few moments. Then Jonathan said, "That's the classic example of how not to treat your children."

"She doesn't want to live, does she?"

"No, she doesn't. And hope, in congestive heart failure, is the most potent drug. She hasn't any. What was I saying? Mrs. Winters is another of the 'old settlers.' She's a widow. She was attached to her husband, in a way, but her whole life was centered on two daughters and one son. She inherited a fortune from her parents and another from her husband. Now she doesn't have a cent."

"What did she do with it?"

"She didn't spend it on riotous living! She let her daughters and her son persuade her to turn her money over to them. They'd take the most wonderful care of dear Mama; Mama was too unsophisticated to manage by herself; dear Mama's sweet head mustn't be bothered by all those nasty financial details; Mama must live and be happy and let lovely Bertha and Grace and Sonny Jim take care of all matters and deal with those old lawyers and banks and other ugly things. Mama Deserved to Enjoy Life now Her Family was Grown."

Jonathan's voice had taken on the viciousness Robert had heard so often before.

"Well, dear Mama listened to all those cooing and loving voices, those dear and darling voices of her children. They were married; the daughters live in Philadelphia and Sonny Jim, when he got his dirty hands on all that cash, moved on to New York. Oh, they don't let her starve! She has a single bedroom in the very hotel where you're staying just now, and they pay her medical bills and remember her with a little— modest—gift at Christmas and sometimes, when they're not too busy spending her money, they send her a birthday card. Sometimes. And once a year they all write her a brief note. They're so busy, you see.

"She let them wheedle and lie her out of her money twenty years ago. They've had children since then. Six grandchildren. She's seen only one, and he was a baby and now he's at Princeton. She never saw the others. They didn't encourage her to visit. Mama was too frail, they said. And they never came back to Hambledon. Why should they? They have what they had set out to get. Right from the moment their father died. She hasn't even a photograph of her grandchildren.

"She knows. She's not a mawkish fool. She doesn't save the cards and the infrequent letters they send her—when they remember she's still alive, which they regret. She did have a photograph of the three greedy and accursed devils. Up to about five years ago. Then she destroyed it. When people ask her if she has children, she says 'no.' She really doesn't. In fact, she never did. She gave them too much of her love, too much of her time, too much of her devotion. She gave them her life. So naturally, they took everything and returned nothing. And she knows. She also knows it is entirely her own fault, and she doesn't blame them. She did it to herself. She understands that if she had kept her money, they'd be rushing around her all the time and smothering her with affection.

"And she doesn't want that affection. She doesn't want bought kisses and bought remembrances and lying, loving letters. If she can't have the real article, she doesn't want anything else. In a way, it's a relief to her that she isn't fooled any longer. If she blames anyone, it is herself—not for giving them the money, but because she wasted her life and wasted her husband's life. What she gave him—the remnants left over after she had given most of the cloth to her children—wasn't enough, and now she mourns for her husband and wants to hurry off to him to beg his forgiveness, for her own blindness and selfishness."

"Tragic," said Robert, much depressed. He thought of his mother, who kept a hard closed hand on her purse and he said to himself, Good for you, old girl.

"The most tragic thing in life is not losing those you care for most, or suffering loss or pain. It's making a damned fool out of yourself—when it wasn't necessary. That's the hardest thing to bear." He looked at Robert and smiled a little. "That's what I did. And I'm paying for it."

"I wonder," said Robert, the young and now depressed, "if I should ask my mother to visit Mrs. Winters. She does love the 'old settlers,' you know. And she's great on what she calls 'visiting the sick,' provided it doesn't cost more than a few flowers or a scented handkerchief or a pot of calves' foot jelly."

"No," said Jonathan. "I haven't met your mother yet, but I've a good idea of what's she like. She'd probably tell Mrs. Winters that she's been a fool, and she'd be quite right. But telling a person that she's been a fool only brings the fact closer to home, and it's not calculated to do the patient any good."

"She's determined to die," said Robert.

"So she is. And as for me, I'll be glad to be the one to close her eyes and wish her Godspeed. I've a standing order to be called when she's in extremis. Someone has to be on hand when the boat unfurls its sail, and cheer from the dock. She'll like that."

A child who was dying and who should live; an old wicked man who was not dying and wished to live; an old abandoned mother who wanted to die. As Jonathan had said, "There's no sense to anything."

In the two last cases Robert failed to diagnose one correctly. He was slightly more successful with the last. When he went out into the sunshine, he felt he had become quite aged. He felt very old and worn and used up. He was not as yet able to be objective.

This afternoon he had to watch three operations, none of which was Jonathan's. He watched Jonathan walk rapidly away and he said to himself, A most ambiguous man.

CHAPTER EIGHT

Four nights later, almost at midnight, Father Francis McNulty came to see Jonathan Ferrier. The lights in the big house were out, but the lights in the office were brightly shining. The moon was icy and glittering for again the weather had turned cold. The priest went to the offices, knocked and entered. He found Jonathan sprawled in a chair, more than slightly drunk, with a bottle of whiskey on the spattered desk

before him. So that's it, thought the young priest sadly, but
made himself smile with a glow of his golden eyes. "Surprised to see me?" he asked, and remarked to himself how
inane that was.

Jonathan, who had long ago removed his collar and tie and
was now in shirtsleeves, had a rumpled and disheveled appearance. He scowled drowsily; his eyes were bloodshot.
"Trust the devil to turn up when least expected," he said. He
waved at the bottle. "Have a drink. There's an extra glass."

"I think I will," said the priest. He sat down. He tried to
keep the dismay out of his voice, and his pity. He poured
some whiskey into the glass and drank it slowly, attempting
to keep Jonathan from seeing his consternation. But Jonathan
was not looking at him. He was yawning heavily and glumly.
He reached for the bottle. "Not just yet, Jon," said the priest.
"I want to talk to you."

"At this hour of the night?" Jonathan looked blearily at his
watch, then snapped the case shut, fumbled for the pocket,
could not find it, and let the watch hang. "Where've you
been? Carousing?" He put the bottle down. He tried to focus
his eyes. "What's up?" he asked. "Somebody died, thank
God?"

"Yes."

"Congratulations."

"Don't be childish, Jon—"

"If you're going to set up a Confessional here, Frank, you
can get the hell out. I'm not up to listening to some sad tale."
His voice was slurred and sluggish. "Nor are you listening to
mine." He became a little excited and his drunkenness appeared to increase. "Wasn't it you who asked me last December
over and over, if I was 'guilty'? Yes, I've not forgotten, you
know."

"I only did my duty, Jon, and you know it. There was always the danger—"

"Of me hanging, in mortal sin. Now, why don't you go
home and say your prayers and let me go to bed?"

"I didn't believe you killed Mavis—"

"Well, not after I'd finally convinced you. In the beginning,
yes."

The priest was silent. He said a private mental prayer. He
said, "I want you to forgive somebody. I'd like to tell him—
her—tonight that you did."

Jonathan forced himself upright and groaned and snatched
at his head. "Who, for God's sake? And why? And what do I

care? Do you mean some pigs have actually become convinced I didn't kill Mavis and have sent you here at this hour? Can't they fry a little in their consciences until tomorrow?"

"They're waiting to hear, Jon. Right now. By telephone. It is bad enough for them just now. It's worse, thinking of you."

"Fine. Let them fry. Tell them 'no.' "

Now he did pour more whiskey for himself and gulped it stolidly.

"Jon," said the priest, "little Martha Best died three hours ago at the hospital."

Jonathan lifted his heavy arms, let them drop on the desk, then dropped his head upon them. He didn't really hear, thought the priest, with compassion. He's fallen asleep. He looked at Jonathan's slack head, at the dark disordered hair, at the side of the sallow cheek, which was as still as wood. Then Jonathan said in a voice that seemed to come from a long way off, "I didn't know. I haven't seen her for four days. They'd given orders, the Bests, and old swinish Louis Hedler, that I wasn't to go near her. Hadn't I 'done enough,' lying to them, scaring them to death, trying to make them suffer? That's what they said. Even her nurses were forbidden to tell me anything about her."

"Yes. I know, Jon. I know. But after the first shock of her death Howard and Beth said to me, 'Can he possibly forgive us?' I said I didn't know. And they asked me to come now, not tomorrow. They can't bear waiting. They've got to know."

"At this time, when Martha's just died? They can think of that now?" He lifted his head and his face was changed and distorted. "What's the matter with them?"

"They knew this morning that she was dying. It was obvious. But you weren't in the hospital then. They looked for you."

Jonathan wet his dried and swollen lips. His eyes seemed full of blood. "So, it seems you've got a Mass of the Angels to celebrate."

"Jonathan, please."

Jonathan said, "Don't talk like that to me, in that pained tone of voice! As for Martha, she's well out of it. What does anyone have to live for?"

"You don't know what they're suffering, Jon."

He stared at the priest in an ugly fashion. "Let them get their consolations from that old fraud, Louis."

The priest stood up, sighing. "So, you won't forgive them?"

He waited. But Jonathan said nothing. However, in a moment he did speak. "I'm to be the saint, am I, forgiving every son of a bitch who digs into my bowels and turns the knife? Why? Just tell me why."

"Because, Jon, though you've turned away, you are still a Christian. And, I hope, a man."

Jonathan laughed. "Words, words." He waved heavily at the telephone. "All right. Tell them. Tell them that I grovel before them and beg their forgiveness—" He stopped. "Hell. Tell them that my heart is broken for them, and then get the hell out of here."

The priest reached for the telephone and took the receiver from its hook.

Marjorie Ferrier sat with her son Harald in her small and private sitting room on the second floor of the great old house. Here no one came except by her invitation. She would quote, without apology, " 'In solitude, when we are least alone.' " Jonathan understood this, but Harald would remark in the new jargon, "It is really selfishness and an indifference to others." He had made this remark, regrettably, to Jonathan, who had snorted. " 'I to myself am dearer than a friend.' Shakespeare. A man never betrays himself unless he is a fool or a saint, and what's the difference? Mother can't really stand people, which shows that she is a very wise woman, indeed."

The soft June rain was falling again, but as it was warm, Marjorie's casement windows were open to the air and the piercing scent of roses blew into the cozy little room. She was knitting serenely; she made many woolen garments each year for her sons and friends, and for the indigent. Harald sipped brandy; he had refused the tea, which stood on the low marble table near his mother. He did not like this small room, with the white paneled walls, the ruffled voile curtains, the rose-colored rug and the delicate mahogany furniture. It reminded him too keenly of the times Marjorie had brought him here as a child to speak to him quietly and firmly after some transgression. It had made him cringe, for she had known him only too well. He preferred his father's infrequent cuffings; at least the old boy didn't understand his children and that had been a blessing.

Harald looked at his mother, at her aloof face, her patrician features, her smooth duck skirt and her severe white-silk shirtwaist. She wore a brown belt about her narrow waist; her clever hands flashed with needles and with her engagement ring. The long lashes of her hazel eyes, so like Harald's, fluttered duskily on her pale cheek. Her dark head was slightly bent. She might have been alone.

But she said, "You know, dear, as I've told you before, I've asked Jenny to come here and live with me. She refuses."

"I know. Well, the island was her father's dream and delight." He spoke with light bitterness. "She has a passion about it. She thinks I'm a dastardly intruder." He smiled. "I hate the damned pretentious place, and she knows it, and she knows that I don't dare stay away from it more than five months out of a year. I bet she counts each day! More than five months, even a couple of hours—" He moved his finger across his throat in a slicing gesture.

"It was a silly will," said Marjorie. Now she looked at her son. "Jenny believes you overheard her mother say to Jenny, just before she died, that she was about to make a new will."

Harald hesitated. He took another gloomy sip from his glass. "Well, I did. She's quite right. But I didn't know that she knew I'd overheard. I was glad, Mother. I knew the terms of Myrtle's old will. I hated them. I thought perhaps she'd come to her senses, after my long arguments with her. So Jenny knew I'd heard, eh? What did she tell you?"

But his mother was regarding him with an intense if secret expression. "She only mentioned it, Harald. She, too, thought it was a stupid will, and unfair—to her."

"Well, it was. Myrtle ought to have divided the money equally between us. I could have left then, kissing Hambledon good-bye forever, and Jenny could have had her damned island all alone and live like the recluse she really is."

Marjorie was still watching him. Harald did not hear her faint sigh. He was pouring a little more brandy into his glass. He was the more handsome of Marjorie's sons, as everyone was constantly pointing out. "You know," he said, "I've wanted Jenny to marry me, Mother."

"Yes, dear. She told me."

"It's not the money, Mother. After all, what does she have until I die or something? One hundred wretched dollars a month. I love Jenny; I want her."

"Yes," said Marjorie. She paused. "Who do you think is spreading nasty tales about you and Jenny, Harald?"

He did not answer for a moment, and Marjorie became a little sick. Why, Harald, she said to herself. You did! You want to force Jenny to make her position there with you less scandalous! Oh, Harald, you were always a devious little boy! But this is dreadful. She felt very ill.

"I don't know," said Harald.

"But everyone believes them."

He shrugged. "More fools they. How could anyone believe anything disgusting about poor Jenny? She's about as seductive as a prim stone statue."

"Jon believes those stories, Harald."

"Oh, Jon. He always ·believes the worst of everybody. He always did." He smiled at her winningly. "When we were kids, he never asked who broke something of his. He took it for granted that I did, and hit first and asked questions afterward. Not that he was invariably wrong. I did like to tease him; he was so solemn most of the time."

Marjorie let the knitting fall to her knees. "Jon was a relentless little boy, dear. To him things were either totally black or totally white. He never saw the gray places. There was a kind of fierceness about him. He could never compromise. Once betrayed, he never forgave. Now you—"

"I live in the gray places. Like you, Mother. Like everybody who's sensible."

"Yes."

He smiled at her affectionately. "If he were a fool, I could understand. But he isn't. Well, not much, anyway. I could forgive and forget. My father always preferred him, though, even if the old boy was more tolerant and understanding. He'd sometimes forget I was alive. It was 'Jon this, and Jon that. My son Jonathan.'" Harald still smiled, but the smile had subtly changed. "My father never took me seriously."

"Perhaps not, Harald. Your father was a very serious man himself."

Harald yawned elaborately. "I know. He was always quoting Thomas a Kempis: 'Everywhere I have sought rest and found it not except sitting apart in a nook with a little book.' He and his little 'nooks!' He'd pull Jon into them with him for hours. Perhaps that is what is wrong with my glum-faced brother."

Marjorie's hands were very still on her fallen knitting. "Let's not belittle Jon's troubles. After all, there was Mavis, and the—the—"

Harald looked thoughtfully at the open casement windows. Twilight, purple and vague, was beginning to tinge the raining sky. "He never knew anything about Mavis at all. He'd known her almost from the moment she had been born. But he never saw her in reality. I did. She was shallow and stupid and plotting and frivolous and sly. You know that, Mother. You never said anything, but I know you could not endure him marrying her. However, there's something to be said in Mavis' defense, too. Jon had set up an impossible standard for her. She was suddenly to acquire intelligence and patience and devotion, and she couldn't do it. She'd lived for Mavis Eaton all her life and now she was expected to live for Jon and his interests! She was to acquire a taste for books and science and for that boring hackneyed art he loves, the pre-Raphaelites. She was to grow four inches taller, at least, metaphorically speaking. But all the time she only wanted to dance, gossip, discuss clothes and people, travel, sing, play, and have a good time generally. If Jon had his complaints, Mavis had them, too, and I think I pitied her the most. Butterflies have to live, too, as well as granite busts."

But Marjorie said, "The town won't forget. In spite of all that Jon has done for it, and his really ferocious care for the sick and his hatred for pain and his devotion, it won't forget. They never say anything, but they still think he killed Mavis."

"They want to believe it, Mother. People always want to believe the worst of others."

Oh, God, Marjorie prayed in herself, please stop me! But she said, "You never believed it for a moment, did you, Harald?"

"Not for a moment! Don't I know Jon? I didn't need those medical witnesses from Pittsburgh to tell me! Jon's word was enough." He hesitated.

Marjorie took up her knitting again. She was afraid that Harald would see the trembling of her hands. "Please pour me some fresh tea, dear."

She watched Harald's deft gestures as if all her life depended on his smallest movement. "Cream, again? Sugar? Well, here you are. You didn't drink the first cup."

"Thank you, Harald. Harald, all those months in prison, for Jon! Oh, it's gone and past and the past is better buried! But it won't stay buried for Jon. People still drag out the corpse for him. He thinks I don't know, but I do. He often spends the night out in the offices, drinking—"

"Jon?" Harald stared. He frowned. Does he really care? Marjorie asked herself.

"He thinks I don't know. And I know something else.

When the little Best girl died, he was inconsolable, for all his surface cynicism. And I heard that her parents rejected his diagnosis, and all the hospital rang with contempt for him. The nurses, and some doctors, had heard poor Howard Best's ravings and threats when Jon told them. But he was right, and the poor little thing died soon after. Sometimes I can't sleep, Harald. So I know that Father McNulty went to see Jon in his offices the night of the death. I don't exactly know why. But Jon wouldn't go to the funeral. I've heard he won't speak to Howard or Beth. Two weeks ago. He really loved that little girl; he loves children. It's very strange, isn't it?"

Harald had been listening with deep interest. He said, "I don't think it's strange. I don't blame Jon. I thought they were among his best friends and had always stood by him."

"What is a 'best friend,' Harald? Sometimes I don't know. I never completely trusted anybody. We are truly alone. But Jon had a way, until recently, of expecting the best from people, or at least decent human behavior. Howard had visited him in prison, and it was Howard who found good lawyers for him and always fought furiously with anyone who said Jon was guilty. Then this." She put down her teacup. "If Jon had any doubts about leaving Hambledon, he hasn't any now. I hope he hurries. I hope he leaves soon!"

And so do I, thought Harald. He can't go soon enough for me. He reached out and patted his mother's hand. "Darling, don't be so upset. It's been a miserable time for everybody. It's over. People will forget. Jon will set up practice in a better place."

"Jon won't forget, Harald. He won't forget those months and the trial."

She picked up her knitting, though the dusk in the room had become almost opaque. "No, dear. I can knit without a lamp. If Jon ever finds out the truth, I'm afraid he might—he might—"

"Oh, he was always violent. What 'truth'? Some hack injured Mavis, and then when she began to be infected from the injury, she went to her darling uncle, old Eaton, and he rushed her to the hospital and tried to save her life with an operation. But it was too late. That's what he testified in court, wasn't it? It all happened when Jon was in Pittsburgh. If old Eaton still believes that Jon bungled, or something, and then sent her to him, no one can change his opinion. Everybody wants to believe what he wants to believe. Including Jon."

Please stop me, Marjorie prayed. She said, "Everyone knew that Jon wanted children. He wouldn't have performed such an operation on Mavis."

The silence was suddenly intense in the room. Then Harald said, too softly, "Unless he wanted to kill her."

He waited. His mother said nothing. She was only a pale shadow in the room.

"But I don't believe that," said Harald. "We know the truth. He was not in Hambledon for five days. It all happened when he was away."

"Yes," said Marjorie. She thought she was going to faint. Her heart was thumping erratically and there was sweat on her calm forehead. "That is why he was acquitted. The medical testimony even from Dr. Eaton, Martin. And Jon's witnesses. It was impossible."

"How did we get on this gloomy subject?" Harald now stood up as if the dusk were too much for him. He struck a match and lit a lamp. He stood in his tall and elegant handsomeness and stared at the lamp for a long time. "We've gone over this so many times. You mustn't be so morbid, Mother. I thought it was agreed that no one must mention this again."

"Yes, dear." She looked at him with passionate love and sorrow. "But it all came back with little Martha's death. It keeps coming back. And Jon's drinking. He was usually moderate. Harald, I'm afraid for him. He is the desperate kind."

"Oh, come. You don't think he'd kill himself, do you?" Harald laughed.

"I don't know. If the worst comes to the worst, the truth will have to come out."

Harald slowly turned and looked at his mother.

"What truth, Mother? The name of the hack who botched the job?"

"Harald. Before Mavis was taken to the hospital, she told me Jon had—had—done that thing to her."

Harald's color diminished. "I can't believe that!"

"She told me, Harald. That was even before she went to see her uncle. I knew she was sick—and then she told me."

"But that's impossible! Jon wasn't even here!" He studied her intently.

"And she told her uncle."

"She lied," said Harald. "Mavis was always a liar."

"I know. But that's what she told me and her uncle."

"If so, why didn't old Martin so testify?"

"I've thought about it. Was he trying to protect Jon, even if he hated him after all that? You know how doctors stand together. But I did read that he protested when the verdict of acquittal came in."

Harald still stared at his mother. Then he said with quiet violence, "I hope to God you haven't told anyone else about this!"

She raised her large hazel eyes to the eyes so like her own. "No, dear. I haven't told anyone. And, if I should hear it rumored about, Harald, I'll know where it comes from."

Mother and son regarded each other without moving. Then Harald said, "It won't come from me. How could you think that? Why do you look at me like that?"

"Because, dear, I know that you hate Jon. I've known that for years. You disliked each other when you were children. I blame your father a lot for that. Harald, if things get worse—"

"They won't." He spoke reassuringly and with quickness. "Let the dead bury the dead."

"But the dead often won't stay dead."

She stood up. She was very tall and thin and straight and she looked at her son intensely. "Harald. Don't try to force Jenny to marry you. I know you love her. But don't make life too intolerable for her. She doesn't want you, Harald."

He felt threat in the room. He said with lightness, "How can I force Jenny to marry me, Mother? These aren't medieval days."

"Harald, you musn't force her. She isn't as strong as she appears. She's a very sensitive girl. You mustn't force her."

The feeling of threat increased. Harald moved a step backward from his mother. He said, "If Jenny ever marries me, it'll be her decision. I promise you that."

"Yes, dear," she said, and wanted to weep. "Yes, dear." She put her arms about him and it was as if she held, again, her very vulnerable little boy, the little boy who had always laughed when he was hurt. But she had loved Jon the most. How could she forgive herself?

"Well, I really don't know, Robert," said Jane Morgan in her usually discontented voice. "The rooms aren't very elaborate."

"But, Mother, they are excellently proportioned, and the house isn't that old."

"I thought we'd live elegantly and up to our station."

"We haven't any yet—here."

"Oh, dear Robert! How can you say that? This wretched little town!"

"It isn't wretched and you've liked the ladies you have already met and you told me yourself that they were very 'civil.' Most of them have Main Line relatives in Philadelphia," and Robert added to himself, Whom you don't know and would love to. He stood with his mother in the parlor of the really attractive Georgian house, and, as he had said— prompted by Jonathan Ferrier—the rooms were excellently proportioned, with high molded ceilings, fine balanced doors, white marble fireplaces and beautiful bright wood floors. Robert resembled a red-gold bear more emphatically and stubbornly each day.

"And the lawns," he said, "magnificent old elms, hickories, oaks, and a view of the river from the morning room and bedroom windows. You won't find any better in Philadelphia at the price."

Jane Morgan, leaning on her canes, again studied the big room with discontent, her widow's weeds heavy and black this hot day, her white silk and lace cap set firmly on her hair in defiance of "modern ways." Her long thin nose twitched; her hard mouth moved with pettish but unspoken thoughts. Her small gray eyes slipped coldly over the sun-shadowed walls, looking for faults and cracks.

"I can't say," she said, "that this is a soffiscated town."

"You mean 'sophisticated,' Mother."

"Robert! I'm growing very weary of your impertinent remarks about my use of the Queen's English!"

"It's King's English now, Mother, remember? King Edward."

The cold little eyes studied him. "You were never like this in Philadelphia! Something has happened to you here—probably that dreadful Ferrier man. I knew I wouldn't like him, and since I've met him my opinions have been confirmed. What a repulsive creature! Haven't you noticed how those thick white ridges spring out around his mouth for no reason at all?"

"That's when he's impatient with people—as he usually is, I admit."

"Bad temper, that's all. Bad blood. I've been hearing a number of things," and she nodded significantly and tapped her canes on the bare wooden floor.

"I suppose you have. Hambledon's as bad as Philadelphia

for gossip. Now, Mother. We must decide. This house, you can see, isn't far from the Ferriers, and it is very close to the offices I will be renting. I like it; it is cheaper than the other houses you've seen and we are lucky. It would be much higher priced if the lawyers weren't anxious to close an estate."

"I visualized a more sumptuous home. I can't say I like this home—"

"Mother." Robert was weary. "This isn't a 'home' yet; we don't live here yet. So, it is still a house."

"Home," repeated Mrs. Morgan. She sighed with her discontent. She was really impressed by the house, but it was not in her nature to approve of anything. "Very well," she said in a grudging voice, "if it pleases you, it'll have to please me, I suppose. But I know I won't sleep well living so close to a murderer— I told the ladies—"

"Mother!" Robert spoke harshly. "For God's sake, I hope you haven't been calling Jon Ferrier a 'murderer!' My God! That's libel. Not here in Hambledon, for God's sake!"

She saw that he was genuinely aghast. She smiled knowingly. "I do hope you can trust my discretion, Robert. I'm not a fool. And many important people think well of him, and I wouldn't offend them, for your sake. Don't take the Almighty's name in vain; that's blasphemy. I don't like your new manners. But not everyone admires him as you do, and I gathered, from a word here and there— Well, it doesn't matter."

"Mother, don't lend yourself to gossip here. That would be the one thing that would ruin me forever."

"Robert, you forget that though I am the mother of a physician, I was the wife of one, too. But I can hardly shut my ears and pretend that I don't hear. That would be most impolite."

She uttered a faint shriek and Robert turned quickly. A large fawn and brindle dog, almost as big as a mastiff, was entering the room, sniffing alertly, its pointed ears high and quivering. "Oh, that's just Jon's dog," said Robert, and squatted on his heels and snapped his fingers at the animal.

"Take the brute away!" cried Mrs. Morgan, forgetting that she had arthritis, for she sped briskly to the windows and almost crouched there in extreme terror. "Robert! Don't touch it! It may be mad. It may have fleas. It may kill us!"

"Nonsense," said Robert. The dog had now thrown its great front legs and paws about Robert's neck and was kissing him with enthusiasm, its big liquid eyes shining delightedly. "Look at the boy," said Robert, parrying the kisses with not too much success. He laughed. "A boxer. Jon imported him from Germany. His name is Montgomery Sears Ward Roebuck. That's one of Jon's little pleasantries, because Monty came in a Sears crate, when he was three months old. Now, boy," he said to the dog, who was taking a sudden interest in Jane Morgan. He had never heard such curious sounds before, a shrill bleating. Moreover Jane was fluttering her handkerchief threateningly at him, and with terror. Robert held his collar tightly, for Monty had decided to investigate this interesting phenomenon. "Do stop screaming, Mother," said Robert. "Jon must be around someplace; he never roams without Jon."

At that beloved name Monty lost his curiosity about Jane and opened his mouth in a great grin and looked at the door. He barked commandingly. Jon, dressed for riding, strolled into the echoing parlor. "So, there he is," he said, and he bowed briefly in Jane's direction, and then smiled at Robert. "He must have heard your voices; he shot off like a bullet. There's nothing so inquisitive as a boxer. They're terrible gossips and such, and always want to know what's going on everywhere."

The dog was standing on his hind legs now, his paws on Jonathan's chest, and he was licking Jonathan's cheek with passionate love. Jane shuddered. "I do wish, Dr. Ferrier, that you'd put him out. I feel quite faint. I'm terrified of dogs."

"Are you? Sorry. Here, Monty," and Jonathan led the dog to the door, expertly pushed him out, and closed the wide double doors. "He wouldn't hurt a mouse, honestly. He makes a big noise about rabbits, but since he tangled with a skunk a year ago he's wary of anything in fur. But a wonderful watchdog."

Jane had partially recovered. "I do hope he isn't permitted to roam freely. I'd be frightened to go out into my own garden, and I'd feel that the home was threatened."

Robert winced. But Jonathan was smiling smoothly. "You mustn't worry. Besides, he'll be going away with me eventually." He looked at the woman and tried to conceal his dislike and contempt for her. He turned to Robert.

"You'll be glad to know I waved old Mrs. Winters out this morning," he said.

"Did you?" Robert's face was still warm. He said to his mother, "Mrs. Winters was a patient of Jon's. She died this morning."

Jane was horrified at both Jonathan's "levity" in the face of death and his look of satisfaction. "One of your patients?" she asked in a meaning tone. "She died—and you're glad?"

"Very, very glad, Mrs. Morgan. I was very happy for her." His eyes were flat and expressionless as he glanced at Robert's mother.

She swallowed, then put her handkerchief daintily to her eyes for a moment in acknowledgement of what she called "the Grim Reaper." "She was in much pain, perhaps?" she suggested.

"Not really. Except the pain of living, and now it's all over for her, and I haven't been so pleased for years."

"A poor woman?" said Jane.

"No. She had been an heiress and had inherited a lot of money." It was evident to Robert, who was flushing again, that he was enjoying himself at Mrs. Morgan's expense. "And she wasn't very old, either. Probably your own age, Mrs. Morgan."

"And you're glad she's dead!" But Jane looked with import at her son.

"Very. I'm usually glad when people die. Dying is nothing. It's pain that is intolerable."

Jane considered death the ultimate of terrors and superstitiously never entered a house where it had recently visited and never went to cemeteries. She stared blankly at Jonathan and then her eyes squinted as if she were confirming something she had long ago guessed about him, something exceedingly unpleasant and unspeakable. She nodded, quite perceptibly, agreeing with herself. This dreadful man! she thought. This, really, monster. What had she heard recently from some newly met ladies? He had had another patient, a little girl, and there had been something quite mysterious about her death—Jane shuddered again and now it was not pretense.

"I do feel faint," she said to Robert, and then quickly simpered at Jonathan as though trying to placate him as one would attempt to placate a demon, before fleeing. "You must really take me back to the hotel."

"Yes, Mother." Robert sighed. "Well, is it settled about this house? I must let the lawyers know this afternoon."

"I'm not overly pleased with this home," said Jane, cautiously edging around Jonathan, tapping her canes smartly. "But I am only your mother, Robert. What pleases you must please me. You mustn't consider me in the slightest."

Robert gritted his teeth. He did not know whom he detested more at this moment, his mother or Jonathan. Jonathan was smiling idly and striking his leg with his crop. He went to the door and opened it for Jane, but she shrank back. "Coming, Robert?"

"Yes, Mother," he said. It was extraordinary how he was quite regularly, these days, desiring to hit something very hard. He gave Jonathan a murderous look, but Jonathan merely raised his black eyebrows questioningly. "I hope your dog won't annoy my mother," said Robert. "Where is he now?"

"Monty? Off inspecting squirrels, I suppose. I'd better go first and corner him. When you hear me whistle, it will be safe. Safe." Jonathan touched his bare head with his crop, in salute to Jane, and went quickly from the room.

"Oh, dear," said Jane. "I can't stand him, I really can't stand him. He frightens me half to death with his peculiar smile and—"

"His smile isn't peculiar, Mother. He is just trying to get a rise out of you, and he's succeeding. I'll take you back to the hotel at once." He heard a sharp whistle.

Jonathan was waiting, holding his dog. The broad steps, fanning out, shone like marble in the hot sunlight. It was a charming house, laced with the frail shadow of the leaves, standing calmly alone on its lawns and among its trees. Jonathan said, "I thought you might like to see another patient of mine, Bob. My very last one, the last I'm taking. You ought to look her over."

He smiled at Robert with broad innocence. But his black eyes were tired and appeared dissipated. "Where shall I meet you?"

Robert was curt. "At the hospital. St. Hilda's?"

"Not this time. The Friends'. My patient isn't rich."

Jane made a mouth at Robert, commanding him to refuse, but he said, "In half an hour, then." He did not look back as he led his mother down the long and winding walk to the street and his buggy. Jonathan watched them go. Poor devil, he thought. We'll have to work on this very strenuously. He studied Jane's gaunt black back as she hobbled painfully beside her son. A fraud. If she had arthritis, he, Jonathan, had leprosy. He was quite accustomed to these hypochondriacal women who ruled their families with pretended illness and, unfortunately, usually succeeded. One of these days, he said to himself, as he patted Monty, who was showing a desire to accompany Robert, we'll have to expose her and that will be very pleasant. One good kick in the ass and she'd be cured. But we must do it more diplomatically.

He took Monty to the white fence below the lawns which separated the house from the offices, thrust the protesting dog through the gate, and closed it. "Go on home," he said. "I think Mary's got a bone for you. Stop grinning at me." He reached over the gate and pulled one high ear affectionately. Then, whistling, he went down to the street, where he had tied his horse. It was a great black gelding who remembered more puissant days, for he arched his neck, showed large teeth, and stamped when he saw his master. "You're another fraud," said Jonathan, who mounted dexterously and rode off to the hospital.

Robert was still sullen when he met Jonathan in the lobby of the large grim building. It was bad enough to have a foolish mother; it wasn't very courteous, however, to make game of one's mother to one's face. Jonathan greeted him kindly. "Miss Meadows will be glad to see you," he said, and tucked Robert's stiff arm in his.

The Friends' Hospital was strictly utilitarian, but thanks to Jonathan it had become what the older doctors said was "entirely too modern and stark." Jonathan, it was, who had reformed the somewhat archaic system of teaching nurses and had established a nursing school under rigorous discipline. He had also insisted on halving the wards so that none contained more than twelve patients and he had opened windows, ordered dark brown walls to be painted in more cheerful colors and had commanded clean white linoleum on all the floors. The four operating rooms had come under his critical eye, also. Witnesses to operations, he said, must be gowned, capped and masked to avoid contamination of the air. This was all folly to the Chief-of-Staff, Dr. Humphrey Bedloe, and the others on the staff, but as Jonathan had offered to pay for the modernizing of the operating rooms, they consented with smiles of indulgence.

However, as in St. Hilda's, he had not been successful in his insistence that some of the older surgeons must discard their traditional frock coats and striped trousers and that they should use modern methods of asepsis. The younger ones, trained in better schools, sympathized with him and assured him that time would take care of their elders. "In the meantime these hacks literally get away with murder," he had said. "We should call this place the Morgue."

The hospital had no spacious grounds as did St. Hilda's. Its hard granite walls jutted straight up from a busy street, and its windows were tall high slits, rounded at the top in an older style. But it was clean, or as clean as Jonathan's constant nagging could make it. It had two floors of private rooms, small but sun-filled now; the other two floors contained the wards, the laboratories, the operating rooms, the kitchens, and the offices and a meeting room for nurses. The doctors had their own quarters, and they also had a restaurant of sorts, forbidden to interns who were usually given a meager tray by student nurses—if the latter happened to remember.

When Jonathan came here now, he came, he felt, as a stranger, no longer involved. He was not as popular here as he was at St. Hilda's, possibly because he and his family had given the private hospital more money. Very often he encountered resistance and sulky hostility and watchful eyes. He ignored it all. He said to Robert now, "One of these days hospitals will be worse than this. Oh, they'll be cleaner and more modern and very, very big. But they'll be totally indifferent and impersonal. We are already beginning to think of patients as stomachs, livers, colons, uteruses, rectums, gall bladders, and what all, and not as people. You can't ignore a man's manhood without making him less than a man. You can't insult his humanity by thinking of him as a mere collection of organs without injuring him spiritually and even bodily. An anthill is a fine place for ants, and collective effort is fine for ants. But man is not an ant. I've been reading H. G. Wells recently. He approves of ant life. He also admires Karl Marx, who thought ant communities the most desirable way to live."

He and Robert were approaching one of the big elevators. The wide corridors hummed with activity. Jonathan pursed his lips. "Remember Shakespeare's eulogy of the bees?

" 'The singing masons building roofs of gold.' Well, there'll be masons in the future, millions of them, but they won't be singing and the roofs won't be golden. I don't think I'm going to like this century. It already has the combined stink of a hive, or an anthill, where 'man is diminished and he dies in the shadow of the work of his own hands.' But it's not a new story. The ant heaps of Alexandria, Athens, Rome, Thebes, and the others went the way of human ant heaps because man is not an ant and he will never be one. That is, if he takes very good care in the coming decades. He never did in the past. He probably won't now."

"Cheerful," said Robert, still feeling resentment.

"No. Just a historian. And I've seen the old crowded ruins, built one cell upon another, like a hive, with all the land around them. Perhaps I'm wrong. Perhaps man is, after all, only a bee or an ant. Sometimes I wonder. 'Creatures that by a rule in nature teach/ The act of order to a peopled kingdom.' Shakespeare's darling little bees again. But the 'act of order' declines into chaos; always does. There's something anarchistic in man, and I, for one, don't denounce it. It's our only guarantee against tyranny."

They went into one of the large elevators. "That reminds me. Here, in Hambledon, we have very lively Fourth of July celebrations. In the square. With a band and flags and howling politicians. You might enjoy seeing how the peasants enjoy themselves."

"You really hate this place now, don't you?" Robert was still surly.

"Well, let's put it this way: I don't believe in unrequited love."

His nonchalance infuriated Robert for some reason. The younger man tugged at his reddish mustache and gave Jonathan a sidelong look. He never saw and talked with Jonathan without feeling heated, disturbed, confused, bewildered, sad or angry. There had been times when he had felt awed and touched; there were more times when he had wanted to punch Jonathan. He no sooner felt admiration but that he immediately felt rage. Jonathan was much too protean for him. He was afraid of the day when he would be alone, and the next moment he could not wait for Jonathan to leave. There was no getting close to Jonathan, no way of approaching him. The slightest effort in that direction was met with sudden coldness or a sardonic remark.

The back of the old man who was operating the elevator had stiffened, and as Jonathan and Robert left the operator he gave Jonathan a look of intense hatred intensified by the cunning knowingness of his curled mouth. Robert was not feeling entirely friendly toward Jonathan, but he paused a moment to stare with haughty rebuke at the old man, who immediately ducked his head and closed the elevator door. "What is it?" asked Jonathan, but Robert said nothing.

They walked down a long corridor, then Robert said, "I thought your patient was in a ward."

"She was. I took her out and put her in a private room, at my own expense. She has never had real privacy in her life, but now she deserves it. I didn't tell you about her. She has a terminal case of cancer—rectum and colon. The poor old soul could not afford earlier treatment, though I frankly say that I don't think there is any cure for that disease. You can arrest it—sometimes—and in some cases of skin cancer it can be eliminated—sometimes. They disagree with me, of course, but I think it is a systematic disease and not local, not local even when it appears confined. If Miss Meadows had come a year ago or even six months ago, we might have been able to do something, at least to prolong her life. But eventually it would've caught up with her. What are a few more years of life—when one is old and has never lived at all?"

"Another like Mrs. Winters?"

"No, the reverse. She must have been pretty once; she was my first-grade teacher and I remembered her as pretty and as plump and warm as a muffin right from the stove. She must have had what our parents called 'admirers.' But she had younger brothers and sisters, and parents, and somehow teachers get tied in to support the whole damned family. 'It's their duty,' everyone says, when even elementary common sense, not to mention religion, should teach people that their first duty is to satisfy themselves as individuals before they can march off to do something for anyone else. But teachers, I've noticed, are born martyrs. Otherwise, they wouldn't be teachers. Dedicated souls. I wonder why? I can pick kids out who will end up teachers. They just foam with a quiet sense of responsibility.

"So Miss Anne Meadows, the dedicated, responsible soul who loved everybody, and wanted to 'serve' everybody, in the ineffable way of teachers, supported her parents and put her brothers and sisters on their feet. Nobody was grateful; no one ever thought poor Anne was entitled to a life of her own. She was only doing 'that which was proper.' No one even dreamed that perhaps Anne might like to marry and have her own children and retire from the damnable weariness of struggling with obdurate young things who didn't want to learn anything in the first place. She was just Anne Meadows, a teacher, with a 'duty.' She never complained.

"Well, the brothers and sisters went off, after an education provided by their sister, and insofar as they were concerned, the parents were still Anne's responsibility. She must have agreed. By this time she was fifty and I've noticed that the

parents of schoolteachers seem to live to be incredibly old.
Then she was sixty, and the parents were still alive, but they
were pettish and complaining and senile, and Anne had to endure them after a full day's work. Then she was sixty-five,
and God apparently became aware of her—belatedly—and
took her parents off her hands.

"One brother and one nephew came to their funerals. My
mother and I were there—but I was the only former pupil.
I'd seen Miss Meadows over the years and tried to convince
her that she had a duty to herself, first of all, but the poor
soul was honestly shocked. That's another symptom of the
teacher-malady. Now she is sixty-eight. Her eyesight failed;
she had to retire. On the most miserable little pension you
ever heard of. I did hear of it. I sent her a cashier's check
anonymously every month; otherwise she'd have starved and
done scrubbing or something to make ends meet. She never
hears from her family; they've forgotten she exists. After all,
don't schoolteachers make such 'large salaries'? Anne was
never able to save a cent. But, again, she never complained.

"That's the saga of martyrs. If there are such creatures as
saints, Anne is one; she has all the heroic, pathetic virtues,
and I, for one, have no use for saints. They're such an infernal annoyance to the rest of us. By the way, she thinks my
monthly check is a tender remembrance from her brothers
and sisters, and she thanks them sweetly every month."

Robert was incredulous. "And they never tell her?"

Jonathan halted and looked at him with amusement.
"Why, no. Don't you know anything abour your dear fellowman? They probably think she is senile or that she is mocking them. So they never write to her. She thinks they don't
want to be thanked! So she knits and sews little gifts for
them, and sends them off every Christmas with her love, for
God's sake!

"I can't do anything for her. But I have an operation in
mind which sets the backs up of the hacks who pretend to be
very pious and believe that 'suffering is the lot of man.' I've
done the operation before, but it's tricky. You can watch tomorrow. I cut the nerves which lead to the cancerous regions.
That stops the pain, anyway, and she's in agony except when
she's under opiates. And think of this: She called me only
three days ago—and all those months she's been suffering
hell. But, then, she's been suffering hell all her life and one
more torment was almost nothing to her."

Robert shook his head. "If people won't take care of themselves and offer themselves up for martyrdom, can others be blamed if they take advantage?" But he was troubled.

The hard white ridges sprang out about Jonathan's mouth. "Anyone who takes willful advantage of another, robs another of his substance, lives at the expense of others, and flourishes on another's work and grows fat on it can't be called a man. He's a parasite and he's done a worse harm to himself than he has to his victim. He's become a simple structure, physically and mentally, as parasites always become simple structures, almost primitive. You've seen parasites under the microscope, and even with the naked eye. They lose their means of locomotion, their ability to survive away from their host. In a way the host is more guilty than the parasite for suffering the parasite. Do you remember what St. Paul said: 'He who does not work, neither shall he eat.' That was more of a warning to the host than to the parasite he makes. No one has the right to make others dependent, even in the name of sweet charity. Charity must be an emergency measure, short in duration—or you destroy a man's very soul. The Puritans understood that; they got a man back on his feet fast and made him support himself at the first possible moment. No malingering. He worked or he starved."

Robert smiled, forgetting his resentment. "You should have been a teacher or one of these new sociologists." Jonathan lifted himself away from the wall on which he had been leaning. He seemed exceptionally tired and his eyes were bloodshot. "I have a feeling about this damned century," he said. "Something not very clean." They walked a few more steps and Jonathan stopped before a door and pointed to a neatly lettered sign on it. He chuckled, and by the glare of the naked overhead electric light Robert read:

PLEASE KNOCK AND WAIT FOR PERMISSION TO ENTER.

"Miss Meadows wrote that herself, and I think it's wonderful." Jonathan laughed. "All her life was surrounded by people—her parasitic family—and the thousands of kids she taught and interfering relatives urging her to 'do her duty,' in short, not to bother them. Her life was made up of bells and beds, blackboards and blackguards, pounding feet and pounding voices, dust, chalk, dishes, clatter, clatter, clatter. Now, at last, she has a chance to be alone. Not even the nurses dare come in without the preliminary knock and permission. Alone. That's a marvelous thing—being alone. We don't fully appreciate it. And I have the funniest damned feeling that we're coming into an era where no one will let you alone or have respect for your privacy. All in the name of 'social feeling' as that idiot Horace Mann called it."

He knocked on the door and after a moment a woman's voice said a little forbiddingly, "Who is it?"

"Jon Ferrier, Miss Anne."

"Oh, come in, come in!" They went in to a large, whitewashed room sparkling with sunlight, and Robert saw the small round figure sitting up in the bed, smoothing back astonishingly black thick hair about a plump and very ashen face. He had expected to see some mortal wreck of a poor aged woman, but Miss Meadows looked quite well, and her round features beamed, and only her color suggested desperate illness. As he walked closer to her he saw that her large brown eyes, however, were clouded and glazed with the opiates she had been given, and she suddenly yawned, then smiled, and held out her small fat hand to Jonathan.

Jonathan held her hand between both of his and said, "Miss Anne, this is the Dr. Morgan I've told you about, my replacement."

She nodded at Robert courteously and scrutinized him with the quick intelligence and awareness of a teacher being introduced to a new pupil of whom she must form a concise opinion. "What a nice red-gold boy," she said, and gave him her other hand. It was hot and tremulous. "I don't imagine you ever caused anyone any trouble in your life, did you, Doctor?"

"Come to think of it, I didn't," said Robert. "Perhaps that's what's wrong with me."

She laughed and it was a pleasant, understanding sound. "Now Jonnie, here, was the worst little boy I ever had. Always in disputations with everything. Always certain of everything. A fierce little boy. Born, I always said to his mother, with an outrageous sense of right and wrong and never willing to compromise." She yawned again. The soft muscles of her full face contracted with a spasm of agony, but she still smiled. She had the born teacher's perfect control of herself, even in unbearable pain. "I adored him," she said, "and I thrashed him twice as much as I ever thrashed any of my other children. He was perfectly horrible to his little brother, too. Harald."

She looked at Jonathan tenderly, and the clouded eyes brightened with mischief and affection. "Jonnie, I know that you're paying for this room. I interrogated one of the nurses, and the poor girl, she's a student, was forced to tell me.

Never mind, Jonnie. You know I'd never accept anything for free—ever. So, I asked my lawyer to come to me yesterday, and he did, and I left Papa's old house to you, and the few dollars I have in the bank. Please don't say anything. The house isn't worth more than two thousand; so old and decrepit, you know, but the land is getting valuable. Give it to one of your charities, if you want to. I just want to be sure you have it—and nobody else." Her voice weakened.

"Well," said Jonathan. He said, "How about your family?"

She smiled curiously. "Jonnie, I'm an old woman and sometimes old women get revelations. Or maybe they're inquisitive. I know you're the one who has been sending me that mysterious monthly cashier's check. Please don't deny it."

Her voice, her eyes, her hair and her manner were that of a young girl, and Robert recalled that most of the teachers he had known had had this odd youthfulness into very old age. Was it because they had associated with children so much, or was it an innate quality of the spirit?

She was still holding Jonathan's hand, and now she bent her head and touched her cheek to it, like a mother. "Such a lovely boy," she said. "Jonnie, you must never leave here; you mustn't let them drive you away. You'll never get over it if you do. Don't make me think I was wrong about you. You always had such courage."

"Now, Miss Anne," said Jonathan. "You aren't my teacher any longer. I'm a big boy now. How did you sleep last night?"

"Very well; better than for many months."

"You should have come to me sooner."

She smiled at him with beautiful candor. "Well, Jonnie, I knew that you treated so many people without charging them. I knew you wouldn't charge me. So, I kept away from you. Yes, I know I could have gone to other doctors—but they would have charged me, and I couldn't afford it. What was a poor woman to do?"

Jonathan sat down on the edge of the bed and looked at her with gravity. "Miss Anne, you know I'm going to operate on you tomorrow, and that will relieve you of the greater part of your pain. But you know it isn't going to make much difference in the long run, don't you?"

"Yes. I know, Jonnie. I'm glad you don't try to fool me. You know, I never did have much time to think about God, but now I do. It's very interesting. In a way it's the most exciting thing that ever happened to me, speculating about God and where I'm going. When my eyes aren't too tired, I study that Bible I brought with me. 'Surely man lives again.' That's quite comforting. I just hope," she said with her merry smile, "that they don't assign me to teaching again, not for a very long time. I just hope that they'll let me live in a small wooden house with roses, in the midst of a deep forest, and listen to the birds sing. All alone."

Jonathan said nothing. He just stroked her feverish hand. "You don't believe it, do you, sweetheart?"

"No," he said, "I don't. But I may be wrong. I hope, for your sake, that I am."

She sighed and then quirked her eyebrows questioningly at Robert. "I hope you're a more pious boy than Jonnie is, Dr. Morgan." Then she returned to Jonathan. Her face changed. "Don't leave me, Jonnie, Jonnie, don't leave me!" There was a sudden terror in her voice.

"I won't, I won't. You know I won't." He hesitated. "I know you aren't a Catholic. But would you like a friend of mine to come to see you, just to chat, a Father McNulty? He won't preach at you or sound off periods at you. But he could tell you things that might interest you; after all, it's his specialty."

"Yes, sweetheart, I'd like that very much." The terror had left her voice. "Thank you, Jonnie. And we'll plot together how to keep you where you're needed so much."

A nurse came in with a hypodermic of morphine, but it was Jonathan who swabbed Miss Meadows' arm with alcohol and who inserted the needle. She kept her eye on him, the thoughtful eyes of a teacher. "Now I'll sleep," she said. "And I did want to think."

Robert had seen hundreds of patients during his internship, but he had never before seen such absolute courage and fortitude. He knew that her suffering must be terrible. Yet her concern was for Jonathan. As the nurse settled her on her pillows and smoothed her sheet and blanket she said, "You mustn't go away, dearest, you mustn't. It would kill you forever. It never does to run; you just stand up and face them, even if your back is against the wall. That's what you did when you were a little boy—I want to remember you like that. Jonnie?"

"I'm not a coward," he said. In a moment she was serenely asleep, but now the full furrows of her torment were deep on her forehead and about her mouth. The nurse said, "Oh, Dr.

Ferrier. The Chief-of-Staff, Dr. Bedloe, is particularly anxious to see you. He said it was most important."

"The hell with him," said Jonathan. He looked down at the sleeping woman. "I wish she'd drop away, like that, and never wake up again. This thing can disintegrate the most courageous patient; I don't want to see her at the last, as she'll be."

Robert said, out of his youth and ignorance, "I don't think she'll disintegrate."

"She will, she will," said Jonathan. "She's not the only one who's keeping me in this town. I can't go until she does. And you can't tell with this disease; she may live a week or six months more." He looked bitterly at Robert. "I know it's our duty to keep them alive. I just wonder why, that's all."

The nurse gave him a prim hard look, then said again, "Dr. Bedloe is particularly anxious to see you, Doctor."

"So you said. And I said, the hell with him." He took Robert's arm. "I can't do you any damage now. You've been accepted on the staff. And Bedloe's going to be your particular misery. One of the old diploma-mill hacks with not a tenth of the sense Dr. Bogus had."

Robert recalled Dr. Bedloe as a tall and stately middle-aged man with a pink complexion, cold blue eyes and an authoritative manner and an absolutely positive voice. Like so many of his kind he had a thick and flowing mop of white and silken hair, and he was reputed to be very wealthy from his investments in oil wells in Titusville. Jonathan said, as he and Robert left the room, "I'd call Bedloe an anus, except that would be disparaging a very hard-working and long-suffering part of the body, much abused and rarely giving any trouble except to the sedentary. I think I'll just call him a cloaca, which isn't flattering the cloaca, which always serves some purpose, which Bedloe doesn't. Except that he does, in a way, cleanly carry away a lot of the bloody sewage his pet hacks spew up in the operating rooms. Cleanly away, with no one suspecting except a lot of us younger doctors and most of us wouldn't dare say anything. I always did. He hates my guts."

The nurse twitched her long white skirts out into the hall after them. "Dr. Bedloe," she began, in her admonishing voice, and then she brightened. "Oh, here he is now!"

Dr. Humphrey Bedloe was indeed bearing down on them like an eagle. "Jon!" he said. "I'm glad I caught you! It's very important."

"Well," said Jonathan, leaning negligently against the wall, "what have I done now? You know I don't have but half a dozen patients in this penitentiary these days." Then he looked at the older man with curiosity. "What's the matter— Doctor? Having a touch of angina again?"

Dr. Bedloe was indeed pale and appeared agitated. He nodded curtly at the nurse, who scuttled away. He bit at the end of his silken white mustache. He glanced warily at Robert. "I must speak to you alone, Jon. It's of the utmost importance."

"Speak away," said Jonathan, not moving. "Bob here is my replacement. He'll be cleaning up after your butchers, who don't even have a sense of proportion enough to wear the straw hat of an honest butcher. Speak away."

Dr. Bedloe's agitation increased. He gave Robert a quelling look. Only two weeks ago Robert would have obeyed that glance and would have discreetly moved off. Now he stood solidly on his big legs and did not stir. For an instant Dr. Bedloe openly and actively disliked him and there was a blue glitter of ominous threat in his eyes.

"It's very private, Jon."

"Nothing's private. Not to me, any longer."

Again the older man savagely bit on his mustache. Then he said, "It's my niece, you know her, Hortense Nolan. You were at her wedding. She married the Nolan boy. Oh, damn it, Jon! I can't stand here like this and inform the whole hospital!"

"If I remember," said Jonathan, "you did inform the whole hospital. About me. Even before I was arrested. In fact, you didn't even wait for the indictment before you had me removed from the staff. A very precipitate fella, you. Dear, paternal Humphrey."

"My God," said Dr. Bedloe, and Robert, with interest, saw actual despair on the man's face. "Why do you bring that up now? Isn't it over with? I'm thinking of Hortense. I've thought lots of things about you, Jon. Always did. But I never thought you were malicious."

Now Jonathan was looking intently at him. "There is something wrong, isn't there? Well, what about Hortense? Pretty girl, if I remember. Lots of red hair and big white teeth. Nineteen? Well?"

"It's—you know, Jon. You know all about it! She was pregnant—"

"Yes. I remember. And I recommended young Harrington

to you, when you asked me to deliver her. But young, modern doctors aren't good enough for you and your family, are they? You said old Schaefer would deliver her. That's it, isn't it?"

"Yes." Dr. Bedloe bent his head. "That's true. He did deliver her, at St. Hilda's. Five days ago. A nice baby, a boy."

"Well?"

"It's this, Jon—"

"Now, don't tell me the girl has puerperal fever, for God's sake!"

"Peritonitis."

Jonathan lifted himself from the wall and he looked at Dr. Bedloe with open hatred and disgust. "I told you. Old Schaefer isn't fit to deliver a cow. Never washes his hands; it's a principle of his, since asepsis was introduced years ago. He doesn't believe in germs even now, does he? But he's such a benign old bastard and gives the girls such encouragement and pats their cheeks sweetly before he slaps the chloroform over their noses. Peritonitis, by God! Well, what did you expect?"

"She's dying, Jon. She's like a daughter to me; never had any of my own. And she's dying. They telephoned me from St. Hilda's just now. She—she's been feverish since yesterday, and now today—"

"And he infected her, the bloody old swine, with his patting dirty hands. What had he been doing before? An autopsy?"

Dr. Bedloe spread out his hands. "Jon, they think she needs an immediate operation—to save her life. She—she bled a little more than ordinarily after the delivery. Thought she was out of danger. Jon, she's dying."

Jonathan said in a loud voice, "An operation? Hysterectomy? At her age?"

All at once Dr. Bedloe looked old and stricken and sick. "It's even worse. The—the baby died last night. A—a brain injury, birth injury, I think. Was doing so well, too, in spite of the high forceps. All at once. She's only nineteen, Jon."

"Sweet Jesus," said Jonathan.

Robert Morgan did not even wince. He was too horrified.

"Jon, Louis Hedler said I should call you at once. He said if anyone can save Hortense, it is you."

"Good old Louis," said Jonathan. He shook his head. "Look, Humphrey, I'm not going to get into this, not even for little Hortense. It's your dirty work; you're not going to smear me with it. Where's old Schaefer?"

"He never leaves her for a moment. It's—pathetic—"

"I bet it is. She's his goddaughter, isn't she? No, I'm not getting into this filthy mess and then letting you sing it out that it was all my fault. No, Humphrey. I'm sorry, but the mess is in your own lap."

Dr. Bedloe grasped Jon's arm. "Please, Jon." His voice broke. "Don't think of anything else but Hortense. I promise you—"

"Sure you will. Anything as of now. But if Hortense dies, and she probably will, then it'll be all my fault. Wasn't it your wife who spread it around that there was something mysterious about little Martha Best's death? Yes, it was. My mother told me."

"Jon, I'll be there in the operating room. Half a dozen of us will be there."

"Fine, fine. In your germy frock coats. No, thank you. I'm sorry about Hortense. But call Harrington, Humphrey, as you should have called him in the beginning."

Dr. Bedloe seemed about to burst into tears. "I—I thought about that. He refuses."

"Good for Phil. Look, I'll say a prayer for Hortense, if I can remember who to, but not for me, Humphrey."

He shook his head and turned away, then caught young Robert's eyes. He stared and said with disgust, "Oh, not you, too!"

"I'll be there," said Robert. "I'll help."

"You and your pretty little red mustache!" Jonathan regarded him with contempt. "Let me warn you: Never clean up after the hacks. Or try to. After it's too late, the hacks will sing, 'He did it, he did it!' They never forgive us for having a decent medical education. Come on."

"Please, Jon," said Dr. Bedloe.

"What more can this stinking town say about me? Just that I murdered Hortense. Bob? Coming? We're going over to St. Hilda's."

CHAPTER NINE

Jonathan and Robert arrived at St. Hilda's after a fast ride through the town. They had not spoken, though Jonathan had given Robert many a grim and accusatory glance, as if all this were the younger man's fault, and as if Robert had forced him into this dangerous situation. But Robert smiled under his mustache. They went at once to the luxurious suite of young Hortense Nolan, and there Jonathan found Dr. Emil Schaefer sitting beside the bed of Hortense, who was whining painfully and protesting, while the doctor gently and lovingly urged her to eat "just a little, dear. This good broth. This dainty piece of chicken, this hot buttered muffin. You must keep up your strength."

Jonathan walked in, almost running, swept the spoon from the doctor's hand, and lifted the filled and steaming tray and hurled it furiously against the wall with a resounding crash. "God damn it!" he exclaimed. "Are you trying to kill the girl? Out, out. I want a conference with all of you." Dr. Schaefer, a short and rosy man with a bald head and a thick gray beard, stared at him as at a mad dog, and he rose slowly, his blue eyes blank and staring. Dr. Bedloe, who had followed on Jonathan's heels, looked with dismay at the ruins of the "nourishing lunch" but said as easily as he could, "Emil, I called Jon Ferrier—he's used to these things—and we'd like to consult with you."

"You called this—this—" Dr. Schaefer stammered.

"Emil, she's my niece. There are some modern things, you know—"

The fair fat face of Dr. Schaefer turned very white. "If he touches her, then I must leave the case, Bedloe."

"Louis Hedler has also asked Jon," said Dr. Bedloe, in terror of Jonathan's refusal. "Please, Emil."

"On second thought," said Jonathan, "I want him here. I want to ask him some questions. I also want those two last-year interns, Moe Abrams and Jed Collins, who've been suffering enough under the hacks. I also want Louis. Go and get them, Humphrey." He spoke to the Chief-of-Staff of the Friends' as if he were a lackey. "I won't even look at the girl until you're all here. And you might tell Moe and Jed to bring their notebooks. This is not only for their information but for my own protection."

His dark lean face was very pale and his black eyes flashed at Dr. Bedloe threateningly. Dr. Schaefer took out his handkerchief and wiped the sweat from his face and his hands. Jonathan took one step toward him, seized the handkerchief, stared at the elderly man and then at his hands, then threw the handkerchief into his face. "So, you have a cold, have you? And you've been examining her—how many times today, you criminal fool? With germ-laden hands?"

"I won't stand this!" said Dr. Schaefer. "I won't bear these insults from a jackanapes, an incompetent, who even bungled—"

"Emil, for God's sake!" cried Dr. Bedloe in an agonized voice.

"Deliberately," added Dr. Schaefer, who appeared on the verge of a stroke.

"Never mind him, Humphrey," said Jonathan. "Go and get those people. Let him stand here and blubber. He'll have enough to do to answer questions later."

He pushed his hands into his pockets as if he were sheathing daggers. Does he have to be so violent? Robert asked of himself, then he moved slowly to the fine brass bed and looked down at the young girl there.

Hortense Nolan lay high on a bolster and pillows and sheets of the best and softest linen, and it was evident to Robert that she was almost moribund with sepsis. She was so slender and small and young that she appeared to be hardly more than twelve years of age, and her mass of red hair was in strong contrast to the ashen pallor of her little face. It flowed over her pillows like a flag of danger and fell over her panting breast. Her eyes were half open and sunken in gray pits; their color was clouded by a glaucous film. Her nostrils

were pale and pinched, her lips faintly purple. She was delicately made, with the slightest of arms, the daintiest of hands.
The latter were pulling restlessly and aimlessly at the bed
linen, and Robert felt sick and frightened. Her breath was
slow yet noisy in the suddenly silent room. But Jonathan
would not look at her; he stood at the windows and stared
out, while Dr. Schaefer pressed his fat back hard against the
wall near the door.

Two nurses came in and hurried to the bed. Jonathan said
without turning, "Don't go near that bed or touch that girl!"

The nurses gaped at him, and both their fresh-colored
faces hardened with surprise and knowing significance. They
turned as one to Dr. Schaefer and spoke to him obsequiously,
"Doctor, Mrs. Nolan's parents and her husband are outside
and wish to see Mrs. Nolan."

"Yes, yes," said the overwhelmed man. "Of course. Send
them in."

"No," said Jonathan. "If they come in, I go—out. And I
won't come back."

But the nurses only awaited Dr. Schaefer's orders, smiling
contemptuously, ignoring Jonathan. Dr. Schaefer hesitated.
His effort to come to a decision turned his plump face scarlet. He looked at Jonathan's back with hate. "I—we—we are
having a consultation," he said to the nurses. One of them,
the older, stepped back in astonishment. "With Doctor—*Ferrier?*"

"With Dr. Ferrier," said Dr. Schaefer. The young women
gaped again. They turned their heads slowly and regarded Jonathan at the window. Their astonishment grew immense.
"Please leave," said Dr. Schaefer in a choked voice. The girls
flurried from the room, their long white skirts rustling. They
could not wait to report this incredible scene to their sisters.
Robert could hear their fluting and agitated voices retreating
down the hall. Silence entered the room again, except for the
anguished breathing of the dying girl, who appeared to be totally unaware of the men in the room, the broad sunlight of
afternoon and the corridor noises and the soft wind lifting
the frilled curtains at the windows. She had sunken into that
profound detachment and distance which is the anteroom of
death. But Jonathan did not look at her; Robert saw his pale
and sallow cheek, the hard jutting of his cheekbones and jaw,
the tensity of his whole body, as if he were on the point of
losing control of himself.

The door swung open and Dr. Hedler, accompanied by Dr.

Bedloe and the two young interns, entered hurriedly. "Jon!" cried Louis Hedler. "It was good of you to—ah—attend this consultation! Very good!"

Jonathan turned slowly from the window, but he looked at the interns while he replied, "I want this understood: I came under pressure. My common sense told me to refuse. I came against my will, and because I'm a damned sentimentalist and have a soft heart for young victims of obdurate and medieval old hacks who never heard of Semmelweis and Lister, and who continue to murder at their will. I came to expose you, as the American Medical Association wants you exposed. I want to rid hospitals of you. That's too much to expect, of course, but time will take care of you."

"Jon," said Louis Hedler, "can't we save these insults for later? Hortense is almost in extremis."

But Jonathan continued to look at the interns. "Moe Abrams," he said. "It was your co-religionist, Ignaz Semmelweis, who, in 1847, isolated the cause of puerperal fever in postpartum females. Lack of asepsis, and coming from dissection rooms to maternity wards with the blood of the dead on 'medical' hands. His chief, Johann Klein, drove him from his native land, Hungary, with calumny and hatred, out of his vanity and his contempt for 'modern methods.' He almost drove Semmelweis mad. And then there was Joseph Lister. But he was also laughed at.

"Both these pioneers are still derided by the diploma-mill hacks we have with us today."

"Jon," said Dr. Hedler.

"Louis," said Jonathan, "you and Schaefer here, and Bedloe, too, have no right even to treat dogs. I know I'd never let you touch my boxer, Monty. You'd probably kill him."

The two interns smiled fleetingly at each other and then with admiration at Jonathan.

"I," said Jonathan, "wouldn't permit you to treat me for a first-degree burn." He pointed to the bed. "Yet, you have probably killed little Hortense here." He moved to the bed and regarded the interns with gravity. "Boys," he went on, "I want you to take voluminous notes here. I'll ask my questions slowly so you can take them down. I want you to put down the replies, too."

"Unethical!" cried Dr. Schaefer and looked imploringly at his friends, Louis Hedler and Humphrey Bedloe. But they uneasily avoided his eyes. "Am I on trial here?"

"Yes. You are and all the rest with you," said Jonathan. He opened his bag and drew a chair to the bedside and for the first time gave all his attention to Hortense. He studied her with absolute concentration, leaning forward over her but not touching her. Then he said, "Fetch a nurse with a hypodermic of 15 mg/cc of morphine, at once."

"Morphine!" cried Dr. Schaefer. "When she can hardly breathe!"

"Louis," said Jonathan, not lifting his head.

Dr. Hedler hesitated, then rang the bell for a nurse and, when she appeared, hurriedly gave her the order.

"He will kill her," said Dr. Schaefer in a low and desperate tone. Jonathan glanced at the interns. "Morphine reduces peristalsis, as you know, among other things. This is a case not only of puerperal fever but of extensive peritonitis." Now he began to examine the girl. She moaned feebly. He threw aside the sheets. Then he uttered the foulest oath Robert had ever heard. "A filthy tampon!" he said. "A dirty, filthy tampon! What for? To reduce bleeding? Look at it!" and he held the object up high in the air. "Filled with what our friends here would call 'salutary pus!' Or something. When in hell did her bleeding stop, Emil?"

Dr. Schaefer despairingly noted that the interns were busily scribbling. "Until yesterday morning—she bled quite a little. That's why I ordered the tampon."

The nurse came in with the hypodermic of morphine and handed it with a disdainful flourish to Jonathan, who deftly injected the fluid into Hortense's arm. She moaned faintly. The nurse, smirking, retreated to the door but stood there. She would have such funny news for the other girls! Robert saw the smirk, and his old conviction of the "goodness" of human nature was strongly shaken again. What had Jonathan said? "Man is not good, he is intrinsically malicious and evil and desires only a bad fate for his brother." Well. It seemed there was much truth in it. Too much truth for one's peace of mind.

Jonathan threw the yellowed tampon on a tray and extended it to the interns. He said, as they looked at it with horror, "Now, Emil. Did you sew up lacerations?"

"I did." Dr. Schaefer's eyes burned with humiliation and his pallor increased.

"After the high forceps? Yes. And did you sterilize the forceps? No. Did you use modern methods of asepsis on your hands? No. Rubber gloves? No. Boys, you have all this?"

Young Dr. Abrams said with portentous solemnity, "Yes, Doctor."

"Good. Now, Emil. Were you certain that all the placenta was delivered?"

Dr. Schaefer moved heavily against the wall. "I believe it was. It—appeared so."

Jonathan pounced on him. "You 'believe it was!' Aren't you sure—Doctor?"

Dr. Schaefer spoke in a loud and rapid voice. "I've delivered thousands—thousands—I ought to know!"

"How many died—Doctor? Of hemorrhage? Of puerperal fever? Of extensive peritonitis?"

"I am not compelled to answer that! I will *not!*"

"No," said Jonathan. "The Fifth Amendment protects you from self-incrimination. So—we have here a distinct possibility of remnants of the placenta being retained, which in itself would cause all this damage. Moreover, an ominous situation is that the normal discharge has been inhibited, and pus has taken its place." He looked at Dr. Hedler. "I want an operating room prepared at once."

Dr. Hedler nodded to the nurse and she flurried out, bursting with news.

Jonathan continued to examine Hortense, speaking slowly. He held the chart in his hand and checked it with his examination, nodding at times. "Tachycardia. Vomiting. Rigidity of the abdomen. You will notice, Dr. Abrams and Dr. Collins, that I do not do a vaginal examination. The patient has had six such today alone. With dirty hands."

"I will not—!" began Dr. Schaefer, turning wildly to his colleagues.

Now Dr. Bedloe looked at him with bitterness. "Shut up, Emil," he said.

Jonathan continued. "Fever of 104° since last night. Violent sepsis. Let us hope to God there is no embolism, too, somewhere." He examined the drugged girl's small white legs minutely. "Not yet, at least as far as I can tell."

Dr. Bedloe said, "A hysterectomy?"

"I don't know. Yet. I find an abscess here, adjacent to the uterus. Extensive peritonitis. Fulminating. Let us hope to God the abscess is walled off! Now, no one shall be admitted to the operating room without complete asepsis, gowns, masks, caps, rubber gloves. You, Dr. Schaefer, must not be admitted at all. Your 'cold' has helped spread the infection."

"My patient! How can I know what you will do to her—you young quack?"

Jonathan stood up and stared at him with disgust. "Quack? I? Look in the mirror, Emil. If I save this girl—which I doubt I can—it will be no kudos to you. It will be in spite of you."

Dr. Schaefer spread out his hands to his colleagues. "Louis! Humphrey! You know what happened! To his wife. You'll let that happen to Hortense?"

Robert did not blame Jonathan for what he did then. Jonathan walked quickly to Dr. Schaefer and struck him savagely across the face. The loud crack seemed to explode the quiet of the room. Dr. Schaefer staggered back and put his hand to his cheek. Everyone stood mute and unmoving, and aghast, except for the young interns who regarded their boots demurely.

Dr. Schaefer said, "I'll have you arrested for assault and battery!"

Jonathan said, "And I'll have you sued for deliberate malpractice, caused by your ignorance and stupidity and your unfitness even to enter a hospital room. If this girl dies, Emil, as sure as God I'll tell the husband to institute proceedings against you." He looked at Louis Hedler. "And against this hospital, for permitting this man to use its facilities and in aiding and abetting him." His black eyes seemed on fire.

The stretcher arrived for Hortense; she was snoring heavily under the influence of the morphine. Jonathan did not look at the older doctors. He said to Robert and the interns, "Ready, as soon as possible. With your notebooks."

He shook his head. "Here is Hortense in an open suite in the maternity section! Do you know how dangerous this is? The infection can spread to the other mothers. She must be isolated after her return from the operating room—if she survives the operation, which I doubt. Complete isolation. And no one who attends her must attend anyone else. My God!"

But Jonathan had overlooked something very vital. When he entered the sitting room of the suite, he saw gathered there Mr. and Mrs. Horace Kimberley, the parents of Hortense, and her young husband, Jeffrey Nolan. Jonathan said under his breath, "Oh ——," another unspeakable word to Robert. Dr. Schaefer was already talking to the tearful mother, who had flaming hair like her daughter's and was as fat and round as a middle-aged and amiable hen. Her wet eyes were like big bronze coins, and she was fussily dressed in a welter of pink ruffles to her insteps and wore a huge straw hat bending under a burden of great pink roses. Her husband was almost as small, but he was thin and boyish of figure and face and possessed an enormous black mustache. The husband, Jeffrey Nolan, was a serious young man, all pince-nez, light hair, and clean-shaven nervous face, a very rich young man who had inherited "old" money, which had placed him far above those vulgarians who had just acquired it "through those dirty oil wells."

Louis Hedler and Humphrey Bedloe were disagreeably startled, and the latter put his hand on Jonathan's arm. But Jonathan pushed it off and advanced on the four with a cold and angry expression. Dr. Schaefer had apparently been talking urgently to the others, and his face was flushed and one cheek was streaked with the crimson of Jonathan's blow. It was Jeffrey Nolan who spoke to Jonathan, while the frantic parents blinked in confusion and fear.

"Hello, Jon," he said, and held out his dry and narrow hand. "What's this I hear? Humphrey called you, is that right? But Dr. Schaefer tells us that Hortense is really getting better— Operation! Jon, she's only nineteen, and the baby died!"

"Now, wait," said Jonathan, ignoring Dr. Schaefer and speaking to the other three. "I have to be blunt because there is practically no time, Jeff, Mrs. Kimberley, Mr. Kimberley. No time. Hortense has what is called puerperal fever, and peritonitis. Please let me finish. Didn't Schaefer tell you that? She needs cleaning out, Jeff, what is called a D&C, dilation and curettage—I don't know yet. The abscess also needs evacuating. Drainage established. I have to do it at once, right now. She's almost in extremis, Jeff, do you understand that? She will be dead in less than twenty-four hours if I don't operate. That's certain."

"I don't agree!" shouted Dr. Schaefer. "She is definitely improving! She has longer periods out of coma! Her heart sounds are better! She just needs nourishment for her strength, and good nursing—!"

"Jon?" said the young husband in a voice as dry as his hand. But his eyes were full of beggary.

"She will die, and very soon, unless I perform that operation," said Jonathan. "That I can promise you with absolute certainty. Jeff, I didn't want to take this on; I wanted Schaefer to suffer from the butchery he is guilty of, and the incompetence and the scorn of what he calls 'modern methods.' Young Harrington refused to be involved with this, for excellent reasons. Jeff, say the word and I'll withdraw. It's no mess of mine."

Dr. Schaefer pleaded with the parents. "Julie, didn't I deliver you of two children and did you suffer?"

"No," said the weeping mother. "It was all perfect. Horace, I don't know if we should give the permission. I'm so upset; I can't think."

Jonathan said, "Mrs. Kimberley, it isn't in your hands to give the decision. It's in Jeff's, the husband's. Well, Jeff?"

Jeffrey looked despairingly at Louis Hedler and Humphrey Bedloe, who had come up to them. "It's quite true, Jeff," said Dr. Hedler, and Dr. Bedloe nodded silently. "Oh, God," muttered the young man. He caught Jonathan by the arm.

"Tell me, Jon! If you operate—will she live?"

"I don't know. As of this minute, I don't think so, Jeff. She has sepsis. She's terribly infected. I won't go into the details; you wouldn't understand them, anyway. She will assuredly die without the operation; with it she has one chance in a thousand. That's all I can promise you. She's far gone."

" 'Far gone?' Jon, can't you give us any hope?"

"Not much. Practically none. I can only do what I can to undo this terrible damage."

"I forbid it," said Dr. Schaefer, his voice breaking into a huskiness. "It would be criminal to deprive this young lady of her childbearing capabilities! That's what he wants to do! It will be murder!"

"If she dies," said Jonathan to the young husband, "it will be murder, indeed. But I won't be the one who committed it. I won't remove the uterus if it is possible to let it remain, Jeff. I'll have to see. The choices are desperate, and I know it only too well. Hortense may die, either on the operating table or a few hours later—or she will die without the operation— or she will live, after the operation, unable to bear children in the future. The choices are not mine."

"There's no other alternative?"

"The very faintest one, that she will live after the operation and be able to bear other children. The very faintest one. I can't give you any hope. It would be cruel to do it. I can only offer you my knowledge and my promise that I will do all I can, all that any man can do."

Dr. Schaefer again appealed to the parents. "Does my experience count for nothing in comparison with this man's 'new' and superficial knowledge? Do you want a—" He stopped. But the parents knew what he had almost said.

"I don't know, I don't know!" the mother wailed, clinging to her husband.

Jonathan sighed and looked at his watch. "Each minute that goes lessens Hortense's chances. Give me your answer, Jeff. It's all in your hands."

Dr. Bedloe put his hand on the mother's shoulder. "You've heard, Julie. It isn't in your hands. I know Jon Ferrier. Yes." he added, in a tone of deep shame, "I know him. I wronged him, Julie. I, too, was afraid of him because he knew more, and I hated him for that reason, too."

Jonathan's black eyebrows raised themselves in somber mockery. "Well, Jeff?"

"I give my permission," said the young man. "Where's the damned paper? Hurry, Jon, for God's sake, hurry!"

He signed the paper, the pen shaking in his fingers. "You have condemned that child to death," said Dr. Schaefer.

"No, you did," said Jonathan, folding the paper. "But I'll try to save her from your judgment of execution."

He looked at Robert, who followed him out of the room. In the corridor Jonathan began to race and Robert ran after him. Once in the scrub room, the young men began to wash their hands, over and over, and over and over, while the skeptical nurses stood silently by exchanging meaningful glances. Now Jonathan seemed to relax. "Old Bedloe's a hack and he's always known it. Now he admits it. That's like the sun rising west. There may be some hope for him. How did I get myself into this, anyway? Hortense isn't my patient. Kick me, Bob, kick me hard."

"Do you think there is any chance?"

"Who knows? I don't. Will my horses win at Belmont in September? I can answer that as easily as I can answer your question. Didn't they teach you at Johns Hopkins that a doctor never asks, nor answers, such a question? If they didn't, then I will immediately lose respect for them. Come on, another soaping. Seventeen times, remember. Must be something cabalistic about that, don't you think?"

Then Robert knew that he was deliberately relaxing himself, making himself objective, detached, before facing the ordeal in the operating room. Jonathan confirmed this at once by saying, "The patient has one thing in her favor. She's very young, and youth often confounds physicians." Hortense

Nolan had become "the patient" to him now and Robert felt an easing of the tension in his own shoulders.

"Did I ever tell you the story about the old goat of a surgeon and a student nurse?" asked Jonathan, resoaping his hands. He then proceeded, to the embarrassment of the silent young nurses nearby, to tell a most lewd story, with suggestive gestures of dripping fingers, gestures which only extreme innocence could not have understood. Robert glanced at the nurses, who had bent their heads sternly, and he laughed loudly. "It's an old story," said Jonathan, pleased. "You mean you didn't hear it in your grand Johns Hopkins?"

"They were careful of our delicate sensibilities," said Robert.

"How nice," said Jonathan. "And I suppose they never told you that some nurses might have the clap, too?"

"They implied it," said Robert. The nurses shifted indignantly on their feet.

Capped, gloved, gowned and masked, the two doctors entered the operating room, which was brilliantly and blindingly lighted from overhead. It smelled of whitewash and soap and ether and carbolic acid. Dr. Bedloe and Dr. Hedler and the two interns were already waiting for them, dressed like themselves. It was Dr. Bedloe who was administering ether to Hortense Nolan, whose bright hair was wrapped in a towel and who seemed pathetically small and already dead on the operating table. "That's about the best thing you do, Humphrey," said Jonathan, his voice muffled behind the mask. "You learned one thing, anyway. Oxygen ready, too?"

He looked at the nurses, searching for one infringement of the asepsis technique. He looked carefully at the instrument tray, glittering under the lights. "I assume," he said, "that these have been sterilized?"

"Jon," said Louis Hedler, "don't you think that's enough levity?"

"Oh, I'm full of jokes," said Jonathan, nodding to the nurse nearby. "Solution of carbolic first. That's right, dear. Now, swab the operating field with alcohol, and I hope it's alcohol and somebody hasn't drunk it and substituted water."

He saw the deadly whiteness of Hortense's cheeks and heard the gasping sound she made as she inhaled the ether. Her eyes were shut and the lids had the blueness of death on them. "She's under," said Dr. Bedloe, feeling the girl's pulse. "I don't dare give her any more, Jon."

The nurse at the instrument tray laid a scalpel in Jon's

gloved hand. This was the moment Robert always dreaded. The actual operations never disturbed him, for he had assisted at many and performed over a score of the simpler ones. But to him, still, the fragile outlining, with the scalpel, on the white flesh, and thin red wake that followed, make his heart quake with dread. It seemed to him that only a sadist could be so unconcerned at the first violation of the human body; the very delicacy of the first strokes appeared cruel and gloating. "Did I ever tell anyone here the joke about the elderly matron who thought she was pregnant?" asked Jonathan, as the nurses moved closer with sponges and sutures.

"Yes," said Dr. Hedler. "Last week. Most improper."

The tension in the operating room increased. Now everyone was silent, but the interns dutifully took notes. Dr. Bedloe's forehead had taken on a livid tint, for he was remembering that it was he who had called Jonathan. He watched without a movement; his eyes hardly blinked.

Then Jonathan said, as the instruments clicked in and out of his hand, "There's one thing certain, now. The infection has spread to the endometrium. And look at this abscess of the uterine wall! Thank God it's walled-off. We hardly ever see that. That's youth, for you, and a good sturdy constitution. We'll evacuate it. We'll put in tubes for drainage. No salpingitis or parametritis, thank God again. How did this child escape that, after old Emil's efforts to kill her? More sponges; counting them, I hope? Tie off this artery, Bob, or are you a statue? Come on, come on, move faster! Where's that Johns Hopkins' technique?"

The minutes moved on. Dr. Bedloe said, "I don't like this, Jon. Her pulse is weakening. Her pressure is down, 92/110." His voice trembled.

"She isn't just having her tonsils out," said Jonathan. Sweat was pouring from his forehead. He bent his head aside and a nurse wiped the uncovered portions of his face. He looked at the clock ticking ominously away on the wall. Nearly an hour.

"The blood loss," said Dr. Hedler.

"I know, I know," said Jon. "Quick! This spurt. Damn you, Bob, move faster!"

"I think she's going," said Dr. Bedloe.

Jonathan said, "Look at old Emil's infernal sutures! No wonder. And, as I suspected, placental remnants. Someone should cut his throat, and it would give me great pleasure—"

Dr. Bedloe started the oxygen. "How much longer?" he implored. "I have to try to bring her out, Jon."

"Go on, then. It's one way or the other." His hands flew. He probed and cleaned, sewed. "Anyway, the uterus is all right now. Did I ever tell you—?"

The girl on the table uttered a great unconscious groan. "Good for you, Hortense," said Jonathan. "Stay with me, darling. Bob, you can start tailoring now."

Robert found his hands shaking. The girl's pulse and heart rate and pressure were all increasing, and her belly was beginning to tense. "Ether!" said Jonathan. "Not much, but enough to relax the belly, damn it!"

He watched critically as Robert made his neat stitches. "Good," he said. He did not look at his patient. He appeared to be concentrating on Robert's work. "I'll have to give her oxygen again," said Dr. Bedloe.

"All right. Do it. Watch that flap there, Bob. Girls, you have all the sponges, I hope?"

His hands were bloody, and his clothing. He stood and watched and only his eyes seemed alive, watching everything, darting from the girl's face and then to Robert's hands. Hortense groaned again, and the sound was terrible in the silent room. "She's still well under," said Jonathan. "Don't wet your trousers, Humphrey. She's still relaxed. Don't give too much oxygen for a couple of minutes."

It was two hours before Hortense Nolan was wheeled away into strict isolation, far from the obstetrical floor, and accompanied by nurses who would attend no one else. The four doctors, unaccompanied now by the blatantly admiring interns, went to the sitting room of Hortense's former suite. The girl's parents and husband were waiting, and they started with simultaneous cries to their feet. "Where's my child?" exclaimed the mother, staring at them with dread. "Why didn't you bring her back?" Her hands flew to her mouth. She dared not ask the question.

Jonathan said, "She's in an isolated room now. She can't come back to this floor. Jeff? Now listen to me, all of you. She has a chance; just a chance. But she won't have even that one miraculous chance if old Emil is permitted in her room, with his own nice little infection and his nice old curious hands. If you let him in, even for a second, I'm off the case. Is that understood, clearly understood?"

Jeffrey Nolan had begun to cry. The parents clutched each other. Jonathan's exhausted eyes smiled at them. "A chance," he repeated. "Just a chance. I wouldn't bet too much on it, but you can hope a little. And, there's another thing. If she lives—I still say, if she lives—she'll have other children, but why anyone would want to inflict life on an innocent soul I don't know. It's one of those unsolved mysteries that always plague me."

"Jon," said Dr. Bedloe, and took the younger man's hand. "I can't tell you—"

"Don't," said Jonathan.

"Jon," said Dr. Hedler, "Hortense will be under my personal supervision."

"Oh, God," said Jonathan. "Spare us all that, Louis. If any doctor is allowed in here when I'm away, he must be either Moe Abrams or Bob here or Jed Collins. No one else. Is that understood, too?"

Dr. Hedler, who looked like a very pallid toad indeed, smiled painfully. "All right, Jon. You don't have to insult us. Is it really necessary?"

"Very," said Jonathan. "I didn't go through all that to have some hack undo it all. I know you're nice old fellows, but I don't want you in the room with Hortense. Strict asepsis at all times. Me, Abrams, Collins. Yes, and Bob here. He is careful to wash his hands. He's heard all about Lister and Semmelweis. It might be an excellent idea to read about them someday, Louis."

"We observe absolute asepsis and sterilization, Jon, at St. Hilda's."

"Now, that is very lovely. But the fact still remains that in spite of all that, men like old Emil have access to the delivery rooms and the obstetrical floor. What do all the precautions mean when one single man can ruin it in a single moment?"

Dr. Hedler hesitated. He looked at Dr. Bedloe. "I think," he said, "that we'll take away Emil's privileges. Remove him from the staff."

Jonathan smiled. "If I've accomplished nothing else today, thank God I accomplished that. Some poor girls will live rather than die, though what the hell anyone wants to live for I don't know. If there's any whiskey or brandy in the house, bring it. Jeff and Julie and Horace need it, or we'll have other patients on our hands."

Jeffrey followed him to the door and tried to speak. "Now,

now," said Jonathan. "Save all your strength for your prayers, Jeff. Remember, the girl is still in the utmost danger. We won't be sure for at least two more days. Pray, Jeff."

CHAPTER TEN

The two young doctors went to see Hortense before leaving the hospital. She was rapidly coming out from the anesthetic. Jonathan took her pulse, nodded silently to himself. Young Dr. Abrams was sitting nearby. "She opened her eyes once," he said. "Doctor, I want to tell you that never have I seen such a wonderful—"

"Nonsense," said Jonathan. "You're just an intern, Moe. You'll see much better. And much worse. How's Mrs. Nolan's blood pressure?"

"Excellent. Almost normal. I won't leave her, Doctor, until Jed can relieve me. We're going to take turns, as you ordered."

"And no one must come in, not her husband, not her parents, not another doctor except Dr. Morgan, or intern, until I give the word. And watch those nurses!"

The doctors left the hospital together. "Aren't we the cock of the walk?" said Robert. "Who runs this hospital? You?"

"I'd love to. For a couple of months. Old Louis would be the first out on his ass. Poor old swine. I don't envy you taking my place on the staff, Bob. There'll be times when you'll wish I'd absentmindedly used a scalpel on his throat in the operating room."

The deep purple twilight was all about them on the busy street. Jonathan lighted a cigarette. "Stinking things," he said.

"But I don't have the strength just yet to struggle with my pipe. In a way I'm sorry for old bungling Emil."

" 'Doctors must always close ranks,' " said Robert, lighting his own pipe.

Jonathan laughed. It was a faint and exhausted sound. "Yes, we must, mustn't we? What if our patients saw us as we are? By the way, have you settled on that house yet? I ought to have told you. It was Mrs. Winters'. Her children had put it up for sale."

Robert paused for just a moment. Then he said with firmness, "Yes, I have settled on it."

"Good. They wanted fifteen thousand, but I beat them down to ten. For you. Good night. But go in to see Hortense before midnight. This is your first case, Bob."

The July night was hot and very still. Jonathan rode his horse slowly and wearily homeward. His eyes felt full and aching and his hands were faintly trembling. He had long ago learned to be objective about his cases, but sometimes he could not push them from his mind. He was less certain about Hortense than he had appeared. The chance of her surviving, the chance of the infection having been halted, were very poor. It was now, he thought, in God's hands, as they say. And I wouldn't trust those hands for a single minute! Not after what I've seen them really do when He's in the mood.

The streets of the town seemed full of clinging steam and the gutters were pungent, and the drains. The gaslamps were haloed with rainbowed rings. Jon could hear the rattle of wheels on cobblestones, the sound of laughter in dark alleys, disembodied voices on porches. Hambledon's odors appeared both nostalgic and too heavy to Jonathan Ferrier. He could smell the river, fishy in the heat, and the sweetness of linden trees and the almost anesthetizing fragrance of full-blown roses and the dust on the grass. Footsteps and the clatter of horses' hoofs echoed in the hot night. Doors opened, shut, banged closed. Somewhere there was a thin singing of a gramophone, the distant shout of a young boy, the cry of a child, the call of an anxious mother in the dark; the giggle of a girl. It was all about him, but he felt himself unseen, unheard, unknown. It was as if he were already an apparition visiting old known places, alone and silent. It was well. Soon he would be gone and it would be as if he had never lived. He looked toward the mountains and they were only deeper shadows against a dim sky faintly sparkling with stars. He looked at the houses he passed and saw the yellow light against blinds or caught a glimpse of a small parlor and nondescript furniture, and men in shirtsleeves reading under lamps or a mother rocking a baby, or children at tables playing dominoes. He, Jonathan Ferrier, saw it all, but now it was strange and remote and he had no part in it. He had no home here. He had no one.

Dear Mavis, he thought. I should have killed you, nice and quietly, long ago.

He passed the swinging doors of saloons and heard the raucous laughter in their noxious depths. He was thirsty. He wanted a cold beer. He remembered that it had been many hours since he had eaten anything. He pulled up his horse. Then he went on. He looked down an intersection and saw the distant square with its iron statue of General Sherman. It looked like a dream or a painted scene and not reality at all. The gaslights blinked and shifted. He went on and now as he approached the section where he lived it seemed a little cooler and the air was fresher and there was a small breeze from the river. The houses became larger and more isolated on dark lawns, and half hidden behind clusters of trees. His ancestors had known and had helped build this town, but he had no part in it and never would again.

He was growing more tired every moment. When he reached the stables where he kept his town horses, he could hardly drop down from the saddle and lift his bag. One of the stableboys came to him eagerly. "Good evening, Dr. Ferrier! My, this horse looks tuckered out."

"He is." Jonathan watched the horse being led away. Soon he would not ride this horse. He would have his farms. Would he ever visit them again? He did not know. He hoped not. He ought to sell all but one, and keep that one for his mother, who loved it. He would give the matter thought tomorrow. He glanced up the street and saw the dark Winters house, where Robert and his mother would live, and between his house and the Winters one he saw his offices, unlighted, silent. He had little more to do there. In fact, he had little more to do with living at all. He thought of the whiskey in his offices, and hesitated. Then he went up the long walk to his house, and the shadows of the trees fell over him and these old familiar creatures did not belong to him any longer, either.

The house was old and strong and high and broad and long, and there were lights in a few windows. His grandfather had added this huge porch, which extended all about the house. The porch was secluded and resembled a colonnade, but it was all wood and painted a solid white. Here on rainy days he had played with his brother or had sat alone, listening or reading, or talking with his father. What had they talked about? He did not remember. His father's voice came back to him, grave, thoughtful, musing. But damned if he could remember one single thing his father had said on all those days, through the years! It was very odd, however, that he could recall almost all that his mother had said to him briefly, on the few occasions she had talked to him on this porch. Jonathan stood there now, looking down the long shadowy reaches of the deserted boards and the still chairs and tables in the faint light that came through the windows and from the far-distant streetlamp. It was on a hot summer dusk that she had said to him somewhat sternly, "You really must stop laughing at Harald. You don't know how you hurt him." He had been fifteen then.

And it was on an early spring evening when he was returning from school that he had paused here. It had been raining all day and now the whispering sound of it was on the air, rustling mysteriously through new leaves and a wind was sighing down the long porch, which was empty. Then he had heard a sound of sobbing, dismal and faint, and he had turned and walked a short distance down the porch, which echoed with his footsteps in the fragrant half light, and he had found Harald, then twelve years old, crouched on the floor with his head and right shoulder pressed against the brick wall of the house. He had lifted his head at Jonathan's approach and had stopped his sobbing, but he still crouched there desolately.

Jonathan said, "What the hell are you doing here, crying like a baby?"

Harald did not answer for a moment or two, and then he said, "Father laughed at one of my paintings. He said I had no talent."

Jonathan knew his father's taste in painting. He liked smooth satiny surfaces and subdued colors and artful postures and, even then Jonathan had to admit it, sentimental and obvious subjects. He particularly liked, for instance, a painting called "The Storm," which depicted an overfed youth, all Hyacinthine curls, racing against a background of velvety dusk with a maiden with large plump legs and daintily disposed garments and flowing hair. The youth had arranged a big cloak over the maiden's head and it billowed with silken highlights. Jonathan had not liked it, but he did not know why. A good, and expensive, copy of it had "graced" the living room mantle until Adrian Ferrier's death —when Marjorie had removed it.

Jonathan had said bluntly to his brother, "I don't know if you have any talent. But I do know that Father doesn't have any."

Harald had caught his breath, and then had slowly risen to his feet. He tried to see Jonathan in the wet gloom. "Do you mean that, Jon? Honestly, do you mean it?"

"Sure I mean it. You're such a baby! Crying out here, as if it's important. If you have talent, it will show. That's all it should mean to you. If you start listening to people and their advice, you'll never amount to anything."

"Don't you listen?" Harald had come closer to him and Jonathan had felt his ardent intensity, and he had stepped back with distaste.

"Never," Jonathan had said with total firmness. "That is, I only listen to people who know what they're talking about."

"But how can you tell?"

"Instinct, kid, instinct." And Jonathan had walked away and left him.

He stood alone on this hot July night, completely exhausted and beset, and he remembered that rainy twilight and Harald's shadowy look of hope. It was certainly strange how things returned to a man when he least expected them and when his defenses were down. "Instinct," he repeated with contempt. "Where was my instinct when I most needed it? Where is it now?"

He opened the hall door and went inside. The hall was long and wide and beautifully proportioned and the ceiling was high. It was Marjorie who had painted the dark wood in her favorite shade of pale gray with soft silver moldings, and it was she who had removed the heavy old dark furniture and had replaced it with graceful pieces exquisitely arranged: A marble console with a tall thin mirror on one side, two Louis XIV gilt chairs with white velvet upholstery, a sofa, and a table of the same period bearing an exquisite marble statuette of a faun and a lamb. The curving stairs at the rear had also been painted gray and were carpeted with blue plush in a dim shade. Marjorie had removed the wall lamps and had hung a majestic crystal chandelier, arranged for gas, from the ceiling. A few of the lamps were lighted now, and threw a golden shadow down on the Aubusson rug, which was colored in shades of misty rose and blue and yellow. There was nothing else here but tranquillity and space and unobtrusive hues and silence.

Marjorie came through a door at the left of the graceful stairway, and her thin silk dress in a tint of mauve rustled as she moved. She smiled but her hazel eyes were anxious. "Dear Jon," she said, "I was worried about you. Why, you look so tired." She glanced down at his hands. She saw they were red and the skin appeared dry and so she knew he had been operating—a thing he had sworn never to do again in Hambledon. He saw her glance and he said, "Yes. I did, and I still don't know why. Don't ask me who; I'll tell you later."

She came to him and kissed him on the cheek and she saw how weary he was and how ghastly his color. She said, "I've waited dinner for you, of course. And"—she paused a second —"and I've laid out your whiskey and soda, and you must have a drink before dinner."

"Thank you," he said. "I'll go upstairs and wash and change."

"Oh, don't change. Do you know how romantic you look in riding clothes?" She smiled again. "I never saw another man who looked so in jodhpurs and boots. Just freshen. I'll wait for you in the living room." Her smile was still fixed as she watched him go upstairs. He walked heavily and slowly and he did not look back. His dark head was bent. She sighed, tightened her hands together and went out of the hall.

She sat down in the large parlor and never had it seemed so empty before to her and so lonely. As a bride and a very young matron she had again used her taste here, removing the ponderous and frowning furniture and introducing the delicacy of an earlier age, including painted walls in a silvery shade and a dimmed Oriental rug that almost covered the polished floor. A lovely Florentine mirror hung where the despised "Storm" had once hung, and the white and carved fireplace had no fire and only a basket of pale yellow roses, which filled the room with a cool scent of tea. The silken draperies at the tall windows were the color of the roses and they fell about long lengths of weblike imported lace. The windows were slightly ajar, and the hot wind moved them. Now Marjorie, waiting for her son, could hear thunder prowling among the mountains and she saw a flash of lightning.

There will be a storm, she thought vaguely. She had been

so listless all day, and her head had ached, and she thought, now, I'm really very tired of living. I won't be able to stand it when Jon leaves. He mustn't leave. Yes, I suppose he must. It's too dangerous for him here, too dangerous for— Her mind fluttered away in fear. She looked at the silent and shimmering furniture, at the Empire settees in blue and soft rose, at the waiting chairs in white and yellow, at all the crystal and marble and silver and at the gilded buhl cabinets which sheltered her collections of china and *objets d'art,* and it seemed to her that no one had ever lived here and no one ever would. The restless pain in her heart was not totally physical; it was like a rat gnawing in the dark under her breast.

There were a cook and a maid in the kitchen, but they were far distant behind thick doors. Marjorie could hear nothing in the breathless silence but a surly grumbling among the mountains. Not even the trees stirred in that slight and burning wind. She thought of the empty bedrooms upstairs on the second floor. Two only were used, hers and Jon's, and once she had anticipated the sound of grandchildren there. But there would be no grandchildren. Jonathan would never marry again, and Harald lived, a widower, on that foolish island and dared not leave it for more than five months a year. Even when he left it, he did not come to sleep here. His room had no tenant, and no others did. The domestic staff slept on the third floor and they went up a back staircase and had their own living quarters. How could she, Marjorie, endure it here alone after Jonathan went away, the only living thing on the second floor, the only tenant of these great rooms, the only person to walk the gardens or watch the snow fill up the trees?

She did not think of her dead husband. His ghost would not keep her company.

She started when someone took her wrist firmly, and she said, "Jon! I didn't hear you come in."

But he was counting her pulse and scowling a little. "Heat too much for you?" he asked, laying her hand down on the arm of the chair.

"A little. Will you mix me a drink also?"

Jonathan went to the silver tray on a marble table. He poured a large amount of whiskey into one glass, added only a little soda, then poured a smaller amount of liquor in the other glass but a considerable quantity of soda. He brought the latter to his mother. Then, standing, he drank deeply of his tall crystal glass as if he could not swallow the liquid fast enough. He had almost drained the glass before he took it from his mouth. He smiled down at his mother, then seated himself. Marjorie kept her face carefully bland.

"I cooked the dinner for you tonight, Jon. But I'm afraid it's very heavy on a night like this. Wiener schnitzel; you always liked it."

"I still do. But you shouldn't have bothered."

"It's no bother." She moved restlessly. "I do hope it'll be nice on the Fourth. Whom shall we invite—it's very late now —for our usual picnic?"

"I've already invited Bob Morgan and his mother. I know. She's all whalebone, flatus and fraudulent copperplate."

Marjorie sipped at her glass. "And I've invited people, too. Didn't I tell you? Rose and Albert Kitchener, and their daughter, Maude. She's such a nice girl, and so very pretty and talented, and intelligent. Such beautiful eyes and curly auburn hair, and a delightful figure."

"For Harald?"

"No, dear. Harald left today for Philadelphia. What a bad memory I have! Didn't I tell you that he is to have a show in Philadelphia on the fifth? He's already shipped twenty canvases. You know that private and very exclusive gallery on Broad Street? Yes."

"Yes," said Jonathan. He stood up and filled his glass again. "It will cost him a nice penny."

"He can afford it. And the owner has been advertising for two weeks, and issued invitations and there has been such a wonderful acceptance. It will be very successful."

"Why didn't you go, too?"

"Oh, I don't know. I've gotten out of the habit of going to Philadelphia. Most of my relatives are dead now, and it makes me feel very sad, and I was a reserved sort of girl and didn't make many friends. Many of them have moved away. I should have gone, I suppose."

"And you didn't want to leave me alone on the Fourth."

"Well, dear, it would have been lonely for you." She looked at him. "I also invited Jenny."

"What? Without Harald?"

"Jon. Please don't sneer. It makes you look quite ugly and you are really a very handsome man. Yes, you are."

Jonathan said in a mocking and musing voice, "Childe Harald. I don't understand his impressionistic style, but he may be good at that. He'll shock the hell out of Philadelphia, and so I wish him well. How did you shuck Jenny from that island?"

His mother was watching him very carefully again. "I just invited her, and she accepted. Poor Jenny."

"I know. She'd mourn for our Harald. It's a wonder he didn't pack her up and take her with him."

"Jon, dear. Is it possible that you don't know that Jenny— dislikes—Harald? Are you that blind? You know very well that she grimly stays on that island because it is her home, and her father built that house, and she adored him, and she regards Harald as an impudent intruder. She won't let him have it alone. She just sits and stands there, waiting for the day when he won't come back again."

"Oh, Mother. I don't believe that for a minute. She stays there because of our Harry."

"You really do believe the gossip of the town, Jon? Oh, no, you simply can't! You, above all! Jon, Harald wants to marry Jenny. He told me so himself."

The glass became very still in Jon's hand, the yellow liquid as quiet as stone. Marjorie watched her son's dark face and heavy brows and hidden eyes with great intentness.

"Harry? He wants to marry Jenny?"

"Yes. He's asked her dozens of times."

"I don't believe it," he said. "I've been there very often, and I've watched her. She stares at him as if she's—hungry. She listens to every word he says as if it came from God. She follows him all around with those big blue eyes of hers. She isn't aware of anyone else when he's around. It's not just the town gossip. I wouldn't consider that for an instant. But I've seen Jenny—looking at Childe Harald. And I'm acutely sensitive to people; I have to be. When he moves near her, she actually trembles. And she waits. She's a woman in love."

Yes, thought Marjorie. But she said, "Jenny is only twenty, Jon. And though I don't like to say it, you really don't know much about women, and especially not about young women."

"No," he said. "You are quite correct. I didn't know." He was thinking of Mavis. His mother saw the clenching of his facial muscles. He stood up as if to hide from her and again refilled his glass. Her anxiety came back to her, sharper than ever. He stood by the table and his face was turned away from her. "You ought to have provided me with sisters."

"Well, it's too late for that, I'm afraid." Marjorie smiled painfully. Jon did not look at her. "Dear," she said, "if Jenny does as you say, it is because she hates Harald. She's watching him all the time. I even think she is afraid of him, in a way. I think she thinks—"

"What?" He sauntered back to his chair. "What does sweet Jenny think, if anything?"

But Marjorie sipped at her glass. "What she thinks of Harald is wrong. I can't tell you what she told me. It—it is probably just her imagination. She's so young and she's always been so secluded, and girls have fantasies."

"She certainly has a fantasy about our Harry. Mother, I may not know all the mysterious thoughts that flitter around a girl's head like bats and butterflies, but I do know a woman in—"

But she said with quietness, "In passion, Jon? Most probably. But in love, Jon? I don't think you could ever detect that!"

"I don't want to. I doubt most women could love, anyway. They don't have the capacity. It's all frivolity to them, and pretentious houses and clothes and jewelry and teas." He waved his hand. "And darling little children and places in society and mean little ambitions. Tell me"—and now he turned abruptly to her—"did you love my father?"

The pallor about Marjorie's mouth increased. She said, "I thought I did. In the beginning. Then I didn't. It took a long time."

"Well, what did happen to all that love?"

"Jon, do you want me to tell you?"

"Yes, now that we're in a romantic and melting mood."

"Very well. Your father wasn't very intelligent, Jon. I know that hurts you to hear that. You loved him so much. And he loved you dearly and always wanted you near him. I don't think he cared about anyone else, especially not Harald. I was just, eventually, the gracious mistress of his house. Jon? Does that hurt you very much?"

He went back to his chair. There was a dull flush on his cheekbones. He considered his mother for a long hard moment. "My father was kind," he said at last. "I appreciate kindness. There's so damned little of it in this world. If a man is kind he should be celebrated."

"He wasn't kind to Harald."

"Because Harald is a fool."

"Why?"

"He listened to my father. He had a way of trailing him."

"Yes, I know. Poor Harald."

"Wasn't he kind to you? It seems to me he was the soul of consideration."

"He never saw me, really, after you were born, Jon."

"Were you jealous?" He smiled at her incredulously and with amusement.

"No. I'd long given up caring."

He considered that. Then he said, "If he was such a fool, as you seem to think, then he'd have been devoted to Harald."

"But he never knew he was—a fool—and that makes a difference."

"A fool. What was he to you, Mother, really? Your opinion?"

"It seems odd to say that so distinguished a man, and so aristocratic, had many, many pretensions."

"To what?"

"To taste. To intelligence. To worldliness. To cosmopolitanism. He was really naïve. And naïveté in a mature man isn't so beguiling, Jon. Except to superficial people, and I'm not superficial. He could talk eloquently; he knew poetry, he thought. He had a wide acquaintance with literature and art and music. Yet, he never felt them at all, where it matters. One thinks that only the vulgar are pretentious. But the pseudo-cultured, vaguely feeling some inadequacy, are desperate to be considered more sensitive than they are." She sighed: "It's very pathetic, in an ordinary man, to struggle to be more than he is, and your father struggled. It was wretched for me to know that, and I was so sorry. When he saw he couldn't impress me any longer, he abandoned me and avoided me. I don't blame him. I should have been more tolerant, but I wasn't."

"And you probably think these things about your sons, too."

"Jon, don't sound so hard and unforgiving."

The dinner bell chimed softly, and Marjorie rose and Jon with her. Once he staggered a little. "I only know this," he said, "you were closer to Harald than to me, and yet you imply that Harald is more like my father. Inconsistent. Are you coming?"

Neither Marjorie nor Jonathan was notable for loquacity even when they felt no strain between them, merely passing pleasant remarks or none at all during the hours they dined together. In this, Marjorie had once reflected, Jonathan resembled herself. Harald was more like his father; they both liked conversation. It was as if words protected them in some manner, kept a bright and defensive barrier between them and what it was they had always feared. What had they feared? Marjorie had been reared in an atmosphere where it was considered unpardonable even to speculate about those deep and hidden sanctuaries of the human spirit in others, and worse even to comment about them. The retreats of a beloved child, or wife or husband, were inviolate and it was indefensible to assault them. It was the lowest vulgarity and outrage of all, it was a Peeping Tom voyeurism engaged in only by the obscene of heart. Therefore, if Adrian Ferrier had obviously feared others—though Marjorie admitted that it was wise to fear your fellowman to some extent—the fear had been out of proportion, invariably, to his routine run of living and circumstance.

But then, she had thought, we always turn a façade to others behind which we watch and wait, hope or fear, love or hate, pray or curse. That is our privacy, that façade. We all have our individual approach to the world, and if Adrian fears that is his particular response to life, and no stranger than belligerence, suspicion, amiability, trust or mistrust, responsiveness or unresponsiveness, exploitation or charity. Even animals have their particular reaction to their immediate life and environment, and none is the same as another's.

Tonight, as they ate their dinner together and drank their wine, Marjorie and Jonathan were unusually silent even for them. The thunderstorm had burst out from its lair beyond the mountains and was assaulting the small city and the river with fire and great explosions. Mother and son were not aware of it. Marjorie was already regretting that she had so violated her code as to speak intimately of her dead husband to Jonathan. It was disgraceful. She had held her husband's secret—which he had never guessed she knew, just as he had lived unaware that there was anything at all to guess about him—to herself alone. To reveal Adrian as he had been, even to his son, was particularly shameful, and she was disgusted and appalled at herself. She recalled every word she had said. What had been the matter with her, to descend to such betrayal, such vulgarity? It was all those months of strain, which were not ending but only mounting, and the dread in which she lived and the daily terror, and the obvious decay of Jonathan and his increasing addiction to drinking, and the wild beast which he denied existed but which was mangling him. And Harald, too, and Jenny. The world was full of menace. Of course, she reflected, it always had been full of menace, for it was a mysterious and dangerous place despite all the songs of its "wonder" and sweetness and "love," and all its ridiculous slogans concerning the "progress of man," but its threat remained faceless until it entered one's own house. Then, as the door opened to admit it, one saw the abyss just beyond the garden, the innocent, lying garden.

She saw that Jonathan's exhaustion appeared to be growing. His color was extremely bad, the sallowness accentuated. He was drinking the good wine not with pleasure but with grim absentmindedness. He had told her nothing of the operation he had performed not very long ago, nor who had so suffered. That was not unusual; he rarely mentioned his cases. But Marjorie saw that he had totally forgotten who had lain unconscious under his hands that day, and this was indeed unusual for him.

She wanted to say to him, "Forgive me for telling you what I knew about your father. I have no excuse; it was degrading of me. Why did I tell you? I don't know, my dear. I never told anyone else. Malice didn't inspire me, nor indifference, nor dislike. I liked your father as a person to the day he died, and was often fond of him. I still don't know why I told you. It was very wrong, for you loved him dearly and believed in him."

Her thought suddenly stopped as she remembered that Jonathan had had no objection at all to her removing the absurd and stylized painting of "The Storm" after Adrian had died. In fact, he had remarked—he had not yet been twenty-three—"I've always despised that thing. It's ridiculous and pretentious and a dozen other things, though I suppose our Harald would call it well-drawn." Marjorie put down her coffee spoon in surprise, and stared at Jonathan, who sat in his father's place in the thunder-vibrating soft light and subdued glitter and pale elegance of the dining room. Certainly, Jonathan had said that, and how strange of her not to have remembered. It had been Harald who had always laughed at "The Storm," but not Jonathan. Adrian had disliked Shakespeare and had read poetry to Jonathan by the hour in his secluded library, but it had been Keats and Whitman and Emily Dickinson and Wordsworth and Browning and Tennyson and Longfellow—particularly Longfellow. He had read prose to Jonathan from the latter's earliest childhood, but it had been Dickens and never Thackeray, Dumas never Zola.

There had been plays, too, but Sheridan never Molière or Gounod—and, back to the poets, Byron, with the exception of *Don Juan*, Whitman but not Milton. Music was his particular adoration, he would say, but he preferred Mozart to Wagner, Schubert to Beethoven, Liszt to Bach. In short, he had lacked an awareness of grandeur and terror. It was as if they had been only alien words to him, accepted in the dictionary and in books but never in reality.

It was Jonathan who loved Shakespeare, Milton, Chaucer, Molière, Gounod, and the mighty Teutonic composers. It was Jonathan who, even as a child, had glimpsed the abysses of life and rarely the gardens, who had known the terror of living and the presence of evil. His father had told him nothing of these, yet he had known. Why, then, had he so loved his father and had resentfully turned away from the most amiable, if jesting, remark his mother had made about him? Marjorie nodded to the girl who assisted the cook and accepted fresh tea. Jon had not touched his dinner, but he was filling his wineglass again, and his face was exceptionally gloomy even for him and exceptionally closed. There was a glaze over his eyes. He was almost drunk. His food was congealing on his plate, and the thunder drummed against the tall and shining glass of the windows and the lightning illuminated them at frequent intervals.

I know, thought Marjorie with sadness. He considered Adrian a child, even when he was a child himself, and he thought he must protect him from his family and from living. But perhaps more than anything else he thought that Adrian was kind, and Jonathan has always been particularly vulnerable to kindness in others, because even as a child he knew that kindness, true kindness, was a very rare thing in this world, and he could not bear the knowing. Poor child.

What had Father McNulty said of him only a few months ago? "Jon is not really a complex man, Mrs. Ferrier. Once I thought so, but now I know that is not true. He is very simple, in the most august and touching way possible. He appears complicated to people, and ambiguous, because he is not a liar, and isn't that a terrible commentary on people and unworthy of a priest? But, it is true. The devious man is always spoken of by his friends as being 'candid' and 'frank,' whereas the exact reverse is correct. People just can't believe simplicity like Jon's. It's labyrinthine to them and I'm afraid that is a sad comment on the state of human nature. Jon just is, and no one accepts a man for what he shows the world.

Men believe that others, like themselves, are always hiding. But Jon never turned a false face and a lying one to his fellowman. He has the attribute of both the saint and the simpleton—he is himself. And that is the cause of his misery, and probably the cause of his unhappiness as a child, as you have told me yourself. That is why he cannot accept lies in others or contemptible behavior in others, and forgiveness is not in him."

Marjorie had had to agree, after some thought. "And he doesn't know what fear is," she had said.

"True," said Father McNulty. "The man who is utterly himself before the world, without guile and cruelty and artfulness, thinks he has nothing to fear. But he has. He has his fellowman. I'm afraid Jon is beginning to suspect that he should fear, but he rejects the very idea. He couldn't live in a world of fear; it would choke him. He didn't fear the judge and the jury because, in his simplicity, he believed that lack of guilt would prove itself overwhelmingly. The wounds he carries now are the result of the actions and words of others against him, and he can't forgive them."

"And why should he?" Marjorie had asked with deep bitterness.

Jonathan had never confided in her in all his life but twice, and she still did not understand why. He had told her of two events. Was it possible, she thought tonight as she sipped her tea, that he instinctively understood that only she would understand his indictments of humanity and that his father would not?

The first incident had been when he was nine years old. He was leaving his school grounds when he saw several large boys tormenting a smaller one, a sniveling, disliked, groveling boy, advertising his apprehension of his mates at all times and his frightened desire to placate them so that they would not hurt him. Marjorie knew the boy and his parents, and had once asked Jonathan why he was not kind to the lad. "He is such a measly coward," Jonathan had replied with scorn, and yet with pity.

But, on that wintry day, he had seen the tormenting of the boy and it had enraged him. Without thinking at all—and how often did Jonathan even now pause to think of himself? —he had lunged at the youths, who were all older than he, and his frenzy of disgust for them, and his hatred that they could torment one weaker, had given him abnormal strength and fury. He had driven them off a distance and had rescued their victim, who was sniveling and weeping, as usual, and crying for his mother.

The momentarily vanquished soon became aware that a single boy was responsible both for denying them their victim and their present smartings, and they advanced on Jonathan like a phalanx and had roughly beaten him up, including blackening his eyes and bloodying his nose. Among his attackers, and the most gleeful, had been the boy he had rescued. When he tore away from his schoolmates and ran—prudently, for Jonathan—the loudest and most derisive catcall had come from the lad he had saved from pain and blows.

"Why?" he had asked his mother, standing before her with his thin legs apart and his torn and bruised face both challenging and furious.

She had said, "You had become the unpopular minority."

He had shook his head fiercely. "That don't—doesn't—explain why Timmy kicked me, too, and jeered at me. Why didn't he just run away? Why did he just stay, and—and—"

"Make common cause with his enemies? Against you? Jonathan, that's hard to explain to you now. It's both subtle and ordinary. Human nature isn't a pleasant thing to think about—"

But unfortunately Jonathan's father had just then entered the morning room and he, after one appalled exclamation of sympathy and astonishment, had swept Jonathan to him and had held him richly to his heart, murmurous and clucking. Marjorie had watched and her features, so like her son's, had closed and tightened. She had waited in silence while Jonathan asked his questions of his father. Adrian held the boy on his knee now, and was stroking his head tenderly, and his blue eyes, a little vacant and protruding, were misted. He had stared musingly into space, considering what Jonathan had asked him. Eventually, a radiant smile—the one which Marjorie particularly loathed—suffused his face like a beaming halo.

"It's very simple, Jonathan," Adrian had said. "The children aren't yet civilized, gentled. They don't understand. Children are so dear and so innocent! So pure, so good. If they do what others consider evil, it really is not evil. It is only lack of understanding or perhaps wicked teachings from their parents. You must think of them kindly and forgive and forget, knowing that Man does Progress, and Man does become Good, when reaching maturity."

Marjorie had felt a little sick, as she always did when her husband emphatically and resoundingly affirmed his faith in humanity. Jonathan, on his father's knee, had looked at him oddly—and why hadn't she, Marjorie, remembered that either until now? Then Jonathan had smiled as if at a child who must not be hurt, and then he had given his mother one of his fierce looks as if warning her not to speak.

The thunder seemed to have picked this old and beautiful house for its particular enemy tonight, for there was a stunning crash. Neither Marjorie, sunken in her revery, nor Jon, growing more drunk by the moment, was aware of it. Marjorie was saying to herself, "I was always getting those looks from Jon, but, God forgive me, it wasn't until just now that I remember them and understand them. It was always my damned reticence—I never explored. I thought it unbecoming and indecent. But still, Jon even as a little boy was always protecting his father. He would have resented it if I had let him know that I, too, knew that his father was a fool. How strange is human nature! We guard what is least worthy of guarding and leave vulnerable what it is most necessary to protect—for our soul's sake."

Jonathan never spoke of that incident again, but for a long time he would watch Marjorie acutely until he was convinced that she had forgotten it and was therefore no longer a danger to her husband and his serene convictions that if one just ignored the ugliness of the world, or smoothed it over with platitudes, it would not exist.

He was a coward, and I never knew it until now, thought Marjorie. Or did I?

Jonathan was a very religious boy. He was also an altar boy. On a few occasions he had spoken seriously of the priesthood. "Oh, not that," Marjorie, the Protestant, had said with a light laugh before husband and son. "You aren't up to it, Jon. You'd be the terror of the Confessional. You'd have no patience with human nature. You don't really understand it at all, and you are now fifteen. You hate evil, but you don't comprehend the causes of evil, and how deep it lies in the human spirit. *In foro interno,* to use Latin."

Adrian spoke ponderously. " '*In foro interno.*' I deny that, Marjorie. Evil is external to man, not in him. As Rousseau has said—"

"Why don't you tell that to Father McGuire?" Marjorie had asked, losing her usual patience. "He would tell you that it is a doctrine of the Church that man is conceived in sin, born in sin, and has no merit of his own and can earn no merit. What merit he has has been given to him by God, and God alone. By himself he is incapable of being good or meritorious, incapable of his own salvation—because, as Solomon has said, 'Man is wicked from his birth and evil from his youth.' "

"You seem to be well acquainted with the doctrines of the Church, Marjorie," Adrian had replied with his heavy irony, "and so I often wonder why you don't ask to be admitted. By the way, I've never heard those doctrines, or they are probably now outmoded. Man is Good—"

"Then you believe that God lies when He says that 'None save God is good?' "

Adrian was shocked. "I don't believe that is in the Holy Bible—"

Marjorie nodded, smiling. "Yes, it is. In St. Luke, and you can find it for yourself. It is a strange thing, but I have noticed that at no time did God or His Son ever break into eulogies about the 'goodness' of man. On the contrary! There are constant references in the Bible about the infamy of man and his need for redemption, and his innate evil. But never goodness."

"Nonsense," said Adrian. His well-colored face, so like Harald's, had deeply flushed and Marjorie, with sudden compunction, saw that he was afraid. "Didn't a man, recorded in the Holy Bible, say 'Am I my brother's keeper?' A magnificent question!"

"It was asked by Cain," said Marjorie. "Cain, the murderer, the father of murderers, the rejected of God."

The silence that had fallen in the room had had a little terribleness in it. Adrian had sat, and now his fright was visible, and he was hating his wife openly. Jon looked at him, and he put his hand on his father's cheek, again in that attitude of protection, and Marjorie, for a moment, had irritably despised her son. There was surely a limit to indulging fools and pretentiousness and ignorance! She said, "The answer God gave to that 'magnificent question' was, I believe, 'Your brother's blood cries up to Me from the ground against you.' And so it always was, and so it always is."

"You have no pity, Marjorie."

And there, thought Marjorie tonight, was a perfect example of the perfect *non sequitur*. But people, when concerned in fantasies and sentimentalities, invariably resorted, with hatred and indignation, to it.

Jon that night, at fifteen, had said nothing. But once again he had warned his mother off, had demanded, by a long hard black stare at her, not to hurt his father. He knew, thought Marjorie, as she touched her napkin to her lips tonight and for once becoming aware of the storm outside, and the growing tension and heat in the long and beautiful dining room, indeed he knew, but he rebelled against my knowing that he knew. He's still not over his resentment against me for knowing, and for "hurting" his father, and that is part of his trouble. How singleminded he was, and is! How still he will not accept the obvious!

And there was Harald, who had at first accepted his father as Jonathan had accepted him. But not after he was fourteen years old. Thereafter he had known Adrian for exactly what he was! Was that why Jonathan even today disliked him so? How very contradictory and intricate and secret and manifold mankind was, and how very, very strange! Jon, in these days, was frequently relieving himself of the most bitter comments on his fellowman, even beyond the bounds of decent pity, and he was speaking with cynicism and even hatred. How much of it did he believe himself, or was he speaking in despair and hoping to be refuted? Or at least hoping that it might be hidden from him, thus permitting him to live again in a little peace? Or what, or who, was he protecting? The memory of his father?

Harald, thought Marjorie with unique surprise, was in this way like herself, in that he accepted everything with tolerance and amused understanding and refused to permit the world to make him miserable. If he sometimes spoke in jesting aphorisms, as she did, it was evident that he did it jocularly—evident to everyone but Jon.

When Jonathan was seventeen, he had joined a Hiking League connected with his private secondary school and had set off with a large group on a walking tour of the state. It lasted two weeks. He returned home, more taciturn than usual, cold, withdrawn, speaking only to his father. He appeared wretched. Marjorie asked her husband, "Has Jon told you anything about that walking tour? He doesn't seem himself."

"He is perfectly all right," Adrian had replied with his usual complacent buoyancy. "He had many interesting experiences. Very, very pleasant, and most edifying." His big blue eyes, as usual, were artless and serene. But, then, Marjorie had remarked to herself, Jon really never tells him anything. "Edifying. Yes," Adrian had continued, with that sweet musing look of his which Marjorie found most infuriating. "We shall look at my Audubon collection tonight and try to identify the birds which Jonathan saw on his very enlightening excursion. Most instructive."

Adrian, Marjorie thought with fearful clarity tonight, abandoned me when I finally stopped protecting him, and found him out, and turned to Jon, who fervently received the burden and who still carries it! My God, why don't we see and understand things before it is too late? And how did Jon get the idea tonight that I "implied" that Harald was very like Adrian?

There is so much of me in Jon and so much of me in Harald, thought Marjorie, tonight. Had she been wrong in believing that Harald's easy conversation, so like his father's, had risen from fear, as his father's had so risen? Or did Harald simply keep up a brighter chatter to fend off the dangerous inquisitiveness of others, because though he liked people he did not trust them? Or found them too ridiculous to take seriously? Jon was always taking people too seriously, though he would be the first to deny that, with angry contempt. Who was it who had said, "Life is a tragedy to the man who feels, and a comedy to the man who thinks"? If that was so, then Jon was really a man who "felt" and did not absolutely think, and so Father McNulty was quite correct, and was that not odd in a man so young? Or was wisdom to be measured solely in years? Marjorie recalled many who were old who were still fools.

She returned to the memory of when Jonathan had been seventeen.

It had been an unusually warm spring for Pennsylvania. Secretly, Marjorie had always worried about Jonathan's health, for he was overtall for his age, almost emaciated in appearance, and his sallow complexion seemed dimmer. Compared with him, Harald, the full-blooded and well-colored, appeared offensively healthy and hearty and slightly plump, at fifteen. Jonathan seemed to be irritated by Harald's light and amiable chatter more than customarily, and accordingly Harald was brighter than ever and more loquacious and deliberately annoying. He could not restrain his pleasure that Jonathan would be away for two weeks and he made his pleasure obvious. Marjorie could not help smiling at this. Jonathan, she had thought, was really too serious and preoccupied and took his studies with a firm intensity, and he was only seventeen. His temper, never well restrained under the best of circumstances, was much worse. But his father, who almost frantically refused to acknowledge unpleasantness or troublesome matters, said, "My dear, you are always too concerned about Jon. He is fit as a fiddle. Fit as a fiddle," he repeated, for he loved clichés and found his sanctuary in them. Marjorie thought to ask him, "And what makes a fiddle fit, or what is fitness in a fiddle?" but she recognized the remark as childish and refrained from it. Let Adrian have his platitudes and aphorisms and clichés. They protected him against life and reality and so their existence could be endured.

Jonathan was gone for the two whole weeks and returned thinner than ever, duller of complexion than before, and with a mature darkness on his face which was never to leave it for the rest of his life. Though even for him he was unusually silent, Marjorie saw that he was thinking deeply and fiercely, for the white ridges, newly arrived, kept springing out about his mouth. Marjorie could hear him talking with his father in the secluded study, but his voice, as always when in conversation with Adrian, was agreeable, even soothing. He sounds like a father talking to a child! Marjorie thought with exasperation, and not for the first time. Adrian's voice, in reply, was grateful and mellow— Oh, the damned mellowness of it! (She could abide unctuousness, for one knew at once that unctuous men were hypocrites and liars and inclined to be dangerous, and so one was warned, knowing the fraudulence. But mellow-voiced men were either fools or cowards. In a way they were much more dangerous than the unctuous men, for they could easily and disastrously betray, not out of malice or design, but out of sheer panic.)

Marjorie waited. Jonathan had not confided in her since he had been nine. She had no hope that he would this time, either. But one morning he came abruptly into her sitting room, where she was discussing the Easter dinner with the cook and, on seeing him, Marjorie asked the young woman to leave. She knew instinctively that Jonathan wished to talk to her and not on an idle matter. But she smiled easily at him and said, "Good morning, dear. Have you had your breakfast? I see you have your bicycle clips on; out for a run?"

He sat down opposite her and did not answer. He only stared at her, and she knew that defiant and challenging stare.

She folded the newspaper on her knee and put it aside, and said nothing and only waited.

He said, with a note of accusation in his boy's voice. "You aren't the least damned interested in my walking tour, are you?"

She could not help being tart. "You haven't mentioned a word about it, Jon, except for talking to your father, a conversation to which I was not invited. What's wrong? Did something disagreeable happen to you?"

He regarded her sullenly and crossed his long thin legs. He folded his arms across his chest. The white ridges were out around his mouth again. "I don't see how anything I saw or did could interest you."

"You might try," Marjorie said. "Did it interest your father?"

"I didn't tell him. Yet. But I will."

Marjorie waited again. She did nothing to encourage his confidence. She sat relaxed and handsome, with the morning light on her dark hair and the jet buttons on her severe bodice glittering. The light was full on the wretched boy's face, but hers was in shadow.

Then he told her.

The rains that spring had been notably heavier than usual in the southern section where the walking tour had taken place. The company of boys, and one of their teachers, could walk only two or three hours a day and then had to run for shelter to the nearest town or village, hoping to encounter a small hotel which was reasonably clean. Some were not too intolerable; some were chilly and grubby. They had not taken the mountain route but just the foothills, very muddy and slippery in the almost constant water and the breaking of recently locked springs, creeks, rivers and brooks.

One day they found the narrow road blocked off with a warning sign. Part of a small muddy hill had begun to slide, and travelers by foot or horse or carriage or wagon were warned to keep off the road for at least a mile in either direction for fear of a landslide. The boys, led by their teacher, cautiously left the road and walked parallel to it at a distance of about a hundred feet, in the meanwhile curiously surveying the brown and leaking and glistening hills on the other side of the road. It was a dreary and monotonous scene against the somber gray sky, and very deserted, for the nearest town was half a mile away and hidden to the west behind another range of hills.

Then the teacher shouted and halted and began to point. At a little distance, and right in the middle of the road, at least a dozen children were playing, for the earth all about was soft and soggy and spongy, and the road offered the only firm ground. Above them leaned the brown lip of a slowly sliding side of a hill.

"Oh, my God!" cried Marjorie with horror, and sitting upright. "I read about that in the papers a week ago! Were you there, seeing it yourself, Jon? Six children were buried in the slide and died, and eight were rescued!"

"Yes," said Jonathan. "I was there. I saw it. We had little shovels in our knapsacks, and it was a good thing we did. We sent one of the boys to the village and the rest of us dug into the mud. The eight were lucky; we could pull them out because just their legs or their arms had been buried. But the other six kids were deep under tons of mud and rock and water. The men from the village and the farms worked all night digging them out—and they were dead. All the lanterns were around and lamps, and the parents, the ones whose kids had been saved and the ones whose kids hadn't. And they had fires going, and firemen working and digging, and the police, too. It was kind of terrible."

"Dear God, it must have been," said Marjorie. "I saw drawings of it in the newspapers. Those poor parents."

"Yes," said Jonathan. Now his look at her was fiercer than ever and tighter. "It was bad enough that their children had been smothered to death in all that mud. It was much worse because of the other fathers and mothers. Much worse." He struck his bony knee with his brown fist. "God—damn—them," he said in a low voice, and it was the voice of a man and not a youth.

As each dead child, muddy and lifeless, was lifted from its wet grave, the cries of the bereaved rose harshly in that cold spring air, and they were the cries of tortured animals. The parents of the children who had been saved huddled together and stared at the distraught parents whose children had died. Then when the last child was brought out, white-stained face under the moon, and the weeping became more anguished, the parents of the rescued children moved into action. Their faces split into wide and exultant smiles. They pushed their children to the grieving mothers and fathers, their eyes glowing radiantly and with inhuman satisfaction in the mingled moonlight and lantern light.

They pushed their children around and even over the little

bodies on the dank earth, which lay there so pitifully. In fact, they moved with eager excitement toward the bereaved. Exalted cries rushed from their mouths, and joyous whoops. They pressed their living children against the grieving, impatiently. "Look, look!" they exclaimed. "My Susie, my Mary, my Tommy, my—my—my—my—! They're all right! Look at them! Isn't it wonderful! Look, look. They're alive. Susie, shake Mrs. Schwartz's arm so she'll notice you. Look, Mrs. Benson! Susie's all right! Look at my Elsie! Look, look! Why don't you look?"

"I couldn't believe it," said Jonathan. "There they were, milling with their kids, shoving them at the fathers and mothers of the dead, demanding that those poor things look and rejoice and hug and congratulate—and their own kids lying there as dead as, as dead as—" He stopped. He stared before him. "We walked away. We didn't say anything. I—well, I wanted to kill. It's the second time in my life I've felt that way. I just wanted to kill, I tell you!" and he glared at his mother.

Marjorie said nothing. Her hands were folded tightly on her knee.

"What's the matter with people?" asked Jonathan, after a long silence. "What in hell is the matter with people?"

Marjorie said, "Did you boys and your teacher talk it over together that night?"

"A little. I think we were all kind of sick and shaken. Then the teacher said that the parents of the living kids were just —just hysterical, and just happy, and they didn't mean anything cruel or brutal—" Again he stared at his mother. "I don't believe that. The dead kids were lying there, huddled up and broken and wet and dirty and smashed. You could see them. And you could hear their parents crying and praying and you could see them tearing desperately at each other, and trying to comfort each other, and screaming— What the hell is the matter with people? And those animals, shrieking with joy, as if they were triumphant, and shouting to their friends to look at the living kids, and jostling them, and angrily demanding—"

Marjorie was silent again, suffering for her son. Jonathan said, "There's a lot of silly stuff being printed these days in books about 'understanding' people. And the 'innate goodness' of people. We are getting them in school. Maudlin books. You are supposed to 'understand' everybody—and love everybody. A sweet, sentimental, gooey drip and stench

—that's what is being written now. Putrid stuff. Horace Mann. We read what he wrote, and the things he said, and what he did— Warm pudding. 'Humanity rising, progressing to perfection.' Other bilge. He was a Whig. A Humanist. He bawled over mankind. He loved, loved, loved, the swine!" Jonathan struck his knee again, in a kind of desperation. "What was wrong with him, and all the others like him? Couldn't they see the facts, the truth, about people? Didn't they ever honestly say, 'What in hell is the matter with people?' And that is what I ask you now. Tell me about it."

Marjorie thought of her husband, Adrian Ferrier, and his song of man, his constant, unremitting, terrified song of man, his imploring song of man, his implicit and eternal and anxious demand to be assured that all was fair in the world, all men were brothers, all men instinctively loved each other, all men were good. She shook her head slightly. She looked at Jonathan.

"I'm not going to lie to you, dear. I've never lied to you. I've always told you the truth. Men are not good; they are not kind; they are not just and tender and compassionate by nature. We are the most evil species this world has ever spawned, and I doubt we'll ever be any better. Men like Horace Mann are just—frightened. They really know what their fellowman is, in spite of the oratory and the sweetness and the insistence. They don't want to know. They are frightened to death of the world they know exists—and so they invent a pretty one instead and try to live in it. They should be pitied. But it should be remembered that as they live in fantasy they can extend their insanity to others, too, and help to divorce them from reality."

Jonathan, young and thin and intense and sick at heart and newly embittered, considered what she had said for a long time. His face became darker and darker.

Marjorie said, "I would be doing you a wrong, dear, to say soothing, lying things to you, to ease your mind and send you away with pretty delusions and confidences. That would be the kind thing to do, but I prefer truth. I also respect the fact that you are no longer a child, to be put off with fairy stories and patted on the head and given a cup of hot cocoa and a plate of cookies. But we should tell even very young children the absolute truth so they will be armored against life and be able to endure reality. Lies are always wrong."

Jonathan smiled very bitterly. "You never did have much faith in people, did you? Never mind. I don't either, not much. But you haven't told me what was the matter with those people down there."

"It's very simple. And very human. They were totally self-ish, primitively human. They were exultant and victorious. The fact that others had lost their children and were grieving and despairing just added an extra fillip, an extra gratification, to the mean pride they felt because their own children were not dead. And because they were so delighted and so elated, and so stimulated by the agonies of the others—you see how bestial we really are—they were outraged at the agonized rebuffs they received from the parents of the dead children. Most people, you see, are involved with no one but themselves. It's a kind of wickedness— But, it is understandably human."

"And forgivable?" Jon's face had become taut and derisive.

"No," she said. "Never forgivable. Never to be condoned. Never to be smoothed over and 'explained' in mawkish words. We must just look at our fellows starkly, accepting them for the appalling creatures they are— We have no choice. We few who see without syrup in our eyes and without tremulous throbs in our hearts, and without being liars."

Jonathan sighed, and to Marjorie it was the most sorrowful sound. The boy said, "Horace Mann proclaims that children can be taught goodness and pity and mercy and kindness—"

"The poor man was a fool, a really dangerous fool," said Marjorie. "I haven't any hope for mankind. I haven't had any since I was fourteen. You see, my father was a very intelligent man and refused to lie to me, and he told me all he knew about humanity."

"Was it painful for you?"

"Very. I never got over it. You can never get over a mortal wound, you know. You have to live with it, and there, I'm afraid I have made a contradiction in terms. But there it is. You have to live with your knowledge all the days of your life. That does not exempt you from feeling pity, though, even for the creature that is man. His very terribleness should inspire compassion."

"From whom?"

Marjorie hesitated. "From God, perhaps. From the few of us who refuse to accept sweet lies and fantasies. We very few."

Then Jonathan said the most pathetic thing he had ever said in his young life, and the most pathetic thing he would ever say: "How can a person go on living, knowing what people are?"

Marjorie sighed with sadness, and tried to smile. "What else can we do? You can't escape from the formidable truth except through drink, perhaps, or in moments of rare personal happiness, or in music or poetry, or in the sights of nature—far from men. I've read some of your books concerning the saints of the Church. Many of them 'fled the world,' it is written, in order that they might contemplate God more clearly and live lives of chastity and austerity. I suspect those poor men just couldn't stand their fellowmen any longer. They had to leave them and the world they made if they were to save their souls and their sanity."

Jonathan stood up. But he looked long and hard at the floor between his feet.

"There's another thing, dear," said Marjorie, aching for him and his introduction to reality. "We few who know what men are must rarely let others know that we know. They have a way of going for—for—"

"The jugular," said Jonathan. "Yes, I can see that. They'll try to kill you, one way or another, if they know you've caught on to them and know all about them."

"Yes. That's the unpardonable sin you can commit against your brother: Letting him know that you know exactly what he is. He'll hate you forever."

Jonathan moved slowly toward the door. Then Marjorie said, "Will you tell your father about your experience, dear?"

He turned and looked at her and again she saw that dark and warning look in his eyes. "No. He wouldn't understand. It would hurt him. He's—kind."

And I am not, thought Marjorie as the door closed behind her son. That's what he meant: I am not kind. I only tell the truth.

"Damn this storm," said Jonathan in a slurred voice, and he set the wine bottle thumpingly on the table. "How long has it been going on, anyway? Look at that lightning."

Marjorie's mental return tonight to her pale and shining dining room was almost traumatic in its violence, for she had been so engrossed in her memories. She started. "It does seem pretty wild, doesn't it?" she said.

The fresh strawberries and cream and tea had come, and had been partially eaten and removed, Marjorie observed, though she had not the slightest memory of them. The wine bottle was empty. "Are you ready to leave?" asked Jonathan. His face was very sunken in appearance, and his eyes were glazed with alcohol, and there was a tremor about his mouth and in his hands.

"Yes, thank you," said Marjorie. He came to her chair and drew it back for her. He walked to the buffet then, leaving her standing. "I think," he said, "that I'll take a bottle of bourbon upstairs with me. A nightcap. I'm tired."

The thunderous rain was washing the tall bright windows and the wind was howling in the eaves. Jonathan was laboriously and with considerable careful difficulty fitting a crystal glass over the decanter. He was absorbed in the delicate task. Then, walking with slow caution and putting each foot down tentatively, he left the dining room. His mother heard his heavy and uncertain step on the stairs. She listened, during an interval when there was only the rain and the wind. Jonathan had gone into his father's study. She heard the solid bang of the door.

She said to herself, "Yes, dear Jon, I always told you the truth. I never lied to you. Would it have been any better if I had? I don't know. In spite of all you knew and all I told you, you became a good man and a doctor who simply could not bear pain in others. You did all you could to alleviate it. It was your personal enemy. Was it because the pain was always so awful in you yourself, and you were trying to exorcise it?

"I never lied to you. Except once. By silence. But it was for your sake, Jon, for your dear sake."

It seemed a century, this evening of inner revelation and discovery, a dreadful century. Marjorie wearily climbed the stairs to her own room. She could not face downstairs tonight, the lonely sofas, the empty chairs, the brilliant, lonely furniture, the glittering windows which would reflect nothing but a despairing woman's face.

By silence, I lied. Was that the better way? By not speaking I saved you so much, Jon, so much more than you have already borne. I wonder, if you knew what I know, if you'd be grateful to me? Perhaps. Would the ultimate have been better than this?

She could hear Jonathan speaking on the telephone in the study. She paused, then went to the shut door and listened. "Good, good," he was saying in the precise voice of drunkenness. "Don't let anyone in. Little sips of ice water only, or, better, little pieces of ice on her tongue. Don't let anyone in."

You never did, dear, thought Marjorie. No, you never did. Except for Mavis.

Before she fell asleep, after a long while, she repeated to herself, as if for consolation:

" 'He is wounded, but not slain. He'll lay him down and bleed a while, then rise and fight again.' "

Would he? He had not forgotten Mavis, and only Marjorie knew that, Mavis the dearly beloved, and the hated.

CHAPTER ELEVEN

Jonathan stood drinking in his father's study, drinking slowly and steadily, and he looked about him at the brown, golden and ruddy room, so calm and sedate under the soft light of lamps. He thought of it as an autumn room, for it was warm and quiet and gleaming, the walls hidden by bookshelves and the books, themselves, chosen, he had suspected even as a child, not for their content so much as for their tawny shining leather and their gilt. There was no dark wood here but only fruitwoods and unstained mahogany, russet and polished and lacquered, so that it glowed like brown glass. The rug was a precious Chinese Oriental, in shades of yellow, ecru, cinnamon, copper and buff. The curtains were of gold silk; all the ornaments were of bronze and very masculine in cast, and the lamps were bronze also with parchment shades. The fireplace was of brown marble, veined with yellow, and so was the hearth.

Yes, it was very quiet. It had always been quiet and staid and spacious. Yet, curiously, in spite of the deep leather chairs, the beautifully carved old desk, the bright tables with their little Chinese boxes and ivories, the books, the general air of warmth, the broad mullioned window with its window seat covered with velvet cushions, there seemed to be no real invitation to rest here, to think, to meditate, to browse, to study. Adrian had called it his "retreat," and had spent most of his leisure here among "my beloved books, my dearest companions," yet it did not possess that peculiar atmosphere of contemplation and profound communion and repose that distinguishes the true library, the true study, of an intellectual man. In short, it was empty. It always shone; it was always beautiful; it gave the impression of invitation. The shining beauty remained after one entered here, but the superficial invitation soon vanished, for it had never been truly given. It was a harmonious shell that had never contained life even in the beginning, for Adrian Ferrier had never possessed that life to give. It was no more lifeless now than it had been in his own period of existence. It was not an abandoned room; it just had never been inhabited.

Jon had known that as a child. But from childhood he had indulged his father in Adrian's conceit that this was the throne room of a dedicated and thoughtful and contemplative man, seeking refuge from a hot and exigent world into the caverns of his own brilliant mind. "Always I am refreshed," he would say. "No matter how weary I am, I come to my retreat and think and muse and give rein to my fancy and let my thoughts soar, and soon peace comes to me and strength to bear the burdens of my life." What his burdens had been Jonathan never knew, but he implied them, sighing, and would lift a plump white hand exhaustedly for a moment and then let it drop on the arm of his chair. He would then smile pathetically at Jonathan, his big blue eyes misty and wistful.

Jonathan leaned against the oaken door of the library tonight, drinking slowly and steadfastly, and then with the strange clarity of drunkenness he began to smile and he said aloud, "Dear Papa, you were a terrible but lovable farce, and I always knew all about you. I loved you dearly and still do, and you were kind. You loved me and I never let you know what I knew about you, because I pitied and protected you from sharp and perceptive Mama even when I was a little kid. Sharp and perceptive Mama. You knew she was on to you. She didn't have the humor and compassion not to let you know. But I did. And you were grateful, and in a way you'd never understand you taught me a lot about people. You taught me, for one thing, to recognize a bore at once and to avoid him. Never mind, Papa. You were a little man, more ordinary than most, and you were very pretentious, and wouldn't Mama be surprised to know I know all this! She thinks that I thought you an Intellect, and I let her think that because it amuses me and irritates her.

"You were weak and vulnerable, and for some damned reason the weak and the vulnerable get right inside my vest and cuddle up in my viscera. Mama despises them and is impatient with them, and probably with good reason, which leaves me in somewhat of a dilemma. Am I a little weak and vulnerable, too? Was that one bond between us?"

He frowned at the glass in his hand, then took a gulp of it. He uttered a particularly foul word. "Maybe," he said. "I never thought of that before. Well, hell, Papa. Poor old boy. I knew all the time that your insistent kindness and solicitude for others was only your terrified defense against your fellowman. You probably had a faint idea of what people are, and so you tried to fend them off, prevent potential attacks on you with declarations of your belief in mankind, that it really is good, decent, kindly at heart, bulging with the honey of goodwill and needing only encouragement to sprout wings. You gave money to every whimpering rogue, thief and lying mendicant who asked your help—so they'd think well of you and praise you for a sensitive and compassionate man. But charitable institutions, and even the Church, rarely got a penny out of you. There you were parsimonious. Sometimes you mortified me when the priest or the Sisters came around. Even though you sent them away with a few coppers or a little silver—poor devils—they thought you were the most benign creature in existence. The funny thing is, you really were. You weren't a hypocrite at all, though I suspect dear Mama always thought you were. You dearly loved yourself, but it was an innocent love, like a child's. God, Papa, you made me ache all over when I was a kid myself and you treated me as if I were your father. Did I like that? Probably. Perhaps that was a bond between us, too.

"I knew when I was still in knickers that you were incapable of dealing, foot to foot, fist to fist, with others. At heart, you were a woman, perhaps even a girl. I don't mean that nastily, Papa. I'm a doctor, and I know that every woman has masculine qualities and every man feminine ones; that's our duality. But your feminine qualities were greater than your masculine.

"I think it was your terror of people that made you love

harmless things, birds and trees and gardens. They never threatened you. Of what were you afraid, Papa? I don't think you ever knew. I don't think you even had the slightest suspicion. You just didn't want to be hurt. Who does? Unfortunately, all of us can't run away, as you ran away all your life. You did have loving and tender parents, so they never scared the hell out of you. You were born as you were born, with all your trembling genes and your fear. You couldn't help it. But Mama thought you could."

Jonathan took another big swallow. The glittering surfaces in the room dazzled him. Cautiously he extended a hand and eased himself into a chair. Some whiskey spilled on his knee, and he cursed abstractedly.

"Poor Pa," he said. "Your parents and your friends protected you. Everybody did. You were so easy to be fond of, with your gentle platitudes and clichés; you never said a word to offend anyone. You couldn't imagine speaking harshly, and I doubt you ever had a mean thought, either. You just weren't bright enough, Papa. The only one who refused to protect and shelter you was dear Mama. I think you came close to hating her, as close as you could hate anyone. You ran away from her. She probably impressed you as a gentle and understanding girl when you were both young, and here was a new Mama already made to replace the one you had lost. But Mama never really was a Mama, though she bore you two sons. Except, of course, for darling Harald, the apple of her eye."

There was one last boom of thunder and then the storm retreated and now the rain was steady and swishing against the glass and the wind had died.

"You know," said Jonathan, smiling at the chair where his father used to sit "to receive my child's closest confidences," "I don't think you really knew a bad poem from a good one, a stinker of a picture from a fine one. But you tried. I think that's damned touching, and always did. I particularly hated 'The Storm,' over the fireplace, but you adored it, and though I never looked at it if I could avoid it, I knew that you loved it and found it beautiful. It was just like you, Papa.

"Yes, Papa, you were sweet and kind. Above all, you were harmless, and that's a damned rare and precious quality in humanity. Harmlessness. I cherished that in you. And I never let you know one single infernal thing about me. It would have scared the dung out of you, and I loved you too much, and had too much tenderness for you, to tell you the truth. You couldn't have stood it. So I invented dear little boyish troubles which you could handle nicely with aphorisms and strokings of my head and soothing murmurs. It made you happy. You died thinking kids are innocent lambs, 'trailing clouds of glory.' That's from your pet poet, Wordsworth, and he makes me ill."

Jonathan filled his glass solemnly. He toasted his father's empty chair. "I miss you like hell," he said. "I miss your harmlessness. You were the only harmless creature I ever knew. Papa, your health, wherever you are."

He laughed a little and sprawled in his chair. "Papa, if there is anything to immortality, I just know what you are now and what you are doing. You are wandering around the blue and shining halls of heaven with a feather duster in your hands, and all the angels pat you on the head as they hurry about their business. You are probably about seven years old. God must love you particularly. I bet you never committed a mortal sin in your life. The capital sins were only words to you, weren't they? What did you tell the priests in the Confessional, Papa? Did you have to invent little venial sins? The sins of a child?

"You never knew what Mavis was. You loved her always, didn't you? You didn't live to see us married. You spoke of her as a 'dear girl, a treasure, a love.' Yes, Papa, she was indeed. Indeed. I'm glad you never knew how many times I came close to killing her. I thought of a thousand ways—"

The glass slipped from his inert hand and dropped to the floor and spilled its contents. He neither knew nor cared. He was fully drunk. He stared blankly before him, but his thoughts were not blank. His exhausted face took on the dark shadow of agony.

Mavis, Mavis, Mavis, he thought. Oh, my God, Mavis! Mavis!

He had been twenty-three years old, two years in medical school, when he had first become aware of Mavis Eaton, niece and adopted daughter of Dr. Martin Eaton and his wife, Flora. Certainly, he had seen the little girl from babyhood, then as a toddler, then a running child shrill and insistent, for she was very spoiled. (Her uncle and aunt invariably referred to her, even after they had adopted her, as "That sweet, motherless, fatherless little one!") But so small a child hardly could inspire a boy and a youth with tenderness except in an academic way, for Jonathan even so young liked children. So, he had seen her, had absently noted her, had thought she was exceptionally handsome for a child, had idly admired her, but had not been attracted by her pert ways, her open rudeness to her adoring uncle and adopted father, and her loud and un-expected outbursts of somewhat rough laughter. There had been a period when she had been grubby, and Jonathan, even hardly past puberty, had disliked grubbiness. Still later, she had lost her baby teeth, and her hair appeared lank and un-combed, and though he was polite to her in her uncle's house —which he visited often—she appeared to him to have lost the shining and spotless and rounded sweetness of earlier years.

. She had not liked him. Other visiting young men, studying medicine, had deferred to her ostentatiously so that the for-midable, rich and famous Dr. Eaton would look upon them kindly and, possibly, in the future, sponsor them. But Jona-than Ferrier was aloof and independent, and these the ten-year-old Mavis interpreted as "stuck-up" and "thinks right well of himself, and he's so homely, too." He never brought her little gifts to flourish above her eager hands in the pres-ence of the smiling Dr. Eaton and her Aunt Flora. On sev-eral occasions, annoyed at her vexation that her uncle and Jonathan were going into his study, where they would close the doors, Jonathan had said to her in a peremptory way she hated, "Run along, little girl, and play with your dolls or pes-ter someone else." This seemed outrageous to Mavis, for had not her uncle intended to take her for a ride to the ice cream parlor before "the prig" had appeared? She came to hate him.

When she was between the ages of ten and twelve, Jona-than had rarely, if ever, even seen her, probably because when he was at home, he contrived to visit the house when she was at school, or bicycling or away on the interminable picnics with which her generation were engrossed. He would sometimes hear her demanding voice in the kitchen or in the halls, but he never encountered her in them.

The Eaton house was on a street broad, spacious and filled with trees and exceptionally wide even for Hambledon, which was famous for its expansive thoroughfares. It stood on two acres of land, far back from the street and cloistered in a heavy stand of linden trees, a tree not common in town. It was said that the whole of Hambledon was fragrant when they bloomed, and certainly a warm damp wind carried their scent for long distances. The house rose above all its neighbors, for Dr. Eaton's father had fancied a tall knoll, and so it overlooked the roofs of other houses, and the upper windows, where the servants slept, stared at distant streets and had a long close look at the river. In fact, the deep and rambling rear gardens sloped down to the river promenade, as the townsfolk liked to call the smooth, silvery gray planks that ran at the rear of the big houses very close to the water. But every house's rear gardens were guarded by low fences with doors in them, usually locked, though a tall youth or man could easily have jumped over them.

Jonathan Ferrier thought the house and its neighbors were hideous, though they were considered very stylish with their wide shadowy verandas and shutters and little turrets and small silly towers and fretwork and stained-glass hall windows and double oaken doors leading to small vestibules and to another door. "Dripping with tortured cellulose," he would say of them. "Well, I suppose it gives jig-cutters employment, but that is about all you can say for all that wooden lace drooping from every possible knothole and eave." The Eaton house had even more "wooden lace" than its neighbors, and was made of wood painted a particularly—to Jonathan—repulsive chestnut brown, with bright yellow shutters and yellow shingles. It had two towers in front, one at each end, and the dormer windows of the second and third floors had tiny little spires rising from them, intricately carved, and not only was there a stained-glass window in the front hall door but a huge one, at least twelve feet high and eight across, in the exact middle of the house, indicating the spiral staircase inside.

It was called a "mansion," for it had eighteen rooms and even one referred to as a "ballroom," though it was hardly that even in size. (It became a "ballroom," when Mavis was older.) Its rooms were long, narrow and gloomy even on the brightest day, but that was the style, to preserve the glow of wood and the fabric of expensive brocade draperies and the shimmer of Aubusson and Oriental rugs. When the walls were not paneled, they were hung, in the drawing room (no "parlors" for the Eatons!) with crimson rose damask, and in the dining room, golden damask. Even so, so fearful was Mrs. Eaton and her generation of the burning rays of the incontinent sun that all the windows, except the servants', could be found at least half shuttered even in winter, except on the very darkest days. The fear of the sun and its "harmful propensities" was not the only reason for the murkiness of the house's interior. There was also a belief, generally held, that

only the vulgar threw open windows and shutters all the time
—such as servants—and "had no respect for their privacy."
Servants, of course, were not genteel. They had no private
lives.

The house was richly furnished and was as hideous to Jonathan Ferrier as the exterior, and all the tables and sofas
and chairs were big and heavy and upholstered in dark velvets or horsehair or somber silks, and the fireplaces were
thickly cluttered with masses of ornamental china, elks'
horns, vases, clocks, little gilt boxes, shells, Staffordshire ware
and containers for artificial flowers (waxed or fashioned of
crepe paper, even when gardens were exploding with color).
And, of course, at each side of the fireplaces stood immense
Chinese jars filled with gilded bulrushes or ostrich plumes or
any other exotica the lady of the house fancied, such as pus-
sywillows in the spring, the only sign of any particular season.

Only the broad gardens, with their conservatory, were absolutely beautiful, though even here there was a gazebo of
latticework painted brilliant white and filled with wicker furniture with velvet cushions, where the ladies took their tea on
hot summer days, or their ices. The gardens were formal and
had been designed by an artist who was now long dead. His
successor was a genius of his kind, and managed, on two
acres, to hint of forests of tall pines, grottoes, little wayward
paths, hidden cool nooks and silent recesses. The lawns cunningly appeared immense and endless, for there were no definite boundaries, and the trees, which included an oak or two,
several maples and a cluster of elms and one pointed poplar,
seemed about to advance at any moment on that stretch of
incredibly green grass, meticulously cut and totally without a
single weed. Gardens of flowers, always in bloom, gave the
impression that they had simply dropped from the cerulean
heavens at a gesture of grace, for they were not formal and
were idly shaped. All this was artful, of course, but it was
also charming, and Jonathan loved the Eaton gardens almost
as much as his mother's. "Artistry," he would say, "can be so
superb, sometimes, that it exalts nature."

Invariably, every summer, Mrs. Eaton received the first
prize of the Garden Club, though her labors in her gardens
often consisted of inspecting the work of the gardeners every
morning and speaking to them sharply, and strolling, in a
light frothy dress, every evening to permit the scented rising
wind to play with her thick masses of bright dark hair. She

was a thin woman, too slender for fashion, but her wardrobe was superb, she purchasing all her dresses in New York, and these expensive treasures drew attention away from her dark and predatory face with its big lean nose, her tight and colorless mouth and her small penetrating black eyes. She had great style, everyone said, and marvelous taste, and she had also inherited a great deal of money, which covered many malicious little sins of character and a truly awesome stupidity, not to mention very black and very thick eyebrows that were a single bar over her eyes.

Dr. Martin Eaton, in contrast with his wife, was big, lumbering, awkward and clumsy, except in the operating rooms, where his deftness and delicacy were famous. He had a fat face, almost square, small kind blue eyes, a nose like a peeled potato and heavy nearly Negroid lips, which could give a smile singularly tender, steadfast and sweet, inspiring courage and trust in anyone who was favored by it. Even when he had been thirty, he had been nearly totally bald, and now his head was a vast dome of which he pretended to be very proud. "Houses an enormous brain, Flora says," he would say with a wink. "My friends, however, remark that the feller —what was his name?—who immediately preceded *Homo sapiens* had a brain cage about twice the size of a normal man's these days."

As he had inherited a considerable fortune, a few who did not admire Flora would often wonder why he had married her. It would have surprised these to know that the two had a remarkably compatible marriage, even a serene one, for Flora fully believed that her husband was not only the handsomest of men but a tremendous genius, and Martin Eaton loved his wife for her deference to him, her devotion to his smallest need and comfort, her admiration, her absolute loyalty to her household, and her love for his niece. Unlike other wives, she never suspected that her husband was sometimes foolish and childish and unreasonable and illogical, and so he could relax in his house at night, confident that no wifely comment would be made concerning his appearance, the people he was treating, his particular friends, or his behavior at the last dinner they had given, or the amount of "spirits"—very copious—he had drunk yesterday or was drinking to night. "Gentlemen must have their relaxations," she would say in tones of absolute authority, "and doctors more than most."

This, then, was Mavis Eaton's background, she who had

inherited quite a fortune herself and was to know no suffering whatsoever in her life until the final days of her last agony, when she was nearly twenty-four years old. To some that death appeared more tragic than ordinarily, for Mavis had lived in eternal sunshine, adored, admired, courted, pampered, petted, rich, beautiful and totally fascinating. Still others bitterly remarked that into that "Eden of a lovely life had come the snake of Jonathan Ferrier to destroy it."

"She never said a word, never a word," her broken uncle muttered on his stroke-tortured bed after her tragic death, "never a word against him, ever. Always smiling, always saying everything was wonderful and how dearly she loved him. Until the hour before she died. Then she told me."

"Everything was 'Jon this' and 'Jon that,' and what could she do to make Jon even happier than he was with her, and would Jon like this or that, or she must hurry home for tea for Jon always wanted to see her face first when she opened the door for him. It was her greatest sadness that she had no children, my dear, dear darling!" That was Flora Eaton, weeping. "But Jon never wanted any children, she said."

It was on a hot August day that Jonathan Ferrier, twenty-three years old, became aware of Mavis in her twelfth year. In fact, as he never forgot, it was August 12, 1888.

He had ridden his bicycle over to Dr. Eaton's house, for his horse was being treated for some vague disorder. He was a tall, exceptionally thin, dark young man, still quite lanky, though with a peculiar grace and elegance about him, and a clever, reticent face which could still become open and lively among friends. His dark eyes were restless but kind and the corners were wrinkled with the marks of laughter. No one could quite decide whether or not he was handsome, or perhaps even ugly. A very few had seen the thick white ridges spring out about his mouth, so the general consensus, after some time, was that he was "attractive in a sort of aristocratic way."

Of course, it was said, he could not compare with the rising brother, Harald, who was as gloriously beautiful as a matinee idol, and who already had the girls mad with love for him, and had the "nicest" disposition.

He wore, on that August day, a suit of light gray wool, a stiff straw hat with a gay red ribbon on it, polished black shoes and a shirt striped in pale blue. His collar was stiff, high and brilliant, and his tie was a devilish scarlet, bought at the university and somewhat shocking to Hambledon. He wore no gloves, and this was unpardonable, and his face and hands were burned dark with the sun, which was vulgar.

He leaned his bicycle against the steps of the high deep veranda of the Eaton house, and was whistling some lively tune whose lyrics would not have been admired in Hambledon. He took off his coarse-straw hat and fanned himself briskly and danced a step or two out of sheer youthful exuberance. His movements were fluid and almost professional in their precision as he swung about on the broad flags of the walk. He appeared to float at high moments. His mother considered him too grave and severe at twenty-three, but today, for some reason, he was lighthearted and practically ready to believe that the world might be an enjoyable place sometimes if one had a sharp eye out for it.

He concluded his dance with a flourish, waved his hat high and was about to clap it back on his thick dark hair when he heard a light laugh, so fragile and pure that he thought it was the tinkling of one of the many Chinese glass prisms which hung in clusters from the roof of the veranda. Then he saw a young girl moving on a cushioned swing. Seeing that she had attracted his attention, she laughed a little louder and mockingly clapped her hands.

Jonathan colored with annoyance and dislike, then saw that it was "only that damned kid, Mavis." He put his hat on; she was too young for gallantries, and he jumped up the broad brown steps of the veranda. "Hello," he said. "Doctor home? Almost five, you know."

"He's home," said Mavis. "Hello, Jon. I haven't seen you for a couple of years." She paused and smiled. "You've grown up."

He stopped at this impertinence from a child, and turned his head and stared at her. "You haven't," he said with shortness, then was still. For it was most evident that Mavis had, indeed, approached an astonishing measure of maturity, more even than her twelve years should have shown. And she had a look of deep animal happiness.

She leaned back in her swing, smiling, and he was struck by her smile, for it was utterly beguiling. He thought at once: The Laughing Girl, and it pleased him that he had reached, in only a moment or two, a perfect miniature evaluation of Mavis. She was born to laughter, and to laugh, as others are born to grieve or to work or to be intelligent or to be geniuses. It would not be a contrived laughter or a laughter solely for effect—though it could be that, also, nor a false or

artificial mirth, nor a grudging one. Mavis was laughter. It
was an integral part of her nature, and she laughed as others
merely smiled or did not smile at all. She had lost the little
irritabilities of young childhood, for they had been merely superficial. Now all the innate capacity for finding almost everything amusing and everything provocative of laughter was
the strongest characteristic of her nature. And it was a husky
and gleeful laugh, evoking laughter in anyone she encountered.

Jonathan, staring, thought of something Keats had written.
This was very strange, for Jonathan did not admire the delicate and tragic if somewhat flowery Keats, though he was
much attached to the more sinewy poets. He said to himself,
as he looked at Marvis smiling at him from her swing:

> "Surely I dreamt today, or did I see
> The wingèd Psyche with awakened eyes?"

Jonathan had seen many beautiful young blondes in his
twenty-three years, each one prettier than the last. So, the
round and perfect young face confronting him, with its apri-
cot and milky coloring, would not have made him stand there
so long, gazing with what he long later called "disgusting ox-
like enchantment." He had seen eyes as blue and lucid before, and gilt lashes as profuse and all of a sweet tangle. He
was not startled by such a faintly rosy mouth, full and just
barely pouting and excellently curved and carved, and he had
encountered even prettier noses, though this was admittedly
entrancing, tilted and translucent about the nostrils. The thick
golden hair that fell in a heavy fall far below the shoulders
was, of course, rare in its quality of luminosity and total yel-
lowness, like a buttercup, but he had seen as beautiful before,
natural and dyed. Her teeth were exquisite, somewhat large
but white, and he had seen teeth like this many times.

He had seen riper figures, for all her precociousness of
adorable body and tiny waist and small and dimpled white
arms, Mavis was still only twelve. She was still a child,
though she had reached physical maturity. Her hair was tied
with a blue ribbon and she wore a blue voile dress with a
pink sash, and blue slippers. Childish attire.

It was something else, mysterious and bewitching, that held
him there, gawking. It was a quality of absolute bright assurance, of magnificent soft confidence, of healthy amiability
and endearing seduction, of enormous vitality, perhaps, of

poise. Like many others, Jonathan had tried to describe and understand charm, and had been as defeated as everyone else. Mavis possessed it in overwhelming measure, like a fairy cloak, like a blessing, like the gift it was. It did not lie in any particular feature, nor was it caught in her golden mist of hair or in her smallish blue eyes, shining and glowing. There was not the slightest flaw to be seen in Mavis, but Jonathan had seen flawless girls before and had found them intensely dull. He had a confused thought: Was Mavis stupid? He remembered the shrill and grubby child he had avoided through the years, and it seemed incredible to him that that untidy little hoyden had birthed so gorgeous a young girl. But was she stupid?

Jonathan, above all things, hated stupidity, and beauty never excused it. He found it the matrix for the abominable vices and the explanation for what was most bestial in humanity.

Mavis, never looking away from him, laughed again that entirely captivating laugh, which was not now fragile nor pure, but rollicking with humor and—this was irresistible— verve and joy in living. It was a laugh that invited the whole world to an expression of mirth, and Jonathan found himself smiling. He forgot to wonder if Mavis were stupid. He saw that she loved to be alive and expected others to have that love, also. She rejoiced in life as a bird rejoiced in it, or some small creature of the field, or as a dancing sapling, rosy with blossoms, fluttered in the spring. To Mavis, it was evident, life was to be taken joyously in both hands and eaten like a particularly large and spicy and fragrant fruit. She would rarely find the worm. She would generously proffer the fruit to be shared, and laugh with pleasure.

She was not overly tall and she was not frail, nor did she have the look of raw immaturity. She might have been seventeen instead of twelve, for the breast of the blue dress was daintily rounded above the narrow waist, and though the dress flowed, it intimated nubile curves beneath it and the lace petticoat. The legs, though mostly concealed, were beautifully formed, and the ankles like thin china in their white silk stockings.

She was born to laugh, to sing, to dance, to play in the sun, thought Jonathan Ferrier. She was born never to grow old, no matter how many years she will have. She is the Laughing Girl.

She approached him nearer, her head a little tilted as she

studied him, her squinted eyes a little puzzled at his prolonged stare. Then the puzzled look disappeared, and Mavis
understood. Jonathan might be an old man—but he was exactly like the boys she knew and so she was not shy with
him. Mavis, in her way, was a very wise girl.

The dress was ugly in the fashion of that year, though it
was expertly and deftly made. It bunched in a very pro-
nounced bustle just above and slightly over Mavis' hips, for
all it was a schoolgirl's dress. But the dress could not detract
from Mavis. It did not distort her beauty, which had the baf-
fling quality of illuminating her pervasive and formidable
charm as even the finest beauty often cannot if it is the possession of another sort of female. In short, her beauty was
only the net in which something more iridescent, something,
perhaps, more deadly, and something far more powerful, was
caught—the captive yet the possessor. Mavis possessed what
many ugly women have possessed, and which has driven
kings from thrones and has devastated empires, and was possessed by it. It is beyond explanation, as Jonathan now knew.
The only safety is flight. Jonathan did not fly.

Mavis was smiling now and not laughing. Yet the aura of
laughter was about her, deeper than the aura of her intense
beauty. It was there, a permanent anticipation, waiting to
break upwards like a leaping wave in a calm sea, at the
brightest breeze.

Jonathan did not even suspect he was maudlin when he
thought: "She is Psyche." He did not even smile at himself
when he thought: "She is a golden rose."

"You've grown up, Mavis," he said, and did not think he
was banal. It was a marvel to him that this was Mavis, and it
was Mavis who was the marvel.

"Girls usually do," she said. She had a husky speaking
voice also, which trembled always as if the impatient laughter
was swelling beneath it and was demanding to be heard. She
stood so near him that he could have touched her. And then,
a little to his helpless horror, he had the most profound and
urgent desire to touch her, indeed. He was appalled, for he
was a mature man of twenty-three and the girl before him
was still almost a child, and he knew that what he was feeling
now was a most powerful sexual urge toward her, stronger
than any he had known before in his life. She stood before
him on the quiet porch, looking up into his eyes and he could
not believe that what he saw in hers was complete knowl-

edge and that she was amused. Years younger than he, she was incalculably older and more aware.

"I hope you like what you see, Jon," she said, and chuckled, and he was again fascinated, for the chuckle was deep, warm and rich, the knowing mirth of a woman.

"You've improved," he said, and he fought down his desperate desire for her with loathing for himself. He tried for lightness. "My last memory of you was of a dirty little kid with a runny nose and tousled hair."

"Really?" she said. "And do you know what I've always thought about you, Jon? You're dippy." And again she chuckled, but it was not a taunting, for, as Jon was later to discover about the Laughing Girls, they never taunt idly except when they are bored with a lover or a husband and wish him forever out of sight.

He found himself chuckling with her, but he still wanted to take her in his arms and kiss her with a man's passion and desire. He tipped his hat a little mockingly, then went to the door and pulled the bell. The day was hot and there was the raucous shrilling of cicadas in the sun and quiet, and the distant rattle of a wagon's wheels on cobblestones, and the heated swish of trees. They seemed to roar in Jon's ears like a confused cacophony, and for the moments he stood there, resolutely facing the door with its stained-glass windows, he felt the smiling eyes of the girl fixed directly between his shoulders.

"Daddy's in the garden, and it's Mamie's day off," she informed him, "and Mama's downtown shopping."

He heard her light quick step running down the porch stairs, and he was alone, and when he turned, he saw the flash of golden hair in the sun and that heart-softening chuckle. He went home. It was not until he was entering his parents' house that he was dismayed, and he stood in the cool and fragrant dusk of the beautiful hall and despised himself. His mother came in from the morning room, raising her brows in surprise. "Why, dear," she said, "I thought you had gone to see Martin Eaton. Wasn't he home?"

Jonathan had never learned to lie very well or often, and so he said, "Yes, he was home."

Marjorie came nearer him, and she was puzzled. "Jon, is there something wrong?"

He was impatient. He threw his hat on a chair and it rolled off and he let it lie. Marjorie bent and picked it up and then stood with it in her hands. "What can be wrong?" he said.

"Well," said Marjorie, who was a little worried. It had been established that Jon would do his internship under the wing of Martin Eaton's friends, and that Dr. Eaton would more than sponsor him in Hambledon. She wondered if Jonathan had quarreled with him. It was not a fatal matter but an inconvenient and anxious one. She knew Jonathan's temper, his quick and even murderous rages, his dislike for any quibbling or deviousness, his way of stamping a man a hypocrite under the slightest provocation, and his deadly impatience and intolerance of humbug.

"Come into the morning room," she said. "I have some very icy lemonade and some fresh cake, which I made this afternoon. You look very hot."

"I want a drink," he said, and his voice was rude and his manner abrupt. "And that doesn't mean lemonade."

Jonathan did not drink regularly, as yet, but when he did, it was somewhat disturbing to his mother, for he drank as recklessly as he lived, and always under stress. She said nothing when he went into the dining room to the liquor cabinet, and she put away his hat, then stood in thought for a moment in the hall. She wanted to return to the morning room but decided that if she did, he would not accompany her but might possibly do so if she waited for him. He came back into the hall with a glass of whiskey and soda, and Marjorie noticed the darkness of the drink.

"Where's Childe Harald?" he asked.

"Boating," she replied. "He's gone on a picnic to Heart's Ease." She smiled. "Let's go into the morning room, shall we?" and she led the way, her slender figure floating in the light green voile of her dress, her head high. She hoped Jon would follow, and she hoped this ardently, and she let out a deep breath when she heard his following if reluctant footsteps.

They sat down together in the pure light of the charming room, and Marjorie took up her needlework and bent her head over it. There was no use pressing Jon for an explanation, she thought. There had never been any use, even when he had been a child. He talked or did not talk, at his own pleasure. "Well, since you were so insistent on that damned lemonade, why don't you drink it yourself?" he asked, standing before her.

"Oh. Yes. Of course. Do pour me a glass, dear."

He poured a glass for her, then stood sipping his own, frowning into the glass. She saw that he was sallow under his tanned face, as if he had some unpleasant experience. But she merely waited. After a little he sat down but on the edge of his chair, and this time he was not so careful of the creases in his trousers.

"A hot day," she said. "Martin doesn't like the heat, does he? I remember when we were children—"

"A long time ago."

Marjorie smiled. "Not so long. I was visiting his parents, with my own parents. I was always thin, I remember, and he used to tease me, but then he was a butterball of a boy, and this is why the heat affected him so cruelly." She paused. "Today is the hottest day of the summer. Poor Martin must be suffering."

"Oh, hell, don't beat about the bush," said Jonathan. "You want to know if I saw him and if not, why not. I didn't see him, though he was at home. I didn't want to see him."

"I see," said Marjorie.

"No, you don't," said Jonathan. He drank again. He turned the glass restlessly in his hands. He had never confided in his mother but twice in all his life and he did not intend to now. In fact, the very idea staggered him. What would she say if he said to her bluntly, "I saw young Mavis Eaton, and she's grown into a terrible beauty, and I wanted to drag her away somewhere and tear the clothes off her and rape her, not gently, but brutally and madly." How did a man explain bewitchment and that awful urge he had never suspected lived in him? His mother, too, was a gentlewoman and she not only would not understand but would rise and leave him with disgust and dread and with his own horror. She would not faint as it was the style for ladies to faint when they were overcome. She would not call for smelling salts and fans. But she would detest him. He had never cared what his mother's private feelings for him were, or her thoughts, or at least he had long ago assured himself he did not care. Yet the thought of her glance of repulsion made him shrink inwardly. And quite right, too, he said to himself. He stood up. "I want another drink," he said. Marjorie did not comment. She only hoped he would return. He did not for a considerable time and when he entered the room again, she more than suspected that the drink in his hand was his third, not his second.

"Say it," he said, and sat down. " 'You drink too much, Jon, for your age and your health.' "

"No," said Marjorie. "I promised myself a year ago I'd

never say it again. After all, you are not a boy any longer, you are not a youth, either. You are twenty-three years old and so you are a man and your life is your own. And a man must do what he feels he must do."

"Now, that's a subtle aphorism," said Jon, in the mocking voice he always used when he felt he must protect himself. " 'A man must do what he feels he must do.' Martin Eaton's a sot. Everybody knows it. Is he doing what he feels he must do?"

Marjorie put her sewing in her lap and looked at her son long and gravely. Then she said, "Yes."

"Yes? Yes what?"

"Just 'yes,' Jon. You aren't the only one who can be reticent, you know."

"I'm reticent about my own affairs—"

"So am I."

Jon thought about that and was intrigued. Then he sat at last, grinning, "Oh, no! Not you and old Martin Eaton? Before Dad, I suppose?"

"Martin and Flora are very happily married," said Marjorie, sipping at her own glass. "It was a very suitable marriage."

"Imagine!" said Jonathan in a nasty tone. "He might have been my father!"

"I never considered it seriously," said his mother, smiling a little. "It didn't happen back in the dark ages, you know, Jon. We'd known each other from childhood, and I was always fond of Martin. You wouldn't believe it, but I called him Fancy."

Jonathan laughed. The fearful tension and sickness in him was relaxing under the drink and the soothing voice of his mother. "Fancy! Old Man Eaton!"

"He's only twenty-five years older than you, Jon, and hardly a patriarch at forty-eight. He told me, when we were very young, that he'd wait until I had grown up, and then—"

Very carefully Jonathan put down his glass. "Oh? And how old were you then?"

"Eleven? Yes, I was eleven, or almost."

"And he—"

"Well, he was older. Sixteen, I think."

"A man!"

"Almost. We thought a boy of sixteen was a man in those misbegotten days, though now we don't think they are full men until they are twenty-one. It's so absurd. Men today are no younger in any way then they were then."

But Jonathan was drinking again, though more slowly. "Sixteen," he said. "And a big sixteen, I should think. Probably had already had a roll or two— I'm sorry, Mother."

"I'm not very shockable," said Marjorie. "Coming down to it, I should think so, about Martin. He was always a lusty boy and a lusty man. That's why I really did almost marry him, though I did not take him seriously. He was like a brother. Now, if he had not been so close to me and so brotherly all my life, I might have—"

But Jonathan said, "And you didn't know at eleven, of course."

"Certainly I knew! A girl of eleven is really much older than a youth ten years older! It is said that all men are little boys at heart, but it is very doubtful that women were ever little girls. I knew that Martin—what is the delicate phrase? —wished to make love to me, and I thought it very exciting. Children aren't as innocent as you might think, Jon."

"And you knew at eleven that he wanted to seduce you?"

"Heavens, what an old-fashioned word, dear. In many ways you are quite old-fashioned and unsophisticated—"

"Never mind analyzing me," Jon interrupted, and his mother looked at him with suddenly intent surprise. "Did you know?"

Marjorie was thinking rapidly. It was not like Jon to engage in a long talk with her. He usually found her boring, or at least he pretended so. And it certainly was not like Jon to be so—well, almost fiercely—interested in a light and trivial conversation about her childhood and girlhood. Politeness was unknown to him. He never endured ennui or made casual chatter, especially not with her. It was not the whiskey that was speaking through him, though Marjorie suspected that it had loosened some of the harsh control he usually kept over himself. She looked at him with what deluded him was a mild interest and nothing else, but her maternal eyes were weighing and studying and coming to a startled conclusion, though she did not as yet know the object.

"Yes, I knew he wanted to 'seduce' me." She smiled and her slender face brightened with mirthful remembrance. "It wasn't moonlight and roses for me, as adults think it is with children. Children are earthy. It is only later that they cover the raw exigencies of nature with a pink gauze of romance and accompany it with poetry and music. Adults are really shrinking souls, but children look at life candidly and see it fully, and are not repelled by smells, nastinesses or criminal acts. That is because they have no conscience to confuse things. They are savages, and any aspects of life are always interesting to them, even those we call the dirtiest ones. Well, anyway, Martin didn't seduce me, not even when I was fourteen, fifteen, and so on. By that time he had become romantic and said he loved me."

"You must have been a fatal woman even at eleven," said Jonathan.

"You've been reading Marie Corelli," said Marjorie. "Let me enlighten you, dear. All women are fatal from the cradle but some more than most. The rare woman, the very rare woman, is still fatal even when she is ninety or more. But that's a different kind of fatality, thank God. I've seen only two or three women like that, and they were deadly."

"In what way?"

Marjorie leaned forward and put her elbows on her knees and pretended to consider. But she was thinking more rapidly than before, and she said to herself, Who, for God's sake? A very young girl? A girl hardly past childhood? Poor Jon. But it may be dangerous.

"In what way?" she repeated thoughtfully. "A really frightful way, dear. You see, they never loved anyone in their lives. They were incapable of it. They never got over the love affair they had had with themselves in the cradle. And that made them irresistible. Men, especially, adore women incapable of loving anyone but themselves. They feel sure the women have good reason for all that passionate adoration, and they join the adorers."

"Narcissistic, you mean?"

"What?"

"Oh, that's a term seeping in from Vienna or somewhere. Alienists are using it. It means being in love with yourself. A sort of mental sickness."

"Yes. An excellent word. But those women aren't ill, Jon. You'll find they are unusually healthy and robust and have an atmosphere about them of overpowering zest and love for life, and gusto. Everything is delightful to them, enjoyable; a relish, tang, adventure. They're never openly annoyed. They are always ready for any escapade. And they laugh—always. There's just one thing you must never do to them: You must never bore them. That's the only crime they hold against anyone."

"The Laughing Girls," said Jonathan.

"Exactly." Marjorie smiled, pleased, and nodded. "The Laughing Girls. And they're the only kind, no matter how beautiful, who don't arouse envy and hatred among the other women. They can bewitch women as well as men. They're absolutely female, and that's lethal. Yes. I should say their great charm is that they are entirely female, and know it and exploit it. One of the most formidable Laughing Girls I've ever known was an elderly aunt of mine, who was then at least sixty-eight. A great-aunt. She was extremely ugly, with a big wart on one cheek, a dumpy short figure like Queen Victoria, scanty white hair, piglike eyes and big thrusting lips. Absolutely no style, and little intelligence, I'm afraid. But she had a devastating effect on everybody, in spite of the fact that she was not in the least fastidious about her person and had a way of wiping her nose on the back of her hand if she couldn't find a handkerchief immediately. But everybody adored her, though she had no style and no graces. The whole family worshiped her, including me. I was still a child, however, when I knew her, and I thought the first time I saw her that she was a nasty old woman with a loud hoarse voice and vile manners and dirty fingers. Then I heard her laugh, and I was her slave thereafter, even if I knew she wasn't worth the cut fingernail of one of her five husbands—who seemed to die off very fast and leave her simply enormous bags of money.

"It was her charm, you see, and her zest for life, and she lived to be ninety-five and passionately enjoyed every moment of it and died protesting. She loved herself completely and had a great sense of humor, brutal, but she was never humorous about herself and the things she constantly demanded for herself. There her humor ended. A very bad, wicked old woman, even from her cradle. We called her kind 'adventuresses' when they were kept women or danced on the stage and captured some bemused rich young or old man. The present favorite of the Prince of Wales, the Jersey Lily as they call her, is a good example. They all have huge appetites for everything."

Jonathan was frowning into his glass. Marjorie studied his bent head. Dear God, she thought, where has he met one? Today?

"I think you speak as a woman, Mother," he was saying. "There must be something else they have—besides laughter and zest—which—arouses—people."

"True," said Marjorie. "I call it diabolism. No, wait. I don't mean they are consciously wicked. They'd be shocked to learn that others think they are, really shocked and hurt. The consciously wicked are a different matter entirely, and one gets onto them easily, you know, and avoids them. No, the Laughing Girls, as you have so cleverly called them, have a—well, an innocent diabolism. Like a force of nature. It is themselves. And diabolism—though you have always denied there is such a thing at all—has an awful charm of its own. I've always thought that Lucifer, above all else, must be a most charming angel."

"I myself," said Jon, waving his hand in dismissal, "believe that their charm is that they are so thoroughly alive, so immediate, so eager for experience, so complete. They are full-blooded women. That's why women more anemic resent them so."

"I don't resent them," said Marjorie. "I just know all about them, though I've met only two or three in my lifetime. I think they are interesting phenomena, like a tidal wave or a comet or a tornado." She paused. "I hope this isn't an academic discussion, Jon. You've probably met one or two yourself, and they interest you. As a future doctor."

"Perhaps," said Jon. He stood up. He appeared irresolute. Is it possible he is going to tell me something? thought Marjorie. He said, "I think I'll have another drink."

When he had left the room, Marjorie thought with more concentration. Jonathan had left the house in the heat of the day on his bicycle to visit Martin Eaton. He had had time only to arrive there, give or take five minutes or so, and then he had immediately returned. He had not dallied. Half an hour in all. Where could he mave met one of his Laughing Girls in that short space of time, especially when he had been on his bicycle practically every moment? He had not mentioned Flora Eaton, so it was probable he had not seen her. He had not seen Martin Eaton. He had gone to the house, found the older doctor home—yet had immediately left without seeing him. Therefore, he had received some kind of a shock almost at once.

He had seen a girl. Marjorie knew the girls of all the best families in Hambledon and she skimmed their faces with her mental eyes. Nice, wholesome girls, some flirts but innocent ones, and none calculated to strike Jonathan so forcibly. Besides, he had known them all his life, these potential wives. Jonathan was stricken; there was no doubt about it. He was under some fierce and devastating spell, for his mother had never seen him drink so steadily before and so much. He was pale; he had the aspect of a man under extreme stress. His hands had trembled a few times. It was someone he had not known before, then. Dear Heaven, not some strumpet of the street! thought Marjorie, then almost, even in her distress, she laughed at herself. Jonathan was not the kind, and where would he have encountered such in half an hour, which had been spent almost entirely on a bicycle?

Her thought returned to Martin Eaton. Had there been a young strange patient in the house or some distant visiting young relative? If so, then the bewitched Jonathan would have inevitably stayed for more bewitchment, and he would not now be so evasive. He would speak. Men do not fly from charmers on a bicycle. They stay and grovel, thought Marjorie, with some bitterness. Then stay and offer their necks for a dainty foot. Even Jonathan would do so. More brilliant men had become victims of the Laughing Girls. They loved to be victims. They dedicated their lives to the victimization and thought themselves blest. They fly only when they know the object of all that silliness and stupidity is either not for them, or beyond them, or is very dangerous to them—and often they do not flee even then. Very rarely do they flee.

So, it must be a young girl, a very young girl. Who? Slowly Marjorie remembered something that had happened last week. She had been at the Garden Club meeting near the river, and Flora Eaton had brought her adopted daughter with her though children were invariably forbidden. "She is really so grownup and interested," Flora had apologized. The ladies had not objected after the first affronted frowns. They had been charmed within moments by Mavis Eaton, who had been so deferential, so beguiling, so lovely, so polite and eager to please. She had laughed so often too, with open delight at everything, the flight of a heron, the scuffling run of a young fox. Her delight had been something radiant and completely fascinating. And it had not been false and shown for effect. The girl was what she was. A Laughing Girl. Marjorie, of all the women there, had disliked her at once and with unusual intensity.

"What a charmer!" the ladies had twittered when Flora and Mavis had left. "What an absolute charmer! What she will do to the boys and men when she is older!"

But she was never young, Marjorie had thought. I know her well.

She started now, seeing that Jonathan had returned to the room and was standing before her, drinking again. He was looking a little sick, as if he were remembering in spite of the whiskey. Marjorie spoke carefully. "You say you didn't see Martin Eaton. I'm sorry. I heard last week that he wasn't feeling so well. Flora told me. It was very tiresome of Flora, really, but she had brought little Mavis with her. You remember Mavis, the niece they adopted."

She knew at once, for his hand quite violently shook for a second, and the whiskey splashed on his fingers. He was looking at her fully and the white ridges she always dreaded had sprung up about his mouth. "What," he said, "is wrong with the kid?"

"Wrong? In what way is she wrong?" asked Marjorie, as if surprised.

"I don't mean that, damn it!" He was almost shouting. "I mean, what have you got against the girl?"

"Jon, please. The windows are all open. I don't understand you. Why should we be talking about a little girl, a little girl in the eighth grade, I believe? A child. Aren't there more interesting things to talk about than children? I don't remember that they are so very important at all but rather boring, in fact, and intelligent people—"

"I asked you, Mother, what you have against the girl?"

Marjorie was terribly frightened. She had never known Jonathan to be like this before, even in his reckless childhood. She said, making her voice cold, "Don't talk to me like that, Jon, and shouting, too! What's the matter with you? Shall we close the subject? Besides, there is something about dinner which I must attend to—" She began to get up.

In spite of her fear she was truly angered when he put his hand against her shoulder and pushed her back into the chair.

"I only asked you a simple, reasonable question," he said, and there was a hard, thick quality about him which was alien to her. "Just a simple question."

"Which I think is too stupid to answer, and far too stupid for an adult to ask. I refuse to talk about a chit. Why should I? Why should you? Are you drunk, Jon? I'm afraid you are. I want to warn you about one thing, my boy. Don't you dare touch me in that manner again. You aren't too old for me not to strike you hard—very hard—across the face."

For a moment their eyes held together and Jonathan saw the icy anger in his mother's, and he was ashamed. He put down the drink. "You're right," he said. "I've been drinking too much today. You see, I've met one of your Laughing Girls, or mine, I should say." He tried to smile. "You must be brave, Mother. I'm not going to be like your Martin Eaton; I'm going to wait for the girl to grow up. But unlike Martin, I'm not going to be put off. I'm going to marry her."

He was still staring at her. She knew that she must not let him know that she knew of whom he was speaking. She must only pray, if she could, that something would happen— She was suddenly confused and exhausted and ill. Not her Jonathan, not her darling!

She tried to laugh a little before that frightening face. "Oh, so she's very young? Well." She paused. "And you are twenty-three. That makes you a mature man, doesn't it—and she is a little girl. I wouldn't, if I were you, let anyone know—"

"Do you think I am insane?" he demanded.

Probably, as of just now, his mother replied inwardly. Yes, very probably.

"I know what happens to men when they fall in love with children," he said.

"Oh, Jon." In spite of herself she winced. "Please don't say anything else. You'll regret it when you remember later. Don't say anything else! It's too dangerous."

"Yes," he said. "It's too dangerous. And I can wait." Later, he wondered why his mother had not been outraged, horrified and shocked to death.

He had waited. All that his mother had said that hot August day had meant nothing at all to him. He had never respected her opinion or known her. He had talked to her that day only because his inner extremity had been so great and uncontrollable, and because he had drunk too much. Within a few days, as she never mentioned that talk—assuredly only a rambling affair to her—he was relieved that she had forgotten it. Only fear of himself, of what he was capable of doing, had impelled him to talk so dangerously. But his mother could have not the slightest idea, and he put her out of his mind. She had no imagination. She was really not very intelligent. And she and old Martin Eaton, by God! Martin had not known what he had escaped. It was unfortunate that his own father had not been so lucky.

That is what Jonathan Ferrier thought that August of his twenty-third year.

He saw Mavis Eaton on every possible occasion during the

next five years, and he thought himself exceedingly prudent and subtle at all times. But Mavis had known from the very beginning, and it amused her that this "old man" was interested in her. She teased him artfully when she encountered him in her uncle's house or in his gardens, or demurely tormented him. She was not intelligent, but she had a primitive wisdom. Her uncle and aunt often spoke of the Ferrier money, and as Martin Eaton was as fond of Jonathan as if the young man had been his son, Martin constantly talked of Jonathan's professional future and success and even hinted that he might possibly leave Jonathan a part of his estate. When she was fifteen, Mavis was already picturing herself as a *grande dame* in Philadelphia or New York, presiding over her successful and famous husband's mansion, for Mavis had no intention of spending her life in little Hambledon. She wanted multitudes of admirers and craved influence. At sixteen she was more than attracting the casual attention of young men in New York, where she attended a private school for a year, and at seventeen she knew her great powers, the seduction and fascination of her perpetual merriment, and her beauty.

Very few noticed the smallness of her blue eyes, for they were almost always arched like fringed quarter moons under her golden brows, crinkled and squinted with laughter. There were some women and girls who said she had "little sly eyes," but this was accounted as envy. Fewer ever saw the cold and conjecturing gleam of those eyes, for they appeared almost entirely closed at all times and somewhat sunken in their sockets. This flaw in her loveliness, which would have been serious and even ugly in a less pretty girl, only gave her more bewitchment and, to young men, a naughty flirtatiousness. Among those who were disturbed by Mavis' eyes and their secretiveness was Marjorie Ferrier.

When Mavis was eighteen, Jonathan told his mother and brother abruptly that he was going to marry the girl in the near future.

Marjorie said nothing, for there was nothing to say. But Harald laughed and said, "Not Golden Girl! Why, she's a dragon! She'd eat the heart out of you in a year!"

The totally infatuated and adoring Jonathan Ferrier hardly heard. Later he was to know that the secret of Mavis' charm was her absolute sexuality. It was not overt; paradoxically she was almost incapable of being aroused herself, almost devoid of sensual passion. She knew that she was irresistible to men, and when she had been fifteen, she knew exactly why, and so she had contempt and amused scorn for those she attracted. However, she learned the art of flaunting her sexual attractions in a most delicate way, with rarely a stir in herself. Such flaunting brought her adoration and gifts and abject admiration, and these were all she really desired. If men were stupid enough to dream that she desired them, more fool they. It had nothing to do with Mavis Eaton's real desires, which she kept hidden.

The Laughing Girls, as Jonathan was to learn much later, have but one love and that is themselves, and but one passion, and that was their enchantment and gain. When Mavis petulantly told him—but with exquisite smiles—that she would not "dream" of spending her life in Hambledon, Jonathan fatuously promised her that in good time they would move to Philadelphia or New York or wherever she desired. This alarmed Martin Eaton. He had a long talk with Jonathan. "We need surgeons and physicians of your kind here, Jon," he said. "You can't desert us, can you, even for Mavis?"

"She's very young. I'm just humoring her," said Jonathan. "Of course, I could have a practice in Philadelphia, too—" It was all in the blissful future, and in the meantime there was Mavis, whose touch and laughter and natural gaiety and beauty almost drove him mad. He could not wait for their marriage. To Marjorie Ferrier this abasement of her son seemed tragic, for she had expected more intelligence and discernment in Jonathan and more taste. There was a certain grossness about Mavis, an animal shine and sleekness, which promised many lustful delights. But Marjorie knew that those delights would be an illusion, for the Laughing Girls knew no pleasure but in themselves and their desires, and none of them concerned the happiness and welfare and joy of others. Once Marjorie had said to Harald, "Mavis, under other circumstances and in a different age, would be the perfect—the perfect—"

"Tart," said Harald. "Concubine? Mavis isn't clever enough. Doxy? Perhaps. I think I like tart best."

"Oh, Harald," said Marjorie, and smiled sadly, but she knew he was right. "I really think, concubine. The perfect illusion of the perfect woman."

"With no personal involvement," said Harald. He frequently startled his mother with his perceptive comments, and she was startled now, and thought, as she thought very often, that Harald was much cleverer than most people knew. It was out of character, in some way, that he had this worldly shrewdness which Jonathan did not possess at all.

Harald said, "There are men who find the world contemptible but, being genial men, they also find it amusingly mad. Jon is not genial, and so he is constantly appalled by the world and enraged by what he considers its meannesses and cruelties and stupidity. He never for a single moment finds it mad, and so he'll never be able to laugh at it and enjoy it. And he'll never understand people, either. How else could he consider marrying Mavis, who has claws where a heart should be?"

(He was to marry Myrtle Heger a little before Jonathan married Mavis Eaton, but no one believed that he loved the woman or that he had married her for anything but her money.)

The marriage of Mavis Eaton to Jonathan Ferrier, on a hot and golden June day, was considered a Statewide Event, and the Governor came, and so did Senator Campion, and, of course, the mayors of several cities. The Eatons were rich, and the Ferriers, and Jonathan was already establishing a famous reputation, and his mother came of an "old family."

He was never to forget his wedding night.

Jonathan, lying in a drunken sleep now in his father's study, or rather sprawled in a leather chair, remembered that night in his dreaming. His dark and faintly sweating face was contorted, and his head moved uneasily, and even in his sleep he was conscious of a powerful nausea and enormous discomfort. He felt as if he were one ache, mentally and physically, and somewhere there was a loud and furious shrilling, as if millions of bees had gone mad.

He pulled himself sluggishly and painfully up from his heavy sleep, saw that it was very early morning and that the telephone on his father's desk was throbbing unremittingly. Nothing stirred in the house. The low and slanting light of first morning was pulsing through the leaded windows. Cursing, wincing, Jonathan reached out and took up the telephone.

"Oh, Jonathan," said Father McNulty's voice in relief. "I hope I didn't wake you too early. It's almost seven, a quarter to."

"Don't mind me," said Jonathan in a slow, thick voice. He swallowed. His throat felt swollen and very dry. "I'm always awake, like the perfect doctor. Call me in a couple of hours, and perhaps I'll answer then, and perhaps not." He was not really awake. He blinked and shuddered at the light and his stomach seemed to have a tendency to climb into his chest. "Good-bye," he said.

"Jon!" cried the priest. "Please listen for just a second or two. For God's sake, Please listen. This is a matter of life and death—"

"In which I am no longer interested," said Jonathan. "Don't you ever sleep?"

"I haven't slept all night," said the priest. "I just came home myself, and I have a Mass at seven. You remember young Francis Campion? I heard you treated him for colitis or something three years ago. Senator Kenton Campion's son."

Jonathan yawned in agony. His head appeared to be dividing itself slowly and surely into separate sections. "What about it? I'm not the family doctor. They only called me because their own was away or something, after he almost killed the boy. Why don't they call him if the kid's sick again?"

The priest hesitated. "I think there is a personal reason. Family doctor, you know. There might be some—some embarrassment— You see, young Francis tried to hang himself last night, and only old Tom, one of the servants, heard him and saved his life. Hanged himself with the sash of his dressing gown—"

"You can be sure," said Jonathan with bitterness, "that there is always some busybody around to take matters into his own damned interfering hands. When a man wants to die, let him die, say I." He paused, then said with more interest, "Tried to kill himself? At twenty? I thought he was doing well in that seminary of his, studying for the priesthood. A fine priest he'll make!" Jonathan chuckled, then coughed. "So, they called you to administer the proper spiritual punishment."

"Jon, please listen. Tom called me. No one else would. Not the aunt. And the Senator's in Washington, though he is due home today for the Fourth of July celebrations. You know the aunt." The priest coughed in apology. "No doubt a very estimable lady but not one to know what to do. So Tom called me. But young Francis would not listen to me at all and refused to see me. I did stay at his bedside, and he never turned his head in my direction. I stayed until I had to leave for Mass."

"A very piteous story," said Jonathan. "But has it got anything to do with me? No."

"I thought—I thought—" the priest stammered, "that you should see him. No, not for medical attention."

Jonathan came up from the reddish sick fog in total amazement. "Are you out of your mind, Father? 'Not for medical attention,' you say. For what, then?"

"I heard that the boy—trusted—you. Or something, Jon. It's just an inspiration. He needs something. I think you can give it to him."

"No," said Jonathan. "Besides, if I saw him, I'd have to report it to the police."

"You saved his life once. I think you could do it again, Jon."

"Why should I? Let him go and give him your blessing, Father."

The priest paused. "You will go, Jon, and immediately?"

"No," said Jonathan, and hung up. He fell back into the depths of the leather chair. When he had strength enough, he would take a cold bath, prepare himself a large cold drink, put a cold cloth on his head and go to bed, and inform his mother that no one, under any circumstances, was to disturb him. Preferably forever. He felt profoundly ill and knew, after a moment's reflection, that the illness was in his mind as well as in his abused body. Mavis. Was he to be cursed for all the days of his life by remembering her? She was part of his flesh, like an incubus, beautiful Mavis, laughing Mavis, coaxing, teasing Mavis. He could see her face as clearly as if she were in the room with him, and a heavy weight moved into his eyes, pressing them, filling them with moisture. There were times when he thought he had forgotten her or that he could live with the memory of her, and then when he was off-guard or had been drinking too much, the house was full of her footsteps and her laughter, the rustling of her dresses, the sound of her raucous singing. Then the pain returned, as bad as ever.

He pushed himself to his feet and was dizzy. Why don't I have the courage to die? he asked himself. Why didn't I have the sense to plead guilty and let the state hang me and so save me the trouble? Then he thought of young Francis Campion, twenty years old, who had tried to take his life a few hours ago. Now, what for, at his age? What could so disillusion a man of twenty as to drive him to death, and a budding priest, at that? Jonathan leaned on a table and in spite of himself he was interested. He also remembered the boy and how he had saved his life three years ago. That life had been saved almost as much by the boy's will to live as by Jonathan's skill. Yet, three years later he had looked for death, the only son of one of the richest men in the state, pampered, indulged, allowed to do what he wished at all times.

Jonathan found himself in his bathroom, naked to the waist, sloshing himself with cold water. He looked at his ravaged face with the bluish growth of beard and said aloud, "The hell with it." He dried himself, dressed in riding clothes. He frowned at his shaking hands. He was all parched leather inside and he craved a drink. He knew he dared not drink water, for it would make him vomit. In complete physical misery, and walking carefully so as not to jar his head too much, he left his room.

Still, no one stirred in the house as yet, though it was almost seven. The house had the dry, aromatic odor of a hot summer morning, compounded of heat, a faint drift of dust, and withering flowers. Jonathan went out into the blaze of the early day and then to the stables.

He still did not know why he was going to see young Francis Campion, or what he was doing out so early in the day with a fearful hangover and a sense that life had become unbearable. He thought of Father McNulty with angry disfavor. Interfering young idiot! But these priests had the idea that human life was sacred or something, and should be preserved. He, Jonathan Ferrier, wished he could take some of them through the wards where people were dying of cancer, including little children, or wards of venereal disease, or tuberculosis, a thousand and one diseases of corruption and agony. Let them see for themselves with what respect their God regarded His own creation that He could bring it so low, far down to the base of screaming animalism, and then abandon it to decay and torture and unspeakable indignities. What God did not respect, man should not respect.

CHAPTER TWELVE

Nearly all other houses in Hambledon were "houses," but the Campion house was a "residence," even to those who possessed a sense of humor. Jonathan was one of the few— and he originated the term—who called the house Pike's Peak, because it not only was the highest building on the mountain that overlooked Hambledon but had a curious roof of blue slate, which did, indeed, rise to a peak directly in the top center of that pile of white stone masonry. Perched on top of that sharp peak reared a weathervane, huge and gilt, which could be seen turning from the streets of the town when the sun shone upon it. It had been built forty years ago by the late Mrs. Kenton Campion's father, old Jasper Pike, so again Jonathan had a wry reason for his appellation. Mrs. Campion had inherited it together with a great fortune from her father's coal mines, and it was considered Hambledon's only authentic mansion in the grand tradition of mansions, for it had thirty rooms, all immense, a marble hall and stairway, teakwood paneling in the library, imported stained glass and statuary from Italy, fountains in glorious climbing gardens, furniture from every country including acres of Oriental rugs, silks, satins, brocades, exotic pictures, vases, cloisonné boxes and ornaments, lamps with gold and silver bases, shawls dripping everywhere in streams of color, buhl cabinets filled with crushes of *objets d'art* from the most exotic places, and enormous oval windows at least fifteen feet high and draped lavishly with delicate laces and swaths of material full of sparkling, genuine gold threads. The architect had not been decided upon the exact style he wished to produce, so he added a white marble colonnade along the front of the house which was incongruous surmounted by that soaring peak of glittering blue slate with its slit windows like a tower. Jonathan never glanced up at the mountain without saying, "Every town has its monstrosity. Hambledon has its Pike's Peak, a nightmare of tasteless luxury, the dream of every vulgarian and illiterate in the world."

No one else, with the exception of his mother, held the same opinion of the "mansion," but Marjorie often remarked that that was because most people were more charitable than her son. Hambledon was proud of it, though it affected to laugh at it enviously. There was not a family, except for the Ferriers, who were not elated to be invited to a "soiree" there, or a tea, or a dance or a reception or a dinner. Governors of the state had been visitors, and mayors of various cities and rich, suspect politicians and businessmen and "aristocrats," and even a President.

As a boy Jonathan had often thought how marvelous it would have been if the mountains overlooking the town had been graced by buildings of the Grecian or Roman order, all white porticoes and columns and walls, half hidden by summery greenery. But no one shared his opinion, for all the houses in that "select" area were pretentious, bulky and elaborate, immaculately gardened, and all the roads were private and maintained by the owners even in the winters, and every tree was cherished, said Jonathan, "within an inch of its poor wild life." To his mind the Campion "residence" was the very worst of all.

Mrs. Kenton Campion had died some fifteen years ago, leaving her politician husband with that one small boy of his, Francis, and all her money. At that time Kenton had been a mere Congressman, but later he had been invariably reappointed by the State Legislature, over a period of sixteen years, as a Senator. He was often spoken of as becoming the Governor, and once he had been suggested by enthusiastic—and indebted—friends for second place on the Presidential ticket. However, at that time there had been some unreasonable resentment against wealthy men occupying all the available political positions and, though Kenton Campion steadfastly maintained that he was at heart a poor man—had not his grandfather been a journeyman peddler of pots and pans when he came from England?—no one truly believed that he had a poor man's spirit, least of all Jonathan Ferrier, who

called him the Marzipan Pear, an allusion which Senator
Campion only too well understood but correctly believed that
few others did. Marzipan, in any shape or form, was practically unknown in Hambledon, which was somewhat fortunate
for Jonathan, considering that the Senator never forgave and
never forgot a slight or a gibe.

He had inherited a small fortune himself from his grandfather and father, who had managed to buy out a small foun-
dry in Pittsburgh, but it could not compare with the Pike for-
tunes. It was after his marriage to Henrietta Pike—a small
and terrified little creature who could not believe that so
magnificent a specimen of the masculine persuasion could
look at her for an instant—that Kenton's political future became established. He had been kind to Henrietta, and for this
she was grateful all her life, for her father had not been kind,
and so she had left him all her money without making any
provision for her son, young Francis. A short time after her
death, her husband's widowed sister, a flushed woman then
thirty-eight and childless, had come to manage the Campion
"residence" and bring up the motherless boy. She was now
fifty-three, a big, massive and handsome woman of awesome
stupidity, good-natured in a bucolic way, and, as Jonathan
confided to some as irreverent as himself, "absolutely devoted
to all her bodily functions, even the grossest ones. She enjoys
them all tremendously. A bowel movement or the emptying
of a bladder is just that to everyone else. But not to Beatrice
Offerton! They are delightful daily Events."

He was not her physician, and so his remarks were no violation of the doctor-patient confidence. He had come to his
conclusions about Mrs. Offerton by observing her, the slow
but pleasurable—to her—flow of her great limbs and buttocks and breasts as she walked, the obvious cleanliness of
her large body, invariably pink and fair and heavily scented
and covered by a layer of rose-violet talcum powder, and
the way she stroked her full, rosy and heavy neck as she
slowly talked, or stroked her arms or hands like a lover. Her
face, to all but Jonathan, was quite beautiful, somewhat
larger than the ordinary woman's face, with absolutely perfect features, which included great round blue eyes, a stat-
uesque nose, and a capacious pink mouth with dimples, not
to speak of masses of light chestnut hair like polished satin
piled smoothly in a pompadour over a white low forehead
that was guilty of not a single wrinkle. Her face was totally
without expression at any time. She could smile, but even

that smile meant nothing, for it was unchanging and smug.
She carried with her, though she was not stout, even if massive, an aura of complete self-love and complacency, not the
self-love of Mavis Eaton, which was aware of itself and others, but a self-love of the utmost simplicity and happy satisfaction, almost unconscious. She luxuriated in her body as a
healthy animal luxuriates, and she had not a single thought in
her head about anything, and never had held an opinion beyond the merits of food, soft touches of garments on her
flesh, warmth in winter, coolness in summer, the pleasure of
comfortable beds and the functioning of her body. Only one
thing could exasperate her: Undue delay over meals or any
other physical inconvenience which pertained to herself. She
had never known a moment's illness.

This was the amiable, dull, dimpling, talcum-scented
woman who had been assigned as a substitute mother to an
overly sensitive and physically tense little boy, who found living to be excruciatingly joyous or excruciatingly painful, depending on mood or circumstance. "Beatrice may be a cow,
though I don't really intend to insult a cow, and not have a
brain of any dimension at all," her loving brother had confided to intimates, "but she will be capital for Frank, who is a
trembling little stick of a boy. He's just like my poor lamented Henrietta. He can't be tranquil about anything. He
has rhapsodies or melancholies, all very delicate of course but
unnerving to a steady fella like myself. He can laugh one
minute and cry like a little girl the next, and no one ever
knows why. Beatrice is just the mother for him, placid, easy,
incapable of being disturbed; she looks at life like a damned
picture of herself, and she was always that way even when
we were children. I never saw Beatrice in a temper in my life
except once when the seamstress had put six ruffles on her
party dress instead of seven, and even then it wasn't much of
a rage. Frank will calm down with Beatrice guiding him. No
children of her own, you know, and like all stupid big
women, she loves children."

Beatrice loved nothing but her body and her appetites.
Francis Campion had grown to young manhood and had
made no more impression on Beatrice Offerton than the gardener's puppy. If asked, she would have admitted she was
fond of the boy, and so she was when she thought of him—
which was seldom—or saw him, but it was a dim far fondness without a touch of maternal concern or tenderness. She
was expert in only one thing: she was a wonderful manager

of that bloated mansion on the mountainside, and servants adored her, and she pampered them. They were so necessary to the perfect, warm, flushed and enjoyable functioning of her body. She was ageless. At fifty-three she looked no older than thirty-eight, and the brightness of her coloring and the glowing softness of her hair had not diminished in the least. She attended them with the only passion of which she was capable.

Her friends called her "sweet" or "lovely," and "so restful, so understanding." They would have been surprised to learn that she was hardly aware of them and their existence. She smiled and dimpled when they visited her, or she them, but her mind was always conjecturing whether or not the cook had been careful with the pastry this time or whether her hostess had remembered that she adored maple-walnut layer cake, or rum tarts or English trifle.

Senator Campion had his delicious young female friends in Philadelphia and Washington, pleasant young creatures who were grateful for the first luxuries of their starveling lives, the first regular meals and handsome clothing and carriages and furs and an occasional jewel. They generally occupied flats in discreet buildings which were filled with their kind, especially in Washington, and were devoted to their benefactors and protectors, who were careful not to leave evidences of their regular occupancy and visits behind them or any casual note which could be used for blackmail purposes. All messages were written and carried by clerks, and infrequently telephoned because of "Central." Senator Campion's little friends rarely occupied the comfortable flat for more than six months, or even less, he having a tendency to tire of a current pretty face. But he always sent the girls—none of them over twenty—on their way with a nice thick packet of bills and all the clothes and furs he had bought for them, and the jewel or two, and as they had no means of speaking spitefully to avid newspaper reporters—lacking tangible proof—they remembered him with affection. He was careful, before acquiring them, to have them examined scrupulously by aware physicians, and to have reports of them given to him regularly by the porters in his employ, to be certain that they did not entertain younger and more attractive men in his absence. It was not his intention to acquire any venereal disease.

He was no more vicious than the general run of politicians and was more genial than most, even in that genial profession. He was a rascal and, being intelligent and shrewd, he was a little more of a scoundrel than his colleagues, but this was not accounted against him in Washington, where he was much admired for his wardrobe, his taste in little friends, his grand manners, his appearance, his wit, his reputation for kindliness, his way of knowing the current President intimately, his interesting speeches in the Capitol, his wine cellar and table, his knowledge of horseflesh as well as womanflesh, his generosity with friends, his even temper and bright smile, his sharp sense of finance and the influential brokers, his friendship with powerful men in New York and Washington, and the fact that in a time of ponderous political bores he was never a bore. Nor was he a hypocrite when among close friends, and he could always appreciate a bawdy joke on himself as well as the teller.

It was his appearance, and his deep and musical voice, which had made Jonathan Ferrier call him a Marzipan Pear. He was a big man, as tall as Jonathan himself, and massive, as his sister was massive. But whereas she was possessed of a figure, being carefully corseted at all times, Senator Campion did indeed resemble a large pear in build, and had a big expanse of belly—usually covered by the most expensive and tasteful of waistcoats in soft, subdued weaves and rich colors. His watch chains were finely handmade and clinked with jeweled seals and trinkets, but he always carried his father's big gold repeater watch, which he fondly referred to frequently, and displayed. (This watch was notable for reassuring nervous constituents, and so the cynical sometimes called him "Old Turnip," though he was but fifty-five.) As he was an affable man and hugely enjoyed life—except in Hambledon, which he loathed—he projected an atmosphere of friendship and intimate concern and affection to everyone, invaluable traits for a politician. This was not entirely hypocrisy, though he used these blessings constantly. He genuinely liked most people, especially those who loved him, and was a great favorite in Washington for his gifts of character. Even though it was known that he was exigent, could be ruthless when it served his purpose, and exploited his office even more than did the others, and was inordinately ambitious, and never blinked at lying, these were not counted as detriments. After all, he was a politician, and he himself delighted in repeating what Cicero had said: "Politicians are not born. They are excreted."

Like his sister, he had a face larger than life, flushed constantly and somewhat fat and jowly and with a very fair complexion, and blue eyes and a big, well-formed nose and rich lips. But where Beatrice's face expressed the most profound stupidity, his expressed alertness and intelligence. He had her serenity of forehead and her light chestnut hair—thick and wavy and tended, without gray—but there was a certain liveliness about him which endeared him to most men and almost all women, a certain gaiety of manner which few recognized as the lightheartedness of the true scoundrel. He also had a sharp ear for nuances. He could be utterly grave with a clergyman, involved with an insistent constituent to the exclusion of all else for the moment, and was the joy of any party any hostess wished to give in his honor. Though the present President was not of his Party, he was invited more often to the White House than any other Senator, or even Cabinet officers, and the President and he, he would say, "had a perfect meeting of minds."

There was no man, he would say, but that he could cherish, if permitted, and no man whom he would not understand and with whom he could not sympathize. But there was indeed one, and that one was Jonathan Ferrier, and there was a pleasant mutual hatred between them. "Pleasant," the Senator would say, "for, after all, his father was my dear friend and I always had a sensibility for Marjorie. In fact, I considered marrying her when she became a widow. But Jon is a difficult young man, and then there was that unfortunate affair of Mavis—a lovely girl, I was her godfather. Ah, dear. A little brightness went out of this old world when Mavis—died. A little golden color, a scent— Yes. But if I must admit it, I came at once to Jon's defense. I had many a talk with—" But no one ever knew with whom he had that "talk," if any. However, the impression remained that if it had not been for dear Senator Campion's intercession—at some unnamed level —things might not have turned out so agreeably for Jonathan Ferrier. But was he grateful? Not at all! He never wasted an opportunity to make an unpleasant remark about "Old Marzipan Pear" and "his cello notes. A damned smiling fraud and a really incredible rascal." Jonathan thought he knew all about the doings of the Senator and followed his career avidly. "You have to admire him, he's so monumental a farce and such a dangerous one," Jonathan would say. "He would sell out his country for a few more oil wells or a trade concession. But, then, what politician would not?"

Only Jonathan—and he had no actual proof except his intuition—was aware that the Senator, in spite of his personal wealth, was incredibly greedy and avaricious and that, like his sister, he was incapable of a really tender attachment to anyone but himself.

These were the guardians and the guides and the directors of conscience to the little boy Francis Campion, a boy somewhat too sensitive, inclined to emotionalism, and with a passionate devotion to and an interest in all that was gently beautiful and harmless, and who, in some unnamed and inexplicable manner, had come to love God and had directed his adolescent years to dreaming of the Beatific Vision and unworldly delights, and had desired, finally, to serve his God for the rest of his life. There had been no pious servant to point the way, nor a friend, nor clergyman, nor a relative. He had found his way himself, through only God knew what dark thickets of loneliness and childish despair and silence and friendlessness, through what echoing abysses and frozen fields. Father McNulty had said, "God finds His own," which Jonathan thought total nonsense.

Jonathan had noticed the little boy on the streets of Hambledon, in his father's carriage, accompanied by his queenly aunt, and though he had been but twenty, and even younger at the time, he had been struck by the white hurt of the child's face, the eager, hopeful eyes, the shy ways, the sudden bashful smiles, the grave and gentle politeness. He appeared to need protection, and though Jonathan would have jeered at the idea that he himself could never resist wishing to give protection to the helpless, it was indeed that very protectiveness in his nature which had made him remember a not very attractive little boy over the next fifteen years. He saw Francis Campion very seldom, perhaps not more than once a year or so, and he thought of him as a white mouse, with his pale thin face, his dark eyes always seeking, his thin dark hair, his very slight body and nervous small mannerisms. He had the mouth of a girl in his childhood, a little tremulous, always a little parted. It was not until he was seventeen that it became both quiet and firm and resolute and his expression somewhat exalted as if he were acquainted with visions. Jonathan saw him then, when he had treated him for colitis, and he had barely been able to elicit any recital of symptoms from the reserved boy. At the end, however, though Jonathan did not know it, Francis Campion had come to trust him and had wistfully desired to be his friend. At eighteen, Francis went away to his seminary, to the serene acceptance of his aunt and the ire of his father, who had but this one child. "It is true his mother was a Papist," he would say to annoyed friends and constituents, "but I never encouraged him. But, then, is it not true that our children, in spite of our best efforts at all times and our sedulous prayers, often disappoint us? And don't we deserve a little sympathy?" The sympathy was always forthcoming, and the forgiveness, for many had disappointing children of their own. And the Catholics in the state, through the kind offices of one of the Senator's friends, were duly informed that he had a son studying for the priesthood. This did not vex the Senator.

Now Francis Campion, unaccountably home from his seminary, had tried to kill himself last night in the enormous pile of the "mansion," in his lonely room. He had failed, but just barely.

Jonathan thought of him as his horse climbed the steep but well-kept narrow road, and he angrily cursed his vicious headache and the young man who was the cause of his early exposure to the heat of the day and his sweltering climb up the mountainside. Here there was no sound but that of gently rattling lawn mowers and the hiss of hoses, or the soft yapping of a contented dog far off in some garden. The grind and clatter of the streetcars below and the usual rumble of traffic and the voices of hurrying people did not reach up here to this heat-blazing but fragrant area of great homes, vast guarded lawns hidden by walls or high hedges, hotly scented trees glittering in the slightest of mountain breezes along the road, and an occasional little darting brook running between fallen stones. It was all brilliant and shining hush, with a few sleepy bird twitters or a low rush of wings, or the startled flash of a squirrel or a rabbit in the sun-struck tall grasses between the trees that threw uncertain fretwork on the hot white dust which Jonathan's horse was treading upward. It was so warm that the sky was the color of pale milk, and the sun had an actual weight on Jonathan's shoulders, like the pressing of heated iron. Lawns below might be blasted brown, even this early in the summer, but the lawns he glimpsed on passing were purely green and plushy and the gardens were fervent with color and gravel walks were sparkling with moisture and the careful use of rakes. There was an odor of pine and roses and cut grass and wetted dust in the clean and incandescent air, which was so bright that every object appeared to be touched with iridescence, even the dust of the road.

Here lived the very rich "old" families and the rich "new"

families, removed from each other by long sloping lawns and flowering hedges and firm white walls exploding with scarlet roses and creepers. Sun broke blindingly on distant hothouses and clean slated roofs. Above them all towered the fantastic roof of "Pike's Peak," with its mighty weathervane fiery under the sky. Stopping to wipe his sweating face and blink the dust from his eyes, Jonathan irately glanced down at Hambledon, swimming in a bluish heat haze, and at the river, which resembled white flame in the sun. It was hot enough here, God knew, but down there it was unbearable in the valley. Still, Jonathan was more and more outraged that he had permitted himself—and how the hell had that happened?—to be persuaded to make this climb when he should have been in a cool darkened room in his mother's house with a cold cloth on his head, a pitcher of ice at his bedside and a cold sweating drink in his weak hand.

Jonathan was firmly of the belief that because a man never chose to be precipitated into life, he possessed the innate prerogative of deciding when he should leave it. Once, three years ago, commenting on a prominent suicide, he had horrified his colleagues by saying, "The poor devil attempted it twice before, and some busybody was able to prevent it at the last moment. Now he's succeeded, and good luck to him, wherever he is. Death is hard for anyone to face, no matter how sick, and it takes a special kind of courage to bring it on yourself, and don't whimper to me about 'cowardice.' A suicide is a brave man." He had then grinned and had quoted a stanza from Omar Khayyam:

> "Oh, Thou, Who man of baser Earth didst make,
> And Who with Paradise devised the Snake—
> For all the Sin wherewith the face of man
> Is blackened—Man's forgiveness give—and take!"

This, in 1898, was often mentioned as indicative of Jonathan Ferrier's "lack of heart and human pity" and, of course, "incorrigible blasphemy." One minister had been moved to give a sermon on a Sunday about "the present disregard for the sacredness of life and the tolerance of Sin," and all his congregation had understood he was referring to Jonathan Ferrier. Another had spoken of the Last Judgment and the fiery Pit for blasphemers and suicides and other intransigent types who "insulted the Almighty to His Face," and again all knew this was a reference to Jonathan Ferrier. For had he not recommended that the man's will be honored and that his body be sent to Philadelphia for cremation and his ashes scattered—and without benefit of clergy? Many suspected, with considerable reason, that Jonathan had not been exactly "faithful to his marriage vows," so when the minister had also mentioned a "faithless and adulterous generation, calmly unmoved before the Foulest Crime of them All," most of the congregation had nodded sober heads. It was no surprise to them when Jonathan did not appear at the elaborate funeral of the sinful suicide, who was not only a prominent citizen but had been a patient of Jonathan's, and his friend. He had not even sent flowers. "I'll be no party to a sideshow he specifically did not want," said Jonathan. "To honor his will was the last thing he had ever asked of this damnable world, and he was denied. So, the hell with a funeral, flowers and a monument."

Recalling this, Jonathan was more enraged than ever that he was traveling on a mountain road to the house where a young man had attempted suicide last night. If the boy wanted to die, then why should he not die? he repeated to himself. It was his own life; he had not asked for it, but it was now his own. Jonathan kicked the side of his horse angrily, then immediately apologized to the beast. "You have twice the sense of a man," he said, patting the hot black neck, "and I regret that I'm riding you up here for absolutely nothing."

He reached the iron gates of the Campion house and rode through them to the glistening whiteness of the tall walls and the incongrous pillars and the mounting slate peak. The gardener and his two sons were busy clipping, watering and raking, and they removed their straw hats in greeting to Jonathan, then stared at him curiously. That young priest was here early this morning and now the doctor, but the house was silent and the doors shut and what was it all about and what did it mean? Not a single maid came out to inform them, though they were certain that one eventually would.

A pretty little maid in black silk uniform and with a frilled white cap and apron met him at the door, and she was rosy with subdued excitement. The madam, she informed Jonathan in a hushed voice, was in the second drawing room waiting for him, and Jonathan gave the girl his hat and asked her to have a groom take care of his horse. Then, dusty and sweating, he went through the cool dusk of the great hall and along the marble corridor to the second drawing room, and he hoped to God that Beatrice Offerton was not hysterical and surrounded by maids ministering to her and holding smelling salts to her nose.

The second drawing room was as large as a tennis court, in Jonathan's opinion, but not so large as the first, which was never used except when a host of friends—and wealthy constituents and "scheming politicians"—were present. Here the immense windows were not shrouded but looked like enormous and hotly colored landscapes, as they framed the trees, grottoes, lawns, and flower beds outside. There was something a little Florentine about these views, which included the blue shadow and blue mist of the rising mountains beyond, and something distinctly Florentine about this room, with its tessellated black and white marble floor, Aubusson rugs, pedestals of white and black marble surmounted by exquisite little marble statues and groups, and heavy marble tables and gilt and damask chairs.

Jonathan was astonished to see Beatrice Offerton alone, standing serenely beside a center table and carefully arranging huge crimson roses fresh from the garden. She had a dreaming and absorbed expression, with a faint smile, one with which Jonathan was very familiar. He had said of it, "She's listening happily to her peristalsis." If anything was disturbing that majestic vacancy which was a woman, it was not evident. Clad in a rose and green print silk dress, with a cascade of delicate white lace pouring over the massive bosom, and with her pompadour glinting and glistening in the pure light of the morning that gushed through the windows, Beatrice was the picture of the lady of the manor, peacefully occupied in a household task which required all her pleased attention. She gave the impression of humming, though there was no sound in the large room except for a little clink of pruning scissors as the lady deftly clipped off a dead leaf here or a wilted bud there.

Jonathan was freshly outraged. He had been told of a tragedy. There was no evidence of it here, though even one so stupid and self-engrossed as Beatrice should at least have shown the merest agitation. She was still not aware of him. She moved a little, richly as always, joyously aware of her body as always, and she was a fine woman, though of too much poundage and altogether too big. The dress was tight over her oversize hourglass figure, as was the fashion, and it then burst into soft pleats and ruffles below her knees. It whispered a little with her movements and fluttered about her insteps. Jonathan, near the doorway, caught, even above the swooning scent of the roses, the odor of Beatrice's inevitable talcum, and he saw the faint bloom of it on her neck and full pink cheeks, and, as the ruffles fell back from her wrists he saw it again on her large fat arms.

He wanted to swear. Though he made no sound, standing on the marble in his riding clothes and with his bag in his wet hand, Beatrice became aware of him and looked up, vaguely and distantly startled. For a moment she appeared not to recognize him. She stood with the little scissors in one hand and a great red rose in the other, and slowly and methodically blinked at him and her face was absolutely empty. One ponderous thought seemed to be running through what mind she possessed: "Can that possibly be Jon Ferrier? If so, why? Today?" Her staring blue eyes were like the eyes of a wax doll.

"Jon? Jon?" she said at last, in her pretty deep voice. "Oh! It's you, Jon, isn't it?"

"I think so," said Jon, "though we could both be dreaming."

She considered that and then she slowly smiled. "How nice," she said. "Dear me, you do look warm. Do come into the morning room in a moment and we'll have some strawberry lemonade and some nice fresh pastry. Or perhaps you'd prefer to wait for luncheon? Kenton is expected on the next train, you know. He is to make the speech on the Fourth of July. He'll be so happy to see you, you are quite a favorite of his and he always said you should be in politics, but Washington is so hot, isn't it, and—"

"I think," said Jonathan, "that I was sent for, Beatrice, or am I dreaming that, too?"

Again she was startled and again she considered placidly. Then at last she put down her scissors. "Oh, dear," she said, and smiled that sweet and meaningless smile of hers. "Such a trial, isn't it? I was sure it would be perfectly all right, if one just forgets these unpleasant things and pretends they never happened, and that—that priest—he did not agree with me. He said you really must come. I didn't truly send for you, Jon dear. I was truly against it. Such a bother and embarrassment, and Francis didn't mean it at all, and I am sure it is an accident and can be explained sensibly, but that priest—"

Jonathan was now totally exasperated. "Correct me if I am wrong," he said, "but I understand that Francis tried to hang himself last night in his room, and a servant heard the crash of the falling chair, and he ran to Francis' room and rescued him in time. Hanged with the sash of his morning robe, I was told." He shook the bag at his side. "Well, what is the truth, anyway?"

Beatrice's flush had paled just a little, and she moistened her full pink lips and looked down at her hands. "I'm sure it can all be explained," she murmured. "So tiresome for Kenton, when he hears. I'm sure Francis did not intend—it was looped over a sconce on the wall, it could have caught there by itself, such things do happen——"

"And it made a nice little noose of itself and just threw itself around Francis' neck while he was climbing a chair—no doubt to polish the candle sconce at midnight, he disliking dust so much after the austerity of a seminary, and then by some chance he kicked the chair over—and there he was," said Jonathan.

Beatrice was actually nodding, slowly and massively. "It could well be," she said in a blank tone. Then she stared at the roses, wet her lips again, and blinked over and over. She touched a drooping flower. "I do love roses," she murmured. "And so nice that we still have some left. Kenton adores them. They make a room so cozy—so homelike——"

Jonathan, though he had known Beatrice well ever since her arrival in Hambledon over fifteen years ago, was incredulous. He came toward her, really staring at her, his black eyes ablaze. "Look here, Beatrice," he said in a brutal voice, "you don't seem to understand. I'm a doctor. I am compelled by law to report the crime of attempted suicide to the police. Do you understand? To the police. And then the newspapers will get it."

He had hoped to shock her into some semblance of comprehension and intelligence. At least, he saw that her hands dropped limply to her sides and that she was paling again and that her blue eyes were enormously dilated and fixed with the faintest terror on him. "Police?" she said. "The police? No, that is utterly not to be thought of, Jon! What are you saying? What about Kenton? Kenton! The shame. Oh, no, not the police. That terrible, thoughtless boy— The police. You are joking, aren't you, Jon?"

"I'm not joking, so you'd better pay me some attention, Beatrice. You're Francis' aunt, after all, for God's sake! Haven't you any feeling for him at all? Weren't you notified at once when it happened? What did you do? Why wasn't I called immediately, or at least some other doctor? What did the boy say to you? To the servant? How did Father Mc-Nulty come to hear of it, and who called him? Give me some answers, Beatrice!"

Beatrice looked about her vaguely, then seeing the chair near her knee she slowly sat down in it. Vaguely, she felt for the handkerchief in her sleeve, and she took it out, pressed it briefly against her lips, then looked at it with all the intentness of which she was capable, which was very little, indeed.

"So disturbing," she murmured. "And so inconvenient. Kenton will be traveling all over the state, speaking, and it does wear him so. It's not that he can be elected, you know, it's the Governor who appoints him, and if the Governor hears of this, such an upright man and such a Christian, but a little rigid—I do wish they'd pass that Amendment so that Senators can go outright to the people and get elected without the Governor— Poor Kenton."

Then Jonathan became aware that this large and shapely sculpture of a woman did indeed have some feeling within that self-loving body, but all the feeling was directed toward her brother, and she feared, as much as she could possibly fear, for his career.

"Beatrice," he said, "it's the State Legislature which appoints Senators, not the Governor. Never mind. Answer my other questions."

She ruminated, her head bent, the handkerchief twisting slowly in her hands. "I don't understand it," she said at last. "I didn't understand when Francis came home. I did think he seemed a little tired and worn, but all that study, and I've heard the priests are very harsh to seminarians. But I thought a few days' rest—I never pry, Jonathan. No one can ever accuse me of prying. I am always prepared to listen, and I respect confidences, but if no one confides, I would never insist. That is my code; it was the code of my family. I thought, too, he might be wanting to see Kenton—the only son, you see. And I thought good wholesome food, and peace and quiet at home, and good sleep at night— But it would seem that wasn't the trouble at all. I don't know, Jon. I confess I never did understand Francis. Such a strange little boy, even when he was a baby. Quite like Henrietta; she was quite hysterical, you know. A weakness in the Pike family—"

Jonathan, leaning against the table now, prayed for patience somewhat blasphemously. But he had to wait until the slow and heavy thoughts could give utterance and answer him.

"Kenton is the only real conversationalist in the family," Beatrice went on, with a dim and hopeful smile at Jonathan. She was really pale now. "I am not; talking does bore me so. Francis, I think, doesn't like conversation, either. I can't remember that he ever talked much to Kenton or to me. I respected his—reticences. He never told me anything, and not this time, either. He just—came home. And then he stayed in his room. That was two days ago. He never came down for his meals. He ordered trays in his room, and I was so upset. I had prevailed on Cook to make his favorite dishes. Strawberry shortcake. Chicken baked in wine, I don't like it, myself, but Francis did, and where he got the idea— ham roasted with honey and pureed chestnuts, even though it is summer now. That curious green tea he favors. But the trays came down untouched. Cook told me. I was quite disturbed."

"It probably ruined your appetite," said Jonathan, with a straight face.

Beatrice considered. Then she nodded. "Yes, I must confess to that. Though I was never fond of the wine with chicken, and ham in summer doesn't really appeal to me. But one doesn't waste; it is quite un-Christian. I had heartburn once or twice. Well, dear me. I thought to go to Francis' quarters and ask him the trouble, but, then, there was that reticence and the dislike of prying. I thought it would all be settled when Kenton came home."

The boy had been alone for more than two days, shut up in his room with God only knew what black and terrible thoughts and what conjectures. Then the final decision.

Now Beatrice was flushing and there was actually a gleam in her blue eyes and the gleam was, incredibly, emotional. "It was that interfering servant, that Tom! He found Francis and helped him in that dangerous situation—I suppose it was dangerous, though one never knows, and Francis can be so hysterical at times, and perhaps he intended to be found, knocking that chair over so loudly, it even disturbed me, though I went back to sleep at once. And then Tom was knocking at the door; I think it was about one then, an unearthly hour, and I am never at my best before the sun comes up. I couldn't understand what he was saying for quite some minutes; quite breathless and excited. The common people, you know, always so excitable. I suppose I should be grateful, but I am sure that even if Tom hadn't gone—Francis would have come to his senses immediately."

"And put the chair back under his feet and unfastened the noose," said Jonathan.

"Yes," said Beatrice. She sighed. "Still, one never knows, does one? Tom says—but you can't really believe that class —that he—well—rescued Francis, and then made him breathe again, and bathed his throat with cold water, and put him to bed, and left him for a moment to tell me, and then he said he had called that priest. I'm beginning to think he was insolent—"

"Yes," said Jonathan. He was smoking now. "Tom exceeded his authority, not in calling the priest, but in saving Francis' life. Kick him out."

"Indeed," said Beatrice. "I will consult with Kenton about discharging him—" Then she was staring at Jonathan, and her eyes were protruding glass. She gulped. "What are you saying, Jon, that Tom should have let—have let—"

"Francis die. Of course."

She actually jumped to her feet and the smooth forehead was bunched together like a big white whirl over her eyes. "How can you say that, Jon? Francis die! Let Francis die! Kill himself! How do you think Kenton would feel—" She was gasping. She put her hand to her high and florid bosom. "You can't mean what you said!"

"Oh, but I did." Jonathan was pleased. He was certain that this was one of the few times in her life that Beatrice had become agitated and disturbed. "A man has the right to choose when to die, doesn't he? Francis chose to die last night. Damn that interfering Tom."

Beatrice looked about her wildly, as if pleading with someone to reassure her that she was not hearing insane words and that everything was all right and she had just misunderstood. Then, to Jonathan's surprise and not a little to his gratification, she burst into tears, threw her hands about aimlessly, then ran heavily from the room.

Jonathan thought, I bet that keeps her from totally enjoying her lunch, but I doubt it. He went back into the hall and there encountered Tom, the elderly servant who had been long in the Campion employ and before that had been employed by old Jasper Pike. Tom had evidently and shamelessly been listening, and Jonathan winked at him.

"You have disturbed the madam," said Tom with a grave face.

"So it would seem. I suggest a little soda with her lunch, just before. We can't have Mrs. Offerton not relishing her food, can we? A tragedy. Tell me, Tom, why did you send for Father McNulty before dawn? Was Francis asking for him?"

"No, Doctor. I asked him, and he said no. But they used to be such good friends, and Mr. Francis had almost committed a mortal sin, and maybe he did commit one, even thinking about it, and I—well, I've known that boy since he was born. I know all about him."

"I bet you do," said Jonathan, "and that makes you a minority of one. Go on. Did Francis talk to the priest when he came?"

"No." The old man's face became sad and fallen. "Father McNulty came at once on his bicycle. It's a hard climb on a bicycle, even for a young man, and I've often wondered why none of his rich parishioners, or a few of them together, never bought him a horse and a buggy."

"Don't look at me," said Jonathan. "I'm not one of his parishioners. Save your glares for the McNellans up here on the hill, and the Fandrusses, and the Temples, and such. So Francis wouldn't talk to the priest."

"No, Doctor, he would not. He just lay on his bed with his face turned away and it was kind of like he was dead, not listening, not moving. Father McNulty stayed until it was almost time for Mass, and so he was tired, and hungry, too, and he made me promise not to leave Francis for long, and said he'd call you."

The old man sighed and wrung his dry hands together. "I made Francis promise me something. I made him promise not to—not to do that again. And he said he would think about it. And, and—" Tears gleamed along the lower lids of the tired eyes. "Well, I reminded him of the stories I used to tell him when he was a little feller, and how I'd take him for walks, and bring him little delicacies to eat late at night, and how we'd cut a Christmas tree on the mountain, and how I'd bandage up his cuts and take him to the barber, and everything— And, sir, it don't sound right, seeing he's a man now, but he began to cry. I pretended not to see, not wanting to shame him when he remembered. And then he held out his hand to me and I took it, and he said, 'Tom, there is more than one way of dying, and I'll die, but I won't do it myself.'" Tom implored Jonathan with his eyes. "I don't rightly understand that, Doctor, but I did get his promise."

Jonathan was looking down at his dusty riding boots and was hitting them idly with his crop. "Hum," he said, thinking. Tom waited. Then Jonathan said, "Any idea why he performed this caper this time, Tom?"

"No, Doctor, I don't, except that the boy's been miserable for over a year. He never told me why, though I asked him."

"Perhaps he made up his mind a year ago that he wasn't cut out to be a priest, but he didn't have the courage to tell his superiors."

"No, sir," said Tom, with sudden strong emphasis. "You don't understand Mr. Francis, Doctor. He always had courage for three boys, not just one. Living here alone, nobody caring about him, not even the servants or the gardener, he was a funny little feller, and it would've killed most kids, or they'd have gotten into bad mischief just for revenge or something. But not Mr. Francis. He was the bravest little kid I ever saw, Doctor. And a brave man. If he thought he'd made a mistake, he'd have told the Fathers right out." He paused. "I think he did this time. He didn't say, but I think he did, but he wasn't screwing up his courage for a whole year, Doctor. It was something else."

Jonathan thought again. "All right, I'll see the patient. Having trouble swallowing?"

"Well, sir, his throat's swole up pretty bad, and getting purple and blue, and looking nasty, but he drank some water and it didn't seem to bother him. I tell you, Doctor, when I saw him there—there was just starlight, and I didn't see him at first, and I tell you—" He bowed his head. "The first thing he said to me, 'Tom, damn you' and he meant it, Doctor. He truly meant it. He could speak, though; it was kind of a sick squeak. It's a little better now."

They went up the enormous white marble staircase together. They stood in the long dusk of the cool and cushiony corridor, with all the carved doors shut along it, and Tom timidly put his hand on Jonathan's arm. "You'll want to see him alone, without me, Doctor," he said. "Doctor, I'd like to ask you something, and I seen you often, even when you was a little boy, and then going away to school, and they say hard things about you, that you are a hard man and a—well, Doctor, I never believed it for a minute! Never! I knew all about you, like I know all about Mr. Francis. And so I don't, I think I don't, have to ask you to be sort of patient with him, and kind. And trying to understand."

Jonathan was moved, and angry at his sentimentality immediately afterward. He said, "You're not his father, Tom, and neither am I, but I admit he seems to need a friend or two."

He opened the door, nodded to Tom, and then entered a large and brilliantly shining sitting room with a fine view of the purpling mountains. But the carpet had been removed from the parquetry floor, and the furniture which had been permitted to remain was small and uncomfortable and plain. Beyond lay a bright bedroom as austere as this, the walls bare except for an enormous crucifix, the furniture nothing at all but a narrow bed, a commode, a chest of drawers, a bare table, and a single chair. The floor was partly covered with a straw rug, suitable for a veranda only, and rough to the foot. The room resembled a cell. This was no new matter. The boy had insisted on such Spartan quarters from earliest youth, as Jonathan, who had been here before, knew quite well. It expressed Francis Campion's personality with fervid force, as if he had revolted against the opulence and luxury of his father's house.

The young man was lying on his bed with the white sheet drawn up under his armpits. He was not looking at the great crucifix which faced him on the wall but through the uncurtained window at the mountains. Jonathan heard in himself, "I shall lift mine eyes to the everlasting hills, from whence cometh my strength," and then he laughed at himself. There was no strength in a man except that which he drew up from within his own being, from his experience, his character, the measure of fortitude with which he had been born.

He saw the fine tuft of black hair on the white pillow, the sunken pale profile of the young man, the quietness of his body, the stillness of the colorless mouth. He advanced into the room, his leather heels clacking on the bare wood. Francis Campion did not move, but Jonathan knew that he was not sleeping. His dark eyes shimmered with the light from the window. Jonathan sat down and placed his crop and bag beside him. He lit a cigarette leisurely and began to smoke. He waited. Francis did not move. Jonathan saw this was not obduracy or resentment or sullenness, or even shame. It was pure withdrawal and indifference and lack of curiosity as to who had entered this room. Francis had passed the point beyond caring who spoke to him or even who looked at him. Certainly their opinions, their thoughts of him, were of no interest to him any longer. A dead man could have been no more uncaring, and if it had not been for the sluggish blink of his eyes, Jonathan would have thought him a corpse.

"It is customary for those who expect to die," said Jonathan at last, "that they at least make some provision for others they are leaving, that is, if they are decent. For instance, Francis, you expect to die one way or another and are planning on it. Yet, the one person who really cares about you is to be left destitute, for he will be fired from this miserable job of his, no doubt because he was indiscreet enough to save your life. You don't have one red copper. If you had, and then left it to Tom Simmons, I'd say, 'Go and God speed you, wherever you are going.' But what does Tom mean to you, anyway?"

For a minute or two Jonathan was afraid that Francis had not heard him, that he had really removed all his senses from ordinary life, including hearing. Then the long thin head turned slowly on the pillow and Jonathan saw the deathly young face, still and rigid, and he also saw the thick and swollen bruises on the other's neck.

"Tom?" said Francis, speaking with pain.

"Tom. Auntie is going to boot him out because of you. Seems he was not only worried about your life, which I admit was stupid, but he was more worried about your immortal soul. That's unpardonable. So Auntie, of course, can't forgive him. Perhaps she'll be kind enough to give him a week's pay—how much is it?—in lieu of notice. After all, can't have someone around this place who is human, can you?"

The frozen suffering on Francis' face increased to starkness. He was thinking, and the effort was apparently too terrible for him. He closed his eyes, then opened them again.

"You don't have a cent," said Jonathan. "Your devoted Mama left every penny to your Papa. Papa would take care of their mutual darling. That's what Mama thought. Well, coming down to it, Papa hasn't exactly starved you physically, at any rate, nor beaten you physically, and he has sheltered you and clothed you and let you choose your way of life without a great deal of uproar, and probably keeps you in pocket money. Well, too bad. Perhaps I can get Tom a job as an orderly in one of the hospitals, but I don't think he'd last long at that. Too hard work, and he's pretty old, isn't he? Been with your father for twenty-five years, and then with old Jasper Pike for a quarter of a century before that. Tom must be seventy. Three score years and ten, and most of it spent in service to people like your father. And you, Francis.

That's some sort of an epitaph, but I'm damned if I can say what kind."

Francis was looking at him fixedly, as if the pain he was enduring, both mental and physical, was too great for speech.

"I'm not one," Jonathan continued, "like our Teddy Roosevelt and some of his friends who seem to think that a man has a right to the fruits of the earth just for the stupid reason that his parents conceived him at an odd moment, probably without intending to, and shoved him onto the rest of us. But I have come firmly to believe that not only is a man worthy of his hire but his hire ought to be enough to keep him decently during his lifetime and permit him to save some of it for his old age or illness. And damned if an employer shouldn't be taxed, or something, to see to it that his employees have a pension for the years when they can't labor any longer to fatten up the employer's bank account and investments. Now, if Tom, when he is turned out of here—and he's lived here for nearly fifty years, hasn't he?—it would be a nice thing if your will had left him several thousand dollars, and if he knew that he would have an income besides, until he found another job, or perhaps never again a job. But he has nothing like that, of course. So, it's the poorhouse for Tom, or the state farm."

The palest shadow of despair ran like a ripple over Francis' face and he lifted his head briefly from the pillow. "I won't let them make Tom leave," he said in a hoarse whisper. "They can't do that to him just because—"

"Oh, but they will," said Jonathan most cheerfully. "Now, if he'd been sensible enough to close the door when he saw what you were up to and had gone cozily back to bed, you'd have been found in the morning, and some doctor who's a family friend could have been induced to sign a certificate saying you had died of 'natural causes,' and all Tom would have had to do, to live comfortably the rest of his life, probably without working, would have been to mention to Papa or Auntie, in private, that he knew what he knew and what about it? But the world's full of damn fools, isn't it, including you and me, and especially Tom?"

The young man did not answer. But slowly and with tremendous effort, he began to raise himself up in his bed. Jonathan watched him with no sign of curiosity or interest, and waited until Francis, heaving and gasping, had pushed up his pillows, settled himself upon them in a sitting position, and was looking at him again.

"Damn you," said Francis Campion, struggling for breath. "Damn everybody. No one's going to hurt poor old Tom. If —they do—I'll let the whole damned world know why—"

"Good," said Jonathan. "You might mention that to Papa and Auntie first, though. Save a lot of trouble. By the way, your father ought to be here in a couple of hours. He's making his usual trumpet speech in Hambledon on the Fourth, and, as usual, you won't be there."

He wondered if he had lost the youth again, for Francis' face had become expressionless and remote again, as if he were engrossed in unearthly thoughts. Then, to Jonathan's pleasure, Francis began to smile. It was not a bright and gleeful smile, but, as smiles go, it was at least visible, if faintly. "No," he said, "I won't be there." Then he frowned.

"Unfortunately I will," said Jonathan.

Now Francis was looking at him sharply, for he was remembering that he had not seen Jonathan since the doctor's indictment and trial and acquittal, and he was remembering other things.

"If I were you," said Francis, and now there was actual life in that dim voice, "I wouldn't go anywhere, I wouldn't see anyone in this town, and I'd tell them all to go to hell."

"Nice sentiments for a budding priest," said Jonathan. "But I quite agree with you. However, unlike you, I do have thoughts for others I'd leave behind. I am staying here until my replacement is broken in, for I am not irresponsible like you. I want to make certain that my old patients aren't going to be carved up by some diploma-mill hack or be treated by some nature lover with 'true-blue-pure-herbs-from-nature's-fields-and-dells.' Now, if you were in my place, this town would have seen the backs of your heels a long time ago, and be damned to your patients. That's right, isn't it?"

"You have a sweet opinion of me," said Francis Campion. Jonathan saw that every word caused him pain to speak and that his voice was rough with effort.

"Not as bad as the opinion you ought to have of yourself. Francis, I'm not lecturing you. I don't care if you string yourself up again five minutes after I leave here. But you don't have a right to cause poor old Tom misery, no matter what trouble, real or imagined, decided you last night to spit in the face of God and man and get the hell out of here."

The thin and attenuated nostrils of Francis' nose tightened, and Jonathan was alarmed to see how emaciated the young man was. He had never been buxom and had always been inclined to slenderness, but now most of his bones were visible under the pallid skin, and his fallen upper lip was indented by the teeth beneath. Whatever had driven Francis Campion to this point in time and space was no trivial thing.

But Francis was faintly smiling again. "What if I get myself a job, make enough money to leave Tom in comparative comfort—and then decide—"

"You have my congratulations in advance," said Jonathan. "Cigarette?"

Francis stretched out his hand and took a cigarette from Jonathan's silver case, and Jonathan struck a match and lit it. "However," said Jonathan, watching carefully to see that Francis' swollen throat did not close at the entrance of the smoke, as it was likely to, "that will take a considerable time, seeing that you are not possessed of a profession or a trade and are just about as helpless as Tom is himself. Perhaps, though, you could borrow a few thousand dollars. I'm sure Papa would repay the debt after you had been neatly laid away, with a sigh of relief."

"Maybe you'd lend it to me," said Francis. "I'll give you my note."

"Not I. By the way, you understand I am supposed to report your case to the police, don't you?"

The thin white skin of the boy's forehead wrinkled in dismal wretchedness.

"That would just about fix Papa's little railway express wagon," said Jonathan. "Especially if you try it again."

The boy smoked a minute. Then he said, "For God's sake, don't tempt me!"

Jonathan began to laugh, and after a painful second Francis gave a thin answering croak. He began to cough and his cheeks turned scarlet; he choked. Then he drew a deep crowing breath. "Don't struggle," said Jonathan, alert on his chair. "Let nature take her course, and she'll do the job for you without you lifting a hand."

The crowing and heaving continued for a few minutes longer, until Francis' face was dusky and his eyes starting, and just when Jonathan was about to go to the rescue, the crowing stopped, and Francis wiped his wet eyes. He put the cigarette aside. He said in a strangled voice, "But you won't tell the police."

"I don't know. I ought to, I suppose. However, you didn't send for me, Auntie didn't send for me, and I'm not really the family physician. I'm attending nobody here, so, by a technicality this is none of my damned business. I'll have to look it up in *Medical Ethics*."

"No one sent for you?"

"No. Father McNulty was told by Tom that I had treated you for a couple of months when you were seventeen—when your regular family physician was off in Europe, and Father McNulty asked me to come to see you. To be perfectly candid, Francis, I don't know why I am here. Auntie doesn't want me. Auntie didn't call me. If she weren't a lady, she'd ask the gardener and his sons to come up here and drag me out and throw me on my ass outside. She'd be quite within her rights. I'm an intruder. I have no status. I'm not even a very good friend of your father's, in spite of what you may have heard. Auntie hoped to keep all this quiet and in the family, but Tom had to interfere."

Francis' young face trembled all over. "You came just because Father McNulty asked you to, Dr. Ferrier?"

"That's right. That's the kind of simpleminded idiot I am."

"Why did you come, really?"

"That's really none of your infernal business, but, as I said, I don't know myself."

The quick smile jerked at Francis' mouth again. "Just your sense of responsibility?"

"Maybe. After all, you did have a bad case of ulcerative colitis when you were seventeen, and I did pull you out of it after the hacks had almost killed you. The Chinese say that if you save a man from death or suicide, his life is on your neck as long as you live, and he is your personal responsibility. Harsh but realistic people, the Chinese, and very intellectual, and they do have a point. After all, when you interfere with a man's manifest destiny, as ordained by mysterious Entities, then the curse is on you for interfering. So, perhaps I was cursed for saving you when you were seventeen, and Tom is now cursed for saving you, and it is possible that he and I together can work out a deal with the fates."

A curious darkening touched Francis' overly eloquent eyes, and his white lips hardened. Jonathan watched him without appearing to watch.

"As Auntie says, I don't pry," he remarked. "But, as it is a long time ago, just what did give you colitis? I'm not one of those New York and Boston doctors who are listening far too much these days to that Austrian hysteric and medieval witch doctor, Sigmund Freud, who appears to think that every ailment of the body has its seat in something he calls the unconscious or maybe it's the Id, or perhaps the Superego. Frankly, I prefer to believe that a great many illnesses arise from what I call the Underego—to coin a term. A man just doesn't have enough manhood, or courage, or self-esteem, or pride, to face life and kick the offal out of it but lies down under all the battering, and cries and works up an illness to get out of the fight. Freud has another weird idea, too. He thinks a lot of mental ills, which give rise to physical ills, too, are caused by refraining too much from tossing in the hay with some willing doxy. He hasn't too much respect for what we call Judeo-Christian morality. Can make a man sick in his Id or something. Now I think that continence, if not carried to the point of absolute absurdity, or if undertaken with the full consent of the will, has a lot to recommend it."

Francis was listening with that intensity of his which Jonathan had deplored as excessive three years ago.

"So," said Jonathan, "what in hell was really troubling you when you were seventeen? Say I'm inquisitive."

Francis looked away from him and stared down at his fingers, which he slowly began to flex and unflex. He said, "Will it help you 'work out a deal with the fates' if I tell you?"

"Maybe."

Francis thought for a few moments and then said, "You know we are not supposed to reveal another's sins—"

"I'm not up on doctrine lately, and besides it is no longer any concern of mine—"

Jonathan was a little astonished when Francis lifted his head very sharply and stared at him with a kind of fierceness and passion. But the youth's voice was oddly quiet when he said, "It's no concern of mine any longer, either. I've left the seminary. You asked me about what ailed me when I was seventeen. It was something that had gone on for a year. Perhaps more. Will it be much of a surprise to you to hear that I adored my father—up to then?"

"Frankly it would." Jonathan was more than ever astonished. "I never admired Daddy."

"I know." And again Francis smiled. "I heard you call him the Marzipan Pear and even worse. I think I hated you when I was a child for that. Didn't you also call him a mountebank?"

"Probably. It sounds like me."

"Yes. It certainly does." Francis turned his head and looked through the window. He did not look at Jonathan when he said, "I adored him. I thought he was a—saint. I

thought he had—magnitude. He was never exactly too conscious that I was around, but when he did see me, he was
quite affectionate. I didn't discover for years that that was the
way he treated everyone. Affectionately. Maybe he does
really like people—That doesn't matter, though. I thought he
was a man—"

"Sun-crowned, holy, untouchable, heroic, Hercules in the
guise of St. Augustine," said Jonathan, when Francis became
silent. "I see."

The thin cheek colored. Francis turned to him now with a
little anger. "Didn't you think that of your father, too?"

"No, thank God, I didn't. Even as a kid I had better sense.
I thought my father pathetic, but I also thought he was a
damned fool and a bore. That didn't stop me from caring
about him, though. Apparently you found out something
about Daddy that disillusioned you, and instead of being sensible and saying to yourself, 'My father is no better, or no
worse, than other men,' you tried to kill yourself off with colitis and run away from your disillusion."

"You make me sound like a weakling!" Francis' voice rose.

"Well, aren't you? Never mind that you were sixteen or
seventeen. You were a man, not a child, at that age. You had
lived long enough to know this world has few heroes and
saints and possibly none at all. What did Daddy do except be
his dear old affectionate self, fully revealed to you at last as
human clay? He's too cautious to do anything really heinous,
that is, too cautious ever to be found out. Did you find out
something?"

"I did," said Francis through a tight mouth. "Several
things. It doesn't matter how they happened, how I found
out. It began when I visited him in his suite in Washington
during a holiday when he couldn't come home. I decided to
give him a wonderful surprise," Francis went on with old bitterness, "and so I didn't tell him I was coming. A surprise! It
was, too."

Jonathan put his hands to his head in mock horror. "Don't
tell me!" he exclaimed. "You found Daddy in the Arms of a
Woman who was not His Wife."

"Laugh," said Francis. "It probably sounds very funny to
you, Dr. Ferrier, but it wasn't to me. At sixteen."

"Oh, my God," said Jonathan. "There you were, at sixteen,
and probably had been experiencing your own 'carnal urges,'
as the Church calls them, and doing some hot breathing and
fiddling at night. Did you think your father was a monk? A

hermit? He was and is a full-blooded bastard and has always been known to have a fiery eye for the ladies, and he isn't married. You did your father an injustice. Did you actually believe he should have devoted himself to Memories of Mama and kept himself immured from the world?"

"You make me sound like a young fool," said Francis, leaning toward Jonathan now and showing deep offense.

"Of course. You were and are. Didn't they ever tell you anything in that boys' school you went to in Philadelphia or even in the seminary?"

Francis' face became cold and grim. "Yes. But that wasn't the reason—I mean, it was a shock at first, and then the priests talked to me, and though my father's conduct still seemed disgusting, I realized it was quite normal. No, it wasn't that. It was the other things I began to find out about him."

"Things people told you?"

"No. Things I found out myself. I made it my business to find out."

"What a damnable young prig you must have been! And a little contemptible, too."

But Francis' large dark eyes did not slink aside or wince. They were, at last, the eyes of a man. "I am not going to tell you what I found out. If they had been the average larcenies and manipulations of a politician, the usual skulduggeries, I'd have finally understood about them, too. There's a hell of a lot of compromising we have to do in living and coming of age, isn't there? I would have compromised, as I compromised before, with all the facile philosophies of a cynical world if my father's—crimes—had just been the usual and accepted ones of a man and a politician. Or even if they had been what people call 'peculiar,' as a way of not mentioning the facts."

Jonathan listened acutely. He was no longer smiling.

Francis' expression was again grim. "No, I can't tell you. I thought when I was seventeen that it was absolutely necessary for me to tell—well, say important men, men in government. I thought it was a matter of my—country. My country. The country he speaks so roundly and richly about on the Fourth of July, and Washington's and Lincoln's birthdays, and Decoration Day. The things he has sworn to protect. You see, he never thought I was very intelligent; even when I was sixteen and seventeen, he thought I was a child. So—I heard. I overheard. In his flat in Washington."

He stared blankly at the upturned palms of his hands. "And there was the trouble. My conscience. My country. Above all, my country. Yet, he was my father. What does a person do in that case?"

My God, thought Jonathan, who had a shadowy revelation. Yes, what does a person do in that case? He said, "I don't know. And so you were torn apart inside, and you bled inside, and you almost died."

"You should have let me die," said Francis, and closed his thin hands.

"You never told him?"

"No. To tell him—I'd have blown apart. I'd have had to do what I was afraid to do. It took me a long time to get over loving him. A very long time. Suppose you had found out something very terrible about your father, Dr. Ferrier, something really—monstrous. Something so criminal that in your country's interest it should be revealed, and that if it weren't revealed, he'd go on and on, doing the same thing and maybe much worse? Would you have—"

"Exposed him?" Jonathan shook his head. "I don't know. I don't think so."

Francis sighed. "Well, there it is. I carried that to the seminary with me when I was seventeen. And—don't laugh at me now—I prayed. Anyway, I put it out of my mind."

"You couldn't have been mistaken? You couldn't have been making a mountain out of a molehill? After all, you were hardly more than a kid, and politicians do some very expedient things."

Francis shook his head. "Give me some credit. I tried to tell myself that for over a year. I tried to think he was not doing what other politicians were not doing, only for much more money and that it was a sort of nefarious game with them, only. Like playing dice for high stakes. But men came to that flat in Washington—Senators—others."

"And he let you stay around to absorb it?"

"No, he wasn't that much of a fool. I kept on visiting him at times he didn't expect me. I had to know. And I always arrived at night. Finally he must have suspected something, for when I did arrive, he was always ready for me. My aunt wired him that I was coming. I found that out, too."

"Christ," said Jonathan.

"And now I don't know anything. I do know he made a lot of money out of the Spanish-American War. I do know he goes abroad a lot. That's all I will tell you, Dr. Ferrier. Except that I've been doing a lot of reading the past three years, a great deal of reading on a very frightful subject. Have you ever heard of Zaharoff, Doctor?"

"Yes. He's called mysterious and sinister. I've heard his name. Something to do with munitions, isn't that it?"

But Francis did not answer. He leaned back on his pillows in utter exhaustion, and Jonathan watched him and respected both his honor and his suffering, and with that he was greatly disturbed. What a thing for a boy to have carried about with him for years! Worse still was that boy's realization that in not betraying his father he was betraying something infinitely greater.

Jonathan said with unusual gentleness, "Look at it this way: If your father were not doing it, and others with him, there would still be a man in his position to do it. I know that isn't much consolation, and when it comes to affairs like this, the individual is pretty impotent, but—"

Francis' eyes were closed. He said in the quietest voice, "You don't understand, Doctor. I don't care about that any longer. I don't care about anything. I haven't cared about that for nearly a year. I haven't cared about anything for that long or longer."

Jonathan was more disturbed than ever. He stood up slowly and went to the bare window and stood and looked out at the long sweep of lawns, the fountains, the arbors and the flowers, and then raised his eyes and looked at the deepening mountains, calm and splendid and remote. Jonathan frowned. The room behind him was too quiet, as if the dead lay there. He said, without turning, "You say you haven't cared about anything for a long time. You have been in a seminary, studying for the priesthood. Don't you care any longer about—well—let's say, God?"

"No," said the emotionless voice behind him. "How can I? I no longer believe He exists. Or if He does, He is not concerned with this fleck of dust on which we live. What faith I have is gone. It took a long time dying. Over a year. It died very slowly, Dr. Ferrier. But it did die. I can't be a priest. My faith is dead."

And that's why you tried to die, too, thought Jonathan, and he thought, "What a rotten, disgusting, revolting and sickening world this is, to be sure!"

He walked slowly back to the bed and stood beside it, looking down on the spent and suffering young man who lay there. He said, "If every man who lost his faith, if every man who was an honestly convinced agnostic or atheist, died of it, then there'd be few people left in this world. I'm not saying that wouldn't be an excellent thing. I am merely stating a fact. 'Men have died, and worms have eaten them,' but not for God."

"No," said Francis, still lying there with shut eyes. "You forget the martyrs who did die for Him and the saints who believed to the death in Him. That seems the worst tragedy of all: To die for nothing."

"We all do," said Jonathan. "We live and die for nothing that we can discern, nothing that honestly makes sense to a rational man. Martyrs, saints, heroes, ordinary men, men like you and me, men like your father: we live and die for nothing. We invent gods when we can't stand the thought of the nothingness, the barrenness, the unreason, and we worship them when we can't bear living in a void any longer, when something piteously human cries out in us for consolation for what we see and suffer. Religion is the real Unreason, but, God help us, we can't be absolutely sane for too long at a time or too often. There's a worse agony than faith; there is a lack of faith. There's a worse madness than believing; there is nonbelief."

Francis' eyes slowly opened and they looked at Jonathan straightly.

"You believe that, Doctor?"

Jonathan hesitated. His perturbation was like a storm in him. He did not know what to say, so he said, "I believe that. At times. You will remember the cry of a man to Our Lord: 'I believe! Help thou mine unbelief!'"

Francis smiled drearily. "I have lost even the will to believe, so I don't need any help."

So that is why he would not speak to Father McNulty. Jonathan drew his chair to the bedside. He said, "Have you talked with the old priests at the seminary about this, Francis?"

"No. I didn't want to hurt them."

"You should have talked with them. Do you believe for a moment that those dedicated and blameless men never have their long periods of dryness and despair, of unbelief? Do you think they never knew doubt and still don't know it? St. Teresa of Avila had thirty years of dryness, and she was only one of the many saints who confessed that they were frequently torn by doubt and tortured by the despair of unfaith. Yet, they persisted in the heroic virtues. I've heard it said that their doubt and dryness were a testing to see if they would persevere in the desert of their agonized souls, in spite of everything."

"Do you believe that, Dr. Ferrier?"

"I don't know," said Jonathan. "You see, when I was seventeen myself, I, too, lost my faith, and it never came back. Not once, not for a moment."

"But how can you live, then?"

"I am not a coward. The world is filled with brave men who have no faith. We find ourselves in a senseless maelstrom, and the only thing that has verity is man himself. His very doggedness, his very patience, his very persistence, his very hope, in the face of apparent senselessness, gives him an awful dignity. He is the observer and the participant. He is the builder. He is the artist who makes order out of disorder, brings some frail light to chaos. I don't usually have much respect for my fellowman, knowing him for his weaknesses and crimes and stupidities, and I rail against him for them. But there are moments when I feel an awe for him, that he survives and will not let himself die. He is tragic, and that makes him a heroic figure in the midst of his blind predicament."

"And you think just living is enough to justify living?"

"What else can we do? Curse God and die? Is that the only thing a man can do? It is, if he remains a child, and if he insists on kicking and destroying everything when he discovers there is no Santa Claus, just out of sheer baby rage and vengefulness."

"Dr. Ferrier," said Francis, "I built my whole life, from childhood, on God. I knew, even when I was a kid, that my father didn't really care about me. I knew my aunt didn't. No one did. I couldn't make friends easily. I was too shy, too timid. I liked to read too much. I had—fantasies. I loved to look at the world, and I loved it, and I loved its great Lover for making such a beautiful world and for creating me so I could enjoy it, too. God, to me, was father and mother, brother and sister, friend, companion, teacher—all the days of my life, from the very first day I heard His Name." He lifted a hand, then let it drop. "And now I have nothing, nothing at all."

"You have your youth, and your world is still here, and you have a life before you to be endured if nothing else. As I endure it."

Francis gazed a long time on the dark and weary and dissipated face that hung over him. Then he said, "You only endure it—Jon?"

"I only endure it. I've only endured it since I was seventeen. By the way, what happened to precipitate this crisis in you?"

"That's the worst of it all, Doctor. If it had been some terrible disillusion, or some tragedy, or some upheaval, it would seem better and more sensible. But it wasn't anything. My faith just ran out slowly, and then it was gone. I tried to keep it, but it went."

Jonathan said, out of his deep pity, "Normal. Usual. Commonplace. That's the way it is with most men. That's the way faith leaves us. It seeps away. Small doubts, unresolved, unanswered. A few months of indifference. A tragic experience to which there seems no logical or compassionate answer. Observance of the unpunished crimes of men. The unexplained misery of the faithful. Disease. Cruel death. The joy and satisfaction of evil. The apparently mindless paradoxes. Confrontation of reality with doctrine. Small things, though, mostly. Attrition. New interests. Eventually something else takes the place of faith. Service. Ambition. Excitement in mere living. New revelations for possible pleasure and enjoyment. Curiosity. Science. Experimentation. Marriage and families. Pleasing results when our senses are indulged. The seven deadly sins, too, if you want to put it in a nutshell."

Francis smiled a little. Neither he nor Jonathan was aware that Jonathan had taken his hand and was now holding it strongly. "The seven deadly sins," he repeated.

"Yes. You'd be surprised how entertaining some of them can be, and enjoyable."

Francis laughed silently. "I don't really know how to sin," he said.

"Then, you've got to learn."

There was another silence in the room. Jonathan finally said, "I think what really happened to you was logic. The seminary priests go in for logic, and they do love Aristotle and Plato. But logic can be most irrational, dangerously irrational. Religion employs it at its deadly peril, for religion is built on the deepest instinct of a man's soul, its deepest emotions, its most mysterious urges, which are totally inexplicable in our worldly terms. A man is born with these. He doesn't acquire them. Only logic can be learned and acquired. I think that's something you can think about! I heard a story once, about a schoolmaster who took his class of seventeen-year-old youths out to see the dawn, a sort of scientific expedition."

It was an unusually black night for all the waning moon and the stars. The young men and their teacher stood in a dark and stubbly field, where they could see the wideness of the sky without the interruption of buildings. They faced the east, yawning and chilled, and there was the faintest sparkle of frozen dew on the dead stems and grasses of the field. Then imperceptibly a blue-gray shadow lightened the east, the merest specter of a shadow. Then, instant by instant, there was a brightening, the palest gold brightening, though the earth was as still as if it were the first day of creation and nothing lived yet to see and no glimmer of radiance touched it. The boys began to feel a curious and disturbing awe, and they did not know why, but their instincts shook off the dull sloth of the learning they had absorbed over the years and murmured.

The first flush of gold grew deeper and stronger, then in the midst of it there began a palpitating, pure and august, like wings of light, endless multitudes of them, and the sky glow, speading broader and higher and vaster into the dark sky, had intimations of grandeur beyond the experience or the imagination of those present. Yet the earth remained black and still and hushed beneath the heavens, without form or shadow or shape or sound. It appeared to wait.

Suddenly, into that throbbing gold, becoming more brilliant by the second, the scarlet trumpets of the dawn were lifted, fanned out from edge to edge of the light, and the whole mighty east glowed and quickened and it seemed to the boys that they saw great red flung banners in its midst, and the majestic rising of archangel trumpeters before the sun. The stupendous glory, so silent yet resounding as no mere exclamation or voice or drum could resound, seemed to be proclaiming the imminent arrival—of a King. But still the earth was dark and not the most fragile movement of light was yet upon it.

The schoolmaster was pleased by the struck attention of the boys, and he said, "You can almost feel, can't you, the roll of the earth eastward toward the sun?" But some of the boys involuntarily cried out, "Hosannah!" and others shouted, "Alleluia! Alleluia!" And for the first time in their lives some fell on their knees and lifted up their hands to the dawn in reverent and exalted greeting.

Francis had listened to this recitation with an absorption even he had never felt before, and his eyes glittered with tears.

"You see," said Jonathan, "the schoolmaster spoke logically, and he told the truth, and so he never stirred a heart or aroused a spirit. But the boys knew. They had seen something in themselves, perhaps, as well as in the sky, beyond reason, and saluted something that only divine unreason can comprehend. You can't will faith, Francis. You can't force yourself to believe. You learned at your seminary that faith is a gift of God only. I don't think you ever really believed, as a man believes, but only as an infant does. Now you've got a great adventure ahead of you, the search for what God is, and what you are, and the meaning of your life. That should take a whole lifetime, at least."

"And if I don't find it?"

"The searching will be enough. What could be more important, more worthy of a man? Somehow, though, I think you'll find it." Jonathan smiled. "And when you do, tell me about it. I'd like to know myself. You see, I was one of those boys in the field, but I wasn't one who cried 'Hosannah!' or 'Alleluia!' I had lost my faith, my child's faith, and never did find it as a man. Maybe I didn't look hard enough. I only know that men stood between me and what could be the only verity we need to know." He looked, for a moment, at the crucifix on the wall.

Francis could not speak. He watched Jonathan pick up his crop and his bag, and still could not say anything. But when Jonathan reached the door, the young man said in a breaking voice, "I'd like to see Father McNulty—I think I'd like to see him."

CHAPTER THIRTEEN

No one was in the corridor when Jonathan entered, spent as he had never been spent even after hours in an operating room. Slowly he went down the staircase and at the foot old Tom was waiting for him mutely. Jonathan said, "I think it'll be all right. I'd like to telephone Father McNulty to come to see Francis at once. He wants to see him."

"Oh, thank God," said the old man. He led Jonathan to the door of the telephone booth, glass enclosed, which stood under the stairway, and Jonathan called the rectory. The priest's elderly aunt, who kept house for him, answered frostily. "I'm sorry, Doctor, but Father was up all night, and then there were two Masses, and he's just exhausted and is resting a little before he makes sick calls."

Jonathan, as usual, lost his temper. "Miss McNulty," he said in an elaborately precise tone, "I, too, have been up all night, and I've been working on one of Father's pet cases, at his request, and I haven't eaten today and I have to go to the hospital on my rounds. So kindly call him, if you please."

Miss McNulty did not bother to reply, but in a minute or two the priest was at the telephone. "I haven't been thrown out of this house yet," said Jonathan, "but I expect to be any moment because of your and my impudence. The next time a parishioner of yours has a brainstorm and decides to join the great majority, please don't interfere with his sensible decision. And don't call me."

"Oh, Jon," said the priest in a stronger voice. "Then everything is well with Francis? I knew I should ask you, I knew!"

"You did, eh? Let me tell you something, Father. I didn't examine him. I wasn't called by anyone but you. I have no position in this house, I am not their doctor. So, I didn't examine the boy for the reason that if I'd laid a hand on him or looked at his throat, I'd then have been the attending physician and I'd then have to report the attempted suicide to the police. But you didn't think of that, did you?"

"I knew you could manage it somehow, Jon."

"Then, you knew something I didn't. All right, he wants you, as soon as possible, and as he is now in a very emotional mood, you should come at once before the tears dry and he gets fresh ideas. May I offer some ecclesiastical advice? Don't quote platitudes to him. Don't express any horror about what he tried. Don't, for God's sake, talk about sin. That boy has encountered enough sin in the past few years to keep a whole Curia busy. Don't mouth doctrine or dogma. He's heard nothing but that for years, now. No aphorisms. No cant. You'll only make him desperate. Come to him as a friend who really cares about him, and keep your mouth shut as much as possible, and just listen if he talks, and if he doesn't talk, don't talk either. Get the thought through to him, if you can, that you suffer with him as a man suffers with a brother, and that's a platitude, too, for it's the rare brother who cares a damn about his own flesh and blood. Do you understand me?"

"I understand, Jon," said the priest gently. He hesitated. "He definitely has left the seminary?"

"Yes, and I think it's a fine idea. Later, you can suggest to him that he take a trip around the world or something, and go down into those dens of vice you fellers are always talking about, and kick up his heels and sow several fields of wild oats. What are you laughing about?"

"Nothing. Go on, Jon."

"Let him see something of the world, and the girls, especially. You remember what St. Augustine prayed: 'Make me chaste, O Lord, but not yet!' That's what Francis needs. Afterward, he may decide to go back to the seminary, or maybe he won't, but in either case he'll be a man."

"Like you, Jon. I hope, in any event, he'll be like you."

"That's a Christian thought. Well, I'm going home now and you get here as fast as you can. On your bicycle. By the way, I thought you ought to know that he's lost something he calls his faith, so don't approach him through that, and don't bring any little holy tokens, either. He's growing up now; in fact, he's just about grown up."

The priest said, "God bless—" But Jonathan hung up the receiver. It was stifling in the hot booth. He wiped his exhausted face and hands, opened the door and confronted, with an inner curse, Senator Kenton Campion and Beatrice Offerton. He had hoped to leave the house unnoticed, and there they were, the Senator beaming like a golden sun and extending his hand, and Beatrice standing in the background, her big face still pale and her eyes somewhat reddened. As much as she could, she was registering not only disapproval of Jonathan but fear and resentment and indignation.

"Dear boy!" exclaimed the Senator, taking Jonathan's hand in both his plump warm palms and speaking in his consciously organ tones. "How good of you to come! I arrived less than an hour ago, and Beatrice has told me how you hurried to us in our—ahem—unnerving situation! How can I thank you? And how fortunate it was you instead of someone else—"

"It was," said Jonathan. "Your regular physician would have had to report it to the police, and such things have a stink about them. As it is, I am in a difficult situation, for I am a doctor even if not yours, and Francis was once my patient. But if no one talks, and if you and Mrs. Offerton look only astonished if there is any mention of it, and if you still have your old hold on the police chief here, perhaps it'll all die down. I take it the servants don't know exactly what happened?"

The Senator was less golden and beaming. He said, "Only old Tom, and Beatrice is going to discharge him immediately for disturbing the household for—ah—nothing."

Jonathan wanted to hit him. "Nothing, eh? Is that all you can say, and promise, about an old man who saved your son's life? I know you don't give a damn about Francis. It's been town-talk for years. But what if Tom hadn't saved him? Do you think your friend the Governor, who comes up for reelection this fall, or your friends in Washington, would still think you were a mighty fine specimen of a gentleman, or would they ask what kind of a father would have a son who committed suicide? Your political career would be over. At the very least the gossips would say that there 'must be insanity in the family,' and though there's plenty of insanity in Washington these days, they just don't want to add to it overtly. Now, what are you going to do about Tom?"

Jonathan, the Senator saw, looked dangerous and ugly, and he was swinging his crop in a very nasty and rapid way, as if he were longing to use it. The Senator coughed. He put his hand, his large white fat hand, on Jonathan's dusty sleeve.

"Now, Jon. I spoke without thinking. Why, old Tom will have my eternal gratitude! Old faithful family retainer, and all that. It was just my natural, paternal agitation—Forgive me, a stricken father. I became quite faint when Beatrice told me."

"From what I can smell," said Jonathan, "several big belts of bourbon revived you."

The Senator smiled his rich smile. "And from what I see, several such belts would help you, too, Jon. Do come into my study."

There was nothing more which Jonathan desired at that moment than whiskey, for he had developed an internal trembling in the last few minutes and his head was throbbing again and his mouth and throat were dry. But he looked at the Senator and thought, This bastard is really the cause of Francis' misery and attempt to die. And he hasn't as yet asked me how the boy is!

He said, "No, thanks. I am going home and will try to rest for an hour or so, and then I have hospital calls. I'm glad to see you're so concerned and crushed about Francis, but don't grieve too much."

The florid Senator colored and his blue eyes had a wicked and malignant gleam for a moment as he stood smiling benignly at Jonathan.

"Certainly, certainly, a dreadful shock, the only son, with such hopes for him, and everything, a fine character, it doesn't seem possible, it must have been what the French call a *crise de nerves.* One doesn't know what is happening to the young people these days. So nervous, so agitated, so restless, so dissatisfied. They fly from place to place, without knowing where they really wish to go. Very unsettling to parents, very disturbing. One does one's best—It truly is discouraging, discouraging. A Christian life, upbringing—it all seems to come to nothing. Duty is rejected, and honor, too, and sobriety, and responsibility, and regard for family name. Well. These are things we must endure in this new century, I suppose."

"Yes, mustn't we?" said Jonathan. The vast marble hall, full of the blazing shine of the sun, was making his head ache abominably, and he was now sick at his stomach and shaking internally with rage. He had a thought. "By the way, it was

Father McNulty who called me." To think that his golden
son of politics had not even asked how his son will be, and if
he is badly injured!

"Ah, yes, yes, yes," said the Senator in a crooning voice.
"Very good of the young man, very good. I must remember
to send him a little gift."

"Say five hundred dollars," said Jonathan. "That will help
toward the horse and buggy he so badly needs. He'll be here
soon—on his bicycle—climbing in this heat, and I know, to
show your gratitude to him and perhaps to me, that you'll
have your check ready."

The Senator's large rich mouth fell open, and his eyes
started. "Five hundred dollars!" he repeated.

"Little enough to pay for discretion, isn't it?"

The Senator struggled for lofty rectitude. "I know that the
clergy are always discreet. They don't bruit about private
matters they encounter. Really, Jon."

"But I'm not a clergyman, and as a doctor I am supposed
to report this."

"You—" exclaimed the Senator.

"That I am. I'm a bad, mean, contemptible, corrupt, degenerate character, Senator, as no doubt you have always
heard in Hambledon, and I have no scruples at all, and you
don't strike my heart with the slightest pity. If Father Mc-
Nulty doesn't inform me joyously soon of your magnificent
generosity, then I'm afraid." He shook his narrow dark head
and Mrs. Offerton gasped in the background and put her
hand on her breast. "I'm putting myself in a very precarious
position by keeping my mouth shut, you will understand."

"Are you sure," said the Senator in a silky voice, "that you
wouldn't prefer the five hundred for yourself, Jon?"

Jonathan stared at him. He half lifted his crop, and the
Senator stepped back in horror and indignation. Jonathan
dropped the crop. He said, "I know three Senators in Washington, Kenton, three fine men. Friends of mine. I saved the
life of the daughter of one. One word from me, Kenton, and
a word to the Governor, and a few more to the State Legislature, and you'll be gracefully, more or less, resigning. Do I
make myself very, very clear?"

But the Senator was no cringer. He said, "I regret that I
came to your assistance, Jon. I fear that there was more, behind the scenes, shall we say, than appeared at the trial."

"Indeed, there always is." Jonathan was smiling. "As for
your 'assistance,' you are a liar. If you did anything at all, in

your discretion, it was your disavowal of knowing the Ferrier family 'well.' It doesn't matter. I want to advise you about something. Before you begin to stuff yourself with your usual hearty lunch, I want you to go upstairs to your son, and say at least five decent words to him, not in reproach or condemnation, but in kindness. He has some faint idea of what you really are, I am sure, though he'd die rather than tell. Be grateful for that. Just a few kind words, if you think you can manage it. And then let him alone."

Beatrice Offerton spoke for the first time, and in a surprisingly shrill voice.

"How dare you insult the Senator like this, Jonathan Ferrier! And what are you implying about my brother, my good Christian honorable brother?"

"Why don't you ask the Senator yourself, Beatrice?" said Jonathan, and he swung about and went to the door of the hall. The Senator watched him go, and there was no happy complacency on his face now, no sweetness, no affection. The big blue eyes were so narrowed that the color had disappeared between the short chestnut lashes. Jonathan's footsteps clanged on marble.

Now, there's another enemy, thought Jonathan, waiting for his horse to be brought to him. He did not care in the least.

Once home, Jonathan fell into bed after partially undressing. The house was hot and close, though all the windows were open, and the curtains were slapping softly against the screens. He promised himself to sleep an hour or two at the most, for he was exhausted and sick. Just as he was falling asleep he heard the soft resonance of music. His mother, as she frequently did, was playing the piano in the drawing room. In the brightness of the full July day she was playing a nocturne, dark and lonely and slow. Jon half raised himself on his elbow and listened. She played with deep emotion and sadness, thinking herself alone, and in spite of himself he was deeply stirred. Each note was grieving, somber, contemplative, and it seemed to invade his very flesh and loneliness and loss, and a knowledge of man's impotence before the face of being.

Was his mother exactly what he thought she was? The question disturbed him, for he had long ago acquired the habit of studying other people, tabulating them on mental cards, and then filing them away in his mind, never to be restudied. It saved doubts and second thoughts. The thought came to him, out of nowhere at all: What do I really know about people? I mean, outside their pain and their surface life? He listened to the sorrowful nocturne, which seemed to express all the loneliness of life, all the blindness and wretchedness and lack of hope.

All his likes and dislikes had been set in stone for eternity, uncompromising, permitting no erasures and no additions. He did not like to think of that now, as he leaned on his elbow and listened to the haunting nocturne. He wanted to shout down to his mother, "Stop it! I'm trying to sleep, damn it!"

Then all at once he was really and profoundly asleep, but he dreamt uneasily, and his dream was of Mavis, his dead wife, as his dreams were usually in these days as never they had been before. He awoke, sweating on his bed and grimy. He got to his feet and was amazed that it was late afternoon and that he had slept so long. He went into his bathroom, shaking and empty and gaunt, and bathed and shaved, and came out dressed. His mother was waiting for him, a tall glass of eggnog, laced with brandy, on a tray in her hands.

She said with her usual tranquillity, "You come in late, or early, didn't you, dear? You didn't have your breakfast or your lunch. Do swallow this down. You seem so exhausted."

Without speaking, he sat down on the edge of his bed and drank the eggnog, making his usual taciturn faces. But it began to revive him. Marjorie never asked about his patients, for she knew that it was unethical for him to discuss them with an outsider. She said, "Young Dr. Morgan called, and I told him that you were asleep, after being out so early in the morning, and he said that everything was fine at St. Hilda's, and you weren't to worry. And Miss Meadows died." She looked at him sadly, knowing how grieved he was to lose a patient.

But he said, "Good. I was going to operate on her, but now I don't need to. I'll make the funeral arrangements." He drank the last of the eggnog. "I'll go along to the hospitals right away."

They sat together in silence. They thought of Mavis. She was, even in her death, an intruder in this house, a bright, brash intruder who should never have entered here. Neither one knew of the other's thoughts.

It was just as well. They were both thinking of Jonathan's marriage to Mavis Eaton on a hot June day several years ago.

CHAPTER FOURTEEN

Jonathan Ferrier and Mavis Eaton had been married in the First Presbyterian Church of Hambledon, in a candle-light ceremony, when Mavis was just past her twentieth birth-day.

"Not before a priest?" Marjorie had asked her son when he had told her of his coming marriage.

"Now, why should I?" His tone was irascibly patient. "I am not Catholic any longer, or rather I should say I am a lapsed Catholic, as the Church would call it. I'm not a medi-evalist or a mystic, and it takes both to be Catholic." Mar-jorie had said nothing. Nor had she made any remark to Har-ald when he announced wryly that he was to be his brother's best man. There are times, Marjorie had thought to herself, when it is utterly impossible to do anything about a situation except hold your tongue and smile as if all were well. Old Father McGuire had come to see her, however, under the vague impression that she was the *diabla ex machina.* They had never liked each other, though they had respect. He was a bad-tempered old man.

"It is true," he said to Marjorie as they sipped hot strong tea in the morning room, "that Jonathan and Harald can hardly be called practicing Catholics. I know that well! But a baptized Catholic is always a Catholic, even when lapsed."

"I never had any influence with my sons," said Marjorie, holding before him a silver plate of nutcakes, the sort he fa-vored, flavored with rum. "I have told you that before, Father. Jon was always under his father's influence, and Harald was always alone, and I never understood him."

The fat old man lifted thick white brows, and sipped his tea contemplatively for a moment. "Adrian was a good Catholic," he remarked. "If Jon was so under his father's influence, why has he fallen away?"

"I don't know, Father. I think something happened to him by the time he was seventeen." She smiled at him. "I think he became disillusioned by humanity. Not an unusual reason for abandoning religion. Jon was always a thoughtful boy, too much so, and too fierce and strong in his responses to others. And intolerant of what he considered any trespass against something he called 'civilized decency.' By nature, I think he is really a Calvinist. Perhaps Adrian had a little Huguenot blood in him."

"No. Adrian was most pious. I knew him well, for twenty years." He paused. "I have tried to talk with Jon. He has refused to come to see me in the rectory, though he has always been very generous with charitable donations. Mrs. Ferrier, did you know that Jon is at war with humanity?"

"Yes, I know."

"And so, he is at war with God. I've known Jon since he was a child. I've known Hambledon for many years. There has always been an animosity toward Jon here."

"I knew that," said Marjorie, with some surprise at the old priest's intuition, which she thought was hers alone. "Jon's character is too definite—"

"True. Definite characters are uncomfortable ones in this world, whether they are criminals or saints. People don't like others with strong opinions unless they are opinions they hold themselves, and even then they don't admire vehemence in speech. They don't like vehement actions, either. That's very strange in so young and strong and vital a country. And perhaps ominous. Republics are usually manly and forthright."

"You don't think America is manly?"

He shook his head and thought for a few moments. "I come from a manly country, Ireland. But America is not manly in that fashion, and that is dangerous. Republics are usually masculine, but lately I have suspected that America is beginning to show feminine traits, and that usually means a nation is declining into democracy. What is it Aristotle said? 'Republics decline into democracies, and democracies degenerate into despotisms.' Yes. Populism is becoming popular in America—an old doctrine, though its adherents invariably think it is a new one, age after age. Thank you, Mrs. Ferrier, these cakes are delicious as always. I have a sweet tooth."

"You were saying, Father?"

"Well, America is too fervid over inconsequential things, and she likes William Jennings Bryan and other novelties. Such childishnesses. And that's effeminate. She also likes fads and frivolities. That, too, is effeminate. There is nothing really stable about America, and her politicians are always talking about 'becoming.' I love this country. It has given my people their greatest opportunity, but still I am afraid. Let us come back to Jon." He smiled at her charmingly, his big flushed face very youthful under his white hair.

"The present animosity I detect here against Jon did not come suddenly with his twenty-first birthday. It was not like a clap of thunder, nor is it motiveless malice. Not entirely. It was there, that hostility, for many silent or whispering years. Jealousy of his merits and talents, his family, and his money. Fury that he is exactly what he seems, and that he is uncompromising and loves excellence. He hates mediocrity, and we must confess that most men are mediocre, though considering themselves exceptional. Jon also hates farce and incompetence and even the polite, social hypocrisies. He is also very brave, and men suspect true bravery, being, in the majority, not brave at all. I fear that the town is only waiting its opportunity to crush him and express its resentment of him."

Marjorie looked with melancholy at him, and with a little fear.

"Let us hope," said the old priest, "that he will never do something rash enough to expose himself to the malice of the community. I wish he would leave Hambledon and go to a larger city. Not that larger cities are more tolerant of the confirmed individualist, but such men are less likely to be conspicuous in big cities. I wish," he continued, with the somberness of his race, "that men like Jon were more appreciated and more honored, and understood, for they are rare, even if a little terrible. That's too much to ask, of course."

"Perhaps Jon will be appreciated as time goes on."

"I doubt it, Mrs. Ferrier. Jon has set himself against human nature, and human nature is not going to accommodate itself to Jon's glorious inner picture of what it should be. He will have to learn to compromise without disgust, and at least to endure." He looked at her. "Do you like Miss Eaton?"

The question was unexpected and shocked Marjorie, and

she winced. She made her handsome face smooth, but the sharp old priest had seen her shrinking. She said, "I am not the sort of woman who interferes with her adult children."

Ah, yes, thought the priest sadly. A proud woman it is, and a reticent one. Her children may respect her but hardly love her. Still, respect is often more valuable than love. Unrestrained love can be very destructive; at the worst, it is maudlin.

When he had left, after some courtly compliments concerning her garden and her beautiful subdued house, Marjorie was beset with anxious and premonitory thoughts. She had prayed that some miracle would occur to keep Jon from marrying Mavis Eaton, but no miracle came to his rescue. Ardent in nature, and indeed fierce, as the priest had commented, and she herself, he was unable to detect the slightest flaw in Mavis. He had lived, during the past few years, in a state of bemusement over her, and with a kind of joyful surprise each time he had seen the girl. What did she represent to him?

Marjorie did not know. It still seemed incredible to her that Jon, who saw flaws in everybody and was eloquent in denunciation, could find nothing wrong with Mavis Eaton. Was it the lure of her pretty flesh? But there were scores of pretty girls in Hambledon, fine young women. Marjorie thought of her old aunt, the Laughing Girl, as Jon had called her kind. However, many men felt no attraction for them. Why had Jon? Jon, above all?

The big fieldstone church, austere and dark even in the hot bright afternoon, flared with shadows and candlelight, and the air was stifling and rustled with fans. Those who had been invited to the wedding filled every pew, and the sultry atmosphere became more oppressive with women's scents and the fragrance of banked flowers everywhere. The mayor was present, and Senator Campion and State Senators, and the Governor himself, and other dignitaries, and their wives. It was a gala occasion.

Jon waited with his brother, sweating with embarrassment and expectation, his dark face clenched. He seemed to be frowning. "Quiet," Harald whispered with amusement, and Jon glanced at him irritably and flushed. Then the organ, and the triumphant voices, rose to the entrance music, and there was Mavis on her proud uncle's arm, and she was floating down the aisle to her bridegroom.

Of less than usual height for a woman, she seemed taller today, for her long gown flowed not only to the red carpet of the aisle but had a long train, held by two young boys, distant cousins, pages in blue silk. A little flower girl preceded her, and eight bridesmaids clad like autumn flowers in gold taffeta. But Jon saw only his bride. Her gown was demurely high in the neck, tight lace and pearls upheld with whalebone about her throat, and the same material partially covered her full breast. The white satin of the gown clung to her delectable figure in all its virginal though mature curves, and enhanced the smallness of her delicate waist and her feminine hips, a trifle broad but very stylish. The satin quivered in the candlelight, and there was something both enticing and innocent, though faintly lewd, in that smooth exposure of her body in the gleaming rich fabric. It was a Worth gown, purchased in Paris, and the ladies in the church gasped both in admiration and envy. It was strewn, at the curve below the hips, with sparkling stones and pearls, and the train, heavily jeweled, glittered like sunlit rain. She wore white kid gloves and diamond bracelets, and there were diamonds in her ears. She was one shimmer of light, exquisite, softly pliant, alluring.

A small tiara of pearls and sparkling stones rode high on her golden pompadour, and from it fell her lace veil to far below her knees. The veil covered her virgin face, so that one caught a glimpse only of a faintly pink lip, a glimmer of eye, a shadow of gilt which was her hair. She carried a bouquet of yellow roses with a trail of green ivy.

Jon watched her, stiff and entranced, as she swayed on her uncle's arm and the Wedding March made the hot and scented air tremble. He felt both exultance and joy, and he also felt intoxicated. It was not only Mavis' beauty which fired him, which made him breathe heavily—to Harald's fresh amusement. It was the promise the girl held for him, the hint of new life, of delirious adventure, of some deliverance from the strange and heavy torment which had bedeviled his life from his very early consciousness. He felt that he was on the threshold of being reborn to a more joyous world, to a world of infinite variety and innocence and promise. To a lightheartedness he had never known, to a sort of delirious abandon, and new concepts. With Mavis he would be released from something that had made his existence somber and gloomy. He would be free, finally, from himself.

With Mavis he would be carefree as he had never been

carefree, and he would be young as he had never been young. She would laugh away many of his intensities, and her humor would make him smile, and he would be unburdened. He would, in short, play and be refreshed, and he would even laugh, himself, at some of the things which he now found intolerable. Life would become, not a conflict as it had been all his life, but light and airy and gay, and their mutual love and adoration would be like a garden to him, restful and full of color, serene and youthful, bright and exciting. He might even become innocent, himself, and accepting.

He knew nothing whatsoever about Mavis Eaton, standing demurely at his side, with her beautiful head bent reverently, and her profile hidden from him by her veil. He endured the long ceremony, and his knees shook, and Mavis' scent, also imported from France, was in his nostrils and he felt that it was the natural odor of her youth and beauty and the wonderment she was keeping for him, alone. When her veil was lifted by her matron of honor, and he saw her face in the candlelight he was stunned with his rapture and his delight and his passion and his love. He dared—he felt he was very daring and irreverent—to kiss her soft cool lips, and he tried to look into her blue eyes. But they were only crescents of thick golden lashes, and he thought it was maidenly reserve and maidenly fear.

Then the Wedding March was resumed on a high and exalted note, and Mavis was on his arm, going down the aisle, beautiful as a dream. She did not look up at him. She smiled widely at the wedding guests and swayed expertly so that all could admire her gown and her jewels and the great diamond on her finger, which Jonathan had given her. It was her triumphant day, her hour, her glory, and Jonathan to her was only the accessory. She had married the most eligible bachelor in town, the richest, and she was a queen. If Jonathan knew nothing about her, she knew nothing about him, either. He would have been horrified if he had known of his own ignorance. But Mavis would not have cared in the least. To herself, she had no faults and no flaws. She had considered Jonathan lucky in marrying her, and, unfortunately, he agreed with her. The guests agreed also, with the exception of Jonathan's mother and brother.

The reception for hundreds of guests was held on the lawns and among the gardens of Martin Eaton's vast and hideous house. There was champagne and whiskey and a magnificent feast. Long hot shadows fell below the trees as the day swung toward evening. Beyond the lawns the river shone like a wide path of blue, and in it stood the silly island, Heart's Ease, and beyond the river and the island rose the violet mountains brilliant with the falling sun.

Mavis was gracious and ebullient, and her loud and husky laughter, so joyous and so abundant, was everywhere, as she moved among the guests and accepted their toasts. They pressed about her, stroking her gown, tenderly kissing her cheek, patting her hands. Her sparkling white gown set her apart in all that color. It was her uncle she chose to walk beside her, and Jonathan and Flora Eaton moved in her train, Flora in lavender taffeta, a color most unbecoming. Marjorie stood apart, watching and fearing and aching but outwardly serene in her gown of soft rose silk, her dark hair shaded by her rosy hat of tulle. Her head was aching, and her heart also, and there was a tumult in her ears of congratulations and mirth and merrymaking and happiness. Above all, she heard Mavis' laughter and her sudden whoops of rough glee and it seemed to Marjorie that it was the most insensitive sound she had ever heard, totally crude and distasteful, and even repellent. Marjorie had given the girl a gentle kiss, and then Mavis' eyes, sunken and secret, had opened a little and Marjorie had seen the old blue gleam, the indifferent yet cunning gleam, as far removed from warm humanity as polar ice.

But no one except Marjorie could resist the boisterous laughter of the girl, the gaiety that was indeed coarse. Everyone was as bemused as Jon at the way she would throw back her head, unaffectedly, showing all her big white teeth in her mirth, her eyes crinkling above, her cheek glowing. Her spirits, always boisterous, enchanted them all, for they held no reticence but were bold and teasing. She slapped admirers on the arm with her white and jeweled fan, and pushed her bouquet gaily into faces, and joked coaxingly, and looked about for fresh admiration and affection. She had none of the shyness of a bride. When Jonathan would push to her side, she would stare at him and then grin deliciously.

The bridal couple was to spend the wedding night in the Quaker Hotel in its most lavish suite, waiting now and filled with flowers. Tomorrow they would leave for the races at Saratoga, and then to New York for the balance of the honeymoon.

Jonathan did not like champagne, but he thought it decorous today to abstain from whiskey. He was certain that a whiskey odor on his breath would revolt his dainty bride. The wine made him queasy, for all his delírium and his joy. He tried to keep up with Mavis, claiming her, but she slipped constantly away from him to new groups of loving friends and entranced admirers. He heard her laughter, and it seemed to him that it was the most lovely sound in the world, the sound which would be the music of his life and its refreshment. He kept smiling inanely, his dark face shining a little. He accepted congratulations and new toasts like one in a dream, and everyone remarked how enchanted he was and how so unusually amiable. When Martin Eaton said to him, his voice breaking, "Be good to my darling little girl, Jon," Jonathan could only say fervidly, "Don't worry, Martin. I am going to devote my whole life to her!" This was so unlike Jonathan that Martin blinked through the tears in his adoring eyes. He pressed Jonathan's hand, moved as he had never been moved before. "It is a sacred promise," he stammered. "A sacred, sacred promise." Jonathan agreed, and his own unusual emotion made him suddenly speechless.

He turned—and saw Harald, his brother, standing a little apart in all his hazel handsomeness, and Harald bowed to him ironically and silently toasted him with the champagne. For the first time Jonathan was aware of something a little disagreeable, and he frowned vaguely and walked off looking for Mavis again in her clotted group of worshipful friends. But Flora Eaton appeared out of nowhere, somewhat feverish, her narrow face quivering. She caught his arm in her dark tense hand.

"Jon! Jon! Be good, be kind! Love her, Jon! She is so tender, so young, so inexperienced, such a child! She is a daughter to us, Jon, a daughter to us! Oh, no one deserves our child, no one! Guard her sacredly."

"I will," Jonathan actually said, and went looking for his bride again. Marjorie heard this exchange and she closed her eyes briefly.

Harald appeared at her side, smiling, and she started. He lifted his glass and said, "To the Golden Girl." He laughed a little, his eyes dancing. "And to Jon, who is going to need it."

"Why?" asked Marjorie.

"He's a silly damned lamb," said Harald. "Our charmer is going to teach him a thing or two. Listen to her laugh! Or is it a bray?" He considered. "A bray," he repeated.

"Don't be nasty, Harald."

"I'm not. I'm factual. Jon is always talking about 'stick to the facts.' He wouldn't recognize a fact if it kicked him in the —well, in the teeth." He was very tall and handsome and he smiled at his mother as if trying to draw her into a mutual joke. Marjorie was not amused, and she moved away, full of foreboding. Harald said, "I don't know whom I pity most."

Japanese lanterns were lit at dusk in the gardens, and there was music over the long lawns, for Marton Eaton had hired the Hambledon German Brass Band for the occasion, without the brass overpowering the violins and the cellos. The first dance, on stiff green carpet laid on the grass, was claimed by Martin and he and Mavis whirled together in a sprightly waltz, Mavis' train over her white kid arm, and her head thrown back so that her big white teeth glowed and glittered in the lantern light, and her veil flew behind her and her full and lovely figure gleamed in its white satin tightness. Next, she danced with her bridegroom, and she kissed the side of his face cheerfully and squeezed his shoulder affectionately in her gloved hand, and grinned up at him. He recalled with happiness that never had he seen Mavis in a "mood," or otherwise than her charming, bouncing self, in a cloud of laughter and scent. She was enormously healthy, too, a most desirable trait in a wife, and health had its own enchantment. Her rosy face was damp with heat and exertion, but she did not pause to wipe away the little drops but let them shine on her vibrant skin. Her sleek golden pompadour loosened, and a few ringlets fell from it. Jonathan could feel the soft but vigorous movements of all her muscles, and he thought of the young mares on his farms, silken and fresh and trembling with eager life. He looked down at Mavis and tried to see her eyes, but as usual they were crinkled with mirth and pure animal enjoyment and the awareness of her beauty. Her translucent flesh appeared to palpitate.

At length it was time for the bridal couple to leave for the Quaker Hotel, and Mavis disappeared with her running bridesmaids and her matron of honor and her Aunt Flora, and there were screams of joy from the lighted house when she threw her bouquet from the stairway. The band continued to play and the guests continued to drink and eat and dance and joke and laugh, and this would go on for hours after the newly married pair left. A little later Mavis reappeared, still vibrant but now cool and softly powdered, and dressed in a white silk suit with a flow of exquisite white lace tumbling from her neck down over her bosom, and a broad white straw hat covered with pale blue roses of silk. The hem of her suit just daringly lifted over the arch of her white stockings and hinted of fragile ankles, and she was dazzling and fresh and shining like the moon.

She never stopped smiling for a moment, her great white-toothed smile, and she kept throwing back her head in a boom of laughter and everyone, as usual, was fascinated and forced to laugh helplessly in return. She stood with Jonathan, her hand on his arm, and cajoled, and affectionately slapped a cheek here and there, or squeezed a hand, or gave a swift kiss, and she was never still for a single second. She was all beguilement and vitality and gusto, though to some ears her laughter frequently sounded like a screech, and it rose even above the music and the loving babble of the many guests.

The bridal couple drove off in Flora's own victoria and with her coachman, and to the last Mavis waved and laughed and called back to the guests who gave them Godspeed. Jonathan, beside her, thought it was like sitting next to a dynamo, scented and breathing and strongly pulsing. Once on the street, Mavis apparently became aware of him, and she squeezed his arm gleefully, and said with immense cheer, "Wasn't that a lovely wedding, Jon?"

"Yes, darling," he said, and lifted her hand and kissed it and she looked down on his thick black hair with affection. "I love you," she said. Jonathan lifted his head, deeply moved, and suddenly remembered that never before had she said that to him. He pulled her into his arms, in a cloud of rose fragrance, and kissed her lips with passion. She purred against his lips like a big, contented kitten, then drew away. She said, "I wish we were going to Europe, though, to Paris."

"I told you, darling, that I have several operations in two weeks."

"I know." Her voice was husky and a little hoarse always, but now it was more so. "Uncle Martin and Aunt Flora have told me what it means to be a doctor's wife." Then he saw her deep dimples in the flare of the lamps on the street. "But I'm not going to let you become dull and smell of ether all the time, like Uncle Martin, and never having fun again."

"Perhaps next summer we will go to Europe," said Jonathan. He was exhausted and exhilarated at the same time, and he thought of his coming night with his wife.

"Um, um," Mavis crooned, and patted his cheek, and began to hum the Wedding March half under her breath. "A lovely wedding," she said again. "I'd like to get married every day."

"Why?" asked Jonathan, with adoring fondness.

"It's such fun," said Mavis, again gleeful. He did not know why he felt a touch of disappointment. He looked at Mavis' pretty face, glowing beside him, and there was no shyness on it and no nervousness. When he kissed her again, she responded absently, and her lips were smiling, and he felt that she was hardly aware of him but was indulging in some delightful thoughts of her own, far removed from him.

The bridal suite shone resplendently with crystal chandeliers and was heavy with the fragrance of hundreds of flowers. Mavis had the gift of flattered gratitude, and she went from room to room, exclaiming over the kindness of friends who had sent silver baskets and bowls of rich fruit and bouquets and heaps of little parting gifts. "Everyone loves me," she said, and looked at Jonathan eagerly.

"No wonder," he said. "And I do, too. Remember?"

But she whirled again through the rooms, singing loudly and laughing over some little note among the gifts, and chortled deeply. She had thrown her hat on a blue damask love seat, and her gloves on top of it. Her luggage, and Jonathan's, was in the great bedroom with its enormous brass bed and lace counterpane. He began to tremble. He called to Mavis, "It's nearly ten, darling, and we must be up at six to catch the Saratoga train at eight in the morning."

She came running to him, and she grasped his arms and looked up into his face, winsome and rosy. "I am hungry!" she declared with pleasure. She pressed her cheek briefly but strongly against his chin. "Hungry as a wolf. Getting married did that to me, but I can always eat, anytime."

"You mean—now?" asked Jonathan. She nodded with that immense good nature of hers, and laughed her exultant laughter. "Yes, yes," she said. "I had hardly a bite at home, just half a plate of cream chicken and a slice of ham, and some rolls and cakes. And," she continued with astonished joy and animation, "I want some more champagne!"

So a little table was brought up to the suite with covered silver dishes, steaming, and a bucket of ice with champagne, and Mavis, still in her white silk suit, hovered over the place settings lustfully, and smiled and smiled and smiled and made little joking comments to the infatuated waiter. "Oh, how delicious it all smells!" she exclaimed, sniffing loudly and lifting the silver covers of dishes, and then humming with anticipa-

tion. Her golden head bobbed emphatically, and she looked
at Jonathan, grinning, and he saw the glittering slits of blue
between her yellow lashes. He could not help it. He laughed
back. He remembered that she was very young and extraordinarily healthy. And innocent. Innocent, above all. He must
be patient and tender to one who knew nothing of marriage
and what marriage meant. She was a child.

Before Jonathan could seat himself, Mavis had already
filled a plate with heaping portions of meat and gravy and
potatoes and stewed tomatoes, and was purring deeply in her
throat with ecstatic enjoyment and appetite. Well, he thought,
we'll never have any vapors to contend with at any rate, and
thank God my darling is abundantly healthy. He could not
touch a bite. He drank champagne with Mavis and watched
her eat. She ate daintily, but all at once he had a thought that
she was also gross, a thought he squelched immediately.
Even while she ate she smiled and purred in her throat in
simple animal pleasure. She drank the champagne like water,
and looked over the rim, twinkling, at her husband.

"You aren't handsome in the least," she informed him, and
chuckled. "Not like Harald."

"Does that matter?" he asked with indulgence, and worshiped her with his eloquent dark eyes.

"Um, um," she said. Then she suddenly stood up, raced
around the table to him, and kissed him smartly on the top of
his head. Before he could seize her, she was back in her chair
and eating again. Part of her hair was tumbling down her
back and it caught vivid gilt lights from the chandelier. She
motioned to Jonathan to fill her glass again, and she laughed
aloud as the bubbles tickled her nose. He had never seen such
verve before, and he thought how marvelous his life would
be with Mavis, how lively and gay and refreshing, after he
came wearily home from the hospital. She would be like a
bright effervescent pool of water, fragrant and reviving to exhausted flesh, and the house would ring with her joy in life
and her husky merriment. He was so moved at this thought
that he could only stare and smile at her with the most touching hope. She would teach him so many things, adventure,
new insights, lightness, happiness, peace, and, above all, zest
in living. He had forgotten what zest was, but he would learn
again.

"I wish," she said, with a mouth full of ice cream, "that we
weren't going to live in that old house of your mother's, Jon."

"I know, dear. You've said that before. But it is my father's house, and mine, and not my mother's, and it is very beautiful."

"Your mother doesn't like me," she informed him, and grinned flashingly.

"She loves you, Mavis. Who could help but love you?"

"Well, she doesn't." Mavis spoke like a malicious child. "Not that I care. I can get along with anyone, really. She won't disturb me. And I won't disturb her. I don't care a bit about running a house, and perhaps I should be grateful that your mother will continue to do that and leave me free."

"For what, love?"

She waved her white hand on which Jonathan's diamond broke in light. "Why, for so many things! All the parties we'll be giving, and accepting, and lawn fetes, and dancing, and shopping and being with friends, and teas, and receptions."

Now she was looking at him with the strangest expression, and her little eyes were sly and calculating and a little cruel. But he did not see the cruelty. He saw only her humor.

"There are more things in life than that, Mavis," he said, and thought what a child she was.

"I'd like to know what is more pleasant," she said. "Um. These lovely little cakes! Marzipan." She burst out laughing. "I remember what you called Senator Campion. A Marzipan Pear. Uncle Martin thinks it is precious. Did you know he's afraid of the Senator?"

"No. Is he? And why?"

She chuckled. "I don't know. Who cares? But he is. And the Senator is such a handsome man, and so kind and happy. I love happy people, don't you?"

"I love you," said Jonathan.

Mavis threw back her head and began to sing hoarsely. "Happiness! Happiness! It's a great wide wonderful world, it's a great wide wonderful world, it's a great wide beautiful, wonderful world!"

Teach me how it is, thought Jonathan. Mavis sprang up again and began to whirl about the room, singing, her arms thrown out, her falling golden hair swirling about her, and she was entirely unconscious of her husband's presence. She was staring sunnily at the ceiling and had her own relishing thoughts. She picked up her wide white skirts and he saw the firm and graceful calves and her delicate knees. He got up and tried to take her in his arms, to dance the dance of life with her. But she pushed him off with head-shaking impatience and danced away from him, as if she needed no one but herself for her own joy.

But Jonathan did not know that now, though the faintest coldness touched him as he watched his young wife whirl alone and dance dizzily through the rooms, singing only to herself. He watched her with passion, exulting in her beauty and vigor.

I don't deserve all this, thought the proud young man with rare humility. I don't deserve all this beauty and youth and sheer exultation in living, and all this hope and happiness.

Mavis stopped suddenly, across the room from him, and she shrieked with mirth, bent and clasped her hands between her knees, and shook with her delight and exuberance. She flung back her hair and raced to him, seized him by the shoulders and kissed him heartily. "Oh, what an old man you are, to be sure!" she cried.

He seized her and held her, vibrating, against his chest. "Teach me how to be young, Mavis," he said, his lips in her fresh and scented hair.

But she was moving restlessly in his arms, like a cat. She danced away again. It was hot in the suite, and the odor of flowers and food was overpowering. He caught a glimpse of Mavis' face and he was surprised to see that it was no longer smiling and that she was sullenly pouting even as she danced. Her small eyes, as usual, were hidden in their arched lashes, and she seemed to be thinking furiously.

"Mavis!" he called to her.

She stopped at once, panting, and pushing back her hair. She stared at him.

"What?" she asked, as if disagreeably reminded of his presence.

"It's half-past eleven, almost."

"Oh, who cares?" she cried. "Are you so old that you can't miss an hour or two of sleep without being ill, or tired, or something? Can't you enjoy anything?"

He was startled. He, as a doctor, was always aware of time and its pressing. He was disturbed. Then he thought, I must get used to this, to having someone near me who isn't harassed all the time and can enjoy the passing moments and live in the present. I've been so immured, so shut in.

"Yes, I can enjoy, Mavis," he said in a humble voice. "But I thought you must be tired, after the wedding and everything."

"I'm never tired!" Her hoarse voice was emphatic. "I don't

know what it is to be tired! And I hate tired people! I won't have them around me, ever!" She shook her head with such vehemence that her hair flew. "I detest serious people, such slugs!"

Half alarmed, half pleased, he teased her: "But I'm a serious person, Mavis."

Again her eyes shut cunningly. "Yes, I know," and then she laughed as at some enormous joke. "I don't mind you being serious, Jon. It helps you make such a lot of money, and don't you just adore making lots of money?"

She is only a child, he reminded himself, as yet unaware that women like Mavis are never children.

"Such a lot of money, a lot of money, a lot of money!" sang Mavis, and kicked up one leg like an expert dancer. She whirled on the other. There was something frenzied in her movements.

Then she stopped abruptly and again stared at Jonathan, and again her gaze was cunning and thoughtful. "All right, old man," she said. "I'll tuck you in your bed so you won't be too tired to make money!"

"But you have a lot of money yourself, darling," he said, "and you are your uncle's heir—"

"Nobody has enough money!" she shouted pettishly, then ran past him into the bedroom and slammed the door behind her. He sat down, and the air in the suite seemed fetid to him, as well as hot and stinking with the smell of rich food. He stood up and pushed the table out into the corridor. The champagne bottle was empty. He was conscious, all at once, of the need of a drink of whiskey, several drinks. He was also, he admitted, very tired, and then he was aware of a kind of hollow emptiness and disorientation. The lights in the parlor of the suite stung his eyes and he got up heavily and turned off all but one lamp. Now there was an odor of gas in the suite. He opened the windows and leaned out and drew in the hot air, burdensome with the smell of heated pavements and brick and dust. The lights of Hambledon winked at him, and he yawned, then rubbed his eyes. He saw the far glitter of the river and the dull shadow of the mountains against a dark but burning sky full of stars. There was a rumble of thunder somewhere, and a little dusty wind blew over his sweating face.

Then he became aware that he had forgotten he had a bride in those brief seconds. He looked about him, somewhat dazed. He felt no passion any longer. He was too tired.

"All right!" shouted Mavis from behind the shut door. "You can come in now if you want to! I'm finished with the bathroom."

He went into the bedroom, shamefully aware of the aching in his legs and back. He was only thirty. He felt like an old man.

Mavis had hung up her suit and put away her hat and gloves, and now she stood before him, a pillar of gold and white in her silk nightgown and peignoir, her hair hanging long and flowing down her back. She smiled at him, and she was neither nervous nor shy. Her scrubbed face shone rosily and her teeth were like young ivory, big and wet. She was freshly perfumed, and, weary as he was, he thought how tireless she was, how young, how adorably alive and greedy for life, and again he hoped.

When he had bathed and undressed in the bathroom, he came out. Mavis had dimmed all but one light in the big hot bedroom and was lying high on the pillows in the bed, contemplating something mysteriously. She turned her little eyes to him and said with affection, "I never saw your hair mussed before, Jon. I like it." She held out her arms to him like a child eager for a doll. Her hair was spread over the pillows in a golden stream. All at once he wanted to devour all that juicy life, all that verve and simplicity, and to forget that life was complicated and full of pain, and mostly joyless.

He sat on the edge of the bed and took one of her cool smooth hands and looked down at her. He quoted:

"Ah, love, let us be true to one another,
    For the world which seems
    To lie before us like a land of dreams,
    So beautiful, so various, so new,
    Hath neither joy nor hope, nor help for pain—"

She opened her small eyes wide at him. "I don't like that," she said. "I don't like poetry, anyway. It's too gloomy. Aren't you coming to bed? You wanted that, didn't you? What's the matter? Oh, I didn't understand that poem, eh? Well, I didn't, and don't. Turn off that light. It's nearest you."

He lay beside her in the hot darkness. It was some time before he heard her muffled chuckling, and he turned toward her and she buried her face in his shoulder, and her young and gorgeous body was under his hands. She was laughing at him, and he was happy. "What is it, love?" he asked with tenderness. Now she would tease the weariness from him.

"I'm just thinking," she said. "Old Betsy Grimshaw, one of my bridesmaids. You know. Twenty-five if she's a day, and never a beau! She caught my bouquet, and she almost cried! She'll never get a husband."

He drew away his hands from her. She lifted her head from his chest and tried to see him in the darkness.

"What's the matter?" she demanded. "Too tired? Or afraid of hurting me? You needn't be afraid. Aunt Flora told me all about it. It's something a woman has to stand, she said. And Uncle Martin gave me a book. I'm not scared."

Shallow, mindless, he was thinking with a rush of deadly new despair. There's nothing for me in her. It's not her fault, the child. The fault was in me and my fantasies. All my life has been full of fantasies, and I never knew it until now.

Her hair brushed his cheek. "Poor old boy," she said, and laughed. "Well, you go right to sleep. I'm sleepy, too."

The marriage was not consummated until the second night in Saratoga. Mavis' lack of passion and enjoyment devastated her bridegroom. He told himself that this was new to her and would pass, and she would eventually respond. He did not know for a long time that Mavis was incapable of responding to anyone but herself and that if she were ever to feel passion, it would not be with him. She had submitted herself to him, not with resignation and frigidity, but with indifference. He had been only her means to a larger and fuller joy in life, away from her uncle's home. He had been only a way to adventure, and the adventure did not include him. He was her "old man."

Her easy affection for him lasted nearly a year. She had nothing to give him and never would have anything. She had nothing to give anyone except pleasure in her laughter and her verve and teasing. But, being the man he was, that was not enough.

He continued to love her for a long time, from a distance, but a terrible, yearning distance, and did not know when it also became hatred.

Before the hatred finally arrived—though the helpless, hoping love long stayed with him—Jonathan would take Mavis to Philadelphia, Pittsburgh and New York, and even Chicago and St. Louis with him, for conventions and consultations—and there, as usual, she would charm everyone and awaken envy of him on the part of other physicians. Jonathan could even enjoy her then, and her cheerfulness and her cuddling coyness, and her sudden bursts of affection for him, though he soon learned that that affection was also mocking. Her beauty was like the sun, inciting adoration even on the part of women. When alone with Jonathan, she was like a golden kitten, purring, coaxing, promising delights which never materialized, promising hope of understanding where there was no hope, promising subtlety where there was only animal enjoyment of living, promising adventures of the mind where there was only adventure of the senses.

I must not blame her, he would repeatedly tell himself. She is what she is. But what Mavis was he did not entirely know for a considerable time. He had told himself since he was twenty that there was nothing to expect from others and that it was cruel to expect more than they had to give in love and perception. But when he finally realized that Mavis was not only mindless and shallow, except where it concerned her demands and appetites, but avaricious and hardhearted and callous toward suffering and intolerant of need and loneliness, and greedy beyond measure, he came to hate her while she still fascinated him and continued to make him believe that if he could but penetrate her shining avidity and triviality, he would find a pulsing core of gentle humanity and tenderness.

She said to him once, cuddling against him in bed, "When are we going to move to Philadelphia or New York, Jon dear?"

He said, "We are not. What gave you that idea, Mavis?"

She was outraged. "You can hardly expect me to live in this miserable little town all my life, can you?"

"I am satisfied here." He was astonished and freshly shaken. "This is my home, isn't it?"

She became sly. "Jonnie, Jonnie. Don't you know nearly everyone hates you here? I hate it, for your sake."

"How can they hate me?" He was surprised. "I give all I can of myself to my patients and to the city, in charity——"

"That's the reason why," she replied, and chuckled knowingly. "People who give everything"—and she held out a giving palm—"get nothing. People despise them. You've got to take everything you can in this world, and then people will respect you—for your money and your position." She clutched her hand greedily to her breast and grimaced happily.

He was both sickened and revolted by her then. It never came to him that Mavis had an animalistic but pragmatic knowledge of mankind, which not all his intelligence could

ever acquire, and that she lived on a level of vulgar realism
which he had rejected in childhood as unbearable if one was
to live. He did not know that Mavis was fearless because she
had accepted life for what it was, and men for what they
were, and asked no concessions. He did not know that
though he was brave, he was also expectant and too vulnerable.

Mavis continued, for at least two years, to insist that they
leave Hambledon. When he gave her his final refusal, she became sullen and withdrew from him and came to hate him
with real and resentful hatred. He loved her as helplessly as
always and would listen for her laughter in his house and the
rustle of her dress, and her quick footstep, which never
stopped at his door. As far as Mavis was concerned, Jonathan
ceased to have meaning and verity for her and was only a
means of supplying her with handsome gowns and jewels and
position. She joked with him on occasion and laughed at him
always, but she lived apart in a joyful world of her own,
which was full of admiration for her and had nothing but
love for her.

Finally, total desolation came to him when he fully realized what Mavis was, and would also be, to the very end of
her life. It was then that he began to muse on ways of killing
her and removing her from the heart of an existence which
was becoming intolerable to him. She had betrayed him, he
would think, betrayed him in the only way which mattered to
a man like himself.

Mavis was primitively astute. They had been married only
two years when she realized he hated her. She was infuriated.

A short time before the tragedy of Mavis' death, Harald
said to his mother, "Jon will never get over Mavis. He thinks
he hates her, and perhaps he does, and I'd not blame him,
but he is also still infatuated with her, like a kid trying to
solve an old puzzle and never giving up. He's the kind of a
man who thinks that perseverance will solve everything. It
won't solve Mavis for him. Why doesn't he accept her for
what she is, idle, selfish, good fun though she has the intelligence of a china doll, and is only a laughing, grasping, dense
imbecile with the mind of a kitten and just big sensuous
lusts? I suppose he can't accept her, our self-engrossed laughing female animal. He's sure that in some way she has what
he'd call 'depths,' though she is about as deep as a strawberry
soda. He can't take it in that the omniscient Jonathan Ferrier
could ever marry a woman with such a low but cunning intel-

lect. It hurts his pride. So he still digs away, buying her books of poems and taking her to gloomy plays in New York —Ibsen, for God's sake!—and symphonies and operas!"

"I never knew why she married him," said Marjorie. "He is not her kind."

Harald laughed at her amiably. "She got what she wanted! The Ferriers are more important than the Eatons and have more money. She is now the whole life of Hambledon society, and that's what women like Mavis just love, and she made a splash in Philadelphia and New York, and last year, I heard, she was quite the toast of London while our Jon was there lecturing on a new technique in brain surgery. Yes, she got what she wanted, all that he could give her, though she didn't want him, himself. She's made that plain enough."

"What do you mean?" asked Marjorie, but Harald seemed only to be annoyed with himself for having made that remark, and he faintly flushed. "No, he'll never get over her unless he really falls in love, and that I sincerely doubt. But because of her he hates all women and suspects them of everything mentioned in the capital sins, except old ladies and sick people and children he thinks are so damned innocent. Do you know what he is? A sentimentalist, a silly, yearning sentimentalist, and ever since he was a kid he was out to remake the world and its people in the image he had of them."

"He's so unhappy, so dreadfully unhappy," said Marjorie. "Poor Jon. I wish that horrible girl had never been born."

"Now, is that nice?" asked Harald genially. "Don't blame Mavis for just being Mavis and not having the capacity to be a grave and sedate and intellectual matron after she married Jon. The world's full of grim women. Why didn't he marry one? No, he has to marry Mavis, and then you blame her and not him! He could have had a hundred bluestockings to choose from—but he chose Mavis. More and more, I am compelled to believe that in many ways we are our own hell and our own devils. I pity Mavis far more than I pity Jon, but she at least knows how to make a fine thing out of a bad bargain. She never even knows when he is around, while he has a habit of haunting her. It's enough to make a girl call for her smelling salts. Phantom of the Opera: that's Jon."

Four months later Mavis was dead, and Jonathan Ferrier was arrested for her murder and the murder of his unborn child, and the house never heard Mavis' laughter again.

Now, on this hot July day Jonathan and his mother sat in

his room while he drank the last of the brandy eggnog and they both thought of the years of Mavis and her death, and bees struck the screens at the windows and the last of roses sent their fragrance through the open window.

Marjorie thought: Why can't a man recognize love when it comes to him? Why must he suspect love above all other things and shy from it, and doubt it and perhaps never even know what it is? He never really loved Mavis. He was only terribly infatuated and bewitched, and he still is. Sometimes I believe in spells.

Jon stood up. "Thanks," he said. "Now I've got to go to the hospitals. Young Bob will be moving into my office in a day or two. About time he takes the calls and treats patients directly. It'll be nice to see the waiting room full again." He stopped near the door, came back and kissed his mother on her forehead.

"We have to get used to everything," he said, and she knew that he knew that she was thinking of how bitter it would be to have a stranger in the offices she had built for him, and how helpless people were before pain and change.

CHAPTER FIFTEEN

When Jonathan Ferrier arrived at St. Hilda's, he found a harassed Robert Morgan, who glanced at him resentfully. Jonathan, to him, appeared too insouciant and careless, and Robert had no way of understanding that this was the pose Jonathan assumed when matters were too stressful for him or he was too exhausted. Jonathan said, "Well, how are you managing our mutual patients?" He did not wait for an answer, "After the Fourth, you know, you will take over my offices and outpatients entirely. I've persuaded old Miss Forster to be your assistant, and she will be there on the fifth. Yes, I'll be around, introducing you. The whole town knows the offices will be open on the specified day. By the way, I hope you won't entangle yourself in the hospital war going on in this town."

"Hospital war?" asked Robert.

"Between St. Hilda's and the Friends'. They are overcrowded now and desperately need new wings, but still they compete for patients! And denigrate each other. Don't get embroiled in it all. St. Hilda's wants the well-paying patients, though it has to take the other kind, too, and the Friends' would love the affluent to make up their deficits and charity list, and has a preponderance of the poor. They are constantly puffing up their staff and gilding them. Don't tell me that you haven't heard rumors!"

"Well," said Robert. He looked into Jonathan's darkly sparkling eye, lit with derision. "I hate controversies," said Robert. "I prefer to compromise."

"For God's sake, don't! Take a stand, once and for all. Tell them both to go to hell, no matter what they offer you for favoritism. Sometimes staffs forget that they are there for the sole purpose of aiding the sick, and not for position. If you compromise, appeasing both, they'll both hate you. Just tell 'em that you are more interested in medicine than rival staff brawls, and make it clear. That's what I did."

"I don't like animosities," said Robert with discomfort.

"All right. Tell me how you propose to handle this, then?"

They were sitting in the small sitting room on the fourth floor of St. Hilda's, and the hot July breeze did not cool them.

Robert thought, his flushed young face disturbed, his blue eyes distressed. "Well, I thought I'd say—I'd say—that it is too early for me to—"

"To do what?" Jonathan began to enjoy himself. He loosened his tight tie and crossed his legs.

"I thought I'd say that as I am a newcomer, I'd prefer to remain outside of any local controversies and just do my—well, my duty."

Jonathan contemplated him. "On the fence? Do you know what will happen to you if you keep putting them off? All at once you won't be welcome in either hospital. Where's your backbone?"

Robert became angry. "I have a very good one! I just don't like warring factions, that's all! They're out of place in hospitals."

"What an innocent you are! No matter where you go, you'll find warring factions. In any walk of life. You have to take a stand, and the sooner you take a stand here, the better for you. Let them see your guts. How many of the old fellas here do you think are devoted to medicine solely? They want position. Every damned son of a bitch in the world wants position, to crow over his neighbors. Your only hope, as it is the hope of any prudent doctor, is to tell the boys nicely that you are practicing medicine, not politics, and though they won't love you for it, they will at least tolerate you, if suspecting your true motives. Well, never mind. I hope you learn. How are our mutual patients today?"

"You know Miss Meadows died."

"Yes. That is good news. She's in the morgue, I suppose? I'll have to arrange funeral matters for her. What else?"

I thought he was devoted to her, thought Robert with fresh resentment, yet he speaks of her death as if it weren't of any importance at all. He sullenly—and Robert was rarely sullen —gave Jonathan a brief account of the many patients. "By the way, a friend of yours is on the third floor, private room. Jefferson Holliday."

Jonathan sat up. "Jeff Holliday? I didn't know he was even in town!"

His face became darkly bright. "When did he get back?"

"Two days ago. He said he tried to reach you but couldn't. Are you his doctor?"

"No. His mother is a fierce hysteric and likes old Louis Hedler, and he was always a boy who listened to Mama. We went to school together. He was one of the few friends I ever had. Old Jeff Holliday! Wonderful. Fine engineer, went to South America for the past six years, don't know why. But full of 'advancing our technical knowledge.' An undeclared hero. Or perhaps just in flight from Mama, who hates me as a 'bad influence.' What seems to be the trouble with him?"

Robert frowned. "Frankly, I'm puzzled. He has darkish coppery patches on his skin, face, backs of hands, trunk. Roundish. Low fever. Says he gets them with a fever. I didn't try to intrude," said Robert quickly. "But as he was asking for you, he was told that I—was taking your place. I went down to see him. Just as a possible friend, and to tell you.

But, as you say, Hedler is his doctor. I looked him over, anyway, just in curiosity."

"Good," said Jonathan. "A doctor who loses his curiosity is a dead doctor, even if he tries to continue his practice. Does he seem sick?"

"Well, not very. Just those reddish patches he gets when he has a fever. After the fever goes, the patches fade away. There's just one thing I don't understand. He showed me the sites of old patches—they are thickened and a little nodular but not painful. Now he has a fresh outbreak of patches and that low fever."

"How long has this been going on?"

"About a year. He forgot about the first attack and didn't make much of the second. Had no medical opinion in those South American countries. Thought his trouble was fungus. Was told in New York it was. Some fungus extant in hot damp countries. They gave him an ointment in New York, a fungicide. He was in New York for two weeks, consulting with his firm. When he arrived in Hambledon, he had a fresh —rash. Rash is all I can call it. I can't recall seeing anything before like this—defined, symmetrical patches, some as big as a quarter. Probably some semitropical disease."

"Is he in isolation?"

"No."

"Dear old Louis!" said Jonathan. "He wouldn't recognize a case of smallpox if he saw it. Not that I think this is smallpox. Let's go down and see Jeff." He stood up.

"His mother is with him," said Robert.

Jonathan studied the younger doctor with amusement. "I see you've encountered Mrs. Holliday."

"Yes." Robert paused. "She is putting sulphur compresses on him. She's quite a manager, isn't she?"

"Very rich, too. Big benefactress of St. Hilda's. Inherited a lot of money from her unfortunate husband. If she wanted boiled onion compresses here, the nurses would be running with hot onion stew and flannels, and old Louis would be beaming and saying, 'Yes, indeed, Elsie, yes, indeed, very efficacious.' Let's intrude."

"Should we?" asked Robert.

"We should indeed. At least, I will."

They went down to the third floor and to a large and lavish room. The patient, a man Jonathan's age, was sitting comfortably in a chair near the window, while his mother temporarily was desisting from the compresses and sitting opposite.

He was a handsome young man, with the broad and vigorous face of an outdoorsman, short and pugnacious of nose, generous of mouth, and lively of gray eye. His thick blond hair curled in damp ringlets over his big head. On seeing Jonathan, he shouted with pleasure. "Jon! You damned old hound, you! Couldn't get you, though I tried. Jon, it's good to see you again!" He held out his bronze hand to Jonathan and stood up. He was apparently bursting with health and vitality, and there was no illness apparent in him except for peculiar roundish and coppery patches on his cheeks and hands and throat, and his partially exposed chest.

The two young men embraced each other awkwardly, with blows on shoulder and arm, and obscenities. They shouted incoherently, in insulting terms, while the prim thin woman nearby, in her early fifties, averted her head and showed the tense white cheek of the born hysteric, and the trembling lower lip. Her hair was gray and untidy under a harsh black straw hat, and she wore the grim black clothing of one who will not defer to weather.

Jonathan, his arm about his exuberant friend, looked down at her. "How are you, Mrs. Holliday?" he asked.

She slowly and reluctantly turned her head to him and her cold light eyes studied him with contemptuous disfavor. "Very well, Doctor," she answered. Then she added, "Dr. Hedler is my son's physician and had him brought here last night. It's all nonsense, of course, but Dr. Hedler is so—conscientious. Unlike many other doctors I could name."

"Good," said Jonathan. Jefferson Holliday colored at the affront to his friend, but Jonathan squeezed his arm. "Probably nothing but one of those damned semitropical diseases, anyway."

"Disease?" Mrs. Holliday's voice became shrill and full of offense. "My son has no disease! What a thing to say." She agitatedly pulled at the gloves in her lap, black kid ones. "Nothing but a scruff. That's what I told Louis. I told him that, I kept telling him that—"

"No doubt," said Jonathan.

"Sulphur compresses, hot," said Mrs. Holliday. "Sulphur ointment." She looked up at her son. "I really think you should ask for discharge, Jefferson."

"I intend to." The young man beamed at Jonathan. "Sit down. Yes, I've met Dr. Morgan. He was kind enough to stop in to see me." He exuded buoyant well-being and immense cheerfulness. "I'm on six months' leave, Jon. You'd never guess! I'm going to be married."

"No!" said Jonathan. "What brings on that sad news?"

"Oh, now," said Jefferson, laughing. "The daughter of the head of my concern. You'd never guess. An anthropologist, by God! Mad about it. She was with me for some time down in South America. Those Inca ruins, you know. Studying the natives for signs of the old Incas. Thinks she has a clue. Lovely girl."

"I bet," said Jonathan, thinking of a hardy, striding woman in short skirts and boots, and with a loud harsh voice.

"You're wrong," said Jefferson. He reached to a nearby table—covered with vases of flowers—and took a small framed photograph from it, and held it out to Jonathan. Jonathan saw the picture of a gentle young girl with dark hair, a serious smiling face, soft lips and extraordinarily lovely wide eyes. Her white shirtwaist was open at the neck and showed a throat unusually delicate and slender, with a thin link of pearls about it. "Elizabeth Cochrane," said Jefferson with pride. "She has a quirk. She believes in reincarnation. She thinks she was an Inca princess once."

"That's a change," said Jonathan, studying the photograph. "Usually they think they were Cleopatra or at least Queen Elizabeth." The photograph impressed him. There was a vulnerable look to the girl, which uneasily reminded him of someone, but who that one was he could not immediately remember. "A nice girl," he said.

"Marvelous," said Jefferson, looking fondly at the photograph even when he had put it down. "After we are married, we'll give up all that exploring—at least after a year or so. My work is finished in South America. We've done as much as we can, but now it is up to the people, themselves. I haven't much hope. They lack American bustle and determination. What we value as enterprise they think is ridiculous."

"Sensible," said Jonathan. He was looking at the reddish patches on his friend's skin. "When did you get that affliction?"

"A year ago."

"Dr. Hedler is his doctor!" said Mrs. Holliday in a shrill voice and she moved spasmodically on her straight chair as if about to go into a fit. The hot room, in spite of the large opened windows, stank with the odor of sulphur ointment.

"Mama," said Jefferson.

"I don't care!" cried Mrs. Holliday. "I don't want him saying things—things—"

"Mama," said Jefferson.

"Never mind," said Jonathan. "I'm just curious. Mind if I look at it? Just academically, not as a physician."

Mrs. Holliday sprang to her feet like a wild young girl and plunged her thin black-clad body out of the room in a rush. "There she goes, after old Louis," said her son in a rueful tone. "Can she cause you trouble, Jon?"

"Not more than I already have," said Jonathan. "Bob, come over here. We'll look at this together."

The two doctors bent over the indulgently smiling patient and carefully examined the blotches. One of them was noticeably thickened, and there was a nodule in it. Jonathan pressed. Jefferson winced. "Hurt? How old is this patch?"

"It's a new one, in the place of the old, which disappeared."

Jonathan felt around the nodule and pressed the flesh. "Hurt?"

"No." The young man frowned. "In fact, I don't feel anything there."

Jonathan lifted the eyelids of Jefferson Holliday, stared at the membranes. He examined the nose and throat tissues. His normally darkish-pale face became sallow and tight. He shook his head. He glanced at Robert Morgan. "Well?" he asked.

"I can't diagnose it," said young Robert. "I never saw such a skin disease before. Did you?"

But Jonathan did not answer. A look of sickness settled about his mouth. Then he took out his pocketknife and gently and carefully scraped the surface of one patch, and noticed that the patient showed no signs of pain. He held out the blade to Robert. "Go to the laboratory, stain this, and look at it," he said. To Robert's surprise his hand was trembling a little. "The stain for tubercles."

"My God!" exclaimed Jefferson with great alarm, and pulled away to look up at the face of his friend. "You don't think I have tuberculosis of the skin, do you, for God's sake! Listen, I don't have a cough. I'm as hearty as a horse."

"No," said Jonathan, "I don't think you have tuberculosis of the skin." I wish, he thought, that was all you had, Jeff, I wish to God.

"Or cancer?" asked the patient, trying to smile.

"No. What gave you that idea?" Jonathan sat down and

stared at the floor. "Under what conditions did you live in South America?"

"Conditions? Oh, sometimes crude and primitive. Most of the time. We had a camp, where Elizabeth and the others stayed except for occasional explorations. But I had to go often into the interiors, among the natives. Sometimes I slept in their huts, during the rains. Sometimes in the jungles with what cover we could cut. Machetes. Why? Do you think I have a parasite of some kind?"

"Maybe," said Jonathan. "Did you see anyone else with this kind of skin disfigurement?"

The young man frowned. "Yes, I did. Two or three. A child. A woman. An old man. In fact, I stayed in their hut during the rains for several weeks, before we could get out and back to the river. Why? Do I have something contagious?"

"Perhaps," said Jonathan. "Mildly so."

"My God! Elizabeth!" said Jefferson. His bronzed face paled. "Do I have something I could give her?"

"I wouldn't worry about that. You aren't married to her yet."

Now the young man darkly colored. "If you think I've picked up a venereal disease, it's possible, between you and me. My God, I can't stand the idea! The woman in the hut —she was young and wasn't blotched then. After all, Jon, I'm a man—What's that arsenic thing they are using?"

"You're thinking of syphilis," said Jonathan. "I don't think you have it, though it's always been endemic among Indians. That's where the white man picked it up in the first place. Let's not worry until we know."

"What did you do to me with your pocketknife?"

"Took a sample of your skin cells."

A thick hard silence fell in the room. Jefferson was pale again. He kept glancing with dubious fear at his friend. He remembered the old stories of Jonathan Ferrier. A fanatic. Always looking for the worst. Everything complicated, nothing simple. One of those new scientists, finding trouble in the mildest things.

"Microscope?" said the young engineer, trying to control a strange tremor along his nerves. "Will it show anything?"

"I hope not," said Jonathan. He looked at the photograph of Elizabeth Cochrane again, and was again sickened.

The broad door swung open and Mrs. Holliday returned with white and vindictive triumph, bursting into the room before Louis Hedler. "Now!" she exclaimed. "We'll stop all this nonsense!" She breathed loudly and victoriously and went to her son and put her hand on his shoulder. Dr. Hedler smiled widely and mechanically at Jonathan and said, "We're happy about Hortense, Jon. We owe it all to you, of course, and the skilled care she is getting. I talked with old Humphrey this morning— Well, never mind. We're all grateful, Jon, believe me. Never mind. What is this Elsie is telling me? Usurping my patient?" He continued to glow indulgently.

"No," said Jonathan. "No usurpation. Just curiosity."

"Curiosity!" said Mrs. Holliday. "Asking my son questions! It's unethical!"

Dr. Hedler put his hand tenderly on her visibly shaking arm. "Now, Elsie. Let's be calm. John is a very talented— yes, indeed—talented, physician, and Jeff is his friend, after all, and doctors do get curious, you know. Nothing wrong, my dear, nothing wrong. In fact, I'm pleased. Always like a new opinion." He glowed upon Jonathan, though his big, froglike brown eyes showed suspicion and caution. "Well, what do you think? Nothing serious, of course. One of those nasty semitropical fungi. Isn't it? Some of the patches are already fading. What do you think?"

"I've sent a scraping down to the laboratory," said Jonathan.

"Scraping? Why? Oh, to show the fungi?" Dr. Hedler was relieved. He turned to Mrs. Holliday. "Nothing more serious than fungus, my dear. Like, er, like the blisters one gets on one's feet. Nothing to worry about."

But Mrs. Holliday was staring with large angry malice at Jonathan. "Look at him! He doesn't agree with you, Louis! He's thinking up something terrible about my boy! Something terrible. Stop him, Louis!"

"Now, Elsie. How can I stop anyone from thinking?" Dr. Hedler's voice was like a sweet ointment. "Thinking doesn't make a thing so, you know."

"I believe it does!" said the hysterical woman with passionate emphasis. "You can do terrible things with your thoughts! I've heard you can even bring death—"

"Let's not be superstitious," said Louis. "Here, my dear, sit down. Do stop trembling."

But Mrs. Holliday pulled her chair as far as possible from Jonathan and then reached out and took her son's hand, her own cold and sweating. She said to her son, peering desperately into his face, "You mustn't listen, my darling, you mustn't listen! It's a lie! You know what this man is, you know what he is!"

"Mama," said Jefferson.

Her voice rose almost to a scream. "Jefferson! Tell him to go away! Jefferson, you mustn't listen! You must just laugh at him!" She laughed suddenly and fiercely and looked at Jonathan with ferocious hatred and mad scorn. She tossed her head at him, and bit her lip, and laughed again. "Louis! Make him go away!"

Louis Hedler was deeply disturbed. He could not upbraid Jonathan, remembering how he had saved the life of little Hortense Nolan only the day before, yet he could not offend Mrs. Holliday, to whom the hospital owed so much. He met Jonathan's eye and saw his hard sympathy, and his plump cheek colored. He said, "In a moment, Elsie. We'll just get the laboratory reports." He said to Jonathan, "Can you tell me what you were looking for, Jon?"

"I'm not really looking for anything specifically," said Jonathan. "I'm just trying to eliminate—something."

Dr. Hedler was relieved. "What?"

"Let's wait."

"I was worrying about isolation," said the older doctor tentatively.

"And the newspapermen coming any minute!" said Mrs. Holliday, with fierce pride. "To interview Jefferson! All the wonderful things he's done in South America!"

Jonathan said, "They can't come in here until we know."

"Know what?" asked Dr. Hedler. He was newly dismayed. "You suspect contagion?"

"I'm not contagious!" said Jefferson, aghast. "Why, I've been with Elizabeth and her father for two weeks in New York, and months in South America! Contagion! My God, Jon, you don't mean—an infection?"

"I don't know," said Jonathan. "Here's Bob Morgan. Now we'll know for sure."

But Robert did not enter the room. He merely stood on the threshold and all the color was gone from his fresh young face. He mutely gestured to Jonathan, and Jonathan rose easily and said, "Want to go outside with us, Louis?"

"Why? Why?" screamed Mrs. Holliday. She jumped up. "I won't be cast aside! I want to hear! No one can stop me!"

Jonathan did not look at her. He went to the door, looked back. Louis was taking the trembling woman's arm and bringing her forward. "Of course, Elsie, you must hear—"

"What about me?" asked Jefferson with irony. "I'm only the one most concerned. But don't mind me, lads, don't mind me."

Jonathan stopped on the threshold. Then he slowly went to the middle of the room. He looked down at his friend. "You're right, Jeff. You should know, above everyone else. I'm not the kind to keep news of any kind from a patient. Come in, Bob, come in. Let's have a consultation." Robert Morgan implored him with his eyes, but Jonathan obstinately looked away from him. "We have a grown and intelligent man, here, Bob," he said. "A brave man. He should know, no matter what it is."

"Indeed," said Louis, lovingly forcing Mrs. Holliday back into her chair.

Robert Morgan came into the room, and his look was desperate. He spoke only to Jonathan. "There's no doubt," he said. "I've only seen slides before, but I'm sure." He paused and again silently implored Jonathan. "Hansen's disease."

Jonathan spread his legs and took a deep breath. His face was taut and bony. Mrs. Holliday looked malevolently from one face to the other and took her son's hand. "What! What!" she cried. "What is that? Hansen's disease. What is it?" Her glance was again full of hatred, directed at Jonathan. "What does this stupid, wicked man mean?"

Louis was bewildered. "Hansen's disease," he said slowly. He nodded his head. "I'm afraid— Jon, you are sure?"

"Bob is. I don't think the laboratory should know— Nor anyone else. Do you understand me, Louis?"

The older man was baffled. He turned to Robert. "Hansen's disease. I'm afraid I haven't encountered it before," he said. "Something new, tropical?"

"Something as old as hell," said Jonathan. "Louis, do you want me to give you the old and ancient name of it?"

"No need at all!" said Louis with haste. "One understands. We can't disturb patients, you know, Jon." He saw Jonathan's face.

"What I'd like to know," said Jefferson, "is just what is Hansen's disease."

Jonathan said to Louis Hedler, "I wish you'd persuade Mrs. Holliday to go into the waiting room and have a cup of tea or something."

"No!" shrieked Mrs. Holliday. "You are not, I say you are not going to lie about my boy, to kill him with fear, to lie, to lie, to lie! You bad, wicked man! You—you murderer! Everyone knows what you did to your poor wife, everyone knows what you did to that poor little child, Martha Best, everyone knows—"

"Mama," said Jefferson.

She turned on him with white fire, then stood up and took him in her arms and pressed his face into her meager breast. Over that tawny head she glared at Jonathan and actually spat at him. "Go away, murderer!" she cried. "Go away!"

"Elsie!" said Louis Hedler.

"Oh, I'll take him home, I'll take him home!" groaned the woman. "Away from murderers! Louis, you'll never see another penny of mine, not another penny!"

Then Jonathan went to her and took her away from her son, loosening her arms with controlled but steady violence. "Get away from him," he said. "Don't touch him." He pushed her off, and she staggered a little, and Louis caught her arm.

"I don't understand," said Louis, jolted. "It can't be that contagious, Jon. Elsie, do stop screaming. Please, my dear. Jon, it can't be that contagious."

Jonathan looked at him steadily in bitter silence. Then he said, "Louis, tell me. Do you know what Hansen's disease is?"

"Certainly."

"You lie," said Jonathan. "I should have known. Take that woman out and put her somewhere, then come back."

He turned to Jefferson, whose face had become strangely gaunt and still. He put his hand on his friend's shoulder. "Jeff." he said. "Tell your mother to leave, to let you alone for five minutes. Please, Jeff."

But Mrs. Holliday had pulled herself away from Louis and was standing stiffly and hysterically in the center of the room, her hands clenched in fists at her side, her face thrust forward. "No one is going to put me out of this room so you can lie and lie, and kill my boy with fear! I am his mother, I'm going to protect him from murderers!"

Jonathan had been through too much the night before, and too much this morning, and the woman's repetitious and even gloating epithet had reached him finally. He said to her with conscious cruelty, "Very well. I'll tell you the ancient name of what your son has, Mrs. Holliday. He has—leprosy."

"Oh, my God," whispered young Robert, and turned aside. But no one heard him.

Louis Hedler goggled at Jonathan, and his whole body and

face became limp and flaccid. "Leprosy," he said in a croaking voice.

"Leprosy?" said Jefferson Holliday. He bent his head and said nothing more.

Then a most terrible scream came from Mrs. Holliday. She flew at Jonathan. Her clawed fingers reached for his eyes, his ears, his nose, his mouth. One of them sank into his lip and tore. She breathed and gasped frenziedly. She fought with him as he tried to hold her, and to the dazed horror of old Louis Hedler she shouted obscenities he had never heard before. She struggled with Jonathan and panted. Finally he flung her from him and Robert caught her. But she was beside herself, mad, frightful as a holocaust. At last Robert dragged her from the room and was gone a little while.

"God help us," said Louis Hedler, and watched Jonathan wipe the blood from his mouth. "Oh, Jon. It can't be true. Pardon me. I do feel a little ill. I think I'll sit down. Jefferson. We can't be sure—" He started to reach out to take the stricken young man's hand, then shrank and pushed his chair away.

"I'm sure," said Jefferson, and his voice was very quiet. "I should have known. I saw the child— It isn't very rare down there. Not down there. Not as bad as in Africa and Asia, but bad enough."

He looked at the photograph on the table, then took it in his hands. He began to cry. "Elizabeth," he said. "Dear Elizabeth." Then he replaced the photograph and looked at Jonathan.

"What do we do now?" he asked. "But, first tell me. Is there any danger to Elizabeth?"

"No," said Jonathan. "It takes prolonged association, intimate association. Jeff, you have the nodular type. Sometimes it takes a rapid course, sometimes it goes on—for years. The sooner you are treated for it, the better."

He could not look at his brave friend, but he had heard, for the first time, the hoarseness in his voice and he knew that the disease had invaded his throat. He said, "I've seen two cases, in New York. It isn't as rare as we like to think, in America. But the old terror of it persists, and perhaps rightly so. Jeff, in Louisiana there is a sanitarium. You must go there at once. There's an old Indian drug they are using now— chaulmoogra oil. It often arrests the disease. There's no known cure yet, Jeff, but they may find it. You must go quietly. Some way, you'll have to keep your mother quiet.

I'm sorry. I lost my head and told her, and that's inexcusable. But there were too many things—I'm sorry. You'll have to silence her one way or another. You know how people are. There'd be a panic in this town, and we can't have it, and hysteria in this hospital. People are ignorant. They don't know that Hansen's disease is only very mildly contagious, and only after prolonged contact. We can't have panic. Did you ever see a mob?"

"Yes. Often." Jefferson spoke indifferently, too overcome by his personal tragedy to feel deeply as yet. "I know what mobs are. I saw them in various parts of South America." He squeezed his eyelids together. "What shall I tell Elizabeth?"

"You could tell her the truth. I hear that people can go to Louisiana to be near those who have—what you have—even to see them and visit them. If she cares enough about you."

"And we can never be married."

Jon hesitated. "I've heard of arrested cases. Not many, but a few."

Jefferson lifted his head. "No, I can't do that to Elizabeth. I can't ask her to waste her life with me. No. I'll write to her —I'll tell her anything but the truth. I hope she hates me. It'll help her."

Jonathan went to him then and put his arm about his friend's shoulders and bent over him. Jefferson laughed a little. "What should I have? A bell? A 'Unclean, unclean!' Jon, aren't you afraid?"

"I'm afraid of a lot of things," said Jonathan. "I'm just beginning to find out. But this isn't one of them."

"I'm afraid, too," said Jefferson. "I'm afraid of this. A leper. Isn't that enough to make you laugh?"

Louis Hedler had recovered his wits. He said, "Jon, it's not that I'm disputing, but shouldn't we have a consultation, with Philadelphia or New York doctors? It isn't possible to believe —a leper. A leper! What is to become of this hospital when it is known?"

"Have as many consultations as you wish," said Jonathan. He was surprised by the other man's docility. "I'm afraid there'll just be confirmations. But let me write to a friend in New York, an expert on tropical diseases, though God knows this disease is more widespread in America than we dare admit. Then we can arrange for Jeff to go to Louisiana, where they are treating scores of these cases. Don't let anyone in this hospital know, Louis, or tell anyone in this town, not even doctors. Just imagine the newspapers!"

"Where shall I go? What shall I do?" asked Jefferson, totally desolate.

"You can go home at once," said Jonathan. "Don't be afraid, Jeff, don't be afraid. You can't infect anyone. Wait for us to tell you when to leave. Keep your mother quiet, Jeff. We have a whole town, a whole state, to think about."

"I've never been able to keep her quiet yet," said Jefferson.

He lifted his hand and Jonathan took it and held it, and Jefferson began to cry again, deep dry sobs of complete anguish. He stammered, "Will I have much pain?"

"Probably," said Jonathan. "Nerve pain. For a while. I won't lie to you, Jeff."

"And I'll be isolated from everyone forever," said his friend.

"I tell you, Jeff, they are doing some wonderful things down there. They've often stopped the infective process, arrested the disease, so that many are outpatients and are living with husbands and wives around the institution, and even having children. The causative agent has been isolated, and that's half the problem, and it's just a matter of time until we have the cure. At least, I'm sure they can arrest the disease in you. It hasn't gone far enough to have caused you much permanent damage.

"There are all kinds of people there, men, women, children, teachers, doctors, former missionaries, people like yourself, from every class and walk in life. I've heard about it. They say it is the most hopeful place in the world. You can do a great deal there for the others, Jeff."

But Jefferson's head had fallen on his chest in incredulous despair.

"Let me write to Elizabeth," said Jonathan. "She's an intelligent girl, you say. She has the right to make a choice for herself. Let her decide if she will go down there with you and stay until they have arrested it. It's her life, as well as yours."

"I don't have the right to ask her to make the decision," said Jefferson, but he lifted his head a little. "Imagine isolating herself down there, with a—a leper, for God's sake!"

"She still has the right to decide. Give me the address, and I'll send her a telegram at once. That's better than a letter."

He added, "It isn't the end of the world for you, Jeff. Nothing ever is until they shovel the dirt on you." He thought, You're a fine one to talk!

"A telegram to Elizabeth?" said Jefferson, and for the first time there was a little hope in his voice. "Jon, I'd appreciate that, I honestly would. But what if she doesn't come, or can't stand the thought of me any longer?"

"Then, you've lost nothing but a trivial woman, and that isn't a loss at all."

He suddenly saw Mavis' face clearly but now the internal vision did not bring its usual spasm of anguish. It brought nothing at all but self-disgust and the blank realization that she had, indeed, been totally worthless and had not deserved all the pain he had suffered. How could he ever have desired her? There were all the years he had known her before their marriage, and he had refused to look at her realistically for a single moment, and then when he had finally known, he had almost lost his mind. That howling laughter, since childhood! She had not concealed it from him or had denied him that she was anything but what she was. He had been the fantasy maker, not Mavis.

He felt that something crippling had fallen from him and that something was beginning to stretch in him a little. The effect was both exhilarating and painful, but he was not sure that he liked this new dimension he had just glimpsed.

"What did you say Jeff?" he asked.

"You've given me a little hope, Jon. I immediately thought of suicide."

"Don't be alarmed at that. No intelligent man never thought of it. The world isn't a sweet place. We know that. It's a damned, ugly, painful, wretched place of existence, but we must come to terms with it somehow." Something I never did myself, he thought with ruefulness. "I saw a young man this morning who had lost his faith, all he had in the world, and wanted to die of it. His affliction is worse than yours, Jeff, for now he must find out how to live without the only thing which mattered to him, or refind it."

"You believe I can refind—something?"

"I think we all can," said Jonathan, and felt surprise.

Dr. Hedler had been listening to this with considerable surprise of his own and he stared at Jonathan, who had forgotten he was present. Well, well, thought the old doctor, this boy isn't as harsh and brutal as we have thought, and I, for one, am ashamed that I had thought it myself.

Before Jonathan left, he said to him in the hall outside, "Jon, don't leave Hambledon. I know, I know! I've been as bad as everyone else, dear boy, as bad as everyone else, if not worse. Forgive me, if you can."

"Good old Louis," said Jonathan, and shook his head and went away.

That evening he sent a telegram to Elizabeth Cochrane, a long and detailed telegram of several pages. He had little hope. Women were not particularly intelligent and though they were emotional, their emotions were superficial, and they were instinctively selfish, and their ability to love was very shallow. At midnight he received Elizabeth's reply:

COMING TO HAMBLEDON AT ONCE TO JOIN JEFF AND WILL GO WITH HIM TO LOUISIANA STOP HAVE SENT HIM SIMILAR TELE-GRAM STOP WE MUST WORK TOGETHER TO GIVE HIM A REASON FOR LIVING STOP THANK YOU DOCTOR AND GOD BLESS YOU

Well, thought Jonathan. This must be a rare creature, in-deed. A rare and unusual creature. How many women would abandon a young and happy life to go into isolation and mis-ery and despair with a man? How many women can love that way?

When he saw Jefferson at his house the next day, the young man was almost jubilant. "I've gained something, Jon. I used to look at Elizabeth and wonder what I had to offer a girl like that! I must be something very special, don't you think?" and he laughed.

"I think we all are," said Jonathan. "In a way," he supple-mented in reluctant qualification.

CHAPTER SIXTEEN

"You've said that so often before, every Fourth," said Marjorie, as she worked in the kitchen with the cook, prepar-ing the picnic baskets. " 'Tribal rites. Sentimentalism. Chau-

vinism.' I know them all. Perhaps you are right. But there will be children there, and young people. They have a right to learn to be proud of their country. What was it Sir Walter Scott said?

> " 'Breathes there a man with soul so dead,
> Who never to himself hath said,
> This is my own, my native land?' "

"Mother," said Jonathan, "do you think the speeches of the mayor and that damned crafty Campion will inspire the youthful mind and enlarge it and make it proud? As for Campion, he never speaks anything but lies and banalities. I don't know why I'm going with you—under my present circumstances. Just a farewell appearance."

The blue and white kitchen, big and airy though hot even so early in the day, was full of odors of frying chicken, potato salad, fresh bread, baking cakes and coffee. Jonathan picked up a small chicken leg and began to gnaw on it. This was so unlike the fastidious and formal Jonathan that Marjorie glanced up with pleased surprise. Something had changed Jonathan, relaxed him a little. He was actually licking his fingers like a small boy. He had never done this before in her memory. He had never seemed to care for food at all and usually ate it with impatience as a necessary gesture to living.

"I'm just thinking of what Thomas Macaulay said," Jonathan remarked, idly considering the chicken again as piles of it lay on white napkins. "About America. 'Your Constitution is all sail and no anchor. Either some Caesar or Napoleon will seize the reins of government with a strong hand, or your republic will be laid waste by internal barbarians in the twentieth century as the Roman Empire was in the fifth.' He said, and wrote, that in 1857, forty-four years ago. It's now the twentieth century. I think he was an excellent prophet. Something's knocking on the gates of America and it isn't nice. Or hopeful."

"Macaulay was a pessimist," said Marjorie, brushing aside a wisp of her dark fine hair with the back of her hand. "Don't you remember what Abraham Lincoln said even earlier: 'Shall we expect a transatlantic military giant to step the ocean and crush us at a blow? Never! All the armies of Europe, Asia and Africa combined with all the treasures of the earth (our own excepted) in their military chest, with a Bonaparte for a commander, could not by force take a drink from the Ohio or make a track on the Blue Ridge in a trial of a thousand years.' "

"You forgot something," said Jonathan, finally taking a wing of chicken. "Lincoln added something else to that: 'We shall be betrayed from within.' The new Vandals. The same mobs which stormed the Tuileries and tore up the stones of the streets of Paris. The same people who in Germany supported Bismarck and the Socialism he picked up from Karl Marx. Now, there was a nasty tyrant for you: Bismarck! Almost as bad as the French Communist, Robespierre, during the French Commune in 1795."

"We have a sensible man in President McKinley," said Marjorie. "Jon, if you really want some of that potato salad, sit down and have it on a plate. Don't fish out the egg with your fingers. It isn't sanitary." But she was delighted.

"My hands are always sanitary," said Jonathan. "President McKinley. Yes, a sensible man. But that riotous Vice-President of his: Roosevelt! Dear old rambunctious Teddy! What a calamity it would be for America if he were ever President! It takes a rich and pampered man to exalt something he calls the masses, probably because he knows nothing about them. The people are much more realistic. I differentiate people from mobs, of course, and the American people, in the majority, are pretty sound. Suppose I skip the celebrations today?"

"And let me go alone? Harald isn't here, and he never came with us anyway on the Fourth. Do you want people to pity me, especially that odious Mrs. Morgan who is so smug about her boy? And the Kitcheners, and their nice little daughter Maude?"

"And Jenny," said Jonathan.

Marjorie bent her head over the bread she was cutting, and she sighed. Dear, stupid Jon, she thought. She said, "Yes, Jenny. She has given the domestics the day off, and she is all alone, and she was pathetically grateful for my invitation. She has so little pleasure, poor child. That is because she has a grim streak in her. She went to school in Hambledon, but knows no one. Her whole life was a kind of dedication to her father, who never lived on his island after all. She can't get over the sorrow of it—and Harald to her, as you know, seems the interloper who has no right on the island at all."

"Not the interloper," said Jonathan. "Mother, don't be naïve."

Now his face was ugly again, and he left the kitchen.

He went to his offices and walked through the hot closed rooms and then stood staring at his files. He no longer hated his dead wife. She had receded into unreality for him. But he hated those who were making it impossible for him to stay in his city, who were driving him out with uttered violence, lies, innuendoes, distrust and malice and hostility. He had asked nothing but to serve them and they had repudiated him. He found a bottle of whiskey in a drawer and drank deeply of it, not using a glass.

He went to a window which had a distant view of the river and he could see a portion of that ridiculous island, Heart's Ease, its tall trees glittering with greenish silver in the sun. Then he had a strange thought. Why was it ridiculous, a dead man's dream of beauty? Innocent dreams of joy and loveliness should not be despised. The "castle" was an anachronism, but then most blameless dreams were, for they were tranquil and full of peace and beatitude. Peter Heger had created an Eden, with love and tenderness for his wife and his daughter, and if it were a little grotesque, it had had the potentialities of an Eden. Who should deride a man's yearning dream and vision of beauty, no matter how absurd it seemed to others? And what was the true measure of beauty or absurdity?

It was possible that Peter Heger could not endure his contemporary world and had tried to make a harbor for himself where he would not have to face it. Was it possible that most men had to make such harbors for themselves so that they could continue to live?

I have no harbor. I never had, thought Jonathan Ferrier. He looked at the bottle in his hand and then put it down. He stared at the bottle. Only this, since I was twenty-one. Who was the greater fool, Pete Heger, or me? I couldn't endure my world, either. Pete at least tried to make a refuge for himself. I never tried. Who was the silly coward?

He looked at the island again and saw the face of Jenny Heger, the "Lilith" of Hambledon. He saw her face and her great blue eyes and the shining forehead and the black hair and the wild gestures and awkward movements. He felt a savage and angry fury and a sharp nudge of pain. She and his brother had desecrated a man's innocent dream, had made it a name for laughter in the town. The pain increased, became almost unbearable, and he took up the whiskey again and drank. His telephone rang.

"Dear," said Marjorie, "it's time to help me load the baskets in the carriage."

It was so banal, in the midst of his misery, that he laughed.

"You are looking very handsome," said Marjorie as Jonathan helped her to place the picnic baskets in the surrey. "I like that blue and white striped blazer. But why do you men wear such stiff high collars, especially on a hot day like this? And stiff white cuffs and studs and collar buttons, and that remnant of little thin tie?"

"Why do you women wear stiff corsets of whalebone and dresses dragging in the dust? Fashion, woman, fashion." He took off his straw sailor and wiped his forehead. He eyed his mother approvingly, and she was startled. She could not remember that he had ever admired her before. She wore a slender lawn dress printed in gray and rose and a broad straw hat with soft gray flowers and green leaves bending down its supple circle. Her aristocratic face, so like Jonathan's, was flushed with heat and her hazel eyes were gentle and contemplative as she smiled at him. But there were mauve circles under her eyes and her lips were pale and a little drawn. Jonathan frowned. "Are you taking that digitalis I gave you?" he asked.

"When I remember. Please don't fuss, dear. Forget you are a doctor, just for today. What a lovely day it is. It usually is, for the Fourth."

"Unfortunately. It encourages the liars and the demagogues to come out." But he still studied her. He seemed to see her in an unusually clarified light, and for some reason his uneasiness increased. She was tucking white napkins carefully about a basket and he saw the slight tremor of her hands. "We're not leaving here until you go back into the house and take your digitalis," he said. He laid his hand on the silken shoulder of his favorite mare and she turned her head and nuzzled his fingers.

"Very well," said Marjorie. "But I am feeling well, truly." She returned to the house, walking slowly up the walk, and her thin figure appeared too weary to him. He frowned again. He had felt for his mother the usual concern of a physician, but now that concern was intensified. He lit a cigarette and stared up and down the wide and quiet street, not seeing it, nor the deep blue shadow of the trees, nor the glow in the sky. The roofs of the houses were still in the sun, and windows glistened, and there was a scent of wetted dust in the silent air, and new-cut grass, and leaves glittered where they caught the light.

He became aware of the distant crackle of firecrackers and the odor of punk in the hot breeze, and an occasional childish shout. He heard the noisy explosion of giant crackers, and the laughter of women in a garden. Here and there he could see the flutter of brave flags on lawns, red and white and blue. It was very peaceful, very shining, very happy, as a nation celebrated its Day of Independence. It reminded Jonathan of the days of his own boyhood, when he sat on this very curb or walked along this very flagged walk, lighting firecrackers and holding smoldering punk and seeing the flags unfurled to the sun. He could even see today, his brother Harald walking carefully behind him and wincing at the noise he evoked. Harald preferred sparklers at sunset and watching the fireworks in the town park. He would hold his ears when Jonathan lighted a giant cracker. "You can be blinded that way," he would protest when Jonathan held the cracker a little too long and the fuse almost spluttered to its end. Then he would shrink at the explosion and start up on the lawn, and Jonathan would laugh.

He always loved safety, thought Jonathan with the old disgust. And pleasantness and nice little voices and amiability and jokes and laughing. Nothing contentious for our Childe, nothing controversial, nothing dangerous. Just easiness, acceptance. Was he, is he, a coward? It's a strange thing: People seem to love cowards and hate bravery or daring. They can be brave enough with fife and drum and flags and celebrations and patriotic songs, and they can even be brave enough for war. But moral courage is something else, indeed, and principles. The men who were willing to die for their God are no longer being born, and Tom Paine and Erasmus and Savonarola wouldn't even be permitted to speak today, nor would the writers of the *Federalist Papers*, nor old Tom Jefferson. "Governments are invariably the enemies of their people," Cicero had said, and Jefferson had echoed him. No one remembered that any longer, certainly not the sort of people who loved cowards.

"Why are you glaring?" asked Marjorie at his elbow.

"Was I?" He helped her into the surrey and she sank on the seat with a sigh. "I was just thinking that Americans haven't any guts now. They are beginning to clamor for legislation for 'reforms' these days, when the reforms should begin in themselves."

"A new world brings new problems and demands new solutions," said Marjorie. "Isn't that what Mr. Roosevelt is always saying?"

"Governments have said that ever since the beginning of history," said Jonathan, taking up the reins. "It's the first step to tyranny. The old problems never change because human nature is not changeable."

"Except through religion," said Marjorie. Jonathan snorted. He held the reins tightly as he drove the mare down the street, for one had to be watchful of mischievous children who might throw a firecracker in the path of a nervous horse. Marjorie was waving to an occasional friend on the walk, and then between the houses they could see the glitter of the river and the green and blue flanks of the mountains.

"So peaceful, so tranquil," said Marjorie. "What a lot we have to be thankful for these days! No more wars, just plenty and hope and peace and industry. We are a blessed nation."

Jonathan snorted again. "I wouldn't count on its continuance," he said. "We are beginning to flex our muscles, like the old Roman Republic. We are no different from the old boys."

But Marjorie was smiling at the sunlit quiet, which was broken only by the short explosions of the fireworks and the warm voice of the trees in the hot wind. "We are so prosperous now," she said. "The Grover Cleveland depression is over. People are so hopeful, so enthusiastic, over this new century."

"You sound like the Marzipan Pear," said Jonathan, and turned the horse down the street leading to the square. They could already see the high flags rippling against the sky and could hear the distant hum of the crowd and there was the long booming of a cannon on the lawn of the city hall. This marked the beginning of the yearly festivities. The air was permeated with the smell of powder and a great deal of punk smoke lifted in the breeze, creating a bright little fog. Now the German Brass Band struck up a martial song, a Sousa march, and there was a prolonged cheering.

Jonathan tied up the horse near a water trough, and in the shade. The mare snorted anxiously. She was answered by other horses tethered up and down the street. Jonathan patted her again, spoke to her quietly and gave her a cube of sugar. She rolled her eyes at him apprehensively. A policeman strolled up. "I'll be watching them all, Doctor," he said,

touching his cap to Marjorie. "No firecrackers on this street."
He laughed. "Lots of manure, though."

Jonathan helped his mother down and again glanced at her
face. It was no longer flushed. She looked increasingly tired.
He gathered up the two big baskets and permitted her to
carry two smaller ones. They walked along the street toward
the square. The houses, on their long silent lawns, were shuttered against the sun on the upper floors, and the big porches
were empty. Chinese wind-crystals made a frail music, heard
even above the hubbub in the square, their tinkling nostalgic and thin. It made Jonathan think of the silent and
sun-filled Sundays of the summers of his boyhood, when
everything appeared to be suspended in clear light and lonely
shadow and there was no sound at all but that delicate and
vagrant chiming, and only an occasional clopping of a horse
on cobblestones. How endless those Sundays had seemed!
From dawn to twilight—they were long days, hushed and
still. Were they peaceful? He could not remember that he had
ever truly felt peace, even as a child, but only agitation and
as strong if nebulous longing. High Mass, with his father, had
begun that restlessness even during the scent of incense and
the solemn chanting and the lost sound of bells. Returning
home, there had been the vast hot dinners in the big dining
room with the shades half drawn against the sun, and then
his parents had napped—and the loneliness had begun and
the more acute restlessness. No children ran in the streets,
playing. The birds spoke sleepily in the hot and dusty trees,
and the Chinese wind-crystals chimed and the sun, striking
here and there through branches, had been like fire on the
walks and the stones. Endless hours, unbroken hours. To
please his father he read only religious books on Sundays,
and little homilies, and had stared at the pastel pictures that
alleviated "pious writings," and he had been bored to death,
and the disquiet had begun to feel like actual pain.

What had he wanted? He tried to remember when there
was nothing to remember but that keen yearning. What did he
want now? Nothing. Nothing.

"Jon!" said a voice behind them, and Jonathan started and
he turned with his mother. Father McNulty, plump and radiant, was at their heels, golden eyes glowing, and young face
shining with sweat. He, too, carried a small basket with a
blue-checked napkin covering it. He beamed at them. "It was
very kind of you to invite me, Mrs. Ferrier," he said, shaking
her hand. His shabby habit had a greenish tint. Then he

laughed joyously at Jonathan. "I have my own horse and buggy now!" he cried. "Senator Campion insisted. Five hundred dollars! I have only two hundred more to pay. The Senator is really very generous. He is paying the livery bills."

"How nice," said Marjorie.

"Dee-lightful, as Teddy would say," said Jonathan. "Why don't you scrounge the other two hundred from your rich parishioners?"

Marjorie said with haste, "How kind of the Senator. Isn't it a lovely day?"

"Marvelous," said the young priest, wiping the wet forehead under the black hat. "I haven't very much here, Mrs. Ferrier. My aunt thanks you for the invitation, but she has one of her headaches. Unfortunate. But she baked a very nice chocolate cake."

"I love chocolate cake," said Marjorie. "It will be delicious with the iced tea." She looked at him fondly. He was such a nice young man, so innocent, so kind. She hoped the Kitcheners would not snub him, nor that frightful Mrs. Morgan. There were such unkind things in the press these days about the "Roman Menace." That is, in what Jon called "the yellow press." Only two weeks ago three newly arrived Irish laboring families had had the windows of their little shacks broken, here in Hambledon, and filthy things scrawled on their sidewalks. No one had protested except Jonathan, in an angry letter to the local newspaper, which had not increased his popularity.

Father McNulty ambled along with them, talking with filial deference to Marjorie. "I like these celebrations," he said. "Small cities are much warmer than larger ones, and more personal."

"That they are," said Jonathan. He could smell the sweet fragrance of chocolate.

"Now, dear," said Marjorie.

"So much kinder and more brotherly," said Jonathan. "So much more loving."

Marjorie was startled to see the strangely keen and compassionate glance the young priest gave Jonathan, for it was not young and not innocent. Then it faded into sadness. They were all silent, their footsteps echoing thinly.

The square opened before them, its lawns spread with crowded picnic tables, and the whole area alive with shouting and running children. It was far hotter here in spite of the thick trees and the open space in the center, with its bronze

statue of General Sherman flanked with old cannon. The City
Hall, the pride of Hambledon, stood far back on its green
rise of grass, its white Grecian pillars blazing in the sun, its
flags flying, and its broad steps, filled with chairs, waiting for
the dignitaries. There was a lectern, waiting but empty. Everywhere flags spread to the burning blue sky, and the German Brass Band, in its round wooden stand near General
Sherman, was playing with fervent gusto, and boys threw firecrackers into the air and their parents gossiped at filled tables, and babies shrieked, and young girls sauntered looking
at the closed shops, their dresses and hats bright with color,
and young men, in blazers and stiff straw hats, watched them.
The light poured down blindingly on the band, turning tuba
and trumpet to painful gold, and the stout uniformed men,
with eyeglasses and blond mustaches, puffed so fiercely that
their faces were scarlet. Drums thundered, flutes shrilled,
children shouted and ran, women called comfortably from tables in the shade. Men laughed hoarsely. They had removed
coats and collars, and some were furtively drinking beer from
cold bottles beneath great and ancient elms. Some even sat on
the steps of the First Presbyterian Church, which faced the
City Hall from across the street, and drank defiantly, and
called back and forth to friends fanning themselves at a distance. It was a lively and jubilant sight, full of noise and
voices and brazen music and startling color, bobbing with
women's flowered hats, feverish with young faces flashing
into the sun and then into shadow. The heat was already pungent with the odor of crushed grass and gunpowder and food
and dust and sweating bodies and aromatic leaves.

In places of honor, near the bandstand, sat row upon row
of middle-aged men in blue uniforms, the Grand Army of
the Republic, the veterans of the Civil War, and behind them
sat the young veterans of the Spanish-American War with
their jaunty Rough Rider hats. They alone seemed without
joy, sitting sternly in their sweltering uniforms and staring at
General Sherman as if at a tribal god, and disapproving of all
the uproarious vivacity about them. Many of the young veterans were affecting a Teddy Roosevelt mustache, especially
the more boyish ones, and some even had his pince-nez, the
lenses brilliant in the sun. The Civil War veterans were more
hirsute, with brown, red, blond or gray or dark beards, with
an occasional white one marking an older officer. They all
wore their ceremonial swords and many had ribbons and
medals of valor, and too many had crutches beside them and

canes, and here and there was a blind veteran with black patches over his eyes.

"Can you find our table, Jon?" asked Marjorie Ferrier. Father McNulty had taken one of her baskets, and she had not protested.

"I think I see a crow," said Jonathan, nodding farther down the crowded lawns. "Yes, it's Mrs. Morgan."

"Now, Jon," said Marjorie.

They walked among vehement tables, and Marjorie smiled and nodded but Jon walked alone with the priest. Jonathan's face was full of distaste, and the priest was diffident. Only occasionally did someone greet Father McNulty, the men rising shyly, the children becoming silent, and then the men sat down and did not, for a while, look at their neighbors but appeared apologetic and pretended to be absorbed in the food on their paper plates. The German Brass Band detonated in its deafening rendition of "The Stars and Stripes Forever." The crowd roared and scores stood up to look at the dignitaries of Hambledon, who were now filling the seats on the City Hall steps, and hats and caps were shook in the air and boys yelled, and firecrackers exploded in long cacophony. The cannon boomed, and the smoke rose in yellow spirals. The veterans stood up and saluted. The flags seemed to ripple more enthusiastically and the sun to become hotter and brighter and the various odors to increase in intensity. Women fluttered handkerchiefs, children shouted, babies in their buggies screamed. Agitated palm fans made a waving confusion of their own, catching the sun like round mirrors.

"I don't know why I stand this, year after year," said Jonathan, picking his way among tables, and trying to avoid dishes and glasses on the grass, and little children.

"It's very innocent. And harmless," said Father McNulty. "There must be several thousand here. It's very happy."

Jonathan looked at him sharply. Then he said, "Isn't it, though?"

"Naïve, perhaps," said the priest, and stopped to acknowledge a sheepish greeting. "But public celebrations go back to man's deepest spiritual history."

The noise was more tumultuous. "I see old Campion has arrived, in all his magnificence," said Jonathan. "Prepare, as usual, for a mellow ripe speech full of glory. There's Beatrice with him, anticipating goodies. But no Francis."

"He left last night for New York," said the priest. "He's going to France."

"Good," said Jonathan. "That should be a full education for him."

"He's going to a monastery in the Alps," said Father McNulty.

Jonathan stopped abruptly. "The hell you say," he said. "Did you contrive that?"

"Now, dear," said Marjorie, seeing the darkness on her son's face. "Oh, here we are. Isn't it nice."

The band became less martial and more lively. "Tell Me Pretty Maiden," it pleaded in strident trumpet tones, and the crowds began to sing and cheer and laugh boisterously. The Ferrier table was a little apart, in deep shade, and there were fewer children running on the grass. A small silence seemed imposed on the table, an awkwardness. Two men stood up, young Robert Morgan and Mr. Albert Kitchener. Robert seemed uncommonly flushed and he had a wide vacant smile and his blue eyes appeared bemused, and he was more of a gentle golden bear than Jonathan had seen him only yesterday. He wore a gray alpaca summer suit and a blue-striped shirt, and his white high collar and stiff cuffs seemed to glitter.

Mr. Kitchener and his wife, Sue, were distant relations and they matched each other remarkably in that they both resembled bright rosy baked apples, even to the cinnamon-colored hair. Mr. Kitchener's mustache was also of that color, very large and bushy. Both were short and round and sweet and inviting in appearance, with brilliant gray eyes like crystal, dimpled chins and pink cheeks, and both had an air of comfortable innocence, placidity and affection. Their daughter, Maude, twenty-two, was their only child, as small and dimpled and pink as themselves, a trifle plump but endearingly so, and her hair was a vivid auburn and escaped in thick glossy waves and ripples from under her wide gauzy hat. The girl wore a sprigged muslin frock with a lace collar and wide lace cuffs, and apparently their dressmaker had been enamored of the girlish theme, for she had made an identical one for Sue Kitchener except that the sprigs were pale lavender. The three had an old-fashioned and contented appearance, as if nothing in their lives had ever disturbed them. Mr. Kitchener was a prosperous lawyer who never accepted a criminal case. He had cozy offices with five clerks and an assistant, and had inherited considerable money. Jonathan Ferrier was fond of the three Kitcheners but found them dull if pleasant and soothing company. It was obvious that they were fond of him also, for Albert Kitchener chuckled at him, shook his hand heartily, Mrs. Kitchener smiled happily and Maude gave him an absent gray look and smiled shyly. Jonathan wondered at that absentness but soon found the reason. The girl was fascinated by Robert Morgan, and even as she smiled at Jonathan her eyes moved mistily to Robert and stayed there.

Mrs. Morgan had the small cold and secret smile of the naturally malicious woman, and it merely became colder as she haughtily acknowledged the newcomers, without a glance, of course, at the priest, whom she ignored even when he was presented to her. It did not surprise Jonathan and his mother that she was dressed very unsuitably on this hot day, and in an old style. Her black silk poplin dress was obviously uncomfortable, with its short mantle that swathed her angular shoulders, and she even wore a widow's bonnet and white ruching at the top of her collar, which was so high, so boned, that it seemed to be pushing into the withered flesh under her chin. Her light eyes examined Jonathan severely, and even with contempt, then withdrew from him to dwell even more severely at the other guest, Jenny Heger.

Jenny, Jonathan saw at once, was dressed as bunchily and as unprettily as always, in a blue and white checked shirtwaist, a heavy blue duck skirt, black-buttoned shoes and a broad black patent-leather belt. Her hat, a big coarse cartwheel of yellow straw, was useful for shading her from the sun but for no other purpose, certainly not to enhance her appearance, with its dusty black ribbon and despondent bow. She sat in stiff silence on her part of the bench after the introduction to Father McNulty, and stared at the table, her hands clenched together in her lap. Unlike the other ladies, she wore no gloves, and her fingers were tanned and her nails were not slightly tinted as were the Kitchener females'. But nothing could really dim the white luster of her face, the extraordinary blueness of her eyes, the stern loveliness of her palely colored mouth, the delicate aquilinity of her nose, and the mass of glistening black hair rolled impatiently under her hat and allowed to droop in a large bun at her nape. Not even the starched wide blue and white checked collar of her shirtwaist could hide the slenderness of her long neck, the contour of her superb young shoulders, and the classical lines of her breast. She made pretty little Maude, who had been a belle in Hambledon since she had reached puberty, appear almost common in her rose-sprigged muslin, white gloves and laces, and charming hat.

Jonathan felt that all the others retreated into mere colored photographs in the presence of this strange girl, and had but two dimensions, and that even her silence was electric in the midst of the friendly remarks and light laughter about the table. This annoyed him fiercely, as it always did, and he was even more annoyed that his neck felt hot and moist and that his hands were becoming tense. She said nothing to him, and he said nothing to her. But Marjorie said, "Jon, do sit next to Jenny, and I really must sit next to Albert. I have so many things to say to him."

Jonathan wanted to say, "I'd prefer to sit across from Maude," for the girl always delighted him with her cheerful inanity and soft conversation, and her air that the world was a truly lovable and romantic and exciting place. But Marjorie was already smiling along the table at Mrs. Morgan, who bent her head as if being gracious to a lady-in-waiting, and smiling, too, at Mrs. Kitchener, who had gently patted the spot next to her for Father McNulty. Unfortunately, he would have Mrs. Morgan on his left, and she ostentatiously withdrew to the limit of the bench to accommodate him. Jonathan gave her a hard look and was somewhat surprised to see that Jenny gave her a similar one. He sat beside Jenny, almost unbearably conscious of her nearness, careful not to let his sleeve touch hers, and feeling, as always, that indescribable tenseness not only in his hands but in his whole body, and a curious sense of being unnerved. He had never tried to explain it to himself, though often he had thought it was revulsion and, sometimes, detestation for what she was in spite of her youth, and her lack of feminine graces and social amenities and ugly dress. He did not know that Jenny had been long convinced that she was most unattractive, awkward, ungraceful and undesirable. Had he known, he would have been incredulous. He did not know that Peter Heger had recognized his daughter's disturbing beauty even when she had been only a child, and had jealously, and knowingly, informed her that she could never expect to be courted for, as he said, she was most unlike other young ladies and ought to have been his son and not his daughter. Jenny, who had adored him passionately, had never once in her short life, not even when looking in the mirror, doubted him for a moment. Her father had recognized her physical disabilities and had wished to shelter her from the harshness of a world that loved only dimpled prettiness, and she was too tall, even as a child, and too slender, and her hands and feet were too large.

Only Harald Ferrier had called her "lovely Jenny," and she had thought it mockery. His insistence on marrying her, of course, was to insure that he could leave the island at will and stay away as long as he desired, for though the money would then be Jenny's, it would, to all effect, also be his.

It was Marjorie Ferrier who, in her long and tender conversations with the girl over many years, had guessed all about Peter Heger and his infatuation with his beautiful daughter and his wish to keep her with him and isolate her. There was no ugliness with which Marjorie was not familiar in human nature, and what she did not know from experience she intuitively guessed. She had tried, as subtly and as skillfully as possible, to assure Jenny that she was remarkably beautiful, but the girl had no self-confidence and as yet, no inner fortitude. She had been grateful for Marjorie's suggestions that she dress more becomingly, but had replied with heartbreaking simplicity, "But why, Aunt Marjorie? Nothing will help. Besides, I don't want to get married, really, and I don't like to be in the company of other people, anyway. They frighten me so. I prefer the island and the gardens and my books, and thinking of Papa, and taking care of his roses. I wasn't popular at school in Hambledon, you know. I was head and shoulders over the other girls and they used to laugh at me. I'm still as tall as most men. No, I must be contented with what I have."

But what Jenny had was nothing, Marjorie would sadly reflect, and it was only because she was so pure of heart and so distressingly honest and so courageous—though in the wrong directions—and so adamantly untouched. All the reading she had done, the studying, the reflections, had not broken into that marble tower and had not touched poor Jenny with flame and longing and desire. Marjorie had gone so far as to send Jenny some books by Zola and others of earthy richness, and Jenny later had reported, "They were very interesting, I think, but a little crude, and besides, they were French—or Italian or Roumanian or Russian—and they didn't seem quite real to me. Maupassant? Well. Was it necessary for him to write *that*?" Poor Jenny's face had become quite red and she had been overcome with discomfiture and had changed the subject.

Damn Peter Heger, Marjorie would think. I hope there is a

special hell for fathers who distort their children's minds like this and destroy their natural impulses, and lie to them.

Marjorie looked at Jonathan's face, where the white lines of flesh had come out around his mouth, and where the facial bones were sharper than usual. He was conducting an apparently casual conversation with that young Dr. Morgan—who was staring so abjectly at Jenny and with so much ardent fascination and so there was really no reason for Jonathan's seeming so overwrought and physically rigid, as if about to spring up and run away. But Marjorie smiled secretly to herself, and she hoped for some overwhelming catastrophe, or something, to reveal to Jon what he really should know about himself. Look at him there! As taut and unbending as Jenny, with his straw hat pushed back from his sweating forehead, and his jerking cheek and lip muscles, and his hands perched tightly on his thighs and his overattentiveness—as if his life depended upon it!—to the very commonplace remarks young Robert was making to him. He was saying, "Aha, aha, yes," in a very emphatic voice, and at length the bemused Robert became aware of this exaggeration and turned to him and said, "Eh? Oh, yes, it was very interesting." He seemed a little puzzled. He became silent. Now he stared openly and helplessly at Jenny, who was no more aware of him than a bird.

Marjorie saw that Robert Morgan was much "taken," as the saying was, by Jenny. Robert interrupted Jonathan's remarks by saying to Jenny—as if Jonathan had not been speaking at all—"Miss Heger, I often look across the water at your marvelous island, your charming island." His voice actually trembled. "I wish you would permit me to visit it again, soon."

Jenny started. She turned her head slowly and met his eyes, and a painful scarlet ran up from her throat and breeched like fire into her white cheeks. "I—" she said, and swallowed. She was in misery. "Perhaps you could—perhaps someday—"

"Soon?" he pleaded, and colored himself, astonished at his presumption.

She tried to smile. She could only nod, then look again into the distance, past Mrs. Morgan, who was greatly shaken and had turned quite ashen, and past the tumult everywhere present on the grass. Maude Kitchener, who was sitting next to Robert, looked dismayed. She timidly touched his arm, and he turned to her, bemused, his blue eyes excited. "We

have the same gardener as the island," she said in her sweet
voice. "Our gardens are very similar. I hope—I hope—"
Then the poor girl blushed at her own boldness. She had
been sitting in bliss near Robert. Once she had believed herself in love with Jonathan, but she had been very young then,
before he had married that awful Mavis Eaton. Yes, she had
thought of him again since Mavis had died, and she had had
her dreams. But she had met Robert today and had since
been delirious, overcome by the sudden light in the scene, a
sort of feverish incandescence, and her heart had been doing
very odd things indeed, and everything had appeared to be
exquisitely radiant and musical and trembling with delicious
agitation. Even the raucous German Brass Band had been
playing, to her ears, the most remarkable and enchanting
music, sensual and insidious.

"Very nice," said the bemused Robert, who had not heard
her stammer. He returned again to his rapt contemplation of
Jenny's averted face.

Then Jonathan became aware of all this. He looked at the
helpless longing on the young doctor's face, and the passionate intensity and slavish desire, and he looked at Jenny, beside him, and her cold withdrawal and her obvious misery.
Jonathan could not believe it. Wasn't the Childe enough for
her, that she must set out to bedazzle this hulk of gold and
rosy innocence? And what was there to bedazzle in the
frump? At the very least she should dress like a young
woman and not an old, poverty-stricken witch. Then he was
struck by his own thoughts and considered them and was
more in a rage than before. He wanted to take Jenny's shoulders in his hands, hold them, and then at this appalling
thought he felt suddenly and distinctly ill and heavily shaken.

Marjorie stood up and said, "Now, let's spread the tablecloth, shall we? Sue, dear, push those folds down to Mrs.
Morgan, so it will be straight. I do hope that everyone will
like what we've brought."

"Quite adequate, I am sure," said Mrs. Morgan in a stilted
voice as she pushed a fold in Father McNulty's direction. He
was talking to Mrs. Kitchener and finding her a most agreeable and sympathetic lady. Mrs. Morgan was most upset.
What had come over Robert? Why was he staring at that
frightful young woman like that? Everyone in town knew
what she was and spoke about it as a "scandal." She, Jane
Morgan, had heard quite sufficient, thank you! The girl had
been bad, bad from the very beginning. There had been that

schoolmaster when she had been only sixteen, in Miss Chiltenham's School, right here in Hambledon. (Jane had heard that story but yesterday.) The schoolmaster had left under hushed and furtive circumstances, but the girl had remained serenely at school! Money! It always came down to that. The Heger money; it would buy anything, even immunity against the town's indignation and shame. How brazen she was! To be cohabiting with her dead mother's husband, in her mother's own home on that island, flagrantly, without regard for decent Christian public opinion! Shameless, shameless. And here was Marjorie Ferrier, of the Farmington's of the Main Line in Philadelphia, *the* Farmingtons, the mother of a murderer who had escaped judgment only because he was rich and powerful, and the mother of another son who lived with his dead wife's daughter, flaunting his sin, his adultery, in the Face of High Heaven! "We don't understand Marjorie," some of Jane's new friends had said with sadness. "Such a fine family. But we have heard—mind, it is only gossip, you know—that she actually drove poor gentle, sweet, kind Adrian to his death with her coldness and hardheartedness. Everyone knew that only Harald mattered to her. Well, it was very dreadful, of course, but then blue blood did run out and become depraved and vicious. The Ferriers were the best example of that. Yes, and that's why Marjorie cannot only tolerate that Heger hussy but invite her to her house! Perhaps"—soft laughter—"she hopes to persuade her son Harald —that silly painter—to marry the girl and get her money, too, or something, or at least to stop the scandal."

Marjorie and Mrs. Kitchener and Maude were spreading the picnic dinner on the table and laying out the silver and napkins and glasses. "Cold lemonade," said Marjorie, "and an old-fashioned strawberry shrub—dear Maude does like that —and, on ice, beer for the gentlemen."

"Robert does not drink," said Jane Morgan. She gave Marjorie a reproving and significant glance. Marjorie smiled. "Perhaps he will make an exception today," she said in her quiet and lovely voice. Jane gave Robert a quelling look, but he was still staring at that hideous trollop. What was wrong with him? Could it be that he was horrified by her, having confronted Evil for the first time and finding it hypnotizing? Poor innocent boy. She must speak of it delicately tonight. "I like beer," said Robert, but did not look away from Jenny, who again seemed as far away from this place as the edge of the ivory moon which was peering like a ghost from the sun-lit sky.

Can it be that it was only a year ago that Mavis had been here with the family? thought Marjorie. Only a year ago, on such a hot and brilliant and noisy day? She and Jon, with all the other dignitaries of the town, had then sat for the speeches on those broad, chair-filled steps of the City Hall. How beautiful she had looked that day, all gilt and rose and white lace and white parasol and white lace gloves and white silk slippers, laughing as usual, tapping men's arms coquettishly, and laughing, laughing, laughing, and Jon beside her, constrained and dark and silent and brooding. Everyone seemed turned, on those stairs, toward Mavis, like sunflowers to the sun, eager for the gift of her beauty and her laughter and her hoarse jokes and her affectionate taps and recognition, delighting in her coaxings and cajolings, her joyful teasings, fawning at the very shimmering sight of her, a gold and white rose of a girl, her snowy tulle hat laden with pink flowers and ribbons. Near her, her fatuous uncle had grown crimson with pleasure and love as he watched her, and even Flora, that sallow stick of a woman, had looked maudlin. But, then, so had everyone else—except Jonathan Ferrier. Now all that beauty and lust and life and verve and laughter were closed forever in the black earth, and no one would hear that boisterous laughter again or feel the patting of her hand.

Marjorie sighed. She could not feel sorry that Mavis was dead, she who had been such a plague to the Ferriers and such a calamity. But it was sad when the young died, however wicked they were, and heartless and grasping and lying. Hambledon was less bright since Mavis' death, even though it had been a false and brassy brightness.

Jonathan was looking at Jenny's hand lying near him on the table. She had made no effort to help his mother, and he was contemptuous and angry, for he could not know that Jenny was shy to the point of agony. But he looked at her hand, long, slender, tinted by the sun to a golden color. And then he wanted to press his own hand hard on hers, to press it so strongly that his flesh, and hers, became one flesh, moving together, inseparable. Such a stricken hunger for this consummation sprang up in him that he again stiffened with real physical pain, and stunning disgust at himself, and new hatred for the girl. So, she could entice him, too, could she? Compared with her, Mavis had been an innocent schoolgirl, an amateur. Was she laughing at him secretly, knowing that wild impulse in him? He looked at her white profile, so stern and remote, and he thought he saw a satisfied glint in the corner of her eye. She was not yet twenty-one, but she was already lewd and lascivious and without shame, already practiced. He looked at that quiet hand and did not see its vulnerability, its helplessness.

Why doesn't Dr. Morgan look at me? Maude Kitchener was thinking. Why does he stare at Jenny Heger that way? She isn't even pretty; quite plain, to be sure. So big, so pale, and so cold. She, Maude, had not believed a single word said about Jenny since she had been almost a child, nor had Sue Kitchener, for there was really nothing wrong to believe. Jenny had always been a retiring girl, turning miserably red if someone spoke to her unexpectedly, and her clothing awful and thick and unstylish, but a wonderful scholar, winning all the prizes at school. Maude, of the gentle heart, had tried to be a friend to that reserved and silent girl, and Jenny had been diffidently grateful at first but then had seemed to find all social intercourse painful in the extreme, and so had frightened off Maude and some of the other girls who might have been her friends. Poor Jenny. But why was that wonderful young Dr. Morgan staring at her so and ignoring herself?

Robert was thinking quite mawkishly, "Why, she is alabaster and fire!" He was taken by the thought, repeated it to himself with intense pleasure and sentimentality. Alabaster and fire. That described Jenny, his Jenny, his beautiful alien Jenny, like a classic statue in the midst of all this hot and blazing hubbub, concerned with things not of this world. She finally felt his staring and looked up at him and saw his kind blue eyes, and she blushed, tried to smile and could make only a grimace.

Mrs. Kitchener thought: How lovely it is when dear friends get together like this! Everyone is so happy and at ease, even that poor young Jenny. Sue was so gleeful at this thought that she smiled at her husband, beside her, and pressed his warm plump hand, and was pressed affectionately in return. Lovely, lovely world, sweet world, thought Sue.

How sorrowful it is that men cannot gather together, even on so innocent an occasion as this, without undercurrents of darkness, malice, hatred and bitter hearing and misunderstanding, thought the young priest, whose wise eyes had seen everything.

"We might as well have our dinner now," said Marjorie, "before all those awful speeches begin."

The German Brass Band sprang violently into "Ta-ra-ra-boom-de-ay!" For the mayor, Emil Schuman, was greeting fresh arrivals on the steps, ladies with big hats and parasols. There was Louis Hedler and Humphrey Bedloe and other members of the staff of the two hospitals, and several clergymen, and Colonel Jeremiah Hadley, late of the Grand Army of the Republic, sixty and gray but tall and stately in his Union blue and medals. He bowed to the ladies, and was seated next to the Senator and his sister, and then folded his military arms and looked at the veterans across the square from him. His severe face changed and he dropped his head for a moment.

"I've heard," said Jane Morgan, giving Marjorie her usual cold and knowing look, "that there is a much more refined gathering today in the park near the river, without all this noise and these howling children and the more vulgar classes."

"Yes," said Marjorie, laying the warm rolls on a silver dish. "But this is the traditional place and the traditional celebration. We in Hambledon have been meeting here for this picnic every year, from far back before the Civil War, ever since Hambledon was a village and not a town. You will notice that Senator Campion is here, and the mayor, and other important people of Hambledon, though I did hear a rumor they are joining the others near the river after the speeches."

"And no wonder," said Jane Morgan. "Such a fearful noise! And that horrible band! Why can't it be quiet even for a minute?" The band was once again begging the noisy mob if "there are any more home like you?" and in falsetto the flutes were replying that indeed "there are quite a few, kind sir!" Firecrackers affirmed this in violent chorus.

Last year I was sitting on those stairs with Mavis, Jonathan was thinking. I was one of the town's honored "dignitaries." Today I am the pariah, the outcast, the nobody, the despised and the rejected. A man may be innocent until he is proved guilty, but no one seems to have taken that seriously at any time. Mavis. He glanced at the City Hall steps and could see Mavis there among all that colorful gathering, shining and sparkling and laughing, nodding gaily to admirers, unfolding her white lace fan, laughing naughtily behind it while her small blue eyes twinkled and flirted. She had ignored him, as she always ignored him, but when her glance did touch him, it became full of ridicule and contempt and genuine dislike. It never failed to chill him, that glance, however much he detested her and knew her for what she was. It did not abash or cow or sadden him. It was just that he remembered his wasted years with Mavis, and his appalling former infatuation for her, his dismal love and passion, his hopes, his longings.

Today, he did not feel his old hatred for his dead wife. He felt only miserable regret that he had endured those years in proud silence. Pride. Was it pride to keep silent and to do nothing? If he had done—something—Mavis might be alive, not in his house but somewhere else, and he would not be here now, still suspected of an enormous crime. He might even have divorced her. He had thought of that very often during the years with Mavis—but on what grounds? Or. had he been afraid of scandal? I was a coward, he thought. What was it that damned priest said to me one day? "Jon, you are a brave man, but you are not a courageous one. I remember an old poem—can't think of the author: 'Courage is the price that life demands for granting peace. The soul that knows it not knows no release—from little things.' "

Perhaps he was right, thought Jonathan with anger. I probably never did have much courage, and that's a hell of a thing to recognize when you are thirty-five and your life is more than half over! I've backed away from things all my life, such as conspiring with my father that he was an intellectual man, and conspiring with him that my mother was brutal and insensitive—and all the other things that no man of courage would have endured for a second.

The roaring of the crowd, the bursting explosions, the band—all the screaming and singing and laughing—disappeared from his consciousness, and he was again in the courtroom, before the judge and the jury, listening to the prosecuting attorney, seeing the dull averted faces, the harsh and cuning faces, against a background of grimy snow hissing against the dirty windows. He had not been afraid of any of them and had even smiled grimly at the prosecuting attorney's denunciation of him as a "ruthless, cruel, bloody-handed murderer of his young and beautiful wife and his unborn child. A calculating, callous murderer! Gentlemen, shall this man go free, and live, with that blameless blood on his hands? Dare you to dismiss him to laugh at you and our Great, Noble, Free American Justice?"

No, he had not been afraid. I should have been afraid, he

thought now. I should have been scared out of my wits. Had I lacked fear because I heartily believed that innocence would never suffer unjust punishment? I've called others naïve. I was the naïve one. This is a disastrous world. I always knew it was, even when I was a child, yet I did not believe it until now.

He looked at his mother, so smiling, so calm and attentive to her guests, so proud and graceful, and he saw her sick paleness, the shadows under her eyes, the lines of patient pain about her patrician mouth. He was ashamed. He had no words to say to her to ask her forgiveness. He had never listened to her, rejecting her even before she spoke, yet she had always been right. Had her very rightness antagonized him, her very serene acceptance of the enigma of living—which he had found it impossible to accept, though he was not blind and not stupid?

I am my father's son also, he thought with scorn. I had to have my shiny little playthings too, my sweet little delusions. I am pretty much of a mess.

The band crashed into "Hail, Columbia, Happy Land!" and the crowd rose in a mass of hot color and cheered and sang lustily and waved small flags and saluted and lit fresh firecrackers, and the sun beat down and all the air was heavy with the smell of food and beer and dust and crushed grass and gunpowder.

Jonathan, too, stood up. In doing so he accidentally lurched against the rising Jenny at his side, and he instinctively caught her as she stumbled, and his arms was about her waist and her cheek near his lips. They stood like statues, stricken into stillness, and then, very slowly, she looked at him, lifting those enormous blue eyes to his, and turning even whiter than before. They could not look away. He felt the girl's body trembling under his hand, and then, to his amazement and tremendous emotion, he saw a blaze of light pass over her face and he saw her lips part.

He dropped his hand. He muttered, "Sorry." But he, too, was trembling. He looked at her again. Her face was now averted from him. She was looking at the courthouse stairs. Jenny, he thought. I must have imagined it. Not Jenny! Not Jenny, his brother's doxy. There was a sick and broken disintegration all through his thoughts and body.

CHAPTER SEVENTEEN

Senator Kenton Campion, in all his florid handsome-
ness, his chestnut handsomeness, followed Mayor Schuman to
the lectern, and everyone cheered and clapped, for he was
very popular. "The friend of the people." The town loved
him for his appearance, his money, the little scandals about
him, his smiles, his geniality, his repeated stories—and his
constant excellent press. He bowed to the crowds, gravely acknowledged the salutes of the veterans, bowed to his fellow
dignitaries, lifted his hands like a loving father to still the
shouts and the screamed greetings and the flurry of flags. His
sister, Beatrice, glowed like the sun behind him, proud to the
point of tears, which she wiped away with a lace handkerchief.

The Senator shone upon his acclaimers when they became
smilingly quiet. He wore a long frocked coat and dignified
striped trousers and an old-fashioned soft, white rolling collar
and a broad black tie, neatly fastened with a diamond pin.
His bare head, with its smooth chestnut waves, was vivid in
the sun. He was every inch the Senator, the dignitary, the beloved native son, the son of his people, the one who preferred
to live in little Hambledon instead of Philadelphia, where he
rightfully belonged. The crowd loved him dearly. He, the familiar of Presidents and Governors, yearly condescended to
speak to them here, not as their superior but as one of them,
a prince among his subjects, not patronizing them but honor-
ing them in himself.

His voice, big and mellifluous, filled the whole square, and
it was rich with emotion.

"Dear friends," he said, "dear neighbors, dear brothers and sisters! Again, on this glorious Fourth, this noble Day of Independence from an old tyranny and oppression, I come to address you, your servant, address you humbly and with gratitude for the love you have shown me, the support you have showered on me, the trust you have bestowed on me. How can I express to you what this means, what this does to my heart as a man, to my immortal soul, to all my emotions and sensibility?" He struck his broad chest with his fist.

"Oh, God," muttered Jonathan, and refilled his empty glass with beer. But no one heard for the crowd was cheering thunderously again and the flags were again flurrying and the band struck up an exultant chord, and everyone was clapping. Even the Senator's cynical friends on the courthouse stairs were applauding and beaming at each other in approval, and Jonathan, seeing that, snorted. He leaned his cheek on his hand, not in the boredom he affected, but in order to control himself, to understand that bounding passion he had felt when he had held Jenny, and to swallow down his wretchedness and horror and dismay and revulsion, and to analyze that sense of sorrow he was knowing beyond any sorrow he had ever known. Jenny was sitting near him again, rigid and unseeing as before.

The Senator, having overcome his sensibility and his natural delicate rapture at being home with his dear friends again, had resumed his speech, his arms lifted for emphasis, his white hands fluttering to accent a point. He was eloquent and powerful, and the crowd became utterly silent. Jonathan had missed some flowery periods.

"—and so, on this glorious day, dedicated to our freedom, our liberty, our sacred honor, our nobility and heroism as Americans, our ancestry of proud and fearless men, our vows to our God and our country, our pledges to all humanity of peace and love and tranquil relations, I speak to you, dear friends, out of the depths of my overflowing spirit, to prepare you for the destiny awaiting you in this magnificent, exciting, sunlit century, your destiny, beyond which the world has never known before!"

"What's that?" muttered Jonathan, and now he forgot everything and concentrated on the Senator's speech, which was oddly unlike any he had given before on this day.

"Our destiny!" sang the Senator, and his voice broke, then rose to glorious heights. "Our immutable destiny, written in the stone of ages, inscribed from the beginning in the heart

of God, prophesied in sacred books! This is our nation, the
new Jerusalem, land of milk and honey, the new Israel, the
new world! Oh, what glories await us, what prides, what ac-
complishments, what accolades, what ecstasies of selfless progress, what inventiveness, what leadership—in this new century of ours, this newly minted century pressed into our
hands by the Hosts of Heaven!"

"What the hell?" said Jonathan, moving quickly on the
bench. But no one heard him. Robert Morgan was still staring raptly at Jenny, who stared at nothing, and Jane Morgan
stared at her son, and Maude stared at Robert, and Marjorie,
overcome by heat and noise and illness, was quietly dozing
on the bench, leaning against a tree trunk, and the Kitcheners
were politely and dazedly listening, trying not to sleep and
trying to be polite to the resplendent Senator, and not caring
or understanding a word. Only Jonathan listened, and the
priest, and the priest's face was uneasy and grave.

"Are we ready for our destiny?" demanded the Senator,
turning from side to side to pierce the crowds with his burning eyes. "Have we prayed humbly enough, have we dedicated ourselves enough, have we understood enough, have we
sacrificed enough, to be worthy of this, our destiny before the
face of history, our destiny which throws into shadow the
empires of Greece and Egypt and Babylonia and Persia and
Rome? And, yes! The passing empire of Great Britain, the
challenging empire of Germany, of Austria-Hungary, of the
little yellow men beyond the Pacific? Have we prayed,
friends? Have we comprehended the scepter extended to us
by the Lord of the Ages, the crown offered to us by endless
millions of the oppressed and homeless in expectation, the
jeweled path laid before us by the Russian Empire, the palms
spread at our feet by the pagan Spice Islands, the pleas raised
to us by the toiling masses—everywhere in the world?"

"My God!" said Jonathan aloud. He looked about the
table, at the glazed Kitcheners, at his dozing mother, at the
still profile of Jenny, at the staring Robert, the staring Maude
and the staring Jane. But no one replied. Then his eyes encountered the alarmed golden eyes of Father McNulty, and
for a long moment they gazed at each other in mutual perturbation. They still looked at each other while the somewhat
puzzled but enthusiastic crowds roared in response to the
Senator's words. They disliked the word "empire," which
they had been taught in their schools was a noxious and suspect word, synonymous with European and Oriental despo-

tisms, and from which America had escaped in 1775. They
knew they should show their disapproval of the fatal word,
and they did, and leaned raptly toward the Senator.

He smiled in ripe satisfaction. "Let me quote America's
great poet!" he shouted. "Walt Whitman—about America. 'I
hear America singing, the varied carols I hear!' Ah, most
moving words, most triumphant, most glorious words! 'I hear
America singing!' How poignant they are, a great democratic
empire singing, from coast to coast, from border to border, in
exultation of power and glory in the name of freedom for all
men! Have we been deaf to these exalted words? Have we
sunk in personal aggrandizement that we are deaf to our destiny?

"No! No! A thousand times No! We know what we are,
we know our manifest destiny, and let the cowards shrink,
the puling whimper, the weaklings hide! We know what path
we must take! Shall we recoil, heed clinging hands, hear trea-
sonable voices, pause in our mighty giant stride into the future? A thousand times No!"

The crowd, more puzzled than ever, but enchanted by all
the ringing periods, roared a thunderous "No!" But the veterans were sitting up now, and Colonel Jeremiah Hadley was
upright, and he stared at the Senator as if at a basilisk or a
Gorgon.

The Senator was rolling again. "We are a great, tremendous,
peaceful country. The land has not been recently disturbed
by war except briefly for the Spanish-American conflict,
which we fought only under the most awful provocation and
to free Cuba and the other oppressed. But that is past history.
William Jennings Bryan and his sixteen-to-one, Single Tax
and fiery exhortations, have come to nothing, though the
corpse will twitch now and then. The dawn of the new century has come. The day of multitudes of automobiles, which
will soon crowd our roads and demand of us greater roads,
greater than the roads of Rome, which led everywhere. The
dawn has arrived when a weak government in Washington
must rise and undertake new responsibilities, for the new empire, for the new America!"

"Christ!" said Jonathan in a loud voice, but only the priest,
and perhaps Jenny, heard him.

The Senator was shining like the sun at all the plaudits he
was receiving, and if he saw hundreds of baffled faces, he did
not care, nor did he care for Colonel Hadley's deep frown
nor the perturbation of the veterans. He had the public ear,

the naïve and accepting ear, the easily deceived ear which loved grand sounds and mighty slogans.

The Senator resumed. "Let the world beware! America is on the march! The growth of our nation can be heard like mounting thunder. The gawky and bashful maiden has grown to gigantic stature, and is looking with arrogant confidence at an amazed Europe. Behind her millions of mighty acres, smoking mills and foundries, tremendous cities whose like has never greeted eye before, the power of our mighty right arm is visible! In our veins is the tumult of resistless blood. In our hearts is the strength of centuries. Little wonder now, when we raise a jubilant shout, challenging and joyful and young. Europe listens!"

"I bet," said Jonathan. "And she'd better listen hard. The whole damned world had better listen to this mountebank, whose name is legion in Washington now."

"Yes," said the priest, and looked with greater alarm at the Senator.

Jonathan thought of what young Francis Campion had told him, and a hot thick rage rose in his throat and he said to himself, Is it really possible that a man will conspire against his own country for power, for money, for lust of position, for hatred of the human race? Yes, it was more than possible. The wrecks of ancient civilizations were littered with the names of such evil men, who had brought down their world to destruction and death and had reveled in it, out of some diabolic ambition or mad enthusiasm. Satanism. Jonathan had always jeered at the word. Now, reluctantly, in his disturbance, he wondered.

"What an inheritance is ours!" exultantly shouted the Senator. "I have spoken of humility. But let us not be humble any longer! To pretend to be so is to reject our God's plan for us! And what is that plan? Let me quote a great British poet—though I do not admire the British. Tennyson is his name, and he was very prophetic, though he wrote several decades ago:

" 'Men, my brothers, men the workers, ever reaping something new;
    That which they have done but earnest of the things that they shall do.

" 'For I dipt into the future, far as human eye could see,

Saw the Vision of the world, and all the wonder that would
  be;

" 'Saw the heavens fill with commerce, argosies of magic sails,
  Pilots of the purple twilight, dropping down with costly
    bales;

" 'Heard the heavens fill with shouting, and there rain'd a
    ghastly dew,
  From the nations' airy navies grappling in the central blue;

" 'Far along the world-wide whisper of the southwind rushing
    warm,
  With the standards of the peoples plunging through the
    thunderstorm;

" 'Till the war-drum throbb'd no longer, and the battle-flags
    were furl'd,
  In the Parliament of man, the Federation of the world!' "

The sonorous music of the poetry delighted the crowds except for the veterans and Colonel Hadley, and Jonathan Ferrier and the priest. They delighted, simply, in resonance and
harmony. They roared their approval and did not understand
in the least. To the simple American the music was enough,
and they did not hear anything ominous.

"And who shall rule that parliament of man, the federation
of the world?" cried the Senator, pacing back and forth like a
tiger on the step on which he stood. "America! America!
Who will challenge us? Who will dare to challenge us?"

"Somebody, I hope to God," said Jonathan. "Somebody in
Europe or America, somebody sane."

"Let me tell you, friends and beloved Americans!" roared
the Senator. "The heavens, filled with commerce, as the poet
said, is no illusion any longer, no dream! 'Heard the heavens
fill with shouting—from the nations' airy navies, grappling in
the central blue!' What a vision, but what truth! Fifty-nine
years ago a great French writer, Victor Hugo, said of this day
and age, concerning the heavier-than-air machine, on which
we are now working in America: 'That very instant frontiers
vanish, barriers are effaced, the entire Chinese Wall around
industry, around nationalities, around progress, falls down.
Man was crawling along the earth—then he will be free. Civilization becomes a cloud of birds, and flies and whirls
around and perches at the same time on all points of the

globe. No more hatreds, no more self-interests devouring one another, no more wars! A new life made up of harmony and light prevails!'

"That, friends, fellow countrymen, was said fifty-nine years ago, by Victor Hugo, in 1842! What a prophecy! And who will bring it to pass! America! It is our aerial navies which will be grappling in the central blue—to bring universal peace and freedom to all men! The cost may be enormous, the suffering great, but the destiny must not be refused, the covenant with God not challenged! The parliament of man, the federation of the world! Where will be its alabaster capital? Its emperor? Its heroic man of peace, justing the nations, accepting their homage and their tributes, imposing his beneficent laws on the entire earth, flowing his standards beneath every sun and on every nation and isle? Washington is that alabaster capital, its emperor and man of peace a democratic ruler with tenderness in his heart for all men, and with reverence for tradition and our God! This is America the golden, the new Rome, the blessed empire, gathering her multitudinous nations beneath her shining cloak, granting them eternal peace and prosperity and song and feasting and love!"

Jonathan, no longer jeering but deeply frightened, had listened to all this. Hambledon was only a small city, hardly larger than a town, and this man was but one Senator. But, was he repeating what was being whispered these days in Washington, by men of lust and hate and ambition? Would he speak so boldly, even to these simple people, if that had not been spoken even more boldly before, in the secret corridors of government?

"All this, perhaps, can be brought about by peaceful words and persuasion," the Senator was crying. "But, if not, sterner measures must be resorted to, for the sake of a world growing smaller by the moment, and closer and closer. How can this be accomplished, and remember, we do this not for our sake—for we have no ambitions—but for the sake of those Jesus so greatly loved, the poor, the deprived, the hungry, the homeless, the oppressed, the wandering, of foreign nations. We can do this with power, and power must be bought with money.

"Soon, dear friends, an amendment will be asked to our noble Constitution, an amendment which will permit Congress to impose a personal income tax on the whole nation. We have had such a tax during the Civil War and again during the Spanish-American War, but an ignorant and greedy

minority of the people—who care nothing for our destiny—
soon had that tax repealed.

"What stupidity! What lack of love of country! What lack
of love for all men everywhere! Shall we huddle between our
two oceans, content with our own fatness, while hundreds of
millions starve and look at us yearningly, asking us to deliver
them from their tyrants? A thousand times No! No! Our destiny calls us! Is our wealth more to us than that which has
been graved for us throughout history? No! No! Sacrifice!
Duty! Unity! That is the call of the future—that is our call.
The sun rises west, friends! The sun rises west!

"As we were delivered from oppression, so it is our duty to
deliver others, from whatever nation we receive the desperate
call. Our gold is nothing. Even, perhaps, our lives are nothing, nor the lives of our sons. With gold and blood we shall
establish the parliament of man, the federation of the world,
and let no man deny us!"

"He's mad," said Jonathan to Father McNulty.

"No. I don't think so," replied the priest, and his round
young face was pale. "I wonder how many other small cities
are being treated to this speech today?"

"I wish some foreign correspondents were on hand," said
Jonathan.

"—a truly democratic, benign empire!" the Senator was
shouting. "Perhaps we shall not see it, but our sons will see
it! Destiny will not be denied!"

"God help us," said Jonathan.

"Amen," said the priest.

The people were in an uproar of excitement and jubilation,
though few had understood the terrible prophesies of the Senator and what implications they had for America. They
bounded across the square to shake Campion's hand, and he
reached down, palpitating like the sun, to seize each eagerly
upraised hand and piously to bless it, and to murmur a loving
word. Every man whose hand was shaken felt himself honored and uplifted, though he did not quite know why. He
dazedly smiled at his neighbors, clapped neighbors on the
shoulder, said, "Wasn't that a wonderful speech for the
Fourth?" No one said, "But what did he mean?" It was
enough to be part of the sweating and enthusiastic crowd, the
crowd beloved of the Senator. It was enough to be shouting
with everyone else in a fine hot spirit of brotherhood and
zeal.

"Something like the Tuileries again," commented Jonathan,

and no one heard him but the priest. "Now, whence comes our Caesar, or our Napoleon? Not with flags and drums, I bet. He'll come with pious sayings and a mealy mouth, a drab little bastard full of 'love.' And hatred, and blood lust, and ambition. No lordly Caesar, no Little Corporal. Probably a eunuch."

"What did you say, dear?" asked Marjorie, coming awake and shivering a little. The Kitcheners were frankly asleep, with their eyes open. But the watchful Mrs. Morgan was still watching the impervious Robert, and he was watching Jenny, who was now gazing at Jonathan, and Maude was staring only at Robert.

"Nothing, Mama," said Jonathan, and at that childish word Marjorie blinked. Was Jonathan mocking her for her weary and involuntary slumber? No, he was smiling at her and he had never smiled at her like that before. But, while he smiled, his eyes were narrow and thoughtful, as though thinking of something else.

Trumpets sounded. Applause and cheering and shouting died. Colonel Hadley was approaching the lectern.

He stood silent and tall and thin, and the crowd resumed its clapping but with less enthusiasm than before. They knew these old soldiers. They had nothing but platitudes to say, unlike the Senator, who could really arouse emotion and make a man feel splendid and big and powerful. Besides, the crowd was full of beer and food and cake and lemonade and sluggish with sun and heat and wanted to go home. The dignitaries were whispering together behind the Colonel, and the ladies were impatiently flapping their fans and yawning, and there was some scraping of chairs on the stone.

The mayor introduced the Colonel, whom everyone knew. "Our great hero, in the Civil War," said the short fat mayor, Emil Schuman. "He has a few words to say to us on this glorious Fourth. A few words," he added, glancing imploringly at the Colonel in his uniform. He wiped his glistening forehead and then his yellow mustache.

People were already leaving many of the tables, gathering up baskets and offspring. The band played louder. The people hesitated, then dropped down at tables of friends and yawned. But many streamed out of the square, wheeling carts and buggies and trailing little children, who howled strenuously.

Then the Colonel's voice rose, manly and strong and quiet

and firm, and even those on the streets paused and stood and waited, in spite of the sun and the heat.

"Fellow Americans," he said. "You have just heard a ringing speech by our Senator from Pennsylvania, Mr. Kenton Campion." He paused. He lifted his thin hand. "I have heard many speeches in my life, my friends, but none so dangerous, so mad, so cruel and so irresponsible, and so sinister."

His voice rang through the suddenly silent square, and now the silence was deep and stricken and aghast. Men came forward to the curbs to listen and then onto the grass. The scufflings and whisperings and chuckles and giggles behind the Colonel, on the stairs, stopped abruptly. The Senator's broad and sunny smile disappeared. The mayor sat upright in his chair.

"I don't believe it!" said Jonathan. "Not old Jerry!"

"An empire," said the Colonel, "is bought with one price only, through all the centuries: aggression against other nations, gold, blood, death, tears, sweat and pain, and slavery. Always the ultimate: slavery. An empire cannot be created nor maintained without that crime against God and man, without bankruptcy, without war, without perpetual armies, without chains, without threat and prisons and firing squads and the sword.

"America is a peaceful country. She has no ambitions—yet. She has no international aims—yet. She does not desire to impose her form of government, though it is a free one, on other nations—yet. She is willing to let other countries live and prosper, to rise or fall, by their own will. She wishes only to present an example of liberty and democracy and peace to the whole world. As of this day, friends, as of this day. She remembers the warnings of George Washington to engage in peaceful trade with other nations but to refuse foreign entanglements and dangerous alliances. She has learned her lesson, which all history has proclaimed—that interference in the name of whatever sanctimonious slogan in the affairs of other countries is the way to power, perhaps, but is also the way to extinction and ruin and catastrophe. It is the way of ruthless and ambitious men, who pervert the nobility in the heart of free men to evil uses, men who lust for wealth and desire to rule their fellowmen."

The Colonel's voice rose and shook, and he lifted his clenched hand.

"Listen to me, my fellow Americans! No nation ever embarked on the road to empire—with heroic slogans and noble banners and drums—without dying in her own blood! It is the justice of God. It is the vengeance of an outraged humanity. I, too, perhaps like the Senator, have glimpsed the future. We have two choices: peace, internal harmony, eternal vigilance. Or—war and blood and bankruptcy and embroilment in the endless quarrels of other nations. It is our choice. I, for one, pray that we will not go mad, that we will not listen to liars and mountebanks and men of ambition. But when men are led on the course of empire, they lose their minds, they become drunk on platitudes, they thunder on the drums of insanity. Their dead fall about them, the young dead, and they call those dead heroes. They are not. They are sacrifices to Moloch, and always they were and always they will be.

"I am a soldier. I obeyed my country's call to arms. The Union won my war, in which many others here today were also engaged. What have we now? A divided nation. How long will these wounds take to heal, and a brother's blood forgotten? How long will it take before the men at Gettysburg are forgotten, and their cannon rusted into the ground? What did it profit us that we fought that war? It was said that it was to destroy slavery, but slavery was already vanishing in the nation, and a few more years would have seen its end. It was said we fought to preserve the Union, but if we had not had *agents provocateurs* in the North and South, that Union would never have been threatened."

He paused. Then he said, "If this be treason, make the most of it."

He bowed his head. "These are not the words I wished to speak today. I wanted to celebrate the peace and safety and grandeur of our free country, our blessed country. But I have heard the words of ancient evil and a sword has entered my heart, and I can only lift my voice in warning: The course of empire leads only to death. May God deliver us."

There was no applause as he turned. He did not sit down again. He walked down the steps, reached the flagstones, then turned straightly and left the square. The crowd watched him go, baffled. They whispered together. The dignitaries wore outraged faces. They whispered and shook their heads and smiled derisively. Some gathered around the Senator to bend and offer him congratulations or condolences at the insult he had been given. He laughed ruddily. "These old soldiers!" he said with indulgence.

The band struck up "The Star-Spangled Banner," and everyone sang, and there was a feeling that something very portentous had happened and something very threatening, but now the premonition was lifted, and everyone could go home in this late afternoon and rest, and sit on porches and yawn contentedly, and then put the children to bed and brew the coffee for a late supper.

They spoke amiably of the Senator. But few mentioned the Colonel.

"One of your more inspired speeches," said Dr. Louis Hedler to the Senator. "I've heard Bryan, even at his best not half as eloquent."

"Thank you, Louis," said the Senator, as he assisted his sister down the steps, and waited amiably for her to finish a little chatter with her friends. "But Hadley! Almost in his dotage, isn't he?"

"Your age, Kenton," Louis Hedler could not resist saying. "And now he's retired."

"Ah, yes, Louis. It's fortunate for the country that most soldiers do not believe as he does. We'd have had the Vandals in on us long ago if they did."

"Now we just have to wait for them to rise from within," said Louis. Kenton laughed. "Then we'll massacre them. We Senators won't be like the old Roman ones who repaired in a stately fashion to the Senate Chamber and sat there, robed and silent, until the Vandals roared in and sliced off their heads. No, indeed. By the time our internal Vandals feel strong enough to strike, we'll have a governing elite who won't be forced to wait for public permission or the vote or anything else in order to act. We won't have public opinion then. We'll have governmental opinion. This is a new age, Louis, a new age!"

"I don't like it," said Louis. "Well, I doubt you and I will live to see America become a despotism; that's one thing to be grateful for."

"Yes, isn't it? My dear, you almost tripped on your hem," said the Senator to his sister, Beatrice Offerton. He bowed to the lady who was engaging Beatrice's attention. He turned to Louis and his handsome eyes had a peculiar glaze over them, as if they had been covered by glass. "Louis, may I ask when young Ferrier is leaving Hambledon?"

"Jon?" Louis' froglike face colored. "I don't know, Kenton, I don't know. Frankly, Humphrey and I are trying to persuade him to remain. After all, he was ac—"

But the Senator's face had lost all its geniality and became vindictive and quiet. "Louis, I want that man out of this town. In fact, I want him out of this state. I have influence in

Pittsburgh and Philadelphia. He won't get hospital privileges in any other city. Get him out, Louis."

Louis had the obstinacy of his Teutonic forebears, and he had never liked the Senator for all they were the dearest of friends. He said, "He saved little Hortense Nolan's life a few days ago, Kenton, and her parents are the best friends you have in this town. He's saved more people than I like to remember. He is a splendid surgeon and physician, and we need him——"

"Get him out, Louis," said the Senator in a soft and deadly voice. "Is that understood? Out of your hospital, out of Bedloe's. Do you know what he did to my son? He made it impossible for him to continue at his seminary. I objected to the seminary in the first place, but I bowed, like an indulgent father, to the boy's decision. Then this Ferrier almost destroyed him, filled his mind with the most unspeakable things, and the boy has run off to France. I have heard some more about his cases. Didn't little Martha Best die under mysterious circumstances, for instance? And only yesterday my dear and delicate friend, Elsie Holliday, was put under sedatives by you, Louis, because your Ferrier drove her son, young Jefferson, out of town, out of his home state, and to some pesthole near the Gulf of Mexico, after some alleged treatment, or diagnosis, which no one else has confirmed and which is probably false."

Louis' face tightened. "Now, listen to me, Kenton, you've heard very filthy lies. Little Martha had a very rare disease, cancer of the blood, and it's incurable and Jon diagnosed it at once. My God, man! You can't blame Jon for an act of God or nature! I don't know about your boy. I didn't know Jon was his physician——"

"He wasn't. He forced himself, uninvited, uncalled, into my house and talked alone to my boy, and the next thing I and his dear aunt knew he was off for France and places unknown. Is it ethical to insist on treating a patient against his will, against the will of his family? I thought not. But what about Jefferson Holliday?"

Louis hesitated. "I can't tell you exactly, but he has something the government designates as a 'loathesome and contagious disease.' That'll have to satisfy you, Kenton."

The Senator chuckled, glanced sidelong at his sister, who was still chatting. "Venereal, eh? Well, young men. What about the new arsenic treatments? Why, Louis, if all the young men who had syphilis or the clap were driven out of the cities, we'd have no one left."

He tapped Louis on the shoulder. "Get him out, Louis. Is that understood? Come, Beatrice, we'll just have time to drive down to the park and dine with our friends and than see the fireworks at night."

Louis watched him go, then slowly lit a cigar and walked down the stairs and contemplated the hot litter and silence of the square, now almost deserted. The heated gold of very late afternoon shimmered in the tops of the trees and on store fronts. "Yes, Kent," Louis Hedler muttered, "it's understood. By you, of course. But there are others."

The ladies of the Ferrier party had discreetly retired, "for refreshment," into the interior of the City Hall, and the gentlemen also retired for the same purpose into the convenient basement of the First Presbyterian Church. They met again at the table. "We're practically alone," said Jonathan with pleasure.

"Well, we still have the chocolate cake dear Father brought us, and there is still ice for the tea," said Marjorie. She sank down on a bench as if very weary. "Isn't it getting a little cooler? What time is it, Jon? I didn't bring my watch."

"Nearly six. Campion gassed so long that you fell asleep, Mother, and nearly everyone else at this table. What a fraud and dangerous farce he is! What did you think, Bob?"

"I?" asked Robert, and his fair cheeks turned very pink. "Candidly, Jon, I don't enjoy listening to politicians. I heard enough of them in Philadelphia. I just let the Senator's words slide easily, without penetration." At this word his color became extremely bright and Jonathan wanted to burst out laughing, for the young doctor had glanced with wincing at Jenny Heger, who was not listening at all and had so far overcome her fear of strangers that she was helping Marjorie fill clean glasses with ice and tea.

"You didn't miss anything," said Jonathan. The men were not yet seated. They stood in a little group together, Jonathan, Robert Morgan, the priest and Mr. Kitchener.

"I didn't listen, either," said the latter. "What for? It's bad enough around election time. Did you listen—sir?" he kindly asked Father McNulty.

"I'm afraid I did," said the priest. "I found it very disturbing. I've never heard a speech like that before, though I've been hearing hints of such things in editorials in many newspapers since the new century arrived. There's a sort of exuberance in the air—"

"Well, that isn't very bad," said Mr. Kitchener.

"An approaching madness," said Jonathan. "I just remembered what Henry James said recently, to the effect that our world will have pretty well gone to smash about midcentury. I believe him. Some of the old boys are very good prophets."

"In what way will it have gone to smash?" asked Mr. Kitchener, and he looked at his daughter.

"Wars. Revolutions. Nihilism. We've already smelled its stench in America. Coming events send their stink ahead of them, as well as their shadows. Populism. Teddy's Progressivism. William Jennings Bryan. Eugene Debs. I've been reading a lot about Debs lately. At midcentury I'll be eighty-four, and dead, thank God."

"But our grandchildren," said Mr. Kitchener, very unhappily.

Jonathan shrugged. "I won't have any, and that's a blessing. Let our grandchildren take care of themselves. Sufficient unto the day— Well, we still have comparative peace in the world just now, though I doubt it is going to last much longer, considering our Campions in Washington."

"Wars?" said Robert. "Can you imagine America embroiling herself in any foreign war? Impossible."

But Jonathan had turned his head to look at Jenny. She was leaning over the table, her back to him, and he saw the extended long slim length of her and her small and slender waist, and the stretch of cheap checked cotton over her fine shoulders. Marjorie caught his eye and the gentlemen, all of them troubled now, returned to the table and the tea and the cake. But now Jenny was sitting far opposite Jonathan, next to Marjorie, and other of the ladies had changed their seats and so Jonathan found himself near Mrs. Kitchener on one side and Maude on the other. Maude was not pleased at this, for Robert was sitting next to Jenny on the opposite bench and was not looking at Maude at all.

They ate and drank desultorily, idly watching the stout German Brass Band put away its instruments. The hot early evening air was so quiet that those at the table could hear the guttural accents of the musicians. They could hear the dry rustling of the trees and the movements of carriages in streets beyond the park as the celebrants drove home. Men were clearing away the flags and the chairs on the City Hall steps, and the draped banners of red, white and blue, and other

men were walking over the grass gathering up the larger litter. No one moved quickly. A man laughed. A distant dog
barked. The sun fell lower and lower into a reddening sky.
There was a scent of old roses and hay from somewhere,
even over the smell of heated stone, and a breath from the
river.

"How peaceful it is," said Marjorie. "I'm just drugged with
sun and air. I'm sure I'll be asleep before we get home. I've
enjoyed this day, in spite of the Senator. You must tell me
what he said when we get home, Jon."

"I've forgotten," her son replied. Now the old sick restlessness was on him again, the blankness, the wanting to go he
knew not where, the intense desire for meaning and fulfill-
ment, which he had known as a child. He looked at the
golden glitter in the tops of the trees and the blue shadows
under them, and his restlessness deepened to an old pain, an
old desire, and his disquiet submerged his thoughts in darkness. He looked at Jenny, shyly talking to Mrs. Kitchener,
and again he was tense and tingling and again he felt sorrow
and bitterness and the deepest anger. But now the anger was
against himself because he knew, finally, what had ailed him
for nearly four years.

"Robert?" said Mrs. Morgan. "I really think we must be
getting home. My arthritis, you know."

Robert seemed rebellious, and then he sighed. "Very well,
Mother." He stood up. He bowed to Marjorie. "Mrs. Ferrier,
it was most kind of you to invite us, most kind. You have
done so much to make us happy in our new home. When we
have moved into our house, I hope you will visit us often."

"My dear, I've done nothing," said Marjorie, and her hazel
eyes sparkled at him with affection.

Robert stood and hesitated. He had the strongest yearning
that Jenny look at him, say a word, or simply smile. He
could not leave without that. As if she felt his urgent desire,
she did glance up across the table, for he had moved to help
his mother, and she gave him her faint and shrinking smile,
then glanced away. It was enough for the young man. He
was quite hearty in his last good-byes.

"Such a nice young man, so devoted to his poor mother,"
said Sue Kitchener. "She has led a life of such trials. Quite a
martyr. Is he—I mean, has he spoken—"

"If you mean, Sue, is there a girl lurking in the shadows—
no," said Jonathan. "He's disengaged. I hope he keeps that
way."

"Now, Jon," said Marjorie, and yawned deeply and richly.

Sue giggled. "Well, I hope he finds a lovely girl, right here in Hambledon." She smiled tenderly at her daughter and Maude blushed.

"And I have Benediction," said Father McNulty, "not that I expect many visitors to the Blessed Sacrament today."

He rose and made his farewells and trotted off, and everyone watched him go, even Jenny Heger. "At any rate, Kenton was good to help him buy his horse and buggy," said Marjorie. "I suppose that was because of Francis." She looked inquiringly at Jonathan, but he said nothing.

"And now I am afraid we must leave, too," said Sue Kitchener. "We are having just a light supper—if we can find any room for it—and then we are going down to the river to watch the fireworks in the dark. Are you going, too, Marjorie?"

"I think not," said Marjorie Ferrier. "I'm really too tired. Jonathan?"

"Certainly not," he replied.

"Well, that's too bad. I thought you might like to take Jenny."

Jonathan was amazed. The very idea was grotesque. The Kitcheners took their leave. Now the last yellow glitter had left the trees and a coolness was rising, and the Ferriers were alone with Jenny, who was sitting in her usual anguished silence with her head bowed and her hands in her lap.

But when Marjorie began to gather dishes and glasses and silver and napkins together, Jenny stood up at once and began to help her, her young hands deft and quick. Jonathan filled the baskets neatly. "Jenny," said Marjorie, "will ride with us to the river. She didn't bring her bicycle today."

"Oh, no, I can walk!" cried the girl. "I like to walk! It isn't far!"

"Nonsense. A young girl walking alone on the streets—it's getting quite dark now—and on a holiday, could be misunderstood," said Marjorie.

"Mother, you're in the twentieth century now," Jonathan said. "Young ladies are understood these days, not misunderstood. Isn't that so, Jenny?"

When she did not answer but only hurried more, he added, "It is all the 'new woman' now, isn't it, Jenny, the free woman, free to do as she likes under any circumstances. Bold and free, like a man."

"Don't be unpleasant, Jon," said Marjorie. "Jenny, I'll hear no more. You must ride with us, among the baskets, I am afraid. Will your servants have returned by the time you arrive?"

The girl blurted, "No. I told them they need not come back until the morning. It is a holiday for them, too."

Marjorie let her hands fall. "Jenny! You mean to spend the night entirely alone on the island! Why, that's not to be thought of! It's too dangerous. Anyone can row over there and molest you or rob you. Say no more. You must stay with us tonight."

"Oh, no!" The cry was purely desperate. "I'm not afraid, Aunt Marjorie. I'm not afraid when I am alone." She looked, in the blue twilight, as if she were about to cry. "I want to be alone," she added. "I didn't mean to say that, Aunt Marjorie, but I did mean it—I mean—"

Jonathan had listened to this with surly amusement. Was she planning a new rendezvous, with Childe Harald away, on that island? She looked distracted enough.

"I won't hear of it," said Marjorie. "What if something happened to you?"

"It won't," said Jenny. "It never has before. I've often been alone like this."

Oh, you have, have you? thought Jonathan, and remembered a recent story now avid in Hambledon, alleged to be directly from one of the servants herself. It was related that the maid had often seen Harald leaving Jenny's bedroom early in the morning, and once or twice had detected Jenny leaving Harald's at dawn. It was a delicious story. There was still another—that Jenny's favors were not Harald's alone and never had been. The girl was only twenty, yet there was hardly a woman more notorious in Hambledon than she.

Who had muttered the sniggering story to him only a few days ago? He could not remember. "But I can vouch for it," someone had said. "It is true enough." Then he remembered. It had been in St. Hilda's lobby, and one of the young doctors had told him. Jenny had discharged the maid, who was now working for his mother. "The wench had seen too much," the doctor had said. "But that Heger trollop is a fine piece! I'd like to—" Jonathan had walked away, full of his chronic rage and full of his hate. He did not see but only guessed the young doctor's obscene gesture.

There was a desperate resolution about Jenny now, as she pushed aside Marjorie's pleas. "I really am not afraid. I really like to be alone. I have locks on the doors," she said. "Please don't insist, Aunt Marjorie."

"I'm really too tired to oppose your willfulness," Marjorie said with severity. "And I'm very angry with you, Jenny. Jon will drop me at home and then will take you to the river. And then," she said in a clear hard voice, "he will row you over to the island and inspect every room for you, and the grounds, and then wait until you are locked up. No, Jenny, I won't hear anything more. I'm very tired. I'd like to sleep tonight and not worry about you. Jon?"

He was delighted to make the girl more distracted than she already was. "It will be a pleasure, dear Jenny," he said, and gave her a low bow. She looked at him with mute wretchedness and her mouth shook and he was elated.

CHAPTER EIGHTEEN

It was deep twilight when Jonathan let his mother out of the surrey and led her to the house. "Hurry back," she whispered, "I'll go in alone. It would be just like Jenny to get out and run away. Jon, be kind to her, will you? Don't tease her so."

"Kind? Jenny doesn't want anyone to be kind to her. She's sufficient unto herself, a very haughty and sullen young lady with a mind of her own. At least let me unlock the door for you."

Marjorie stood in the lighted doorway and watched the surrey drive off. Jenny, apparently, had refused to leave the back seat and still sat crowded among the baskets, which Marjorie had forgotten. It was just like the poor child. Intellectual, intelligent, proud, but shrinking and afraid. Marjorie thought, Intellect isn't enough for a woman, or even intelligence. A woman isn't really a man, though so many militant women seem to think so these days, and say "there is very little difference." They don't understand that that little difference is the most important thing in the world. There's little difference, I heard, between lead and gold—until it reaches the marketplace. A woman stripped of her "difference," in mere mind, was still not a man. Even those deprived of their generative organs were not men. The mysterious and inexorable "difference" remained, and, thought Marjorie, closing the door behind her, let the world beware when it forgets that. A woman who was not distinct from a man in a spiritual way could betray the whole race.

The surrey clopped through the quiet dark streets. The lamps were already lit, and burned in yellow straightness, for there was no wind. A few voices sounded sleepily from dark porches, and there were the creakings of rockers and an occasional scolding as a woman addressed herself to dilatory children inside the houses. Now the refreshed grass exhaled its sweetness and the trees murmured a little, and at a far distance there was a clatter of one of Hambledon's few streetcars going toward the river park. It was a somnolent early night.

Jonathan drove in silence but acutely aware of the girl behind him. He knew that she hated him, but he had never cared, until now, to know the reason why. He had seen her in childhood and young girlhood, and then in early womanhood, and it was not until she had been sixteen—and still untouched, he had presumed—that he had sharply noticed her. That had been six months after his marriage to Mavis. She had reminded him of a young white swan sailing alone in a pond, quiet, shy, nervously smiling when spoken to, rarely speaking. Her mother had been alive then, foolish Myrtle, and had recently married Harald. No, it had not been that marriage which had changed the girl from a touching young softness to a steely witch, for though it had been evident that she had at first thought her mother had violated the sacred memories of Daddy, she had regarded Myrtle as a child who must be given what she desired to make her happy and to keep her protected. Jenny had not changed until her mother had died. Myrtle had been on digitalis for a considerable time, then six months before her death her condition had worsened. Jonathan had told her then that her days were counted, and to his surprise the silly woman had not become hysterical or maudlin but had accepted what was to come. But Jonathan, she had said, must not tell dear Harald or darling Jenny. It would destroy them. Jonathan had been freshly surprised. Myrtle had not seemed to be a woman capable of strength to carry her affliction alone.

Myrtle's death changed Jenny violently. The girl who could speak so gently in her sweet strong voice—when pressed by kind insistance—and could even laugh a little, though she was always so grave, became cold and hard and remote and silent. It was her foolish mother's will, of course, which had changed her. She had probably felt herself betrayed. It was odd, but not so very odd—considering human nature—that money could transform people. Yet, at her early age, she had become Harald's mistress, and not long, if one was to credit reports, after her mother's death. Was it to hold Harald to the island? If he left for more than seven months at a time, the money would be hers, but it was possible that it was not only the money she wanted but Childe Harald, too.

It was a mystery which Jonathan had not been able to settle satisfactorily in his own mind. There was a dimension here which eluded him, which was stark and brutal, yet hidden. Certainly, in the presence of others she was deadly silent and did not speak to Harald, and, if he spoke to her so directly that she was forced to notice him, she looked at him with what appeared to be actual and deep aversion. It was all very elusive. Of course, they could have conspired together to give this effect to others in order to deceive, for there were times when Jenny could not take her eyes off Harald and watched his every movement like a woman possessed, and it was very evident, then, that nothing he said was not heard by her intently and probably weighed and measured. Jenny was the weighing-and-measuring kind; that had been evident from her very childhood, for she had always been thoughtful and contemplative and had answered the most casual question as if she had given it her deepest consideration and had not replied until she was certain her answer was correct in all respects. When others spoke in her presence and Harald's, she was totally indifferent and gave the appearance of deafness, but when Harald spoke, she came alive.

Only an infatuated woman could behave so and have such an immoderate reaction to a man's every gesture and every word.

Jonathan remembered the first time that Jenny, as an awkward girl approaching womanhood, had become more than a child to him and had invaded the wretched cloister of his life with Mavis. It had been a spring day and he had visited Myrtle and Harald on the island—they had not long been married—and Jenny, the devoted daughter, was pruning her father's roses. She had never dressed well but always frumpily, as if deliberately trying to offset her mother's very fashionable and elaborate clothing. Jonathan, strolling over the grounds and silently laughing at them as usual, had come upon Jenny in the pale spring sunlight, bending solicitously over the steaming dark earth and tenderly cutting here and there as careful as a surgeon cleaning up after an operation. She wore a brown wool dress and an ugly brown coat and her hair was bare to the cool crispness of the wind and it rolled in long black waves over her shoulders and her back.

She had looked up at him, startled, for she had not heard him come, and the sunlight had suddenly struck the exquisite pale contours of her face and the carved rose jade of her lips and had made her blue eyes blaze like illuminated sapphires. Knife in hand, still bending, she had turned her head, and the wind lifted her long black hair and blew it about her in a tumbling cloud of deep shadow and sparkling light. She was like a nymph, he had thought without originality, faintly smiling, still startled, shy, ready to run but afraid to offend, her hands stained with mud, her immature body as delicate and pliant as a white birch sapling.

"Hello, Jenny," he said. "I thought you were over in Hambledon today."

"No. No, Uncle Jon," she answered, and for the first time he was conscious of the promise of rich sweetness in her voice. She straightened, and tried to control the tossing masses of her hair. "I didn't know you were here, either. I— I'm pruning my father's roses. It should have been done long ago, I'm afraid. So much dead wood from the hard winter. I think his best old-fashioned one died." She looked down at the bush sadly. Jonathan inspected it, too. "No," he said, "there's a leaf or two, very small, near that dead crotch. Just cut off the top."

She was joyful and bent with him for a closer inspection. "Four leaves!" she cried. "I don't know how I missed them! It's such a wonderful bush; the roses are like little cabbages, and their scent is much deeper than the others. My father loved it best."

He saw her profile now, childlike and radiant and softly

smiling. She cut expertly. Her lips were parted and he saw her teeth, small and pearly, unlike Mavis', which were so large and so lavishly displayed in her wide laughter, and which just narrowly escaped being called "buck" or "horse teeth." Jenny's were like white ivory, barely showing between her lips, yet perfect and feminine. Too many girls these days were producing teeth as big as a young mare's, and they seemed to be proud of them, which was mystifying, and flared them out on all occasions. Jonathan thought that it was very inexplicable that two such arrant vulgarians as Myrtle and Peter Heger had brought forth such a daughter.

Jenny's hair fell over her cheeks as she bent for a last clipping, and she seemed clothed in that brightly black cloak, living and soft and shimmering in the sun. Then she stood up and flung her hair back unaffectedly and laughed at Jonathan with delight, as if he had given her a priceless gift. The sound of her laughter rang through the gold and frail green quiet of the spring gardens, and it was laughter unlike Mavis' boisterous and bursting mirth, for it was very musical and shy.

Jenny, Jonathan had thought, as he stood there easily and smiled at her with his chilled hands in his pockets and his polished boots already muddy. Sweet Jenny. He had forgotten, since his marriage, that there were such girls as Jenny in the world, tender, simple, honest, gentle and diffident, who could be so happy when a dead bush proved it was not dead at all but was importantly and exuberantly alive. Here was no avaricious flirt, no schemer, no liar, no grasping woman with tiny eyes and a huge grinning mouth, which could express the utmost in callous cruelty. Jenny's mother was rich, yet Jenny was unaffected and her joy in a rose could never have been known to a Mavis.

She stepped back from the rose bed and her shoe stuck in the mud and she hopped on one foot. Jonathan retrieved the shoe and he never noticed it was several sizes larger than Mavis' dainty slippers. He scraped the mud off on the new green grass, then gallantly insisted on putting it on Jenny's foot again. To support herself she leaned her hand on his bent back, and all at once a fiery thrill ran through his shoulder and then through his body. For an instant he could not move. Then, his hands shaking, he put the muddy shoe over the coarse brown stocking and he saw that though the girl's foot was large, it was also miraculously slender and beautifully molded. She was murmuring something, but he did not catch her words. He was still stricken by his response to her touch, and now felt the heat in his flesh, and a sudden incredulousness, and a sudden rush of happiness and buoyance. He had never known these before, and he was dazed at his own beatitude.

"Thank you, Uncle Jon," said Jenny. He stood up, his face darkly flushed. He said, "I wish you wouldn't call me 'Uncle Jon,' Jenny. I'm not really your uncle. Call me Jon."

She studied him seriously. Then in her shyly blunt way she said, "But, Uncle Jon, you are so much older than I am! I'm only sixteen. It wouldn't be respectful."

"What's fifteen years between friends?" he asked, trying for lightness because his breath was coming too fast. "You call Harald 'Harald,' and he's only two years younger than I. Come on, Jenny."

She considered him with that young solemnity of hers. The blueness of her eyes seemed to fill her face, that immaculate face of absolute purity and without any guile at all. Then her expression changed after long moments. It became startled, very frightened and confused, and she turned her face aside and her cheeks were suddenly awash in brilliant scarlet. Without a word she flung herself away from him and ran back to that ridiculous castle. Her long black hair floated behind her like a mantle, catching the light.

Jonathan watched her go. He was too involved with his own emotions to wonder why the girl had run like that and why she had colored so and had been so silent.

He did not see her again that day. But as he lay awake that night with Mavis sleeping blissfully beside him—she had not as yet moved to another room—he could not forget Jenny. Academically, he knew much that was to be known about humanity and human emotions, for he was a doctor, but as young Father McNulty was to later say, he was essentially and amazingly a simple man who could not, as yet, translate his knowledge into personal objectivity. If another man had told him of this experience, he would have said with a broad smile, "There's nothing mysterious about it. You've fallen in love with that girl, and probably you've fallen in love for the first time, and never mind that you're married."

His marriage took a change for the worse in the next few days and then he and Mavis had gone to Europe for the summer, on her insistence, and he had agreed in a last desperate hope that he could change Mavis and save the marriage and persuade her to begin a family.

He had not seen Jenny again for nearly a year, and incomprehensibly he only saw her at a distance. In the following years he saw her exactly three times before her mother's death. He would have jeered to learn that he was a rigidly upright man in his soul, yet for a long time he not only tried to devote himself to Mavis and to change her but he suppressed that day with Jenny in his mind. He had removed himself from his Church, but the moral teachings and doctrines had sunk irrevocably into him. Whenever he remembered Jenny, he choked the thought at once and did not know that the heavy sadness he always felt was connected with that spring day in the castle's gardens.

He had not known it until this Fourth of July, 1901, on a peaceful hot day in a peaceful and joyful and busy country. He remembered it now, with all its first poignancy and longing and sharp delirium and passion, and all its sense that something incredibly novel and beautiful had happened to him and had lightened his whole somber world, had made him young and expectant and unbearably happy, for a few hours at least.

But the girl in the garden and the girl behind him in the surrey were not one and the same any longer. One had been innocent and beloved, and this one was besmirched and unclean. To him that had been long unpardonable and worth only his hate. For a second that afternoon, when he had caught Jenny at the table, it was Jenny of the garden again, Jenny of sixteen years, and the look she had given him had recalled that whole day.

The surrey turned toward the river, and down the long street the dark water was glittering and the bulk of the island stood up in it against the sky and the opposite mountains.

"You can let me out here," said Jenny. Her voice was rough and low.

Jonathan said, "You heard my mother. I promised her to see you safely home, and on your island, with the doors all locked." He did not turn to look back at her in the dark. Jenny was crouching on the cushions as if deadly cold, hugging herself with her arms. She was crying silently, great noiseless sobs that shook her body and tore at her throat. This was an anguish familiar to her, for it was compounded of grief and despair, of longing and loneliness, of monstrous desolation. Her tears ran down her cheeks without a sound and dropped on the plain blue and white check of her shirtwaist. She looked through the watery mist of them at the back of Jonathan's arrogant head and then she closed her eyes and pressed her lips together.

The first flare of the evening fireworks rose in the sky at the left, above the houses and this long street to the river. It flowered like a huge rose in green and red, spreading with a thunderous roar that rolled along the water, breaking into vivid stars against the deepening dark of the sky, in which the ivory curve of the moon was embedded and in which the stars were beginning to tremble and change. Jenny was too absorbed in her misery to see, but Jonathan saw and remembered again the last Fourth of July when he and Mavis were guests of the gay party of dignitaries in the park near the river. Mavis, as usual, had been given the seat of honor and each blaze of the fireworks lit up her luminous face, her smiling face, her constantly tossing golden head, her quick and lively gestures. She had appeared to be enjoying herself, surrounded by love and adulation, and her French perfume had been a cloud of delicious fragrance all over her so that it seemed not to appear extraneous but a part of her smooth and beautiful body and the white lace dress she was wearing. Jonathan's latest gift to her, a necklace of aquamarines and pearls, hung about her throat and seemed to gather color and warmth from her lucent flesh.

Yet, that night, when they were alone in her dressing room, she had risen to cold and contorted fury. This was not new. Her rages were very frequent when with Jonathan. She had ordered him from her bedroom and dressing room. But he had stood there, somber and silent, just staring at her with a kind of incredulity which further outraged her, for she knew by now he still could not reconcile the lovely-lady-among-strangers with the uncontrolled virago who was his wife and who had the most cruel of tongues. He could not reconcile the lady-of-love with this greedy and empty woman. He was always in a state of desperate wonder.

She was sitting at her dressing table in a peignoir of white lace and satin, with her golden hair streaming over her shoulders and her face as ugly as death, and livid. She screamed at him and beat her fists on the table and her eyes were full of glittering hate.

"You are such a fool! Such a bore, bore, bore! Do you know how boring you are, sitting like a clod among your friends and not speaking or, if speaking, making some disagreeable remark! Bore! Bore! Old man, old man, old stupid man! If you weren't so stupid, you'd have left this dull and silly town long ago! They can talk about your 'brilliance,' bah! but I know how stupid you are, how boring, how tedious, how tiresome, with no conversation and no fun. You keep me here in this horrid town, in this horrid old house, among these horrid people, and all you can say is that it's your 'home,' and these are your 'people,' and I'm like to die of ennui and yawn myself into a stupor! What fun is there for me, here—and with you? Tell me! Just tell me!"

He could speak now, slowly and without emotion. "I'm sorry I bore you. Yes, this is my 'home.' This is my city. These are my 'people.' You know it. You've known it from the beginning. I take you to New York and Philadelphia and Boston and Chicago on medical meetings. You know of the offers I've had, in great hospitals and clinics—"

She had listened to him, her furious breaths making her breast lift and fall rapidly, and her rage rising. Again she beat her fists on the table. "How long do you stay in those wonderful cities? A few days, a week or so, letting famous men flatter you while they are laughing at you out of the other side of their mouths! They know what you are, a small-time, small-town fraud, with no ambition, no imagination. You can't even dance properly. You hardly ever laugh. You're a clod, a farmer, a dullard, a fool! I wish I'd died before I married you!"

"So do I," he said. Now his voice was heavy and full of thick anger, murderous anger he rarely felt—and then only with Mavis. "I wish you—or I—had died before we were married. Indeed."

She became silent then, her hands unclenching on the table, and she looked at him and what she saw frightened her and made her turn very white. She half rose. The mirror reflected her pale and fallen mouth. Her tiny blue eyes opened as wide as they could and they were sharp with wary fear. She clutched the edge of the table, and then her pink tongue darted out to wet lips suddenly dry. She blinked and she watched.

"Do you know how many times I've wanted to kill you, Mavis?" he asked. "Do you know what I think at night when I can't sleep? I think of ways of killing you. Poison? Cutting your throat? Smothering you? Strangling you? You tempt me all the time, Mavis, you tempt me."

She knew it was true and she let out a deep gasp, and then, inch by inch, she moved away from him backward, her dressing gown glistening in the lamplight, her hands pressed tightly against her smooth thighs. She began to whisper. "I—I didn't mean what I said—it's just that I'm so bored here—I'm alone at night—you are out on call, or the hospital. I know you're a doctor—I know—I know— But I'm young!" Her whisper lifted to a thin and venomous wail in spite of her fear. "I'm not an old crone, ready to die. But I'm withering in this house, I'll be old before my time. I'm only twenty-three, but I feel ages, ages. I go out, but it's the same old thing, among the same old people, and the same old talk. No fun—"

"Life isn't 'fun,' " he said. He swallowed the sick and infuriated lump in his throat. "You should know that. You aren't so very young any longer. You knew when you married me that you'd never be able to coax me away from Hambledon. I've given you all I could, bought you everything you wanted, have taken you abroad and to the big cities frequently. That wasn't enough for you." But nothing would ever be enough for the Mavises of the world, nothing would ever satisfy them or fill the gaunt lust with which they had been born. "Fun." They lived only for that. Some said the Laughing Girls had a tremendous "lust for life." But it was an empty and superficial lust, demanding tinsel and endless amusement and endless mirth, and dancing and rich food and wines and money. Above all, money, and adulation and flattery and fawning.

What made them think they were worthy of all this, of worship, of jewels, of fine carriages and furs and silks and masculine attention and adoration? Or were they capable of asking themselves this merciless question? To them it was sufficient to desire. The world was their servant, created just for their pleasure and entertainment.

"You won't even give me a child, you trivial, mindless wretch," Jonathan went on. "You selfish imitation of a real woman. But, then, I should be grateful. What kind of a mother would you make? What kind of a human being would you produce? Yes, I should be grateful."

He stared at her with his violent black eyes. "I should have killed you before this, when I found out what you were. One of these days I may do it. Don't tempt me again." She saw the hunger to murder her in his face, the pallid shine of his face, the glint of his teeth between his lips, the fire in his eyes. She backed away from him still farther, then suddenly whirled in a rush of gold and white and ran into her bedroom, slamming the door in real terror behind her, and locking it. Then she leaned against it and closed her eyes and

breathed rapidly, listening for a sound behind the door. But
Jonathan went away and she heard his own door close, and
all was soft rosy lamplight in her charming bedroom, which
she had decorated in pink and blue and silver. "I'll tell Uncle
Martin," she whispered with vindictiveness. "I'm not safe
here any longer." She was not afraid now. She was only
amazed, horribly offended, aghast that he had dared speak to
her like that. She wanted revenge for such an insult to her,
Mavis Eaton, who could have married anyone—anyone. It
was not to be believed! That wicked old man, that nasty old
man, who had betrayed her by marrying her, and who was
keeping her a prisoner in this awful dull town which she
hated and where she was not appreciated!

Tonight, as he drove Jenny down to the river, Jonathan
fully remembered that night when he had wanted to kill his
wife, when just a few more words from her would have precipitated him into fearful action. But she had had the cunning of an animal which she was, and she had not railed at
him again.

The rockets were blossoming in noisy and rainbow profu-
sion in the dark sky, and the river carried the sound of music
along the shore and far faint laughter. Ahead, at the end of
the street the water moved silently and blackly, and the island
stood there, not a single light in any window, not a light on
its rising bulk. Jonathan said to the silent girl behind him,
"You didn't have the sense to leave a light burning, did you?"

Jenny did not answer. She knew if she said a word, that
she would burst out into open agonized sobs. But she looked
at the fireworks scintillating against the sky, and heard, even
above the incoherent internal stammering of her old pain, the
voices and the music. Jonathan, for the first time, turned his
head and looked over his shoulder. He could barely see the
girl as she huddled in the rear, but he caught the outline of
her thin body and her face turned to the fireworks. She was
only a mute shadow there, but he felt something very odd.
He felt a lonely wistfulness in that shadow, a hunger, a silent
yearning.

Nonsense, he said to himself. But still he was surprised.
Why should the grim Jenny Heger want to be part of that
noisy celebration and to be among people she had rejected
years ago and who laughed at her openly now and repeated
lewd tales of her? Still, he was surprised, and with that surprise the old sadness and bitterness came back to him. She
knows what I know about her, he thought, she knows what

she is, and she knows what the town says of her. Above all, she knows what I think of her and that is why she is always crude and rough with me and runs at a look from me.

They reached the water's edge and Jonathan left the surrey to tie up his horse. Jenny flew swiftly past him down the shallow bank; she was like a moth. In an instant she was in one of the three waiting rowboats. She was actually pulling away, after strongly shoving the boat from the shore, when he leaped over the widening black water, half fell into the boat, recovered his balance and raised himself on a knee. "You damned fool, you stubborn fool," he said. "Get over here. Give me those oars." The broad boat rocked from side to side and some water splashed in and Jonathan swore. He reached for the oars and the girl raised one and its wet side caught silver from the brightening moon. He knew she wanted to hit him, and knew that she would, so he pushed himself to the stern and said, "All right, I love a show of manliness."

She rowed with firm young strength, bending and straightening, and the oars were urgent, and Jenny's body moved in perfect rhythm and the boat fled over the quiet water. Now, to the east, the bursting fireworks reflected themselves in the river in gaudy splashes of orange and scarlet and gold and blue, infinitely beautiful and weird, exploding into points of falling light. The boat creaked softly, the oars dipped with hardly a sound. A particularly elaborate fireworks display represented an enormous head of President McKinley, important and solid, and loud applause clamored over the water. Jenny turned her head toward the massive display, which was painted on the black sky in fiery color, and Jonathan saw her face, the smooth white forehead, under the brim of her great ugly hat. It was the face of a child.

The approaching island's dark bulk loomed against the mountains beyond, and on the flanks of the mountains Jonathan could see the climbing lights in the windows of the houses built there. The warm night air flowed over his face and he could smell the flowers and the fir trees of the island and its heated earth. But Jenny still watched the fireworks, forgetting her unwelcome passenger, and the oars moved more slowly. Once one of them was dyed crimson from the reflected fire, and another time it was deeply blue. Jenny sighed. She took off her hat and tossed it into the bottom of the boat, right at Jonathan's feet, and her black hair lifted in the river breeze, unrolled from its hasty knots, and fell about her shoulders.

When the boat grated at its island landing, Jenny did not wait to pull it ashore and tie it. She jumped over the two feet of water, and ran up the bank. Jonathan cursed again, tied up the boat, then searched for the little wooden shelter that held lanterns. By the time he had found one and lit it, Jenny was gone, finding her way like an owl in the night. He ran after her, the lantern throwing yellow light all about him, and soon he was on her heels. Immediately she stopped running but kept several steps ahead of him, moving like a flying shadow in spite of her long skirts. She had already unlocked the door of the castle when he reached it. She turned to him, panting a little. "That's all that's necessary. Thank you." Her voice was shaking.

"I'm going to search the damned place, as my mother asked me," he said. "Anyone could have rowed over here during the day or even during the last hour. Haven't you any sense at all?"

She blocked the way stubbornly, leaning against the wide bronze doors which caught golden glints from the lantern. Then with a sigh of resignation she went into the hall, her footsteps hard on the black and white marble squares. She lighted a lamp, which was waiting on a Spanish commode, and it brightened on the laughable suits of armor against the walnut walls and threw long shadows up and down the medieval stairway. The stained-glass window on the first landing glimmered into sections of rose and purple, red and yellow.

Jenny turned and faced Jonathan. "Thank you," she said. The hall, as usual, smelt musty as if ages had passed here, and the banners hanging along the walls lifted in the light wind which came through the open door. Jenny's face was bleak and still and she stared at Jonathan with formidable bitterness.

"Not yet," he said. "I must still search this monstrosity." He knew his remark would hurt her, but he was not prepared for the deep and quivering pain that ran over her face, and he was surprised at the trembling of her mouth. Then she turned and ran up the stairway, her steps clattering and loud, and he called after her, "When I'm finished, come down and shoot the bolts." A door banged upstairs and he heard a lock slide. He laughed shortly. He looked about him and found a candelabra and lit the candles on it and held it high, feeling ridiculous. No gaslight here, and, of course, no electricity.

This preciousness annoyed him and made him shake his head. He went down a rear passage to the dining room and glanced in carefully, and the candlelight struck the peaked and timbered ceiling, brought out a glow of rose on the damask walls, struck against the thin mullioned windows, and raced across the vast old table and the beautiful Aubusson rug and sparkled on the lavish silver displayed on the big black buffet, and showed the cavern of the white granite fireplace. Everything was deathly silent, and musty and still.

He next went into the vast drawing room in the tower wing, and again all was quiet, and the candlelight showed nothing but the Oriental rugs, the green damask of the walls, the tapestry at the windows and the frivolous French furniture all gilt and velvet and silk. The light brought the faces in the portraits on the walls into sudden life, and they gazed at Jonathan coldly and watchfully, the eyes seemingly following him as he came farther into the room. He stumbled over a velvet footstool and loudly swore, and one of his elbows knocked against the glass of a buhl cabinet and the candelabra was almost thrown from his hand. His elbow went numb for a moment or two. Unfortunately, the glass had not broken. For an instant Jonathan wanted to rectify this injustice, then laughed at himself. He climbed the stairway, careful to keep his footing on the polished wood. Now he was on the second floor and facing a long narrow hall carpeted in Oriental rugs. He knew Harald's studio and went to it and opened the carved wooden door. He could smell paint and turpentine and airlessness, and the candlelight glanced at easels and on canvases stacked against the wooden walls. He could hear the river gurgling secretly below, and it had a sinister sound. He climbed a much smaller staircase to the third floor, where the servants lived and slept, and he examined each quiet room and even the closets and wardrobes. The voice of the river was louder here for some reason, and the explosions that still continued in the park. Jonathan retreated down the stairway and passed the shut doors along the hall, reasonably certain that no intruder lurked there. However, he went back and did open other doors. One of the rooms, very large and exquisitely furnished, was Harald's bedroom, where he had slept with his dead wife. He had not bothered to remove certain furbelows and ruffles and pink draperies, and it still possessed a wan feminine air, mutely pathetic and lonely. A quick search showed it to be empty. Another search of other rooms verified Jonathan's opinion that no unauthorized person was present. He tried a last door, far down the hall. It was locked. So, this was Jenny's room. The old-fashioned handle was brass and polished; it turned in his hand but the strong door remained shut to him.

He made considerable noise clattering downstairs. He examined the breakfast room with its plain but beautiful Amish furniture, then he went into the morning room and wrinkled his nose at the dark oak and chintz. He last came to the library and set the candelabrum on a table while he lit two or three oil lamps. This was certainly the gloomiest room of the house, he thought, narrow, cold, and tall, lined with books and furnished with leather sofas and chairs in dull dark blues and blacks and crimsons, and here the air was definitely dank. The lamps flickered on the bearded portraits of Victorian men and prim ladies in their huge golden frames, and they eyed Jonathan with expressions of pure resentment at his intrusion. He opened one of the windows and the long crimson velvet draperies bellied inward into the room.

Where was that stupid girl? Why hadn't she come down, hearing him descend, to lock the doors behind him? He debated on calling her, then saw that there were several books on one of the black oak tables, and pencils and paper. He picked up a very slim book bound in soft leather. Villon. The book fell open in his hand and he saw that it was well-read and that verses, here and there, had been marked as if particularly poignant. Jonathan's eye fell on one:

> "I have a tree, a graft of love,
> That in my heart has taken root.
> Sad are the buds and blooms thereof
> And bitter sorrow is its fruit."

I bet, he thought, and slapped the book shut and wet his lips wryly. So, that was a favorite of Jenny's, was it? Harald had never cared for poetry. These were all Jenny's. He threw the book down and picked up another. Emily Dickinson. Again there were heavy markings.

> "There's a certain slant of light,
> On winter afternoons,
> That oppresses, like the weight
> Of Cathedral tunes."

Well, thought Jonathan. So we can be melancholy, can we?

> "As all the heavens were a bell,
>   And Being but an ear,
>   And I and silence some strange race,
>   Wrecked, solitary, here."

All at once the quiet around Jonathan became enormously oppressive and mournful and he heard the sad lapping of the river and he thought, quite involuntarily, of the lonely girl who lived in a dead man's dream and loved such poetry. He put down the book more slowly than he had replaced the other. His hand touched another, worn and bending. Elizabeth Browning.

> "How do I love thee? Let me count the ways—"

"Sentimental claptrap," he said aloud, and now he was sick again with his old anger. He could see Jenny here in this clammy library, mooning over these ardent and sorrowful love poems—and thinking of Harald. Did she read them to him, on winter nights, perhaps, before they climbed the stairs together, hand in hand, laughing secretly? Then he could not imagine Jenny like that, laughing secretly or at all, with Harald.

He picked up still another book, a selection of poems, and at once it opened to Matthew Arnold and he read:

> "Ah, love, let us be true to one another,
>   For the world which seems
>   To lie before us like a land of dreams,
>   So beautiful, so various, so new,
>   Hath neither joy nor hope, nor help from pain—"

Jenny had enclosed this in blacker markings. Jonathan stood still, the book in his hand, and remembered his wedding night, when he had quoted this to Mavis. He saw Mavis' translucent face and wide laughing mouth and all her large white teeth, and he heard her pettish rejection of the poem and her sullen remark that she did not like it. Well, it was considered rather puerile these days, like all truths. It struck on his thoughts, however, with a kind of dull misery, and again he thought of Jenny, who liked this poem as much as he did.

He put the book down. Near it was a notebook. He opened it curiously. He had never seen Jenny's handwriting before,

and he felt a sharp internal sting. The writing was small but
not schoolgirlish nor affected. Every word was clear and
strongly written, even angular and very firm. The pages held
poems, and some of them were infernally bad and amateurish, and so Jonathan knew that these were Jenny's own essays
into poetry. His eye stopped on one, and as he read he
stopped smiling.

> "I had shaken the world to its heart's centre,
>   And when it was sobbing and crying like a harp,
>   I knew my Love and looked upon His Face—
>   Calm and stately as the morning, and as still.
>   I touched His Hand and said to Him in wonder:
>   'But You I always sought and never knew 'til now!' "

For God's sake, thought Jonathan, and shook his head,
and frowned uneasily. It was a young and passionate poem of
deep and simple love and devotion, addressed, as all such
poems should be, to God. It disturbed Jonathan. His inner
conception of Jenny seemed reflected in water, and as it was
so reflected a wave shattered and dispersed it and dissolved it
away. He forced himself to read other lines, unfinished
poems, or just sentences:

> "Sweet rush of April skies—of cloud and wing—"

> "Ripe days of wine and apples, blue shine of noonday sun!"

He closed the notebook, slapping it loudly together. Then,
as he did so, he heard a quick gasp and after that a rustle. He
turned quickly and saw Jenny in the doorway, staring at him
in the lamplight, unbelieving and alarmed.

She wore nothing but a long nightgown of some light white
cotton with a childish collar of lace, and her hair tumbled
down her back and her blue eyes were wide and glittering
and her feet were bare.

"I thought," she said, "that you had gone!"

Then she looked down at herself and turned a vivid red.

CHAPTER NINETEEN

The voice of the river appeared to roar into the room like a torrent of tumultuous water, and Jonathan and Jenny stood and looked at each other. "Jenny," he said. "I didn't mean—I was just waiting for you to come down and lock the door after me, as I asked you to." He heard his own voice, thick and ponderous, and the heat was in his neck and throat again, and the pain was knifing into his temples, and then, with primal instinct, he felt the stab of excruciating desire. It was so intense that he bent a little, and he knew that he had never forgotten this girl at all and had always loved her and wanted her.

"Jenny!" he said. He took a step toward her.

She retreated, and the fright was big in her eyes, and she covered her breasts, in that thin cotton, in the ancient gesture of a startled woman, her arms crossed. Her long thighs drew together stiffly. She had never seemed so beautiful to him, not even in the garden, nor so desirable and beloved, in her present disheveled state and with the color leaving her face and her lips parting in embarrassment and shame.

"Jenny," he said, and took another step toward her. She fell back, and she made a little sound like a faint cry. She began to turn. Then he was upon her, catching her wrists, swinging her around to face him. She tried to resist; he had known she was strong, but she was like a young man in her sudden resilience. She bent backward to loosen his hands, and he bent over her and tried to kiss her mouth, holding her with violence, but she swung her face from him so that his lips touched only her cheek. She screamed sharply and it was

345

the sound of frantic rage. Again she swung her head and her soft cloud of black hair swept over his face. It fell back. Her exposed white throat gleamed in the lamplight, and he bent over her again and pressed his mouth into its soft warm hollow.

Their bodies cleaved together, Jenny's arching back, Jonathan's following hers. Then Jenny was very still, no longer struggling. He felt the long sweet length of her against his clothing, the pressure of her breasts, the slender rigidity of the wrists he held behind her back. He exclaimed, "Jenny, sweet Jenny!" and kissed her again, and he was determined, in the shout of his desire, to have this girl and to have her at once. She was not resisting now. Her flesh clung to his, languid and weak, and now he found her mouth eagerly and with ruthless demand. He began to groan, to pull her farther into the room, and her stumbling feet followed him. "Sweet Jenny," he said, and he let her wrists go and his hand fumbled for her breast and found one and closed tightly about it. It was like a sun-warmed apple in his hand, and the scent of her flesh was in his nostrils, fresh and maddening and young.

Then she came to wild life. Her hand knocked away the hand that held her breast with a force that amazed him. Then both her hands were on his shoulders and were pushing him away from her. He was so surprised that he fell back from her.

Her eyes were one furious blue blaze of hatred through great tears, and her teeth could be seen, clenched, between her white lips. He came to her again, lust pounding in him, and when he had almost reached her, she lifted her hand, swung it in a large circle and struck him viciously across the face. She jumped back and faced him, and her breast rose up and fell in frenzied outrage.

"Murderer!" she shouted. "Murderer!"

Her voice rang in the library. It was the ugliest sound he had ever heard, and the most terrible. She was no longer afraid, and her hands were clenched at her sides. She trembled with fury.

The strong lash of her hand had made his face burn with throbbing pain, and had rocked him on his heels. It had the effect of increasing his ferocious desire for her, and he also wanted to inflict the same pain on her and subdue her, and conquer her, and lie upon her and take her brutally and at once.

If she had struck him only and had not thrown that hateful

word at him, he might have controlled himself. But he was aroused. His dark face was a dull and heavy red, and his features thickened.

"I'm not good enough for you—is that it?" he said in a slow and malevolent voice. "It's just for my brother, isn't it?" And he motioned at her loins in a gesture he had never used to any woman before. "And for a few others, too?"

Jenny's white face flushed with horror and it quivered visibly. Her mouth opened and she gasped. "Your brother?" she said. "Harald?" She could not believe it. She stared at him. She had not understood at all. And then she understood. She uttered a fierce cry. "Get out of here! Why, you murderer, you—you—! You filthy monster!"

She turned again and ran from the room, and after a second he ran after her. She ran down the corridor to the hall and reached the oaken stairway in the murky fluttering of the lamplight. She lifted her nightgown and ran up the stairs like a terrified young animal, and her long white legs flashed in rapid movement. He lunged after her, trying to catch one of her ankles or a fold of the floating nightgown. But she was faster than he, and her long hair rippled behind her like a banner.

If he had felt lust before, it was nothing to what he felt now, this urgent passion and rage, this desire not only to take her but to hurt her violently for the things she had screamed at him. She could hear his hoarse panting behind her, and she ran even faster when she reached the upper hall, and raced for her room, full of dread and fear and hate.

She reached the door of her room and pushed it open and tried to close it. But his hand flung out and held it. They struggled for the door, and Jonathan began to laugh through his teeth, wondering at her strength and sweating. They battled ridiculously for it, swinging it back and forth, Jenny on the inside pushing it toward the lock, and Jonathan on the threshold, pushing it upon the girl. Her strength continued to astonish him; she thrust her shoulder against the door and almost reached the lock, and he had considerable difficulty in preventing its closure. He could hear her loud and struggling breath, her broken exclamations, but he said nothing now, intent only on winning this battle which was beginning to appear absurd to him. His pride was turbulently affronted that she denied to him what she gave so freely to his brother. "Don't be so coy, Jenny!" he exclaimed.

He gave an extra heave and the door flung itself back on

its hinges and Jenny was also thrown back into the room, which was dimly lighted by only one lamp near her bed. Instantly Jonathan was upon her, seizing one arm. He used his other hand to grasp the neck of her nightgown and to rip it down her body to her knees. Before she could move, his hands closed about her slender damp waist and he had pulled her to him and was kissing her mouth in a rapturous storm of desire. She struggled frantically. She tried to kick him with her bare feet and he laughed, and his fingers pressed themselves into the warm flesh of her body, and his mouth held hers, forcing her lips apart. He felt her breath in his own mouth and he grunted, "Jenny! Jenny! Jenny!" His ecstasy was like an agony in his own body. He pushed her backward toward the bed, and her struggles became even more frenzied. The torn nightgown impeded him, and in one movement he tore it completely from her and she was naked.

He pushed her against the bed, and her knees bent from the pressure, and she fell backward upon the white narrowness and he fell on top of her, his mouth still holding hers. "Sweet Jenny," he whispered, and his knee fumbled at her body, trying to separate her legs.

Then her body arched in one last desperate attempt, and so strong was that effort that he was almost flung from her. He fell beside her on the bed, still half straddling her, and the lamplight struck down on her face, and he saw it.

What he saw was utter and complete terror, unaffected terror, virginal terror. He had seen it but once before in his life, when he had been nineteen, and he never liked to recall that episode and had always felt shame at the memory. It was not to be mistaken for anything else but what it was—the affrighted woman faced with the unknown and recoiling from it and preparing to fight to the death against it.

He held her but did not move, and he looked down into her eyes and saw the awful and shivering fear there and the blue and fainting cloudiness, and he saw her stricken lips and heard the chattering of her teeth. He leaned over her, all desire gone, and with only shame and remorse.

"Jenny," he said, "my God, Jenny."

She looked up into his face and she lay very still and tears began to roll from her widely opened eyes and she uttered a whimpering sound of total defeat. He took the edge of the sheet and pulled it over her nakedness with tender care and shaking hands, then stood up and looked at her as she lay with the sheet under her chin and her eyes now closed, and weeping, her girl's young body outlined under the covering.

Dazed and infuriated with himself, and ashamed beyond anything he had ever felt before, he looked about the room and saw that it resembled a monastic cell in its small and quiet simplicity. The walls were white, the polished floor bare except for one small rug, and there were only a desk, two straight chairs, a painted wardrobe, a table, and one single lamp in the room. There were no ornaments here, no womanish daintinesses or ribbons or silks or taffetas, no intense scent of perfume. There was not even a dressing table with a mirror. In fact, there was no mirror at all. It was the cell of a nun, the bed the narrow hard bed of an ascetic woman.

If Harald had ever occupied that bed, he had occupied it alone! That was the foolish and humiliated thought that came to Jonathan as he clumsily rearranged and smoothed his clothing, which had been rumpled in his tussle with the girl and his attempted rape of her. He detested himself. He wanted to take one of Jenny's hands, now so flaccid on the sheet, and kneel beside her and beg her pardon for his animalistic attack on her, which seemed completely monstrous and unbelievable now. How was it possible that he had tried to do this thing? How was it possible for him to have believed the lies about her? Now his hate for himself was mixed with pity for the girl, and abyssmal love.

"Jenny," he said. "I wouldn't blame you if you never forgave me. No, don't ever forgive me. I'm so ashamed, Jenny." His voice was humble as his voice had never been humble before in all his self-confident and self-assured life. "Jenny, I wish there were some way I could tell you— But I suppose there isn't."

He leaned his palms on the bed beside her and stiffened his arms and bent over her. She continued to cry helplessly with her eyes shut. "Jenny, I want to say just one thing: I love you, darling. I've always loved you, since that day in the garden, when you were sixteen. Think about that, dear, and perhaps you'll be able to forgive me, someday, sometime." But she continued to cry silently, far removed from him.

"Jenny? I really love you, my darling. That's no excuse for what I—well, what I tried to do. Don't be afraid, Jenny. I'm going away now. Watch for my lantern through your window," and he glanced at the little bare casement, innocent of any draperies at all "Then when you see I've gone, go downstairs and lock the door. Jenny?"

But she did not answer him. She only lay there rigidly, her black hair flung about her in complete disorder. There was a growing bruise near her mouth and when he saw it, he hated himself more than ever and he had to hold back to keep from bending and kissing it gently. He wanted to do this with a passion greater than any lust he had felt for her, and he hesitated. Then he straightened up and went from the room.

Jenny heard his footsteps dragging slowly and wearily down the stairs. She heard them echoing in the hall. Then the bronze doors opened, and she could hear him close them behind him. She saw the faint reflection of the lantern on her window, and then she heard him going down the flagged marble of the walk, and finally she could hear him no more.

She sat up in bed, then sprang from it and ran to her casement window and flung it open. She saw the flickering lantern light retreating down the length of the island, twinkling through bushes and trees, dying away into the distance.

She dropped her head on the wide windowsill and burst into anguished little cries. "Oh, Jon, Jon, Jon! Oh, Jon!" She cried for a long time, until she slipped to the floor, and then pressed her cheek against the stark wall and mourned over and over, "Jon, Jon." She was exhausted and desolate. She slept there, crouched in nakedness on the wooden floor, and when she awoke, it was a dim and purple dawn.

When Jonathan let himself quietly into his father's house, he hoped that his mother had gone to bed, but he was no sooner in the soft and silvery hall than he heard her voice from the morning room. "Jon? Is that you? I'm in here, having a cup of tea. Do have one with me."

He cursed silently to himself, and hesitated. Then he went into the dining room, and by a very dim light he filled a glass full of whiskey and soda and carried it into the room where his mother was waiting for him. She looked extremely fatigued, but she smiled at him affectionately. "Was everything safe on the island?" she asked. Then she uttered a consternated exclamation. "Jon! What's wrong with your cheek, all puffed and red, and with that long scratch on it?"

Lies were unfamiliar things to him, and so he felt his face and tried to think of one. He finally said, "Oh, that. I bumped into something in the infernal dark on the island."

Marjorie stared at him thoughtfully, and then she smiled inwardly. Jenny! She felt a real pang of happiness. Was it really possible that at last he had admitted to himself what she had known of him and Jenny for several years? Her tired hazel eyes began to shine. "Do sit down, dear, and talk to me for a minute before I go to bed. I just didn't have the strength to move until I had some tea and a little quiet. What a noisy day, wasn't it?"

He had seated himself reluctantly on a chair in this charming and restful room, but he could not force himself to look at his mother, so he examined the contents of his glass and frowned at it. "Awful day," he said.

"I do believe," said Marjorie, "that your young Robert has what we used to call a crush on Jenny, but Jenny is oblivious. Such an innocent girl. She never learned to flirt or be young or gay or lighthearted. Poor child. It was that awful Peter Heger, you know. Wouldn't it be nice if Robert and she—What's the matter, Jon?"

"That's nonsense," said Jonathan. The little white ridges had come out about his mouth. "Mother, you know Jenny well. She's often here. Is there anyone?"

Marjorie made her eyes very artless. "Oh, yes, indeed. There is someone she dearly cares about. Quite a bit older than herself, of course, but eminently suitable. She's loved him a long time. I know you don't like the word 'love,' Jon, and think it is absurd and that there's no such thing, but only 'love' can describe the way Jenny feels about that certain man."

"What's his name?" asked Jonathan. "Do I know him?"

"She never mentioned his name, and I never asked, and I only know about it because I am a woman, too, though that, too, will probably surprise you, my dear. But there are certain things a woman can't conceal from another woman, and among them is when she is in love. I know all the signs."

Jonathan drank half his glass of whiskey and soda in one breath. He shook the glass. His black brows drew together. It was unbearable to think of Jenny in love with a stranger. He had tried to take her forcibly tonight, had intolerably insulted and attacked her, had gone away certain that he would never be allowed to see her again and knew it was all he deserved.

"It's possible that you're mistaken, Mother. Do you have any idea who he is?"

"Yes."

He stared at her formidably. "Who?"

"Why don't you ask Jenny yourself?"

He stood up and began to walk slowly up and down the

room. "If she never told you, she certainly would never tell me. That's ridiculous. Does Harald know?"

"No," said Marjorie, with slowness. "He doesn't. As I've told you before, he wants to marry Jenny. But you always laughed when I told you."

Jonathan stopped and looked at her. "Mother, who has been spreading those disgusting lies about Jenny in Hambledon?"

If Marjorie had had any doubts before, she did not have them now and she almost laughed with joy. "I don't know, Jon." But she dropped her eyes to her teacup.

"Does Jenny know—about these vicious tales?"

"Jenny?" Marjorie was shocked. She put down her teacup. "She's never once suspected! You don't know Jenny very well, Jon. She's as simple and innocent as an infant, and it would seem incredible to her that wicked people would make up vile lies about others. She just wouldn't believe it. It would have shaken Jenny to her very heart. She avoids people because her father told her, when she was a child, that she was ugly and unattractive and that no one, except him, of course, could ever love her, and so she must stay at home with him." Marjorie's pale face colored, but she looked Jonathan straight in the eye. "I'm not a simpering, old-fashioned woman, Jon. I wasn't brought up in a velvet-lined box and put away with Mama's pearls in a dark and secluded place. My father liked the very idea of the 'new woman,' and what he called 'the new candor.' Personally, I think he carried it a little too far sometimes.

"Well, I know all about Peter Heger, Jonathan, from the perfectly innocent things Jenny said about him. I think he—"

Jonathan smiled nastily. "He had incestuous thoughts about our little gosling?"

"Well, yes. It isn't a word you hear very often; it isn't a word 'nice' people use all the time in polite conversation. But that is it, exactly. Jenny once told me that he had 'flattered' her by saying she looked exactly like his mother, her grandmother, who died in Germany when he was a young boy, and that he had always dreamed of building a schloss for his mother. But, as she was dead, he was building a castle for Jenny in which to live, as he had dreamed of his mother living in such a castle."

"I follow his ideas," said Jonathan. "Yes."

"Jenny thought it very touching. She is such a simple

young woman. There are times when I'm sure that Jenny thinks children are procreated by osmosis or something."

Jonathan could not help laughing. He sat down near his mother and eyed her with genuine pleasure. Then he said, and he stopped smiling: "Somehow, I don't think Jenny believes that. No, I don't think she believes that."

So, you did teach her something, then, Jonathan, thought Marjorie. A rather strenuous lesson, from the look of you.

"So," Marjorie continued, "Jenny believed her father and so she became abnormally shy with people, thinking she offended them with her 'ugliness.' Then she was much taller than the other girls at school, and this is the day of the little dimpled darling, Jon, and the cupid's bow lips, and 'the head no higher than my heart.' You are really a stupid race, you men! Never mind. Then she was secluded on that island, even though her father was dead. He had built the schloss for her, contrary to the popular notion that he had built it for Myrtle. She not only feels compelled to live there but she loves the fantastic thing. I don't think Jenny ever once considered that a man might want her—" She stopped, for Jonathan was looking at her grimly.

"She does now," he said. "All right. I must tell you something before Jenny does, or even if she doesn't, you'll wonder why she never wants to come here again. I tried to rape her tonight. Do you understand me?"

Though Marjorie more than suspected that and was delighted at the thought, she knew that propriety demanded some quite contrary reaction from her. So she sat upright, arranged her features into an outraged expression, and exclaimed, "Jon! How could you, how dare you, a defenseless young girl alone and unprotected! How terrible, how dreadful, how unbelievable of you!"

He waved his hand wearily. "Very well, I'm a blackguard, a dog, a despoiler, a stinker, a hound—think them all. I'm all of them. Well. I didn't succeed. Jenny fought me off like a wildcat, like a female cougar. Partly, it was her fault. She called me—something. I think that precipitated the whole thing, though perhaps not. So, while we're being so bloody frank, as our English cousins call it, I might as well say that she convinced me that she was what is prissily called a 'pure' girl, and that I was particularly loathsome to her anyway. That stopped me. Of course, had I continued the little wrestling match, I'd have discovered the whole truth in a minute or two for myself, and that, of course, would have been beyond repair."

"Yes," said Marjorie, "it indeed would have. Women don't like to be taken by force."

"Like hell they don't," said Jonathan. "Mama dear, I'm not a little boy. I've known a considerable number of women. But Jenny wouldn't have liked it, to use an understatement. Did you say you didn't know the name of the man she's in love with?"

"I didn't say." Marjorie considered what Jonathan had told her and now she felt a trifle disturbed. Would Jenny ever forgive her son? Yes, she would, eventually. She might even look into a mirror and study herself very soon and wonder what there was about her that had aroused Jonathan so and had incited the attack upon her. Once let a woman suspect she has charms that could drive a man to assault her, and she will love him then—if she had never before—for desiring her. Things were progressing very nicely, thought Marjorie. She gave a great yawn and then regarded her son seriously.

"Jonathan, you have behaved atrociously, as you know yourself. I don't have to tell you that. If Jenny were not fond of me, she might prefer charges against you. This isn't a light matter. Poor Jenny. By the way, what *did* make you lose your head like that?"

"It's not important," he said. "Men are always losing their heads over some damned woman, figuratively or literally." He smiled at her. "You've called us men 'a stupid race.' No doubt. Say I lost my head. Jenny's a very beautiful girl and a very desirable one, and I was having one of my moods today, and tonight, and there Jenny was, apparently available, though I don't suppose you understand that."

"Yes, I do. Still it was an abominable thing. Jenny's only twenty, and a very young twenty, and you are an experienced màn of thirty-five, and a widower. You're almost old enough to be Jenny's father. In some cultures you would be." She paused and watched him closely. "I don't suppose, while this joyous caper was going on, that you gave a single thought to Mavis?"

He looked at her blankly. "Mavis?" He was more blank than ever and Marjorie thought, Thank God, then, it is all over. "What has Mavis to do with it?"

"Nothing, to be sure!" Marjorie almost sang. "Dear, do let me bathe that ugly scratch. I presume Jenny did that to you, and it's all you deserve."

He carried a fresh glass of whiskey into his bedroom, then looked at it with distaste and put it down. He went to the window and looked out at the hot and breathless night, so still now that all festivities had ended and the fireworks already forgotten. He craned for a glimpse of the river, which held the island in a watery moat, and he thought of Jenny. Then he thought of Mavis.

The old misery and despair did not return to him now, and when he thought of Mavis, he could hardly remember her appearance, though she was dead much less than a year. He could only faintly recall her raucous laughter. He was amazed. She was like someone he had not thought of for many years and whom he had hardly known. He stood quietly and waited for the sickness of mind to come, as always it had come, but it did not. Where the memory of Mavis had lived there was an empty place but not a wretched one. It was like a room being prepared for a new guest, for the first stranger had gone forever. Mavis no longer had the power to make him suffer and hate and turn away from living.

He felt intoxicated with relief and gratitude. The infection of Mavis had been dissipated. He could even think of her now with a kind of remote pity, recalling her youth and the swift ending of her life and the grave which he never visited but which was always covered with flowers from her aunt and uncle and others who had loved her. He went into her dressing room and then her bedroom, and lit a lamp and looked at the beauty there and the rosy lamps and pretty furniture. The very ghost of Mavis' perfume floated toward him, but Mavis would never wear it again. He closed the door upon her room as one closes the door on someone who would never wake again.

Now he could think of Jenny. It was possible—though he did not actually believe it—that he would never see her again, or that, if seeing, she would never speak to him. He had done a violent and unpardonable thing to her, but women have rarely held that against a man. He dismissed the thought of her loving someone else as totally inconsequential and not to be given serious consideration. What did young Jenny know of love, anyway? He would contrive means of putting himself near her. She would not be able to avoid him! He chuckled. Then, after many months—but not too many —she would be forced to take him seriously, she would begin to think about him. How long would it take? A year, perhaps, if he could wait that long. Sweet Jenny. He remembered how she had felt in his arms and the touch of her mouth and her warm breath and how—how could he have forgotten that for a minute?—she had not resisted for a few seconds in that gloomy library and had let him kiss her throat.

He turned from the window, smiling. He felt young as he had never felt young even when he had been a boy. He felt rejuvenated, alive, tingling, excited and expectant. For the first time he considered the thought that it was probable that life indeed had moments when it was desirable to be alive, and even rapturous. He was thirty-five and so he was not really young, and he could never give himself enthusiastically ever again to joy, or even truly believe in it, but there could be some contentment, some purpose, some infrequent happiness, in existence. Above all, there could be a purpose, and that was even more than enough for any man and much more than the majority of humanity ever could know.

CHAPTER TWENTY

When Jonathan entered his offices whistling the next morning, he found, as he expected, young Robert Morgan already there studying the files, which the elderly spinster "typewriter" had laid before him on Jonathan's desk. Robert stood up, easily flushing as always, and said, "Good morning. I didn't mean to take over your desk when you are still here, but the lady placed the files here and—"

"Perfectly all right," said Jonathan. Robert stared at the court plaster on his face. He said, "An accident?"

"Just a romp with an unusually spirited lady last night," said Jonathan. He appears very lively this morning, thought Robert Morgan. He watched Jonathan as he flipped through the files, and nodded.

"We enjoyed yesterday, my mother and I," said Robert. Jonathan lifted his black eyes quickly to him, and the whites of them were very clear and bluish as if he had slept well. "Good, Bob." He was brisk. He was the teacher. This was to be a strictly business session. Jonathan thoughtfully whistled as he kept glancing through the files. But he did not sit down at his desk. He had tacitly turned it over to the younger man.

"I see you've separated the goats from the sheep," he remarked, "the hypochondriacs from the authentically sick. Don't underestimate or despise the goats too much. They are the backbone of a doctor's practice, and his bank account, for invariably they have money. They are even interesting. They can produce the most bizarre and fascinating of illnesses and symptoms—and pay well for your fascinated attention, too. Just a word of advice: Don't discourage them overtly. Don't underplay their complaints or lose patience. More than anything else, don't be too quick to assure them that they are as sound as a dollar. That's indefensible in a prudent physician. They'll only take their purses to a more sympathetic man, and then where will you be? Harassed and bedeviled by the really sick, who have too much bad luck and misery to remember to pay the doctor promptly—if they ever pay at all."

Robert laughed. Then he was grave again. Jonathan continued: "The difference between a hypochondriac and the really sick is that the former wants to believe he is ill—but not frighteningly ill—and that his doctor takes him seriously and is attentive to his suffering—but the really sick wants to be reassured that he is in good health or soon will be, and that he is in excellent hands. The hypochondriac wants to brood sentimentally about death, but the sick man can't think of it without terror and demands an assurance that it is still far from him. That's your clue. Watch your patient's face while you consider him and talk with him. If he has a little tear in his eye, even before you examine him, you'll find him in fine shape. If his eye looks at you imploringly and with fear, then you can get down to the ugly bare roots of the matter, and you won't be disappointed."

"You're pretty cynical," said Robert, laughing again. "I never heard that at Johns Hopkins. There were even some doctors there who said that hypochondriacs really are sick—in their minds. And that their sickness is caused by psychic distress."

"A man," said Jonathan, "or even a woman, who has psychic distress is not in straitened financial circumstances. He hasn't time for such illness, unless he is a mental case. But a hypochondriac, you will learn, is usually highly intelligent and sane and pleasingly solvent. He can afford holidays and self-pamperings. The authentically sick, on the other hand—and in most cases—don't have psychic symptoms too often in any measure. They are too busy trying to save their lives, and to pay their bills, and to keep their jobs. I'm not speaking of genuine anxiety, of course, which can frequently kill, but we don't encounter that very often, and it never rises out of affluence, boredom, discontent and cravings for different pleasures, as pseudoanxiety rises in the hypochondriac. Someone told me once that when a man feels 'divine discontent,' he needs a change of chefs or a change of mistresses. You won't find 'divine discontent' in the honestly ill. He just wants to get well and back to work. But the hypo lad wants his doctor to tell him that he's overworking and needs a long, long rest, preferably an extended sea voyage, and preferably with a lady who isn't his wife."

Robert shook his head, smiling. "I still say you are a cynic."

"No. I just know people, and what I know about them doesn't keep me in a state of glee."

Robert glanced cautiously at the shut door behind which the clicking of the typewriter was very emphatic. "I've noticed that," he said, lowering his kind young voice. "I noticed it yesterday. You didn't seem to be enjoying yourself much."

"Well, I wasn't."

Now Robert's easy color was rising again, but he affected to be studying a new file. "You didn't seem to like most of the people there. Not even that lovely young lady, Miss Jenny Heger."

Jonathan, sitting in a comfortable chair which was reserved for patients, stopped in the motion of lighting a cigarette. Then he slowly blew out the match.

"Jenny? My niece-in-law, if you can call her that? What about Jenny?"

His voice had changed so sharply that Robert was startled. "I mean," he said, "that she's exceptionally—well, comely, winsome. Any man would be charmed."

"And I wasn't charmed?"

Robert turned and looked at him. He did not understand that tone, and now Jonathan was regarding him with what could only be cold displeasure. Robert was bewildered.

"I shouldn't have been so personal," he apologized. "Excuse me. Now, this Mrs. Summers—"

"No, no. Go on. About Jenny."

"There's nothing to 'go on' about, Jon." He was remembering the first time he had seen Jenny, on the island, and he also remembered Jonathan's derisive attitude toward her and his sneering, enigmatic remarks. Above all, he was thinking with anger of the ugly stories his mother had been sedulously relating to him on every opportunity concerning the girl. He had repudiated them with indignation, but the memory of his mother's significant and malicious smiles, and her head-noddings, stung him. He could hardly punch his mother, but he would have liked to punch Jonathan now. He said, "I was only trying to be pleasant, and trying to thank you for a pleasant day and pleasant company." Then he was angry as seldom he was angry. "Does it offend you that I find Miss Jenny pretty and attractive?"

"Why the hell should it offend me?"

Robert laid down the file very carefully. He stared down at it. He said, in a very precise voice, "I find Miss Jenny very pretty and attractive. I hope she will let me visit her on that island. I hope she won't find me too repulsive and that she will let me take her, soon, to a concert or a play. You do have concerts and plays in this town, don't you, or have I flattered it?"

"No flattery. We have a decent little orchestra, which calls itself The Symphonic. Or is it the Philharmonic? We don't entirely subsidize it but almost." Jonathan had begun to smile but a trifle disagreeably. "The members of the German Brass Band you heard yesterday are members of it, and then there are some college boys from Scranton who are quite 'gifted,' as the ladies say. Sometimes the music is recognizable. I've heard them do a Chopin nocturne that didn't entirely defeat them, though Brahms can make them hysterical. They do have courage. And if they are a little heavy on the brasses and the cymbals and the drums—that makes a hearty sound, good for the corpuscles. They're best on Sousa, though, and I defy any orchestra, even yours in Philadelphia, to get more out of 'The Star-Spangled Banner' than our boys do. As for plays, we have stock companies condescending to visit us in the summer from New York, with only a third-rate cast, and Chautauqua casts its tents on our fertile grounds in the summer, too. And once the divine Sarah passed through here and paused for a single performance. Even New York can't beat all this, not to mention Ringling Brothers or Barnum and Bailey in the spring. That's really a fragrant occasion."

In spite of his anger Robert was laughing. "I see this is a very cultured town and not barbarous. I'll enjoy taking Miss Jenny to some of these extravagant events."

"I hear—what is that delightfully coy expression, so loved by the ladies?—'her heart belongs to another.'"

Robert looked at him with quick and open dismay. "Who?"

That's what I'd like to know, thought Jonathan. "Who knows? It's only a rumor. However, that is a very unapproachable as well as an irreproachable young lady. Somewhat like a porcupine. By the way, do you know how porcupines mate?"

Jonathan was about to give an indecent explanation when the telephone rang. Robert looked at Jonathan, but Jonathan nodded at it, and Robert took it up. "Dr. Morgan speaking," he said, with young gravity. His thick reddish eyebrows frowned. "Yes, Dr. Morgan. I am Dr. Ferrier's replacement, you know. Oh, yes, indeed, Mr. Kitchener! I didn't recognize your voice. You wish to speak to Dr. Ferrier? Indeed, sir," and he held out the receiver to Jonathan. Jonathan put his hand over it. He said, "A doctor shouldn't call any layman 'sir' unless he is an elder and prosperous clergyman, a very rich and older patient, or a celebrated mountebank, or a President of the Republic of the United States of America." He said, into the receiver, "Yes, Al, no one ill at home, I hope?"

"No, no, Jon, thank God," said Mr. Kitchener's warm and friendly voice. "It's a matter of a friend of mine, a very dear and valued friend, Dr. Elmo Burrows. You may have heard of him, though I don't think you've met him. A very brilliant scholar, and one of the heads of the English Department at New York University. Very distinguished; has written several fine textbooks on Chaucer and some minor poets of the Middle Ages. Very distinguished, received a number of awards and citations—"

"From other scholars, I presume," said Jonathan.

Mr. Kitchener laughed. "Well, yes. Like all other professions, scholars give each other awards. Who else would? Elmo's a very modest man. He took a sabbatical a few months ago and moved to a pretty little house here which he had inherited from his wife, along with a pretty little amount of money. He's writing a novel about Chaucer."

"Now, that's a subject which should set the whole country afire," said Jonathan. "I can see our burly tycoons and our farmers and our mill workers buying such a book in the millions."

"Well, he's no Booth Tarkington or Frances Hodgson Burnett, that's for sure," said Albert Kitchener, chuckling. "And not even a Jack London or a Joseph Conrad or a Mark Twain. I've known him for years. Elmo. His daughter is keeping house for him, a very devoted girl, devoted to him, and goes with him everywhere. She's his secretary, too, and researcher. A bright girl, Maude's age. They're very close friends, the girls. Her name's Elvira, old-fashioned name; it was my mother's, too. She's good for Maude, and even though I'm Maude's father, I must admit my child can be a little vague sometimes. Elvira's giving her an interest."

Jonathan yawned and rolled his eyes. "Very edifying," he said. "Elvira's sick, I suppose? Anemic, probably?"

"No, no, Jon, please let me explain. It's Elmo. Everything was fine until two weeks ago. Then he had a stroke."

"What hospital is he in?"

"That's the point. He isn't in any hospital."

"Just a little stroke, eh? Who's his doctor?"

"That's the point again. He hasn't any doctor in Hambledon."

Jonathan sat up in his chair. "No hospital, no doctor, and the man had a stroke two weeks ago? Who the hell said he'd had a stroke?"

"Elvira. Now wait, Jon, and that wasn't a very nice word to use over the telephone, and Central might be listening in, and you can't be too careful about offending those nice girls, can you? Elvira told me, just this morning. She's begun to worry about him—"

"Dear Elvira," said Jonathan. "And who told Elvira?"

"Nobody. But she's a very intellectual girl, Jon, one of these 'new women.' She took up nursing for a year or two, not really to go into it, but just for any emergencies. She's seen a lot of people with strokes. Anyway, I went right over to their house—237 Rose Hill Road, not far from the cemetery, you know the street, very pretty and exclusive—you got that number?—this morning, and there was Elmo, lying absolutely still in bed and quiet, as if he was already dead. He'd had the stroke two weeks ago, and took to bed and has been there ever since, and five days ago he couldn't speak, though Elvira says he understands every word she says." Mr. Kitchener cleared his throat. "He can use the commode Elvira bought for him, and which he has beside the bed, but that's about all. He can drink a little milk with porridge, and broth, or a little vegetable soup and cocoa, but nothing else. For two weeks. And he doesn't even want to do that. I tell you, Jon, I'm very worried about Elmo."

"And so you should be. Apparently two cerebral accidents in two weeks. Why didn't that stupid girl call a doctor two weeks ago, for God's sake?"

"Well, I told you. She's had nursing experience, and she nursed her mother before she died, and she told me she knows exactly what to do about these things. But now she's a little worried because Elmo isn't speaking anymore. I told her about you, and she consents to let you come right out and see what you can do. As a favor for me," added Mr. Kitchener cunningly.

"You know, Al, that I'm leaving this town soon, and Dr. Morgan is my replacement. He is taking over all my old patients—those I have left—and any new ones, too. So, I'll send him along at once."

"Jon," said Mr. Kitchener, "Dr. Morgan's a nice young boy, but he's just a boy, and we like him very much. But this is his first practice, isn't it? News gets around. I wouldn't have anyone for Elmo but you, Jon, he's too valuable a person and scholar, and we don't have enough of his kind in America."

Jonathan sighed with exasperation. "All right. I'll send an ambulance from St. Hilda's for him at once, and I'll meet him there in an hour, after he's signed in."

Mr. Kitchener said, "And that's another point, Jon. Elvira won't let him go to a hospital. She says she's seen 'too much.' A very determined and resolute girl. She says that when she even mentioned it to her father, she knew that he was as against it as herself. She's willing to have a nurse or two here, if you insist, but that's all."

"God damn it, I'm not going to take care of a man with two recent strokes outside of a hospital!" shouted Jonathan. "He needs extensive and constant and professional care, not the tender hands of Elvira! Get him ready for the ambulance."

"Now, Jon, don't get on your high horse. I'm right here in the house with Elmo and Elvira, and I've been trying to per-

suade her to take her father to St. Hilda's, but she's adamant.
Jon, Elmo will die right here if he hasn't any medical care,
and since I've told Elvira all about you she won't permit another doctor to come into the house. I had a hard enough time
as it was to get her to consent to you. She doesn't trust doctors."

"The more I see of women," said Jonathan with wrath, "the
more I think the Almighty should have made men bisexual,
like snails. But that wouldn't be much fun, would it?"

"I hope Central didn't understand that," said Mr. Kitchener, but he chuckled.

Jonathan hung the telephone receiver up and said to Robert, "Come along. No office hours until two. You might as
well get to know the women called Doctor's Little Helpers.
Or, perhaps it would be better to call them Doctor's Nemesis.
They can undo more good work by an expert physician than
an officious nurse can accomplish."

"You forget," said Robert, picking up his straw hat. "I
have a Managing Mama."

On the way to the house of Elmo Burrows, Jonathan gave
Robert much advice concerning women, hardly any of which
could be found in standard textbooks on the subject. Robert
found some of it risible and some of it lascivious.

"The age of chivalry," said Jonathan, "pretended to deify
women and regard them as too precious for ordinary congress, but that was to keep them 'pure' when the boys were
off murdering Saracens or searching for the Holy Grail—
which is a pretty poetic way of saying they were looking for
rich real estate. Eventually, however, when woods colts began
turning up the boys invented the chastity belt. After that
women weren't deified any longer, until the late lamented
Victoria, who managed to change the Merry Men of England
into industrial tycoons or mill slaves, and brought a gloom on
the country which almost reached the heights of Cromwell's
reign. Or depths. The Regency girls, with their thin muslin
dresses—and nothing underneath—used to wet down those
gowns with water to achieve something which wouldn't now
be permitted on our most raucous stages in the New York
Bowery, or on Whore Row in Hambledon, or in an other city
where the ladies of joy are untrammeled. Victoria decided
she didn't have the physique for such general exposure, so
she led the movement to petticoats, bustles, mantles, iron corsets, chastity, and deification of women. A dreary regime,
though, as Disraeli said, one needs only to put a roof on En-

gland to make it one whorehouse. However, the hypocrisy persists that women have no ginger in their souls and no blood in their veins, and that good women don't like romps in the hay. We do them an injustice. Women don't want deification. They don't, really, even want the franchise or equal rights. They're just discontented—and they have a right to be —at being deified and considered above the grossnesses of copulation. Give a red-blooded woman a red-blooded man— in short supply in this new century—and the hell, she'll say, with the vote or a pedestal or standing shoulder-to-shoulder with her mate, and braving the future together, hand-in-hand."

"Naturally, you speak from experience," said Robert. "The suffragettes should lynch you as a menace."

"I don't like men jeering at them when the poor dears parade," said Jonathan. "They should just invite them home for a little intensive instruction, in a horizontal position. Is your Mama an advocate of Votes for Women?"

"In the context you've just used, I refuse to answer. I'm a respectful son," said Robert.

"I really have hopes for you," said Jonathan. "If you ever marry, and I hope you won't, treat her gently but firmly, and never tell her anything. And give her detailed instructions in sex, repeatedly. She'll love you forever. I made a mistake with my wife. I thought she had something to give me besides her pure white body. She never forgave me for that, and I don't blame her."

"You denigrate half of the human race," said Robert laughing.

"Don't you fret. They denigrate us, too, with a lot more imagination. Have you ever overheard the ladies discussing their husbands? It's an education every boy should have before he marries. Fortunately, though, he'll never get it. If he did, he'd never marry. It was, and is, the primitive men who invented the awful taboos about women, and they knew what they were about, though doubtless the ladies objected. Modern man has lost his fear of women and that's a calamity. For him. There's nothing like a few deadly taboos for making bedtime the most exhilarating time of the day."

They approached Rose Hill Road, which was a wide and quiet street with little traffic, for at the end of the street was an old cemetery, white and silent in the hot July sun. The houses on the road were called "cottages," probably for the reason that they were enormously expensive and the owners were using euphemisms in reverse. All were built of tan fieldstone, in rough imitation of "modest homes," but all were surrounded by large lawns and secluded behind masses of great dark trees, and all possessed lavish and intricate gardens. As the houses were "cottages," they were one architect's dream of old English village cots in the sort of English villages which had not existed, to any extent, for nearly one hundred and fifty years. "He could never quite bring himself to thatch the roofs," said Jonathan, as they rolled past the houses and Robert admired the flower-scented quiet and the deep shadows and the rich lawns. "It must have broken his heart to have to compromise on slate. But he's gone wild on the unnecessarily high chimneys, as you'll observe. And the darling little gates in the hedges. I've heard he even put in a few mazes in the rear, but that may be a vile canard. English 'cottages' or not, every owner is an Anglophobe, as aren't we all in America today? Somehow, I have a feeling that will soon pass. We'll need England and her empire for our own ambition one of these days, and then God help the British Empire. She'll be hauling down her Union Jacks everywhere in the world, one after another. All in the name of liberation, of course, which will mean liberation from civilization, while America will nobly take on the white man's burden and collect the ducats, and the power. The power above all. This is going to be a grand century for the man with a sense of sardonic humor. I've already detected the signs. Haven't we already 'liberated' Cuba and the Philippines? This is small pence. Wait until we start liberating the whole damned world!"

"That's a wild dream," said Robert.

"Never underestimate the nightmares of men," said Jonathan. "They're the only authentic prophesies. Well, here we are, and isn't that the prettiest sight you ever saw?"

The "cottage," a simple structure of no more than twelve large rooms, nestled sweetly far back from the cobbled road in a crown of tall maples, and the flagged walk, of varicolored rough stones, meandered between clipped hedges and fragrant flowering bushes, bruised within inches of their blossoming life by stern shears. At the end of the walk there was a black iron gate, attached to no fence and having no other function but to add an air of protection to the small estate. Jonathan pushed it open, and they stepped on a wide fieldstone terrace, filled with potted plants and white iron furniture on which no one would ever sit if he had any regard for his buttocks. A carved wooden door, on which was surmounted a brilliantly polished and brazen lion's head, was warm to the touch. Absolute silence enveloped the house and the whole street, except for a faint rustling when a heated wind touched the trees, or a clipping of scissors indicated the presence, in the rear, of an industrious gardener. Jonathan banged the knocker vigorously, and protesting echoes went wandering up and down the road, and probably even disturbed the sleepers in the cemetery.

The door was opened by a trim little maid who almost curtsied, in the English manner, and admitted them to a deep stone hall with English furniture and old fine rugs. Albert Kitchener emerged from the dusky depths at the end, and with him came Maude, sweet and fresh as a rosebud in her blue voile dress with its crisp ruffles slipping over her pretty little arches. Her auburn head caught a ray of light from the open door and burnished her pink cheek and showed her dimpled little mouth and white chin and big, soft eyes. A little doll, thought Jonathan, who loved pretty women. Robert was bowing to her gravely but showed no admiration, which annoyed Jonathan, who gently pinched her cheek and pressed her hand. She smiled at him but could see only the oblivious Robert, and the pink in her cheeks deepened to a blush. Can't he see what a lovely waist she has, and such a deep breast? thought Jonathan. And the dimples in her wrists and elbows? She's a sweet morsel for any man, even if his mind is occupied by another woman. He's probably one of those single-minded bastards.

"Good of you to come, dear Jon," said Mr. Kitchener, shaking hands and beaming at the two young men. "Dr. Morgan. A lovely day yesterday, wasn't it? Maude, will you tell Elvira our friends are here?" He led them into a reception room of noble proportions and furnished, unfortunately, in a cluttered Victorian style, all polished tables and vases and settees and chairs of horsehair and black marble fireplace and heavy draperies of bluish brocade over the handmade lace curtains. "Charming, isn't it?" said Mr. Kitchener. "Very authentic. Mrs. Burrows inherited it from her parents, who used it as a summer home when away from Boston, and Elmo inherited it from her. He isn't fond of it, sad to say, but then he's an austere man, like most scholars and intellectuals."

"Dr. Johnson was a lusty son of a bitch," said Jonathan, "yet I think he had quite a reputation as one of your intellectuals. In my opinion, the more truly intellectual a man is the more he can appreciate the raw winey goodies of life, and the tankards, and the girls. The fraudulent intellectual, the poseur, pretends to prefer the ascetic life, the hypocrite. Probably he has atrophy of his—" He stopped suddenly as Maude came into the room with another girl about her age, whom she introduced, somewhat extravagantly, as "my dearest, dearest friend, Miss Burrows."

Maude had a sweet high voice, and she spoke always as if she were a little short of breath, but Elvira Burrows had the clear, no-nonsense voice and inflections of a boy. She was taller than Maude and she wore a starched dress of gray cotton with a plain round collar, and no ruffles even at her wrists, for her sleeves came all the way down even on this torrid and humid day, and the hem of her frock fell stiffly over her slippers with no promise of a revealed ankle or arch. But her black leather belt cinched a waist of extraordinary lissomeness, and the black buttons marching grimly from her collar to her soles had a sweet and rebellious way of rising over the proper little hills and indicating where her torso joined her swathed legs. There's much to be said in favor of concealment, thought Jonathan, keenly noting these interesting facts. She has a splendid, if lean, figure, this girl. He left the figure, so definitely cut and neat, to look at Elvira's face and head. Her face was long and pale, her features sharp yet curiously harmonious like a statue's, and her brow was a smooth petrification, and her eyes were a clear hard gray between thick black lashes. Her mouth had little color but was of an excellent shape, one which Jonathan particularly admired. No cupid's bow here, full and small in the fashionable manner, with what was called "a bee-stung lower lip." Elvira's mouth was wide and thin and firm with indented corners, very determined and resolute. Her hair was not dressed in the prevailing way, pompadour and combs and "rats," and flourishes. It was dark brown and it was pulled back from the planed and clever and classic lines of her thin face, tightly braided then rolled into a severe crown on the top of her small head.

Maude, beside her, suddenly became one of those execrable dollies now so very popular, the fat little naked dollies, totally sexless, with a porcelain or bisque curl on the top of a round head, tied with a coquettish bow. Elvira was an aristocrat, unbending, scornful of furbelows and oramentation. She was all razor assertion and awareness. In a few years, when she had lost her youth, thought Jonathan, she would be a harridan, the terror of male relatives, the suzerain—female—of unfortunate lady connections. Unless, of course, some courageous man took pity on her soon and introduced her to softer delights than ruling everyone and everything on which her marbled eye fell. Apparently no such valorous man had as yet approached her, which was a pity, for such women could be very ardent when awakened, as Jonathan had learned before. He himself preferred a dry wine to a sweet, and he knew how tasty was the flesh around stony pomegranate seeds. He had a moment's strong desire to alleviate Elvira's sorry condition, if only temporarily, as a purely beneficent act.

She was looking at him and Robert Morgan with a sort of cool umbrage and disfavor. "Thank you, gentlemen," she said in a clear, plain enunciation without, of course, any gentleness or consciousness of her sex. She shook hands like a busy man, quick and short. "I wish to make it emphatic, however, that I hold doctors in no high regard."

"Neither do I," said Jonathan, with an excessively humble smile, which, for some reason, made those narrow cheeks color faintly. Now Elvira gave him her exclusive attention, but it was not kind. "Indeed," she said, and the thin highbred nostrils of her nose flared a little. She paused, and gave him a keener and even more distasteful study. She was no fool, this girl. She swept her cold eyes over him, like a schoolmistress surveying a student who had been reported to her as incorrigible and worthy only of harsh dismissal and punishment, and she saw his dark and polished competence and his elegance, and the debonair way he stood and his dapper clothing. Then she looked fully into his eyes and slightly frowned and turned away. Her firm mouth had taken on a reluctant color, as if someone had kissed her forcibly.

"It was only through the importunities of Papa's dear friend, Uncle Albert, that I have permitted medical"—she paused and made an unpleasant and contemptuous moue—"consultation. Papa really needs no one but me, and other nursing attention. However, gentlemen." She had reached the hall again and was leading them, her very starchy frock rustling briskly, her heels clacking before them.

She took them past a regrettable drawing room so smothered in velvets and brocades and tapestries and glassed cabinets and draperies and horsehair that it seemed almost a travesty of the crowded Victorian era. She led them upstairs—a stairway of brick and Oriental runners—to the upper story, where the choked bedrooms lurked. It was darker here, for curtains were drawn against the few rays of the sun which could penetrate the maples, and it was distinctly cool. Jonathan and Robert were close on her heels, with Mr. Kitchener following and puffing a little, for the steps were steep in a "cottage" affectation, and Jonathan, catching Robert's eye, made a deplorable gesture at Miss Elvira's round but encased little bottom, and Robert murmured, "Tut, tut." Behind them all came Maude, lifting her skirts high about her ankles. Unfortunately, Robert did not glance back at this delectable sight.

Elvira smartly opened one narrow door and entered without invitation to those following her. They entered another room of fine proportions, with white plastered walls and little casement windows open to the scented air and the green luster of leaves. A jade dusk filled the room, a luminous dusk. In the center stood a large, carved poster bed of ebony with a canopy of white muslin, and in it lay an absolutely immobile long figure which hardly raised the quilted counterpane. Here the room was less crowded and contained only a walnut and marble wardrobe, a highboy, two rocking chairs, a little rosewood desk, and one or two tables, and the floor was covered in a dark Brussels rug surrounded by darkly polished wood.

Elvira stood squarely and straightly beside her father's bed and addressed, rather than talked to, the intruding physicians. "My father has had two strokes," she announced, and Jonathan involuntarily looked for her notes. "One, two weeks ago, which almost completely paralyzed his entire body except for his hands. He has some control over his legs and—"

"His bodily functions, I hope," Jonathan interrupted. "Very important, that control."

Miss Elvira turned very white and the gray eyes glittered upon him, not with modesty or embarrassment, but with cold anger. She repeated precisely, "His bodily functions. In good and controlled order—Doctor. Please do not interrupt for a moment or two. I will be brief. Doctor." She made the word sound like an imprecation, one a lady used only on the most extreme occasions. "He was able to communicate his wishes to me, though haltingly, until a few days ago. Thursday, to be exact. Then apparently he had another stroke, which cost him his voice. He cannot speak at all. We converse through his slight gestures—of his hands. He understands what I say, however, which is fortunate. He takes little nourishment, and that only liquid. I give him camomile tea or catnip tea at bedtime so he will rest comfortably. He sleeps without incident. I rest in one of these chairs so I will be able to hear his slightest movement. He does not stir—except for using that commode which you will observe beside his bed." She stopped as if clipped off and regarded the doctors impersonally.

Robert spoke for the first time to her, and with indignation. "You never considered calling a physician, Miss Burrows?"

She did not look at him but only at Jonathan as she replied. "No. I have told you my opinion of doctors. This opinion does not rise out of ignorance but out of knowledge. My father's condition is familiar to me. He needs only excellent nursing care and passive movements of his—his members—and quietness. In time we shall know if he will regain control over his muscles and speech or if he will be condemned to lifelong invalidism and be confined to his bed."

"Of course," said Jonathan, waving at Robert, who was seething visibly, "you know the proper medications to give him."

"I am an advocate of herbs," said Elvira with firmness. "Dandelion root for muscular stimulation. Sassafras bark for blood. Foxglove for circulation. Hot milk and honey for agitation of the mind. Lemon for appetite. Sulphur for intestinal cleansing. Cinnamon bark for restlessness, brewed in hot tea. Ginger in hot water for gastric upsets. Soda bathings. Foot baths."

"I think," said Jonathan, "that I will advocate taking your license to practice away from you, Miss Burrows. That, of course, will be only envy on my part. Have I your permission to examine your patient? For consultation purposes only, naturally. Then later, we will have a full medical discussion."

Elvira gave him a killing glance and motioned loftily to the figure on the bed, then stood with her hands folded together, her expression coldly contemptuous. Robert approached the other side of the bed at Jonathan's gesture. The two doctors bent over the recumbent man and began to examine him. Elvira disdained them. She went to the casement window and gazed out calmly, as if no one were in this room but herself and her father. Mr. Kitchener and Maude hovered near the doorway, ignored by Elvira.

The emaciated tall man on the bed was not more than fifty, if that, with rough brown hair and a livid face like a skull, but an aristocratic skull, all fine hollows and protuberances. with a high nose and definite planes. His eyes, gray like Elvira's, and alert and intelligent and extremely conscious of everything, looked up at Jonathan somberly. Then, all at once, he smiled faintly and humorously, and Jonathan liked him at once, as he liked very few men. Elmo Burrows had sardonic thick dark eyebrows, and as Jonathan expertly examined him those eyebrows lifted with a most knowing expression. Then, after a second or two his expression became melancholy and withdrawn and bitterly sorrowful and despairing, and he rolled his head aside on his pillows. He lay totally inert, with no movement of what Elvira had called his "members."

Jonathan began to frown as his examination continued. He said to Elvira, "Was your father ever in a coma? Did he become unconscious after his first stroke?"

She replied indifferently from the window, from which she was studying the leaves of the tree, "Certainly not. He merely, one morning, could not get out of bed. He told me so. He said it was very difficult for him to move his arms and legs. I first thought of arthritis, but he had no pains in his joints and they were not swollen. The next day he said it was even more difficult to move, and so it continued."

"He did not complain of dizziness, nausea or headaches?"

"No, indeed. We are not subject to those ills caused by dietary indiscretions."

"He had no stiffness of the neck?"

"No. He had had no cold or catarrh."

The patient's limbs were not flaccid nor flattened; they were as round as the legs and arms of any healthy man who was somewhat too thin; they were cool to the touch. Jonathan suddenly gave a bicep a hard tight pinch, and the arm involuntarily jerked away. He subjected the other arm, and the legs, to this treatment and in every case the limb recoiled and a faint protesting sound came from the sick man. His temperature, pulse and respiratory rate were absolutely normal for a bed-bound patient who was not really ill or in danger of his life. His blood pressure was normal. "How old is your father, Miss Burrows?" "He is not quite forty-nine."

"Excellent pressure," said Jonathan to Robert, who was looking perplexed as the examination continued. "A trifle low for his age but excellent. And no signs of recent cardiac infarction or auricular fibrillation. No spasticity. Reflexes a little sluggish but within the range of normal. He seems undernourished—"

"I am cleansing his system with a liquid diet," Elvira said without turning toward the room. "But he cannot swallow easily, and indicates he does not desire nourishment." Her voice was dispassionate.

The sick man had lain with his eyes closed, as if not present or not conscious. But now he was looking up at Jonathan with an intensely devastated expression. Jonathan bent over him again. "You can hear me, Mr. Burrows? Good. I see you can move your head a little. Can you speak? No? You can see well? Good. No pain anywhere?"

The gray and sunken eyes became more anguished. "Head? Legs? Arms? Neck? Back? Chest? No? Good. Then, where is the pain?"

Mr. Burrows' eyes filmed over and he turned aside his head and dropped his eyelids. Jonathan straightened up and looked down at his patient thoughtfully. "No paralysis," he said to Robert. "No conjugate deviation of the eyes, no lateral signs. Neurological responses within the range of normal. No cerebral symptoms of any kind, not even a mild meningitis, which I first suspected. Aphasia, yes, but I wonder what kind."

"In short," said Elvira bitterly, from the window, "you find my father in perfect health! He has had no strokes, yet he cannot rise from his bed and cannot speak!"

"I did not say your father was in perfect health," said Jonathan. "On the contrary. I should like a consultation with you in another room, if you please, Miss Burrows. Come, Robert. Al and Maude, would you please stay with my patient?"

The two young men followed the energetic Elvira out into the hall. Then she stood there with a look of cold defiance. "Will this not do, for what little you are able to tell me out of your medical ignorance?"

Jonathan reached for the nearest doorknob and Elvira said sharply, "That is my room, if you please—Doctor."

"Don't be alarmed," said Jonathan. "I've been in more ladies' bedrooms, invited and uninvited, than I can remember, both as a physician and as—shall we say visitor?"

"It is not necessary to be lewd," said Miss Burrows very clearly, "though I am not one of your namby-pamby misses, but a modern woman of the twentieth century, frank and candid—"

"And I bet you know all the words, too," said Jonathan, with an air of great admiration. "Well, if we're not to invade your vestal chamber, where shall we go?"

Elvira looked as if she had a very pertinent suggestion she

would like to offer, then merely pressed her lips together and marched down the hall and pushed open a distant door. With an imperative gesture she motioned them inside. There was a streak of high color on each of her prominent cheekbones. "And," said Jonathan, "I bet you know all the euphemisms of the words. If not, I'd be glad to instruct you, my dear young lady, at your convenience. Alone."

"I am sure you would!" said Elvira, and her eyes became wintry lightning. "Pray, will you enter this room, Doctor, which was once my dear, dead mother's little sitting room?"

Robert had thought Jonathan's remarks hardly pardonable, but he had not been able to help smiling under his golden-red mustache. She was really a very spotless young lady, with pretensions of modernism, and it was fortunate that she had not really understood Jonathan's naughty insinuations. There was no one quite so pure as a lady who affected to be emancipated and free of inhibitions. The real trollop was usually very dainty in her speech and pretended to be insulted at the slightest jocular remark, and was very retiring and lip-licking in the presence of strange men. Elvira, on the contrary, was a veritable grenadier.

They went into a very stuffy and musty little room, overpoweringly redolent of camphor and lavender flowers and hot heavy draperies and mothballs and heated rugs and cumbersome furniture. The mirrors over the dresser and the dressing table had been sheeted, and the few pictures had been turned to the brown-painted wall. A small window looked out on branches of trees and nothing else. It was a most unpleasant room and Jonathan decided to stand, whereas Elvira sat down as straight as a ruler on a small armless rocker covered with horsehair.

"I will ask you a few serious questions, Miss Elvira," said Jonathan, and now he looked forbidding. (This expression of his had always been highly successful with neurotic or hysterical or intractable ladies before, and had the effect of quieting and subduing them. But Elvira merely gave him a cool smile of scorn and waited.)

"I wish you to be frank—as all young ladies of this age are," he added.

She inclined her head.

"First of all: When did your mother die?"

Elvira, for the first time, seemed a little taken aback. "My mother? What has my dear, dead mother got to do with Papa's illness?"

"Miss Elvira, I am asking the questions. You don't want your father to die, do you? He is certainly on the steady way to death. If you care about him, please don't waste my time."

The girl had become ghastly in color, and her eyes were flickering with fear. But she had fine control of herself. "I don't believe he is dying, not in the least. However, I will answer your questions as briefly as I can. Mama died eleven months ago, in New York, in our small town house. Quite unexpected. She had seemed in good health, though at her age—forty-two, anything could have been possible. Elderly people— They are subject to many afflictions. I suppose you agree, Doctor? Indeed. She had had a good dinner—I had cooked it myself, our cook having her twice-monthly evening off—and as I am partial to health foods, I can assure you it was a very wholesome dinner."

"I am sure it was," said Jonathan. "What was it, by the way?"

"Whole browned rice with crushed nuts and chopped spinach, broiled in a little butter. Formed into chops."

Jonathan visibly winced. Elvira's color was returning, and she had the elevated appearance of a fervent fanatic. "We began with a light broth, bean-stock lightly flavored with nutmeg and thyme."

"I see, I see," said Jonathan with haste. "That's quite enough, please. I see that the meal could not have disturbed your mother had she been in superb health. She was, I assume?"

"I am not sure that I care for your tone of voice, Doctor," said Elvira, who was a very keen young lady. "Nor for your insinuations that my mother could only survive health foods in the event that her health was superb. I will let it pass, considering that these remarks came from a prejudiced mind. My mother said she had enjoyed the food very much, and I was pleased, as I had been trying for a long time to get her to eat more sensibly. She preferred rich food and corpses—"

"Corpses!" exclaimed Jonathan with a slightly overdone air of revulsion.

"You know very well what I mean, Doctor. The innocent corpses of innocent beasts, slaughtered to satisfy our lusts."

Jonathan opened his mouth to say a very indelicate thing, then thought better of it. "Quite right," he said instead. "Go on, please."

"I am sure," said Elvira, her voice becoming more inflected and clear every instant, "that you really aren't interested in poor Mama's diet. At any rate, she woke at midnight, calling me, saying she had acute indigestion. Very severe. She claimed she felt as if she had been poisoned."

"No doubt she had," said Jonathan but almost inaudibly.

"What did you say, Doctor? No matter, it really isn't very important, though I suppose it was impolite. You are a very rude, uncouth man, if you will pardon my candor.

"I gave Mama my usual remedies, ginger in hot water, hot soda water, hot tea with a little cream of tartar. They are usually quite enough. Mama had had these attacks before and always came out of them splendidly under my care. But she continued to complain. She asked me for a doctor. To soothe her mind—though, of course, I have no trust in doctors—I telephoned one. It took me quite a time, through Central, to find one near our house, and so it was an hour or more before he arrived."

She suddenly squeezed her white eyelids together hard, and her inflexible mouth trembled very slightly. Then she opened her eyes again. "When he arrived, he said that Mama had had a heart attack and that she was dying. I don't know what he gave her, but it must have been something murderously drastic. She died half an hour later. I always held him responsible. Had he not been there, Mama would be alive now and with us."

Jonathan was a little sorry for this obdurate girl. "And how did your father take her death?"

"I did not tell him until the morning. He had been very fatigued for over a week and needed his rest. I sat with Mama from the time she died until I knew that Papa had descended to the dining room and had been given his breakfast by Cook, and that he was quietly reading his newspaper before leaving for the university. That was about eight o'clock."

"And you had stayed alone with your dead mother all that night?"

"Yes." For the first time the young voice was not so crisp. Elvira bent her head for a moment. "When I told Papa, he said nothing. Nothing at all. He just sat there in his chair, looking at the last of the coffee in his cup. Then he quietly folded his newspaper and went up to Mama's room and closed the door behind him—forgetting he had a daughter at all—and he did not come out until the undertaker arrived. I was so relieved to see him. He hadn't shed a single tear, while my own face and eyes were swollen. He looked quite calm, almost his usual self. He spoke to me calmly, too, and patted my head. He kept saying, 'It's all right, Elvira. It's quite all right.' He was a tower of strength to me. He and I—we had been like parents to Mama—"

"Had your parents been fond of each other?"

"Oh, very. Mama was a little too young for her advanced age. She was never very serious, though she had had a good education and she had a superior mind. She and Papa were always having their private little jokes together. Papa is a very sober man, but Mama could make him laugh like a boy. There was hardly a night, no matter the weather, but what they went alone on walks together, and they would go far up into the country—even as far as Central Park—in our carriage, alone, for Sunday drives, and sometimes they would take a lunch with them. They would come back laughing like children, sunburned and grass-stained and sleepy, and very happy."

For the first time she was faltering, and her throat kept forming little spasms as she struggled with her grief. She looked not at Jonathan now, but at the floor, and she was crushing a plain linen handkerchief in her long and pretty and competent hands.

Jonathan's voice was actually gentle when he said, "Did your father have other relatives, those close to him?"

"No, he had no one. He had been an orphan for years. He had no brothers or sisters, and only distant cousins he rarely saw. They lived hundreds of miles away; they didn't even correspond. He had no one but Mama and me." She paused. "Sometimes I think he thought he had only Mama!" Her voice broke.

"I'm sure you're wrong," said Jonathan. He thought of that quiet scholar whose only joy and laughter came from his wife. "I'm sure he knew, and knows, that he has a very devoted daughter, one of the best."

She looked up at him, startled and suspicious, but his face was so kind that she swallowed quickly and tried to keep from bursting into tears. "Thank you," she murmured. "I had only Mama and Papa myself, no sisters, no brothers, though I have gone out into the world far more than ever my parents did. I believe in wide associations and participations, and being part of humanity and events. I belong to many charitable committees and boards, and we do a great deal of good."

"I'm certain of that," said Jonathan, and refrained from wincing again. "As I see it, your father took your mother's death very calmly and sensibly."

The girl hesitated. "Indeed he did. Except he did one strange thing. He did not go to her funeral. In fact, on the morning of her funeral he disappeared. He was gone for two days. I did not notify the police. After all, I knew Papa would never be guilty of anything—exaggerated, if you follow me. I had never seen him much disturbed in all my life. He had a most equable temper and a consistent way of looking at life, and was very balanced. Once there had been a fear that he would lose his eyesight; that was four years ago. Mama went quite to pieces and we had a frightful time with her. But Papa never lost his equilibrium. Mama almost lost her mind with joy when the doctor notified us that he had been mistaken in his diagnosis, but Papa only smiled. He always had perfect control of himself and stability. I think I resemble him a little there."

"Yes," said Jonathan. "Yet, he disappeared on the day of your mother's funeral and stayed away two days. How did he appear when he returned, and what did he say?"

"He was very pale and exhausted but very calm, as usual. He gave me no explanation and I asked for none. He never spoke of Mama again. Not once, in eleven months. It is as if she had never lived and he had never known her, and she had never been in this house or in our house in New York. He went back to the university and then decided on a sabbatical to write his novel about Chaucer. My father is a very distinguished man," the girl added with pathetic pride. "He has received many honors and awards from famous scholars and their committees. He has spoken in London, Paris and Berlin, and he is a brilliant linguist, speaking foreign languages perfectly. He was much acclaimed everywhere he went. He has thought of this book for years and discussed it almost every night with Mama. They were like eager children about it. I'm glad that I can take Mama's place in this one thing, at least."

"Has he never visited her grave?"

The girl looked up at him, startled. "It is very odd that you should ask that! No, he has never gone to her grave. He has never even asked in what section of the cemetery she is buried. I never asked him to go with me at any time, for he was healing so nicely and I did not want to open his wounds again."

The trite words and clichés did not seem unpleasant to Jonathan but only very sad, for they had the freshness of devotion and grief. This girl was not so strong-minded as she believed she was. In her own way she had been as lonely and deprived as her father. What was wrong with such ostensibly independent and equable people? Were they really too sensitive to endure living without the safeguards of love, protective love, about them, and without the strength of others? Were they too proud to admit their terrible need? Must they condemn themselves to death in silence when the one reason for their living had vanished?

"And your father has seemed in good health, and sleeps well, since your mother died?"

The girl thought. "No," she said at last. "Of course, Papa never complains. He was never stout, but now he is quite gaunt. I'm sure you've noticed that. He eats very little, even of his favorite dishes. And I hear him walk up and down for hours in his room every night, back and forth, without saying a word. I thought he was thinking of his book. He was, wasn't he?" Her tone was suddenly girlish and abjectly pleading, for she had begun to follow the torturous way Jonathan was talking.

Jonathan went to her and took her hand and held it warmly. "Miss Elvira," he said, "I wish you were my sister. I truly do. I need a sister like you. I'd like to have a daughter almost exactly like yourself. Please don't look so incredulous; I mean it.

"Do you know what is wrong with your father? He is deliberately dying of grief for your mother. Everything else is shut out from him—you, his book, his work, his students, his friends. He has locked himself in a cave and is dying in darkness. Do you understand?"

"Yes." Now she was crying and did not know it.

"Tell me," he said, "what kind of a woman was your mother?"

"Oh, she was gentle and sweet and loving. A little woman, not tall like me." The girl snuffled frankly into her handkerchief. "Soft, plump. Papa used to call her his little bird. She was like a bird, to tell the truth. Not chirpy, but singing and gay. She used to tease me that I had no sense of humor at all, and I suppose I really don't. It wasn't that Mama was frivolous. She just accepted life and everything in it, and thought the world was wonderful even when it manifestly was not. She was very religious, too. She wanted everybody to—love God. Papa and I are agnostics, but sometimes, because of what Mama was, I thought there might really be a God, and I think Papa sometimes speculated on that, too. But it all left when Mama died. It was as if—as if—everything had been washed over with gray, so that there wasn't much color remaining in the world."

Robert had been listening in silence and in pity, and in surprise, too, at Jonathan's comforting of the girl, who had seemed such a formidable piece of self-righteous and narrow-minded intensity. Live and learn, thought young Robert.

"Your father," said Jonathan, "has been desperately trying to suppress his grief, to override it, to surmount it. He never gave it a chance to spend itself, and so he is still wounded, still suffering, perhaps more than he was at the very beginning. It is poisoning him. It is killing him. He wants to die. He sees no reason for living any longer."

The girl was shattered. "And I thought he was so very brave, and I was trying to measure up to his bravery myself, and all the time poor Papa—"

"And poor you," said Jonathan.

"Oh," cried Elvira, "what does it matter about me! But Papa is everything, important, needed, not to be replaced. Why can't he understand that?"

"Because I am afraid he always thought he never had anyone but your mother. I know that sounds harsh. But if you had been openly grieved, he would have comforted you and grieved with you, and you would have both been healed together. He thinks you are very strong and do not need him or anyone else. Isn't that the most ridiculous thing?"

"But, I'm not strong at all!" the girl blurted, and then she colored and looked abashed and sheepish. "I'm the ridiculous one. Do you know, Doctor, I always thought I should protect my unworldly parents!"

"One of these days," said Jonathan, "you are going to be a wonderful wife and mother, and I hope you have a dozen children, except that you'll probably spoil them to death. I envy the man you are going to marry, though I hope he will be the kind you won't have to protect and would be outraged if you tried it."

"No," said Elvira, "Papa needs me. I have dedicated myself to him."

Not if I can help it, thought Jonathan, and patted the hand he still held. He said, "Do you have some spirits in the house? No. Well, I keep a flask of brandy in my bag. Elvira, do you trust me now?"

She looked up at him in hesitating wonderment. Then she said, "Why, Doctor, I believe I do. I really believe I do!" And smiled weakly through her tears.

Jonathan said to Robert, "Would you mind staying here alone with Elvira, Bob? I want to talk with her father."

He went back to the sick man's room and asked Mr. Kitchener and Maude to leave. Then he drew a chair to Dr. Burrows' bedside, and carefully poured a good round drink of brandy into a glass. "I want you to drink every drop of this," he said. "All at once. No sipping." He smiled kindly.

Dr. Burrows made a slow negative movement with his head. Jonathan put his arm about the thin shoulders and forced them upright and plumped the pillows under him. "Take your choice," he said. "You can swallow it or I'll give it to you as an enema. Either way is effectual, but one is less pleasant than another and a little messier."

The very shadow of a smile appeared on the high and unworldly face. Jonathan put the glass to Elmo's mouth and held it there until every drop was swallowed. It took considerable time. It had been a redoubtable amount. Elmo's face was quite suffused in consequence, and Jonathan then let him lie back on his pillows. "A little water? Though it would be a shame to spoil the after-bouquet. No water? Good."

He sat back in his chair and crossed his elegant legs and looked at his watch. Then he stood up and walked about the room, picking up a book here and there and examining it. "Isn't Chaucer a little rich for innocent American minds?" he asked. "Remember, we have Anthony Comstock and other little Cromwells here. We're an awfully naïve people, and a very simple one, and not too bright as yet. We still don't like to admit that ladies have legs and bowels and bladders, and are as avid after what is called 'carnal knowledge' as we are. We still don't want to admit that the world is a very evil place, and a bloodthirsty one, even a frightful one. We'd prefer to believe that it is sweet and lovely, full of laughing children and women who live only for others, and rulers who have the best interests of their people at heart. History, I read in some editorial a few weeks ago, is the evil page of the past, the far past. But from now on history will have nothing to record but the happiness of races and brotherly love and festivals and meeting-of-hands-across-the-sea, and the flowery dells of May, and songs, songs, songs. No more czars, no more kings, no more emperors, no more kaisers. Just one long lovefest of harmonious nations. That's what I read. Do you know what I call that?"

Dr. Burrows was watching him with eyes which were miraculously clearing. He shook his head. So Jonathan told him in a few pungent words. Dr. Burrows was very still a moment. Then he laughed. It was a low and uncertain laugh, but it was certainly a laugh.

"Have another drink," said Jonathan, and this time Dr. Burrows did not protest. He even lifted one tremulous hand to guide the glass more carefully. "Ah," he said, when every drop was gone.

Jonathan sat down again. "A real lively book about Chaucer, with no Latin passages to save the sensibilities of the innocent, and with ye olde Saxon adequately and lustily translated so even a 'pure' child could understand most of it—I favor the *Canterbury Tales* myself—would be spectacular in America. Of course, the censors would be howling after it and you, and you'd probably have the exciting experience of being thrown into jail for a time, with every judge and every emancipated woman and every self-righteous man screaming for your blood. Isn't it strange that so many want to keep the rest of us from what they call corruption, when the only real corruptions are politicians, governments, liars, hypocrites, and the new breed who are calling themselves 'the lovers-of-men'? That's true corruption for you! Nothing that is real and honest is corrupt in itself. Isn't that what St. Paul said? Yes. It is what comes out of a man which soils him, and not that which goes into him."

Then Elmo spoke for the first time in days, and in a strong voice. "I quite agree with you, Doctor. I emphatically agree. You don't know the struggles I have with my students. Very uninformed and simpleminded, faced with true corruption every day and never recognizing it until it is too late, and then most of them think it is the noblest thing in the world and not the vilest."

"We need a lot of brave men to help fight the authentic corruption which is growing in America," said Jonathan. "This is going to be a very corrupt century. The signs are all here. But I will give you my theories, and my fears, some other time. You know, of course, that you never had a stroke at all?"

"I know." Elmo's eyes were strongly bright now, and his color had changed for the better. He even hitched himself higher on his pillows. "It was just that—" He stopped.

"You didn't want to live any longer after your wife died. I know. I've had a long talk with your daughter, a marvelous girl, one in a blue moon. America would be the better for several more million like her."

The dark sorrow and suffering had returned to Elmo's face, and the tragedy.

"Elvira? She is a very strong and brave girl, Elvira. She needs no one but herself."

"She needs you,'" said Jonathan, and now he was not smiling but was stern. "I talked with her. It's funny, but she thinks you are the strong and brave one, needing no one but yourself. Did it ever occur to you that the poor child is suffering terribly over her mother? But she is trying to keep a stiff spine—for your sake—so you won't suffer for her and so distract yourself from your precious work."

"Elvira?" Elmo was flabbergasted and then passionately interested.

"Elvira. I suppose it never crossed that secluded mind of yours that she might grieve for her mother, that she might have loved her mother. No, you thought only of yourself. Did you ever really look at Elvira, or have you always thought of her as only the by-product of your marriage? She is a person in her own right, selfless, devoted, sacrificing, ready to give up all promises of the future just to serve you. What do you think will become of Elvira if you kill yourself this way?"

"I never thought," said Elmo, and turned his face away. After a little he said, "You don't know what it is to lose your wife, Doctor, especially a wife like mine. We were closer than breathing; we were truly one flesh. I never had a thought apart from her, nor she from me."

"That's very poetic," said Jonathan. "But it just happens that it is not true. We live alone in our own flesh. Not even those closest to us can guess our inmost thoughts, and when I consider that, I think it's damned fortunate for everybody."

Again Elmo smiled that shadow of a smile, but it was more certain now.

"And keeps most of our minds comparatively clean. I am a surgeon, Dr. Burrows. I've been in dozens of operating rooms. It would astonish you to hear what the most gentle, most Christian, most genteel, most reserved and well-bred and soft-voiced ladies say when under ether. Quite edifying. At first I was shocked. But not now. Nothing shocks me any longer, not even when a woman murders her child, or a child a mother. We're abominably human and I don't know how God can stand us much longer."

"Neither do I," said Elmo. Then he relapsed in his melancholy again. "My life has gone to pieces. There's no purpose in it, no goal, no promise, now."

"I'm not going to dispute that," said Jonathan. "My purpose, when I was younger and more zealous, was to save lives and cure pain. I'm still all for stopping pain, but saving lives? I don't know. What for?"

Elmo was surprised, and he pushed himself to a sitting position and regarded Jonathan keenly. "Isn't a life worth saving, any life?"

"I don't know. Do you?"

"It would seem to me," said Elmo, "that a good man's life is worth saving in this contemptible world! A good life is the only redeeming quality on earth, the only inspiration." He had a very resonant and vital voice now, full of warmth and emphasis. "It is the only salvation. If that good life is also endowed with genius, or even with just talent, then we are rich indeed to have it among us. It is a faint picture of what men can truly be if they become more than men." He hesitated. "With the grace of God," he added in a quieter voice.

Jonathan let him think about that for several moments. Then he said, "Your wife was an inspiration to you. She was a good woman. You were an inspiration to her and to your daughter, who adores you. You are a good man. So, am I going to let you lie here and selfishly die, when the world needs you so much, that world you think is worth saving?"

Elmo tried to prevent a smile. "You are very eloquent, Doctor." Then he sighed.

"Let us delude ourselves that there is a purpose, a higher purpose, in every life, which we don't as yet know," said Jonathan. "We live in delusions, anyway, and illusions. The world is a very mysterious place, and the more scientists reveal of it the more mysterious it becomes and the more unfathomable—and so more exciting. We are on the trail of something, though I can't imagine what it is. Call it God, if you will. In the coming terrible days which many of us now foresee, we'd better keep a purpose firmly in our minds, and a knowledge of the mystery of life, and our faith, whatever it is—or all of mankind is certainly going to lose its mind. The point is, do you want to be part of the army of the sane?"

"I think I'd like another drink," said Elmo. So Jonathan gave him another. Elmo sipped it, his eyes averted, his scholar's face absorbed in his thoughts.

"What do you think your wife thinks of you now?" asked Jonathan.

"Grace?" Now Elmo looked up in astonishment. "But Grace is dead."

"How do you know that?"

"Doctor! You are a physician and you can ask that? You and I aren't children."

"Well, let's put it this way: We don't know. No one ever returned from the dead to tell us, though it's alleged there was One. We can't prove that there is a God, but we can't prove that there is not. The bad man fervently hopes there isn't, and the good man just as fervently hopes there is. Whose hope do you prefer?"

Elmo smiled. "You are quite a Christian, aren't you?"

"I? No one has ever accused me of that yet. I've never met a Christian except, perhaps, for one or two. Still, it would be a nicer and safer world, wouldn't it, if there were about two or three million honest Christians in it? Granting that it would be a nicer and a safer world, then Christianity has considerable to recommend it, hasn't it? Perhaps you could explore it at odd times—when you aren't eulogizing Chaucer or battling the feeble minds in your study rooms. A scholarly research and exploration, from the vantage point of skepticism and without passion or prejudgment."

Elmo clasped his thin hands behind his head and thought, his eyes and lips sorrowfully drooping. Then he said, "You've opened an exciting vista for me, Doctor, or maybe it is quite puerile after all. Still, it's worth pursuing. All the ancient and modern religions. There must have been an original source to faith— Or something spontaneous in our nature. Personally, I shouldn't like to contemplate a world without the idea of God. As Voltaire said—"

"Yes, I know. A bright old boy. I have sad news for you, Dr. Burrows. We are rapidly approaching a time when men will utterly banish God. That's been evident for over two hundred years, and the pace is accelerating. Did you ever wonder why?"

"No. Why?"

"Now, that's something I don't know, either." Jonathan stood up. "I'm going to call Elvira in, your very efficient young daughter. She will be pleased."

He went out and came to the room where he had left Elvira. She was talking earnestly with Robert, and when she saw Jonathan, she started up and said, "How is Papa?"

"Come and see for yourself," said Jonathan, and he took her hand and led her like a child into her father's room.

Elmo had removed himself from his bed. He was sitting in a chair with his dressing robe and slippers on. Elvira stopped on the threshold, disbelieving, struck.

"Papa!" she cried, and then her face dissolved and shook, and she was only a bereaved girl now and not a young lady with opinions and convictions.

"Dear little Elvira," said Elmo, and held out his arms to her, and, sobbing, she ran to him and knelt beside him, and he took her in his arms. They began to cry together, and Jonathan shut the door silently and went back to Robert.

"Talk about raising Lazarus," he said. "And this one, too, had already begun to stink in his grave clothes."

"Just hysterical?" said Robert, as they went down the stairs to join Mr. Kitchener and Maude.

"Aren't we all, one way or another?" asked Jonathan. "Poor, damned world. And I don't use that expression advisedly, either." He added, "Somehow, I don't think our Elvira is going to be so devoted to health food any longer, and, I hope, she won't remain emancipated."

"A really fine girl," said Robert. "A good mind."

Jonathan stopped on the landing. "Now, that's a despicable thing to say about a nice young lady! The very worst."

CHAPTER TWENTY-ONE

As the doctors drove back to their offices Jonathan said, "Burrows exactly illustrates what I earlier said: That it is only the financially secure who suffer uncontrollably from 'psychic distress.' Oh, the poor have their worries, but those worries are concerned with bread and shelter and clothing and survival—honest things. If Burrows, after his wife's death, had had to scrounge to pay her doctor's and undertaker's bills and hire a woman to care for several children, and then had had to continue, no matter how grieved, to work hard for a living, he'd have soon been, if not reconciled, too pressed to sorrow much. He just would not have had the time. But because he had money and had inherited a great deal more, he had the leisure to indulge his selfish grief, and the hell with his daughter and the hell with everything else, including his own life. It's a strange thing, too: Those who truly enjoy living are those who work sweatily to make that living and have small leisure, but those who work little and have much leisure, and need not worry where their next dollar is coming from, are generally the ones who find life unbearable and joy nonexistent. They are also the ones who appreciate gloomy poetry, gloomy plays, and desperate—and revolutionary—philosophies.

"It wasn't the working man of France, or the farmer, or the miner, or the artisan, who started and maintained the French Revolution of 1795. It was not the hungry. It was the idle men, restless and discontented and envious and bored, the men with gold francs in their pockets, the men of education and philosophy—in short, the men who had nothing to do and nothing to worry about, and so could harbor pains in their souls. *Weltschmerz*, to shift to German for a moment, is the sole possession of those who have uncallused hands, who never knew a plow or a sail or a machine or the reins of a workhorse. Karl Marx is the prime example of this modern age. You will notice that those who are most enthusiastic about him are those who never dirtied their little pinkies with honest work. Woodrow Wilson, professor of jurisprudence and political economy at Princeton University, is noted for his peculiar revolutionary and socialistic philosophies, and the nearest he ever came to an honest element of the world is ink. If I had my way, I'd never let a man teach a class or write a book or be elected to even as lowly a post as garbage superintendent who hadn't worked with his hands—by necessity—on a farm or in a mill or in a mine. It is those who scream the loudest about 'justice to the working man' who despise him, and it was the abolitionists of the North, who had never seen a Negro or employed one, who shouted the most vociferously for an end to slavery. These people love what they call 'ideas,' which lack the power to deduct one cent from their pockets. But let them be asked to pay for those ideas, out of their own purse, and they have a change of heart. Ideas, they maintain, are not to be confused with something they designate as 'filthy lucre.' It would hurt their purity."

"Yet," said Robert, "you were sorry for Miss Elvira."

"I'm always sorry for the victims of the men of ideas. I must get her away from her eminent father, who is doubtless the soul of nobility and therefore not to be trusted."

Robert laughed and shook his head. "I don't understand you."

"You don't understand anybody, and no one else ever did, either."

He seemed in high good humor, and Robert, who did not know of the intervening events between the uneasy holiday of yesterday and the reality of today, thought that Jonathan was a very volatile man whose moods could shift like the shadows of clouds racing over a range of hills. Mercurial, thought Robert, who had never been accused of having a totally original conception of anything. In his turn Jonathan thought that Robert would be an excellent physician and a careful, conservative surgeon but would never introduce a novel method of treatment or dare a unique operation. He would never be reckless but he would also never initiate. A good sound man, young Robert, but no genius, no innovator. He would save the lives of many through care and devotion but would never rescue the almost moribund through boldness. The middle way had a lot to recommend it, even if it never opened a new world or lifted the horizons of men or brought the stars nearer, and never considered if there was another dimension to man not yet discovered by the philosophers or the scientists.

The waiting room was crowded when they returned, and Jonathan greeted old patients with affection and smiled at the new. "We are in business again," he said to Robert when they went into the office. "It's like old times. Hear my clichés! I will leave you to it all and make my rounds at St. Hilda's," and he went out whistling.

Everything, now, to his eye looked fresh and new and interesting, and those who encountered him at St. Hilda's thought that they had never seen him in such good spirits, not even before his marriage to Mavis Eaton. He was actually affable, a very rare thing. He could be heard humming. When he encountered a young gynecologist—a new breed —in a hall, he stopped him. But young Philip Harrington said first, "Jon, may I congratulate you on your operation on young Mrs. Nolan? I hear you performed a miracle. You know I refused to intervene after I heard what old Schaefer did to her?"

"I tried to get out of it myself," said Jonathan. He looked at Dr. Harrington with a reflective eye. "Phil, you aren't married. And you're thirty, thirty-one? Yes. You once told me that you'd never marry unless you found a woman young and handsome and rich and with intelligence and independence, and who had some original ideas. Correct?"

"Correct," said the young doctor, smiling. He was a tall, somewhat beefy and very blond young man, with a cheerful face and a light manner.

"I've found just the girl for you," said Jonathan. "Keen as horseradish, tart as a good old wine, devoted as Penelope, patient a Griselda, innocent as an angel, pretty as Venus, rich as Croesus' daughter, smart as turpentine, not strong-minded but strong-principled, limpid as honey, and with a figure that would grow a eunuch a second pair of testicles. How is that for a combination?"

Dr. Harrington laughed. " 'Why don't you speak for yourself, Jon?' " he asked.

Jonathan struck his chest dramatically. "My heart lies elsewhere," he said. "If it did not, I'd be galloping around the young lady like a centaur, though I assure you she is not a mare."

Dr. Harrington eyed him curiously. "What gives you the idea that such a paragon would look at a poor doctor who is still paying off his debts for his education?"

"I told you. She is a girl of high principles. Moreover, the thought of money has never entered that lovely head. I know these unworldly girls, though she thinks she is very 'modern.' Her father is an eminent scholar and has more money than he knows or she knows. Go to her in the guise of Sir Galahad and you can sweep her up on your white steed whenever you say the word. She 'loves to serve,' and while I usually find that phrase a curse word, in Elvira's case it sounds very pretty, coming as it does from such pretty and unkissed lips."

"What's wrong with her that she's never been kissed?" Dr. Harrington was suspicious.

"Devotion to parents, dedication to 'duty,' and horrible, isn't it? However, her mother died not long ago, and as Papa is only forty-nine or so, he will inevitably remarry, and where will that leave Elvira? Not only permanently unkissed but un—"

"Hey," said Dr. Harrington, as a pair of young nurses began to pass them. "Watch your language." But he grinned.

"Somebody's got to rescue Elvira," Jonathan went on, "and if it isn't you, it is going to be some scoundrel, for she hasn't a single idea of what men are, and isn't she lucky? I prefer to see her in competent and conscientious hands, which will guide her gently to the marriage bed and instruct her in all the things every good woman should know."

"I know one end of women very well," said Dr. Harrington. "I'm not up on the other end; just an amateur."

"You have enough knowledge for Elvira," said Jonathan. "She'll think you are a veritable rake—and adore it. She's the kind of a woman who can become very fiery, and aren't they loves? Well?"

"How do I meet her?"

"Very simple. Her father was suffering from hysterical paralysis and aphasia. I cured him with brandy in about half an hour." Dr. Harrington raised his eyebrows at this. "It's a fact," said Jonathan. "His wife was devoted to him and he to her, and you may have noticed that when a man has lost a good wife, he rushes out soon to find one exactly like her, and usually succeeds. My erudite conversation, and my brandy, got him out of bed almost immediately, and I'll be sadly mistaken if he isn't married again in six months, or if he is not thinking of that very thing at this very minute. A dependent sort of cuss, who can't live without a loving woman. If he marries before Elvia is engaged, or interested, or something, she'll feel abandoned and will remain an old maid.

"So, all you have to do to meet Elvira is to drop in on her father in my name, my kindly name, to see how he is getting along."

"I'm a gynecologist, and though I could perform some spirited schottisches with Elvira, I'm afraid I couldn't do that with Papa," said Dr. Harrington, who was now very interested. "But, how do I explain that your replacement didn't come? How do I explain my coming at all?"

"You have no imagination," said Jonathan, shaking his head. "You aren't going there as a physician; you are doing this out of your Christian heart, as my friend and my emissary. My replacement is too busy for casual calls. And, by the way, you mustn't explain, on the first visits, what you really do, or Elvira will want to know details and will be looking up the word in a medical dictionary—and I'm sure she has one. There is nothing which will turn a woman away from a man so fast as when she discovers he knows all about women. Amorously is fine; women love rakes. But clinically, no. She'll suspect that such a man will lack ardor and that in the very midst of licit lovemaking she will wonder if he is thinking of her parts in an objective fashion, and that's death to romance. Get in a few first kissings and a few soft fumblings, and then you can admit your criminal specialty and assure her that you are first a man then a physician. Convince her that you can rut at least as well as the driver of a beer wagon and that you can't wait to demonstrate. It won't be hard. These intellectual women can truly inflame and gratify a man, and I don't mean intellectually, either."

"You put it eloquently," said Dr. Harrington. "You entice me."

"Let Elvira entice you," said Jonathan. "By the way, she told me she doesn't trust doctors, and she may try to make you a convert to homeopathy or health foods and 'nature's way.' Don't groan, please. Teach Elvira that there's one 'nature's way' in which you are an expert, and she'll want you to demonstrate, but after the wedding bells, of course. But you are certainly imaginative enough to incite her own imagination, aren't you, with a few deft words and teasing touches, and raise up those naughty anticipations even the nicest girl feels?"

"Don't get thee behind me, Satan," said Philip Harrington. "What's her address?"

Having accomplished this worthy deed of righting a young lady's affliction, Jonathan proceeded down the corridor. Near the doctors' lounge room he encountered Dr. Louis Hedler. "Well, Louis," he said, "I've been in to see young Hortense Nolan and she's coming along splendidly and in about a year she can start a new baby. But, for God's sake, get young Harrington for her or someone like him. What's the matter?" he added.

Dr. Hedler was looking very solemn and high-minded. "Come into the lounge, Jon," he said. "No one is there just now. This is private." He importantly seated himself and regarded Jonathan portentously. Jonathan knew that expression. Louis had something to impart to him which was personally unpleasant but which could give Louis pleasure. Too bad, thought Jonathan, that a grateful man can't remain grateful. He sat down and neatly arranged the legs of his trousers, and crossed his knees. "All right, Louis. What did I do now which has raised the dust on Olympus?"

"You have done nothing 'wrong,' nothing at all, Jon. You will recall that you made a very loud uproar not long ago about surgeons performing operations when it was more than suspected that they were taking drugs?"

"I do. No man under the influence of heroin or morphine or any other derivative of opium should touch a scalpel under any circumstances, nor should such a man ever practice the most innocuous medicine, nor should his diagnosis ever be accepted. We're not running a slaughterhouse here, and God knows enough surgeons like that have slaughtered, and in recent history, too."

"Well, now, Jon. I always did think you were too harsh. You have new-fashioned ideas about the dangers of addiction on the part of doctors. I still don't quite agree. Nothing, so far, has been definitely proved that those drugs are harmful or can impair a man's efficiency. A doctor is under stress most of the time. If he takes something to relax him, there is some evidence that this is not only supportive but beneficial. I'm sure that some doctors are what you call 'addicted,' and it has been my opinion that they did no harm and that the unfortunate events in the operating rooms here in St. Hilda's, and in the Friends', would have occurred anyway even in the hands of a nonaddicted surgeon. But I gave this opinion before, before the Board."

"I disagree," said Jonathan, flushing with anger. "I investigated the last two 'unfortunate events' myself. They were uncomplicated and simple operations. The victims—yes, they were victims of men made incompetent by drugs—died needlessly. I am working with a large committee of doctors now, from all over the United States, to have the Federal Government proscribe the indiscriminate giving of narcotics by practicing physicians to patients, and to bar addicted doctors from surgery or the practice of medicine until they are cured."

Louis smiled indulgently. "I doubt that even politicans would be stupid enough to pass such a law," he said. "In my opinion those drugs are no more harmful, or dangerous, than aspirin or bicarbonate of soda. I never tried them myself, but neither am I addicted to alcohol." He looked meaningly at Jonathan, who laughed shortly.

"So, it is rumored around, as well as other rumors, that I am a drunkard, too? Where did that come from? Dear Mavis?"

Louis was shocked. "Jonathan! How can you speak so contemptuously of that lovely girl who was your unfortunate wife?"

"Come on, now, Louis. Mavis spread that rumor. There was some grounds for it, I admit. But I never enter an operating room if I have had a drink within the past six hours, and I never drink the night before an operation, except for a little beer or a glass of wine. I drink very little at social gatherings, and everyone knows that. So only Mavis could have told it around that I can punish a bottle as well as the next man, if I have no following responsibilities. And you surely aren't insinuating that alcohol—to a man who isn't alcoholic—is no more dangerous than narcotics?"

"I consider them all narcotics." Louis was righteously pompous.

"I consider gourmandizing addiction, too," said Jonathan. "Anything to excess is dangerous. But drugs are in a special class by themselves. They aren't self-limiting. A man who is a gorger at the table does arrive at the place where he can't eat any more, and an alcoholic does drop off into a stupor, where he can do no harm. But drugs aren't like that. More demands more, and the appetite increases, and eventually the man dies or goes mad. I'm no humbug, Louis, no self-appointed busybody about my fellowman. I believe in minding my own business. Let a man kill himself with food or women or drink or drugs. That's his own affair. But when he becomes a menace to the innocent who trust him in an operating room, or in his offices, then he has no business there, and it is our business to put him out of business." He paused. "A man who is drunk is soon detected by patients, and his practice vanishes. But what layman can tell when his doctor is dangerously ill of drugs and incompetent?"

Louis frowned. Jonathan went on, with increasing anger: "An addicted doctor fools himself that his addiction is just a pleasant way of releasing his strains, and is harmless, and so he prescribes them freely for any patient with a headache or a backache or a toe ache or an ache in his soul or his ass. And the patient is free to have that prescription filled and refilled indefinitely, and also free to give the stuff to others. Haven't you read the latest warnings, Louis? Four out of every ten doctors are now addicted, and so a disaster to their patients. Three out of every fifteen American laymen are also addicted. These are facts, Louis, facts compiled by responsible doctors and sent to the proper Senators and Congressmen in Washington, and it won't be long before there is a Narcotic Drugs Act, and you can bank on it!"

Louis still said nothing. Jonathan stood up, pushed his hands into his pockets, and began to pace the room. After a few moments he stopped in front of the older doctor. "Louis, we've had patients here, scores of them, unfortunate men and women addicted to drugs prescribed by their physicians. You've seen some of them, many of them, when we've taken them off the lethal things. Some of them die in convulsions. All of them suffer tortures. We have to institute a slow withdrawal program, and it isn't permanently successful. The poor devils leave here 'cured,' and within a few days there they are again in the drugstores, with a new prescription, given to them either by a doctor who refuses to face the truth or an addicted one. Haven't you been reading the new articles in our very own medical journals?"

Louis moved restlessly. "There were a lot of warnings about aspirin, too. Adults, and children, have taken overdoses and have died."

"Louis, for God's sake! Aspirin doesn't cause addiction, nor does the taker of a few tablets, even regularly, need desperately to increase his dose. You can die from an overdose of anything—even water, and you know it. But addiction isn't merely an overdose. It is a craving, a deadly, destroying appetite, which only more and more will satisfy, until the man is killed or kills, or loses his mind. Law authorities are reporting with alarm that drug addiction is one of the main causes of crime. And then you talk about aspirin!"

Louis took out a fretted-silver cigar case and slowly and carefully lit a cigar, not looking at Jonathan. After the cigar was drawing fully, he said, "It was you, Jon, who insisted that six of our best surgeons here at St. Hilda's and ten of our best attending physicians have their privileges revoked. You had all your 'facts' and your figures and your quotations. You impressed the Board; you were very passionate. A majority agreed with you. They were removed from staff. Eight of them were my very good friends."

"I'm sorry about that, Louis, but I only did what I had to do. I liked those men, personally. But their patients' welfare had to come first."

"You might not have been so virtuous, Jonathan, if you had had, among them, a very dear and valued friend. That would have been a horse of another color."

"No, Louis, it would not. Private emotions end where public welfare begins."

"Good. I'm glad to hear that," said Louis Hedler. He smiled, and Jonathan did not like that smile. Louis stood up. "I regret I must tell you this. Tom Harper, one of our most talented and respected surgeons, and one of your closest friends—I believe you lent him money during his last two years—is a drug addict, as you would call him."

"Tom Harper?" Jonathan was stunned.

"The very same. He had a hard time getting through medical school, didn't he? His father sold the family farm to finance him. The farm was mortgaged, wasn't it, so the sum after the sale wasn't very large. Tom had to work hours after his studies to pay the difference in the fees. His parents died in the most extreme poverty—malnutrition, I think it was. But Tom is one of those dedicated doctors who could never have been anything else, and his family sacrificed, even to their lives. Still, when he was studying surgery, he got married. A nice girl, one of our nurses. She, too, worked to put him through. A desperate situation. He was already thirty-six years old when they were married, and he was still here, interning. Then they had children— Very unfortunate. Four of them. You'd think a doctor would be more careful. How old is he now? Middle forties? Yes. Unfortunate. Let me give you the facts of his 'addiction,' Jonathan, and his accidents in the operating room. Perhaps you will find it in your heart to be more tolerant, as I wished to be tolerant about my own close friends."

Jonathan could not believe it. But the older doctor, with enjoyment and relentlessness, gave him the undeniable and the dreadful facts.

"In here," said Jonathan to Tom Harper. They went into an examination room with its table and a desk and two chairs, its bright lights and windowless walls covered with white paint, its cabinets of instruments. Dr. Harper sat down, and Jonathan noticed his stiff care. Jonathan closed, then carefully locked, the door. "What's this?" asked Tom. "Don't want to be interrupted?"

"That's correct," said Jonathan. He stood near the door and looked intently and closely at his friend, the long thin body, the unusually slender wrists below the stiff white cuffs and the cheap cuff links, the shabby but polished boots, the sleaziness of his suit with the long old-fashioned coat at least eight years old. But more than that he saw the bony and yellowish face, the sunken darkness under the clear gray eyes, the clefts about his mouth, and the curious lack of luster of his light brown hair. His ascetic nose appeared unusually sharpened and pointed and his mouth was bloodless, the humorous, kindly mouth that could express so much sympathy and pity and patience. He had a little brown mustache, and its ends were waxed. For some reason this struck Jonathan poignantly. Then he tightened his own mouth and looked sternly at his friend.

"I'm not going to run around the mulberry bush, Tom," he said. "You know I'm on the Board, here. Dear old Louis Hedler has told me he more than suspects you're taking morphine from the supplies, and as doctors have easy access to drugs anyway—there being no law as yet to register drugs and control them—this spells just one thing to me. Tell me if I'm wrong."

Tom Harper's sallow face had begun to sweat, though the room was not hot. The drops of sweat became larger on his forehead, as if they were tears. He said nothing. Jonathan went to him then, roughly took his chin in his hand, and tilted Tom's face to the ceiling light. He looked down into the eyes and saw the pinpointed pupils. He looked at Tom's hands and saw the muscle tremor. Then he angrily seized the other man's arm and pulled up the coat sleeve, tore out the cuff link of the worn but meticulously starched cuff, rolled up the sleeve—it was darned—and saw the needle marks. He dropped the lifeless arm. Dr. Harper had not offered the slightest resistance. He had become flaccid.

"A week ago," said Jonathan, watching the other doctor slowly and dreamily pulled down his sleeves, "you operated on an old man, Finley. Gallbladder. A nasty, bloody, dangerous operation, I admit, but you're famous for your cholecystectomies, Tom. You do things I'd hesitate to do, and you do them with flair and success. You haven't lost a patient yet. People come even from Philadelphia for your operations. I've seen you in action. Old Finley had a routine case, calculi, no inflammation, no complications. Field pretty open, I'm told. Yet, you tied off his common duct, Tom, and even when his resultant symptoms were urgently called to your attention, you said it was 'nothing.' And so, he died. It was told me that you were 'airy' about the whole matter."

Dr. Harper scrupulously fastened his cuff link. His head was bent. The drops of sweat were falling down his cheeks now, one by one, and Jonathan thought he could hear them drip.

"Old Finley hasn't been the only one, has he, Tom? Simple operations—not your usual kind—but four patients have died in the past month. Louis insisted on autopsies, unusual around here. He'd been suspecting you for a long time, months. And in every death there were the signs of carelessness, stupidity, incredible clumsiness. Louis doesn't like you, Tom. You're one of 'us,' and so to be wary of, and guarded against, and watched, and triumphantly found out and disgraced, if possible. But Louis, to give him credit, now won't let a surgeon operate when he suspects he is an addict. Drug addiction among doctors and surgeons is common these days and they all say it is 'harmless.' When they merely bungled, but the patient didn't die, or they managed in spite of the drugs, Louis used to say nothing. He let them go on. But now Louis draws the line. Tom, aren't you going to say anything?"

Dr. Harper spoke in a far voice, as if nothing mattered. "I did my best. I don't know how it happened—I didn't even know about the autopsies. I suspected—yes, I suspected how it had come about. I warned myself not to operate." His voice died away as if he were infinitely weary.

"Then, why did you?" Jonathan was both enraged and horrified and could hardly control himself. "You've murdered five innocent people! Yet, you still operate! You're a murderer, Tom. If we didn't close ranks, you'd be up on charges of malpractice at the very least. Tell me, why did you, damn you? Knowing your addiction and unreliability, and the danger, why did you?"

"Are you going to revoke my privileges?" Dr. Harper brushed away the falling sweat and then looked stupidly at the back of his hand. "You won't do that to me, Jon." He shook his head over and over. "You won't do that to me." He began, to Jonathan's awful exasperation and increasing horror, to cry. He bent his head on his chest and stammered, "No, you won't do that to me, Jon. There's Thelma and my four children."

Jonathan sat down in a straight chair and thrust his own shaking hands violently into his pockets. "Tom, I am going to do just that. I'm going to prefer charges against you, with Louis, and you'll never operate again until you can give us all assurances that you've stopped taking the drugs. And you'll never see the inside of another hospital."

The stricken doctor continued his dry soft weeping as if he

had not heard. "You won't do that to me, Jon. I need the money. I'm forty-six years old. In the past six months I've made five thousand dollars. Five thousand dollars! Four of them went to pay off old debts. I have six operations scheduled. Next week. One hundred dollars apiece—six hundred dollars. A fortune. I must have that money, Jon." He spoke with quiet and desperate firmness.

"You're not going to make it. You're not going to murder anyone else in this hospital or anywhere else." Jon spoke heavily, for his instincts were informing him that rage could not shake this unfortunate man, nor threats, for something more terrible was destroying him, even more terrible than the morphine he was giving himself. "Listen to me, Tom, if you can. Try to focus on me. Look at me, damn you, and stop that ridiculous womanish crying! Tom, I'm your friend. I know how hard it's been for you and Thelma."

"No," said Dr. Harper. "You don't know, Jon. Look at me, Jon. I'm dying."

"I don't believe it!"

"It's true. I have what you call the Beast, Jon. I have gastric cancer."

"Who told you?" Jonathan's voice was rough because he did not want to believe this monstrous thing.

"Jon, I'm a doctor, too. You know how we are. If we suspect something is wrong with us, or we have a few symptoms, we are the ones who get medical advice last, and besides we're too busy. Then, we know all there is to know, and that makes cowards of us. It isn't ignorance that makes us cowards, contrary to the old saw. It's knowledge. It started several months ago. For a considerable time I'd been having epigastric pain, and I thought, 'Oh, if I don't stop taking on so much, I'll be developing an ulcer,' so I took the usual antacids. I began to lose weight, and Thelma said I was working too hard, which I was—all those debts. Then I lost my appetite and started to vomit—and about three months ago I had that famous coffee-ground vomitus. I examined my blood. Anemia, and then I found occult blood in my stools. The classic picture; nothing vague. My mother died of cancer, you know. Now I don't sleep very much—except—"

He made an exhausted and vague movement of his thin and trembling hands and then dropped them on his knee.

"You know the prognosis of that, Jon."

"Would you mind if I examined you?" Jonathan still did not believe it. Tom Harper silently stood up and removed his clothing. Jonathan was aghast to see his rib cage clearly visible; his legs were only bone covered with a thin layer of muscle and skin. Tom lay down on the examination table, and Jonathan silently examined him for the most part, asking questions only when necessary. Once he said, "If only to God we had an X-ray machine here in town!"

"What if we had? It would just be interesting to doctors but not for me, Jon. Well?"

"Get dressed." Jonathan carefully washed his hands so that he would have something to do and so calm himself. He wiped his hands on a clean towel, then sat down near his friend.

"I suppose you know that it's already metastasized to the liver? And to the supraclavicular lymph nodes and peritoneum?"

"Yes, I know. As a doctor and as a patient—I know."

"Why the hell didn't you come to me months ago?"

"To have you tell me the truth?"

"I've seen two rare operations, Tom—resection. I can do it myself. I assisted at one, in New York."

Tom smiled drearily. "How long did the patient survive after that?"

"A year longer than he would have done without an operation. But another is still surviving, not in a rare and roaring state of health, but he's still alive."

"If he were a doctor, would he be able to keep up his practice?"

"No. Frankly, no."

"You see," said Tom, "it would have been worthless to me, even if I had survived. What would I do without medicine? I can't do anything else. And there are my children and my wife. Well. Now you know. I can keep going on morphine, Jon. It keeps the pain down enough. I'll be making enough money to give Thelma a little breathing space. There's five thousand dollars in life insurance—all I could afford. The boys won't have much chance, but at least they're healthy. I've got to go on, Jon. I can't stop."

Jonathan looked down at his narrow, polished boot. He swung it back and forth, his lips pursed as if whistling. His manner was nonchalantly thoughtful, but he was thinking rapidly. Tom Harper finished dressing. He, too, washed his hands mechanically at the basin, then, sighing, he smoothed his damp hands over his thick brown hair.

"Tom," said Jonathan, "you are a country-born boy. You

lived on your father's farm until you entered medical school. And twelve or fourteen years ago he sold the farm so you could continue? But you know farming.

"I have three farms. One of them is about two hundred acres. I have a tenant farmer there, in a house by himself. The farmhouse is big, with running water, and comfortable and has been renovated. It's very old, but it's a fine house. The farm is stocked with some truck. Three hundred head of cattle, Holsteins. My bulls have won a lot of prizes, and my cows, too. The farm's perfectly equipped; it brings me a good income, even after my tenant farmer gets his share, and he gets a very generous share. Excellent man, with a family, and his house isn't far from the main house. A good school two miles away. Highway nearby—less than an hour's drive to Hambledon. A church a mile away. Rolling country.

"I want you to go and live in that farmhouse, Tom, and take Thelma—who's a country girl herself—and your four children. A healthy and tranquil life for all of you. And I guarantee you this, and will sign a contract with you to that effect: Thelma is to occupy that house during her lifetime, unless she marries again, and the children with her until they leave permanently for marriage or career. And the income from the farm, after the tenant farmer's share, goes to you, as long as you live, and to Thelma, as long as she lives, or until she marries again, which I doubt she will do. There'll be no fine print, Tom, but just as I've told you.

"I've seen temporary remissions in what you have, Tom. A life without strain and with peace, and with the knowledge that your children are provided for—Thelma can save from the income for their education—and your wife, too, will prolong your life for a few months, perhaps. You'll have peace of mind, above everything else. And, Tom, I will, within the next few days, arrange that all expenses of the farm be paid by me, and all improvements, even to the seed and fertilizer, new machinery, and everything else. You'll have no extraneous expenses. If Thelma dies prematurely, your children will live there under the same provisions.

"Now, what do you think about that?"

Tom said nothing. He merely looked at Jonathan with tortured stupefaction, his emaciated face working without a sound. His hands knotted together, and then he wrung them over and over.

Jonathan said, "There's the little village of Russellville down the road, and old Dr. Jonas lives there and practices what he can practice. But he is a good man, a Dr. Bogus himself. Occasionally, when you feel well enough, you can help him out—once in a while. No night calls, no deliveries, no operations, of course. Simple diagnoses. You know the farming regions, and people.

"Tom, your addiction to drugs comes from your pain, and I know that only morphine can relieve it. So, take a good supply with you, a very good supply, but use it only when absolutely necessary. For you know as well as I do that as long as it's possible for a cancer patient to function even a little adequately, it's best to keep the dosage as low as it can be. Or later—nothing will help the pain except death. And we want to postpone that as long as we can for Thelma's sake and the sake of your children. On the farm, without stress and the necessity to work as a surgeon, you will find that you can keep the dosage pretty low for a long time and save its real benefits—for the last."

He stood up. He could not look at his friend's face now; it was too much for him. "Do you want me to tell Thelma for you, Tom? Will it be better that way? Or shall I go with you now and we'll tell her together? She's a sensible woman, Thelma."

"Jon," said Dr. Harper, in a very low and rusty voice.

"Yes, Tom?"

"I've got to tell you something, Jon. I can't accept your offer without telling you first, and perhaps after I've told you, you will withdraw it, and I wouldn't blame you."

Jonathan smiled. "All right, tell me. It can't be very important."

Tom threw back his head so that his thin and contorted neck reared out of its high stiff white collar. He stared at the ceiling and groaned. Then he reached up his hand and covered that straining face and spoke from behind them.

"Jon, weeks before you were arrested—it was accepted that you had been—away, I went to Humphrey Bedloe and spoke to him in private. I swore that if he repeated what I said to anyone, or called me in before witnesses, I'd deny I ever said it, and I'd deny it on the witness stand.

"Jon, I told Humphrey Bedloe that I had seen you, right here in Hambledon, on the day your wife told her uncle that she had had that criminal abortion which caused her death."

Jon stood as if struck in the center of the room, and slowly his face became terrible.

Tom continued. "Humphrey went to the sheriff and told

him but did not give my name. He knew it was his duty. He said only that he had 'information.' It was on that little 'information' that you were arrested, Jon. It doesn't seem possible that in this day and age that would happen, without a sworn statement before the proper authorities, and questioning, but it did. This town hates you, Jon. It's always hated you—that is, the important part of it if not your patients, and even some of them do, also. They wanted to believe the worst of you, Jon. Out of envy, and because you—you have an abrasive way sometimes, and you have no patience with lies and hypocrisies and pretensions, and malice, without which most people could not live a full life. And you let people know what you think, and that's not forgivable."

He had dropped his hands heavily to his knees again, and he inclined his head like a man totally undone and broken, but his eyes looked at Jon unflinchingly and with anguish.

"With what I told Dr. Bedloe, and what Martin Eaton did, too, it was enough. Perhaps one without the other wouldn't have carried weight. My weight carried, Jon, it carried weight."

"What really did you tell Bedloe?"

"I—well, I said that I had seen you not far from your house, as I was in the neighborhood. I said I had seen you walking along the river bank, deep in thought. You—you had a bag with you, a piece of luggage. And then you walked in the direction of the station. Bedloe didn't doubt me, Jon. He never had reason to doubt me before and has had no reason to doubt me now. Don't hold it against him, Jon, that he removed you from the staff of the Friends' even before you were indicted. It was my doing."

Jonathan said with soft wonder, "You son of a bitch. You son of a bitch."

He went to the door and unlocked it. Tom said behind him, "Yes. Yes. I'm much worse than that. You canceled the five thousand dollars I borrowed from you, Jon. You called it a 'gift to medicine,' and 'a public duty.' I tried to think it was only that, Jon; I would not let myself think for a moment that it was the greatest generosity and kindness in the world. I even persuaded myself that you did only what you ought to have done and that in a way I was your benefactor, and not you mine. That's the way people are, Jon, that's the way they are, but I don't think you ever knew that."

Jonathan's tall back was to Tom Harper. He put his hand on the doorknob and began to turn it.

Only a few weeks ago, perhaps less, he would have turned it and would have gone out, and that would have been the end of it and there would have been nothing left to do but to make certain that Tom Harper was removed from staff and his patients taken from him. But there had been some dark and still unknown unrooting in the deeper places of his mind lately. He stood at the door and faced Tom Harper again.

"Why?" he said. "Just tell me why. I want to know."

Tom sighed despairingly. "Jon, my father sold his farm to help put me through medical school, and there was very little left after the mortgage. Your father bought that farm, Jon, about fourteen years ago. It's yours now. And you've always been rich, and that was another thing, and you didn't have hundreds of cold black nights going through medical school, when you wondered whether you'd make it or not, and you were hungry, and you couldn't afford to sleep because you had to work outside to make expenses. It wasn't your fault, Jon, that I went through that, and my father, too, but there it was. That is the way people are. I took your five thousand dollars—that's the way people are."

"Yes, so it is," said Jonathan. "I always had a low opinion of humanity and now you've dropped it down another thousand or so fathoms, Harper. I was ten years—more—behind you in age. I didn't know when my father acquired the farms he left me. You have no accusations to throw at anyone, Harper. My father bought that farm because it was offered for sale through a county agent. He neither knew nor cared why it was being sold. Why should he have? If it had not been your father's farm, it would have been another. My father liked land. I knew nothing about it. My father was the only one who wanted to buy that farm and he paid the money asked. He wasn't guilty of 'exploitation' or deliberate cruelty. But that's what you thought, wasn't it?"

"That's what I made myself think, Jon. I must have been insane all those years. Thelma thinks you are the most wonderful man in the world, and sometimes I'd say to her, 'Sweetheart, if you only knew!'"

"Well, it was a nice boost to your ego! It put you on the level with Jonathan Ferrier or even made you his superior. The funny thing is that I never considered you 'below' me, Harper, and I never considered you inferior! To me, always, you were a fine doctor and surgeon, far above the average. We were at least equals. I was proud to help you—because

you were a member of a profession which seems to me to be
the most important in the world.

"Now that I've seen some specimens lately, I'm not convinced. And you've helped, Harper, you've helped."

"I know, Jon, I know. Say anything you want to me. It
isn't half what I deserve."

The sick man bowed his head on his chest. Jonathan
looked at him with the greatest hate and bitterness and
thought: He wants me to feel sorry for him, to pat his shoulder, to laugh heartily and say it's nothing, and the farm arrangements will go on!

Then another thought came to him. Tom Harper had had
no compulsion but one of conscience to tell him what he had
done. He had had only to keep silence—and accept. Yet, in
this desperate business he had deliberately risked what could
have been the answer to his catastrophic situation. He had
sacrificed himself, his wife and children in order to feel honorable again and in order to right an injustice.

Jonathan slowly came back into the room. "Why did you
tell me, anyway?"

"I had to—after your offer. Do you think for a moment I
could have accepted it, even for Thelma and my children,
knowing what I had done to you out of envy and malice and
resentment, when none of it was your fault at all and you
had given nothing to me but kindness?"

"I see," said Jonathan, and frowned at the floor.

"Men don't reason with their minds," said Tom Harper.
"They reason with their guts, their emotions. That's why the
world is what it is. I took your friendship and all that went
with it, but because you are rich and I was and am poor, I
think I hated you, Jon, while, at the same time, I liked and
respected you and was your friend. Complicated, isn't it?"

"Not very," said Jonathan. "We're a pretty ambiguous
race, and all at once I'm beginning, halfway, to believe in the
dogma of original sin."

It was absurd, but a fraction of an old prayer he had
learned as a child came to him, as if spoken aloud: "And forgive us our trespasses as we forgive those who trespass
against us."

A lovely sentiment but unrealistic and, in a way, snide. If
you don't forgive an appalling crime against you, and one
which might have caused your death if it had been successful,
then you won't be forgiven your tiny venial sins, either. Mad
idea, thought Jonathan with harsh amusement. Justice, in a

rational world, should always be measure for measure. The old boys were more sensible: an eye for an eye, a tooth for a tooth. If I remember rightly, you are now supposed to forgive the sons of bitches the worst offenses against you and not only forgive them but ask that they be forgiven, too. That was doubtless all right for Christ, but men are not God. No wonder there were practically no Christians in the world. The whole thing was against reason and logic and, above all, against human nature.

Jonathan said with hard contempt to Tom Harper, "All right, get off your knees, I've absolved you and you can leave the Confessional. Let's go and talk to Thelma. And if you tell her one word of what you've told me, you'll regret it the rest of your life. You're not going to burden Thelma with your crime so that you can wallow in her forgiveness, too, and perhaps even get her to pity you, for Christ's sake!"

"Jon," said Tom, "I swear this to you, and you know I am dying: I would never have let you be convicted. It was in my mind—I must have been crazy—that your arrest would pull you down a notch, as they say, and make you less haughty and proud and arrogant. You weren't those things, I know. I just thought you were. Because, God help me, in your position, that's just what I'd be and so would ten thousand other men."

"Shut up," said Jonathan. "I don't know who's forgiven you. I haven't. I'm going to do what I suggested but not for you, Harper. If it were you alone, you could rot along with your disease, and I'd never give you another thought. But why should your innocent wife and children suffer?" His dark face had flushed with rage and his eyes sparkled.

"You know what this is going to do to me the rest of my life, Jon? It's going to make me do penance, and perhaps sometime you can be superhuman enough to forgive me."

"That will be a long summer day in my dotage, Harper. When you are dead and forgotten, even by me."

"Did you hear what Jon Ferrier did to that unfortunate Tom Harper—his best friend, or almost that—the other day? He forced him to resign his hospital privileges just because Tom took a little morphine occasionally, for heaven's sake!" This was said by Jonathan's colleagues and "friends," with head-shakings and compassionate cluckings. "But, then, Jon was always a vindictive man. I'll never forget the time he refused to testify in behalf of Jim Spaulding, in court, when poor Jim was sued for malpractice by that worthless laborer who had the wrong infected arm taken off. Almost ruined Jim. Jon stood right up there in court and said that Jim should have every damned cent taken away from him in damages—and Jim one of the finest surgeons in the country, and who was that laborer with the foreign name, anyway? Well, that's Jon for you. Glad he'll soon be getting out of this town."

Later it was rumored that Jonathan had given Tom Harper a job as a hired hand on one of his farms, and the resentful hatred and envy of Hambledon against Jonathan became more vociferous than ever. Senator Campion was particularly vocal. He marked the incident down in his little black record book and smiled with satisfaction.

CHAPTER TWENTY-TWO

When Jonathan came into his offices six days later, he was gratified, for Robert Morgan's sake, to find every chair taken in the waiting room, Robert busy in the examination room, and even a few standees in the hall outside. He went into the office and Robert came in and said, "We have a rush. Was it always like this?"

"Yes. Nice, isn't it? The news that you are not married and that you are handsome and rich must have gotten around, for I see quite a number of well-dressed mamas out there, all, no doubt, equipped with marriageable daughters, and there are two or three young ladies, too." Jonathan removed his hat and wiped his ridged forehead. "Four o'clock, and the evening rush hasn't begun."

Robert picked up a typed card from the polished desk.

"Now, here's a young lady who interests me. A Mrs. Edna Beamish. Beautiful, and apparently with money. She insists on seeing only you. Hints she has something quite extraordinary wrong with her."

"Never heard of her." Jonathan took the card and read the address. "Kensington Terraces. That's one of the few places in this town which can really be called an apartment house —unpleasant things, harbingers of the bright new future when men will be living in anthills. But this, so far, is a nice and very expensive group of flats—why do they call them 'apartments'? Flats. I've been in one. Lavish, surrounded by gardens. Hum. Edna Beamish. Twenty-two years old. Any idea what is wrong with her?"

"No. She looks very well to me, naturally good color, very pretty and stylish. And with a gay eye. I've told her you are taking no new patients, but she says she has heard so much about you and will see no one else. Take a look at her, anyway. She probably has a fat purse," and Robert grinned. "She's worth looking at, and from her manner I gather she wouldn't object too much if I invited her out for a decorous evening."

Jonathan went into the waiting room. "Mrs. Beamish?" he asked of the crowd. A lissome young lady rose, dressed in a simple but obviously costly lavender silk dress, which sheathed her figure tightly and dropped in a mass of rustling ruffles to the floor. She wore a broad silk lavender hat to match, with pink roses, and her hands were gloved in white and she carried a beruffled parasol the color of her hat and dress, or gown would more properly describe it, thought Jonathan. She had a very attractive bosom, indeed, on which reposed a long string of amethysts set in gold, and the same gems enhanced her ears.

Her hair was fair and abundant and beautifully coiffed under the hat, and she had a small and mischievous face, very piquant and lively, with large light brown eyes and impressive lashes, and a dimple in a pink cheek. The eyes flashed seductively at Jonathan, roving rapidly from his face to his feet. She sighed and smiled. "Mrs. Beamish," she murmured.

Jonathan was intrigued. He said, "I am taking no new patients, Mrs. Beamish. You were told that. But Dr. Morgan will see you." (That would be a nice figure to examine.) He waved to her to precede him and she swept by him in a sweet rustle and embowered in a rich and enticing perfume, which Jonathan appreciated immensely.

Once alone with him in the office, she turned, gave him another view of the deep dimple, sighed and smiled. "Oh, Doctor." Her voice was light and caressing. "I'm so sorry, but I just couldn't see anyone but you—after all I have heard." The fine eyelashes fluttered like moths and threw a dainty shadow on her round cheeks. "I really couldn't."

"That's nonsense," said Jonathan, inspecting the figure again. "The town is full of good doctors, and Dr. Morgan is one of the best. He'll admit it himself."

She trilled with delight, then coquettishly tapped Jonathan on the arm with her parasol. She shook her head. "No, only you, Doctor. I heard Dr. Morgan isn't married—" She dropped those wonderful eyelashes modestly.

"Oh," said Jonathan. "I'm not, either. By the way, I've never had the pleasure of seeing you before."

"I've lived in Hambledon only a few months," said the young lady, waving a little gloved hand and so setting the perfume in motion again. "I have a slight—chest. I was told, in Scranton, that the air here is very good for such things."

And the chest is very pretty, too, thought Jonathan approvingly. "That's silly. Of course, Scranton is smokier, but not too much. So, you are from Scranton?"

"Yes. I'm not well-known there either, Doctor. You see, I come from a very unimportant working-class family. Poor but honest. But I married well. A gentleman from—from Chicago. He was visiting in Scranton, and liked it, and so we were married."

"But he likes Hambledon better?"

Again she sighed, and the lively face became sorrowful. "I am a widow, sir."

"I'm sorry," said Jonathan. Her sigh was very beguiling.

"A lonely widow," said Mrs. Beamish.

"Oh, I doubt that!" said Jonathan gallantly. But she shook her head and gave him a sidelong vision of her lashes and tilted nose. A very alluring baggage! Jonathan was beginning to have some idea about the lady and he doubted she was inconsolable and that she would reject the suggestion of a quiet and private little dinner somewhere, with good wine. He knew just the place and knew it well.

"It is very hard for a lone woman to become acquainted with genteel people in a strange city," said Mrs. Beamish with a sorrowful but fetching glance. Now Jonathan heard her accent, common and uncultured, but nice for all that. Commonness was not to be despised in a very pretty woman; on the contrary.

"Well," he said, and looked at the card as if considering. "If you insist, Mrs. Beamish. But I warn you that if your condition demands long treatment, I shall have to turn you over to Dr. Morgan."

"What a treasure you are!" she exclaimed. Robert appeared with his patient from the inner examination rooms, and seemed surprised and pleased to see Mrs. Beamish. "I shall examine Mrs. Beamish," said Jonathan with a grave voice, and winked at Robert. "If you don't mind, Doctor. Then she is yours."

"That," said Robert, "will be my pleasure." The girl tittered but not disagreeably, and gave Robert a flirtatious glance. Jonathan opened the door and let the young lady go in. Robert shook his head at him and smiled.

"Disrobe, please," said Jonathan, and removed his coat and put on a white jacket. Mrs. Beamish surveyed the immaculate room with its table and its formidable array of cabinets with fearful instruments in them. She seemed a little daunted. "Disrobe?" she said.

"Well, I can hardly examine you with that dress on, and your corsets, can I?" Jonathan asked with reason. "I'll go into the other examination room, while you at least take the dress off and loosen the corsets."

When he returned, she looked more fetching than ever, in her white silk and lace petticoats and what was known as a camisole, all white ribbons and embroidery. The bosom did excellently for itself without the whalebone. She had taken off her hat, too, and her hair was very bright and fluffy. Most appealing, thought Jonathan. He sat down near her and took one of her small plump hands. "Now, tell me what you think is wrong," he said. "Chest, again?"

She dropped her eyes. "Well, no, Doctor. I'm afraid it's female trouble. Inwardly."

"That's where it usually is," said Jonathan. "I've never seen it elsewhere. Now, my dear, I am a doctor, and I'm sure other doctors have examined you before for one thing or another, so shall we put aside the modesty for a few minutes and get down to questions?"

She laughed at him demurely. She answered the questions readily enough. She had pain in her right side very often, every month. "Probably just ovulation," said Jonathan.

"Quite often a little painful." Oh, but this pain was agonizing! It tore her apart. She screamed, really she did. Nothing helped at all. It went on for days. She couldn't sleep or rest or eat. It was frightful. Her face became quite awed and pale.

Ovarian cyst? thought Jonathan. He asked more questions. She was a little vague. Her knowledge of her own anatomy was very sketchy and grotesque. When he said "ovary," she stared at him blankly. "You know," he said in a jocular voice. "Where the eggs are."

"Eggs? Doctor, I'm not a hen!"

"Nevertheless, you do lay an egg every month, I assure you," he said. She looked offended. He gently slapped the white silken thigh and said, "Now, I'll examine you. Just lie down on this table, please. And here are the stirrups. Put your feet in them."

"Stirrups?"

"Have you never been examined this way before?" asked Jonathan.

"No. It was always just my chest."

"We'll examine that, too, after this. Now, just don't be so stiff. Lie down. That's a nice girl. Cover yourself with this little sheet. And up with the feet. I won't hurt you."

But she looked at the dilating instrument with real terror, half concealed though it was with a napkin. She pulled her knees together. "It won't hurt you," said Jonathan. "Perhaps a little discomfort, but you're a big girl now, and you've been married."

His amused voice reassured her, and she endured the extensive examination with only a wince or two. After the first flurry she appeared to lose her modesty and concentrated her attention on the instrument, and didn't mind Jonathan's careful peering.

"All right," he said after about five minutes, "you can sit up now." He carried the instrument away to a basin to await sterilization. The girl sat up and arranged the sheet very carefully over her legs. Jonathan came back to her, smiling.

"I have good news for you," he said, "though it's sad that your husband is not alive to hear it. You are nearly three months pregnant."

"Oh!" cried Mrs. Beamish, and fell back on the table and began to cry. "Oh! Oh, poor Ernest! Not to have known about it, and he did want a baby so! He died two months ago, Doctor."

"Unfortunate," said Jonathan with real regret, both for the

deceased Mr. Beamish and for himself. "Well, now, you must
take the best of care of yourself, and rest as much as possible, and be brave, and walk quietly every day. I will give you
a little booklet—"

Mrs. Beamish suddenly gave vent to peal after peal of tearing and tortured screams, so loud that even those in the waiting room could hear them. While Jonathan, stunned and mo-
tionless, looked at her in absolute amazement, she rolled back
and forth on the table, howling.

"Doctor, please, please, please! Oh, Doctor, you are killing
me! Oh! Oh!"

There was a loud knock on the door, which Jonathan did
not hear, being petrified by the screams, and then Robert
rushed in, very agitated. He looked at the convulsed and
half-naked girl on the table and then at Jonathan. "What the
hell?" he asked.

"Hysterical," Jonathan could manage at last. "She's a
widow and pregnant. Legitimately, I assume. Here," he said
to Mrs. Beamish. "Stop that!"

"My God, you can hear her on the street," said Robert,
quite shaken.

Jonathan deftly slapped the girl's face and she stopped at
once. Tears ran down her cheeks. She looked at Robert imploringly. "He hurt me terribly when he did it," she sobbed.
"Hurt me terribly. I didn't know it would be that bad."

"Nonsense," said Jonathan. "You never let out a whimper.
Go on, now. Get dressed." He said to Robert, "Just the usual
pelvic. A robust piece."

Robert looked at the girl, frowning. "I think you'd better
leave her to me," he said. But the girl was hastily dressing,
crying quietly and shaking. She did not put on her hat or
gloves, but instead she galloped out of the examination room,
raising her voice in loud and frenzied sobs and staggering visibly. She rushed past the astonished spinster at the typewriter
and the aghast and staring patients, and she exclaimed at the
door, "He almost killed me, and he said it wouldn't hurt!"
Then she fled outside.

"For God's sake," said Robert. "What did all that mean?"

Jonathan shrugged. "We get all kinds," he said. "I just
think she's upset, knowing she's pregnant and her husband recently dead. She'll calm down and be back in a week or so."
He heard a carriage draw up outside and looked through the
window. "And a very nice vehicle she has there, too," he
said. "A good pair of mares."

Robert was uneasy. "You never saw her before? Where has she been hiding?"

Jonathan explained. "I still don't like it," said Robert, perturbed. "If she goes yelling like that to another doctor, it would hurt your reputation."

Jonathan laughed. "Nothing can hurt my reputation any longer," he said. "No. She'll be back. If only to look at you."

But Mrs. Beamish never returned, and after a few days the two young doctors forgot her entirely. The elderly spinster did not, however, nor the other patients present. It had been very dramatic to people with drab or uneventful lives. Gossip spread through the city.

Marjorie Ferrier read all the newspaper clippings pertaining to her son Harald's show in Philadelphia, and she almost cried with gratification and sadness. "Wonderful, dear," she said to Harald. "How very successful! I am glad you were so appreciated and sold so many. We must send these clippings to the local newspapers."

"Three thousand dollars," said Harald. "Not too bad. But, then, there were collectors from New York who know the coming trend in painting. By the way, I was offered five thousand for one—five thousand!—but refused it."

"But why?"

He smiled at her with her own fine hazel eyes. "I saved it for you. I want you to have it. It was the only portrait, and one of the few I ever did."

He lifted a large canvas and carefully removed the several burlap coverings, and then exposed it to the vivid July light in the morning room.

It was a portrait of Jenny Heger. It depicted her in profile against a faintly umbrian interior, like rich but muted sunshine. She wore a dress of bluish-white of no particular style, except that her throat was visible and the top of one smooth shoulder. A small high casement window, mullioned, had been thrown wide open and the girl appeared to be looking out at nothing at all but a bleak and glaring light, a nothingness stark and empty. There was not a shadow, not an outline, of a single thing in that remorseless and almost blinding illumination, at once desolate and haunted. Her expression was brooding and quiet and very still, as if she knew that she was contemplating a barren glow in which nothing would ever move or live. Her black hair had a wild and disheveled appearance, suggesting that she had thrown it aside in haste when she had run hopefully to this casement, only to let it fall heavily down her back in her devastated realization. One hand was lifted in a gesture intended to smooth that hair, and then she had left it in that lonely gesture, halfway to her cheek. Her mouth was only slightly colored, and apart in childlike wonderment and sorrow, and the blue of her eyes appeared to shimmer in the abandoned brilliance.

The whole impression of the painting was of coldness, of forsaken and solitary dejection, of faith left forlorn and deserted and betrayed in a hollow light. Harald had not used the traditional bland style of painting. The paint was rough and strong and bold and full of vitality and passion, very moving and exciting, conveying powerful emotion both in the girl and in the viewer.

"Oh," said Marjorie, and she winked strongly several times. "How very beautiful. And—how very terrible. How you have caught poor Jenny! When did she pose for you, dear?"

"She never did. I didn't need her to pose, Mother."

"No," said Marjorie, still looking at the portrait, enthralled and deeply moved. "I suppose you didn't, Harald. No, I suppose you didn't. It is just like Jenny and conveys so much. I —well, I must confess that I never knew how much you—" She stopped.

"How much I understand and care for Jenny?" Harald's handsome face smiled easily, but his eyes were ambiguous. "I thought you knew. Anyway, it is yours, Mother, because you are so fond of Jenny, and I want you to have it."

I will hang it in the drawing room, thought Marjorie, and then she had a quick and disturbing thought. Jonathan must never see what his brother had painted of Jenny. Marjorie wanted to cry in her sudden wretchedness. She watched Harald place the portrait against the wall of the morning room, and she saw all his slow and absorbed movements. Then he stood off from the portrait and looked down at it, his head bent as if he had forgotten her. He said, his well-tailored back to her, "I've watched her so often, with that very expression. She's had a miserable life—Jenny. Like a recluse, and she's only twenty. That was Pete's doing. Then Myrtle did not care about Jenny with the strong love Jenny had for her mother. Myrtle was incapable of anything strong in the way of emotion or attachment. She accepted everyone's affection graciously and kindly, and appreciated it, and was fond in return. But love—no. She wasn't very intelligent, but she had gentle ways. I liked her very much. I really did. I tried to get her to do something about Jenny, to send her abroad for her own good, to meet her contemporaries, to force her to dress better, and Myrtle did try, with her soft persuasiveness."

Harald laughed shortly. "If she had suggested to Jenny that she hang herself, the girl wouldn't have been more horrified! No, she said. She had to stay—to take care of Mama and watch over dear Papa's castle, and his rose gardens. Particularly his rose gardens. I've seen women possessed by men, and jewels, and pleasure, and vice and all the passions, but I never knew anyone possessed by a rose garden before! Did you?"

"No," said Marjorie, wanting to cry more than ever. "Perhaps the rose garden means something—someone—to Jenny, who is immeasurably dear to her. She haunts it."

"Pete, probably," said Harald. "What a gross little fat beast he was! And crass about everything but his foolish castle."

He turned to his mother, and his highly colored and appealing face was serious. "I've asked you before: Isn't there any word you could put in about me to Jenny?"

"No, dear, there isn't, and I've told you that too, before." Marjorie shook her head and looked at her son with pity. "Harald, dear, I think you'd better look elsewhere."

"I don't want anyone but Jenny, Mother. I never will. I'm not very young. I'm thirty-three. That's old enough to know what you want." He sat down beside her and sipped at the brandy near him. He regarded his mother thoughtfully. "Something just occurred to me. Is there something you haven't told me? You are so sure Jenny will never be reconciled to me or consider me."

Marjorie hesitated. "Perhaps," she said, "there is someone else. Jenny hasn't told me, but there is something—something about her that makes me feel there is, indeed, someone else."

"That's not possible. Jenny never goes anywhere, never meets anyone, hasn't seen half a dozen men in as many years! And only one or two young men." Harald smiled confidently. "It's something else. Pete's memory."

Marjorie was silent. Harald's light eyebrows dropped over his eyes as he studied his mother, and his suspicions increased. "Mother, have you any idea?"

"Jenny has never said a word to me."

"That's not exactly what I asked you, dear. I asked if you have any idea, yourself."

"I'm not a mind reader, Harald."

"No, but you're evading the question." He smiled at her with affection.

"Harald, I can't conjecture without absolute knowledge. And Jenny has—"

"Never said anything to you. I know. You haven't seen her anywhere, with anyone else, have you?"

Marjorie looked at the portrait. "She was at the Fourth celebrations with me and Jon and Dr. Morgan—such a nice boy—and the Kitcheners, and Mrs. Morgan."

"Now, that's a lively gathering if I ever knew one! The Kitcheners are like soft, rolled breasts of chicken cooked in cream, and about as pungent, and Mrs. Morgan, I have heard, is a harpy, and young Dr. Morgan is very innocuous, with all that boyish charm. Our Jenny, who constantly reads Pascal's *Pensées,* and Molière and Walter Pater, and St. Augustine, and God knows what else, can't be interested in Dr. Morgan."

"I think he was quite smitten with her," said Marjorie, glad that one name had not been mentioned by Harald. "He stared at her as if bewitched all through the fried chicken, the beer, the chocolate cake and the iced tea, not to mention the potato salad, the hot rolls and the green onions. He looks like a hearty young man with an excellent appetite, yet he hardly ate a thing, and when he got chocolate icing all over his fingers, he quite simply sucked them—and stared at Jenny, enraptured."

Harald laughed, seeing the picture vividly.

"And how did our Lady of Shalott respond to that?"

"Well, you know how unaffected and unworldly Jenny is, and how little she appreciates her beauty or even knows she has it. She kept blushing. Robert made her uneasy, I am afraid."

Harald stopped laughing. "When a man makes a woman uneasy, even if he is sucking chocolate off his fingers or nibbling at fried chicken, then it is serious. That uneasiness can grow into interest, and interest into something stronger. Has she seen him often before?"

"I really don't know, dear. You know that Jenny comes into town once or twice a week, on that deplorable bicycle when she could have a buggy of her own or hire a hack, and it's possible she's encountered Robert on the street here and there or in a shop. He's looking for a special mirror which his mother wants, and some old paintings, preferably of London in a foggy rain. That's Mrs. Morgan's taste."

But Harald was not diverted. His fair forehead knotted, and he considered. "He's just the sort of red-gold lamb who could appeal to a woman's cradle instincts. Such men end up with blue ribbons in their hair eventually, put there by Mama."

"He's not that soft and weak and unmanly, Harald. He gives the impression of virility and a lot of stubbornness and other masculine qualities. I had invited him because of Maude Kitchener, who was enraptured as much by Robert as he was enraptured by Jenny."

"And who do you think Jenny was enraptured by?"

The sharp and sudden question affected Marjorie unpleasantly. She said, "I'm sure I don't know, dear, as I told you before. It is just a—tenuous feeling I have. But, could you really imagine Jenny that enraptured by anyone, so that she might be present in person but far off in mind, dreaming?"

"I do indeed," said Harald in that same sharp tone. "I do, indeed! She is just the sort. Now that you mention it, I *have* seen her in that absent condition, staring into space almost by the hour. Reminds me of that silly old poem, 'A woman dreaming of her demon lover.' The point is, who's the demon?"

Marjorie sighed. "Do you really have to talk about poor Jenny so much?"

"Mother," said Harald, "she is the only thing I ever think of, most of the time." He sat near his mother and though he had considerable of Jonathan's appearance of containment and control, just then he gave the impression of urgency. "I can't keep on just trying to change Jenny's mind about me any longer. I have to bring her to realizing—well, that I love her and want her. I've told her dozens of times! It doesn't seem to penetrate her mind, shall we say? That's why I thought you might be able to help me, to put in a word—"

"Harald, I couldn't. You know I never interfere, and I'm absolutely no good at hints or insinuations, and I wouldn't want to offend Jenny by seeming to be minding her own business." She bit her lip a little. "It's possible we'll know soon enough, if there is anything to know."

"And that'll be too late for me. You're hiding something from me, aren't you?"

"You've been home three days, haven't you, Harald? You've seen Jenny. Have you shown her those clippings?"

Now she saw Jonathan clearly in him for the first time, concentrated and annoyed at her attempt to change the subject. "I've seen her," he said, in Jonathan's own hard and impatient voice. "I've talked to her. I might have been talking to a statue, a statue which finds me particularly revolting, if a statue can feel anything. Show her the clippings? She'd throw them in my face! And what in hell did I ever do to her to merit all that hate?"

"Did it ever occur to you, Harald, that a young girl like Jenny might find it a little—well, repulsive—to think of marrying a man who was married to her mother?"

"Not in this case. I told her frankly after Myrtle died that —what is the delicate little euphemism?—we had not lived together as husband or wife, though we manifestly occupied the same bed."

Marjorie did not know whether to laugh out loud or to express horror. She rounded her eyes at her son. "Dear me, I didn't know. How—very confusing. Why on earth," asked Marjorie, "did you two ever get married in the first place?"

"It was simple." Harald was smiling now. "I needed money, and Myrtle needed a flattering, courteous, attentive man with whom to travel and whom to display—and an attractive one whom other women might envy her. She couldn't travel with Jenny. After all, even an unimaginative woman like Myrtle would find Jenny a little rocky to take while traveling and among company. Myrtle was considerably older even than Pete. She had been nearly forty when Jenny was born. She was one of those nice, inoffensive, agreeable little women, and full of affability, which men like Pete—bustling, offensive, determined little brutes—adore. But after one child —that was enough dallying in love's arms for Myrtle. So, we came to a pleasant arrangement. She loved art, she said. She wanted to be a sponsor for my art. She needed a winsome escort—that was me. And, she liked me and was fond of me, and I liked her and did not find her in the least objectionable. Her will was a shock to me, I admit, under the circumstances."

Marjorie was fascinated. "And what did Jenny say to all this when you told her?"

"I think she wanted to kill me, and for the life of me I don't know why. Do you?"

"Surely. She thought you had married her mother for her money."

"Well, I did. Though it wasn't so bald as all that."

Mirth glittered in Marjorie's eyes. "You know, Harald, you may find it incredible, but sometimes you are as single-eyed as Jon. Not very often, for you know a great deal more about people than he does, and they never surprise and stun you, as poor Jon is always stunned. But still, you were a little naïve in telling all this to Jenny."

"I don't think so. She's the forthright sort, and so I was forthright. And by nature I'm not at all that blunt, so please don't compare me with Jon. He's like a sledgehammer and throws himself at everyone he decides isn't being candid and honest enough for him, or just possesses the little ordinary human weaknesses that everyone but himself, of course, possesses. That's why his—trouble—was worse than it was. All he had to do, in court, was to defend himself respectfully, gently, modestly, and sincerely, with an eye to impressing the judge with his blameless sweet nature and the jury. Instead of that he showed every sign of contempt for them all, as if he thought them below the status of mankind for even daring to believe he had—done that to Mavis. He was outraged at them! He lacks finesse, the ability to slide around rough edges. He lacks diplomacy."

Harald's ruddy hair caught a beam of sunlight and it sparkled on his fine teeth and Marjorie, as always, thought how endearing he appeared and how charming.

"Yes, I know," she said. "Jon was like that from babyhood."

"You can't go around in this world telling the truth," said Harald. "It's a very bad, disgraceful habit and deserves all the uppercuts it gets, and all the infamy and hate. Besides, what makes Jon think that everything he thinks about people is the exact truth? For instance, he called me a 'lute player' years ago—"

"A lute player?"

"Yes, an idle singer of poetic little songs to amuse the ladies with. Of course, I'm using my painting seriously, for the simple reason that the almighty Jonathan Ferrier never understood it or wanted to understand it. To him I was as trivial—as—Mavis, and just about as useful in the world. Not to be useful in the world was to him a cardinal sin, one of the worst. I strolled around the fringes of the grimy and industrious world; I laughed when I should be deadly solemn. I sauntered when he thought I should be running. I lacked 'purpose,' he said. He was always bursting with purpose, until he married Mavis, and then he started to wander in a dark wood, like Dante. But you can be sure that under all that he was seething with his infernal purpose or trying to recover it. He couldn't live without it."

"Yes, I know," said Marjorie.

"He never found out that the real purpose of living—if there is one at all—is to enjoy yourself as much as possible and have as little pain as you can. It's a very interesting and beautiful world, and I like to roam it and paint it, my own impressions of it, and mingle with people—I like people and can't live without them—and drink and dine with them and laugh with them. It's harmless; it's enjoyable, and if there is some plan for us here, I think it is purely to have pleasure in a world made for pleasure. There's every enticement, God knows."

"And that's always been the contention between you and Jon."

Harald shifted in his chair. "Partly. At least, that's what started it. Then, he's possessive. Do you know that he thinks you never cared for him in the least and that all your maternal devotion was centered on me?" He laughed at his mother's astonishment.

"Now, really, Harald!"

"Oh, he does. I used to watch him when we were kids, and I used to torment him about it. He wanted everyone and everything centered on himself."

"Jon never cared about anyone but his father."

"Don't believe it, Mother. He took good care of dear Papa's tender little sensibilities, but you were the object of his real affections. He thought he didn't have yours, so he decided that you weren't very intelligent in not appreciating the golden salver he was offering, containing his heart's blood or something. Maybe his head."

Marjorie was still disbelieving and she smiled at Harald in denial. "Perhaps you are as wrong about Jon as he is about you. You two were always incompatible. I think you both try very hard to find something tangible to dislike each other about, when it's only a matter of—a matter of—"

" 'I do not like you, Dr. Fell,
The reason why I cannot tell.' "

"Exactly," said Marjorie. "It isn't uncommon between brothers or anyone else."

Harald stood up. "When is he leaving Hambledon, with

that rasping tongue of his? To afflict some other community?"

"I suppose soon, when young Robert is well established. But, it's a very strange thing. He hasn't talked much about it lately." Then Marjorie looked at her son with her hazel eyes darkening and becoming deeper and more watchful.

In turn, he lost his amiable look. He went over to the portrait and affected to be studying it, and his voice was careless when he said, "I wish he'd leave very soon. It would be better for him. Much better. And very much safer, safer above all."

Marjorie was silent. When Harald turned to her again, her face held nothing but pain, and she showed every sign of intense weariness. "You mean Hambledon has robbed him of purpose?" she said after several moments.

"No," said Harald. "I don't mean that at all. I mean Mavis."

CHAPTER TWENTY-THREE

"Where, in God's name, did you buy that suit?" asked Jonathan on a very warm Saturday late in July. He surveyed Robert and laughed.

"You provincials," said Robert. "I bought it in New York last spring. It is jealousy, my dear man, which suffuses your cheek with yellow, and envy which has jaundiced your eye. Your remark was poltroonish. Consider the fit, the style, the flair."

"I can't," said Jonathan. "I'm partially blinded as it is. What did the morning's patients think of it?"

"Stunned," said Robert. "Stunned to awe."

"I bet," said Jonathan. Robert's suit was of lightweight wool in a gigantic plaid design embracing black, white, a splash of green, a quick run of red thread here and there, and even a shy hint of orange. The long coat was stylishly cut back. With this he wore a high white collar, the points of which were open just below the chin, and flared outward, and he had crowned the whole attire with a lavish silk tie repeating the plaid and fastened with an enormous pearl tiepin. His pointed boots shone like black coal, and a pair of yellow leather gloves and a pearl-gray fedora completed the costume. He slowly pivoted to allow Jonathan to survey all the glory, and he touched the tips of his red-gold mustache and jauntily struck a pose.

"Not even lascivious little Perry Belmont ever dared to wear a suit like that," said Jonathan. "You look like an overgrown jockey. All you need now is an automobile. I'm thinking of getting one, myself, from England."

Robert was impressed. "Do you know Perry Belmont, personally?"

"I not only know the stocky little lecher but I know most of his ladies, too, who are mad for him and why I never knew. He does have a Nero sort of appearance, a wicked eye and a fat nose. Maybe these are attractions to the ladies. The short men seem to enchant them, especially if the Little Corporals look Napoleonic, and Perry does." Jonathan shook his head. "He was Minister to Spain, and that cost him a fortune and I hear he upturned the señoritas like a cyclone through a forest. They all fell down and pulled up their skirts at the mere sight of Perry. Or, at least he says so.

"He and I were guests of Cornelius K. G. Billings, the racing boy, last year, and we both belong to the New York Riding Club, and I bought a mare for fifteen thousand dollars from Cornelius, and she wasn't worth five thousand. Never trust a rich man; he'll flay you with pleasure and sell your hide and call it Morocco. Well, Cornelius gave the club a banquet at the famous restaurant, Sherry's, and damned if he hadn't sodded the floor with earth and grass, and we arrived on horseback, were taken up to the banquet hall in elevators, still on horseback, and we still sat on the horses while we were served caviar and champagne and a dinner cooked by the best chefs in the world, and all on heavily gold-plated fine silver, complete with solid gold dinnerware. And there were lackeys, of course, to clean up the manure behind the horses and wash down the sod, and there we sat, on our prize animals, in formal evening wear. I thought it was the most outrageous, the most depraved, the most infantile and brutish affair I ever attended in New York, and I have attended some marvels. I hear it cost Cornelius about twenty-five thousand dollars, which would have helped to found a hospital somewhere for tuberculosis." His face had turned contemptuous. "The only animals there who could really boast of aristocracy and decency were the horses. I felt embarrassed for them and wanted to apologize to them. I did apologize to my own horse."

"I've read a lot about those things, in New York," said Robert, "and what they call the Four Hundred. That makes good subject matter for William Jennings Bryan—the lavish and degraded and vulgar spending of enormous amounts of money, and the overgrown crowded mansions, and the gaudy jewelry and the vice—and the social diseases, as they are discreetly called. It's not folly; it's cheap garishness. The average workman is lucky to have a wage of twelve or fifteen dollars a week! No wonder half, or more, of his children die before they are five years old! And he's an old man at forty."

"True," said Jonathan. "But let's not glorify the workingman either. I admit his state in America is far worse than anywhere else in the world except, perhaps, Egypt and Arabia and the darkness spots of Africa. But he's human, too. He is beginning to utter loud and bitter cries over his condition —and I'm glad of that and I'd like to see him strongly unionized—but let him get power and he'll be just as bad as the bluebloods, as they like to call themselves, in New York or London or Paris or Berlin. It's that old thing called human nature. You can't trust it. Well. Who is the lucky young lady who is going to be paralyzed by your costume today?"

Robert carefully pulled on his yellow gloves. It was obvious they had never been worn before. "Miss Jenny Heger," he said, giving much attention to the buttons of the gloves and seeming to have a small difficulty with them. "I wrote to her last week and asked if she would care for a ride along the river, and a picnic, in my company."

"Jenny?" said Jonathan.

"Miss Jenny. I am not on less formal speaking terms with her," said Robert. "I received a kind little note in reply, and I must confess I was both pleased and surprised, and she accepted my invitation."

Jonathan leaned against his desk and crossed his ankles. "I don't believe it," he said. "Jenny has never accepted any young man's invitation before."

"She accepted mine." Robert was very relieved that Jona-

than had shown no intense interest or annoyance, though
why he should do either Robert could not understand. He
only knew that any mention of Jenny heretofore aroused Jonathan to inexplicable emotion or lascivious remarks. He
smiled a little and looked up at Jonathan, who was lighting a
cigarette. "I know she is a very bashful young lady, and I will
try to gain her confidence."

Jonathan's polished black eyes surveyed the suit and acces-
sories contemplatively. "That ought to scare her to death,
rather than reassure her," he said. "What if there is an emergency at the hospital?"

"Don't you remember?" asked Robert. "You kindly offered
to attend to that for me, seeing that I haven't had a day's leisure since I arrived. And we doctors do need recreation, as
you've said yourself, or we'll soon not be worth anything to
our patients."

"Did I say that?" said Jonathan. "One of my more careless
moments." He seemed casually amused. "You'll quite out-
shine poor Jenny, who doesn't possess, I have heard, one single pretty gown."

Robert ran his hand over his fine gold watch chain and
took out his watch. He was more and more relieved. He said,
"My mother once remarked that it seemed strange that Miss
Jenny did not employ a companion, an older woman, *in loco
parentis,* as it were." What his mother had really said was, "It
is an affront to the morals of the whole community that that
young woman is so brazen in her conduct, and so careless of
public opinion and the sensibilities of gently bred young ladies, that she does not have with her some elderly female of
impeccable background and position in this city to protect
her from gossip and give her respectability." Remembering,
Robert blushed, and Jonathan saw it.

"Jenny? An elderly female companion?" Jonathan laughed.
"Jenny, I can assure you, can take very good care of herself."

"But there is, after all, your brother living in the same
house with her, and he a young man still, and only the servants."

"Isn't he protector enough for Jenny?" asked Jonathan.

The term, Robert recalled, was ambiguous. He began to
feel a little heat of anger against Jonathan. "Just what do you
mean by protector?" he demanded.

Jonathan said, "Now, what do you think I mean? Technically, he's her stepfather, the husband of her dead mother.
Don't develop an evil mind, Bob."

"I'm not the one with an evil mind!" said Robert, and felt a hard constriction in his chest. "I've seen Miss Jenny only a few times since the Fourth of July, on the streets and in the shops, and a more lovely and innocent young lady I have never seen in my life!" He seemed to swell. "We've talked a little, here and there, and she's very shy and timid and seems afraid and awkward. I—I like Miss Jenny very much! I do, indeed. Eventually, I hope that she will take me seriously."

Jonathan whistled. He eyed Robert and not with kindness, and then with a slow thoughtfulness. "We have progressed, haven't we?"

"I hope so. I fervently hope so!" said Robert, and shook an invisible speck of dust from his hat and prepared to leave. Then he had another thought. "Why doesn't your brother supplement her income so she can leave the island for a more —a more—protected residence?"

"I hear he did," said Jonathan. "But she refused. I told you. She regards him as an interloper, a criminal blackguard who married her mother for her money—and she is quite right, Harald makes no pretense otherwise, and it was an amiable marriage—and she considers the island hers, as it was her father's, and she stands guard over it. She'll never leave it unless she is first sandbagged and blindfolded by someone, and somehow I can't see you in that role."

"Hardly," said Robert. "But still, if she marries, she may change her mind."

"My dear noisy-suited friend," said Jonathan, "I should not blow up my hopes if I were you. Jenny and my mother are almost as close as mother and daughter, and my mother has hinted to me several times that Jenny's affections are firmly fixed on some mysterious stranger."

Robert's face actually paled, and Jonathan frowned. "If that were so, she would not have accepted my invitation," he said.

"Perhaps the gentleman is unattainable," said Jonathan.

"Then, all the more should she be diverted," said Robert, and took himself off in his sartorial glory.

Jonathan had not seen Jenny since that evening when he had tried to seduce her somewhat strenuously. He had often rowed over to the island on the pretense of amusing himself by mocking his brother, but when Harald was there—which was infrequent—Jenny appeared to be absent, or at least she made no appearance. Jonathan had idly asked about her once or twice and Harald had shrugged, had remarked that she was "in town," or was not feeling well, or, "God knows, I don't know where she is!" Harald seemed less easy lately, less nonchalant and less smiling, and to be absorbed in some thoughts of his own. He was restless. If one so affable and pleasant could be said to be brooding, then Harald was brooding. In view of what Marjorie had said, this was interesting to Jonathan. He wanted to say, "Insofar as Jenny is concerned, sweet brother, you might as well give up, and perhaps I should, too, though damned if I will until the day I die."

When she visited Marjorie, Jonathan did not know, though he suspected. Marjorie did not mention the girl except to remark at one time that Jenny was not visiting her as often as usual. This was understandable, considering that she probably feared his unexpected arrival in the house.

There was one thing which had relieved him excessively: It was most evident that Jenny had never told Harald of his brother's attack on her. She could easily have done so. Harald would then, at her insistence, have forbidden Jonathan to come to the island any longer. (It would have been interesting to see if he could summon up a rage or engage in fireworks or threats for the first time in his life.) But, for some strange reason, Jenny had not told him, and this was exciting in itself, nor had she written asking him never to go there any longer, nor had she asked Marjorie to convey the message.

But he had not seen her. The infuriating thing was that Robert Morgan had seen her on the streets and in the shops he was prowling for his mother, and she had actually accepted an innocent invitation from him. The implications of this nagged at Jonathan. He liked Robert immensely; he felt for him the strong brotherly affection he had never felt for his own brother. It annoyed his pride and his opinion of himself that he should, this hot Saturday afternoon, think many uncomplimentary things of his young replacement, and also of Jenny.

If Jenny had been elusive before, she was far more elusive now. Jonathan had planned a nice strategy of coming across her in the gardens of the island, where she was eternally working, or alone in the castle, and then forcing her to listen to him, even if he had to hold her. He had planned, to the last comma, what he would say. But Jenny eluded him. He never even caught a glimpse of her. He was not a patient man. He had planned that tomorrow he would see her, or perhaps later today. He had never failed in a wooing of a woman yet, and had even married one—the only one he had wanted to marry. For this pursuit he had an engaging mixture of flattering impatience and even more flattering bullying, mixed with a real gentleness. No lady, except Jenny, had outrightly rejected him, not even married ladies of genteel reputations. He had not had to buy them with gifts, not even glittering courtesans who could command stupendous prices. In Hambledon, he had been more circumspect, though not entirely. The ladies of New York and Philadelphia knew him well, and often too well.

He had never, for a moment, doubted that in the wooing of Jenny Heger he would be successful. He loved her, and he had never loved a woman before, as he realized now. He had everything to offer, such as himself and marriage. Not even when pursuing a particularly difficult lady had he hinted marriage as a possibility, nor had he ever called Mavis "darling" as he had called Jenny.

Now, out of nowhere had come this naïve young Robert Morgan, with his gorgeous raiment and his ability to get Jenny to do what it had been impossible for any man before him to do. What of the man Jenny was alleged to be attached to—unless Marjorie had been entirely mistaken? Could it be —it was impossible!—that Jenny had been detached from that stranger by Robert Morgan? It was absurd. It was not to be thought of for a moment. Jenny was a girl of intelligence; she was unlikely to be attracted to a man of limited imagination. But one never knew about women. They were capable of the most bizarre revulsions and attractions.

The telephone rang.

A high and breathless female voice rushed to Jonathan's ear. "Jon? Jon! This is Prissy Witherby! Oh, Jon, I'm scared to death!"

"I shouldn't wonder, being married to Jonas," said Jonathan. "Anything specific wrong, Prissy?"

"Jon, please come at once! He's out driving today—he goes every day. But all at once I can't stand it! I'll lose my mind!"

Jonathan would have smiled indulgently at this from another woman, but Priscilla Witherby, the former doxy, had the common sense of her calling and the realism, and so hysteria was unlikely. "What's he up to now, Prissy?"

"I don't know! That's what makes it so frightening, Jon. But it is something, I know. Since he came from the hospital, he sits smiling all alone, like a damned satisfied spider, spinning, plotting— Oh, I know I sound fanciful, but you know Jonas."

"I do. I'll come as soon as I can, Prissy. How long does he stay out, driving?"

"From two to three hours in this weather. Jack drives him to the park and around." The girl caught her breath in a sob. "He's been gone fifteen minutes. That should give us time to talk."

After he had finished his conversation with Prissy, Jonathan thought about Jonas Witherby, the soft, smiling, loving evil of a man. The gentle-voiced, charitably speaking, mild, tender-eyed evil. Damn them, these dangerous ones! Jonathan remembered the dead wife, the ruined sons, all the victims of this monstrous corruption, this man who had never been known to speak evil, to see evil, or to hear evil, at least overtly—this man who had deceived almost an entire small city into believing in his goodness and kindness and pure-hearted sympathy. If Jonas Witherby were to testify in a court of law against or for a man, the judge would inevitably believe him, listening to his affectionate voice, looking at his saintly face, and so would a jury. Jonathan prepared to leave for the Witherby house when he heard the bell ring in the waiting room. He frowned with annoyance as he went to the door. There were no office hours here on Saturday afternoon except for emergencies and fixed appointments.

Two well-dressed gentlemen in their thirties, strangers to Jonathan, stood in the deserted waiting room. He said with abruptness, "I'm sorry. Dr. Morgan is not in, and there are no office hours on Saturday afternoons except by appointment."

One young man spoke, a tall and pleasant man with shrewd light eyes and blond thick hair and with a humorous face. "Dr. Ferrier? Thank you. I'm Bill Stokeley, from Scranton," and he gave Jonathan his card. Jonathan looked at it: William Sebastian Stokeley, attorney-at-law. "And this other gentleman," said Mr. Stokeley, "is Dr. Henderson Small, also of Scranton." Another card was given Jonathan in identification.

"Well, what can I do for you?" asked Jonathan.

"We'd like to discuss a former patient of yours, Doctor," said Mr. Stokeley, "and to pay you for her examination. I understand that you never sent her a bill."

"What was her name?"

"Mrs. Edna Beamish."

Jonathan considered. The name sounded familiar to him, but he could not recall the patient. He shook his head. The two men glanced at each other in satisfaction. "You may not know," said Jonathan, "but I have—had—a large practice, not only in Hambledon but from surrounding villages and townships, and even from Scranton and Philadelphia. My replacement, Dr. Morgan, has been handling most of them. I am merely here now to help him establish himself, before I leave the city permanently."

"Mrs. Beamish lived at Kensington Terraces when she visited you, Doctor."

Jonathan shook his head again then went to the files, opened one and withdrew a card and studied it. Then he laughed. "Oh, Edna. Yes, I remember now. She was here almost a month ago. Charming young lady. She did not let me complete my examination and became a little—disturbed— and ran out after creating a scene. She was understandably upset, for I discovered she was at least ten weeks pregnant, and her husband had recently died, and so he would never know his child. I didn't send her a bill because the examination was incomplete." He looked at the lawyer.

Mr. Stokeley said, "I am here to pay her bill, Doctor. You see, my firm manages her late—husband's—estate. Ernest Beamish. So, she reports all bills to us, and we pay them for her. She is very young and inexperienced herself, and incapable of managing the rather large estate her husband left her. He appointed us executors." He smiled. "In fact, we are *in loco parentis* to her. So when she returned to Scranton to live two weeks ago, she told us that she had consulted you and that you had sent no bill."

"Don't bother about a bill," said Jonathan. "I expected Mrs. Beamish to return for further examination, and possibly prenatal attention, and possibly for obstetrical purposes, at the hands of my replacement. As she did not return, I don't think she or you are obligated to pay any bill, and I certainly won't send one."

He looked curiously at Dr. Henderson Small, a short slender man, very dark and grave and inconspicuous. "Are you attending Mrs. Beamish, Doctor?"

"I did," said Dr. Small in a significant voice.

"Did she run out on you, too?" Jonathan smiled, noting the past tense.

Mr. Stokeley intervened. "Mrs. Beamish is—er—a rather

difficult girl. I happened to be in town with Dr. Small today, and I thought it well to stop in to see you and ask for a bill."

"No bill," said Jonathan. He was becoming irritated. The afternoon was hot and fine. He intended to ride out to one of his farms and see how a certain filly was doing, one who was showing all signs of being a remarkable racer. "If that is all, gentlemen—"

Mr. Stokeley said smoothly, "As I told you, Doctor, we act *in loco parentis* to Mrs. Beamish. Obviously she needs continued treatment. Dr. Small, here, is not a gynecologist. He is a general surgeon, and certainly not an obstetrician! He told Edna he has had very little training in obstetrics—I think that is the new science of doctors who deliver babies? Yes. However, she insisted on him examining her, and he discovered a—slight—abnormality." Mr. Stokeley gave Jonathan a genial smile. "He referred her to an obstetrician in Scranton, but so far she hasn't followed his advice. By the way, did you find any abnormality, Doctor?"

"None," said Jonathan. "At least not during the pelvic examination, which was as thorough as I could give, considering the fact that she was squeamish and resistant, not an unusual thing in young ladies under the circumstances." For the first time he saw that Dr. Small was discreetly taking notes on a very abbreviated little black notebook. "What is this?" he asked.

"Just for reference, Doctor." Mr. Stokeley was very pleasant. "You see, there is that large estate, and naturally a—er—natural issue would be important, wouldn't it? We feel every responsibility for Edna. Now, Doctor. Would you mind telling Dr. Small exactly what your examination showed?"

It was almost two o'clock. It would take at least an hour for Jonathan to ride out to his farm after seeing Prissy. He glanced at his watch.

"I found no abnormality," he said, with increasing impatience. He looked at the reserved Dr. Small. "What did you find?"

"No abnormality in the pelvic regions," said Dr. Small. "But something unimportant in the pancreas. We did want your opinion before sending Mrs. Beamish—insist on sending her—to a competent man in Scranton."

"It isn't necessary," said Jonathan, more and more impatient. "I found her approximately ten weeks pregnant, a healthy young white female, widow, with no previous history of disease of any kind. She did complain of 'terrible pain' in the lower right quadrant of her abdomen, which she gave as the reason for her coming to me in the first place. This usually occurs during ovulation, a common thing. I examined her for a cystic ovary and found everything normal. I then examined her for chronic appendicitis, or blind bowel, as the laity call it. Nothing pathological there, either. I intended examination for possible kidney involvement or—"

Dr. Small interrupted. "But insofar as the pelvic examination was concerned, there was no abnormality?"

"None. Didn't you say that was your opinion, too?"

Mr. Stokeley gave Dr. Small an enigmatic and unfriendly glance, and the doctor said at once, "I saw no evidence of a natural—a natural—abnormality."

Jonathan found this ambiguous. He looked intently at Dr. Small and said, "We don't usually speak of 'natural abnormalities,' Doctor. A contradiction in terms."

"And of semantics," said Dr. Small.

"Yes. So, what did you mean?"

"Oh," said Mr. Stokeley, "let's not get into a medical discussion, gentlemen, on this fine day! Our train leaves in half an hour for Scranton." He held out an expansive palm to Jonathan and said in a rich but slow and emphatic voice, "So, you did not receive payment for your examination?"

"I told you, no." Dr. Small quietly wrote that down.

Mr. Stokeley grinned and shook his head. "That Edna! She is always complaining that she never has any pocket money. Let me be frank, Doctor. She claims she paid you two hundred dollars for your examination! In cash, and not by check, on which we usually insist."

Jonathan laughed. "Had I completed the examination as I had wished, I'd have sent her a bill for ten, perhaps fifteen, dollars. I'm afraid our little Edna is attempting a financial wheedling from you. She never paid me a cent and I never sent her a bill. Now, if you will excuse me—"

"Thank you, Doctor, thank you," said Mr. Stokeley effusively. "I shall really have to castigate our Edna, I really shall. I suspected it all along. Good day, Doctor."

The two men left, and Jonathan saw that a station hack awaited them outside. He watched it drive away in the direction of the depot. He forgot the episode at once in his hurry. After all, it was not unusual. Pregnant ladies with money were understandably, and expensively, concerned with their state. He was about to replace the card in the file, then thought about it. Mrs. Beamish would not be his or Robert

Morgan's patient. He tore up the card and threw it away. He liked to keep his files neat and up to date, and have no dead and useless information in them.

He went off, whistling. He was usually whistling these days. He felt such vitality lately, such an awareness of life and strength, such a consciousness of joy in living, in spite of all that he had suffered and endured since his marriage.

It seemed to him that food had never had such a vivid taste before and such delightful odors and enticing bouquets, that wine had never had so much body and richness, that sleep had never before been so profound and waking so eager, and that the mere goodness of soap and water and coffee had not been fully appreciated by the world of men, and that in the main—including himself—mankind was not worthy of all these blessings. Sometimes he laughed at himself and accused himself of being jejune, like a middle-aged man suddenly discovering, and for the first time, the allurement of women. The golden years of youth! They had not been "golden" for him at all. They had been years of anxiety and despair and uneasiness and bleak and shadowless light— from the age of seventeen. Now his real youth had come to him, in the hands of an obdurate, wild, hating, pathetic and appallingly innocent girl. (Jonathan Ferrier, unlike others of his generation, did not entirely admire innocence of mind. He preferred chaste women, but he also preferred them with a touch of worldliness.)

In the meantime, it was joyful to be alive and he wanted to prolong this unique experience.

He had almost reached the street when a uniformed messenger approached him. "Dr. Ferrier?" asked the lad, then touched his cap, gave Jonathan an unstamped but sealed letter, and rode off on his bicycle. Jonathan looked at the writing on the envelope and it was unfamiliar to him, and for some peculiar reason he thought, This is a feigned writing and not the real one of the writer. Perhaps it was the elaborate curlicues, or the change in slanting, or a "t" crossed differently from another "t," or a baroque circle over an "i" when following "i's" were merely dotted with a tiny dash or not dotted at all, which made the writing appear hidden or contrived. Jonathan opened the letter.

"*Murderer!*" it shouted. "*If you are not out of this good city by September 1st, at the latest, you will be ridden out on a rail, tarred and feathered! Do you remember the effigy of you which was hung near the courthouse when you were*

*falsely acquitted of the murder of your wife? The next time
the rope will hold your neck and not an effigy. Beware! Your
crimes are all known."*

Jonathan could not believe it. His first impulse was to
laugh, then destroy the letter, for only a madman could have
written it. But then he was impressed by a sense of malig-
nancy in the writing more than in the wording, a deep and
terrible hatred of him, a personal hatred. He had received
hundreds of vicious letters from not only Hambledon but
from Philadelphia and Pittsburgh, and even from New York
and Boston, when he had been acquitted, and after his initial
rage he had begun to laugh at them and destroy them and
forget them at once. A sensible man did not give any of his
attention to the sly and anonymous wicked ones of the world,
or he would go mad himself. But this letter caught his attention as none other ever had. Someone in Hambledon had sent
it. Jonathan went back into his offices and called the messenger service.

A youthful male voice answered him. This had been a very
busy Saturday, it informed Jonathan, with many people coming in and leaving packages and messages, and no record was
kept except in cases where a reply was expected. Yes, indeed,
sir, he did recall a letter for Dr. Jonathan Ferrier! But, was it
a young lady, or a gentleman, who had brought it in for delivery and had paid the fee? Jonathan waited and could almost
see the avid ear of Central listening in. Confound the girls.
They were always eavesdropping on his calls these days, and
he must complain about it. The young male voice was obviously ruminating, if one could imagine such a thing. Then
it returned with apology. It could not remember at all. It was
"someone," it was sure, but who that one was escaped it entirely, and it was very sorry. It was also sincere. Jonathan
hung up. He went back to his private files, opened one and
took out his bottle of whiskey, and drank a considerable
amount. He knew again the desire to kill with his own hands.
He stood with the glass in his hand, his elbow leaning on the
files, and his face was again stark and hard and pale under its
darkness, and his mouth was set and harsh. He drank again.
Then he remembered that he had promised to see Priscilla
Witherby almost immediately. He put the bottle away and
locked the files, and once again left the hot and silent offices.

He went to the livery stable for his horse, and spoke absentmindedly to the groom, who watched him canter away.
What was wrong with Doc Ferrier now? He hadn't seen such

a look on his face for a long time, and now it was back. They called him a tough man in Hambledon, and the groom could well believe it for the first time. No, sir, he wouldn't want to cross Dr. Ferrier!

Jonathan tied up his horse before the handsome white brick and stucco house of rich old Jonas Witherby, careful that the animal was in the shade of the great elms. He went up the flagged walk; the stones were colored rose and faint blue and yellow, in a very artistic pattern. But today everything looked malign and hurtful to him, and too sharp in outline and tint and shade. He had often wanted revenge. He wanted it now with a terrible hunger he had never felt before, except for a few times with Mavis. The brilliant white door, with its polished brass knocker, opened for him and he was confronted by Priscilla, who took him at once by the hand and pulled him quickly into the large and pretty hall with its scent of jasmine, a perfume Priscilla favored and which she always wore and with which she always permeated her environment.

"Jon, dear!" she gasped. (Prissy always gasped, as if unbearably surprised, outraged, delighted, overcome, amazed, startled, or aghast. It was considered very intriguing by her admirers.) "Oh, Jon, dear, I wondered if you'd forgotten me! I watched by the windows every second!" She was out of breath. She had a dear little voice like a very young girl's, or a breathless child's. "Do come into the drawing room, where it is so nice and cool! I have your favorite whiskey. Jon, you get handsomer every time I see you, I swear it! And you should never wear anything but riding clothes and boots, and carry a crop!" She burst into tears. "Jon, I can't bear it, not for a single minute more, not for a single minute!"

She threw her arms about his neck, standing on tiptoe to do so, and she kissed him fervently on the lips, and hugged him harder, pressing her face into his neck. He held her by the arms, gently, then put her off. "All right, Prissy, did the old bastard put arsenic in your coffee?"

Prissy was at least thirty-two and had been a whore since she was fourteen, and a very jolly and appreciative and expensive one. She was a little woman, small even in an age which preferred little women. She was a perfect miniature of a female, lovingly formed, a figurine of porcelain, softly but brightly colored, smooth and glowing with porcelain lights. There was a sleek polish about her which transferred itself by magic to her clothes. She was always svelte and clean and perfumed and exquisitely and fashionably dressed. Today she wore a flowing lawn dress with pink dots sprinkled all over it, a pink sash, and a pink ribbon, broad and satiny, tying back her pale shining hair. She even wore pink slippers of an incredibly small size, and narrow and pointed, and her arch showed the glint of a silk stocking. Being a lady of taste, and fastidious, she rarely wore much jewelry except for the great diamond which old Jonas had given her and little pearls in her pretty ears. Her dainty features were childlike and guileless and frank, and she had very large, pale blue eyes as innocent as an infant's, with golden thickets about them. She reminded many adoring men of a lily, and they had spoken of it, and Jonathan, who was very fond of her, had always made a ribald remark. He had often been one of Prissy's patrons before she had married old Jonas and had never discovered anything gross or repellent about her. But, then, as he had frequently said, and with approval, there was no one quite so refined as a whore who knew her own worth and respected herself, and enjoyed her profession. Prissy had not been "forced into selling her pure white body," as the current phrase was, but had chosen her life's work with full deliberation and realism, as she had often confided to Jonathan. Golly, she *liked* men! Was there anything wrong with that? And if gentlemen wanted to give her a little gift, or a small fur, or a pretty piece of lingerie, the dears, whose business was it? Her bank accounts, long before she had incomprehensibly married old Jonas, had caused her to be received with bows and enormous respect in the banks of Hambledon. Prissy was prudent. She was also modest and never let anyone use "rude" language in her presence, or pass a "naughty" remark or tell a pungent story. In addition to all this, she was intelligent.

She owned considerable property in Hambledon, including a lumber business of increasing prosperity, and was known as a very shrewd businesswoman. She was a scandal. The ladies hated her, though since she had married Jonas Witherby, she was often invited to the "best" houses. "For Jonas' sake," the hostesses would apologize. "Dear, darling old Jonas." They were certain that Jonas was Prissy's victim, though gentlemen held exactly the reverse of that opinion and wondered often and loud, and resentfully. Had old Jonas gotten "something" on Prissy? a very few asked each other, including Jonathan. Jonathan was certain he had, though Prissy denied it vigorously. He was very rich, and she had liked him, honestly she had, and she had thought him so good and kind, and after all a girl had to think of her future, too, didn't she? Prissy was never the legendary "prostitute with a heart of gold."

The drawing room was most tastefully furnished—by Prissy. She had removed the huge and sullen furniture it had once possessed, and now it reflected Prissy in its small and gay and colorful chairs and settees and really good paintings on the white walls. She led Jonathan to a chair, and, with fresh tears rolling prettily down her cheeks, she poured him a large drink, hesitated, tossed her head, and prepared one for herself. She sat down near him, a delicious china figure, and stared at him hopelessly.

"Come on, Prissy, what's the trouble?" asked Jonathan, after a pull at his crystal glass. "I have an appointment later in the afternoon."

"You know Jonas," said Prissy, wiping away a tear with the tip of a rosy finger as small as a child's, and as vulnerable in appearance. "Ever since he came home from the hospital — Jon, you never did believe that I tried to poison him, did you?"

"No, dear. But I often hoped you would."

Prissy giggled abruptly. "Well, I've thought of it, but I'm not a fool, Jon. You know who they'd first suspect, and maybe with good reason, him with all that money, too. Not that I'd grieve much now if he'd drop dead. But he'll live to be a thousand, Jon! A thousand! He's just that bad—he'd live to spite me."

"And spite others, too," said Jonathan.

"Well." Prissy sighed. "Jon, I know you won't believe me. But I'm sure now that Jonas was really poisoned. I'm sure he did it to himself. Go on, laugh at me."

Jonathan shook his head slowly. "No, dear. I won't laugh. I believe it myself. Oh, he didn't take enough to kill him, of course, the old devil. But just enough to make him interestingly sick—and make people ask questions. About you."

"But why, Jon, why?" The girl cried again.

"He wants people to remember his 'illness' in the hospital. I hear he talks about it constantly so they won't forget. Then, when he does die, there'll be ugly conjectures. Nothing positive will be proved about you—but they'll talk. Perhaps there'll be litigation over his will. Perhaps he's already arranged that. Perhaps there's something rotten about you in that will; it wouldn't surprise me. Perhaps he's left you nothing, saying that he had always 'suspected' you tried to kill him before and that you were thwarted by fast medical attention. To be truthful, his record on admission does say that he 'showed all symptoms of poison.' But he didn't vomit in the hospital, and so we had no samples, and don't make such a nasty face, Prissy. However, he insisted, the dear innocent loving old man, that he had eaten nothing you hadn't eaten and that it was surely only 'acute indigestion.' He actually cried when I questioned him. I wasn't his admitting physician. I was away when he came in. Perhaps he made sure of that, too, fearing that I might be too sharp for him and too cynical.

"But he did need a fella who'd suspect poison after all, and so I did. He didn't want soothing-syrup doctors who wouldn't make good witnesses. He handled it very cleverly. No overt evidence. I saw him forty-eight hours after he had been admitted to the hospital under emergency. He was suffering the aftermath of poison all right, but what kind was not clear. I think myself it was arsenic."

"I still don't understand, Jon, why he should do that!"

"Prissy dear, like all sanctimonious brotherly-lovers, he hates people. I don't know why. There are still some hellholes in the human psyche that baffle me even now. It could be that the brotherly-lovers are afraid they might be detected in their luxurious hatred and then others wouldn't love them, and they do cherish the regard of others! They know all about themselves, probably, and secretly despise themselves, and their only defense against the horror of their whole being is to see the deceived love-light and admiration for them in the eyes of other people. We all have our methods of self-defense against the world. The brotherly-lover probably more than most, for he is a weakling and can't accept what he is, and is afraid that if found out, the world would punish him —as it ought to do, by God! He's a menace.

"The brotherly-lover is not only cruel, beyond the cruelty of less talented liars, but he loves to see people suffer. He doesn't dare be overt to them and cause them to suspect him of their misery, for they might punish him as he deserves. So he slides around them, like an oily snake, making loving sounds as he inserts fangs—which they don't know are his alone."

Prissy had listened with her fair brows in a knot. She shook her head. "It sounds very strange to me, Jon. I've always been decent to others and always thought they'd be decent to me in return. Until I knew Jonas. Why should—what do you call them?—brotherly-lovers enjoy seeing others suffer?"

"Because they are crazy, my dear, absolutely mad. And they're evil. In some cases evil and craziness are the same thing. Well, you know the history of Jonas' wife, who killed herself, and his wretched sons. They hadn't injured Jonas. But they were handy for his malice. He'd call that 'reforming' them. You'll notice that it is the haters of humanity who are always trying to reform it. They want to feel superior to the general run of mankind. Besides, they're malevolent to the very heart of them. What did Christ call them in one of His less benign moments? 'Hypocrites, liars, sons of the Devil.'

"Well, that's what old Jonas is. And so, he wants to make you suffer. I don't think he has anything against you. In fact, I think he likes you in his perverted way, and is very fond of you. But, you are handy. If he can make you totally miserable, then he'll be contented and beam like a rose.

"I think his little play-acting with the arsenic was to frighten you, to make you fear the whole city and the whole city to suspect you. Some do, you know. You know that.

"He is bruising you mentally. He keeps you simmering with terror. I don't know how he managed to do that with his first wife, but he did it, and so she killed herself to escape him, and his sons escaped him, too, one way or another. Prissy, you won't take my advice, but I'll give it. Pack up and leave at once. Unless, of course, you have the strength of will to pretend to great serenity with him, and if you can make yourself wink at him sometimes and imply that you're on to him and that you're not in the least disturbed."

"Golly, Jon, I've stood more than three years of that old wretch! Don't you think I deserve something after he's dead? If I left him now, I'd get nothing. Though I admit I do get restless sometimes." She gave him a pretty and significant smile through her tears. He patted her hand. "I'm sure you still have—friends," he said. "If you can manage it discreetly."

"Oh, I couldn't. He watches me all the time. If I go shopping, I must give him a detailed account of every damned minute, Jon. And what I bought, and if the clerks were slow. He times me. And Jack drives me, you know, and he gets reports from Jack, too. I know it."

"He isn't concerned with your fidelity, dear. It's just his little way of making you miserable. I agree you deserve something for enduring him for three years—and he'll probably

live forever. You must make up your mind as to whether or
not it is worth it, for you."

"Oh, my God!" exclaimed Prissy, glancing through the
window. "Here he is now, and he's looking at your horse and
he knows it is yours!"

"Let's pretend we didn't know he had returned," said Jonathan. "That'll be his first disappointment—not to find us
romping in your bed, not that he really cares or is capable of
romping, too. Let's smile at him sweetly. Then leave us alone.
Perhaps I can put the fear of God into him, though I've noticed that the brotherly-lovers don't believe in God at all."

Old Jonas Witherby came into the house, elaborately assisted by his coachman, who handled him as though he were
extremely fragile. But Jonas was vigorous and strong, even if
he permitted his servant to pretend that he was not. He came
in beaming and rosy, all silken white hair and holy smiles
and happy eyes. "Jon, my boy!" he said, holding out two soft
warm hands and taking one of Jonathan's and pressing it tenderly. "How delightful to see you! But, is Prissy ill?" He
looked at his wife with enormous concern and affection.

"No, she isn't, and aren't you glad?" said Jonathan. "I was
passing by and I thought I'd drop in and see how you were,
and to find out if you were interested in giving me a check
for the new tuberculosis hospital we're still plotting about."

Jonas cackled happily and shook his head as if Jonathan
had perpetrated a wonderful joke which was greatly appreciated. He sat down with a rich sigh of pleasure. "What a
marvelous day it is!" he said. "So comforting to old bones.
Prissy, love, would you give me a drink? My usual. Just a
little, a very little, whiskey, but plenty of cool soda. I see you
have both been celebrating in my absence."

"Yes, we have," said Jonathan. "After all, how often do
you leave this house?"

Jonas chortled. He pretended, all at once, to be very
watchful of Priscilla. "Sweetheart," he said, in a very wistful
and timid voice, "is that the whiskey you and Jon have been
drinking?"

Priscilla looked up with a start and her lovely face became
strained. She did not see Jonathan shake his head at her in
reproof. "Yes, it is," she answered, and her hand trembled as
she poured the liquor. Jonathan watched idly. He said, "You
know, Jonas, I wouldn't blame Prissy a bit if she dropped arsenic in it—though, how could she get arsenic?"

The old man was still intent on the pouring liquid, pretending to helpless concern. Then he said, "Eh?"

"You heard me. You know that arsenic isn't easy to come by, though it is used for insects in gardens. Not the pure stuff, of course. To get the pure stuff you must buy it from a chemist and sign for it. That's the law. So, how could Prissy get it without throwing suspicion on herself?" Jon sat down and smiled sweetly at the old man. "Perhaps you could tell us, Jonas."

The old man's face was cherubic with infantile bewilderment. "Eh? Another of your jokes, Jon? Really. Very bad taste."

Jonathan leaned back in his chair and studied the high white ceiling. "Of course, one could give a story about rats. Or send someone for it—in another town, with a false name and address. Prissy, have you been tampering with Jack, the gardener-coachman?"

"Jon! What are you saying?" Poor Priscilla stood with the bottle in her little hand and regarded Jonathan with terror.

"Just speculating, Prissy. I'm a great speculator. Besides, I'm curious. Jonas, what do you think?"

"I wouldn't poison even a rat," said Jonas in a sad and trembling voice. He took his glass from Priscilla's hand, gave her a courtly bow of his head in thanks. "I love all that lives."

"Oh, I'm sure you do. You have a reputation for that, Jonas. Prissy, would you give me another drink—from that very bottle, dear—and then leave us for a minute? I'm still concerned about Jonas' health and would like to ask him a few questions."

Priscille was very pale. Jonathan saw how her hands shook. When she caught his eye, he winked at her broadly, and for the first time a little smile appeared on her mouth. Her fingers touched his urgently as he took the glass, and he pressed them deftly in return. Then with a murmur she left the room, walking with tiny grace, her dress flowing behind her. Jonas watched her, allowing Jonathan to see his wide soft smile, his air of indulgent adoration. "Dear girl," sighed Jonas. "How she has brightened my days and brought new life to an old, helpless body."

"I bet," said Jonathan. "But what does Prissy get out of it?"

"My all," said Jonas, in a deep tone. "My all. My worship, my protection and, at the end, my money."

"Good. I love precious marriages like this. So rare. Prissy will still be young when you are gathered to your ancestors, Jonas. That should give you happiness, knowing that she can enjoy your money for a long time—though without the delight of your presence, of course."

A dark and ugly look sparkled in the old man's eyes, and Jonathan saw his spirit, treacherous and lying. Then it hid itself behind benignity again. "Ah, yes," he sighed. "It is really one of the satisfactions of my days to think of that."

"I really love you," said Jonathan. "In a naughty world you are a shining light of virtue, Jonas. A light of peace and goodwill toward men, blameless, tender, trusting, generous. Innocent, above all. Now that we are alone, Jonas, where did you get that arsenic?"

Jonas regarded him with smiling soft hatred. "Now, Jon, please don't joke about such serious things."

"I'm not joking, I assure you. Jonas, stop being so damned sanctimonious. I'm a doctor. Remember? I have only to make a few inquiries here or in other cities in the state, and I'll get the information I need. It will take a little time, and a few descriptions, and a little pressure, but I'll get it. Do you understand?"

Jonas smiled superbly. "Really, Jon. If anyone bought any arsenic, anywhere—"

"It wasn't Prissy. I've already told that about. What's the matter? Do you feel ill?" Jonathan rose with pretended sudden alarm.

Jonas waved him back. He pulled his linen handkerchief from his pocket and wiped a sagging old face, which was no longer pink. "No, no, there's nothing wrong, Jon. Just a touch of the sun, perhaps." His breath was now honestly harsh. "I don't know what you're talking about, Jon. What is all this about arsenic? I wasn't poisoned."

"So you weren't. I know you'll mention that occasionally. We have you down for acute indigestion with a touch of the liver. I made that emphatic on your chart." He remained standing. "Unless, of course, you wish it to be known that you tried to poison yourself—you couldn't stand the wickedness in this old world or something—and so took the arsenic in a moment of noble desperation."

"I've thought of it!" Jonas' voice was all tremulous and full of dolorous music. "I have thought of it!"

"Well, we all think of it occasionally. Only the stupid

never contemplate suicide. But don't think of it again, Jonas old boy. Try to enjoy life."

Jonas was much moved. He looked at Jonathan with gratitude. "Dear boy, what a comfort you are to a poor old soul."

"Indeed I am. I won't mention a word of this conversation, poor old soul, unless it becomes absolutely necessary, which I am sure it will not."

"It will not, Jon, I give you my word. After all, it would not sound very nice if I mentioned that my doctor hinted I had poisoned myself, would it?"

"Oh, by then I'd have proof," said Jonathan, with an airy gesture. "Names, dates, descriptions. You know how people would laugh, don't you?"

Jonas drank slowly and appreciatively from his glass. "Jon," he said, wiping his lips, "I don't think you truly love, do you?"

"Indeed I don't," said Jonathan with affability.

Jonas sighed. "I have devoted my whole life to humanity, nurturing, offering, comforting—"

"Well, you can do that again. Send me five thousand dollars, by check, tomorrow, for that tuberculosis hospital we have been discussing all this time."

Their eyes locked together, Jonathan's amused and hard, the old man's vicious.

"Five thousand dollars," said Jonathan. "Not made out to me, but to the Hambledon Tuberculosis Hospital. Why, we'll have a plaque on the wall for you, dear heart! 'Gift of Jonas Witherby, Founder.' In the most prominent place, naturally. Perhaps with a bas-relief of you, with your fine patrician features, smiling your benevolent smile. Isn't that a lovely thought?"

A tear moistened Jonas' eye as he considered, but the evil light in it did not diminish. He nodded. "Tomorrow, Jon, I give you my word."

"Good. And let there be no more talk of poisoning, even by innuendo, dear heart."

Jonathan saluted amiably and left the room. He met the fearful Prissy in the hall. He whispered, "Don't worry. I've stopped him. I think." He kissed her cheek lightly.

After he was gone Jonas, with a very sprightly walk, went up to his bedroom. He gave a number to Central, speaking in his unctuous and loving voice. A few moments later a voice answered him, and he said, "Kenton? Jonas Witherby here. Yes. When can we have our little talk?"

The still apprehensive Priscilla, not quite reassured by Jonathan, and always nervously suspicious these days, had followed her husband discreetly and when he had closed his bedroom door, she pressed her ear against it and listened.

CHAPTER TWENTY-FOUR

Jonathan rode rapidly out of town on horseback to his nearest farm, which began on the outskirts of the city and which was now being managed by Dr. Thomas Harper. He rarely talked much to his former friend, not out of continuing resentment and hatred and contempt, but because he was fearful that if he showed kindness, Tom would become maudlin and overwhelmed again by his own guilt, and this was something Jonathan found extremely embarrassing, to the point of anger. If a man had been a villain and an ingrate, let him then feel remorse and repentance in his heart, and not infuse them into his ordinary daily communications, particularly when talking with the object of his former malice. It was Jonathan's firm conviction that while repentance was theoretically good, it could also have a repercussion dangerous to the victim: The repentant aggressor, being human, and desiring to relieve himself of his painful state of mind, might look for more reasons to hate his victim and end up being more malignant than before. From both sentimentality and malignance Jonathan wished himself to be delivered.

He hoped to ride about the farm and talk with Thelma Harper and her four engaging children, for he had known Thelma as a nurse at St. Hilda's when he had been a lowly medical student and her husband an intern. He had had no status at St. Hilda's as yet and was snubbed by nurses and indulged by interns, but Thelma had been kind and motherly, though she was but four years older than himself. She had also—and this was more important to Jonathan than anything else—been an excellent nurse in a day when nurses were only drudges and exploited and regarded with more than a small contempt by hospitals in general.

Jonathan took the narrow riding path and rode along the river, not only because it was cooler here but because it was the shortest way to his farm. His horse did not like water and pretended fear of it always, rolling back an eloquent eye at his rider in reproach and apprehension. "Nonsense," said Jonathan. "Even if you are gelded, you still have enough manhood in you, and stop being such a farce." The horse bent his head in piteous resignation and pranced along at a sedate pace. "I suppose," said Jonathan reflectively, "that as most men now seem gelded in spirit if not in actuality, I shouldn't call your state to your mind. It's a universal and melancholy fact. Only the boys roaring out into the territories seem to have any gumption these days, but when they have the West well settled and the cities rise up, then they're gelded themselves, too. A man can't live in the city with testes. What was it Socrates said: 'A hamlet breeds heroes. A city breeds eunuchs.' Vicious ones, too, for eunuchs are always shrill and iniquitous and full of murder. And never mind Charles Lamb and his 'thither side of innocence.'"

Thelma had written him recently that Tom seemed much improved, "and able to take short rides every day." What had the poet, William Blake, said: "Cruelty has a human heart, and jealousy a human face." It took a poet to be pithy and full of verity, and only the ignorant called them decadent or ladylike or other demeaning terms. They were a virile breed. Jonathan recited some of his favorite poems to himself and looked at the river. The island was partly behind him now. A little mist was rising from the water into the heated air, and the island seemed adrift, a fairy place, and Jonathan thought of Jenny and Robert Morgan, and chuckled but not very agreeably. He would have to corner the elusive Jenny very soon and no more delicate approaches. Jonathan remembered what Ibsen had said: "One should never put on one's best trousers to go out to battle for freedom and truth." Nor should he put on his best trousers to fight for love, either.

The river had a dreamlike quality today, its current hardly visible, hardly running, its surface like pale blue silk and as smooth. The ferries chugging from side to side were busy with holidayers, and there were boats out with sails, and rowboats moving placidly with picnickers looking for a likely spot along the shore, and the sun was a yellow haze and the mountains on the other side of the river were gauzy shapes of green. It was what countrymen called "a pretty day." Humid and hot, but languorous and peaceful, and voices called and laughed from the river and from the gardens that bordered the narrow road. But now the houses and the gardens were becoming farther and farther apart, and the country was approaching, smelling of dust and hay, and the peculiar excitation of the lovely and carnal earth.

Here and there along uncultivated stretches of land little humpy and jagged roads tumbled out to join the River Road, and as Jonathan approached one on his left a buggy came smartly hurtling toward him, and his horse, predictably, reared in pretended fright. For an instant he stood against the sun with Jonathan standing in the stirrups and raised from the saddle, then he dropped his legs at a quick touch of the crop. The buggy also came to an abrupt stop, and there was young Father McNulty's face peering out from under the dusty top.

"Jon!" exclaimed the priest, and against all knowledge of horses he flung down the reins of his own and jumped from the buggy. "I've been calling you! What a Godsend you are to appear like this!"

"For God's sake," said Jonathan, and alighted, and went to the buggy and caught and fastened the reins. "Your horse could bolt, you damned city man! Good thing she's a tame mare and I'm not riding a stallion." He stood in the hot yellow dust of the road and regarded Father McNulty with no pleasure at all.

But Father McNulty was too fervid with gratitude to care. He grasped Jonathan's arm and pointed up the little road. "You know the McHenrys."

"No, I don't, and moreover I don't want to know them."

"Young manager of the Hambledon Lumber Mills. From Michigan."

"Good. Hope Prissy Witherby pays him a good salary. She was the town doxy, you know, temporarily reformed. Prettiest legs between here and New York, and as for her other qualities, what is it the advertisements say? 'One trial will convince you.' "

"Jon." The priest smiled. "Don't try to shock me." He stopped smiling. "It's young Mrs. McHenry I've been visiting.

Peter called me. I'm afraid the girl is going mad. I could do nothing with her at all. Matilda is the loveliest girl."

"What's wrong with the rites of exorcism? Out of business in this scientific twentieth century?" He moved toward his horse, and the priest grasped him again.

"Jon, I prayed to find you. I've been calling you. This is a terrible emergency. I want you—"

"I'm no alienist," said Jonathan. "I've had no training in mental illness. Send her off to Philadelphia. I know just the man."

"You did wonders with young Campion."

"Oh? Matilda tried to commit suicide? Well, why did you interfere—again?"

"Please, Jon. No, she didn't try to kill herself, but she is distracted enough to think of it. I am afraid she is losing her mind, and Peter is desperate. They have such a delightful little girl, too, Elinor. It's a tragedy."

"I told you I'm no alienist, for God's sake, and besides, I don't much believe in them. No, I'm on my way to my farm, and if you'll kindly let go of my sleeve, I'll be obliged."

"You are the only one who can help her," said the priest.

Jonathan stared at him incredulously. "You must be out of your mind yourself!"

"I've always had a certain feeling about you, Jon, and you are so compassionate."

Jonathan burst out laughing and shook his head and went to his horse.

"Priests have intuitions," said Father McNulty. "That's why I know about you."

Jonathan put his foot into a stirrup and looked back with annoyance. "I've heard about those intuitions. They're invariably wrong. Old Father McGuire, whom you succeeded, was all full of the damnedest intuitions about my father, and not one of them had any reality. We must have a chat about that soon. Besides, if you need a doctor, there's my replacement, Bob Morgan, who's so full of loving kindness that it makes me want to puke sometimes. Call him for Matilda on Monday. He's out riding with my lady at the present time. I hope they aren't indulging in the pleasantest pastime of all, the only one that matters."

"I prayed to find you," said the priest in a voice of such urgent humility that Jonathan paused. "And then there you were. It was God's answer to my prayer. You can't overlook that, Jon."

"God and I parted company when I was seventeen," said Jonathan, "and one of these days I'll tell you about that, too, and make an agnostic of you." He mounted his horse. Father McNulty caught one of the reins, and the horse stepped back, almost on him, and Jonathan, with an oath, had to apply the crop again.

"Christ!" Jonathan exclaimed. "Don't you know anything about horses at all? You are a menace. You shouldn't be driving that buggy for a minute."

"I know about people," said the priest with pale resolution. "I know about you."

"No."

"Yes."

Jonathan looked down at him with amused wonder. "You're a persistent devil, aren't you? What's the matter with their own physician?"

"They've been here only two months. They came for Matilda's health. Please, Jon. I can't wait until Monday for Matilda, and besides I doubt young Dr. Morgan could help that poor girl. You need only to talk to her for a few minutes. Please."

"They're well off, I suppose?"

"Moderately so. What—"

"And servants?"

"A housekeeper, and a second maid, and a gardener. What—"

"I have the perfect cure for the lady," said Jonathan, "and it will cost her husband—unfortunate devil—nothing. Let him discharge the servants and make the young lady roll up her sleeves and pin up her skirts and get to scrubbing, cleaning and cooking and washing and ironing, and tending the garden. Then her megrims will be gone—presto—overnight. Nothing like hard grim work to cure a sick mind."

The priest said, "Not always, Jon. And there's that darling little girl, Elinor. Think what this is doing to the child—and she is only nine years old." He smiled up at Jonathan pleadingly, but also with artfulness. "She reminds me of little Martha Best."

"That's a lie, and I hope you confess it," said Jonathan. He sighed. He looked at his watch. "All right, considering that I'd have to ride you down if I don't. I'll look at the delicate, pampered lady for exactly five minutes and that's all."

With more expertness than Jonathan would have believed, the priest turned his buggy around on the narrow side road and rode off in a spume of yellow dust and Jonathan followed. The road climbed, and then at the top where it leveled there was an old farmhouse, restored, mellow and warm in its nest of trees and sun, with ancient lawns about it and a white picket fence and a pretty bed of flowers near the door. Cicadas shrilled in the burning heat, but otherwise there was no sound and no sight of any human being. The place seemed deserted. As the leaves moved, the sun struck on small latticed windows and on dark old wood, and laced the stone path with dancing shadows. Jonathan remembered that this was "the old Barrow Place," once a farm, and sold long ago.

"Tie up your horse to that tree," said Jonathan. "It's a good thing she's an intelligent elderly mare, or you'd not have a horse by now. She's patient with fools, I can see." His voice echoed from the lonely land. The priest opened the broad and weathered door and they stepped into a cool and dusky hall with a bare and polished floor and a few good prints on the paneled walls and one Spanish table, dark and impressive with a mirror over it. There was a scent in the air of potpourri and wax. Jonathan looked about him with approval. There was nothing vulgar or modern here, and everything expressed dignity and breeding and the self-restraint of the truly mannered person. His glance into rooms off the hall showed him the same calm and solid elegance and paucity of elaborate decoration, and the distinction of the old furniture, a mixture of early Victorian and Spanish. Whoever the McHenrys were, they were not cheap in any meaning of the word.

At the end of the hall was a noble staircase of very dark wood, as polished and bare as the floors, and now there were hurrying footsteps coming down them and a young man appeared, very handsome, very Spanish in appearance—the Iberian complexion and features but the rugged tall breadth of the Irish—and dressed only in trousers and a white shirt without a collar. His thick black hair was rumpled and when he saw the two intruders he hastily tried to smooth it down with fine hands. Jonathan approved of him at once and shook hands with sincere appreciation when he was introduced to Peter McHenry. "God answered my prayer, you see, Peter," said the priest. Jonathan winked at Peter, but Peter nodded his head with total acceptance.

"Where is Matilda?" asked Father McNulty.

"I persuaded her to lie down. Elinor is resting, too." The young man turned to Jonathan. "We came from Detroit because of Matilda's health, you see, to a quieter place near the mountains, and not so bad a winter. So kind of you to come, Doctor. Matilda hasn't been very well since Elinor was two years old—that's seven years ago. We had a doctor in Detroit, but he was baffled."

"I probably will be, too," said Jonathan. "You have some very good doctors in Detroit. What seems to be wrong with your wife?"

The young man was so anxious and disturbed that he did not invite his guests into one of the rooms off the long hall. He stared at Jonathan. "The doctors can't find out. That's what's so frustrating. It isn't physical, they say, yet she has high blood pressure, at her age! She's only twenty-eight, for God's sake! She's a very equable person, Matilda, and well-controlled, and quiet, and amusing when she wants to be. She can't sleep, and she seems disturbed most of the time."

"Hysterical, too, I suppose."

"Hysterical? Matilda?" Peter McHenry gave a short laugh. "She never was! Never. Not even when she's most depressed."

"Depressed, eh? And what is her chief complaint?"

Peter hesitated. "I don't think she has any. Matilda never complains about anything. She is homesick, I know, and misses her family—wonderful people, better than mine, I'm just a Mick—but she never mentions it. She is used to the city but loves it here in the country. But sometimes she looks at me, sort of distracted, you know. Empty. Frightened. As if there was something she couldn't deal with and didn't rightly know what it was, anyway."

Probably bored, thought Jonathan. He felt sorry for Peter McHenry and felt dislike for his wife. Mick or not, he was possibly too good for her. He looked up to meet Peter's black and shining eyes, so like his own, with the whites a brilliant gleam in the duskiness of the hall. A good and intelligent man, and his wife? A pampered, whining fool. "I'd like to see Mrs. McHenry," he said. "Though I must tell you I am no alienist—never had any patience with their magical abracadabra anyway, and their Viennese incantations, and their high priest, Freud. Certainly there is such a thing as—well—let us call it mental disturbances for the moment—but I've discovered that almost invariably they have a physical basis. To put it more crudely, a man, though of previous sound reputation, can go berserk if aroused, and almost anyone can kill under enough provocation. You see, I'm a pragmatist."

Peter had listened seriously. "And now," said Jonathan, looking at his watch ruefully, "let's go to Mrs. McHenry. Incidentally, I'd like to see her alone after you've introduced me to her."

They climbed the broad staircase in silence, came upon a long hall with six doors leading from it. Peter opened one and said with the false brightness of acute anxiety, "Darling, Father McNulty has brought his friend, Dr. Ferrier, to see you."

The blinds had been pulled against the sun, and the big square room was partly dark, and Jonathan saw here again the elegant mixture of Victorian and Spanish furniture. A thin young woman in a flowing white dress was lying on a chaise longue, and she lifted her head quickly from a posture of utter exhaustion. Peter raised a shade and the green light outside struck her face, and Jonathan saw that Matilda McHenry vividly resembled his own mother in her youth. There were the same clear hazel eyes and fine features and the cloud of soft dark hair and the sensitive mouth and the look of pure candor, and the same restraint in dress. She held out her thin hand to Jonathan, and when she smiled, it was his mother's smile. charming and a little reserved.

"These two shouldn't have bothered you, Doctor," she said, and smiled lovingly at her husband and the priest. "There's really nothing wrong with me except tiredness, and why I should be tired I don't know. It's gone on for years."

"I don't have my bag with me," said Jonathan, "so there can't be much of a physical examination." He glanced at the other two men. "I'd like to be alone with Mrs. McHenry, please." When they had gone, he drew a chair close to the young woman and looked at her attentively. Too pale. The clear dark skin had no color at all, nor her lips. Anemic? He bent forward and gently turned down her eyes to examine the mucous membranes. No, not anemia. He felt her pulse. It was entirely too fast and erratic, as if she had been running for a considerable time. He repeated, "I don't have my stethoscope, so I'll have to use the old method of listening with my ear." She nodded, and he pressed his ear and cheek against her soft small breast and listened closely. The heart sounds were the sounds of a heart under stress, or hysteria.

He asked the young woman some quick questions. She had little appetite. She could sleep very little, and only that fitfully. She tired at everything. "I was never weary before, until Elinor was about two, Doctor. And then—well, I began not to be able to manage things." She tried to laugh. "Things just seemed to slip through my hands, and those acts you do mechanically—I had to guide them consciously, the way you do when something is new to you and you aren't certain how to do it. It's very hard to explain. I was always so competent when I was a girl. Tennis. Croquet. Golf. Swimming. Quite the tomboy, my father used to say. I was never sick. And here I am now, a burden to Peter and Elinor, and I keep bursting out crying at nothing, and don't know why I am crying."

She had a wonderful low voice, soft and clear, but now it trembled even while she tried to smile in self-deprecation. Beset, though Jonathan. Now, what in hell is besetting her?

He said, "Does anything about your husband worry you?"

"Only that I've become a burden to him." Tears came to her eyes and she was ashamed of her emotion and averted her head.

"And your little girl?"

She turned her head back quickly to him and her face suddenly glowed. "Oh, Elinor! She's a darling, though a little too sensitive. I can understand that; I'm that way, too. She's very reserved, even more than I was as a child. But so self-sufficient, and so grown-up! I worried about there not being any children here, but Elinor doesn't mind at all. She goes to a little private school just inside of Hambledon—the St. Agatha School. Do you know it, Doctor?"

"Yes. I know it well." I ought to, he thought. I gave two thousand dollars when it was established. "A very fine school. Elinor has friends there, I suppose?"

"Well, no. I don't think so. She never mentions them. Things that are important to other children aren't of importance to Elinor. She attends dancing school and neither likes nor dislikes it. But she prefers to play by herself. A little old lady, I often tell Peter."

Jonathan did not speak. He continued to look at her attentively.

"When Elinor was about two, I thought to myself: Oh, here's a very strange little miss, indeed! She began to resent the usual kisses and hugs mothers give their children. She even wriggled away from Peter, though I think she prefers him. He tries to play with her, too, and sometimes she obliges him." Matilda laughed feebly. "But only to oblige him! And then she goes off by herself."

A thought came to Jonathan, a most unpleasant thought. "And Elinor's teachers?"

The mother hesitated. "Well, they all say Elinor is very advanced for her age. An excellent scholar. But the past year or so—she seems to have slipped back a little. Much less interest in books. The teachers don't know about the slipping, for we've been here just two months. But I've observed it myself, though Peter hasn't. Perhaps it is just my imagination." Her young face was tight with suddenly desperate strain.

"Does the child seem contented?"

"Yes. At least, she is healthy, though a little thin, and has never been ill, not even the children's diseases. Contented? I never thought of it before, but I don't think so!" She sat up suddenly and stared at Jonathan with increasing bafflement and misery. "It's not just what she does and says. She seems —dissatisfied. She sits for hours, it seems, sometimes, and just doesn't move a finger."

"Does she seem lonely?"

"Oh, never. I told you: So self-sufficient, even when she was just a baby."

The unpleasant thought was growing in Jonathan's mind. He said, "And she never speaks of her schoolmates or teachers?"

"Well, sometimes." A little uneasiness came to the lovely voice. "It's not that she whines or complains. Elinor isn't a talker, Doctor. But I've thought, once or twice, that she was unjust to—others. She accuses—no, accuses is too definite and harsh a word—she speaks of the other children and her teachers as if they didn't like her, and she gives me the impression that Sister Mary Frances, her mathematics teacher, is persecuting her. Of course, that's absurd. Children do get strange ideas. Strange, strange," repeated Matilda to herself, hardly audible. "Always such a strange child. Just a week ago she told me that 'Daddy was watching her and thinking unkind things about her.' Why, Peter adores the child and indulges her all the time!"

"And your husband doesn't think the girl is strange, too?"

"No, not at all." Her voice became emphatic. "I mentioned it once, but Peter said she's just like his grandmother, quiet, retiring, thoughtful. I think he even admires it."

"And you don't?"

Mrs. McHenry looked at him with wide tight eyes for a moment, as if the question had alarmed her. Then she shook her head. "I suppose I don't understand Elinor. I have the feeling, and that is silly, that she doesn't love us at all. Isn't that ridiculous?"

Jonathan reached for the thin wrist. The pulse was bounding furiously, and the pretty breast was rising and falling rapidly. She looked at him with desperate pleading, and he looked away in pity. He laid the hand down gently and said, "If you don't mind, I'd like to see your little girl, Mrs. McHenry."

She brightened again. "Oh, would you? How kind! So few people like children, do they, though everyone is now affirming madly, over and over, that they 'love children.' They don't really. It's just a modern pose and very tiresome. But you'll love Elinor, Doctor. Most adults do."

"Probably because she doesn't annoy them with loud ways or loud chatterings," said Jonathan, smiling.

"Elinor was never like that. We didn't use any strictness with her. It wasn't necessary. She's most obedient." She paused. "And I—is there something seriously wrong with me, Doctor?"

"No, I don't think so." Jonathan stood up and stared at the glittering green leaves at the window. "I think it is just your emotions. Very common. So far as I can see, you're a perfectly healthy young woman, but that was just a cursory examination. Suppose we leave it at that for a little while. In the meantime I'll see your daughter. No, just rest there."

"How really kind of you, Doctor. Sometimes I think Elinor is worried about me. She'd never say so. She should have had her nap by this time. She naps on Saturday afternoons because we take her into town later for a little recreation." She smiled at him winningly. "Please tell Elinor that Mother is perfectly well, won't you?"

Jonathan went out into the hall, where the priest and Peter McHenry were waiting for him. He closed the door and said quietly, "I couldn't give your wife a thorough examination, Mr. McHenry, for obvious reasons. But there seems no physical complaint at all, either on what examination I did and her own words. She's under stress of some kind, and I don't think she even knows that. But, what are the words that the alienists are using so lavishly these days? Yes. 'Feelings of inadequacy. And guilt.' No, they don't mean much to me, either."

Peter's quick Irish temper came boiling to the surface at once. "Matilda? Inadequate? Guilty? Guilty! Of what is she guilty, for God's sake?"

Jonathan held up a calming palm. "You misunderstood.

Those are psychiatric words, and pretty nonsensical, in my opinion. They don't really explain. But it is quite true that very often people take on a job too big for them, and they aren't up to some of the demands of their circumstances and environment or work, or they feel inferior to a brother or a sister, or to anyone for that matter, and so they are 'inadequate.' I think that's the general explanation. The funny thing is that in nine cases out of ten they really are inadequate, and nothing else, and no mystery about it. They just need advice to lower their sights and think more highly of themselves, that's all, or get an easier job, or spruce up, or buy a hat more often and sometimes—it is as simple as that—win a few dollars at a horse race. We all feel inadequate very often. It's only when it gets chronic that it is disturbing to one's emotions and can get out of hand and make you pretty damned miserable."

Peter was listening with bewilderment. "But that doesn't describe Matilda."

"No. Well. Sometimes there's a subtler feeling of inadequacy, which the sufferer doesn't recognize at all. As for the guilt feelings I mentioned, darling favorites of the alienists: Don't we all feel guilty at times? Sometimes we have damned good reason to feel that way! We can overcome it by doing recompense one way or another—or we can hate the person we injured more than ever and persuade ourselves that the reason we ruined him or treated him unjustly was that he really deserved it, after all. There's many a way of washing your hands, including the one Pilate used.

"But there's a subtler kind of guilt which sensitive and intelligent and gentle people often suffer, without knowing they are suffering it. They do their very best, with love and kindness and fervor—and it isn't successful with a person or a situation. So, being conscientious people, they feel it is their fault and it devastates them. Now, what's the matter?"

For Peter's face had darkened with anger. "I don't understand a word of this gibberish, sir! I appreciate everything Matilda does, even when she gives me a smile or touches me! She is the whole world to me, far more than Elinor is, or anything else. She hasn't any reason to feel I don't love her and appreciate her! What gave you that damned idea?"

"Why, nothing at all." Jonathan smiled easily. "I was merely being didactic, like the alienist boys. Well, there's nothing really physically wrong with your wife. But she is under stress. I'd like to find out what it is. I'd like to talk to

your child. Children are far more perceptive than adults,"
said Jonathan, still operating under his pet delusion.

"Very well," said Peter, inflamed and belligerent. He
marched down the hall and knocked at the door and called
his daughter. The door opened at once to show a thin but
almost beautiful little girl with her parents' thick dark hair,
her father's Spanish face and features, her mother's air of elegance, and her meticulous dress. "Yes, Daddy?" she said.

Her frock was of lace and lawn, covering her slender knees
and flaring out, and her hair was tied with a huge blue ribbon
and she wore blue socks and little white shoes. Jonathan
thought, A little love—and tried to suppress his ominous conjecture. He went to the door of the child's bedroom and she
looked up at him with her large moist eyes in their masses of
long dark lashes, and at once he was chilled. He had seen
that look before, that "strange," eerie look, in hospitals but
never before in a child. He felt cold even in the warmth of
the hall, and he held out his hand.

"I'm Dr. Ferrier, Elinor," he said, "and I've just seen your
mother, who isn't well, and she told me about you, and I said
I'd like to meet you. I hope you are liking to meet me, too."
He felt sick, and his love for children made him even sicker.

She curtsied and said with the utmost gravity, "Poor
Mummy. She is sick, isn't she? I knew it all the time. That's
why she's so cross and sometimes mean and says terrible
things to me."

"Elinor!" Peter was stunned. "You know that isn't true!"

She gave him a sly and sliding look and said, "Oh, but,
Daddy, not when you're here."

Peter turned to Jonathan in agitation. "The child imagines
it!"

Yes, thought Jonathan, I know that, my friend. He said,
"I'd still like to talk alone with Elinor, please."

"Not if she's going to—to lie like that!" Peter was now furious. "Elinor, you never lied to anyone before. What's wrong
with you today?"

"It's very hot, isn't it?" said the child in her dainty voice,
and touched her forehead.

"You know Mummy never even slapped you in her life,"
went on Peter.

"I think I'd like some lemonade, Daddy."

"Elinor! Answer me! Did Mummy ever once spank you or
scold you?"

"I think I'll go downstairs," said Elinor.

"Aren't you ashamed?" shouted Peter.

"Should I change my dress before we go to town, Daddy, or will this do?"

Peter was about to explode, but Jonathan took him by the arm and led him down the hall, seething. "Now, wait," said Jonathan. "Have you ever noticed the child talking like that before—not seeming to answer direct questions no matter how often you ask them?"

The seething subsided. Peter's flashing eyes narrowed, and he breathed heavily. He tried to control himself. Then he said, "Yes, I did. Several times. She's been getting worse lately. But kids are like that. I used to try to get out of punishment or scolding, myself, by avoiding a direct answer. And Elinor—"

"Listen to me," said Jonathan. "And think before you answer. Does Elinor only evade and avoid when she is afraid she's done something wrong and might be punished?"

"But, we never punish her! She hasn't any fear of us, for God's sake! Why should she?" But Jonathan waited and Peter was forced to think. Then he said with reluctance, "Yes, she's gotten that maddening habit recently. I tried to get her out of it, but she only makes an equally senseless remark, avoiding the subject. I think she is really a little tease—most children are."

But not this one, thought Jonathan. He glanced down the hall to see Father McNulty talking affectionately to Elinor. Looking at Father McNulty, Jonathan actively hated him. What a hell of a situation that busybody had dragged him into, on a fine summer day!

"All right," said Peter with unfriendly sullenness, "you can talk to Elinor alone."

Jonathan saw a way out. "Now, listen, my friend. I didn't want to come here to your house. I was dragooned here, by Mrs. O'Grady down there, the town helper. He practically kidnaped me. Say the word and I'll go off quietly, and you can call another doctor. I'd prefer that, anyway."

Peter was astute. He looked at Jonathan acutely. "Why?" he asked.

"I'd rather someone else examined your daughter, someone more capable than I."

"My daughter? But it was my wife you came to see! It is my wife who is ill!"

"No," said Jonathan. "It is your child, I'm sorry to say. You need a more competent man. Your wife is suffering from deadly anxiety and inadequacy, most of which she isn't conscious of, but it's deep in her mind and is torturing her. She knows something is wrong, but what it is she doesn't know. I'm not the kind of doctor you need at all—for your child. So, shall we say good-bye?"

"You haven't even examined Elinor, but you can make a snap judgment like that!" The poor father was beside himself. He clenched his fist and bent toward Jonathan.

"Do you want me to talk to her a little—alone?"

"All right, all right!" shouted Peter, waving a big muscular arm at his distant child. "And you'll come out with a smile on the other side of your face!"

"I hope so," said Jonathan. He went back to the girl's room and took her hand and said to her with the special voice he used for children, "Elinor, will you spare me a few minutes of your time, dear?"

"I'm very thirsty," she said.

"Yes, I know. It will take only a minute or two." He led her into her pretty bedroom and closed the door behind him. The child went at once to a buffet and sat down with her hands neatly folded in her lap and her slender ankles crossed. She looked at Jonathan but without normal curiosity, and he stood and looked down at her blank face and eerie eyes. He stood for several minutes and the eyes did not blink nor did the quiet static expression change on the small face.

"Who hurts you and talks cruelly about you, Elinor?" he asked.

The expression remained the same, and the awful eyes, but the child had heard something that had put her in touch with her own fearful reality. "Everybody," she said. "I don't like to go to school because the Sisters and the other children whisper about me, and point at me, and talk about me. Sometimes I want to hit them." For the first time the eyes did move and blink, and there was a sudden peculiar and lusting glare in them.

"And it makes you afraid?"

"No. I'm not afraid, Doctor. Sometimes I don't think I'm really there—"

"Like a dream?"

"Or everybody's dead."

"Does that make you feel bad?"

"Do you have any little girls, Doctor? Like me?"

"Elinor, I'm asking you about school and your friends."

"I'd like to go back to Detroit and see Grandma."

Jonathan saw that he could not break through that wall of glass, and he had suspected it. He tried again, however. "What do you like to play?" he asked.

Again, she touched her reality. Her Spanish eyes glowed at once. "They don't know I'm a princess!" she said. "A real princess. I'm adopted. They stole me from my parents, and I hate them, I hate them, I hate them!" She struck the buffet on which she sat with a passion direful in one so young.

Jonathan knew that children liked to make up fancies to amuse them, but this child was not fancifying. She believed what she said. He bent down and kissed that small and dreadfully distorted face and patted the thin shoulder. "Just stay here quietly, dear," he said. But she had lapsed again into her eerie staring and did not see him go.

He rejoined the two men. Peter looked at him with hatred and umbrage, but Father McNulty was alarmed by Jonathan's expression and took his arm. "Let's go downstairs and sit down," said Jonathan, and left them and went down the stairs and they followed. He found what looked like a sitting room and stood there, and again hated the fact that he was a doctor. How do you tell a loving father that his adored only child is probably hopelessly psychotic?

The others came in, and Father McNulty sat down, but Peter stood in the middle of the room, blackly derisive. "What did you find wrong with Elinor, Doctor? I heard, in town, even before I knew you, that you have a way of finding mysterious things wrong with people, and you tell them so, and they die of fright. Did you tell Elinor something like that? If you did," and he knotted his big fists.

"Shut up," said Jonathan. "I will tell you brutally and frankly. Your wife isn't sick. But her heart is under unbearable stress, and it will probably give way in a year or so, and she will die or be an invalid the rest of her short life. The stress comes from your child. She told me that even when Elinor was only two, she felt the child was 'strange.' Did she never tell you that, too?"

Peter had turned a ghastly yellowish color. "Matilda? Something wrong with Matilda's heart?"

"Didn't you hear me at all?"

The man breathed noisily and he blinked. He finally said, "Yes, I heard you. Yes, Matilda told me that Elinor was 'strange,' even when she was a baby. I laughed at her. The kid is bright beyond her years, but she has a lot of reserve and maturity and imagination—"

"Such as telling you wild stories of who she really is, or something?"

Peter's face relaxed in a fond smile. "Well, you know kids. I told my own parents I was Davy Crockett one time, and was going West."

"But you didn't really believe it?"

"Of course not. But it was an exciting story."

"The trouble is," said Jonathan, "that your child really believes her stories. And there is the difference between—"

Peter seemed to swell with both horror and rage. "Are you trying to tell me that my little girl is—is—crazy?"

Father McNulty stood up and went to stand beside Peter and he gazed with dread and grief at Jonathan.

"The term," said Jonathan, "is dementia praecox, paranoid type. They've coined a new word for it out in Vienna. Schizophrenia. Split personality."

Peter was numb with his increasing rage and shock, and his eyes bulged as he looked at Jonathan.

"Your wife will die," said Jonathan, "unless she is relieved of this burden, though she doesn't know it is a burden, and unconsciously blames herself for not being able to reach her child with normal love and attention. That is the guilt feelings we have been talking about. Whenever I see a man or a woman with no physical complaints but under such terrible stress—normal nice people, good people—then I stop looking at them. I look for the actual person who is creating that disturbance, and unlike Freud, I don't blame every damned thing on a mother or on an 'afflicted childhood.'

"You can't reach a person suffering from schizophrenia in the regular way. In fact, a normal person can't reach him at all. But your wife is trying, God, how she is trying! And it's no use at all. The child needs specialized attention. I know a private sanitarium in Philadelphia—"

"Why, you're insane," Peter whispered, with horror now of Jonathan himself. "You're out of your mind. A child! Psychotic!"

"Your child is already deteriorating mentally," said Jonathan with a detached cold air. "Her mother mentioned it. Do you want her to have no chance at all of a cure? A very small chance but still a chance?"

"You're out of your mind," said Peter, still in that whisper. Then he shouted madly, "Get out of my house at once!"

Jonathan stood up. He put on his riding gloves. He said, "I told you I am no alienist. I may be wrong entirely, though

I'm afraid I'm not. But I've seen a number of these cases, in mental hospitals, in sanitariums, and I could recognize it, though other forms of—insanity—would escape me entirely."

He looked with bitterness at Father McNulty. "You'd better stay a while and talk to these parents—if you can. And the next time you think God has answered your prayers, kindly ask Him to suggest somebody else. Is that clear?"

"Jonathan," said the priest.

But Jonathan turned and left the house, and he was feeling very sick and shaken, and wild with anger against the priest and against his own foolishness in being decoyed by him. He got on his horse and looked for the last time on the stricken house. Yes, it was stricken. A ghastly darkness lived there, and it was seeping into the spirits of two normal good people, and they would not believe it existed. Well, it was a damned awful thing to accept. But it had to be accepted. If not, tragedy and disaster would result, and they'd find it out soon enough, God knew.

Houses, he reflected, as he rode away, are mysterious sounding boards and reflectors. If evil lived in them, it revealed itself in the very postures of furniture, in the very drape of curtains, in the very air of the rooms, but if good lived there the rooms appeared lighted, the furniture inviting, the draperies beautiful and bright, no matter how humble it all was in reality. The house had been "good" to him until he had stepped into Elinor's room. It was the child's presence which had given the house its look of isolation from the beginning.

He could not relieve himself of his feeling of despondency and dread. He had always harbored a whimsical thought which was partly acknowledged superstition and partly fancy: That the mad are in some manner evil, no matter their pathos. It was stupid, he acknowledged, himself, but he had seen madness and evil hand in hand many times, and rarely one without the other. Exorcism, he thought, was perhaps a badly misunderstood thing, and he laughed aloud at himself. But perhaps the alienists were really exorcisers themselves, even if they did not consciously know it!

CHAPTER TWENTY-FIVE

Robert Morgan and Jenny Heger were only a quarter of a mile behind Jonathan. Robert had met the girl at the little dock on the mainland side, though he had wanted to go to the island and row her to the shore. However, when he arrived in his smart new buggy, he found her waiting for him, diffidently smiling and silent. He knew nothing of women's clothing, but somehow he immediately guessed that her apparel was new, and he was delighted that she had gone to this trouble for him and cared enough to do so. She wore a frail white shirtwaist all tinily tucked from chin to waist, with frills here and there of white lace, and her skirt was of expensive white silk with a black patent-leather belt and a glittering buckle. She wore white stockings and slippers, and her ankles were occasionally visible as the wide skirt flared with her movements. Her head was covered with a new hat of Leghorn, a very pale gold, and heaped with snowy roses of silk, and there were actually white gloves on her hands.

Her beautiful face was sunburned, a disgusting defect in ladies, but she carried no parasol as a "proper" young lady would have done. The extra color in her cheeks and on her lips made her appear more vivid than usual. She was "rosy" or "dewy," as his mother called sweating—a euphemism that made Robert laugh—and her upper lip was beaded artlessly with water, and her forehead, too. She smelled of lavender soap and sachet. When she strode to Robert's buggy, still not speaking, she walked like an elegant young man, sure and free, not mincing as other girls minced, setting her feet down firmly yet not hard. She climbed in before he could help her. He thought that she wished to avoid his touch but saw at once that she was acting in full simplicity. He climbed in after her, picked up the reins, then smiled down into the profound and shining blue of her eyes and noticed again the total candor of her heroic face and the dimple in the white chin.

"I brought a really nice lunch," said Robert. "The hotel put it up for me. We aren't quite settled yet, my mother and I, in our new house, so we're still at the hotel. We expect to move into our house on Monday. Well, it's a nice lunch, I think. Cold chicken and salad and buttered new bread and strawberry shortcake and cheese, and a good bottle of white wine, with goblets. I hope you enjoy it."

"Yes," said Jenny. She had naturally accepted the fact of the lunch, unaware that ladies usually prepare the picnic collations. It was the first time she had spoken, but at least she was smiling faintly and shyly at him, and studying him with the frankness of an honest child. Yet, for the first time, he wondered uneasily why she had really accepted his invitation. It was not quite in character for Jenny Heger, the young and frightened recluse about whom such appalling stories were told in the town.

They drove off along the River Road. "A wonderful day," said Robert. "I'm so glad you consented to go with me, Miss Jenny."

She was silent. She was looking at the river as if she were all alone, and at the island. Robert drew the thin buggy cover over her clothing to protect her from the dust and she was not even aware of it.

"I found an admirable spot when I was visiting patients the other day," Robert went on. "Very beautiful, very secluded. Very cool, even in this weather. With a view of the river, too."

"That's nice," said Jenny in her strong clear voice, and then she looked at him with that lovely but uncertain smile. "It was good of you to invite me, Doctor."

He hesitated. His kind eyes smiled down at her. His red-gold mustache was very bright in the sun. "It was my pleasure, Miss Jenny. But I hope it isn't exclusively my pleasure."

She was unaccustomed to gallantries, he saw at once, for she pondered his hint with amusing seriousness. Then she said, "I like it, too. The only picnics I've ever gone to were those given by Aunt Marjorie. Mrs. Ferrier, you know."

"A charming lady," said Robert.

"Yes," said Jenny.

All at once the conversation died, to Robert's disappointment. But it was enough for him that Jenny was beside him, her elbow sometimes touching his sleeve as the buggy rolled over uneven places in the road. She exhaled freshness and youth and innocence. Then Robert knew that he had loved this girl from the very beginning, and he was deeply moved. Because of the dangerous and sudden intensity of his emotions he looked for easiness. He wondered what she liked, this mysterious girl, and what amused her. He had heard she had had a good schooling, and then when she was fifteen, her mother had hired a tutor for her for two years to complete that schooling. (There were tales about that also, in Hambledon.) Yet, she had gone nowhere. She had seen nothing of the world. The only point of reference between him, Robert Morgan, and Jenny Heger, was Jonathan Ferrier. But he did not wish to talk about Jonathan, above everything else.

It was Jenny who indirectly approached the subject. He saw that it was awkward, even painful, for her to initiate a subject, so he was not surprised when she stammered, "Do you like Hambledon, Doctor?"

"Yes. Very much. I could have remained in Philadelphia, and I was offered staff positions in New York and Boston, but I wanted a small town. I don't know why, Miss Jenny. But now I know, I think."

He waited for her to ask for further elucidation, but she did not. She said, "New York. Boston. Paris. London. Vienna. St. Petersburg. I—I think of them often. I'd like to go. I think."

"Perhaps you will someday." He thought with what joy he would take Jenny to those far-off places, and what he would show her. They would explore, for the first time, together.

"Yes," said Jenny, but there was no conviction in her voice. She waited a moment and then with that painful difficulty she said, "So you will remain here."

"Yes." (Damn that monosyllable!)

"And Jon—Dr. Ferrier—will truly go away?"

"Yes." (He was falling into a helpless game.)

"Soon?"

"Yes." (At least she was talking!)

"Where to?" asked Jenny. He was surprised that she was interested in a man she so obviously loathed. However, perhaps she was eager for him to get out of her sight.

"I don't know," said Robert. (Why weren't they talking about himself, and, best of all, their own future?) "I don't think, though, that he'll ever come back to Hambledon. Never again. I have a feeling his mother will go with him, too, for it's doubtful he'll ever remarry. The town treated him abominably, as you know." Now he was curious to know her own reaction to the murder trial. She said nothing. So, he went on, "How anyone can believe that Jonathan Ferrier killed his wife and—er—his child is beyond credibility."

Jenny turned and looked at him gravely, and shook her head. "Jon never did that, Doctor. Never. He—he couldn't have—he was away at the time. Of course, I once read that anyone is capable of anything. But Jon didn't do that, he didn't do that."

He was surprised at her mixture of sophistication and ingenuousness. "I'm glad to hear you say that, Miss Jenny. But you and I make up a minority in this town, you know."

"Yes." She paused. "I didn't think Jon was such a coward."

"Coward?"

"Running away. He should stay—and fight."

"I think so, too. But how can you fight cobwebs, even if they are poisonous?"

"I do," said Jenny. Now her face was exceptionally pale under all that sunburn, and he could see the sudden whiteness around her mouth.

"I suppose you do," he said with sadness. She jerked a little with her own surprise, and then, to his greater amazement, she colored violently and unbecomingly.

"What do you mean?" she demanded.

"The stories," he said.

"About Jon? I don't believe them in the least!" Her voice was vehement.

Then it came to him that Jenny knew nothing about the tales concerning herself, and he was sad and freshly moved, and filled with the desire to protect her. But, why was her face so red now, and so almost challenging?

"Does Jon ever talk about me?" she asked. Her voice was trembling.

"Jon? Why no. Why should he?"

"Oh." The color left her face and she seemed to be relieved.

"He wouldn't talk about his relatives, anyway," said Robert.

"I'm not his relative!" said Jenny. "His brother is my stepfather—but Jon is no relative of mine!"

She looked at the water and said, "Isn't it beautiful? The

sun on the sails, and the color of the mountains and the
water? I've seen so many paintings of faraway places—the
Rhine, the downs of Devon, the Seine, the Riviera, and the
Orient. But none seems to me so beautiful as here, and I
want to spend my life on my island."

She looked at him with that touching candor of hers and
said, "You know, everyone thinks Papa built the castle for
Mama. But he built it for me. It was a secret between us, so
that Mama wouldn't feel neglected." He couldn't tell in what
direction her thoughts were flowing, but he was enchanted
when she smiled a real smile this time and he saw her small
and brilliant teeth. "Mama and I had secrets, too. She said
gentlemen did not appreciate intelligence in ladies and that it
was the duty of ladies to play the fool to keep the gentlemen
happy. She also said that a man never really forgives a
woman for marrying him." She laughed for the first time and
he thought it an endearing and childlike sound. "Mama deceived Papa, and Harald, and almost everyone else, into believing she was only comfortable and fluffy. But she was
really very sharp."

"I am sure," said Robert, "that it would be impossible for
a stupid lady to have a daughter like you."

She blushed and drew away from him a little, and her eyes
were suspicious. Then, they brightened with anxiety. "What
do you mean?" she asked.

"Why, Miss Jenny, you are the handsomest young lady I
have ever seen in my life!" He spoke with deep sincerity and
Jenny watched him closely for a few minutes after he had
spoken. Then she was smiling again.

"Do you honestly think so?" she asked, not in flirtation but
with a real desire to know. "That is, as children say, cross
your heart and hope to die?"

He lifted his yellow-gloved hand and crossed his heart and
Jenny was openly pleased. "Why?" she asked with disturbing
directness.

"Didn't you ever look at yourself in a mirror?"

"Yes. Of course. I am very plain."

He glanced at her with disbelief, but again she was perfectly sincere.

"Who told you that, Miss Jenny?"

"Why, Papa. And he was quite right. They used to call me
a great gawk in school. You see, I am so tall and thin, and
have big hands and feet—and I don't look well in pretty

clothes. I'm not gracious, not charming. I don't know what to do with myself!"

Robert drew up the buggy under the shade of a giant elm, fastened the reins and turned fully and solemnly to the girl, and she instinctively shrank back from him a little. But he did not touch her. He said, "Jenny, I want to tell you now that I've seen many beautiful girls and women in my life, in big cities over all the eastern part of the country, and there is none who could match you. Did you ever ask yourself why I wished you to come with me today? Did you think it was my Christian kindness of heart?" He smiled into her eyes, which were widening slowly. "It was my selfishness. I wanted to be with a lovely woman, a great lady, and that is what you are, Jenny. A great lady."

She pondered over every word he had said, weighing his truthfulness, his actual meaning, and finding nothing wanting at all. She looked faintly incredulous. She adjusted her hat, smoothed her gloves, bit her lower lip, but never took her eyes from his.

"Has nobody ever told you that before?" he asked.

"No. That is," and she hesitated, "two did, but I didn't believe them. I still don't. Oh, yes, Aunt Marjorie told me, too, but she is very kind and so I couldn't believe her. Truly, you don't find me repulsive?"

"Jenny!" He wanted to take this woman, who was still a child in her mind, in his arms and kiss her hard and repeatedly, but he knew that that would frighten and outrage her. He was so sensitive to her by now, so full of the acuteness of love. "Jenny, you are as repulsive as a rose, as ugly as a young green tree, as hideous as a butterfly! Now, is that sufficient?"

She laughed reluctantly. "Perhaps to you, and thank you," she said.

He saw that she trusted him, and he was elated. He said after a moment, "Who were the 'two' who told you what I've told you in all honesty?"

Now her blue eyes left him and she looked down at the dust cover that lay over her knees. "They don't matter. One was Harald, and the other was Jon."

"Well, Harald should know. He's an artist, a painter, and they are very perceptive of beauty. And Jon—well, I understand he is quite a connoisseur of women." He added this delicately, but it was apparent at once that she took his remark on its face, for she nodded.

"Mavis was the prettiest woman I ever saw," she said. "She was like the princess in the fairy tales I read as a child. Rapunzel. The Sleeping Beauty. Cinderella. Snow White. She was all of them, Mavis. Of course, she was a lot older than I was, four years. She was—dazzling. People always stared at her, absolutely hypnotized. I wanted to look at her for hours —but she was never still."

"You mean, jiggling with her hands and her head, the way the ladies all do now—except you, Jenny? The fashionable jiggling, pretending to animation or something?"

She giggled. She actually giggled. He thought it an adorable sound. "They do look as if they have the palsy, don't they?" she said. "No, Mavis wasn't like that. It wasn't that she was quiet. On the contrary. She laughed all the time, boisterously. It was the only ugly thing about her, and I thought how it spoiled her appearance. But others seemed to like it!" She shook her head in wonder. "They always talked about Mavis' laugh, as if it were marvelous. Perhaps I was the one who was wrong. I don't like noisy people."

"Mavis was noisy?"

"Well, yes. I know that sounds unkind, but it is the truth. She was noisy. And cuddly. She was always cuddling against people, and laughing that raucous laugh of hers," and now Jenny's voice rose with honest indignation. "She would do that with Jon when they were first married, and I felt sorry for him, for she embarrassed him. But no one else was embarrassed. I think Jon annoyed Mavis."

"He's too severe, perhaps?"

"I never thought so." She was again surprised. "In fact, I began to think him frivolous, light-minded, superficial, since Mavis—died."

There was no limit to the power she had of astonishing him. "Jon—frivolous? He seems very bitter to me, and I've heard he was harsh, though I know better. He is the most unhappy man I've ever known. But grim men like Jon always make disastrous marriages, and heaven only knows why."

The buggy was jogging along again now and the sweet dusty breeze blew over their faces and Robert was filled with a huge content. So, this was what love was like, was it? A kind of peace, a contentment, a radiant serenity, a quietness and sweetness of the spirit. Sweetness, above all. Everything had a shine to it to his eyes, the sun, the earth, the tall dry grasses along the road, the quiet water, the hills. He saw Queen Anne's lace in the grass and heard the bees and the cicadas, and he wondered at the beauty of the world when it was lit by this inner illumination of passion and tenderness. There was more to love than desire, the Jon Ferriers to the contrary. Desire was the least part of love, though it was its foundation, its earth. Above the roots rose the living tree with the rosy fruit and the jade leaves, the everlasting tree which not even death could cause to decay, for it was changeless and immutable, imperishable and fashioned out of some loveliness deep in the sullen and restless human spirit.

"Yes," said Jenny, "it was disastrous for both of them, Mavis and Jon."

There are some who would call this gossip, thought Robert Morgan. But Jenny is as guiltless of the intent to gossip as an infant. She speaks whatever comes to her mind without malice or cruelty. Now he was afraid for her. She had no one in the world of her own, no way of protection, no wall against her vulnerability. Her only defense would be marriage, and he was more than ready to offer that defense.

"Jon is bitter because his friends believe he killed Mavis," said Jenny. "No one told me, but I know. Otherwise, he is jaunty, if you don't like the word 'light-minded.' You don't, do you? Oh, he was never afraid of anything. He despises everything, and he was that way before Mavis died. He never took anyone seriously."

For the first time it came to Robert disagreeably that their only real conversation so far, on this gorgeous day, had been of Jonathan Ferrier. He could not remember that he had instigated this conversation, but he did not like it. He preferred to talk about himself to Jenny, and he wanted to inspire her regard. So far, she had shown no open interest in him, though at least she was now talking and not merely answering "yes." That indicated trust, and the young man's heart rose as light as a bird.

Unfortunately, a surrey was approaching them on the narrow road, filled with four young women. They had just come round a bend, and now the air echoed with their gay laughter, their little squeals and their high and girlish voices. The horse trotted along briskly, the fringe on the surrey swayed, and the girls held their hats. Robert cautiously guided his horse to the extreme right of the road to let the equipage pass with its pretty burden. Then, as it was beside him, the driver halted it, and he saw the pink dimpled face and auburn hair and sparkling eyes of Maude Kitchener. Her mouth was like a plump rosebud, but it stopped smiling when she saw his companion.

"Oh, Dr. Morgan!" she trilled. "How are you today? Oh, and do you know Betty Gibson, Susie Harris, Emiline Wilson? Girls, this is Dr. Morgan—the gentleman I have been telling you about—" She stopped and blushed furiously. The girls eyed Robert with animated curiosity and some sly smiles, and it was evident, even to the young man, that perhaps Maude had been somewhat too confiding about him to her friends. In their turn the girls openly admired his magnificent apparel and his face, but when they glanced at Jenny, nasty smirks appeared on their young mouths, and Robert saw that, too. He had taken off his hat, and it lay on his knees.

"A pleasant ride, ladies?" he asked.

"We've been to lunch at Emiline's aunt's," said Maude. Her sweet voice was subdued. She regarded Jenny with trouble. "How are you, Jenny?"

Jenny had become stiff and remote again. Her nod was jerky. "Very well, thank you," she replied, and the stammering note was back in her voice.

The other girls said nothing at all to Jenny but averted their eyes from her and talked in a lively fashion with the young doctor, of whom they had heard so much, particularly from Maude, who had hardly stopped talking of him all through lunch. They did not know whether to pity her or to be a little happy that the young man, whom she had hinted was "much taken" by her and practically ready to propose, had found that unspeakable Jenny Heger more to his liking than Maude Kitchener, at least for this day. But, then, everyone knew what that hussy was, and gentlemen will be gentlemen, even such a nice, handsome young man like this.

Robert was not so obtuse that he did not observe the snub given Jenny, and so it was he who put on his hat and lifted the reins and said good-day to the young ladies. He was the one who drove off first. The surrey moved off behind him with less vigor, he thought with some satisfaction. The only nice girl among them had been Maude Kitchener, and he felt warm toward her. Women!

"Really, that creature!" said Emiline Wilson. "Whatever in the world does he see in her?"

"Guess!" said Susie Harris, with a naughty giggle. Betty Gibson hit her on the shoulder coyly and said, "Don't be lewd, Susie."

"If I had any interest in him at all," said Emiline in a meaning tone, "I'd tell him all about her, that I would. It's disgraceful. He probably believes she's respectable. Poor man."

"He hasn't been here long," said Maude. Then she added, "But, of course Jenny is respectable! You mustn't be mean, girls. You know as well as I do that it is all lies, that people say of Jenny. We went to school with her. If—if Dr. Morgan likes her, it's no wonder. She's so very beautiful."

The girls chorused "No!" with loyal emphasis, and Maude was pleased.

"This is really a very stupid town," said Emiline. "I don't suppose anyone has invited Dr. Morgan to dinner except the Ferriers. Have they?"

All but Maude answered in the negative. She knew that her parents had invited Robert on many occasions, but he had been in the hospitals or on house calls or otherwise engaged. But he had promised to dine with the Kitcheners next Monday and had expressed his gratitude to Mrs. Kitchener. So Maude said, "He's been so busy, and he is to have dinner at our house on Monday."

The girls spoke their happy envy of Maude, and they all began to laugh again. But Maude remembered how Robert had looked at Jenny before they had driven away, and she wanted to cry.

Robert found his promised spot a few minutes later. He turned his buggy up a rambling little side road, and it mounted steeply. Then at the top it was like a small and grassy knoll, with one huge oak in the very center. Below them was brush and untended shrubbery, behind them was a lonely meadow, and before them lay the river scintillating in blue lights in the sun, the mountains rising above it like a green barrier. Buttercups and wild daisies and Indian paintbrushes huddled in the thick warm grass, which was not too high, though very dense. Robert held up his hand to Jenny and this time she took it to alight, and at the first touch he had had of her Robert was struck as by lightning and turned very pale. It was a moment before he could help Jenny to the step and then down to the grass, where she stood smoothing her white skirt with her gloved hands and looking about her with shy pleasure.

"Do you like it, Jenny?" he asked.

"Oh, it's wonderful," she said. She took off her hat, and

her hair, hastily pinned as usual, began to drop about her face. She tried to restore her attempts at a pompadour, but it was useless, so with a shrug she merely shook out her hair and let it fall on her shoulders and down her back.

Now she began to laugh uncertainly as she helped Robert anchor the checked tablecloth on the grass, for here it was breezy under the tree. She ran about, finding good stones for the anchoring, and brought them back gleefully in both hands. She showed keen interest in the food, laid the plates and the silver and polished the goblets with a napkin. Then she sat down, folding her legs like an Arab, and laughed again with pleasure.

"What fun picnics are!" she exclaimed. "Mama and I used to have them before she—married—Harald, and I was just a child. On the island, of course. We told each other lots of secrets, and the trees were so thick and the rose gardens were unbelievable. The rose gardens," she added, and her face changed and she was not smiling any longer.

"Beautiful gardens," said Robert. As the host, he filled Jenny's plate first and she stared down unseeingly at the large portions he had given her. He opened the wine bottle and poured the pale golden liquid into the glasses.

"What?" said Jenny, coming back with a start.

"What? Oh, I said your rose gardens are beautiful."

Jenny picked up a fried chicken leg, eyed it absently, then began to eat it. Her mood appeared to pass. Fresh color came up under her sunburn. The weight of her black hair fell across her ears, and her lashes gave another spiked shadow on the rose of her cheek. Robert could hardly eat for enchantment and new and deeper contentment. He had loved her for her beauty from the beginning, and for her redoubtable innocence. Now he loved her, besides, for what he had guessed about her, and her simplicity. He lifted his wineglass high, and her blue eyes followed it.

"To you, dear Jenny," he said.

She picked up her own glass at once, smiled back at him, and said, "To you, Doctor." He wished she had shown some coquetry, and that she had called him by his Christian name. But still he was content. He had not dreamed at first that she would be so responsive to him, and so childishly happy in this picnic. He looked at the river, which was not so blue as Jenny's eyes. He could smell pine near him, aromatic and exciting, and the grass gave off a hot fragrance sweeter than any manufactured perfume. Jenny was part of it. She was alone in this shining silence with him. There was no one else.

She drank the wine eagerly. "Oh, this is delicious," she said. "I don't like it as a rule, but I do like this. Is it a French wine?"

He gave her the bottle to study its label and was gratified to see that she was impressed. "Why, it's—1890," she said. "Eleven years ago. What a long time!"

"To you, perhaps. You were only nine then, weren't you, Jenny? But I was much older."

She glanced at his young face and his luxuriant mustache, and then he saw another side of Jenny, subtle and amused. She smiled at him frankly and shook her head, and the breeze lifted her hair and tossed it. "You are really very young," said Jenny, and he did not know whether to be pleased or displeased. "You believe the world is good, don't you? Do you recall what Machiavelli said: 'A man of merit who knows the world becomes less cheered, as time goes by, by the good, and less grieved by the evil, he sees in the world.' "

He considered that, then nodded. "Don't you believe the world is good, too?"

"No, I truly don't. People think I am foolish and ignorant, but I'm not. I listen. I hear. I see. I think. I read. I walk alone by myself. I am never lonely—by myself. I watch the birds. Nothing very much surprises me."

For some reason Robert thought of Jonathan Ferrier and did not know why. The thought came from nowhere, and it jolted him.

"No one but a fool would think you foolish and ignorant, Jenny."

Again she gave him that amused and subtle smile. "You must chatter all the time, in this world, and be doing something in a rush, or something you call important, or going somewhere very fast, or returning from somewhere just as fast, to be thought clever and sophisticated. But if you are contented with your own self, and don't like confusion and only your own thoughts, and the work you love to do, then you are mad, they say, or you don't like your fellowman, and are even un-Christian." She shook back her hair. "They forget, or never knew, what Shakespeare wrote in *As You Like It:* 'And so from hour to hour we ripe and ripe, and then from hour to hour we rot and rot.' If they gave that a little thought, they'd stop being in such a hurry—nobodys going nowhere, and pathetically trying to be somebodys going somewhere. But very few people are 'somebodys.' "

He had not thought her capable of making such a long statement, but as he saw the flush on her cheek and her empty glass he knew that the wine had taken her shyness from her and that Jenny was herself with him, and he blinked his eyes rapidly.

He refilled her glass and she watched him with that touching pleasure. "As for myself," she said, "I am content to be a nobody, going nowhere. That's the nice thing about being a nobody: You don't feel you have to go somewhere—and there's no somewhere, really."

Now her face changed again, and she looked down into the wineglass with sudden melancholy. "Nowhere," she repeated. "Nowhere at all."

"Oh, come, Jenny. You are young and the world is open to you."

"No," she said. "I'm afraid it opened, once, when I was sixteen, for about three minutes. Three whole minutes. And then it closed again, and that was all there was to it, and all there ever will be."

"Tell me," he said, wanting to know more and more about this enigmatic girl.

She shook her head. "There's nothing to tell. It was all in my imagination."

She put down her plate from her knee, and quickly drank the wine. In a more worldly woman it would have been a theatrical gesture, for effect. In Jenny it was swift desperation. Again, for apparently no reason, Robert thought of Jonathan Ferrier.

"Jenny," he said, "Why don't you go away for a while, to see something of what you should see?"

"Oh, I can't, Doctor. I couldn't leave my island. But if Harald ever leaves permanently, which he won't, then I could leave it for a little while myself."

That sounded strange to Robert, and he frowned. "You see," said Jenny with all earnestness, "I couldn't leave the island alone to him. Could I?"

"Why not?"

"Well, when I came back, it wouldn't be the same to me."

He was baffled. "One day, when you are married, you will leave the island and never go back except for a visit."

"No. I'll never leave the island. And I'll never get married."

A vague dimness came over the earth for Robert and nothing was very bright any longer. He said, "You'll change your mind, Jenny, when you find someone who loves you."

To his horror and concern he saw her eyes fill with tears, and she shook her head. She put the empty wineglass on the cloth and it rolled from her and she watched it.

"Hasn't anyone spoken of—well, love to you, Jenny?"

She only shook her head over and over.

The breeze grew stronger and it lifted away the leaves and the sunshine fell on Jenny's hair in a shaft of pure light, and Robert thought, How lovely is the sunlight on a woman's hair!

He wanted to say, "I love you, Jenny, my sweet Jenny. Let me tell you how much I love you." But he knew it was too soon. He would only alarm her away, send her off into her silences again. There was someone else like that whom he knew. Jonathan Ferrier. The slightest extension of stronger friendship or personal concern given by anyone to him sent him off into one of his cold remarks or a ribald aphorism. He rejected the close touch as much as Jenny feared it and would reject it. Robert did not like the resemblance.

He decided to change the subject. "What do you particularly like to read, Jenny?"

She had swallowed her involuntary tears. "Poetry," she said. "I like Homer, in Greek, and I especially like Ovid, in Latin."

Robert was impressed. Another woman who confessed this would make him recoil, but in Jenny it was quite natural and part of her.

"So much of the essence is lost in translation," said Jenny. "Don't you think so?"

"I'm afraid my Latin extends only to medicine," said Robert.

She laughed suddenly. She looked about her with that frank candor he found so touching and lovely. She stared at the water. Then she said, "Did you like Aunt Marjorie's picnic on the Fourth?"

"Very much. She is a delightful lady."

"It was a ridiculous speech," said Jenny.

"Wasn't it? I'm afraid I didn't listen to it very much. But Jon and Father McNulty thought it 'ominous.' I believe that all politicians are ominous myself."

Jenny had taken a long grass in her hand was was pulling it

through her fingers. Her head was bent and he could not see her face.

"Won't it be very hard for you to take all Jon's practice, when he has gone?" she asked. "It's a very large practice, I heard."

"I hope to do my best," he said, and heard the stiffness in his own voice.

"Yes," said Jenny. She wound the grass over her fingers and pulled it hard.

"He may come back from time to time to help me, if he can."

She looked up so suddenly that he was startled. "Did he promise you that?"

"No. He didn't. He said that when he left here, he was finished with the town forever, and with everyone in it."

"But you feel he will come back?"

"No, I don't, Jenny. Why should he? He didn't abandon the town. The town abandoned him, and for no good and worthy reason."

"Did he—recently—say he would never come back?"

"Only this morning."

Jenny drew a long breath and he heard it. "But, he has his house and his farms."

"I hear he is looking for a buyer for his farms, except for one. The house is really his mother's. No, he won't be back. He is leaving before the first of September, he told me a few days ago."

"Four weeks," said Jenny.

"Yes."

He was bored and unaccountably disturbed by the conversation. He let himself lie back on the grass, his arms folded under his head. He did not know why he said, "Then, again, he may take someone with him. A lady calls him up at least once a week and he sounds very pleased to hear her. It isn't a patient, I know. He used his 'personal' voice when he talks to her."

The sky was suddenly blotted out for him by Jenny's head, bending over him.

"A woman?" she said, and there was deep shadow on her face. "A woman calls him?"

"Yes. I don't know who she is, Jenny. I do know he calls her 'dear.' "

"Oh." Then Jenny said in a flat voice. "Perhaps he is thinking of marrying her."

Robert deliberately yawned. "Who knows? Why don't you lie down, too, Jenny, in this soft thick grass, before we go back?"

She did not hesitate at all. She stretched herself beside him, and he could hear her light breathing and could see her profile. It was blank and pale. Then she closed her eyes and her head was like a fallen statue's in the grass. He felt the poignancy, the lost and broken abandonment of it. Something had gone wrong in this halcyon day, which had begun so vividly and with so much joyful contentment, and he did not know what it was.

He saw her hand near his hip, and he carefully lifted one of his arms from behind his head and let his hand wander to hers, and then her fingers. He expected her to snatch her hand away, but she did not. Nor did she open her eyes or move. Her fingers were cool and flaccid under his, but still it was enough for him, at this time, just to hold her hand and to feel again the sweet contentment of his love for her. He wished they needed never to go home and that they might spend eternity here like this, with the wind blowing over them and the dark green tree arching over them, and the butterflies in the grass, and the faint sound of the lighted river just slightly disturbing the scented air.

He drowsed. He began to have a curious half-dream or fantasy. He thought that he awakened and when he did so, Jenny was not there, and it was autumn, and the bronze and red leaves were falling all about him, and the river roared, and he was full of cold desolation for he knew he would never see Jenny again and that she had gone away forever.

He came awake with a violent start. Jenny indeed was not beside him. But she had gathered up all the dishes and the linen and had put them neatly in the basket, and she was standing, looking at the river and winding up her hair.

Her back was to him. He could see the long and slender lines of her figure, the lithe grace of her waist, the fine modeling of her shoulders and arms. She had forgotten him. What she was thinking of he could not remotely guess, but he knew that she was lost in her own dreams, or thoughts, as he had been lost in his. Her hands pinned up her hair now. Her arms dropped to her sides. She sighed and turned.

"Well," he said. "It seems I fell asleep."

"Yes."

"It must be late."

Jenny looked at the watch pinned to her shirtwaist. "Five

o'clock," she said. Her face was quite still and indifferent, but when he caught her eyes, she gave him again her shy and diffident smile. "It's late."

"Not very." He hesitated. "Jenny, will you have dinner with me?"

She replied with haste, "Oh, I couldn't!"

He did not ask why. He got up, found his coat and put it on. He brushed himself down. He put on his hat. Jenny watched him, and when he glanced at her, she was smiling gently, as one smiles at a child of whom one is fond. "I want to thank you for a lovely day, Doctor," she said.

"Jenny, why don't you call me Robert, or Bob?"

"Very well. Robert." He had never heard his name said before like that, or so it seemed to him. He was quite cheered. They went to the buggy, and found that the horse had eaten all his oats, and they climbed into the vehicle and turned homeward. They were halfway to Hambledon when Robert said, "You forgot your hat! We'll go back at once."

"No, no. Please. It doesn't matter at all. It really does not."

She means it, thought Robert. Had she accomplished something with the hat, and her new clothes? The thought was very queer to Robert, himself, and yet he could not shake it off. He could hardly speak the rest of the way, and Jenny made no remark. The world was less glowing to Robert now, but he was still resolutely planning to meet Jenny again, and very soon.

"You will go somewhere with me again, Jenny, in the near future?"

"Yes. Oh, yes."

He was so elated that he wanted to bend toward her and kiss her cheek. But she was looking at the gardens along the way and seemed to be absorbed in them. They arrived at the little dock, hardly more than a plank or two, where the island boats waited. There was only one left. "Harald must be home," said Jenny, and she appeared disappointed.

Robert was helping her out of the buggy when they heard the brisk tattoo of horse's hoofs, and there was Jonathan Ferrier on his horse, looking down at them and smiling broadly. He touched his hat with his crop and said, "How was the picnic?"

"Splendid," said Robert, and felt less cordial to Jonathan than usual. "Here, Jenny, take my hand." She did so in silence, and Jonathan watched her descend as if her every movement was intensely interesting to him.

"How did you enjoy it, Jenny?" he asked.

Jenny had jumped to the ground. She did not know where
to look. As if involuntarily pulled, her eyes rose to look at
Jonathan. And then Robert saw the deep and ugly crimson
on her face, the heavy tears in her eyes, and her trembling
chin. She stood like that, stricken, and she and Jonathan
could not look away from each other, and Robert saw it all,
and he knew.

Jenny, at last, walked toward the boat and Robert followed
her on legs that felt like stone. Yes, he knew. He knew now
why Jenny had gone with him. She had gone to hear him,
Robert, speak of Jonathan Ferrier and give all news of him.
She could ask him, with openness, things which she could not
ask his mother.

"Let me row you over, Jenny," said Robert, and his voice
was dull.

"No. Please. I like to row," said the girl, not looking at
him. She jumped into the boat. She still did not look at him.
But just as she rowed away she did look once again at Jonathan, and the crimson was still in her face and her mouth
was shaking. Robert watched until she was only a dark figure
on the gleaming golden water of the evening river. He forgot
Jonathan. When he turned, Jonathan was still there on his
horse.

"I wouldn't," said Jonathan, "take Jenny too seriously, if I
were you." Then he touched Robert lightly but smartly on
the shoulder with his crop and rode off.

The jocular blow stung Robert. Had it really been jocular,
or friendly? Robert looked after Jonathan until he had disappeared. Jenny, he thought. Jenny, I'm not going to give up. I
don't know what this is all about, Jenny, but he isn't the man
for you, nor are you the woman for him. I won't give up,
Jenny. I have something more wholesome and something
more of life to give you than a wrathful man who will soon
have no home of his own. I have youth to give you, and
hope, and peace, and some fun and laughter, and travel, and
I have all my love and no terrible memories. From those I
will protect you.

CHAPTER TWENTY-SIX

Jonathan had just left the operating room at St. Hilda's, where he had watched Robert Morgan perform an operation, and had assisted. He met young Philip Harrington in a corridor. The gynecologist put both hands on his shoulders and said, "Congratulate me."

"Congratulations," said Jonathan. "What is it? No, let me guess. You've bedded Elvira Burrows."

"Now, now, Jon. You know Elvira better than that."

"Have you been wasting your time, by any chance?"

"Oh, come on. Anyway, we're engaged, thanks to you! We're to be married on September first and you are to be the best man."

"You thought I'd congratulate you? Aren't condolences more in order?"

"Hey, aren't you the one who contrived all this?"

"So I did. I must have been out of my mind to do a thing like that to a nice, sweet, innocent bachelor. Well, Elvira's got a lot of money and will inherit more when Papa dies, and there's the house, of course."

Phil Harrington began to laugh. "You were right about Papa. A few days after you cured him with brandy and your ineffable advice, he hied himself to New York for a few days for research on his damned book about Chaucer—I read a few chapters. Clean as a frog. Chaucer was a lascivious old boy, yet Papa's quotations are all scrubbed up. I asked him about that and he said he wanted to 'engage the curiosity of young minds first,' so they'd do their own research on Chaucer, and I told him that young minds are invariably prurient and are bored to death by niceness. Well, anyway. At some

477

party in New York he met a very erudite widow—with money—and with what he calls 'a remarkable mind,' and Papa is a very fast worker, for the lady had given him her photograph before he returned to Hambledon. A nice cozy little body with a pretty round face. About forty-five. Elvira and I don't need programs to show us how the romance is progressing, and we are very happy for Papa. Elvira wanted to wait for our own wedding until Papa was married. 'More seemly,' the darling said, and after all Mama hasn't been dead a year. But I said it was far more seemly that we went to bed as soon as possible, and she agreed."

"Did you put it to her that crudely?"

"My friend, after Elvira and I had a few dark evenings together during Papa's absence, she opened one of the guest rooms, with a double bed, and is having it all spruced up. Don't jump to conclusions. We didn't help ourselves to the jelly beans—and we won't until we are married, and you can be sure that Elvira will investigate the minister thoroughly and all his credentials to see that the knot is not only legally tied but firmly double-tied."

"A masterful girl," said Jonathan.

Phil Harrington looked into the distance with a far and dreaming smile. "Oh, I wouldn't say that. I wouldn't say that at all." Jonathan thought he looked asinine.

"I don't think I'll be here on September first," he said.

"But, damn it, it's only three weeks! What's the hurry?"

"Practically all my practice has now been taken over by Bob Morgan, so why should I stay? All right. I'll remain for the wedding and for the first kiss of the bride."

Now Phil Harrington looked troubled. He said, "Jon, you always told me I didn't have much imagination, and you said that imagination was fatal for a surgeon like me. So perhaps I've been imagining things after all, a new characteristic. I'd like to talk to you in private. Let's look in the lounge."

The doctors' lounge was empty, for it was lunchtime, and the two young men sat down in comfortable chairs near the windows. Phil had lumbered to them, and when he turned to Jonathan, his usually buoyant and amiable face was disturbed and uneasy.

"Don't tell me," said Jonathan, "that you have another girl whom you've knocked up and you can't get rid of her."

"Be serious for once," said Phil. "This concerns you, not me."

Since his arrest Jonathan had become familiar with a sudden sick dropping in his middle, something which he had never experienced before in his brave life. He lit a cigarette and watched Phil Harrington. "Well, tell me," he said.

"I wish to God I could come to you with facts and conversations and 'he said' and 'they said,' and all that, and with dates, but I can't, Jon. I began to suspect something was in the wind when the other fellas would stop talking when I came up to them, because they know I am your friend, and once or twice I heard your name. It's sticky. I keep getting side looks and smirks and questions about how you are these days, as if they don't see you in the hospitals as much as I do."

"Hum," said Jonathan.

"It's even more obvious at the Friends'," said Phil. "I wish to God there was something definite I could tell you, but I think there's some danger in the wind for you, Jon."

Jonathan thought of the malignant letter which had been delivered to him by messenger. He said, "I wouldn't worry, Phil. After all, no matter what they say or what evidence they think they have, I can't be tried the second time for the same crime. Double jeopardy. Anyway, I'll be out of here in a few weeks, forever. That ought to satisfy them."

"They know you're going, Jon. But this thing has blown up very recently." He paused and frowned at his big competent hands. "It's worse than months ago, if that's possible. There's a kind of elation in the air among the fellas who never liked you. You know them. They were the ones who were almost out of their minds when you were acquitted."

"I know." The sick and fallen feeling in Jonathan's middle became stronger. Then with it came a deep and bitter anger and the white folds sprang out about his mouth.

"There's nothing anyone can do to me," he said. "I'm financially independent of my profession. I'm a rich man, with sound investments and property. So, they can't hurt me in my pocket. They can't injure my reputation, for I haven't any here, and be damned to reputation anyway. They can't take away my patients, because I have sold my practice. So, what can they do to me?"

"I hate conjectures," said Phil.

"Well, what do you 'conjecture'?"

"Jon, so help me, I don't know. It's just a feeling I have. Maybe I've developed an imagination since I met Elvira. She's a very complicated girl and gives me books to read, books I never had time to read before or even knew existed.

Edgar Allan Poe is one of her favorites, and he's mine now, too, and you can't read Poe without getting your imagination all excited or developing one."

"I bet you had fun with *The Pit and the Pendulum*."

"I sweated, I swear." Phil smiled briefly. He got up and put his hands in the pockets of his untidy trousers and lumbered heavily up and down for a few moments, and Jonathan thought he would be one of the few people in Hambledon whom he would miss. Phil stopped in front of him and looked down gravely. "I smell danger," he said. "It's the kind of inner smell I get about a patient even before I pick up the scalpel. A feeling that something's wrong, though all previous indications have suggested this is going to be a very simple and uneventful operation. I had a young woman last week with what all examinations seemed to show had just a cystic ovary, and the uterus was clean and healthy. But when I took the scalpel and looked down at her unconscious face—a nice healthy-looking face, plump, too—I knew there was something not so pure and pretty going on here. And, by God, I was right. The poor girl had a carcinoma, and the damned thing had spread—way up."

"So, you think there's something cancerous going on around me."

"Don't smile, Jon, but that's exactly what I think."

"And not a single word or hint to prove it."

Phil sat down, thrust out his legs straight before him, pushed out his big red lip and stared at his boots, which, since he had met Elvira, shone like the sun. A shaft of light touched his thick blond hair, and he looked like a troubled schoolboy, for he had round large features full of young health and vitality.

"Well, there was just something a couple of days ago. I was passing old Louis' office and he was talking to someone behind the shut door, and he was yelling, and we always try to listen when Louis yells. He was shouting, and I caught your name, but that's about all, except that he did say 'don't believe it.' If I hadn't been uneasy for some time, I wouldn't have thought a thing about it, but I went back down the hall and waited. And then out of Louis' office came a sweet-faced old man with white hair and that scoundrel, Senator Campion. Old Louis just stood on the threshold and glowered at them, and then he slammed the door right on their heels."

"Good for Louis," said Jonathan, but his voice was absent. "That was all?"

"Thinking back, I heard Louis saying that something was 'beamish,' and that's one of Lewis Carroll's coined words, isn't it, from *Alice in Wonderland*. Now, beamish means gladsome, if I remember, and smiling, and shining, all at the same time, and from the tone of Louis' voice it didn't seem right. He was bellowing then, and why was he doing that when things were so 'beamish'?"

Jonathan suddenly sat upright. "Beamish?" he repeated. "Was he talking about a—a woman? A patient, perhaps of mine?"

Phil shook his head. "I don't know, Jon. I just know that Louis looked as if he was about to have a stroke there on the threshold, and Campion was as rosy as could be, and grinning, and the old man—"

"You never met Jonas Witherby, did you?"

"Witherby?" Phil thought. "Oh. Once. A couple of years ago. I've seen his photograph in the newspapers when he's been sponsoring something or other, or laying a cornerstone. Yes, by God, it was Witherby!" He paused. "Now, look, Jon, maybe it means nothing at all. Maybe I just thought I'd heard your name from Louis. I've been on tenterhooks about you for the last few weeks."

"Perhaps," said Jonathan. He shrugged. "Don't worry. I'm not going in to old Louis and ask him anything and so get you in trouble. It could be nothing at all."

"Sure," said Phil. "Oh, the last thing Campion said before he had the door slammed on him was 'We'll bring you the depositions first. Thought it was only fair.' "

"Well, never trouble trouble until trouble troubles you, as the old saw is," said Jonathan.

"If it weren't for the smirks I've been getting and your enemies asking about you, I wouldn't be so nervous, Jon. But maybe I've been building up something from nothing. You know how it is in a hospital among the staff and other doctors. They hear the slightest rumor, mostly without truth behind it, and they spread it all around fast. Never saw such gossips as doctors. They must do it to relieve the strain or something."

"But it's worse at the Friends'?" asked Jonathan, thinking of Humphrey Bedloe.

"Yes, thicker, but still just that—feeling. Do you want me to scout around?"

The thought of cumbersome Phil Harrington being subtle and indirect made Jonathan smile. "Don't bother, Phil. Just keep your ears open, will you? Though damned if I can think of anything they can do to me now."

"I will, Jon, I will. Don't worry, yourself. By the way, that intern now specializing in neurology here: Moe Abrams, the smart Jewish boy. You remember him. He walked in your shadow until he decided to give up obstetrics and take up neurology. He's with Newcome, and then he's going back to med school for further study. Didn't he help you with Hortense Nolan or something?"

"He did. He'd make a fine obstetrician, but he told me lately that it 'hurt' him to see young mothers suffer, and I couldn't change his mind. Must have what the Freudians call 'a mother complex' or something just as silly. What about him?"

"Well, I'd almost forgotten. I never listen to stories much. He wanted to know if he should tell you something but was scared. After all, he's having a hell of time getting along financially, and he's terrified of being hurt himself, and you can't blame him. He said he'd rather I told you myself and not use his name, but how can I?"

"I'd be the last person in the world to get Moe in trouble," said Jonathan. "I won't even let him know we're having this conversation. What did he say?"

"Well, you know old Newcome, who looks like an elder British statesman, lean and lanky and dignified, and wears a monocle, and affects an English accent ever since he spent two years at Oxford. But a good neurologist just the same. Took it up five years ago. He called Moe in to listen to a case he just had, a little girl. He also called another assistant, in his last year, interning. You know him, too, Walt Germaine. Sharp as vinegar. The kid's parents had brought her in. Name of McHenry—"

"McHenry!"

"You know them? God damn it, I'm sorry about that, Jon."

"Go on!" said Jonathan, and now his voice was more ugly than Phil had ever heard before.

"Moe said that Newcome examined the kid and looked at the reports of two nerve doctors in Pittsburgh about the little girl. Pretty kid, Moe said, and very quiet and dignified. There was also a report from Dr. Berryman, the G.P., you know, a sound man, here in town. Doc Berryman had said the child was anemic and needed more sun and fresh air and maybe the seaside, and then the parents had taken the girl to Pittsburgh for a more complete examination. Moe read the reports. 'Mild anemia, as approaching puberty. No pathology anywhere. Child unusually reserved but equable of temper and devoted to parents, and generally liked at her school. No nerve damage. No sign of any mental aberrations. No hallucinations. Mentally considerably above normal. A little constrained, but that is the result of fine breeding. Obedient. No troublesome traits.' That's the way it went on from the Pittsburgh boys. And the mother cried and kissed the child. It was the father who lost his head. He demanded to see Louis, and so he snatched up the reports and made old Newcome go down to Louis' office with him, and he was raving mad, Moe said, and he said he'd have you up for something or other. Incoherent. And they stamped down to Louis' office. That's all."

Jonathan's cold black rage stood in his eyes. He told Phil briefly about his encounter with the McHenrys. "I'm not an alienist," he said. "I told McHenry that at the very beginning. I was kidnaped into that house by that fool of a priest. I told them all I could be mistaken. I suggested to McHenry that he go to Philadelphia with the child and consult competent alienists and consider a sanitarium."

Phil was a doctor and so he said, "You really thought the child had dementia praecox, as McHenry alleged you had said?"

"Yes, I did. But, again, I could well be mistaken. That isn't my line. But neurologists. Why didn't the idiot follow my advice and take her to an alienist? Well, I could be mistaken. Who among us hasn't made mistakes in his practice? The girl isn't my patient. I was called to examine her sick mother—who is being driven out of her mind by her daughter's—peculiarities. I should have minded my own business, suggested to McHenry that he take a holiday with his wife—alone—for a while, and left it at that. But not Jon Ferrier, the soul-healer! No, indeed, God damn me! Well, Louis knows I'm no alienist, so he can't call me on that. What did Louis say, by the way?"

"Moe wasn't invited to join the conference. But he heard McHenry raving in the hall that he was going to sue for damages, or something, punitive damages against you for mental anguish and suffering, and there was something said about suing St. Hilda's too, because you are on the staff, a member of the Board."

"Oh, shit," said Jonathan. "Let the bugger sue me, the big

Mick. I should have punched his nose in when he insulted me in his house, and while I was at it I should have punched that priest, too. Moe's a good boy for telling you this, Phil, and I appreciate it, and I won't say a word to anyone."

"I think," said Phil, "that the word got around about the McHenrys and you. Not from Moe. He was terrified of even telling me. Maybe Newcome's assistant or Newcome himself. He never liked you, you know."

"No, he didn't. He was all for going into a man's skull after a 'tumor' one time. The man was crazy with head pains and pressures and was scared to death about a brain operation, and I don't blame him. So his wife brought him to me." Jonathan gave a short and ugly laugh. "Do you know what was wrong with him? He was forty-eight years old and refused to wear glasses for reading! He was quite a beau around this town, and still is, in spite of being married. He wanted to give the impression of being a romping boy, and he was afraid glasses, even for reading, would spoil that pretty vision. He also had hypertension, 188 over 110, nothing to fool with. One of the drivers, rushing to the top in his work, wanting to retire 'while I'm still young.' So I had a talk with the lad, told him he needn't wear glasses except in the bosom of his family and behind locked doors in his office, and advised him to calm down or he'd have a coronary soon or a stroke, and then where would the girls be? I also gave him a mild sedative, put him on a salt-free diet, told him to lose ten pounds and take more exercise—restore his beauty and put the roses back in his cheeks—and sent him on his way, blessing me. He never forgets me at Christmas or any other time he can think of.

"The stupid bastard, though, not only called Newcome to tell him the operation was off but gloated over the fact that Newcome had been wrong, and lavishly misquoted me. Newcome's never forgiven me the insult, and in a way I don't blame him. I never complain and never explain—an old aphorism of my mother's, and she is right—so I didn't drop my dignity long enough to tell Newcome what I'd actually said to that ass."

"Well, doctors," said Phil philosophically. "You know how they are."

"That I do, my friend. I've made wrong diagnoses myself dozens of times, and when the patient consulted someone else who gave the right diagnosis, and the other doctor told me, I cursed myself, but I was grateful. But Newcome is too egotistic for that. He never makes a mistake. Well, I'm afraid he has made one this time, though I hope to God he hasn't."

He patted Phil's huge knee. "Even if I made a wrong diagnosis about Elinor McHenry, what harm has been done? Louis's familiar with wrong diagnoses. He's made a few gorgeous ones himself, more than a few. He knows we aren't infallible. Let McHenry give himself pleasure thinking about suing me. On what grounds?"

"Still, even the instigation of a suit, no matter if it will be thrown out, isn't pleasant, Jon."

"I've had my share of unpleasantness, and the worst of all, so nothing else can really disturb me."

He went back to the offices in a murderous state of mind. He told himself that he was imagining things, but now he recalled that for the last two or three weeks his colleagues had indeed either been avoiding him, or greeting him coolly, or not stopping for chats in the corridors. He had thought that was because he was already no longer one of them and that he was leaving. He had few real friends among them, very few indeed. Had he intended to remain, he had thought, they would have treated him as always. But he was a departing guest, and they were remaining at home, and what had they in common now? No more hospital gossip, no more attending at operations, no more joint consultations, no more familiar ground.

He had thought that was all. But Phil Harrington had brought him that sullen sinking illness in his guts again. It was his conviction that in his case it would have been better if he had not known. Being forewarned was all very well for the soldier who was staying in his fortress, but it was irrelevant for one who was already marching away with his battalions to safety. "The hell with them all," he thought. "What can they do to me?"

Then he recalled "beamish." Edna Beamish, the rich and hysterical young widow, who had been so anxious to pay her bill, and which he had refused to tender? He thought of the doctor and the lawyer who had visited him. Well, what about it? He had not accepted any money for an incomplete examination. Phil could have been mistaken. He had listened outside a shut door, a dangerous thing, a thick shut door. Possibly Louis had not said "beamish" at all. Squeamish, perhaps. Campion could make anyone squeamish, and Jonathan now recalled, with a loud laugh, that Louis had not wanted him to be appointed United States Senator, and had so written to the

State Legislature, he having a better man in mind. Campion had probably never forgotten and perhaps was pressing Louis on some matter, and Louis was "squeamish." Old Witherby and Campion were great friends. No doubt Campion had taken Witherby along as support. As for Phil hearing Jonathan's name being mentioned it could possibly have been half a dozen "Johns," and not Jonathan Ferrier at all.

The McHenry matter was something else again. Jonathan could not shake off the memory of the child's eerie eyes, the air of subtle disturbance about and in her, the sense of something hidden and sinister and dangerous. He could not forget the distraction of the mother and the ominous stress on her heart.

The elderly spinster at the typewriter gave him a telegram when he arrived. Jonathan did not like telegrams on principle. He opened it, and his premonition was confirmed.

MUST INFORM YOU WITH SORROW THAT MY DEAR HUSBAND JEFFREY HOLLIDAY DIED LAST NIGHT IN THE SANITARIUM IN LOUISIANA STOP UNSUSPECTED NODULES HAD INVADED HIS THROAT AND THOUGH DESPERATE MEASURES WERE EMPLOYED HE SUDDENLY SUFFOCATED STOP HE HAD BEEN DOING WELL FAR BETTER THAN EXPECTED THANKS TO YOU JON STOP IF THIS ACCIDENT HAD NOT OCCURRED WE SHOULD HAVE BEEN SO HAPPY AS ALWAYS STOP BUT WE HAVE HAD THESE WEEKS TOGETHER AND THEY MUST LAST ME A LIFETIME STOP JEFF MUST BE BURIED HERE AS YOU KNOW STOP PRAY FOR HIM AND FOR ME TOO STOP ELIZABETH

Jonathan stood with the telegram in his hand and he thought of his friend and the valiant loving woman who had married him, and he felt ill with sadness. Only two days ago he had received a letter from Jeffrey, a buoyant letter full of hope and contentment and the surety that he would be eventually cured.

Jonathan thought of Jeffrey's hysterical mother, Elsie Holliday. He felt pity for her. She had lost everything she had. She could not even have the sorrow, beneficial, of seeing her son for the last time in his coffin. She could not arrive soon enough for his burial in the dark swamps of Louisiana.

The spinster lady cleared her chaste throat. "There is a veiled lady waiting for you in your office, Doctor. I told her there were no office hours until six o'clock, but she insisted! Really! Said she was a friend and this was a personal matter."

Jonathan went into the inner office. A small and fragile young lady waited for him in a dark blue linen suit and white frilled blouse and dark straw hat over which she had drawn a thick black veil to conceal her face. But he knew her at once.

"Well, Prissy!" he said. "Take that damned tent from your face, will you? You attract more recognition with it than without it."

She threw back the veil and he saw the real reason for it. Her face was very white and she had given up the paint pots since she had married Jonas Witherby and her eyes were red with sleeplessness and not with tears. He sat down near her and took her black-gloved hand and it was trembling. "Don't tell me the old bastard accidentally took another dose of arsenic and did himself in! That would be happy news, indeed."

She tried to smile. Her nice mouth was very pale and dry. "No, Jon, dear, I'm afraid that's not it. I can't stay but a minute or two. Oh, I wish he was dead! How could I have been such a fool to marry him? Just for money, as if I hadn't enough! That's greed for you, Jon."

"It's the old desire of women to be respectable, though God knows why they should care so long as they're comfortable and having a fine time of it. Well, what is the matter, Prissy? You aren't ill, are you?"

"No." She fumbled in her purse, took out a scented handkerchief and pressed it to her mouth. She regarded him with pain. "It's you, Jon."

He frowned, and again the weak and plunging sickness hit his middle. "What's wrong now?"

"Do you remember when you came to see Jonas recently, when I was so afraid of him? Well, after you left, he went up to his bedroom and closed the door and I don't know why I should have listened to him telephone. I never did before. He was calling Senator Campion, and he said they should have a talk, a little talk. And then he said, 'But we have to make very, very sure, Kent, and build up quite a case, here and there, so Ferrier will be finished once and for all.' That's what he said, Jon. 'Finished once and for all, not only in the state but in the whole country, too.'" She gave a little dry gasp. Then she took out a little golden case in which she kept her violet-scented Turkish cigarettes, and Jon lit one for her. Even over his anger and consternation he remembered the odor of those cigarettes in Prissy's little house, in her tasteful and gracious parlor where she met her friends, and friends they were.

"Oh, Jon, what did you ever do to the old son of a bitch that he should try to hurt you? Oh, you've joked with him and made fun of him to his face, but he always laughed and seemed to enjoy it."

"I don't think he did, Prissy, and I never intended that he should. I let him know that there was one in this town who knew all about his pious lies and sweet mouthings and Christian tolerance and soft pattings-of-arms, and tender voice." He got up, walked about slowly, then stood behind his desk, staring down blankly at it, rubbing a little dust with one dark finger. Prissy watched him with acute and loving anxiety. "A man will forgive you if you catch him in larceny, or even in a great lie, or if you best him in business or undercut him or rob him, or even if you run off with his wife or ravish his daughter. But he'll never forgive you for catching him out in hypocrisy, or calling him a psalm-singing rascal to his face. After all, he's spent a lifetime polishing up his public image as a saint, and garlanding it, and gilding it with a halo, and he washed that image's feet until they are as white as snow and arranged every damned fold in its heavenly toga. From childhood he has practiced the saintly voice as sedulously as a singer practices, until every modulation is full of music and prayerful sanctity and as round as an organ note. Then comes along a suicidal idiot like me and knocks the plaster image over and it cracks, and out crawl the black smelly worms of pure iniquity for everyone to see. No, Prissy. A man never forgives that."

"But, Jon, I've known a lot of bad men, and they even enjoyed being told they were bad—"

"But not one who pretended that he had the personal Ear of the Lord Himself. Old Jonas is a disaster, as I don't need to tell you. He's destroyed more people with his sweetness and light and loving voice and ways than a maniac will do with poison or a gun. And even his victims will tell you, with tremolos, that 'Jonas is such a good man, such a saint!' It wasn't his pawing fault that catastrophe happened to you, or you are sick at heart, or undone, or broken, or despairing, or scared out of your wits by menacing shadows. Oh, no. It was really your own fault. Jonas did everything he could to help you. Wasn't he always there, purring and fondling and sighing, and advising? Yes, indeed."

"I wish there was a way of getting away with murder!" said Prissy through her clenched white teeth. She beat her small knees with her gloved hands. Her large blue eyes flashed.

"So do I. I've thought the law was most unfair about murder," said Jon. "Murder is as deep an instinct in the human soul as self-preservation, or sex, and just as valid and perhaps just as healthy. After all, our cave ancestors practiced it with fervor and thought nothing of it. That still lies under our civilization, in spite of religion, and those who deny it are cowards afraid to face the truth or ashamed of it."

Jon came back to her and sat down.

"Jon, what do you think the old—scoundrel—is trying to do to you?"

"I don't know, my love. I wish I did."

"Why don't you go to him and ask?"

"And cause you trouble? No, Prissy. Besides, he'd just give me that darling haunted look of his, his precious innocent look, and be all bewildered and heartbroken. He might even burst into tears! No, Prissy, don't even think of leaving him. He can't live forever. Even the Devil gets impatient for his own at last and one of these days, soon I hope, you will be a rich and happy widow."

She was so deeply distressed for him that he made himself smile and he took her hand again. "Dear Prissy, I can fight my own battles, and what you've told me is not news to me. They can scheme and plot, but they can't hurt me, dear."

"Truly, Jon?"

"Truly."

She kissed him, and he kissed her pleasurably in return, and saw her out, veiled again, and Miss Forster stopped her typing and was full of curiosity. Before Jon went back into his office, she said, "Doctor, I deposited two large checks in your account three weeks ago for examinations you gave to two ladies last November—before—before—"

"Before my trial, dear. Yes. When did the money come in?"

"Oh, I forgot. They weren't checks. They were cash. Should I have put it in Dr. Morgan's account, seeing he bought your practice?" She looked as if she were about to cry, for she was very devoted to Jonathan.

"Well, no. They were old accounts. How much?"

"One was for fifty dollars, the other for seventy-five." She consulted her books. "A Miss Louise Wertner, and a Miss Mary Snowden. I receipted the bills and they took them away. Then I wanted to make a note in their folders, but there were no folders in your files." She frowned worriedly. "I know you throw away old cards and folders, Doctor, but you should wait at least three years. You never know."

"Never know what? We don't have income tax any longer, dear heart, to pay for any war. No use cluttering up your files." He recalled that he had thrown away Edna Beamish's record, too, and for some reason he felt a vague disquiet.

"Well, anyway," said Miss Forster with disapproval. She was very meticulous. "Do you recall those young women, Doctor?"

"From last November, with this place crowded to the eaves every day? And I also had other things to think about, if you recall. It was a time that could be lightly referred to as 'trying.' "

"Yes. But you must have seen them often, to have such large bills."

"They do seem large, don't they? They were typed on my letterhead, were they?"

"Yes, indeed, Doctor. I typed with this very Oliver. The 'd' is always crooked. It spoils the look of letters, reports and—"

"Take it up with Dr. Morgan and nag him into buying you a fine new Underwood. You deserve it, dear, after all these years with the Oliver."

She smiled at him dryly, and he went into his office and sat down and began to think. He forgot Miss Forster and her worries. Jonathan went over in his mind what Phil Harrington had told him, and Prissy. Vague but disagreeable. There was no doubt that his enemies were plotting something, and he could find no area in which he was vulnerable. Then he thought, But who is invulnerable to malice? He shrugged. Now he found an acid pleasure in speculating on what his enemies were up to, including Kenton Campion. They knew that the town was driving him out or that he could no longer endure living in it. What more did they want? His license had been restored to him the moment he was acquitted. (They had had no right, the State Medical Society, to insist on its revocation before the conclusion of the case, and he could have caused them some unpleasant moments, or he could have sued for malicious mischief and punitive damages, but he had been only too glad to drop the matter, even though the newspapers had been gleeful enough to print the news of the revocation of his license in large type, and be damned to the unlawfulness of it.)

Malpractice. Was some unknown former patient, man or

woman, about to sue him for malpractice? The procedure, in such a case, was for an attorney to approach a doctor and ask for an out-of-court settlement first, "to save notoriety and money and fees and costs." Besides, he could not recall a dissatisfied patient or one who had complained.

Jonathan's uneasy mind tried for ease, and he remembered that he had wanted to be a priest when he had been a boy. His mother had thought it absurd, and he had agreed within a year or two after she had expressed her outright opinion. Now he thought about it. It would have been a life, even in a leper colony or out in darkest Africa with the missions, far more tranquil than the one he had known since boyhood. There would have been no uncertainty but only certitude. No love for Mavis but only love for God. Had he not married Mavis, she would be alive now, probably the curse of some other man's life—or, ironically, probably that man's delight. He had loved God in those days, with a deep and almost terrible love, profound in its intensity. He recalled the quietly passionate transports he had experienced, the unquestioning knowledge, the fiery faith, and longing, the instants of ecstasy at Mass at the elevation of the Host, the depthless gratitude at receiving Holy Communion, the inner grieving cry, "Lord, I am not worthy that You come under my roof—" The High Masses, the rolling music, the incense, the unearthly colors on white walls as the sun struck through the stained-glass windows, the majesty of the ritual, the awe, the kneeling, the bowed head— Yes, there had been absolute certitude, beyond doubt, beyond skepticism.

Jonathan had had an encounter when he was seventeen, even before the episode of the hiking trip through the state, when he had come violently face to face with the God he so adored, and all the questions, and his faith had died at once, not dribbling away in a sickening little stream as it had been with Francis Campion. Could one call that faith, indeed, that it should have been murdered outright in one single hour or two? Or had it been only adolescent infatuation with the idea of God, a frequent affliction of adolescence? In every man's life, he had read in some pious book, there comes one appalling encounter with God—an encounter never to be forgotten —and thereafter a man adores more profoundly to the very death, or he gives only lip service to a lost and beloved memory—such as one gives the dead for whom one no longer sorrows.

Father McGuire had told him that his faith would not

have died so absymally, so abruptly, had it been faith indeed. But the priest was wrong. The irrevocable deaths come to the most vaulting love, the most vehement love, and the most intense faith. It is the lukewarm, contrary to general acceptance, who casually endure in love and faith, and if that love and faith are only coolly milky and faintly heated, they are at least viable, which was more than one could say of the shattered corpse of love and faith, the rotting corpse.

It was only recently that the world had taken on three dimensions again, had rounded out, had become fervent with color and vitality and youth. It had been resurrected with Jenny.

Love was of one piece. It was impossible to love, to know love fully, and then deny any part of it, whether it was love for God or love for a human being. A woman dearer than life, to a man, a beloved woman whom one could trust with one's life, inevitably brought the grandeur of God within the vision of a man again, and he saw again that the endless universes were charged with His glory. There lay all peace of mind, all invulnerability, all power of spirit, all fortitude—the "Shadow of a Great Rock in a weary land."

I wish I had it just now, thought Jonathan. But as if in the corner of his eye, he saw the eternal garden of tranquillity again, and this time there was no chasm at the end of it.

"The hell with the Campions and all the rest of them," he said, aloud.

He thought again of Jeffrey Holliday, and then he wrote out a check for Father McNulty and added a note: "You knew Jeff, I believe, and he is dead now, and so I am enclosing my check for twenty-five dollars as an offering, and hope that you will mention him in your prayers. By the way, I have inherited a large old house on Fordham Street, near St. Leo's, from a former patient, a dear old friend and my teacher, Ann Meadows, and it is yours—for that residence for nuns you are plotting to bring in for your confounded parochial school, if you can raise a bank loan. This is no incitement for you to harass me for further funds."

The mere writing of that flippant note to a young man of whom he was truly fond, and whom he respected, unaccountably lifted Jonathan's spirits. Now he would really have to corner Jenny and persuade her into a quick marriage, and then leave Hambledon with her.

Softly whistling, he went into his examination rooms, clean and empty and white. There, in the left corner of the second room was one of his big shining cabinets. It was filled with instruments, including the most complex for operations. These had been the gift of his father on the occasion of his entering medical school, and each fine steel instrument was engraved with his name in a flowing script. In those days every surgeon had his own personal instruments, engraved like these, which he carried with him, but since then the majority of hospitals supplied their own for surgeons, a progress toward asepsis in the operating room. Now these glittering instruments, for which his father had proudly paid a considerable fortune—they had silver handles, many of them, and silver sheaths—were unnecessary, including the large Morocco leather bag in which they had originally been carried. Jonathan had used them but four times in his surgical practice. They were anachronistic. He had often thought of sending them to some poor priest-physician-surgeon, and now was the time to think of donating the whole expensive outfit to the missions.

As they were so costly, Jonathan kept the key to this cabinet among his other keys. He stood before the cabinet and stared at the brave and shining array. That instrument for opening the skull: Its form had not been changed for thousands of years and was almost a replica of the instrument the ancient Egyptians had used. Fine old boys, the ancient practitioners. Modern medicine had hardly improved on them. They had had a high forceps of a sort for difficult births. These had been reinvented again only a few years ago. Christianity had done marvels in raising the moral stature of men, for helping to abolish slavery, for lifting degradation from women, for showing concern for children, for advancing education to the lowest common denominator—a debatable thing at the best—but it had certainly knocked hell out of the legacy of ancient medicine. It had debased the physician, for centuries, to a mere midwife, or a bloodletter, or a brewer of herbs and nostrums—a scurvy and starving servant fit only for contempt. The art of medicine had been relegated perilously close to the practice of witchcraft or, at the worst, considered as a survival of "Paganism." "Good" Christians did not become ill unless they were also "sinners," and the worse the illness the worse the sinner. You'd have thought, Jonathan reflected now, that the Black Death would have thrown that into the garbage pail, but it did not—until almost within recent memory. We probably owe the fact that there are any human beings left at all to the skill of the "perfidious" Jewish physicians throughout the centuries, who religiously and with loving kindness had disastrously decided to keep humanity alive. For that they had been repaid with hatred, and that was probably a just fate, at that.

What was that from Genesis: "For the imagination of man's heart is evil from his youth." Yes, and William Hazlitt, in the same context of thought, had said, "There is not a more mean, stupid, dastardly, pitiful, selfish, spiteful, ungrateful animal than the public. It is the greatest of cowards, for it is afraid of itself." True. It was that "public" which had condemned him, Jonathan Ferrier, before he had even been arrested or convicted, and had shown not only extreme disappointment when he was acquitted but in resentment was now driving him from his native town. He still did not know why. It had been hinted to him, time after time, by those who cared for him, that perhaps a little diplomacy was needed by him, a little tact, a little evasion, a little creaming-over of obvious ineptitude and stupidity, "in the name of Christian charity." But that "Christian charity" would have cost the lives of many helpless patients at the hands of diploma-mill hacks or it would have permitted some outrageous social wrongs.

For Jonathan Ferrier was the organizer for, and the sponsor for, the Hambledon Association for the Abolition of Child Labor. He had cared for many little children who had been wounded and smashed in the local mills and yards. He had come to them when they had been weltering, dead, in their own blood. He had not used "loving" language to the mill owners, nor creamy words to soothe their sensibilities, nor had he exercised "Christian charity." He had only called them the Assassins of the Innocents. He had spent a large part of his own money to establish other associations throughout the state and had hounded Senators and Congressmen and Governors, and had put huge advertisements in many great newspapers. The associations had grown enormously, and it was predicted that within a short time child labor would be illegal. Needless to say, Jonathan was not loved by those whom he had so deeply offended in their purses—and their morals.

When he had been younger, he had honestly believed that a good cause carried its own good strength with it, that a righteous idea could never be suppressed but must be ultimately victorious. He was not so certain about that now—but unfortunately he still had remnants fluttering about in his mind, and that kept his tongue abrasive, his manner openly contemptuous when among hypocrites, and his temper finely honed.

He came to himself in his examination room, before his glass cabinet of instruments.

Then he noticed a little gap on one shelf. He bent closer. Some instrument was missing. He tested the door; it was locked. But someone had taken an instrument from the cabinet. He went into the other examination room, frowning, wondering if Robert Morgan could have done this, and then he searched the other room, also. It was foolish to suspect Robert. He had high instincts of privacy, and besides, he did not need these particular instruments. The other examination room had a host of ordinary ones for office procedure, though not for major surgery? Jonathan frowned. When was the last time he had opened this cabinet? A year? Two years? Once a year he carefully dusted the instruments himself, because of their value and their association. Had he done that last year? He could not remember.

He stood and frowned and considered, looking at the empty space. Someone had tried to move slender instruments together to conceal the spot, but its impression was on the original white satin which Adrian had insisted be laid on the glass shelves. A narrow long depression. Now, what was it? Jonathan slowly turned over in his mind all the instruments, counting them, thinking of them. Then he knew. It was a curette.

Why would anyone want a curette, and who had taken it? It was a sharp and chancy instrument, and had to be used with the utmost care or a womb could be perforated when the products of a spontaneous abortion or a miscarriage had to be removed. Special training was needed for the use of a curette. Only in cases with threatened sepsis did a man use it, or if there was danger of a hemorrhage.

Jonathan minutely examined the depression where the curette had lain and saw that it was faintly peppered with dust. So, the instrument had been gone a considerable time, and not lately. He went out to Miss Forster and said, "Has anyone unauthorized been in my offices when I wasn't present, or Dr. Morgan absent?"

"Why, no, I'd never permit that, Doctor! I believe I know my duties! Of course, there was that veiled lady who claimed to be a friend—"

"No, no, dear. I should think several months ago, at least."

"Never!" said Miss Forster, with emphasis. "Why, is something missing, Doctor? After all, there are prowlers—"

"Who had my key, of course, and took only one instrument, and then carefully relocked my cabinet and restored my key."

Miss Forster seemed ready to cry, so Jonathan patted her shoulder, told her it was probably a mistake, his mistake, and went out for his horse and his ride to his farm.

CHAPTER TWENTY-SEVEN

A gray heat haze hung over the cities of the valley. No rain had fallen for nearly three weeks and the river was low and tributary streams were dry in their beds, with boulders roundly blazing in the sun. Lawns browned in town, but on the mountainsides, where springs and deep brooks still spurted, the grass was green and flowers burned. There was a tense and breathless expectancy in the absolutely immobile air, as if before a conflagration, but in spite of the constant prophesies of rain and thunder, nothing stirred and trees prematurely dried and filled gutters with crisp brown heaps. A sick languor overcame nearly everyone, and children, afflicted with what mothers called "second-summer complaint," became ill and an unprecedented number of them died.

"We tell them, over and over," said Robert with exhaustion, to Jonathan Ferrier, "to boil the milk and the water they feed their infants, to keep all butter and perishable food on ice, and they smile at us knowingly and talk of 'summer cholera' or 'summer complaint,' even while their children sicken and die or dehydrate themselves with vomiting and diarrhea. We still have diarrhea as the chief cause of death among young children, and even older ones, but we can't make people take precautions."

"Just as Lister and Pasteur and Semmelweis struggled against public apathy and stupidity for too long," said Jonathan. "I've been advocating for years that tubercular cattle be destroyed, and I am called 'the enemy of the poor farmer,' wishing to deprive him of his precious herds just for a 'fad.' I've tried to get the Board of Health to prohibit the sale of all milk that isn't pasteurized and to demand universal pasteurization, and I'm just a 'new-fangled faddist.' I've even been reprimanded by that congregation of imbeciles, the State Medical Society, which tried to revoke my license less than a year ago. If there is one rule this idiot world insists upon it is 'Never disturb people.' Never cause them concern; never bring political mountebankery or malfeasance to their attention; never kick a popular hero in his buttocks; never ask them to do something for the good of their community; never demand that they practice some sort of hygiene; never hint that their country needs a long hard look, especially at Washington. Never preach disaster. Never tell the truth. That's the way to a serene life."

"Well, St. Paul did say, 'Never kick against the pricks,' " said Robert, wiping a round face unusually pale with heat and fatigue. "The pricks are always public opinion, public will."

"Hah," said Jonathan. "In modern words, you mean 'You can't fight City Hall.' Well, I've been fighting City Hall most of my life and it is practically the only pleasure I have, outside of a lady or two. You may not be able to defeat City Hall, but it rouses up your blood, and once in a while you can get in an uppercut. How many kids, in our practice, have died this week?"

"Eight."

"And all we can give them is paregoric, and give their mothers advice. The children's hospital wards are full, but even in the hospital they don't boil the milk and water. One of these days we are going to have a fine epidemic of typhoid unless something is done to purify the water at the source or people boil it. It's a strange thing. We doctors sweat our lives out trying to educate people into staying alive, and invariably they smirk and kill themselves. With the help of the Doctor Boguses. Do you recall that in 1873 Sir John Erichsen, the 'eminent' physician and surgeon, said, 'There cannot always be fresh fields of conquest by the knife; there must be portions of the human frame that will ever remain sacred from its intrusions, at least in the surgeon's hands. That we have already, if not quite, reached these final limits, there can be little question. The abdomen, the chest, and the brain will be forever shut from the intrusion of the wise and humane surgeon.'

"Yet the old boys, thousands of years ago, did so 'intrude,' and many of their patients lived. Now we are 'intruding,' too. Cheer up. In spite of stupidity, we do advance a little. We now have spinal anesthesia, thanks to James Leonard Corning of New York, in 1885, and we are tentatively giving some thought to Mendelian laws, and one of these days, perhaps soon, we'll be able to give blood transfusions safely. Yes, we do advance. And we do have State Health Departments now, so we can look forward to some end to the general carnage of ignorance. But you can be sure that new stupidities will jump up like toadstools as the old ones are destroyed. The human race never learns."

"You're no Utopian, I see."

"Of course not. No sane man ever was or is. That presupposes a change in human nature, but it hasn't changed one iota in recorded history. Besides, it would be damned boring. Imagine a world where everyone is 'happy'! Happiness never created a great picture, a great book, a great idea, a great statue, a great symphony. It never invented anything. It is just mental constipation. But unhappiness, the 'divine discontent,' releases human energy and creativeness—though I must admit it releases the swine of Gadarene, too. If it reveals the face of God, it also shows the Devil in full color. Still, I prefer activity to 'happiness.' Do you remember what Emerson said, 'Every reform is only a mask under cover of which a more terrible reform, which dares not yet name itself, approaches.' True. But I'm all for liveliness, good or bad."

"Iconoclast," said Robert, sighing, and rang for the next patient.

"Well, to follow Emerson's thought, one of these days the old idols will fall, and maybe we'll get a few frightful Molochs in their place."

The island, in the quiet and sinking river, was cooler than the mainland, for what breeze stirred did ruffle the trees and enter the open windows. But the water had a brazen look, molten and still, and seemed to exude heat by itself, though the sky was far and pale blue and burning. The springs that fed the earth kept the grass green and the trees in glistening leaf and the gardens flourishing, but every stone was hot and the little castle seemed to palpitate as if afire inside. Dust ran in little twirls along the paths, and there was a fetid smell from the various ponds. The boats lay on barely wet stones and had to be pushed far out into the water before they floated.

Jenny sat in the library reading, with the shutters half closed. The large long room, in its duskiness, gave the illusion of coolness, but her flesh stuck to the leather upholstery and her face was damp. She wore a thin brown skirt of linen and a severe shirtwaist, open at the throat, and she had pinned her hair high on her head for coolness and it rose in a largely untidy black mound over her pale face. Harald never came into this room, and so to her it was a sort of sanctuary, just as she had small hidden grottoes on the island where she often sat, and about which Harald did not know, he not having much curiosity about the island.

The library door opened, and to Jenny's consternation and anger Harald entered, his handsome face reserved, though he smiled affably enough when his eyes met Jenny's vexed ones. He held a sheaf of paper in his hand. When Jenny jumped up to leave, he said, "Please give me a moment. This is very important—to you, Jenny. To you. They are outlines for legal papers."

"Consult my lawyers," said Jenny, closing her notebooks and preparing to leave.

"I already have. And these papers are the result. For God's sake, Jenny, this is most important for you."

"Nothing you have to say—" said Jenny, but she did not run out. She watched him darkly as he continued to advance into the room.

"It isn't what I 'say,' Jenny, it is what your lawyers and mine say." He sat down near a table. "Sit down. Please." His hazel eyes studied her gravely, and they shone with seriousness, and Jenny was reluctantly impressed in spite of herself. She sat down stiffly on the edge of her chair and tightly folded her hands on her knee. She stared rigidly at a point on his broad white forehead, and waited, filled with revulsion and hatred.

Harald picked up the papers and studied them, and did not look at her. "Jenny, you know I don't like this island. I detest that part of your mother's will which states that I must spend at least seven consecutive months here, or I lose the very nice income from her large estate, which is held in trust for you and which will be yours when I die. My income is thirty thousand dollars a year, sometimes considerably more, depending on the dividends of the investments. That isn't a sum one gives up lightly."

"You intend to give it up?" Jenny was astounded. "You mean, you will leave the island—forever?"

"That is entirely up to you, Jenny."

She could not believe it. The tense lines of her young face relaxed in wonder and tremulous hope. Seeing that, Harald was filled with genuine and very deep pain and sadness. He looked at the papers intently and rattled them.

"You see, Jenny," he said, and his voice was very gentle, "I am establishing myself as quite a famous artist. That doesn't interest you, I know. But I did excellently in Philadelphia. I have five fine orders. I can sell all I produce. But I don't want to stay here, for the place stifles me. I know that hurts you, but it does. When your mother was alive, we weren't here a great deal of the time. We traveled. We were free. We had some happy times—"

Jenny made a curious sound, and Harald looked up and saw the dense bitterness on the girl's face and the sudden aliveness of emotion.

"Yes, we did, Jenny. Your mother and I were very happy together, though you choose not to believe it. It was an arrangement—it satisfied us both. An arrangement. I was very fond of your mother. What did you say?" he asked, as again she made that smothered sound.

"Never mind, Harald. I'm not interested in your 'happy times' with my mother. Go on with your important business. You said you wished to leave."

"Yes." The sadness was like an old sickness in him, and the longing for her was the greatest hunger he had ever known. "Now, if I leave, I forfeit all the income from the estate. I'm prepared to do that under one condition. I have made a contract here—a contract with you. It is true that you are still a minor, but the lawyers will act in your behalf, if you are willing and give your consent." (He knew this was not true.)

"When I permanently leave, you will immediately come into the millions left in trust by your mother. I will make it short. If you, when you come into that money, will give me only three hundred thousand dollars of it, I will sign away my right to the lifetime income from the estate. A lump sum of three hundred thousand dollars. I will then leave you to both the money and the island. Do you understand?"

"Yes." She was more astounded than ever and now began to tremble with her hope and rising joy.

Is it hopeless? he thought. Jenny, Jenny, Jenny! He said, "Do you want to read these two contracts, yours and mine, now?"

"Please." She extended her hand for them, and he reached toward her and gave them to her. Her hands shook, but she read clearly and steadily. "I, Jenny Louise Heger, hereby contract to deliver to Harald Farmington Ferrier the sum of three hundred thousand dollars, from the estate of my late mother, Myrtle Schiller Heger Ferrier, which will revert to me, when the said Harald Farmington Ferrier gives up all his rights to the income of the estate and departs from the residence on the island called Heart's Ease and never returns. He is to leave me in full possession of the residence and the estate, with no later demands and upon his recorded oath that he has relinquished all rights to said residence and estate forevermore, of his own free will and desire."

There was considerably more, and Jenny's rapid eye went over it quickly, suspicious of any fraud. Then she read Harald's contract. "In consideration of the sum of ($300,000) three hundred thousand dollars from the estate of my late wife, Myrtle Schiller Heger Ferrier, I hereby relinquish all rights to said estate and the residence called Heart's Ease, and will leave said estate and residence and never return—"

Jenny let out a long and audible breath. Her intensely blue eyes shone like cobalt. She almost smiled at Harald.

"Tomorrow," he said, "you and I will have to go to the lawyers and sign these contracts before witnesses. Are you willing?"

"Yes. Yes!" She spoke with fervor.

He held out his hand for the papers and she gave them to him. Then he sat in silence and looked at her, and her face was soft and young and sternly sweet, and she seemed to be in an ecstatic dream. He watched her for a considerable time. Of what was she thinking, this quiet and enigmatic girl, so young and naïve and unworldly, which made her face shine so brilliantly, and her parted lips acquire a deep rose?

"You will understand that this is a big sacrifice I am making, Jenny?" he said at last. She started. Her eyes stared at him for a moment without recognition.

"Sacrifice?"

"Yes. That money is scarcely ten years' income for me, from your mother's estate. I will be only forty-three—if I choose to spend thirty thousand a year, as I have been doing —when the money is gone. Do you appreciate that sacrifice, Jenny? I am in good health, and could live into my seventies on this island, and my income would come to me steadily, and would probably increase. Hundreds of thousands of dollars, at the very least. Yet, I am willing to give it up—to please you."

"I—I thought you said this place stifles you—"

He smiled, and his hazel eyes regarded her kindly. "So it does. But still, I have five free months to go where I will— and receive the income and security. A man can endure a lot for thirty thousand dollars a year for life!"

She was confused, and frowned at him, trying to understand.

"You've made it painful for me to stay here, Jenny."

"Painful?" Now she colored unbecomingly.

"Yes. Still, one can stand a lot of pain for thirty thousand dollars a year for life. What is ten years' income—and freedom—compared with that?"

"Then—then, why are you doing it?"

He laid the papers on a table and looked at them, and his profile was somber and she had never seen him like that before, and for the first time his handsomeness did not offend her and she was not revolted by his mass of curling ruddy hair. But still she trembled with eagerness never to see him again, never to hear his voice or his footsteps.

He began to speak slowly, still looking at the papers as if reading from them. "Jenny, I've said you've made it painful for me to live here. You've been ugly and unpleasant and— and almost savage—toward me since your mother died. Before that, you were friendly and even laughed with me. Perhaps you were embittered by her will. In a way, I don't blame you. I should have felt the same under the same circumstances. It was an affront to an only child, an only daughter, and your mother loved you dearly, Jenny. I never did understand that will. I wanted Myrtle to change it—"

"I know!" Now her face became dark and furious and pent. "I know you overheard her telling me, in the hall, that she knew she had done me an injustice and that she was going to change her will! That was only two days before she died!"

He showed no surprise, for he had heard that revelation

from his mother months ago. "Yes, that is quite true, Jenny. And I was glad."

"Glad!" She jumped to her feet, bent toward him stiffly in hard and violent rage, and spoke through clenched teeth. "You were so glad that you and your brother plotted together to kill my mother before she could change her will! I heard you both! And he did, he did! That murderer!"

He turned absolutely white. He stood up, very slowly, and confronted her. He tried to speak, wet his lips, then tried again. His voice was queer to his own ringing ears when he said, "Are you mad, entirely mad? Have you gone out of your mind?" His eyes dilated and became fixed, like amber.

She made a disordered and fierce gesture.

"Do you think I cared about that money? Do you think it was important to me? Do you think I was outraged at my mother's will? It was her money, her money! She could do with it as she wished, as far as I was concerned! It meant nothing to me, nothing at all. But her—her—life—it meant everything to me, and she was killed to prevent her changing her will, and you can lie and lie—what a liar you always were!—and nothing will ever change the truth!"

He looked involuntarily at the shut door, and his pale face was sick and changed. "Jenny, lower your voice. How can you think that of me, and Jon?" He was trembling himself now. "So, that was what has been wrong since your mother died. Jenny, Jenny, you are insane. Believe me, I am convinced you are insane."

"Insane!" She threw back her head so far and with such fury that the muscles in her neck stood out like white ropes. She laughed, and it was a short and awful sound. "That's all you can say, in your guilt—and you know you are guilty! You and your brother, the doctor!"

He caught one of her stiff arms and held her and when she tried to pull away from him, he held her tighter. "Listen to me, you fool," he said in a low voice. "Listen to me instead of your crazy imaginings. Your mother died of a heart attack. She knew she was dying for months, but she didn't want you and me to know, and made my brother pledge his silence. But after she was dead, he told me. She was a brave woman. She preferred not to make us unhappy before it was time. A brave woman. She knew she could die any moment, but she said nothing to us. I won't have your insanity hurt her now, Jenny, I won't have it!"

She tried harder to pull away from him, frenzied, and now

he let her go and she reeled with a sudden release and had to catch the back of a chair to keep from falling headlong. He stood and looked at her with his set face and it was the face of a stranger to her, cold and rigorous and condemning. In spite of her wild rage and hate she became confusedly quiet.

"I'll have a doctor examine you, Jenny, and have you put away until you are cured of your mad obsession. I mean it, Jenny. But before I do that, I want to know how you acquired that twisted idea, for you have a twisted mind, Jenny, a strange and peculiar and inhuman mind."

"Very well, I'll tell you!" she cried, and now tears ran down her face and her breath caught in her throat. "It was the night she died. Your brother came here to see her, and then you both went downstairs into the hall, talking, almost whispering, together, and I was frightened about my mother. I knew she was sick but not very sick. Jon was treating her. He came almost every day. I thought you two were hiding something from me and so I crept down the stairs, you didn't see me, and I heard you both almost whispering together in the hall."

She stopped, swallowed, gasped. A lifetime of grief and suffering stifled her breath. She put her hand to her throat and choked, and then she moaned.

"Go on," said Harald in his brother's own relentless voice.

"I—I didn't hear it all, but enough! I heard him say '—I gave her an injection. Don't give her the digitalis she's been taking. Throw it away. That injection may do it.'"

Harald's face became like Jon's, closed and hard and drawn.

"Go on," he said with quietness.

"She needed that digitalis to keep her alive! But you took it away, and I couldn't find it! And then—and then—two hours later she died—after what he gave her, that injection!"

Jenny put her hands over her face.

He waited. His face was slimy with sweat. When Jenny finally dropped her hands, he saw her abysmal pain and despair, but he was not moved.

"Did your mother ask for her digitalis, Jenny?"

"No! But I always gave it to her at night, the last thing, and I couldn't find it. I wanted to ask her, but the—the thing —your brother gave her—it made her drowsy. I think she went into a coma— Oh, God, I don't know! But she never woke up."

Then Harald shook his head slowly and dazedly and sat down and regarded the floor in silence.

The girl was sobbing now, heaving dry sobs that shook her whole body. She held to the back of a chair and bent her whole body in her anguish. At last the sounds she made penetrated Harald's stupefaction, and he looked at her, and then he was full of pity.

"Jenny, Jenny," he said. "That night when Jon came, he found she was practically *in extremis*. He thought of the hospital but decided she was too ill to be moved. She had been in very bad pain all that day, and she never said a word to us, did she? But I knew she was more ill than usual, and I sent for Jon, and he came. He said there was one last thing he could try, something new. Adrenalin. She was in shock, and dying. Jon stayed with her until she was a little relaxed, but he told me in her bedroom that she could not live, though perhaps there was some small hope. He'd come the next morning. But she died in the night, as you know."

"You lie, you lie! You wanted her money! That's all you married her for—her money!" But Jenny, of a sudden, looked stunned. "And—you had her killed! You wanted her to die before she could change her will!"

"Oh, Jenny, you fool. Jenny, do you remember that your mother's—your mother—was taken to the hospital the next morning? You were so broken that you didn't ask why. But I knew. Jon wanted an autopsy. Autopsies are important to doctors. I gave my consent. I was sorry, afterward, thinking of Myrtle's body— But, by God, I am glad now! God, how glad I am! Your consent wasn't necessary. The husband makes the decision. Your mother's—heart—it was closely examined by at least five doctors besides Jon. It was a classic case of what they call myocardial infarction. I think that means a big blood clot. In a way, her heart disease had had nothing to do with it. It could happen to anyone, but it was worse for her, having a weak heart. They wondered how she had survived those hours before Jon arrived. In fact, one of the doctors wrote about it in a medical magazine—with photographs."

"You lie," Jenny whispered. It was only a whisper. But a glazed look of horror began to spread over her face.

Harald sighed and shrugged. "Jenny, the hospital records are there for you to read for yourself. Go to St. Hilda's tomorrow, see Dr. Louis Hedler, and ask to see the records. As Myrtle's daughter, he won't refuse you. Or"—and now he laughed with something close to contempt—"do you think all the doctors, including Hedler, are in league with Jon and me? Perhaps you think all of Hambledon conspired with Jon to 'murder' your mother."

Jenny collapsed into a chair. She looked at him with huge eyes in a gray face. She could not speak.

"To think," said Harald, "that on the basis of a little suspicious and ugly eavesdropping, you could think my brother, a reputable physician, would plot with me to kill your mother! For what? Some of her money? She was fond of me, Jenny. I know she intended to change her will. She meant to give half her estate to me and half to you—with no damnable provision to jail me on this detestable island for seven months of my life, every year. We discussed it, Jenny, before she even mentioned it to you."

He shook his head over and over, then put his elbows on his knees and dropped his head into his hands.

"It's all Pete's fault," he said, as if speaking to himself. "He twisted you, shut you away from life, from people, and I have a disgusting idea why he did it. You were his princess, he said. Your mother told me. You were his darling. He wouldn't ever let you get away into a sane and normal life, for then you'd see things in perspective, see a whole world you had been missing. You'd leave him, eventually, for somebody else, some other man. Are you following me, Jenny, into the sewer that was your father's mind? Don't look at me like that, Jenny. I might be sorry for you, after all your accusations, and I don't want to be sorry yet. I think I want to laugh at you a little, to despise you a little, though I know it isn't your fault. It is your fantasies, the fantasies your father encouraged in you, so you'd never leave him. He built up a world of madness for you, to make you afraid of others, to suspect dragons in every corner, to mistrust everybody. To keep you shut in. For himself."

He dropped his hands. "I have some letters your mother wrote to me, when I was in New York, before we were married. We were engaged. She wrote that she hoped that the normal life we could bring to you, together, would change and free you once and for all. I'll give you the letters tonight, Jenny. I never wanted you to see them, but I think you need the punishment."

He stood up, very weary and shaken. He looked down at the girl, whose head had fallen on her breast. He dearly wanted to touch that mound of black hair, like shining glass.

He wanted to hold and comfort her tenderly, without passion. She was suddenly a broken child to him. Jenny, Jenny, he thought. This will pass. You're young, and you'll recover. And then, perhaps, there'll be some hope for me, after the nightmare you've been living.

But Jenny was thinking, Jon, Jon, Jon. How can I ever look at you again, Jon? How dare I look at you? Oh, Jon, can you ever forgive me? I must have been out of my mind. I was willing to believe anything of Harald. But how could I have believed it of you?

That night when she could finally go upstairs, weak and quivering, she found her mother's letters on her table, and she read them all, weeping.

If Jenny did not sleep that night, neither did Harald Ferrier to any extent.

His gesture to Jenny concerning her mother's estate was at least partially sincere. He found the island more and more distasteful, and the months he was compelled to spend here were months he designated to his friends in New York, Boston and Philadelphia as "my penal servitude." It was not to his modern taste or habits and he found it oppressive. He was restive every moment he spent there, for since early childhood he had despised Hambledon and had dreamed of a more cosmopolitan existence than the slow tide of the town. Affable and handsome and engaging though he was, he had few or no real friends in Hambledon, for it was not in his nature to become attached overmuch in friendships and society. Moreover the people were inclined to become very partisan in politics or mores, and very emotional over many things, and Harald by temperament was not partisan or emotional. He found both boring. His was the easy way, the pleasant way, the enjoyable calm way—accepting rather than declining, and never at any time taking a definite stand about anything.

But he loved Jenny. At first he was amused at the very idea and found it novel. Later, experiencing its pains, he found the condition of being in love disturbing yet exciting. He truly wanted the girl, but he wanted her without the island. In offering to return the estate to her, he was also returning the detested island. He had believed that her infuriated and constant antagonism toward him since her mother's death had been due to her anger that she had been treated so indifferently by that mother, for Harald, in spite of his agreeable and casual approach to life, valued money above all else. He could not conceive that others would be uninterested. In giving Jenny her mother's estate he believed that he would have removed both her antagonism and her reason for rejecting him. Like his brother, Jonathan, he had found women always ready for light romances and always susceptible to him. He had no reason, therefore, to believe that Jenny was an exception.

Had she not flown at him like a wild young eagle, all talons and slashing beak and blue fury, his next step after her acceptance of his conditions would have been a gentle reminder that he loved her. He had had it all planned, like a stage scene. Her rush of gratitude and joy over the prospect of receiving all of her mother's money, and the island to boot, would have softened her, made her take him seriously, made her think that money was not everything to Harald Ferrier but that she was. No woman could have helped being flattered and touched by such devotion and sacrifice, especially as the obstruction had been removed. In a few days— for Jenny was a thoughtful girl—she would begin to feel kindness for him and regret that she had treated him so vilely and so unjustly. The future would then be inevitable.

His part in the script had been letter-perfect. Then the script had gone mad. Jenny had at first responded as she was intended to respond, but after that she had lost her Harald-written speeches and words of gratitude and begun an impromptu speech of her own. The play was in ruins thereafter, the characters uttering whatever they desired to utter with a total disregard of the playwright—Harald Ferrier. He had intended a comedy-melodrama along graceful lines, with urbane periods and poetic intimations. It had become a tragic farce, a tragi-comedy.

He lay on his bed—or rather, Myrtle's bed—sweltering in the heat, which would not relent, and stared at the hot stars and the hot moon and did not know whether to curse mildly or laugh. Poor old Jon. It was not enough for him to have been accused of two murders but tonight he had been accused of another, and the last so absurd, so contrived in the mind of that poor silly girl, who suspected everyone and everything, that even Jon would find it excruciatingly funny. One of these days, when Jenny and I are married, thought Harald, turning over his hot pillow, I'll tell him about it. He has no sense of humor, only a brutal wit. Still, he should find it funny as well as incredible.

It was not Harald's intention at all to relinquish his dead wife's estate to Jenny and also resign his rights to the island if Jenny should remain adamant to his proposal. Should she continue to refuse him, then he would not sign those contracts. His little speech about seeing their mutual lawyers tomorrow had been only to shock her into noticing him, for the first time, as a heroic and sacrificing figure, attractive, benign, loving, devoted. Well, tomorrow was another day. He would pretend utmost hurt over her accusations, and would not let himself forgive her so soon, and so he would take time to "think" the matter over carefully.

He had indeed been shaken, and considerably frightened and alarmed, at Jenny's mad accusations but not for long. He knew a great deal more about erratic human nature and its irrational storms than did his brother, and nothing much surprised, jolted or bewildered him. So his first consternation was not long in disintegrating, leaving him more and more amused by the moment, and feeling more and more pity for Jenny, who had carried this bloody suspicion so long in her naïve mind. Jenny, Jenny, he thought with affection, if I had indeed wanted to do away with your mother, I'd have done it with far more finesse and certainly would not have trusted Jon, or dreamed of trusting him to help me. How little you know of anybody!

Now his usual urbanity and tranquil spirits returned, and he at last fell asleep, reflecting that if Jenny married him or not, he would still have the income from her mother's vast estate. But he did not permit himself to think that Jenny would actually reject him. After all, who else wanted her, who would marry a girl with a small income of one hundred dollars a month, with only prospects, it is true, of eventually inheriting a great estate? But those prospects were far in the future, and young men had little faith in the future. They wanted the Now.

With Jenny as his wife he would not only have the one woman he had ever wanted to marry with any desire and passion and love, but he would have that lovely money as well. They would sell that damned island or rent it. It meant nothing to Harald as he drifted off into a peaceful sleep. He had a happy dream that the island had been broken and smashed by a hurricane and he and Jenny, aboard a luxurious liner, watched it drift away in chunks. And laughed.

CHAPTER TWENTY-EIGHT

Robert Morgan walked gloomily through the house his mother and he had bought. It was a beautiful house, of noble proportions, and not afflicted by the Victorian "wood lace" which Jonathan Ferrier so despised and which he had taught Robert to despise also. But Jane Morgan, who had been born in that very sort of a Victorian house, deemed it beautiful and "refined" and indicative of "culture" and taste. So she had brought the heaviest and the ugliest of her inherited furniture to this house in Hambledon, and had hung the darkest and most impenetrable draperies at the windows—which she had also swathed in somber lace—and the shining floors had been covered from wall to wall with dim carpets. She kept the shutters at least half shut and so a house once radiant with light became dusky and secretive and cold. Every possible corner was crowded with "antiques" of dubious value, and cabinets leaned darkly against pale paneled walls filled with what Jane conceived of as *objets d'art* but which had been made lavishly in factories in Sèvres in imitation of Dresden and Meissen. Marble fireplaces had their mantel-pieces draped in dull velvet, red or brown or deep blue, with ponderous fringes, and upon this velvet she had placed fraudulent ormulu clocks, false Staffordshire ware, tall vases corroded with gilt and of weird and depressing shapes, conch shells, little china trays, and crystal holders filled with dried flowers or wisps of pussywillow.

Even the big mirrors she installed here and there reflected only swart shadows, dejected images, shut and looming doors. The whole effect suggested dinginess, funereal sullenness. It did not seem the same house Robert had bought, airy, bright, clean, the windows glittering, the doors opening on gardens.

After the second night she had spent in the changed house she said to her son, "Robert, the birds are very disturbing in this town, very disturbing indeed. They awaken me early in the morning and impinge on my nervous state. I have not been able to sleep for more than eight or nine hours a night since we were unfortunate enough to arrive here."

Robert looked about him and was more depressed than ever. Was it possible that he had never noticed before how vile and uncouth his mother's taste was, and how coarse? But he had seen the Ferrier house and other houses of light and comfort in Hambledon, including the house of the Kitcheners, which, though it did not possess the elegance and charm of the Ferrier house still had distinction of color, openness and warmth and innocent gaiety and homeliness. How could he have dreamed of bringing Jenny Heger to this house—which he now referred to as "my mother's house"? His mother had cleverly, and as if with malice, destroyed every perspective, every grace.

He said, "Mother, I don't find the birds disturbing. And you are not an invalid. It isn't normal to sleep for more than nine or even eight hours."

"Robert! Have you forgotten that I am indeed an invalid and have arthritis?"

"None of your joints are swollen."

"You have not seen my—limbs—or my feet, nor have you felt the pain in my shoulders and my back. I do not understand you, Robert. I have done everything to please you, consented to this little town, to this home, which I did not admire from the beginning. There were other homes more suitable—"

"Houses," said Robert.

Jane raised her voice imperatively. "I repeat, I do not understand you, Robert! We were discussing the birds. Can we not trap them or at least buy one or two cats to destroy them! How the Almighty could create such noisy creatures, to disturb the peace of humanity, is beyond my comprehension! Once I rather admired them but do so no longer. They are surely useless—"

"Mother," said Robert, "if all the birds in the world disappeared, man could not survive more than seven years thereafter. That is a scientific fact. You don't like these beautiful trees either, and I believe you mentioned that you 'wondered'

why God had made them, too. If trees disappeared from the
face of the earth, we should soon have only a desert in which
we could not live. Rainfall would cease, grass would die, and
we'd become a barren world. It is only mankind," said Robert in a louder and relishing tone, "who could disappear totally and never be missed by anything which lives. To tell the
truth, he's a worthless creature!"

Jane looked at him narrowly. "I must say, Robert, that you
sound like your dear friend, Dr. Ferrier. Blasphemous. Did
not the Almighty make man to have dominion over this
world and the rule of everything? Then, everything else could
disappear—and in many cases it would be an improvement
—and man would still be triumphantly alive."

"Not at all," said Robert. "He would be dead, and sometimes, during my contacts with my dear fellowman, I think
that would be a delightful consummation. Seeing that you are
quoting the Bible—again—let me remind you that it states
that God made the creatures of the earth, the land and the
sea and the sky, and forests and lakes and streams, before He
inflicted man on them, and He blessed them first. If He did,
indeed, give man 'dominion' over these blameless things, then
it was not to incontinently destroy them or injure them but to
protect them, for surely they are beautiful and man is as
surely not."

"Blasphemy!" cried Jane with horror.

"I have begun to believe," said Robert, looking again
about the large and dreary room which Jane had designated as
the parlor, "that man is the blasphemy by his very existence."

"That is not Christian, Robert!"

Robert was enjoying himself. "It may not be Christian in
your sense of the word, Mother, but it is certainly true. The
cities are beginning to encroach on the countryside all over
the world. If they were at least beautiful, and if they respected the world, and cherished it and guarded its resources,
that would not matter too much, though I dread the thought
that there won't be any quiet sanctuaries in the future, and
no blessed silences, and only the discordant voices of people.
However, I probably won't be here then, and that's one blessing of mortality.

"Incidentally," said Robert, more and more enjoying himself and getting revenge for the destruction of his beautiful
house, "I believe the Bible mentions that only man is corrupt,
full of sin, vicious, murdering for murder's sake, and practically irredeemable. Not even the serpent or the tiger—and

not even the mosquito or housefly—is condemned in such vigorous language. 'Man is wicked from his birth and evil from his youth.' I don't recall that said about tadpoles or the lowly louse or bedbug. Just about men."

Jane had begun to smirk in a peculiar way. "I see that your friend has really changed your Christian attitude, Robert. But—and how grateful I am for this!—he won't be here much longer!"

"True," said Robert, and it came to him that in spite of what had happened, apparently with such lightness between him and Jonathan, he would miss Jonathan more than he had thought it possible to miss another human being. As he was young and optimistic, he had almost recovered from the shock of that day's encounter, and had seen Jenny a number of times on the island, and she had been shyly kind and had welcomed him with obvious pleasure and trust. He had begun to hope. She had not spoken to him of Jonathan again, and Jonathan had not mentioned her recently.

"A wanderer on the face of the earth. He will be that, Robert."

"Possibly for a little while. I know that he has had many magnificent offers from New York and Philadelphia and Boston. One hospital even offered to make him Chief-of-Staff, and another of the surgical division."

"He will never realize any of them, my dear Robert."

Robert turned on her quickly. "What do you mean by that?"

Jane smiled with deep satisfaction. "I do associate for your sake, Robert, to incline people to you. During those associations with the ladies in this miserable little town I have heard —hints."

"Of what?" Now Robert was alarmed and disturbed.

"I am not at liberty to tell you," said his mother, setting her mouth primly. "Moreover, I am not one to gossip, nor do I permit confidences."

Robert was silent, studying her and frowning. He had felt that something was wrong concerning Jonathan in this town during the past few weeks, but he had dismissed it as his imagination. He was treated kindly by new colleagues, but he noticed that faces changed when he mentioned Jonathan, and the subject was dismissed. He had come to the conclusion that as Jonathan was leaving, he was no longer important to the medical world in which he moved in Hambledon, for it was a parochial town and concerned only with its own, and Jonathan was not now part of that closed society.

" 'It is a fearful thing to fall into the Hands of the Living God,' " Jane quoted with pleasure.

"It is, indeed," said Robert. "Mother, if you have heard of anything concerning Jonathan I insist that you tell me, for he is my friend."

Jane nodded grimly. "He is no man's friend, but has set his face against everyone, and so I am most happy that he will indeed be leaving soon, or perhaps he will be forced to leave. That is what I have heard, Robert, and all I have heard, from many indignant ladies, who also hinted that never again will he be permitted to practice anywhere. Certainly—"

"For God's sake!" Robert suddenly shouted. "What in hell are you talking about? What fool women's gossip have you been listening to?"

His mother rose with slow vast dignity, lowering her eyes before this violence, and, forgetting her canes for once, marched as if preceded by heralds out of the room, and in silence. Robert seethed, watching her go. He knew his mother. She would tell him nothing. He had deeply offended her. Now she would not speak to him for days except on occasions of deepest necessity, until he would be forced to apologize or she would find her own silence no longer sufferable.

He slammed out of the house into the hot sunlight of the morning, and it was as if he had been delivered from a dank tomb. But his mind was greatly perturbed and anxious. He wondered if he should tell Jonathan. He recalled that Jonathan had lately seemed very lighthearted and pleasant and amiable, and his tongue had been less abrasive. Jonathan, who knew Hambledon, as Robert did not, would surely be aware by this time if some danger had begun to threaten him, some inconceivable danger. He decided not to repeat his mother's malignant gossip. What had she said, really, except to repeat remarks of spiteful women?

His concern for Jonathan, however, removed the last hostility and estrangement he had felt since that day by the river, and his thoughts of him were again brotherly and full of respect. If no one else missed him in Hambledon, he would be missed by Robert Morgan. Perhaps, thought Robert, when he is established somewhere else, he will send for me. I like Hambledon very much. But if Jon asked me to join him, I would.

Senator Kenton Campion got out of his fine victoria—his sister's—and looked at Dr. Martin Eaton's great and monstrously ugly house and thought, as he always thought, that if "Pike's Peak" was ridiculous for Hambledon, Dr. Eaton's house should be razed in the interest of public beauty, after public condemnation. It was no worse, he reflected, than other houses on River Road, and it did have remarkably lovely gardens and linden trees, and had a fine back view of the water and expansive grounds, but still it was hideous and an insult to an eye that winced at deformities.

He stood on the walk and looked up at the little silly turrets and small absurd towers and the appalling stained-glass hall window that glowered in the very center of the chestnut-colored wood façade and seemed to enhance the putrid yellow hue of the shutters and shingles. Ghastly, ghastly, thought the Senator, climbing the stairs to the cool shadows of the deep long porches and pulling the bell. He was almost always good-tempered. The Eaton house increased his feeling of well-being because it was so repulsive, so rich, so pretentious and so without grace. His eyes shone like polished glass. A maid admitted him to the great parlor with all its clutter of china, elks' horns, clocks, vases and dark velvet furniture, and, of course, its shutters pulled against the radiant morning sun. It was dusky here, though not cool, and the Senator felt his way to the center of the room, considered a deep chair, then decided against it. He was too portly to sink himself into that mass.

Flora Eaton came in hastily, in a gardening apron, her thin sallow face damp and her dark hair damper still and disheveled. She threw aside her gardening gloves and advanced into the room, her dotted cotton dress fluttering about her angular figure. "Dear, dear Kenton!" she exclaimed. "How happy I am to see you! How is darling Beatrice? Do forgive my appearance—my sweet peas, you know, in this weather, and my phlox—not doing well at all—and Martin will be so happy, too, to see you! Iced tea, Kenton, or perhaps"—and her pale lips made a naughty coy moue—"a little drop of something?"

"A little drop of something, dear Flora," said the beaming Senator, as he enfolded her thin freckled hands in his warm, fat palms. "Where is Martin?"

Flora was breathless, as always, and she "jiggled" in the present fashionable way, all jumping fingers, nodding head, and little jerkings of her shoulders. The Senator disliked this fashion, which had been taken from the Florodora Sextette's handsome young ladies, but the lively animation was not too repellent in a girl, though tiresome. However, a lady Flora's age should know better, he commented to himself. She made him nervous. What did she remind him of—and other ladies like her? Some disease. Yes. Parkinson's.

Flora gaspingly informed him that her husband was in his study, as he always was in the morning, but she would summon him and they would have a little cozy chat. Her big, hollow dark eyes rolled meaningly, her big white teeth glittered, her elbows, hands hips, shoulder, jiggled, and she kept rising and falling on her toes.

"No, no, dear Flora!" cried the jovial Senator. "I wouldn't take you from your beautiful garden for a moment! I should have called first. I'll go to Martin's study. Dull business, y'know, my dear, dull business, not fit for a lady's ears. I know the way! Don't bother, my dear, don't bother!" He tapped her affectionately on her sharp shoulder and went off very fast for a gentleman of his girth and size. Flora looked after him languishingly. He was so good, so kind, so sweet, so distinguished. She found her gloves and raced back to her garden, which she was preparing for a tea that afternoon.

The Senator climbed the stairs. Here again all was shuttered and dim, and the shut air smelled of wax and heated varnish and aromatic dust. He passed room after room, with closed doors, until he came to the study, on which he knocked quickly. He said, "Martin? Kent Campion here. Can you see me for a few minutes?"

He heard a creak, a hoarse mutter, then a shuffling, which came toward him. The door opened and the tall and shrunken figure of the sick doctor stood on the threshold, staring at him dully. The once fat face was fat no longer; it had sunken in one year. His bald head no longer shone; the skin was yellowed and parched. The once kind blue eyes had faded and were slitted. Only the big nose and the thick lips remained, ruins among ruins. Martin leaned on two canes, and his left side was almost completely paralyzed.

He wore a wool morning coat, for all the heat, and wrinkled trousers, and a collarless shirt striped in white and gray, and suspenders. He trembled as he stood with the aid of his strong canes. He said slowly and precisely, "Good morning, Kent. Come in." He had regained a good measure of his speech. He shuffled slowly back into the dusky room, which was filled with Mission oak furniture, leather chairs, ugly lamps, and dark blue silk draperies. Here he had held consultations with lesser doctors on important matters concerning an obscure case or a rich patient. Now his precious medical library, which lined the oak walls, was dusty and unused. The rug held no footprints, for few came here any longer. Martin, since his niece's tragic death, had become a recluse, drinking in lonely silence in this room and reading "light" books and magazines, and thinking, thinking, thinking, his own desolate and anguished thoughts.

The Senator glanced about him. Pity was not one of his virtues, but he felt pity now. He remembered hearty convivial days in this library, or study, and manly jokes and chuckles, when a big fire was laid on that black marble hearth and the winter snow hissed on the long windows. There were only echoes here now, and on that desk, once weighted with medical books and folders, stood only a bottle and a glass and a pitcher of water.

The Senator, still beaming, seated himself near the desk and thought, but only for an instant, that he was on dirty business and he wished it was not necessary. However, it indeed was necessary. Besides, in a way, he was doing Martin a favor. No doubt the shattered doctor had been dreaming, for a year, almost, of revenge, and had broken because he could not attain it. His dear friend, Kent Campion, would put it in his hands. So the Senator became cheerful again. "Yes, yes, Martin, I will indeed have a drink. Thank you." He watched the crippled man reach for another glass, survey it for dregs, and then fill it with whiskey and water. "Thank you," repeated the Senator, and leaned forward and took the glass. "How are you, dear old friend?"

"Waiting for death," said Martin very slowly.

The Senator laughed heartily. "Oh, dear me, how morbid you are! But, of course, you are joking. You're a young man yet, Martin. World before you. Two years younger than me. Why aren't you sitting out in the garden, your wonderful gardens? So pleasant in this weather, with cool breezes from the river."

The doctor had painfully and carefully seated himself. He put aside his canes. He folded his right hand over his paralyzed left one, which now resembled a claw. He gazed at the Senator with eyes so sunken and so narrowed that they appeared lifeless and of no color at all.

"I care for nothing," he said. He lifted the bottle. When the Senator would have helped him, he waved him aside exhaustedly. He filled his glass, added only a dash of water, then put the glass to his lips and drank like a man dying of thirst. The Senator watched him, marveling that he could drink so much, and not for the first time today, either.

He said with his usual buoyancy, "Now, Martin, we must pull ourselves together, we really must. For the sake of our—er—friends. Our—er—community. Our—er—loved ones. We owe it to ourselves, to others. We are not unimportant. We are revered, admired, needed, We—"

"Shut up, Kent," said the weary voice, and the right hand tilted the bottle over the glass again. "What do you want? You always want something."

"Is that kind?" said Kenton Campion, chuckling richly. He drank of his own glass and tried not to notice the mass of fingerprints on it. "We've had many a happy hour in this room, dear Martin, many a happy hour. We miss you. We miss those hours. We shall have them again. I promise you that—when all this is forgotten, and —er—consummated."

One lean broad shoulder rose and fell under the morning coat. But now the dying eyes fixed themselves attentively on the politician. They actually peered in the dusk, and the Senator, perceptive as were all politicians, was aware of a concentration on him, a sudden watchfulness. He pulled his chair closer to the desk. "I am here to bring you the satisfaction you've been dreaming of for months, Martin, for months. And then a miracle will happen, and your heart will be at peace, and your health restored."

"Go on," said the faltering voice, but it had quickened.

"Jonathan Ferrier," said the Senator.

He expected some show of emotion now, at the sound of that hated name, a quickening, a trembling of the side of the face which was not paralyzed, an exclamation, a faint cry, perhaps, a clenching of the living hand, an involuntary movement. But nothing of this occurred. Martin Eaton continued to stare at him with those frightening eyes for several long moments, and he said not a word. Finally he stiffly turned his big head, with its glinting yellowish baldness, and he looked at the shuttered windows. He appeared to have forgotten the visitor.

"Jonathan Ferrier," said the Senator, wondering if Martin's mind had gone also, and if he had forgotten that name.

"I heard you," said Martin, and still looked at the windows and did not move.

The Senator coughed. "The man we all still believe killed

your niece and her unborn child." (What the hell was the matter with him, anyway?)

Martin said in a vague and distant voice, "They believe that still?"

"Indeed, indeed, dear friend! They never believed he was innocent. There are rumors he bought some members of the jury."

Martin closed his right hand over his left again. He rubbed the dead flesh slowly, slowly, and did not look at the Senator. His ash-colored mouth fluttered uncontrollably, and the Senator was pleased, for now he was surely expressing his grief and inconsolable sorrow. Then Martin said, "He did not buy the jurors. They were honest men."

The Senator frowned. "Ah, well, you know rumors, Martin. I never heed them myself. But who can stop tongues? And—old stories? But we know Ferrier was guilty. You know, too. Didn't you stand up in the courtroom, when the verdict was given, and didn't you cry out, 'No! No! No!' "

The fallen chest, once so massive and strong, heaved visibly, and the Senator smiled a little. So, the old hatred still burned there, in spite of the dead and passive face, the averted head, the hidden eyes.

"Yes," said Martin. "I did."

"So you know he was guilty."

There was a long sick silence. Then Martin mumbled, "He was guilty."

"Well, then," said Campion, freshly pleased. "And now I have some news for you. Do you hear me, Martin? Yes. I hear that Ferrier has decided to remain in Hambledon after all, to destroy and injure at will. To flaunt his crimes in our faces. But—we, shall we say 'we' at present?—have decided that this little city must no longer be defamed and shamed by his presence. We—have been working not only to revoke his license in the whole state but to revoke it permanently, and everywhere. Who will give him shelter and privileges when the sovereign Commonwealth of Pennsylvania will no longer permit him to practice but will drive him out?"

Now the ruined face turned almost quickly to the Senator and for the first time there was a sharp burning deep within the hollows of the lost eyes, an intense and focused burning. The Senator nodded richly.

"Yes, dear old friend, yes."

"He is a doctor," said Martin.

This was not exactly the reply the Senator had expected.

"Well," he said, waving his hand. "He soon will not be." He watched Martin as he lit one of his heavy cigars and then deposited the match in a bronze tray. Martin watched his every movement as if powerfully fascinated. "With your help, Martin."

Martin had fixed his gaze on the cigar. The lips were shaking again. The Senator said, "All you have suffered in your sorrow will be avenged. Poor lovely Mavis will be avenged. I promise you that, my friend, I promise you that."

Then, to the Senator's consternation, the big ruined head began to move negatively from side to side, in denial. "He is a doctor," said Martin again.

The Senator wet his lips. "Yes. But what a doctor! And how he repaid you for the paternal affection you gave him, the patronage, the introductions, the pride, the kindness! He repaid it all with hatred—and the murder of that lovely thing, your heart's joy and delight."

Now the fiery spark in Martin's eyes dimmed with moisture.

"No," said Martin.

The Senator took the cigar from his mouth, blew out a cloud of smoke, and said gently, " 'No' what?"

"You shall not have my help," said Martin.

The Senator raised thick and chestnut eyebrows. "But, Martin, why not?"

The shaking lips firmed and again the slow denial began.

"Come," said Kenton Campion, and smiled. "I know it is painful for you, dear friend. I know you do not wish old sorrows to be exhumed again. But you must be brave. Have you forgotten Mavis? Ah, who could forget that vision of beauty and joy and laughter? Not her devoted—uncle. Who adored her. Be brave, Martin. This is the last battle, and Mavis will be avenged."

"What do you want of me?" asked Martin.

"I will bring witnesses to you, here, Martin, Louis Hedler, Humphrey Bedloe, for your testimony, which you did not give in court. We have long known that you knew something which would have convicted Ferrier but suppressed it, perhaps because of your old—interest—in his mother. Old friendships. A tender heart that had suffered enough. Your heart. Yes, we knew that you deliberately did not testify in a crucial matter, that you kept your silence. I do not want you to keep it any longer, dear friend. I want you to tell your friends of it, to unburden your heart at last, to bring justice to bear on that murderer finally."

The reply was a dry whisper. "Double jeopardy."

"Yes, I know," said the Senator with impatience, and again waving his cigar. "He cannot be tried again for the same crime. But your testimony will convince Hedler, who is proving a little fractious in spite of what he has suffered from Ferrier's hands, to allow us to bring in two prominent members of the State Medical Board from Philadelphia. They already have many—proofs, shall we say?—but yours will be the most convincing of all."

"Proofs?"

"Oh, not of that crime. But of others. Enough to drive Ferrier out of the country. To the ends of the earth."

Again the eyes were bits of fire. The slow voice came without intonation: "What did he do to you, Campion?"

The Senator started, looked with keenness at the broken doctor. His smile became pinched. "Enough, Martin, quite enough. He did me a great injury. I, too, want revenge. But I will not bother you with my troubles. Yours are sufficient. When shall I bring the witnesses to you?"

Was that a bitter and sardonic smile on Eaton's dying lips?

The Senator could not tell. But he did hear the one word, "No."

The Senator was angry and astounded and incredulous. There had been such finality in that word, such strength.

" 'No,' Martin? After all he did to Mavis, and to you, out of cruelty and viciousness and hate?"

"Please go, Campion," said Martin.

The Senator's eyebrows rose again and stayed there. He studied the end of his glowing cigar. He smiled, reflecting. His big red mouth moved and twisted as if he were thinking of something very delicious.

"You will not help us, Martin?"

"No. No. That is all."

The Senator sighed. He leaned back in the leather chair and contemplated the ceiling. "In my profession," he said, "it is most necessary to know the secret hearts of people, their thoughts, their emotions, their desires. Mavis was a dear girl. But, she had her faults, her little perplexities, her small defects. Always, Martin, she was shielded by you, upheld by you, devotedly guarded by you. She was dearer to you than anything else in the world, above everything else in the world. You would never hear a word against her, not even

from dear Flora, who is a paragon of a woman. Yes, yes, my
ears are always open. I never forget anything. To you Mavis
was an angel of light, to be worshiped and honored, her
name kept inviolate. You would have died for Mavis."

A steady hoarse breathing began to fill the closed and
dusty room. "Yes," said Martin Eaton, and again the living
hand clenched on the desk. "It is true."

"Not an ugly word must ever touch Mavis, mar her or dim
her."

"No," said Martin. The breathing was louder and quicker.

The Senator sighed and shook his head. "Martin, it breaks
my heart to say this, then. If you will not help us, I must, in
my stern search for justice, bring Mavis' name into public
view, to public laughter, speculation. Calumny. And yours,
also."

The great shattered figure behind the desk stirred and
shook as if a hand had seized it furiously. The dead lips
parted, closed silently. The fallen eyes opened wide and
blazed.

So, I have stirred up the wrecked bastard, thought the Senator with pleasure. He continued to shake his head, sighing.
"You know how women gossip, Martin. My wife was the
very close friend of your brother's wife, Hilda Eaton. They
endlessly confided in each other, and in no one else, and in
letters. They were like sisters, closer than sisters. My wife
was overcome with sorrow when Hilda died. Dear soft-
hearted Henrietta. Dear gentle soul. I comforted her, as any
good husband would. And then she told me."

"What?" The word was a hard rasp.

"That," said the Senator with an air of delicacy, "Mavis
was your daughter, not your brother's. That Mavis was the
result of—er—adultery. I do not condemn you, dear old
friend. But Hilda did resemble Marjorie Ferrier, did she not,
and you always—admired—Marjorie Ferrier and had wanted
to marry her. Let us be thankful that your brother died not
knowing, and that you adopted Mavis, you and Flora, and
made her your daughter openly, as well as naturally. It was a
noble and loving thing, Martin, and I admire you for it. No,
no. No one else living, except you and I, know the truth, and
the truth is shut behind my lips and will never come forth.
Unless you force me to it. I will not be denied, Martin."

Now he looked at the crumbling man with a baleful light
in his eyes, and his wide smile was evil.

It was as if all the last strength of Martin Eaton came to

him violently. He said—and his voice was almost normal and loud—"You have no proof. I will sue you for libel." The blaze was deep in his eyes and cold with hate.

"Ah, yes, but I do have proof, Martin. A politician, you will understand, garners all little matters which may be useful to him in the future. It does not matter how trivial. It may be a nugget later. So, I persuaded Henrietta to write it down for me, in her own handwriting, as a kind of 'confession' that she had withheld the truth for so long. Henrietta was a very virtuous soul. She had not been moved that Hilda had been infatuated with you, and that you loved her. There was some sternness in my dear Henrietta's soul. She felt that you had 'betrayed' pretty Hilda, had seduced her from her husband's side. Need I elaborate? So, I induced Henrietta to write down her own indignation over her beloved friend's fate and the fact that she had not dared proclaim abroad the true paternity of her child. Henrietta did not blame Hilda. She did not blame the wronged husband. She did not blame Flora. She blamed only you"—and the Senator chuckled indulgently—"the seducer of the innocent, the breaker of a loving home, the despoiler." The Senator laughed softly. " 'Thou shalt not commit adultery.' To my Henrietta that was a crime above murder, above all the other Commandments. Hilda had not committed adultery, no, not Henrietta's friend! But you had forced yourself upon her. How Henrietta had come to that conclusion is a great mystery, but you know the chaste hearts of women," and he signed unctuously. "They cannot believe that a good wife would betray her husband, no, not unless she was 'forced.' "

He clasped his hands over his silk and patterned waistcoat and looked at the stricken doctor with an air of sadness and benignity. "Martin, unless you help us, tell us what you know, the name of Mavis will be darkened forever. You do not care about yourself, but you do care about Mavis. It is your choice: The memory of Mavis, or Jonathan Ferrier's punishment." He sat up in his chair. "Knowing what you do about him, how can you refuse to help us? How can you deny to Mavis the justice her soul must crave against her murderer? I cannot believe it! I cannot understand it!" He struck the desk with his meaty fist in outrage.

The doctor's face was a gray portrait of extreme agony. His mouth had fallen open, and it was twisted, and his teeth could be seen, dimly glimmering in that dusky light. His panting was rough and deep in the room. He stared at the

Senator in his extremity of fear and hatred and despair. The Senator stared back, assuming severity and indignation.

Then, very slowly, the live hand opened a drawer and withdrew a piece of white linen, and laid it on the desk. The two men regarded it in silence. Finally, the doctor made a feeble motion toward it, and the Senator reached for it and took it in his hand. It was at once light and metallic, within its piece of linen. The Senator unrolled the cloth and found in his hand a curious tool or instrument. He bent forward to examine it more closely. A knife? A curved knife? A medical affair? Then he saw the name in a flowing scroll on the silver handle. Jonathan Ferrier.

"What is it?" he asked. He noticed that the edge was rusty and smeared with an old smear.

"Curette," said Martin Eaton, as if expiring.

"Curette? What is that?"

"An instrument. Surgery. For emptying a woman's womb." The breathing was more discordant and shrill.

"Ah!" exclaimed the Senator.

"Mavis' blood. On it," said Martin Eaton. "She brought it to me. Gave it to me. Before she died."

He sank back in his chair and groaned. He rolled his head and his eyes stretched toward the ceiling. "It was used on her. Her blood. She brought it to me. He—he had put it down. She took it." He pointed blindly at the cloth, and now the Senator recoiled. The cloth held old rusty stains.

"Good God," said the Senator in a subdued voice. He had wanted proof but not one so horrible as this. He rerolled the curette gingerly. Then he said in a voice of genuine disgust, "And he used that on that helpless girl, to kill her and his child!" He had not believed it before, but he believed it now, or forced himself to believe it.

The live hand of Dr. Eaton darted to the cloth and the instrument and seized it and then thrust it back into the drawer. The drawer was quickly locked. The two men looked at each other, the doctor panting as if he had struggled a long time with something formidable, the Senator with curiosity.

The Senator stood up with an air of satisfaction. "Thank you, Martin," he said. "Please forgive me for pressing you. It was necessary, as I am sure you know now. Very necessary. for Mavis' sake, and yours, and Hambledon's. As soon as the witnesses can come, I will let you know, and they will wish to consult you personally."

"Get out," said Dr. Eaton, and he closed his eyes.

Smiling urbanely, the Senator left. He met no one in the lower hall but the maid, who respectfully led him to the door.

For many minutes after the Senator's departure Martin Eaton sat in his chair, clenching and unclenching his right hand and staring into space. His heavy breathing subsided, but his mouth remained partly open. He began to look about his gloomy study as if he had never been here before and was examining everything. Then he said aloud, "Mavis. Mavis." Again his eyes filled with moisture. Then he said, "Jon. Jon."

He looked at his telephone, and he reached for it, and then he remembered the Senator and he snatched his hand away. But he continued to stare at it for a long time, a very long time, and his sick mind was turbulent.

Then he groaned. "Hilda. Marjorie. Marjorie!"

CHAPTER TWENTY-NINE

Jenny Heger wandered hesitantly onto the terrace where Harald Ferrier was smoking and reading the morning paper. She looked at him with diffidence for some time before he became aware that she was there. Then he glanced up smiling, stood and laid aside his newspaper, and motioned her to a chair in the shining and golden heat of the morning. She shook her head and clasped her hands before her on her rough brown frock.

"I suppose," she said in a very subdued voice, "you will never forgive me?"

"Jenny," he said with the utmost gentleness, "I never held it against you. I was only sorry that you could think such things of me." His hazel eyes sparkled largely on her with genuine love. "But I was a little—hurt. That's why I refused to go with you to our lawyers and sign those contracts. I wanted to think, to get over my hurt."

Jenny sighed and peeped at him shyly. "I've been thinking, too," she said in that same uncertain voice. "Mama wasn't very fair to you, and she realized it. So, I want to do what she should have done, and which she would have done if she had lived. The contract you made out—that wasn't fair. So —so if you want to—we'll go to our lawyers, and we'll divide the estate equally, and then you can—go. I don't know just how large the estate is. I never gave it a thought before. But it must be quite a lot?"

"Yes, Jenny. Several millions of dollars, and still increasing from investments." He still smiled at her, but he was alert. "Even divided, it would provide enough income for both of us, a rich income, for the rest of our lives, with the residual estate still intact for our own heirs."

"I'm glad," said Jenny with humility. "So you can go. I will stay here, on my father's island, and I will be able to keep it up as he wanted. We can see our lawyers whenever you want to, Harald."

He was elated, but he did not let it appear. He said, "Jenny, I want to talk to you. Please, Jenny, sit down for a minute. It won't take long."

She was too ashamed of her old prejudices and suspicions to refuse. So she sat on the edge of a wicker chair and colored a little, and looked at the rushing azure of the smiling river, and waited. The island was swept by a soft breeze, and held the scent of pine and cut grass and flowers and water. Jenny's eyes were the eyes of a child, wondering, content, questing. The light wind ruffled the masses of her hanging black hair, which was caught back from her face by an untidy blue ribbon. Jenny, Jenny, thought Harald. He had never seen her before like this, quiet, without tenseness and hostility. Once he had thought her simple and without complexities, but now he knew that Jenny was a very elusive personality, and secret.

"Jenny," he said, "will you listen to me for just a little, without jumping up and running away?"

She looked at him with that directness of hers. "I've finished with running away," she said. "I've been running away all my life, and now it is over."

He knew it was true. She had lost her shy fear of everything and everyone lately, and there was an air of proud reticence about her now. Her eyes did not dart off from anyone's gaze any longer, nor did she blush very easily, nor did she flit away at the slightest sound of curiosity, or probing, or amusement. Jenny had become a woman. She had acquired courage, and Harald had no doubt that she could now face any hostility or ridicule with fortitude or deserved contempt. That part of her nature had been suppressed too long. Harold had even heard her laughing in the house and had seen her playing with kittens on the grass.

"I'm glad," said Harald. "There was never any reason for you to run. When I was a child, I used to run, too. It was stupid."

"Did you?" She smiled at him with interest.

"Yes, I did. I wanted my father to like me and to like my painting. I thought he was quite wonderful. But I found out he never had any real taste, such as my mother had. He liked stereotyped art, for he had no imagination to judge anything else. So, when I showed him my early attempts, he would look pained. He always had a way of looking pained, and very delicate and bruised. He was a silly man. My brother, Jon, never found that out. He thought Papa was the acme of everything, the final resort, and so he didn't like our mother because she was onto Papa herself. Jon doesn't like my paintings because Papa didn't."

Jenny frowned seriously. "That doesn't sound like—Jon."

"Oh, but it's true! Jon hasn't any imagination, either."

Jenny said nothing. She looked down at her hands. Harald laughed gently. "The only perceptive people in our family, Jenny, are my mother and myself. Jon's idea of something interesting and beautiful is a corpse." He laughed again. "He never appreciated Mavis' beauty, for instance, and never understood her at all."

"There was never anything to understand," said Jenny with her old bluntness. "I knew that even when I was very young, four years ago. It was Jon's trouble that he thought she had —had—well, other things that weren't obvious. But she didn't have anything that wasn't obvious. She was what Mavis was."

Harald was astounded. He was not sure that he liked this acute Jenny.

"What do you mean?" he asked.

Jenny actually became quite animated. "Mavis was very simple, really. She wanted just what kittens want, food, play, amusement, sleep, fun, a soft place to curl, petting, pampering, and what used to be called 'cosseting.' Admiration, strokings. And to give nothing in return. And to fight for her luxuries, which she felt were deserved."

Harald pondered this, narrowing his eyes on this Jenny he had never recognized before. He knew that what she had said was quite true. He only disliked it that Jenny had not been deceived by Mavis.

"Mavis hated anyone who wouldn't indulge her or who expected anything real and human from her," Jenny went on.

How true, thought Harald. But how beautiful she was! He said, "I'm suprised at you, Jenny. You're being uncharitable."

"No," said Jenny, with a return of her old earnestness. "I'm just telling the truth, which Jon found out eventually."

"How do you know he found that out?"

Jenny looked away. "I just know."

"He treated Mavis abominably."

Jenny swung the profound blue of her eyes to him again. "How do you know? Did she tell you?"

Harald became immobile in his chair, but his hands tightened on the arms.

"I knew," said Jenny, "that you were with her often."

"How did you know, Jenny?" He was terribly alarmed and now he sat up.

"I saw both of you along the river at night, talking."

Harald inhaled slowly and carefully. His fingers twitched on the arms of the chair. Then he said, watching Jenny, "She had to have someone to confide in. And I was sympathetic."

"I suppose so," said Jenny, and one look at her ingenuous face convinced him that there was no danger to him in this girl. "It was very sad, all around," said Jenny. "But I am more sad for Jon."

Harald took out his scented handkerchief and carefully wiped his forehead. He said, "Mavis, though perhaps you won't believe it, had a great interest in art."

"That's nice," said Jenny with indifference. She had already dismissed Mavis. "But you wanted to talk to me about something, didn't you?"

"Yes." Harald pulled himself out of his fear. It had struck across the sunlit terrace like the shadow of a black and avenging wing, but now it was gone. He leaned toward Jenny, his hands clasped between his knees, his smile charming and winsome. Then he became serious.

"Jenny, you never used to believe it when I told you I wanted to marry you."

She stiffened. Her face became cold and distant.

"Jenny, it usually isn't considered an insult when a man declares his love for a woman!"

"I—I suppose not." She shifted to the very edge of the chair.

"Don't you believe me?"

It was ludicrous, but she was considering, her thoughts going back to the past. Harald found himself smiling again. Jenny was embarrassed, and the faintest flush rose in her pale smooth cheeks. "I believe you. Now," she said. "I wish you wouldn't talk about it."

"Why not? It's the most important thing to me, Jenny, and it doesn't concern money."

"No. No. It doesn't concern money," said Jenny. Her color brightened. "I'm sorry I ever thought that."

"Well, Jenny? What do you say now?"

She looked at the tangled fingers on her lap, and she was distressed.

"I—I can't think of you like that."

"Because of your mother?"

"No. It—is something else."

"Jenny, I've noticed that that young doctor has rowed over here to see you occasionally. Jon's replacement. You aren't taking him seriously, are you?"

"He's very kind," Jenny was miserable.

"And very puerile." Harald spoke indulgently.

"You're wrong," said Jenny with some heat. "Kindness doesn't mean you're a fool. I like to talk to him. He doesn't have—hidden—places. He's honest. I like his company. We like the same things."

"Enough to marry him?"

Jenny said nothing. Her appearance was wretched. Then when she saw that Harald was waiting, smiling, for her answer, she said, "I haven't thought of marrying him."

"Well, that's encouraging. So, Jenny, what is your objection to me?"

"I told you. I can't think of you like that." She stood up, and looked desperate. "You mustn't ask me. Never again. I could never marry you, Harald."

He stood up, too. "Jenny, would you at least think about it, in justice to me?"

She looked about her as if searching for some hiding place. "I can't think about it."

"But there's no one else. Jenny, I understand you. I've loved you for a long time. We could be very happy together."

"You'll have to excuse me!" cried Jenny, and before he could say anything else, she had run off in her old manner. He watched her flying away down the stairs of the terrace into the gardens. He felt some encouragement. At least she had not rejected him outright, and she had shown considerable confusion and distress. That must mean something. A man who disturbed a woman and sent her flying off had a lot in his favor. Moreover she pitied him because she had wronged him in her thoughts, and pity was first cousin to love.

When Howard Best entered the large office of Dr. Louis Hedler at St. Hilda's Hospital, he found not only the doctor there but Father McNulty. They all shook hands, and Howard sat down. He saw that Louis was very grave and that his large froglike eyes gleamed with consternation. Louis said, "Thanks for coming, Howard. I know it's late; right at dinnertime. But I wanted you and Father McNulty here when the hospital isn't teeming as usual, and the corridors rushing, and too much curiosity aroused. This is a very serious and private matter. Private," he emphasized, looking from one to the other slowly and pointedly.

"You can rely on my discretion," said the priest, his golden eyes quietly alarmed.

"Yes. And you, Howard?"

"Give me a dollar," said Howard, smiling. Dr. Hedler stared a moment, then took out his billfold, extracted a dollar bill from it and laid it before Howard, who said, "I am a lawyer. You have just given me a retainer. So anything you say to me and anything I hear in this room is completely private and confidential." His kind boyish face stopped smiling. He put the bill in his pocket and settled his rangy body in the leather chair. He could see the shimmering mountains in the distance, deepening slowly to purple in the evening sky. The weather was still very hot though it was the latter part of August.

"Howard," said Louis, "you were Jon Ferrier's lawyer, weren't you?"

"Yes. Here in Hambledon. I was the one who moved for a change of venue, as you know, and it was granted, considering the atmosphere in this town against Jon. Then I got it moved to Philadelphia and found the best lawyers for Jon there." His face became as grave as Louis'. "Why, Louis?"

Dr. Hedler looked down at a thick folder on his desk. He

sighed. He rubbed his eyes and stared through the windows, and his finger tapped the folder. "There is one thing," he said, "Jon can't be tried for the same alleged crime, can he? Double jeopardy."

Howard sat up alertly. "No, he can't. What the hell is this, Louis?"

Louis said, "But it would ruin Jon, wouldn't it, if fresh evidence were unearthed that he had really 'bungled' the abortion on Mavis—perhaps deliberately so—and killed her and his unborn child? It could result in the revocation of his license to practice anywhere?"

"I suppose so," said Howard, and now he was as alarmed as the doctor. "You know more about that part than I do, though. Come on, Louis! Tell me."

"Let me begin at the beginning," said Louis, wiping his face with his handkerchief. He lit a cigar and Howard saw that his hands were shaking slightly. He opened the folder and stared at it grimly, nodding his head from time to time. "It begins with Kent Campion."

Now the quiet priest sat up very straight in his own chair and both he and Howard fixed their eyes on the doctor.

"Jon," said Louis, "made a very bad error when he began to oppose ambitious politicians in Washington a couple of years ago. He joined the Anti-Imperialist League founded by George S. Boutwell, former Senator from Massachusetts, former Secretary of the Treasury under Grant. I remember that Boutwell said, 'Our war to free Cuba must not be turned into wars for empire. If America ever does seek empire, and most nations do, then planned reforms in our domestic life will be abandoned, states' rights will be abolished—in order to impose a centralized government upon us for the purpose of internal repudiation of freedom, and adventures abroad. The American dream will then die—on battlefields all over the world—and a nation conceived in liberty will destroy liberty for Americans and impose tyranny on subject nations.' Boutwell also said, if I am repeating him correctly, and he quoted Thoreau: 'If I knew a man was approaching my house to do me good, I would flee for my life.' Then he went on to say, 'Every ambitious would-be empire clarions it abroad that she is conquering the world to bring it peace, security and freedom, and is sacrificing her sons only for the most noble and humanitarian purposes. That is a lie, and it is an ancient lie, yet generations still rise and believe it!' "

Howard hesitated. He rubbed his long jaw. Then he said,

"I belong to the Anti-Imperialist League, too. I joined when that scoundrel lawyer, Albert Beveridge, now a Senator from Indiana, shouted that 'Who dares to stop America now, now when we are at last one people, strong enough for any task, great enough for any glory destiny can bestow?' He also yelled, 'Our dream is the dream of American expansion until all the seas and nations shall bloom with that flower of liberty —the flag of the United States of America!' He wasn't the only one, Louis. He even had the antiwar Populists applauding him! Yes. So, I joined the League. I didn't know Jon was a member, though."

"It seems," said Louis with a wry smile, "that not only did he join but he gave thousands of dollars to it and wrote little anonymous leaflets for it. Campion found out. He's hated Jon ever since. Calls him un-American, antipatriotic, antidestiny, and such. Even a traitor. Yet I understand that all the League wants is peace at home and abroad, and needed social reforms put into practice, so as to end, justly, the war between labor and capital, assure the soundness of our currency, abolish unjust taxation, advance the cause of the American Negro and the Indians in the West, outlaw child labor, and punish and banish from office all corrupt politicians. I am quoting your League, of course."

"Those are our objectives," said Howard, "and very decent and worthy ones."

"Yes. But that doesn't help Jon. He made a terrible enemy of the empire-loving Campion and his fellows, though he doesn't know. I also think there is something else—personal. Campion has complained that Jon induced his son to leave his seminary and 'flee abroad to some disreputable place where a father cannot reach, comfort and sustain him.'"

The priest uttered an exclamation of anger. "That is most untrue, Doctor! I hope I am not violating a confidence—well, even if I am—but Jon saved young Francis Campion's life! I know where Francis is. He could assure you of the truth, and not lies."

"Then," said Louis, "get him. Bring him back as soon as possible."

The priest said, "He is in France. I will cable him tonight."

Louis sighed. "At the best, he will be able to return in ten days. Send for him, Father. Tonight."

"I will do even more than that," said the priest. "I will explain, in my cable, why it is needed that Francis not only return at once, but that he send me a cable refuting the—er—

errors of his father. That should arrive in less than four days after my cable is sent." His young face was greatly disturbed.

Howard, equally disturbed, said, "What is all this, Louis? Why is this necessary?"

Louis looked down at the folder. "I am endeavoring to lay the foundation for what I must tell you." He folded his arms on his desk and held Howard's eyes.

"Jon has always been a contentious man, and controversial, in Hambledon, even from boyhood. We all know that. Even worse, he was always honest." He gave his guests a rueful glance. "There were times when I could have smote Jon thankfully. There were times when I accused him of practically everything. He has no tact, no diplomacy. Unfortunately, too, he is usually right, and that's unpardonable, isn't it? You will remember little Martha, Howard."

"Yes, God forgive me, I do."

"Do you see him often, Howard?"

"No. I suppose he's forgiven me. He told me so, anyway. But he doesn't forget. He's a relentless man and won't forget a wrong. We—Beth and I—kept inviting him to visit us, and he always refused in his blunt fashion. He informed us he wished to have nothing more to do with Hambledon. Yes, I know he is bitter. My parents do invite Mrs. Ferrier, and she accepts our invitations, but when she has dinner guests of her own, Jon always has an excuse not to be present. He won't forgive Hambledon—not that I blame him. But what about that new 'evidence' you mentioned, Louis? What has it got to do with Jon?"

"To be brief about it, Howard, Campion has declared a vendetta against Jon, all very smooth and righteous, of course, and for the good of the town. The plot has been under way for some time. The Senator and quite a number of other people—you'd be surprised—not only want to drive Jon out of town but want to deprive him of his license to practice anywhere. And to subject him to new criminal proceedings."

"But they can't do that!" cried Howard. "He can't be tried again for the alleged murders!"

"No. Perhaps not. But he can be tried for performing abortions, can't he?" Louis opened a desk drawer and drew out a slender piece of linen, stained, and laid it on the desk. Then he opened it silently, and the two other men saw a long curved instrument. "A curette," said Louis. "For the scraping of a uterus. It is used for legal—and for illegal purposes. It is a lifesaving instrument after a spontaneous abortion, and it is also used by abortionists. Look at it, Howard."

With horror Howard picked up the instrument, and then he saw the script on the silver handle. "Jonathan Ferrier!" The priest looked at it and shrank.

"Yes. I've talked with Martin Eaton, Mavis' uncle, at the Senator's request. I went to Martin's house. He gave me this curette. He said Mavis had brought it to him—after Jon performed the abortion on her. She told him that Jon had insisted on performing the abortion the night before he left for Pittsburgh. He did not want children. She was heartbroken—"

Howard looked at him wildly, then ran his freckled hand through his bush of auburn curls. His light eyes bulged. "Why, that's an infernal lie if I ever heard one! I think old Eaton's lying! He heard the medical testimony of doctors from this very hospital, Louis, and the testimony of doctors in Pittsburgh, that Jonathan was there two, three, days before —" He banged his fist on the desk. "For Christ's sake, Louis! How could you believe their lies for a moment? Your own surgeons, your own doctors, in this damned hospital, said she had been—aborted—at least forty-eight hours after Jonathan left Hambledon!"

Louis shook his head slowly and painfully. "I know, I know, Howard. Calm down, if you please. But why did old Martin—old indeed!—he's years younger than I am—lie like that? I have his solemn statement in this folder. He's a doctor himself. He was here in this hospital with Mavis and he had admitted, before she died, that Jonathan had been in Pittsburgh for several days. I heard him myself while we were trying to save her life. He was distracted. He did say, over and over, when she died, 'He's guilty! Guilty as all hell!' Well, we can put that down to his distraught state. The girl must have lied to him—he was alone with her when she died. That's the only explanation."

Father McNulty spoke in a hushed and shaken voice, "Nothing in the world, even if he confessed it himself, would convince me that Jon ever had anything to do with that crime, that frightful crime."

"Nothing in the world, Father," said Louis, "would convince me either. I know Jon. I've hated him more often than I've liked him, and wanted to get him off the staff and do him other mischief when he openly insulted me and called me 'Doctor Bogus.' " He smiled sadly. "But I know him for a good man, even when I wanted to cut his throat." He hesitated. "The—committee—went to see Dr. Humphrey Bedloe of the Friends', too. You know old pompous Humphrey. The committee, I might mention, was composed of Senator Campion, Mr. Witherby, and Dr. Schaefer—whom Jon called a butcher and a murderer, with some reason—and a few more prominent citizens who have, to put it kindly, encountered Jon before in some of his less benevolent moods, in and out of the hospitals.

"Well, they went to see old Humphrey and showed him the curette, and he was aghast. He had admitted that he had thrown Jon off the staff, and Board, even before he was tried. He also admitted he had been 'hasty' and that he had never really believed in Jon's guilt. Then they showed him the curette, and he almost had a stroke. He then confessed that he knew someone who had told him that he had seen Jon in town the day the abortion had taken place."

The large froggy eyes moved from one face to another. "It was on that frail little evidence—though you never knew it, Howard—that Jon was arrested in Hambledon. Humphrey refused to give the name of the man, but when the committee called on him—with his evidence—he blurted out the story. It was Tom Harper."

Howard glared at him with incredulity. "Tom Harper, who's dying of cancer, and whom Jon is helping so wonderfully now?"

"The very same," said Louis, and he told the two men. They looked at him, dumbfounded and sick. "Of course," said the doctor, "it isn't possible that it is true. I have my own means of information, and I know they went to Tom. There was a rumor that Jon had been very harsh and cruel to him, had driven him from practice, and then had, even more cruelly, gave him a 'menial' position as a hired overseer on one of his farms. I see you both know the real story. At any rate, Tom then admitted that he had lied to Humphrey out of envy and resentment for Jon, and he was brokenhearted. They tried to inveigle him into making a false affidavit, I heard. Thelma, his wife, told me. But he absolutely refused, and threatened to go to Jon with the tale." Louis' sigh was very deep. "Unfortunately, Tom died at six o'clock this morning, of a massive internal hemorrhage, caused by his disease. So, we have only Thelma's word that Tom had told the committee that he had lied to Humphrey. The rumor remains of Jon's 'cruelty' to that unfortunate man. If Thelma tries to help Jon, it will be brought out, to Jon's injury, that he had given Tom and her a contract, most generous—amazingly kind and charitable and generous—assigning the income of the farm to Tom, or to Thelma, for life, and Jon also has paid for their children's education in the future. The committee is already calling that a 'bribe to stifle the truth.' "

"Dear God," groaned Howard. "What kind of people live in this world, anyway?"

Louis was so disturbed that he could not help saying, "Don't be too hard on humanity, Howard. We—you—are part of it. You will recall the day when Jon told you about your little girl, Martha. I believe you called him a 'murderer' yourself. This was dutifully repeated all over the town."

The priest looked at Howard compassionately. Howard said, "I deserved that. I really deserved that. I thought it was the truth. Or perhaps I did not. Perhaps I was shouting at the threat to Martha and not really at Jon."

"We all try to excuse ourselves, myself included," said Louis Hedler. "I'm sure this is a familiar story to you, isn't it, Father?"

"Very familiar," said the priest. "Even in the Confessional, people will try to defend themselves. And even on their deathbeds sometimes." He had suddenly begun to look much older and wearier than usual. Louis took a sheet of paper out of the folder and studied it. "Yes," he said, and folded his hands over the sheet.

"I don't know if you know Peter McHenry, Howard, though Father McNulty does. It seems that Father McNulty had practically kidnaped Jon on the River Road one day to bring him to Matilda McHenry—"

Howard sat up very straight in his chair. "I know the McHenrys," he said. His pale eyes began to sparkle wrathfully, in anticipation.

"Good. Then perhaps you know that Mrs. McHenry was in frail health and had been so for years. Jon examined her, then demanded to examine their child, a little girl of nine, named Elinor, for he was convinced, he said, that Mrs. McHenry's illness had a psychological basis and not a physical one. Peter objected to Jon examining his child, or even talking to her, but I think Jon insisted—" He glanced at the priest, who hesitated.

"He didn't exactly insist," he said. "You must pardon me. The events of that day are painful to remember. It was all so unjust to Jon, and I was the guilty one who cajoled him into seeing the McHenrys. It is true that Peter objected—at first. Then, if my memory is not failing me entirely, he reluctantly consented."

"Yes," said Louis. "He told Mr. McHenry that his child was—psychotic—and that she was the unconscious cause of her mother's illness, though no one, not even the young mother, suspected that. Mr. McHenry"—and Louis looked at Howard piercingly—"was as infuriated as you were, Howard, when Jon told you about Martha. The truth is very hard to accept, isn't it? At any rate," he continued, when Howard's face darkened with heavy color, "they took the child to neurologists in Philadelphia, I believe, and all examining doctors said she was quite normal. Then Mr. McHenry came to me, shouting that Jon was a troublemaker, an incompetent and a cruel liar, and demanding his removal from staff and Board. He was accompanied by Senator Campion and Mr. Witherby. He said his child had not been Jon's patient at all, had not been called for the child, had insisted on examining her and giving his amateurish opinion—which had caused her parents devastating worry and mental anguish—and acted, in all ways, unethically."

He lifted the paper on his desk. "Mr. McHenry's affidavit, sworn to three weeks ago."

Then the priest spoke through pale lips. "I think Peter will ask for the return of that affidavit, Dr. Hedler."

"Yes?"

"You see," said the priest, and there were tears in his eyes, "little Elinor had an episode that even Peter could not overlook. One of the gardener's boys was teasing her one day, the way boys will tease little girls, and she picked up a scythe and—well, she tried to kill him with it. When her father, who was nearby, tried to take it from her, she turned on him, screaming that he wasn't her father, that he and Matilda had stolen her from her true parents. She was quite—wild. Out of her mind. She struck at him with the scythe, then when he attempted to catch her, she raced for the house, shrieking that she was going to kill her false mother. Peter ran after her. They caught her at the door, and she was—Peter's own words—like a demon. Then she collapsed. When she awakened a few hours later, she claimed not to remember the event at all, but Peter says there was something in her eyes, cunning and watchful, which frightened him even more than her violence. He took the child a few days later to the alienist in Philadelphia whom Jon had recommended." The priest looked down at his shoes. "Dementia praecox, as Jon had diagnosed. Paranoid type. The girl is now confined in a private sanitarium."

"Dreadful," said Louis. "The unfortunate parents." But his voice was a little relieved. He wrote something quickly on the paper. "Perhaps you can induce Mr. McHenry to say he was mistaken in making this affidavit, and to tell the truth."

"I am sure I can," said Father McNulty. "He wrote to Jon, I believe, asking his pardon, but Jon never answered him. You know—Jon," and he looked at Howard. "Very unbending. And proud. Peter would have always repudiated that affidavit, Doctor, if he had remembered it. But he's very distraught just now, and consoling his wife."

"To be sure, to be sure," said Louis, but he did not sound too sympathetic. He lifted another paper. "A similar complaint by Elsie Holliday. She complains that Jon was not the doctor of her son, Jeffrey, but only a friend. However, she swears, Jon forced himself on the case, insisted on diagnosing it. I am not at liberty to tell you what his diagnosis was, but Jeff did die a short time later in a sanitarium in another state, of the disease Jon diagnosed correctly. It still remains, however, that Jon did examine Jeffrey without permission of Jeffrey's physicians and under the protest of the mother. She claims that Jeffrey did not give Jon permission, either. Of course, it is a technicality but an unpleasant one, but if the facts are so, it does not reflect comfortably on Jon. But hardly enough to cause the revocation of his license. However, we know the town, and we know Jon's enemies, who insist on repeating the scandals against him, and this is just one more, such as the Harper rumor, and then the accusation spread by Peter McHenry among his associates before he discovered that Jon was entirely correct. One thing piles on another. It makes for miserable reading in the mass, though individually it means little. Cause only for a reprimand, if that."

"And all that, on top of what Martin Eaton is now swearing, and the curette, is a lovely story," said Howard, making a sick mouth.

"Yes. Yes, indeed. Martin's story and the evidence of this curette is very damning, in spite of what we know to be the facts. I wish Tom Harper were alive to repudiate the rumor, which the Senator and old Witherby heartily believe. Or, at least they pretend to. Incidentally, Old Jonas told me—swore to it, in fact—that Jon had accused him, without proof, and on later examination, of trying to commit suicide. Jon was not present when Jonas was admitted to the hospital. I think he was out of town. Jon is his family physician, however, and returned a day or two later to take charge of Jonas. Now, it was really very reckless of Jon to tell his patient later that he believed him to have attempted suicide. We all know old Jonas. His one terror is of dying. He wants to live forever. I don't know the true story or what made Jon accuse Jonas of a crime, but that, too, is a sorry tale. It could have serious repercussions, you know, for a physician is supposed to report an attempted suicide. Jon did not."

"It smells," said Howard. "It smells to high Heaven."

"That is my opinion, too," said Louis. "But everyone in Hambledon is certain that old Jonas is a saint, and his word would be taken against Jon, who is not regarded as much of a saint." Louis smiled briefly. "I have Jonas' affidavit here. 'As a good Christian man, as my friends can all attest, I deeply resent Dr. Jonathan Ferrier's accusation, to me, that I attempted to kill myself with a dose of arsenic. This is libelous in the extreme. Et cetera, et cetera.' "

"You know," said Howard, "I feel as if I am in a crazy, malignant dream."

"It has been my experience," said Dr. Hedler, "that this is a most malignant world. What did Pope say of it? 'Where every prospect pleases, and only man is vile.' Yes, indeed."

Howard was thinking. "Coming back to that—that curette. Anyone could have taken it from Jon's cabinet. It's in his examination room." He paused.

"But, they will ask, if Mavis visited an unknown abortionist, why did she take the curette with her? He'd have had one of his own."

"Perhaps he asked her to bring Jon's."

"There is that possibility, yes. But that will hardly be believed, you know. People will ask, 'Is Dr. Ferrier actually accusing a doctor, an abortionist, of asking for another man's instrument? Aren't abortionists more circumspect than that, or is Ferrier implying that there is a deep-laid plot against him, and that the abortionist deliberately killed Mavis to involve Jon? That is what they will say, and no one will believe it. We don't even believe that ourselves, do we?"

Howard shook his head dismally. "No, I don't believe it, either. Mavis is dead. I suppose we'll never have the real story."

The priest said. "Murder will out."

Louis replied, "I am sorry to disillusion you, Father. It often is concealed forever."

Now he was frowning. "I am approaching the really serious matters, and these cannot be explained and are totally damning if true. I have here the affidavit of one Mrs. Edna Beamish of Scranton, formerly of Kensington Terraces, in Hambledon. She alleges that on a certain day—the date is here—Jonathan tried to perform an abortion on her in his offices. She had come to him for that purpose, she swears, because she is a young widow and did not wish to bear a child without a living father. She is very penitent. She claims that she was distracted with grief for her dead husband and hardly knew what she was doing. However, the pain she suffered in Jonathan's offices caused her to scream so loudly that she was heard not only in the waiting room but on the street, also. She was in such pain and so terrified that she would not let him proceed, and left. He had demanded two hundred dollars, she swears. She left for her home. Unfortunately—and there is an affidavit from a certain doctor in Scranton to this effect—the injury to her was so extensive—something about the complete dilatation of the uterus—that she did in fact abort later. Two days later, in Scranton, while visiting friends. The doctor, who swears in his own affidavit that an attempt had been made to abort the young lady, is a man of high reputation and standing. He was forced to operate on her. She was hemorrhaging. It is doubtful that if she remarries, she will ever be able to bear children, the damage done by the abortionist was so extensive and the resultant inflammation so widespread."

Louis looked at the two appalled men. "Gentlemen, that was a crime. There is no extenuation. It was a serious crime. The young lady was slightly over three months pregnant. Moreover, we now have affidavits of patients who were in Jon's office that day. The affidavits were reluctantly given, and how Campion and company discovered who those patients are I simply do not know. But they are here—sworn to by simple, honest people of good reputation in Hambledon, who like Jon and only gave these affidavits under pressure. They testify to the young lady's screams and her protestations of agony, and her accusation that Jon was 'hurting' her. They have described her disheveled state and her denunciations as she 'fled from his inner rooms.'

"The affidavit from Mrs. Beamish was sent to Senator Campion, who, as her Senator, was outraged. It seems that he had had a warm acquaintance with the late Mr. Ernest Beamish and esteemed him highly. So Kenton, of course, investigated. The young lady's affidavit, on the face of it, and her doctor's affidavit, then can be considered genuine."

"I don't believe it," muttered Howard. "Something smells again. I don't believe it."

"Knowing Jon, I do not believe it, either," said Louis.

"I don't believe it," said the priest, and shuddered.

"Nevertheless," said Louis, "there are the hospital affidavits, the attending surgeon's affidavit, and the fact that Mrs. Beamish was indeed in Jon's office, and that indeed other patients heard her screams and saw her flee. Moreover, we now have affidavits from Mrs. Beamish's husband's executor, and from that doctor in Scranton, that they visited Jon, alleging that there was a bill due him. He pretended, they said, not to recall Mrs. Beamish immediately, and then admitted that he did. He told them frankly that she had been three months pregnant, but had 'incontinently,' run out before he had completed the 'examination,' and that therefore she owed him nothing." Louis smiled his wry smile. "On the face of it, that sounds absurd. No other doctor would have refrained from sending a bill. After all, he did partially examine her. Even if the examination had not been completed, there was still his time, and his good faith in proceeding with an examination she had requested, herself. So, Jon stands damned there, too."

"But he will have his records of Mrs. Beamish," said Howard Best, the lawyer. "And no abortionist keeps records of his patients."

"True. Let us hope he has his records still. Of course, before a judge and jury, the showing of such a record will not carry much weight, but it will still carry some. Now, let us go on.

"I have here two affidavits from two other young women, a Miss Louise Wertner, seamstress, of Hambledon, and a Miss Mary Snowden, milliner, also of Hambledon. The young ladies—if one can call them such—were indiscreet, indulging in premarital experiences, as they admit themselves in their affidavits. One girl is nineteen, the other twenty-one, and in poor circumstances. They had heard, they say, of some 'rumors' in connection with Dr. Ferrier, and in their extremity had gone to him, and he readily consented to perform the abortions, even to declaring that he detested children and did not blame the girls for wishing to rid themselves of their 'burdens.' "

The froggy eyes surveyed the two silent men on the other side of the desk, both looking cold and a little shriveled and despairing.

"The young ladies do not know each other. But one paid fifty dollars for the alleged abortion, the other paid seventy-five. Jonathan had his office clerk send them bills to their homes, one dated November 10th, 1900, the other November 21st, the same year. I have those bills here. They went to his office lately, the clerk recognized the bills, accepted payment of them, and receipted them. Would you care to look at them, gentlemen?"

They examined the damning bills, and the receipts. Howard put them down quietly on the desk, clasped his hands together and studied them. Then he said, "There is no proof that Jon aborted them, as they claim, is there?"

"In a way. They both suffered some slight ill effects a few days later. They went to separate doctors, who, in affidavits I have here, swear that the girls had been pregnant and that a recent abortion had been performed on them. The doctors are reputable. Neither knew that Jon was the 'culprit.' One of them is on the staff of this hospital itself. Dr. Philip Harrington. I have had Phil in here, told him none of the things in the affidavit, and asked him about Miss Wertner, his patient. He readily stated that indeed the girl had had a recent criminal abortion, that her condition at no time had been serious, but that she had complained of cramps. She stayed one day in the hospital. You both know Phil Harrington. As I already have an affidavit from the other doctor, I asked Phil to make one also, and he did so. He is about to be married. He says he would like to meet the 'criminal' personally, who had killed those embryos, and deal with him himself."

Howard said in a dull voice, "Wasn't that indiscreet of Jon to send the girls bills—if he really did perform the operations?"

"Not in ordinary reasoning. The girls did not have the money. He was sorry for them, or even wished to abort them for some twisted reason or other. Or, he wished to conceal criminal activity and sent them bills for 'complete physical examinations,' as the bills themselves state clearly. There is another thing: the usual fee for examination, conducted for patients who are in such poor circumstances, is usually far smaller than this. The best physicians ask only fifteen dollars, for such examinations take several days, of at least one hour a day. Quite often, under the rule of charging less for the poor, and charging more for the rich, a doctor will charge only a very few dollars."

"How did it happen, Doctor, that you received those two affidavits?" asked the priest, who appeared quite ill.

"It is the rule, Father, that when a girl goes to a physician and he discovers that she has had a recent abortion, he must report it. Phil reported it to the Board of St. Hilda's. The other doctor reported it to the Friends'. This is to protect the attending physician, who must have witnesses during the examinations. It is also the law. It is very necessary to run to earth those despicable creatures, the criminal abortionists, who put the lives of young mothers into terrible jeopardy. The girls often die, you know. The girls were much afraid to report Jon, for fear of legal reprisals, for they are parties to a criminal act. They were given assurances that if they did report the name of the abortionist, they could be protected and not prosecuted. Still, they returned to their miserable habitations to consider the case. Then they both made affidavits and sent them, one to this hospital, one to the Friends'."

Howard considered long and deeply. Then he said, "I don't believe it. Call that an emotional statement if you will, but I don't believe it. My lawyer's instinct tells me that it is a lie they are telling of Jon."

"I do not believe it, either," said Louis, and Howard and the priest smiled at him weakly in gratitude. "But still, there are those receipted bills, there are the affidavits of the doctors. Under other circumstances, Howard, what would you say?"

The young man hesitated. Then he admitted, "Guilty."

"So." Louis sighed.

"Campion does not know of these second and third abortions?"

"Of course not. He knows about Mrs. Beamish only." Louis closed the folder. "Campion and company are demanding that I call in some members of the State Medical Board to review the 'facts.' The 'facts' he has given me. Now, Howard, as Jon's friend and his former lawyer, what do you suggest I do?"

Howard rubbed his auburn curls wearily, then examined his nails, then scratched his ankle. "How long is Campion giving you to appeal to the State Medical Board?"

"Ten days."

"Then, you must ask for a longer time. I am going to investigate these serious cases, the Beamish, Wertner and

Snowden ones. The other affidavits are only malice and not worthy of consideration. Except for Jon's curette. I'll try to see Eaton, but he's rabid against Jon. Everyone remembers the Philadelphia papers reporting that he shouted, 'No, no!' when the verdict of not guilty was brought in. Then he had a stroke. They also remember that he had loved Jon like a son and was delighted when Jon married his niece, Mavis. Men don't turn against such 'sons' unless for cause, everyone will say. The cause seems obvious. Or, is it so obvious?"

"I do not understand you, Howard."

"It is a rule among lawyers to ignore the obvious unless it is written down in black and white as a sworn statement or a confession. Even then we are suspicious. That's why we scrutinize everything, and that's why we are so often successful in defending a case. The incredible is more often the real explanation."

"I hope you are not catching at straws," said Louis. "Are you going to tell Jon now?"

Howard considered a long time. Then he shook his head. "No, it would only make him furious and even dangerous. You know Jon. No. I want to have some substantial refutation before I talk to him. And, by God, I am going to get it!" He thrust out his long sharp chin belligerently.

Louis was silent for a few minutes. "You know," he said at last, "I am endangering my position here by telling you any of this, Howard. This is all confidential, you see, as Campion warned me, and he is very powerful on the Board, the only layman. They, too, are preparing the case against Jon. He wants to face Jon with complete iron facts and resolutions, and the State Medical Board members. He wants it all done ruthlessly, like a knife cut."

"Typical of him, the damned radiant scoundrel," said Howard with bitterness. "Such men can't stand honest men, men who oppose them. I'd rather face a tiger than a politician who is after my hide." He looked at the pale and silent priest. "Father, what do you think of all this?"

"I think that Jon is surrounded by vicious and vindictive enemies, who will do anything to destroy him, Howard. How he earned those enemies lies in his nature, and in their natures, too."

"Well, he has friends, too, Father, including Louis here. Louis"—and Howard smiled at him—"I'd never have thought it of you!"

"Perhaps," said Louis Hedler, smiling back but not with

much amusement, "you would have no reason to think that of me even now, Howard, if I were not financially independent! It is very strange and sad, is it not, that the mere matter of economic independence can make a man brave, whereas a man not so fortunate would not be brave at all?"

"Courage is always the price that life demands for granting peace," said the priest.

"A worthy sentiment, Father, and perhaps true. But if a man jeopardizes everything in his life for the sake of the peace of his conscience, he often has reason to regret his nobility. Heroes are lauded in story books and in history, yet even in history they frequently come to a sad and inglorious end. Later, of course, they are eulogized, but that does them no good at all when they are in their graves."

"Then only God remembers," said the priest, and Louis looked embarrassed. He thought that he might begin to believe that if Jon were saved from what was planned for him.

CHAPTER THIRTY

Today, thought Jonathan Ferrier, I will hunt Jenny down if I have to take Hambledon, and the island, apart with my bare hands.

He had not been sleeping well lately, partly because of the heat, which did not abate, and the sullen hot days, and partly because as the time approached for his departure from Hambledon he was feeling a strong depression, which never lifted. He knew he could not stay in his town under present circumstances, which became worse day by day rather than better, but a heavy sadness had come to live with him which he could not philosophize away nor laugh at in his usual man-

ner. Then there was the elusive Jenny, and her elusiveness
had at first irritated him and then had become a source of
impatient anger. He had heard rumors that Robert Morgan
was visiting her more and more frequently, in spite of the
smart warning he had received from Jonathan, and was even
seen at local public gatherings with her, including Chautauqua and the circus, of all things. Jonathan was finding it
harder and harder to keep from making kindly and derisive
remarks to the ingenuous Robert, who no longer spoke of
Jenny Heger.

He had been calling at the island at least three times a
week, usually between five and six in the afternoons, and
Jenny was always "not at home," according to Harald and
the servants, or totally invisible and not to be found. Jonathan had thought of writing to her in plain terms but was
afraid that Harald might recognize his handwriting and that
was intolerable. Worse, Jenny might refuse to answer. (Coy?
thought Jonathan. No, she's anything but that.)

He decided, early this morning as the sun came up, that he
would see, or find, Jenny at noon on the island, before she
had time to hide or whatever it was she did when he appeared.

He stood at the bedroom window and looked to the east,
hoping for rain. But there was only a brilliant scarlet glittering in the east, sparkling through the long dark fronds of a
great willow, and a harsh dusty odor of parching land. The
mountains seemed to heave and pant for moisture and coolness; their green had become brownish and burnt. If there
was ever a downpour of any magnitude, Hambledon, in its
river valley, would be in the same position as some Spanish
towns on waterless plains which suddenly experienced a del-
uge and then flash floods. Even the river was sinking more
and more visibly each day, and at noon the sky was brazen.
At night everything seemed to gasp feebly.

Jonathan cursed as he struggled into clothing already damp
with his own sweat the moment it touched his body. He
would make his hospital calls early, overseeing what Robert
Morgan had done. He called Robert's house and said with
curtness, "I don't want to be out in this heat more than I
have to, Bob, so I am going to the hospitals as much before
noon as possible. Will you be there?"

Robert yawned, glanced at his bedside clock, and said,
"For God's sake, it's only a quarter to seven! You don't

usually start until nine. Very well. I'll meet you at the hospitals. St. Hilda's first?"

"Don't I always?" asked Jonathan, and hung up, feeling again a huge irritation against practically everything and everybody, and waiting for the heavy depression to fall on him again. It did as he went downstairs to the morning room, where breakfast was waiting. But Marjorie had not as yet arrived, and Jonathan sat down and gloomily contemplated the warm prunes in a dish before him. He rang the bell and the little waitress came in and he said, "Haven't we a slice of cold watermelon, Mary, or a cantaloupe, or perhaps a chilled orange?"

"For breakfast, Doctor?" asked the girl, astounded. "It's always prunes for breakfast, isn't it, or stewed figs?"

"I'm starting something new," said Jonathan, "beginning today. Bring me some cold fruit if we have it."

"It will disturb the stomach, Doctor," the girl said. He could not help smiling at her.

"It's my stomach, Mary, and if I get cholera infantum at my age, it will be my own damned fault, won't it?"

A few moments later the cook arrived, disbelieving, and sweltering in her bulk. "Doctor, is Mary right? Do you want some fresh fruit—fresh—and cold, for breakfast? I never heard of such a thing!"

"You've heard of it now, dear."

"It's against nature, Doctor."

Jonathan surveyed her kindly. "Emily, I've been against nature most of my life, but now I'm really getting into the battle."

Mary, her face doubtful and averted and a little afraid, brought him a cold little melon and he attacked it with pleasure and with unusual appetite. Mary peeked at him around the swinging baize door, expecting him to have convulsions at any moment. Then she brought him his poached eggs, bacon and coffee and marmalade. By the time these arrived, Marjorie had come downstairs. "Aren't you early, Jon?" she asked. She appeared more wan than usual, and thinner.

"I thought I'd make an early start and finish before the worst of the heat," he said as he helped her into her chair.

"Is that cold fruit you have been eating?" she asked, looking with mistrust at the remains of the melon.

"Yes, and very good, too. Why should fresh fruit be served only at the end of a meal, and dinner at that? If I don't drop dead of it by tonight, then I'll have exploded another fallacy of the hacks, that fresh fruit on an empty stomach can cause the flux, dysentery, colic, colitis, and assorted ills. Never believed it anyway. Have a piece for yourself."

"It looks inviting," Marjorie admitted, and when Mary arrived, she gave her own order, to fresh consternation in the kitchen. "Dear me," said Marjorie, touching her forehead with her handkerchief. "It is very hot, isn't it? I can't recall it being like this in Hambledon before. When the weather breaks, it will be quite violent."

She told him then that she intended to go to Philadelphia in a few days to visit old friends and distant relatives. "And perhaps I'll go to Atlantic City, too, for a look at the sea, and some coolness. I've never really got accustomed to living in a land-bound town like this."

Jonathan said, "When I leave, which will now be very shortly, why don't you return to your home in Philadelphia? After I've done a little wandering, I may settle there myself."

Marjorie's lips trembled as she smiled. "That would be nice, dear. Let me consider it. After all, I've lived here so long, a lifetime, thirty-six years, and I knew it, too, as a child. Still, it never really seemed my home, though I love this house of your father's. It is hard for a woman of my age to be moved easily."

"Fifty-five or -six isn't ancient," said Jonathan. Now he looked at his mother and saw her pale and dispirited appearance. "When you are in Philadelphia, why don't you stop in and see Dr. Hearndon?"

"I may," said Marjorie, who had already decided to visit the cardiologist. Her body seemed very thin in its light batiste embroidered shirtwaist and high lace collar, which rose to her chin.

"Why don't you women wear sensible clothing in the summer?" asked Jonathan, with some uneasiness. He did not like his mother's color and her air of lassitude. "That duck skirt of yours—it looks like iron."

"Your high stiff collar is even worse," said Marjorie. "Well, I hope you won't miss me too much when I am in Philadelphia. Incidentally, Harald is going with me. I do wish Jenny would come, too. So lonely on that island, though I hear she has made some new friends." Marjorie gave her son an artless glance.

"If you mean Bob Morgan," replied Jonathan, "he is quite harmless."

"They have been to dinner several times at the Kitcheners'," said Marjorie. "Poor little Maude. She is really very smitten with Robert, and he is exactly right for her, though as men are so very foolish, he probably does not realize that."

Jonathan stood up. "But, I'm sure that Maude, in the old way of women, will soon enlighten him," he said, and left the room and the house. He went out into the hot light of the morning. He looked at the shriveling trees, at the burnt grass, at the dust in the gutters and between the cobblestones. It would be one hell of a day.

He looked over the lawns to his offices, still shut and closed and silent, and the depression became a hard rolling in him. They had been more of a home to him than his father's house, which his mother had made so elegant and charming. There he had hung his first shingle and had contemplated it with pride. There he had settled the new furniture, and put in his cabinets and arranged his examination rooms. He knew every corner, every window, intimately. The sun glanced off the clean windows and glimmered on the polished wooden doors. The offices were now no longer his. They belonged to a stranger. They had abandoned him and had driven him away. For the first time in many days he thought of Mavis and was disagreeably surprised to feel a lunge of the old murderous hatred for his wife again in the very pit of his stomach. He had thought he was all finished with that, and he ran hurriedly down the steps of the deep wide porches and went to the livery stable.

He chose his buggy today, which would give him some shelter from the probing sun. He drove off through the hazy streets. It was still very early, but from open windows he could hear the unmelodious and—to him—obscene shrilling of the new phonographs and the new popular songs. Edison was truly a genius and a blessed man to his countrymen, but why he had invented the phonograph was a mystery to Jonathan, who detested popular music and its cheapness. At least three exuberant phonographs were grinding out a particularly detestable song, "Under the Silvery Moon, I like to spoon—"

Brash, lightless century. Who had called it the Century of Light? There were such marvelous things prophesied for it in practically the immediate future: A four-hour working day (while men still worked ten to twelve hours a day!), flying craft for every family by 1914, the total disappearance of disease and poverty "within our foreseeable lifetime," large airy houses for a pittance for everybody, great parklands surrounding every city, automobiles which would race over enormous roads at a hundred or more miles an hour by 1920, an extension of life to at least one hundred and twenty by 1925, and, among the other fragrant bouquets of the politicians, absolute peace and no more wars. "Fraternity, liberty, equality!" they sang, picturing the "new" world on the threshold. "No hatred, no bigotry, no tyrants, no old despotisms, no hunger, ever again! Only love and light, forevermore! The Millennium!"

Jonathan, by nature, did not believe in millenniums, politicians' promises and dreams, and love and light. He also believed, with Ibsen, that "When everybody has everything no one has anything" of value. But he did not doubt for a moment that the politicians would soon find a way of buying a country through gigantic bribes, for their own power, and that way would be the way of a personal income tax, an evil which had inevitably destroyed every nation in the past. It was a ludicrous spectacle: politicians buying the souls and bodies of the people with the money stolen from their own pockets! But mankind never learned. No, it never learned, and even when faced with the ultimate and inevitable catastrophe, it could only look at it with dazed eyes and say, "How did this happen?"

The old tyrants and the old despotisms would soon arise in the world again. It was history. The world was due for the reappearance of the great dragons. They would arrive on schedule. I hope, thought Jonathan, not in my own lifetime, but I may not be so lucky. The grinding of the phonographs, or gramophones, as some called them, seemed to mock him like little shrieking demons.

Robert Morgan was not at St. Hilda's yet when Jonathan arrived, now in a bad temper. But he met Philip Harrington, who never lost an opportunity to remind his friend that he was to be best man at his coming wedding with Elvira Burrows and to give Jonathan some fresh, and fatuous news of his bride. "That girl," he said today to Jonathan, with pride, "you should see her linens!"

"Have you been sampling them before the wedding?" asked Jonathan. "To test their smoothness?"

"Don't be crude," said Philip.

"Wrinkles in a sheet can distract any girl's bottom," said Jonathan. "Never mind. But it's a fact anyway and a curse on a honeymoon. What's the matter?"

Philip's large and good-tempered face had changed. "It's Dr. Brinkerman—again."

"Old Claude? What's he been doing now?"

"Telling everyone I don't know a uterus from a burlap sack. But I'm used to that now. You know what he thinks of us younger doctors. A nasty, surly brute, big as a house, and mean as a red-eyed bull, and as arrogant as an ignoramus."

"I like your metaphors," said Jonathan. "You should be of help to Elvira's papa. But what's the swine—not to mix metaphors—been up to lately?"

"He had a case, a young mother, first baby born at home, as usual, then something went wrong. Child premature; detached placenta. Her own doctor rushed her to the hospital and called Claude, who calls himself 'the senior gynecologist' around here. I and my friends are just butchers, according to him, or in our first year of med. Well, he operated on the girl —to save her life, to quote him—and removed the uterus. Twenty-two years old. Isn't that pretty? While he was at it he also took her ovaries, and that's the prettiest of all. Plunged into old middle age in her early twenties."

"Were they diseased?"

"No, of course not. And the uterus could have been saved with a little skill. But you know Brinkerman. The Marquis de Sade would have loved him. He hates women and their functions."

"You were in the operating room with him?"

"Yes. And a couple of others. I tried to intervene. For a minute, there, I thought he would deprive me of my manhood with his scalpel. That would have been hard on Elvira, not to mention myself, so I said nothing more. You know old Louis, what a stickler he is for etiquette between the old doctors and the young."

Jonathan said with disgust, "Did you tell Louis?"

"Yes, I did. I thought he'd blow up at me, but he has something on his mind these days, or he's coming down with something. Subdued. Abstracted. He only said, 'Let's have a little peace here. Claude probably did what was best in his own judgment.' "

"Good old Louis," said Jonathan. "The Golden Brotherhood hangs together, probably because they know that if they didn't, they'd hang separately—with the judge wearing a black cap. I'd like to spring the trap. Well, what is done is done, unfortunately. Don't brood on it."

"I want your help," said Philip. "An ectopic pregnancy

was brought in here this morning. Claude's case. He'll mutilate the girl, as sure as hell, just as he did the other. I can see him licking his chops right at this minute. He's a great hand at mutilation, Claude."

"That's because he has a young wife, his second, who could teach Prissy Witherby a few delightful tricks. All other women are proxy for Ethelyn. I've often thought that doctor's first practices should be confined to members of their own immediate family and closest friends before they went into general practice. That should not only teach them discretion and care but would help them get rid of secret resentments. A few discreetly murdered wives, for instance, would make a doctor love all other women thereafter, in forgiveness."

"I wish you'd be serious," said Philip, and the two young men paused a moment to nod at passing doctors.

"I'm deadly serious. Phil, I can't help you, and you know that. Brinkerman hates me like poison, and that's funny because I never had cause to cross his path except for twice, and that was five years ago. Told him he was unfit."

"That should make him love you, or he should have a short memory."

"That was five years ago. I rarely see him. We don't speak, but we do exchange the most telling glances. We meet socially here and there, or we used to when I mingled, and we were very, very polite to each other. How could I possibly get into his operating room?"

"You could ask old Louis—for a study."

"Won't you be there?"

"Yes. But the old bastard scares me to death. He looks at you like approaching nemesis if you venture a remark or an opinion. Powerful old bugger. Now he can't intimidate you."

"It's all unethical. He'd probably order me out at once."

"Louis still has the say, in spite of his new preoccupation with some damned problem or other. Brinkerman's getting a rotten reputation among us younger fellas, and we're spreading the word. That's bad for St. Hilda's, and Louis knows that, or he should. Jon, this is a very young woman, only twenty, for God's sake!"

"I don't know how I get into these things," said Jonathan. He thought of Dr. Brinkerman with loathing. He knew more about the older doctor than did Philip Harrington. Yes, a sadist, a lusting hater of women, helplessly infatuated with his gay young wife, and rabid. To him, a man of fifty-two or -three, all pretty young women were secret whores, though he was famous for his attachment to them. He had a way of painfully pinching or squeezing student nurses, then laughing in their grimacing faces and assuring them of his affection for them. They feared and avoided him, running at the sound of his roaring, brawling voice and his oversized presence. They dreaded encounters with him in the corridors and in quiet places. He had what the girls called "a dirty mouth" and dexterously tormenting fingers. He could inflict more torture on a young woman in his examination rooms than any Inquisitor. Yet, for some unknown reason, he had a reputation as a fine doctor and surgeon, to the younger doctors' bafflement. Jonathan believed it was because he was very rich and influential, and a shameless egotist.

Jonathan found Louis Hedler in his office. He was struck, when he entered, by Louis' worried and drawn expression, and his sluggish manner. He was also surprised when Louis, instead of looking apprehensive as usual when Jonathan entered, smiled at him almost paternally. "Jon, my boy," he said.

"What's the matter, Louis? Are you sick?"

"Well, no. Sit down, Jon. I'm just—concerned—about a member of the staff." The bulging brown eyes studied Jonathan with a peculiar expression. "A fine man, rather young. I'm afraid he's in a little trouble—of his own doing, in a way. Rash. Impetuous. A little indiscreet at times. But I happen to be fond of him." Louis smiled. "Personally, he offends me often, but I have to admit he knows what he knows, and in a superior manner. If you had told me," said Louis, "a year or two years ago, or even six months ago, that I'd be concerned over him now I'd have laughed tremendously."

"You're mellowing, Louis. Who's the mellower?"

Louis contemplated him, then smiled enigmatically. "I don't think you know him, Jon. No, I don't think you know him at all." He rubbed his lips. "You never come in here, Jon, without bringing me contention or alarms or worries. Which is it now?"

"Every single one." He told Louis about Dr. Brinkerman and Philip Harrington. He did not know why Louis' face became more and more dismayed as he talked. "So," said Jonathan, "if you have no objection, I'd like to be present in the operating room."

"That's impossible! You know how Claude hates you."

"Just because we had a difference of opinion? A long time

ago? Don't we all have differences of opinion with each other? I'm not pretending that Claude loves me, but he's surely forgotten my clash with him."

On the contrary, thought Louis, very much on the contrary! He said with some malice, "Jon, wasn't it a few of you bright young lads who insisted that the operating surgeon have the privilege to refuse to have anyone present he did not desire to be there? Yes. In the old days any physician who was interested, and even his friends, could enter an operating room and observe to his heart's content. But not you lads. All for asepsis and no theater atmosphere."

Louis smiled at the tight strong face opposite him, and the dark and amused eyes. "Touché, Louis. But, we are right. Who is the young lady, by the way, and who is her family physician who sent her here?"

"Um," said Louis. He shook his head, then said, "Mrs. Jason Hornby. Attending physician, Summers Bayne, friend of yours."

"Splendid," said Jonathan, and reached without permission for the telephone on the desk and called Dr. Bayne and then spoke in his most ingratiating way. "I'd like to be present, Summers, when Claude Brinkerman operates on your patient today, Mrs. Jason Hornby, at two o'clock. Oh, ten is it? Even better. I am here at St. Hilda's now. You see, Dr. Phil Harrington can't be present," said Jonathan cocked his black eyebrows at Louis and smiled. "So, Phil has asked me to be there in his place. There's a little difficulty, Summers. Old Claude doesn't love me as he should. You'll mention that I am there at your request if he should object? By the way, who picked Brinkerman?" Jonathan listened and frowned. Then he said, "I quite agree with you. I wouldn't let him clip my dog's nails. Don't worry, Summers. I'll be right there, and you will be, too, and we won't let him do any fancy hemstitching or let him waltz around the vena cava. He does so love that vena cava, and why the Board doesn't throw him out is something perhaps only old Louis can tell you." Jonathan winked at his indignant elder. He replaced the telephone receiver, and said, "The young lady chose Brinkerman herself. Insisted, so what can poor Summers do? He was quite relieved when I said I wanted to be present."

"You're an impertinent rascal, Jon."

"Oh, I know that. Incidentally, why don't you throw Brinkerman out?"

"Jon, he's an expert surgeon, if a little—radical—at times.

He is as bad as you about asepsis. If his judgment occasionally fails him, who among us can plead that we are never wrong? If the average layman fully understood into what vulnerable weak hands he was trustfully submitting himself, and to what fallible judgment, we'd have no more hospitals, no more operating rooms."

"And many people would still be alive instead of rotting peacefully away in some pretty cemeteries. That's just confidential between ourselves, of course."

"You don't keep that very 'confidential' very often, Jon." Louis was very disturbed. "I wish I could dissuade you. I have my own reasons for suggesting you not be there. You have enough enemies, Jon, and Brinkerman is a man who cherishes his enemies and never stops until he has cut their throats."

"He can't hate me more than he already does."

Louis was silent, gazing at him, and then he said in an odd voice, "You are quite right."

Jonathan went out to inform Philip Harrington that he was "taking your place. You have an emergency." Philip was relieved. "Mrs. Hornby is a nice rich young lady, or Brinkerman wouldn't look at her, and isn't it fortunate for a lot of people that they can't afford some operations? Poverty has done more to save lives than wealth has done, and if that isn't heresy what is it?"

"It's truth," said Jonathan, and went on his rounds. At half-past nine he was in the scrub room adjacent to the operating room and, whistling, was beginning to scrub when Claude Brinkerman came in with a blast like an attacking Minotaur. "What the hell is this, Ferrier, you being my assistant on the Hornby case?"

"Didn't you hear?" asked Jonathan, very mildly. "Phil has an emergency. He asked me to do him a favor and—"

The hard and flaming face seemed to radiate irrepressible hatred and fury, and the little pale eyes sparked with a murderous glow. Jonathan, who was well aware of their mutual dislike and mistrust, was still surprised at this overwhelming and vehement attack, for the cause of their old disagreements had been trivial. But Brinkerman appeared beside himself as he stood and breathed rage at his junior, clenching and unclenching his huge hands at his sides, his broad chest heaving. Had Jonathan been his deadliest enemy, he could not have betrayed more savage irrationality, no more incipient violence.

"I won't have you!" shouted Brinkerman. "I want no mur—" He stopped, visibly and painfully swallowed. But his rage grew. "I won't have you! Is that clear?"

"Summers Bayne asked me," said Jonathan. "He has that right. Or would you prefer to let Phil Harrington to the job for you in an hour or two, when his present emergency is over? This case isn't an on-the-minute emergency, I understand." He looked at Brinkerman. "What was it you were about to call me, Claude?" He shook his wet hands and now as he looked at the other surgeon there was something in his eyes that was frightening. Dr. Brinkerman looked back at him and a curious malign flickering ran over his large coarse features, and there was a twitching of his long thin mouth.

"Never mind," he said. His forehead was purplish red, but now the doctor began to subside. He lowered his voice. "Ferrier, I don't like you and I never did. I don't trust you and I never did."

"I can repeat those laudable sentiments about you, too, Brinkerman."

"You can be of no help to me in that room, Ferrier."

"But I can be of help, perhaps, to the patient," said Jonathan, and again their eyes met like boulders meeting.

"Are you questioning my professional competence?"

"Are you questioning mine, Brinkerman?"

The other doctor again raised his voice. "I don't want you!"

"Summers does. Louis knows, too."

Dr. Brinkerman was suddenly silent. Then he smiled very slightly. "Old Louis," he said, "may have reason to regret this very soon."

Jonathan shrugged and went back to his scrubbing. Two young nurses near the doors, forgotten by the two men, smiled meaningly at each other. then gave Dr. Brinkerman, whom they detested, a sympathetic glance. Jonathan saw this in the mirror on the wall and shook his head. These girls would not have been in the room alone with Brinkerman, but there was another man here whom they disliked more, and that man was Jonathan Ferrier, who had given them no cause at all to hate him, and if he had often been rudely jocular with them, he had also shown them his respect for their profession and was frequently kind. But he was a "foreigner" to them, even to one of the young ladies who was an American citizen by naturalization. He watched them make moues of sympathy at Dr. Brinkerman. Encouraged by this, Dr.

Brinkerman pinched the breast of one roughly as he passed her to another sink. She winced, and tears of pain came into her eyes, but she still tried to smile at him.

Human nature, thought Jonathan, who had seen this and strongly wanted to hit Claude Brinkerman, is something I will never understand. But then, as Mama once told me when I was a kid, I am the "unpopular minority." Yes, indeed, minorities generally catch hell. Yet, how are unpopular minorities formed, and by whose judgment and whose decree? Who has the right to decide who shall belong, and who shall not, to the general "loving brotherhood of man?" By what standard? Personal integrity, worth, honor, intelligence, charity, goodness, harmlessness, dedication, decency? It has been my experience that these virtues are held in very low repute by majorities, so they cannot be the frame of reference for judgments.

He became aware, and through the mirror again, that Dr. Brinkerman was giving him even more curious glances, satisfied, hating, gloating, and his instinct for danger was alerted. But, what was the danger? What damage could Brinkerman do him? He looked at the thick red neck, a neck as muscular and almost as heavy as a bull's, and at the meaty, soapy hands. He had no doubt that Brinkerman would enjoy murdering him, and he returned the compliment. Still, he wondered. When he had encountered Brinkerman infrequently in the corridors, they had exchanged cold nods and nothing more. This new wild violence was inexplicable.

"I want you to know, Brinkerman," said Jonathan, "that I did not exactly force myself into this situation. My presence was requested."

"I am aware of that, Ferrier. I shall deal with Summers Bayne in my own way at my own leisure."

Jonathan considered this. "I am not without friends," he said.

"You would be surprised," said Brinkerman, and chuckled hoarsely.

Jonathan frowned. He was remembering what Philip Harrington had told him recently, and the odd way his former friends were treating him in the hospital corridors and in the lounge rooms recently. But he made himself smile, knowing that Brinkerman was watching him closely.

"Very ambiguous," he said. "But I have enough friends to protect Summers, and I am famous for protecting my friends." He motioned to one of the nurses, who came forward to powder his drying hands and to help him with his rubber gloves. "Moreover, Summers' brother is a State Senator, close to the Governor, or did you not know that? I also believe that brother is on the Medical Board. If I am wrong, please correct me."

Dr. Brinkerman had forgotten. He gave Jonathan another vicious look but remained silent. The young nurse assisting Jonathan held her mouth prominently disapproving of him and avoided his eyes, and Jonathan again wondered at human nature, for he knew that Dr. Bayne was very popular with the nurses and Brinkerman's ugly threat against him should have vexed the girl. Jonathan mentally checked another black mark against mankind.

The patient was ready when the two surgeons went into the operating room and Dr. Bayne, already scrubbed and masked and covered, was waiting for them. He gave Jonathan an inquiring look and Jonathan winked at him. The patient was under anesthesia, and all was in readiness. Jonathan looked at her pretty unconscious face, the face of a child. Then he looked at Dr. Brinkerman, who was also studying those soft and childlike features, and his eyes were lustful and hungry as a torturer's, and as the sadist's they were.

There was no denying that he was a competent surgeon, and he made the incision with a preciseness and skill and smoothness that won Jonathan's admiration. It was a routine matter. The pregnant tube was large and bulging but was not unduly inflamed, nor had it ruptured. The girl was lucky. Dr. Brinkerman neatly excised it, and then he said to the watching interns, ignoring Dr. Bayne and Jonathan, "I will now closely examine the uterus for deformities, and the other ovary. I have not yet decided if this one should be removed, and possibly the uterus."

The men exchanged troubled glances. But Jonathan said, "I can see for myself that the uterus and both ovaries are in prime condition, and there is no need for an extensive exploration."

Dr. Brinkerman paused. He turned his head slowly and his pale eyes glowed with evil fire. "Am I the surgeon, or are you, Ferrier?"

"I am your assistant, if you wish to call it that, and I am also bound by the Oath of Hippocrates and am a defender of the public weal. Therefore, if you do any damage to this girl's reproductive system, I shall do everything I can to prevent you from ever operating on anyone again."

He spoke clearly and sharply and with assurance, fully aware that he had now done the irrevocable: he had deliberately insulted and defamed the operating surgeon in his own domain, before the faces of witnesses. But to him the young girl on the table, so unaware, so trustful, so helpless, was more to him than any consequences to him, though he knew they could be grave. However, only the strongest of threats could stop this sadist, and Jonathan had used them.

"For this alone," said Brinkerman, in a terrible voice, "you could have your license revoked."

Jonathan laughed. "I should like to see you try it. I will bring witnesses against you, and be damned to professional ethics and always protecting the bungler or the intentional mutilator. Well? Aren't you going to suture the girl or are you going to permit her to bleed to death?"

He nodded to Dr. Bayne and, still watching Brinkerman closely, he went to the tubal pregnancy on its receiving basin, and he dipped his hand in water and baptized the exposed embryo. Some of the interns smiled indulgently, but at least two looked grave, and Dr. Bayne blessed himself. Dr. Brinkerman laughed lewdly and made a low indecent remark to the nurse nearest him. But the girl was unexpectedly near tears.

"After your vindictive remarks, Ferrier," said Dr. Brinkerman, "I have no recourse but to report you to the Board. Moreover, if this patient of mine suffers unfortunate results, the blame rests with you, for interference and overt intimidation."

Jonathan came back to the table. "I shall protect myself by watching every move you make, Brinkerman, so you don't do the girl a sly mischief, which I would not put past you. You have a reputation for that." He looked at Dr. Bayne, whose eyes showed his worry and alarm. "Don't be too concerned, Summers," he said. "Just watch the child carefully."

Everyone was convinced that Dr. Brinkerman was about to have a stroke. His hand trembled and shook. Jonathan dared not take the needle from him, for his hand had become contaminated, he believed, even in the presumably sterile water in which he had dipped it. He did not, however trust the sterilizing of very much in the operating room, and so refrained. But he watched every movement of Dr. Brinkerman's. The older surgeon had considerable self-control when he wished, and he recovered himself and his awful color receded, and he completed the stitching without incident. Then he strode, without a word, from the room, viciously stripping the gloves from his hands and banging the door behind him.

"He'd kill you if he could, Jon," said Dr. Bayne, as the interns and nurses tenderly covered the girl closely with the blankets and sheets and wheeled her out. "That is a very bad man."

"And a man who should not be permitted to operate on any woman under the age of fifty," said Jonathan.

"Jon, be careful."

"In this business it is a crime to be too careful of a colleague's delicate sensibilities," said Jonathan. "I've never covered for a man like Brinkerman before and I do not intend to do it now."

He expected to be called to Louis Hedler's office, but though he remained in the hospital for another hour, he received no call. He went down to the river, and to the island.

When Jonathan was half across the unusually quiet water of the river, he noticed that the sky had a disturbingly hot brazen quality, actually saffron, and burning. It reflected itself on the small blue ripples of the water, not with the clarity of sunlight, though the sun shone hot enough, but with a dullness. He looked down the river and saw the white steeple of a little church on the winding mainland, and for some reason it appeared bleak to him and hard and cold. It's only my depression, he thought. He had seen that steeple countless times, and never had it affected him so before with a sense of lonliness and removal.

Damn it, he thought, I had such dreams for this town. I'd have an X-ray in one of the hospitals. I'd have a store of radium. I'd induce famous doctors to come here to lecture our bumpkins. I'd build a tuberculosis wing on St. Hilda's, and a cancer research laboratory. That's what I, the great Samaritan, wanted to do for Hambledon—to make a small, compact, modern medical center, which even Boston wouldn't despise. God knows we—I mean they—need it. Farewell, dreams. Farewell everything except Jenny.

He had taken off his tie and his tall stiff white collar and his coat, yet he was sweating profusely by the time he reached the island and had tied up the little boat. He noticed that the river had fallen again, and more stones were bare. He looked at the sky. When this extraordinary weather broke, it would be hell. He had already forgotten Claude Brinkerman. All his thoughts, as he climbed toward the castle, were of Jenny Heger. He carried his coat on his arm, and his hat in his hand, for his skin was so naturally dark and of an autumn color that he did not fear for sensitivity to the sun. He began to whistle.

The mica in the stone of the little castle glistened and glittered in the brassy sunlight, as if the whole edifice had been erected of mingled cement and diamond dust. Jonathan could see its small turrets and its thin high windows and its bronze doors. He heard the silence all about him except for the weary chirping of an occasional bird. Not even a gardener was about, and the whole pretty island and its granite walls and its flowers and brilliant grass had an abandoned air, as if the sleeping inhabitants had awakened and had left it forever.

Jonathan was informed at the door by old Albert, who had a curiously sly look today, that Mr. Ferrier was not at home, Doctor, no, I really don't know where he is. Miss Jenny? It was believed that she had gone into Hambledon, though not certain. Would Dr. Ferrier like a drink? Dr. Ferrier declined and went away glumly. Where the devil was the girl, if she was on the island? There were all sorts of cool nooks, of course. Then Jonathan remembered that only one boat had been tied up on the opposite bank, in Hambledon. That meant that Harald had left it there before going into the town. Three, including the one Jonathan had used, were now on the island. He began to smile. When Harald arrived across the river, he would find no way to get back unless he signaled and someone saw. Of course, he could be away all day, and even the evening, and by that time Jonathan would have returned to the mainland and left a boat for him.

So, Jenny was on the island, hidden away as usual. Jonathan began to explore. He knew the island fairly well, for it had intrigued and amused him from the beginning. He toured the island, peering into every hidden grotto, into every trellised arbor. The scent of pine was very fresh here of a sudden, for a slight breeze had risen. After he had searched one side of the island, Jonathan, feeling hotter and hotter and more and more irritated, began on the opposite side. He saw the mountains clearly against that yellowish sky, and they were ochre-colored or bronzed, except for sharp islands of green where the lawns flourished about houses which appeared tiny and white from this distance. Again he thought of the plains and mountains of Spain, and what would happen here if there should be a flood and the water rose in this valley. Everything was parched enough.

His whistling became a little shriller and now a few birds answered peevishly. The light on the river was blinding and it had a torpid, oily look smeared with metallic blue. Little paths crept down the "fraudulent" woods, as Jonathan called the stands of expensive, rare trees, but he was grateful for their brief shade as he passed into it and then out of it. He could smell damp earth, rich and carnal, and old fallen leaves, and the rank odor of the few wild flowers permitted to grow here. He saw the tiny artificial bay in which Peter Heger had intended to keep tropical fish. It was covered with algae, another thing which was unusual, and the confined water stank unpleasantly. But a wild duck or two sailed its surface placidly.

The stone walls that surrounded most of the island were overgrown with glossy green leaves of ivy or climbing rose-bushes which, though their time was spent weeks ago, still bore a scarlet blossom here and there which looked like blood in the sun. Now, as if at a signal, cicadas began to whirr and shrill loudly in the hot silence. Jonathan passed a single apple tree and noticed that an apple or two looked red and ripe and he plucked one and chewed on it. It was a mistake. It was still green, and he threw it away.

He stopped to mop his face, and turned his eyes from the river and the walls and saw a grotto practically hidden by honeysuckle bushes and untended shrubbery. He saw a yellowish movement, quick and alert, beyond the bushes, and then it was still. He had found Jenny. Had he not stopped to sample the apple and then to throw it away, he would have missed this natural grotto, this small cavelike place sunken into the rising bank of the island. A curtain of wild wisteria drooped over it like a frail banner. He was certain that Jenny had heard his approach and his whistling. Yet now she crouched on the big stone in the grotto like a hunted thing, avoiding pursuit. This made Jonathan more annoyed than ever.

He pushed through the shrubbery and lifted aside the wisteria, and saw Jenny indeed crouched on the stone, with books and papers about her, and in a yellow cotton dress as plain as a shift. She looked at him in a white, mute silence and her eyes were very large and blue as a sudden little ray of sunlight touched them. She said nothing in recognition. She merely sat there and regarded him, not with anger or aversion or indignation, but with no expression at all.

"Hello, Jenny," he said, and in spite of his annoyance his

voice was very gentle, and he was surprised at the emotion that took him at the sight of the girl, and the tender desire for her, and his longing. He stood and looked at her, and smiled, and after a moment Jenny turned her head and her beautiful mouth trembled. He saw her profile, and it was dearer to him than anything he had known before, and he wanted to put his hands to her face, turn it to him and kiss that mouth and those long black lashes and the slender white throat. "Jenny," he said. Her black hair was not dressed. It tumbled over her shoulders and back like the hair of a very young girl.

He was afraid that she might jump to her feet and run past him, as she had run that July Fourth, and so he blocked the passage with his tall body, but easily. However, she did not move. Her hands were pressed one on top of the other in her lap, and her face was still averted. But her lashes had begun to blink, as if she were about to burst out crying. Jonathan could see the quick lift of her breast under the plain yellow bodice of the frock, and then its fall.

Very slowly, so as not to frighten her, he let the curtain of wisteria drop and it immediately made a living dusk in the grotto. Jonathan approached Jenny, and again with infinite slowness he sat down on the dark clean earth and hugged his knees and watched her. She did not look at him. He saw her knee near his cheek, and he wanted more than anything else to lean his cheek against it; he could see the coarse threads of the frock and the outline of her long thigh and calf, and then the arched foot in its sturdy slipper.

"I've looked for you for weeks, Jenny," he said. "But you avoided me. I wanted to know that you've forgiven me."

She spoke as if to the stony earthen wall of the grotto: "I forgave—you." Her voice was so quiet that he could hardly hear it.

Then he remembered something he had forgotten concerning that night. When he had thrown Jenny on her bed and then she had fought him off wildly, he had seen her great terror of the unknown about to be thrust upon her so brutally and with such violence. But with this was another terror: the terror of her own desire to surrender, the weakening of her legs under him, the sudden brief softening of the muscles of her thighs. It was then that she had arched her body in total resistance and had pushed him off, and had broken into tears.

He had been confident in these weeks that he could make Jenny love him. He was startled and overjoyed to know that

Jenny had loved him even then as she had fought him off and had struggled with him. She would not have him as he was then, fighting with her, about to take her by force. And, of course, he thought with indulgence, without benefit of clergy.

"Well," he said, "I'm glad you've forgiven me. But, as I told you then, Jenny, my darling, I've loved you for a long time. Didn't you know that?"

"No," she said.

"And you didn't believe me that night?"

Her head moved farther from him and she dropped her chin on her shoulder. "No, I didn't."

"Do you now?"

She pushed back a heavy fold of her hanging hair and he saw her hand, tanned by the sun, long, elegantly made, like his mother's hands.

"Won't you tell me, Jenny?"

But she pressed her lips tightly together and he thought of a shy but stubborn child, and he smiled again.

"Jenny, I'm going away. I am never coming back." He could smell the green life about him, and the earth, and the faint scent of the soap Jenny had been using, and the natural warm fragrance of her body and her hair. He put his hand on her foot. The foot jerked, but to his delight she did not remove it. Then his delight went away, for he saw that a few tears were running down her smooth pale cheek.

"I want you to come with me, Jenny," he said. "I love you. I've loved you for years. I want you to marry me. Soon. Tomorrow if possible. I want to take you away from Hambledon, where we'll have some peace. I want to show you the whole world. My darling."

He had never spoken to any woman like this before, nor had he felt this tenderness mixed with desire, and gentleness and even peace. He felt the warmth of her foot under his hand and through the cotton stocking. He wanted to kiss it. "Please don't cry, Jenny. Please answer me."

She said in a voice almost whispering, "Robert Morgan asked me to marry him yesterday," and she raised her hand and childishly wiped away her tears with the back of it. She still would not look at him.

"Bob Morgan?" He almost laughed. "That boy! Well, I admire his taste if I don't care for his impudence."

She turned suddenly to him then and her cheeks flared into color, and her blue eyes flashed with anger. He had always suspected Jenny of a deep temper, and he saw it now.

"What impudence yourself!" she exclaimed. "I can tell you this, Jon, he's an improvement on the Ferrier men!" Her voice was strong and direct and clear. He was delighted again. He squeezed her foot and very softly he let one of his fingers rise to her slender ankle and caressed it. He felt the flesh start a little under his touch; she did not snatch her foot away as he expected.

"Oh," he said, "I have no doubt that almost any man would be an improvement on us. We're a bad lot, as the English would say. Harald's an idiot, and I have the worst disposition in town, as you've probably discovered yourself. We are no gems on the matrimonial market, and there I agree with you. I wonder how you will endure being my wife. I really pity you." Now his whole hand was about her ankle. He wondered how much higher he could dare to raise it. It was a delicious thought. Then he was aware that she was very still, and he looked up and saw she had a tremulous, be-mused expression, as if all her awareness was directed to the ankle which he held. He watched her closely. Then he leaned his cheek against her knee. It stiffened, jerked, but she did not draw away, and his hand slid upward to the slim round calf, warm and firm and smooth.

A deep heavy flush swept into the girl's face. Her eyelids trembled, then dropped slightly. She began to cry again, soundlessly. Very slowly Jon rose to his knees, looking into her quivering face, then took her into his arms, hesitated, and pressed his lips into the hollow of her throat. Her head fell back helplessly. He felt the sudden bounding of her pulse against his mouth.

"Jenny, Jenny," he whispered. Her body was young and soft in his arms. He dropped his head and pressed it against her breast. She stirred once, then was still. He felt her rapt and virginal passion. She was not afraid, though she had begun to shiver. The duskiness of the cavelike grotto appeared to enlarge to him, to be filled with unbearable excite-ment, pleasure and happiness, and to be waiting. The quiet was not disturbed except for the distant sound of the cicadas, the faint whispering of the trees, and everything was height-ened to the senses, the fragrance of earth and leaves and young flesh.

Jonathan thought, in the intensity of his now rising desire, that there were worse places in which to take a beloved woman, who was surrendering. He kissed her bare throat again. His hand fumbled at the buttons on her bodice, little

plain white buttons, which he saw as large as plates. He unfastened one, two, three, and then she caught his hand and
her own was strong.

"No," she said. She burst out crying, not cries of fear or
protest, but sounds of desolation.

He immediately stopped. He held her as gently as before,
and then he pulled her head to his shoulder and let her cry.
What else had he expected of this inexperienced girl? He was
terrified that he had ruined everything and had confirmed her
previous bad opinion of him. "Jenny, my darling," he said.
"I'm sorry. But I love you more than my life, Jenny. I won't
annoy you again or disturb you. Until we're married. Jenny?"

"I can't marry you!" she cried, and his shirt was wet with
her tears. "I want to, but I can't!"

"Why not?" He was elated.

"I've done something terrible to you!"

He paused. He laughed a little. He held her more tightly.
"For God's sake, Jenny! What 'terrible' thing could you do to
me, a child like you?"

She rolled her head despairingly on his shoulder. "I can't
tell you, Jon. Please go away. Forget you ever saw me. Go a
long way away."

At this point an alien voice intruded, full of amusement
and contempt.

"I hate to end this touching, pastoral scene," said Harald
Ferrier at the entrance to the grotto. "There is nothing so
lovely as true love, is there? And what a scene! All the ele-
ments of dramatic seduction, immaculate surrender, tremolos
of dulcet tones, manly force, blandishments—everything. I
should have been a playwright. I'd make my fortune."

Jenny literally leaped in Jonathan's arms, and he let her go
and got to his feet, his furious temper rising, his dark face
thick with blood. He saw his brother leaning negligently
against the entrance to the grotto and smiling his broad and
amiable smile. Harald winked.

It was that lascivious wink, that indulgent smile, which
made Jonathan feel acute embarrassment as well as rage, and
a sort of juvenile shame. "What the hell are you doing here?"
he shouted.

Harald raised his ruddy eyebrows and beamed. "Why," he
said, as if surprised, "I believe I live here. At least, I thought
I did. Don't I?"

"Spying on us!" shouted Jonathan, feeling foolish.

"Oh, I'm sorry. Perhaps I should have waited for the final

scene, but I confess I'm a little too prudish for that. There
would have been a final scene?" He looked at Jenny,
crouched on the stone, her head turned away. "I'm surprised
at you, Jenny," he said in a mock reproving tone. "A nice
girl like you." He regarded his brother again in a friendly
way and his eyebrows cocked humorously. "Quite a dog, you,
Jon. No girl is safe with you, not even an untouched morsel
like Jenny. I really should be very outraged. After all, I am
her natural guardian. At the very least you should have observed etiquette and asked for her hand, and not have tried
—er—to take it robustly, if I may put it in a euphemious
form?"

Jonathan wanted to kill him on the spot. He also hated
him. He also felt ridiculous, a little contemptible, and wholly
sheepish.

"Button your frock, Jenny, my dear," said Harald in a paternal tone. "Quite extreme, the way it is gaping open. You
should be more careful when you dress. And do drop the
hem of your frock. Young ladies are not supposed, I believe,
to expose themselves almost to the thigh—in broad daylight,
too. But that happens during a romp, I have heard."

Jonathan's fists clenched. The heavy blood was still in his
face. Then he looked at his brother's eyes and saw that they
were not smiling in the least, and that their usual handsome
hazel had turned an ugly dark brown, and were glinting.

Harald laughed softly. He stared fully at Jonathan. "Let's
end this comedy, shall we? It distresses me to catch frolickers
in an—indiscreet—moment. But I heard voices and I was
looking for you, Jon. I was told you were still on the island. I
was resting in the castle, and it was believed I was in Hambledon. So, I was searching for you. It was not my intention
to force my company on you and Jenny. Had you both been
talking nicely and politely in genteel fashion, conversing as is
customary when a gentleman calls upon a lady, or perhaps
have been drinking tea—Jenny, did you forget the teacups?
—I should have withdrawn to a distance, made some com-
motion, called to let you know of my approach. But there
was something in the sounds I heard—scuffling? kissing?—
that alarmed me." He spread out his hands pleadingly. "So,
what else could I do but to hurry to save Jenny's honor,
which was apparently in the direst danger, or rescue her from
—what do the ladies call it—'a fate worse than death?'
Jenny, you should be very grateful."

The poor girl had buttoned her frock and dropped the hem

of her frock and now sat rigidly and very still on the stone, her hair fallen partly over her face.

"Now that you've had your little moment of fun," said Jonathan, restraining himself from hitting his brother only by the greatest effort, "suppose you let us alone."

"To continue the seduction of an innocent and helpless girl?" Harald recoiled in a parady of horror. He grinned, showing all his large fine teeth, and struck himself on the chest dramatically, "Not I, the protector of my stepdaughter!"

Again Jonathan saw the ugliness in his brother's eyes above that wide smile and he thought, He hates me as I hate him. He would kill me as easily as I could kill him. Now, this is a pretty situation.

"You don't need to protect Jenny," said Jonathan. "We are going to be married, practically immediately."

"Before or after?" asked Harald.

"Oh, go to hell," said Jonathan. He looked at Jenny, who was too silent, too stricken. "Jenny? I'll have my mother invite you to stay with her until we are married. You will come, won't you, Jenny?"

Harald shook his head sadly. "No, I am afraid she will not, Jon. I truly am afraid not."

Jonathan ignored him. For some perverse reason he now wanted to laugh explosively. He wanted to comfort Jenny, too, and make her laugh. "Tomorrow, Jenny?" he asked.

"Ah, no, dear brother," said Harald, when Jenny did not answer. "Jenny has her reasons, don't you, my dear? A very upright and valid reason, too. Jenny is all honor, or at least she was until about half an hour or so ago. You see, Jon," said Harald, assuming a mournful air, "Jenny thought you were a murderer until quite recently, when I enlightened her out of the deep charity of my heart."

"What!" said Jonathan. "You're lying, of course."

"Not at all! Ask Jenny herself. She believed that you murdered her mother. Tut, tut! All these murders you are accused of! Bluebeard was a tyro in comparison. What a reputation you have! And what a black face you have, Grandpa, all at once."

Jonathan was looking at him with a daunting expression, but Harald was enjoying himself too much to be overly alarmed. However, he did step back a little. "Why don't you ask Jenny yourself?"

Jenny was now sitting upright on the stone. She had pushed

back her hair. Her face was very white in the green gloom of the grotto.

"Jenny?" said Jonathan, turning from his brother.

"It's quite true," she said in a muffled voice. "It was very stupid of me. I—I thought you—and Harald—had conspired together to kill my mother, for her money." She suddenly put her hands over her face. "How could I have been so stupid, so ignorant? I thought, that night just before she died, that the injection you had given her—I didn't know she was already dying and that you tried to save her."

"And all this time," said Harald in an affectionate voice, "the poor child believed we were brother-murderers. At least Jenny had not thought so badly of me; she thought I was guilty of only one murder, or the instigator of one. You were the real brute. With your little deadly needle."

"Christ," said Jonathan. He stared at the girl with disgust. Then he said sharply, "Jenny, you can't have been that big a fool, can you, not even you?"

His tone made her shrink. She could only sit with her covered face and dolorously shake her head. Even when Jonathan picked up his coat and hat and pushed past his brother, she did not look up. Harald had lit a cigarette and was smoking it tranquilly. Jonathan stopped a short distance from the grotto and said with harsh contempt, "So that is why you were always running from me, Jenny, like a whipped mouse! If you hadn't conjured up that wild fancy in your mind, Jenny, would you have let me share your bed with you that night?"

"Oho," said Harald. "What a lovely vision arises in my brain! When was 'that night,' Jenny? Was our Jon too ardent, too pressing? He has no finesse, you know."

Jonathan raised his hard brown hand and slashed his brother across the face, and Harald fell back against the side of the grotto. Then Jonathan went off, the sound of his enraged departure slashing through the silence for several moments.

Jenny was weeping. Harald smoked and watched her kindly until she could cry no more. She fumbled in her pocket for her handkerchief and blew her nose fiercely like a child. Harald said, "Nature can be very dramatic and heroic, but she inevitably ends on a ludicrous note. We weep out our hearts, then have to blow our noses or pay a visit to the water closet. Very banal. Jenny, this isn't such a tragedy as you now think. You've seen Jon at his worst, if that's possible. He never waited for explanations; he never does. He makes up what he considers his mind and never hears the defense. Think what you've escaped, Jenny."

She blew her nose and glared at him with anguish and anger.

"I know, my dear. You're blaming me. But I did it for your own good. You see, Jon wasn't treated so unjustly by you, after all. Perhaps you never knew it, but there are some very vile tales going the rounds about you, in Hambledon, and he—"

"About me?" shouted Jenny, springing to her feet. "Me?"

"You, my sweet. That you are my mistress and probably the playmate of many other gentlemen, too."

"Oh, what a filthy liar you are!" Jenny screamed, advancing on him.

"Jenny, compose yourself, pray." His mocking tone halted her. "Jon believed them all, every one. He has made many obscene jokes about you, Jenny, in my company and in the company of others. He has made them, with some slight reservations, to my mother, too. If you don't believe me, ask her. You might ask others also, in Hambledon."

Jenny's long black lashes, wet and matted, blinked rapidly at him. She was thinking, even while fresh tears ran down her face. She remembered the covert smiles she had been enduring in Hambledon since her mother had died, the avoidances, the snubs. She had always been miserably shy. She had thought that her increased shyness had brought out the half-hidden sneers she had detected in the town and that her "plainness" was becoming more and more evident and was arousing hostility. Her father had told her she had no "graces," and she had come to think of herself, in her early maturity, as a clodhopper, quite deserving of smirks and indifference. She recalled Jonathan's perverse remarks, too, which she had not understood.

Then on July Fourth, Jonathan had attacked her in her father's house, where her mother had died, when she was alone and with no defender. She had forgotten what he had said to her in the library, and while he struggled with her in her room, for she had been too guilt-ridden later, and too remorseful to remember. Now she recalled, with sick cold horror, his taunt that she was withholding from him what she gave so freely to his brother. She remembered that she had struck him across the face as he had just struck Harald. How could she have forgotten? How could she have forgotten his manifest contempt for her, his jeers, his laughing accusations that she was "coy"?

Her face turned scarlet now as she faced the smiling Harald, who was dabbing carefully at his cheek, touching his lips with his handkerchief, then examining it for blood. "Are you thinking of confirmation, Jenny?" he asked. "If so, I am glad. If Jon had any respect for you, he would not have tried to force himself—as I gather he did—on you 'that night,' nor would he have attempted to do the very same thing today in this grotto, when he thought you were alone on the island, without me to protect you, and far from the house. He treated you like a trollop, Jenny, a drab, a slut. Surely even you are clever enough to realize that? A gentleman does not try so crudely to seduce a young girl, especially a girl like you, unless he believes her beneath respect. His offers of marriage—Jenny! Had you—er—succumbed to him, let us put it nicely, he would have laughed in your face afterward. Believe me, I know my brother. He has a bad reputation among women."

"Jon could think those things about me?" muttered Jenny in pathetic wonderment.

"Jenny, Jenny, haven't you been listening? Isn't it evident that he did and still does? Isn't his conduct enough for you?"

"Oh!" cried Jenny, and put her hand to her cheek and turned her devastated face aside in shame and sorrow and bitter loneliness.

"I know this is hard, my sweet," said Harald, exultant. "But how much better it is for you to know it now than later, if I had not come to your rescue. Think of what you would have endured then. Jon's a bad man, Jenny. He was cruel to his wife, Mavis, and drove her out of his life, though you choose not to believe it. He is ruthless with women, absolutely ruthless. A woman serves but one purpose for him. The female part of the whole damned town adores him, except when it has reason to hate him. Now, isn't that strange? I will forget modesty for a moment and remark that compared with me he has no charm or appearance."

"I hate you both," said poor Jenny. "I despise you both." Then she flung back her hair and marched to the archway of the grotto. But Harald smiled at her, shaking his head and not moving.

"You don't despise me, sweet Jenny. You despise what I've told you, and is that fair to me? You wronged me terribly in your thoughts, and I've forgiven you, and wasn't that magnanimous? Who else would forgive such an awful accusation so easily, except someone who loves you?"

"Please," said Jenny in a broken voice, "please let me go. I —I can't stand it any longer. Please."

"Of course," he said with gentleness, and moved aside and she passed him in a rush and he heard one loud sob from her as she ran toward the castle.

"Dear Jon," thought Harald. "One good turn deserves another. I do believe one of my teeth cut the inside of my cheek. At any rate, I think you've seen the last of Jenny, and she of you. Will I invite you to the wedding? I must give that long and serious thought."

CHAPTER THIRTY-ONE

*Miss Amelia Forster regarded Howard Best with hor*ror and disbelief as he sat opposite her in the deserted waiting room, for this was Saturday afternoon and Robert Morgan was in the hospitals and Jonathan was not to be found. Howard had called Miss Forster, whom he knew well—his father had been a schoolmate of hers and she was a friend of the family—and asked her if he could consult her in Jonathan's offices. Miss Forster, as the daughter of a minister and a member of the Ladies Aid, had been accustomed to taking orders all her life and so, though she had had plans for a picnic lunch with her sister's family, it never occurred to her to mention that she had a previous engagement. Moreover, Howard's voice had been properly grave and insistent and resembled her father's voice in his sterner moments.

So Howard sat alone with her on this hot and dusty afternoon, the latter part of August, and gave her a circumspect outline of that section of Louis Hedler's story which intimately concerned the office and herself, and asked that the matter be confidential.

She began to cry silently, her thin white nose turning quite red. She removed her spectacles and wiped her eyes. Her stiff muslin leg-of-mutton sleeves took on a wilting air for a moment or two. Then she briskly patted her gray pompadour and sat up straight and folded her lean hands on her desk. She said in a very quiet voice, "Howard, you know that it is all lies about Dr. Ferrier."

"Yes, Amelia, I know. But it is going to be very hard to convince others."

"But to think Dr. Ferrier, who is so kind and so good—a little strait-laced, but I like that in gentlemen—so old-fashioned but so *good,* could be the victim of so much *hate,* and *malice* and lies and *cruelty!* To think there could be a plot to take away his license—"

"And to send him to prison," said Howard.

Amelia gasped. "What a wicked, *wicked* world!"

"I never heard much to the contrary. But it's not surprising, is it? 'The children of darkness are wiser in their generation than the children of light.' Isn't that what the Bible says?"

The minister's daughter said, "The wicked flourish like a green bay tree. A rich man's wealth is his strong city. I have seen servants upon horses and princes walking as servants upon the earth. —Money answereth all things.' Yes, the Bible says all this, and it makes one wonder, does it not?"

"I wonder all the time," said Howard. "But—we—believe that great error arises from private interpretations of the Bible, Amelia. Please don't take offense and bridle that way. We aren't going to have a discussion about sects. Now, please look at these receipted bills, November 10th and November 21st of last year, made out to Miss Louise Wertner and Miss Mary Snowden, of this town, respectively, one for fifty dollars, one for seventy-five. Did you receipt these bills a short time ago?"

The spectacles now in place, Miss Forster examined the bills closely and said with firmness, "Yes, indeed. I remember the young ladies well, on that day, rather small and pale."

"Did you recognize them at all? From an earlier date?"

"No. But Doctor has a large practice, you know. It is impossible to remember all who come and go within these walls, especially if they are not regular patients. To my own knowledge I never saw these young ladies before they came in to pay their bills, and I accepted the money in cash and receipted these bills." She rested an angular forefinger on them.

"I see." Howard pondered with some melancholy. "And this is your handwriting?"

"Indeed, yes. And the bills were typed on this Oliver, and in my fashion. No one forged those bills, Howard," and she gave him a faint smile. " 'Complete physical examinations.' "

"So, these bills were sent out last November, as dated, after Jon examined the girls?"

Miss Forster frowned. "Why no, Howard. The girls did not bring bills with them."

Howard sat up, catching his breath. "What do you mean, Amelia?"

"They came in, hours apart, and they both said they had forgotten to bring the bills, but the amount was so-and-so, and the bills were dated on those dates. Now, I accepted the money, of course, and I typed out fresh bills, and I receipted them and—"

"Three weeks ago?" shouted Howard and jumped to his feet with a wild expression.

Miss Forster stared at him, somewhat frightened. "Why, yes." she stammered. "I told you so, Howard. Was I wrong to accept the money when they had no bills? Is it absolutely senseless to believe that people would come into this office and say they owe the doctor money, and offer it, when they don't owe it at all, and you simply must not—"

"Wait!" Howard was breathlessly elated. He sat down and regarded Miss Forster with a beatific smile. "Let me understand this clearly. You, to your knowledge, never saw these young ladies before, but they came in a short time ago, told you they owed Jon money, mentioned the amount, and claimed they had forgotten to bring the bills? But the dates were for last November?"

"Quite correct," said Miss Forster.

"And three weeks ago—on that very date—you made out new bills?"

"Quite correct."

"And receipted them, then and there, and accepted the money?"

"To be sure."

"Then, as far as you can recall, you never sent out bills for those amounts last November?"

"Not as far as I can recall, but it was so long ago, nearly

nine months, When I accepted the money, I went for the young ladies' files—to note down the payment, of course, so no new bills will be sent."

"Darling Amelia! Let me see those files!"

She blinked at him. "But there weren't any, Howard."

"There weren't any?" He was incredulous, but deeply smiling.

"No, indeed. It worried me a little too. I mentioned it to Doctor later, and he wasn't disturbed. You see, he often destroys records which are no longer active. I think it very incorrect myself, but we'd need a warehouse, considering his practice, and if the bills are paid and the patients do not appear again within six months or a year, he destroys the records and—"

"He often does that?"

"Usually. He says it isn't necessary to keep old obsolete records because there isn't any income tax any longer—"

Howard was still breathless. He leaned back in his chair and regarded Miss Forster with love. "So, it wasn't unusual at all not to have a file on those young ladies?"

"No. Though he doesn't throw away files unless they have been paid, of course, or he has decided not to charge the patient—he is so very charitable, you know, Howard, so *feeling,* so pitiful toward the poor—"

"Yes, yes, I understand that. Amelia, if called on, would you swear that these bills, though dated last November by you, on demand, were really made out only three weeks ago, because the patients claimed to have forgotten the original bills, though they knew the amounts?"

"Swear, Howard?" Miss Forster was aghast.

"You know what an affidavit is?"

"Yes. I do know, certainly. No one has ever doubted my word in this town, so—"

"Dear, sweet Amelia. If I make out an affidavit for you in my office, will you swear to it—all right, don't shake your head—will you affirm that it is true, all these facts you have given me?"

"I will do that, Howard." Miss Forster looked resolute. "But I do not understand what this all means; you have given me only a brief sketch of some nefarious plot against Doctor—"

Howard considered her. "Those young ladies, Amelia have already made out affidavits to the effect that on those dates last November, Jon aborted them right here in his examination rooms."

Miss Forster's thin and colorless mouth fell open and her eyes bulged on Howard, and then a dark crimson rushed over her dry face. She looked away and blinked rapidly.

"I thought you understood, Amelia, when I told you that certain females have alleged that Jon performed upon them —well, what is considered illegal surgery."

"No. I did not," said Miss Forster in a stiff voice. "I thought you meant surgery which should have been performed in a hospital, but Doctor decided to do it here without anesthetic— This is very wrong, you know, and not to be justified, if true, but—"

"I was talking of something called criminal operations, Amelia."

Miss Forster stood up, very agitated. "You must excuse me. Howard. I feel quite ill. I must lie down for a few moments."

Howard stood up also. He took her arm. "I'm sorry, Amelia. I understand. But now you see what this all really means. All right, dear, cry if you must, but try to listen. You see the enormity of the dangerous charges against Jon?"

"Yes, yes. But surely no one could be so evil? Those girls —they were pale and poor and very gentle, and talked to me so nicely, and were so apologetic about not bringing the bills, and I thought how well-mannered they were for their station in life, which was obvious."

Howard smiled at the stilted language. He hugged Miss Forester very gently.

"How is it *possible*, Howard, for such meek little things to be so *wicked*?"

"Well, I've heard that demons often disguise themselves prettily."

"I—my father—we didn't believe in demons, Howard."

"They certainly exist. Never mind. But if it will help you, I can almost assure you that those girls did not think of all this by themselves. I think their names were furnished to certain parties. It doesn't matter, dear Amelia. Perhaps some force was exerted on them, or threats, to make them perjure themselves. We may possibly never know."

She blew her nose, which had become quite swollen, and mutely nodded her head. She still had not grasped in full the extensiveness of the plot to ruin Jonathan Ferrier, though now she could see the dim outline.

"And on Monday, Amelia, you will come to my office to —affirm—that affidavit?"

"Yes. But what excuse shall I give Doctor? I can't lie, Howard, and I have promised you not to tell him of these—matters."

"You must tell him that you have a matter of business with a lawyer, which will take but a few minutes. After all, my office is only ten minutes walk from here."

She clasped her hands tightly together with new agitation. "Oh, Howard, what a frightful thing to do to Doctor! These people must be punished, punished, punished!"

Then Howard said, "Do you recall a Mrs. Edna Beamish, Amelia?"

She frowned and thought, then nodded. "Oh, yes, a most hysterical lady."

She told Howard of what he already knew, and her voice rose indignantly. "Such a vulgar display! Rushing out with her hat in her hand, and waving her parasol as if demented. Really!"

"She did not appear to be in pain, or hurt?"

Amelia looked at him in astonishment. "Why, no, not at all. I did hear her scream that Doctor was hurting her, and then Dr. Morgan went at once to the examination rooms—he was across the hall, and I saw him, because I was so alarmed that I opened the door, and I heard their voices, and Doctor was laughing as if at a joke, and Dr. Morgan swore a little. I did hear that. And then I hardly reached my desk again—I was truly astounded—when she burst out into this room and screamed at all of us here, the patients and myself, that Doctor had hurt her, and I almost laughed, for he has never hurt anyone—"

"You are a jewel, Amelia." Howard patted her shoulder. "I will include that in the affidavit, too." He had another thought. "Do you know if Jon still keeps the instruments his father gave him?"

"Yes. In a locked cabinet."

"No one has the key but him?"

"No one. Not even Dr. Morgan, who would not need them anyway. There is another cabinet, quite complete, in the other examination room, and Dr. Morgan has the key to that. Not surgical instruments, however, but just for examination. Our hospitals are modern, you know."

Howard went into the white and deserted examination room and studied Jonathan's cabinet and saw the expensive instruments on their white and silken beds. He saw where the curette had lain, and he saw the dark pepper of dust in the empty indentation. Who had taken Jonathan's instrument? Who had had access to his keys? The only answer was—his wife. Howard stood, rubbing his chin, staring absently through the glass doors of the cabinet. Mavis. So, Mavis had taken the instrument. The question was, why? Mavis had been a stupid young woman. She would not have known the name, or the use, of the curette—unless it had been described to her.

Miss Forster was still waiting for him, for she must lock up the offices.

"Amelia," he said, "several people, both men and women, were here in this office on the day Mrs. Beamish ran out accusing Jon of 'hurting' her. Some parties have sought them out, and they have—with some reluctance—made affidavits of the affair, as much as they remembered of it. I haven't been able to understand how they found the names of Jon's patients on that day."

Miss Forster stared, then leaned forward. "Why, Howard, I think I can tell you that. At least, I do think so. A gentleman, who said he was a police official—I have no doubt but what he was, for he showed me his credentials—said that some lady claimed to have left her purse, containing a considerable amount of money, in this office. I do not recall the particular lady in the least. There were so many, many, on that day. I was told the exact date, and I did get out a few cards and gave the police officer the names of four or five people. It was the day, I remembered later, when Mrs. Beamish was here. The police official said that perhaps a lady had mistakenly picked up the purse, or a gentleman had taken it, believing it was his wife's, and I remember being puzzled, for with the exception of Mrs. Beamish on that day there were no absolute strangers waiting to see the doctors, and I *know* that there were no thieves among them! I gave the official a piece of my mind, and I told him—"

"Would you recognize him if you saw him again?"

Miss Forster considered, then shook her head. "No, I do not think so. A very nondescript little man. Howard, do you think he was a fraud? Do you think he lied to me?"

"I don't think he was a fraud," said Howard with grimness. "But he lied to you. He wanted those names for affidavits against Jon. Of course, he probably told the patients that Mrs. Beamish was making some claim against Jon, and he was trying to protect Jon, so would they just please say so and so, about the woman shrieking that Jon had hurt her? They were reluctant, I see now very clearly, not because they thought they were hurting Jon, but because they have the ordinary citizen's aversion to dealing with the law in any form." He thought a moment. "Of course, that is what it was! And all the time I've been thinking something else. Everything, Amelia, is not always what exactly meets the eye."

Once out in the street, he climbed into his trap and sat and thought long and hard. He had considered going to "the young ladies" who had made affidavits alleging that Jonathan had performed criminal operations on them but had discarded the idea. They had unseen but powerful friends, and of that he had no doubt. There were large and shadowy figures behind them, and they would report to these figures at once.

There is something worthwhile about living in a small city like Hambledon, he thought as he drove away. Almost everyone knew Miss Forster, whose ancestors had helped found this city. She and her family were held in the highest respect, and though they were in rather poor circumstances now, the word of a Forster would not be challenged. Her brother was minister of his father's church and had a considerable reputation everywhere. Miss Forster's word—and affidavit—would be accepted in any court of law, and even Campion understood that. Howard considered again. The Senator had claimed no acquaintance with the seamstress and milliner, nor had they claimed any knowledge of him but Howard's lawyer's intuition assured him, without the slightest proof, that there must be some connection. Still, he dared not approach them directly or indirectly, for they would run in terror to those who had demanded their perjury.

At the proper moment, however, they would be confronted. Howard had a plan of his own in mind, and it was broadening moment by moment.

Howard Best was well known to the police in Scranton, and the chief of police was one of his best friends, for they had known each other from childhood.

So Howard went to see William Simpson confidentially. "It's just a little matter," he said. "A small claim against a Mrs. Edna Beamish, who used to live in Scranton. I am doing it as a favor." Friends though they were, Howard was enough of a lawyer not to be too forthright and honest.

William Simpson laughed. "Oh, Edna. A girl from across

the tracks, as we say. Pretty little trollop. Prettiest little thing who ever picked up her skirts to show off her wares to the highest bidder—on the right side of town."

Howard laughed, too, genially. "That sort, eh? And all the time I've heard that she was married to a rich man in Scranton, one Ernest Beamish."

"Well, that's true, too. Old fool, Ernest. Never married in his life, and when he saw Edna, he decided he'd found the girl of his dreams. She wasn't cheap, Edna. No common whore. She had style, too, and nice sweet little manners. Almost a lady. She married him when she was eighteen and had been in business for at least three years before that."

"Very enterprising," said Howard, trying to keep the intense interest off his face. "Have a cigar. Twenty-five cents apiece. What this country needs—"

"Yes. I know. A good five-cent cigar. What's this about a small claim against Edna? Old Ernest left her quite a lot of money when he died two years ago and—"

Howard sat up. "Two years ago?"

"That's right." The chief of police chuckled. "Perhaps Edna kept him too busy." Now his sharp eye studied Howard thoughtfully. "Come on. Tell me the truth. Why do you want to know about Edna Beamish?"

Howard was annoyed at himself. But he smiled and waved his hand. "It is a small matter, Bill. She lived in Hambledon, and there's a matter of a confection, some millinery, she forgot to pay for."

The chief of police pursued up his mouth and gave Howard a skeptical look. "Now, that's quite a story. Edna never lived in Hambledon in her life, so far as I know, and I keep up with the gossip in this town."

"Why, that's impossible, Bill. I have the bill of sale right in my office. Thirty-five dollars."

William Simpson shook his head, and for some reason he began to laugh deeply to himself, and Howard watched eagerly. "Howard, someone's pulling your leg. I repeat: Edna never lived in Hambledon. Old Ernest Beamish was well known to me. We played poker together. He never lived in Hambledon, either. They had a nice house in town, very stylish, and they gave fine parties, and I was there. After Ernest died—"

"Yes?"

But the chief continued to smoke and shake with silent laughter. Then he said, "That Edna," in an admiring tone.

"What about her?"

"I thought," said the chief, "that your sole concern for our local Jersey Lily was purely in behalf of a millinery claim, and Howard, I'm ashamed of you, a prominent lawyer like you making up a ridiculous little story like that. I thought better of you. Can't you trust an old friend?"

Howard considered him long and steadily. "I want to know her connection with Senator Campion, one of our unfortunate Commonwealth's two Senators."

A closed look came over William Simpson's face. He carefully deposited cigar ash in a tray. He said, "Why didn't you say that in the first place, instead of trying to make me believe that you believed Edna had lived in Hambledon?"

"She did. She lived in a place called Kensington Terraces. Not for as long as she claimed, however, but for a few weeks. Recently. Very recently."

The chief said, "One of the things a political appointee learns very early—if he wants to survive—is not to talk about powerful politicians, that is, repeat gossip about them. But hell, a few people know, and I'll tell you if it goes no further, Howard."

Howard hesitated. "It might have to, Bill. I'll try to keep it as quiet as possible and look for information which will be a result of your information without revealing the source."

"I know you lawyers," said the chief, and looked at Howard with large cold eyes. "When it comes to a client, you'd betray your best friends—for a good fee, of course. You haven't been exactly candid with me, and why should I be candid with you?"

"For no reason except that if I don't hurry and get some information—and not just about our little Edna—a good fine man will find himself unjustly in prison, not to mention the loss of his reputation and profession."

"Oh. Why didn't you tell me? Has Edna gotten him into some mess?"

"Yes. She had an abortion, a criminal abortion, only a short time ago."

"Ha," said the chief, and began to laugh again. "The Senator won't like that! Little Edna playing house when the master is away. Sneaking away from Washington to kick up her heels in a dead-dog town like Hambledon, at that! Papa won't like it, not at all."

"I don't suppose he will," said Howard, pretending to laugh deeply himself, though he felt intense exultation.

"And little Edna found herself with a cake in the oven which didn't belong to the Senator, eh?"

"Maybe it did."

"I thought," said the chief, sober again, "that you were implying that Edna went into the bakery business with that friend of yours in Hambledon?"

"Let me put it this way, Bill. Edna has let drop a few remarks that my friend is—responsible."

"I can hardly believe that of Edna! She knew how to keep her mouth shut!" The chief's eyes were hard and suspicious again.

"Oh, not that. I mean that she is accusing my friend of performing an abortion on her."

"Edna? Doing that openly? The Senator will kill her! He's a Hambledon boy. Keeps his reputation all glowing and sweet-smelling. Come on! What is this all about?"

"Just what I've told you. Now, would you advise me," said Howard, with a great air of earnest artlessness, "to tell the Senator?"

"My God, no! He'd murder Edna if it ever even got out that he was playing Papa and Mama with her in Washington! She's the latest of his little friends and has lasted the longest, and only a few in Scranton know about it and they know that if the Senator ever caught them scandalizing about him, they'd land in a pitch pit. Powerful boy, the Senator, and never forgets his friends or his enemies. Look here, Howard, I don't want any of it!"

"People must know, in Washington."

"People know a lot of things in Washington. But they don't talk about them."

Howard stood up, affecting to be disappointed and downcast. He sighed. "Very well, Bill, I should have thought about your position before coming here. You have told me nothing and I am not going to ask you anything. I can appreciate your need to be discreet."

They shook hands, the chief very relieved. It was only when Howard had left that William Simpson began to wonder sourly if Howard had been entirely candid in his disavowals, and if he himself had not been led up the garden path. In the meantime Howard was considering how best to prove Edna Beamish's liaison with Senator Campion, the fact of her manifest pregnancy by him, and her resorting to an unknown abortionist either in Hambledon or Scranton. He also needed to know why she had appeared in Hambledon and in the offices of Jonathan Ferrier, though he now had a rather clear idea of the circumstances—to his incredulous horror—and the use to which Edna Beamish had been put, and the reason. As a pragmatic lawyer and paradoxically an honest man, he had always discounted the conspiratorial theory of both history and human conduct, but now he admitted freely that both were not only possible but probable. In Jonathan Ferrier's case they were actual.

Howard thought of Senator Campion very thoroughly. He knew that the Senator regarded Hambledon privately as bucolic and simpleminded. We'll show him how really crude he is, thought Howard, on the train home. What a striking, amateurish plot he had thought up! However, it had been Howard's experience, amateurs could often display a boldness experienced plotters could well envy, and by their very clumsiness convince.

During the next few hurried days Howard made several other discreet investigations, and was well satisfied as well as infuriated.

CHAPTER THIRTY-TWO

Flora Eaton said, "Howard, it is very sweet and kind of you to call to see poor Martin, but he is very sick, you know, and needs his rest and peace and quiet."

"Yes, I understand, Flora. But, you see, this is a matter of extreme importance to someone very important to Martin."

They sat in the huge dim drawing room of the ugly house near the river, and Flora eyed Howard Best dubiously, plucking at her gray linen skirt and biting her lips. "Howard, Martin hasn't been at all well since Senator Campion called on him. Visitors seem to disturb him very greatly."

Howard sat up quickly. "The Senator was here?"

"Yes, indeed. So concerned over Martin, they are such good friends, you see. But it was too much for Martin, too much stimulation. He quite collapsed after Kenton had left and I had to call the doctor for him, and the doctor said he was not to be disturbed or upset, or even stimulated again. After all, it has not yet been a year—"

"I know, I know! But I think it will do Martin a lot of good to see me, Flora, I really do."

"Legal business, Howard?"

"In a way. I know Martin has something on his mind, and if he tells me about it, it will be a relief to him. Please ask him to see me for five miutes, Flora."

Still doubtful, she lifted her thin flat figure from the chair and left the room and Howard felt a sense of excitement and elation. So Campion had been here, had he, and had "disturbed" Martin Eaton? What had he threatened or said, to make Martin give up that damning instrument to Louis Hedler? This was very interesting, indeed. In spite of the closed shutters and draperies, the room was very hot and Howard, restless and more and more excited, wiped his face and his hands and looked impatiently at the door. He could hear the voice of the river, rustling softly in the morning silence, and the whirring of lawn mowers, and the bark of a dog, and he thought how peaceful the world was, or could be, without mankind.

Flora Eaton returned, uncertain and hesitant. "I've talked with Martin, Howard. He's been writing and writing and is so exhausted. But when I told him you were here, he consented to see you for a few minutes. Howard, please don't stay long, will you? He needs to rest."

Howard stood up. "Writing? Is he writing a book?"

Flora simpered and made a foolish little gesture with her hands, crossing them at the wrists and then fluttering them out. "I am not at liberty to say, Howard." The idea had not occurred to her before this, but the suggestion intrigued her. "But I do know it is quite voluminous, and not a letter. Such a secret!"

Howard Best had not seen Martin Eaton for months and even in his preoccupied state he was shocked at the change in a once powerful and robust man with presence. He could smell the acrid closeness in this room, and the higher odor of illness and mortality. Martin was a dying man, shattered, ruined, cavernous of face and appalling of color. He looked dully at Howard as he advanced across the room toward the desk, and sat there unspeaking like a crumbling Buddha sifting into dust in some lost temple.

Howard was so full of pity that he forgot to smile and did not wait to be asked to sit down. He sat down across from the desk and Martin, and he said, "Forgive me, Martin. I know you are ill. I should not have imposed on you if the matter were not so important and so immediate, and concerned—"

"I know," said the faint and empty voice. "You were always Jon Ferrier's closest friend. You moved for a change of venue and succeeded. You procured the best lawyers in Philadelphia for him."

Howard studied him and listened to the voice to catch any echo of animosity or hatred or hostility or contempt. But there was none. The tone was lightless and unaccented and indifferent.

"So," said Martin, "I know why you've come. It is about Jon Ferrier."

"Yes," said Howard. "He is in terrible danger, and he is innocent. I know you don't believe that, but it is true."

Martin Eaton looked down at the desk again, and now Howard saw that there was a sheaf of papers there, closely written upon, neatly stacked. Martin's hand still held a pen.

"I do not know what is truth," said Martin, "or what is lies any longer. I do not know even what is guilt."

"Martin, surely you know in your heart that Jon did not kill Mavis."

"You are wrong." The voice was louder but still indifferent. "He killed her. I knew his guilt. I've always known it."

A little chilliness ran over Howard's warm cheeks and hands. He looked at Martin intently. Then he said, "Guilty of killing her—how?"

For the first time Martin smiled, a dreary, painful smile. "You lawyers. I made a simple statement which would be accepted by anyone but you. I said Jon Ferrier was guilty of Mavis' death; that should have satisfied you. I don't lie. But you say 'how?' "

Howard's hopes rose. Martin lifted his living hand, which held the pen. "Kenton Campion has been here and has told me everything, so it is not necessary for you to tell me the detestable tale of the plot against Jon. I assume Louis Hedler told you. Poor Louis. I know there are other ramifications of this plot not concerned with me and Mavis. So, spare yourself, Howard." He looked again at the papers on his desk and sighed a long and gusty sigh.

"I have written the whole story here, lest it die with me and evil again be done. I am glad you came. I did not know to whom to intrust this story. But, as you are Jon's friend, I know I can trust you. I have but a few more lines to write, and it is finished. Then you may read it for yourself and save both you and me from copious explanations and words. I am so weary these days. So—beset."

Howard felt that this was a momentous time. He sat in silence as the pen painfully scratched its way across the page. He saw it dipped into the ink, saw it write, saw it dipped again. The dead hand lay on the paper, unmoving. The shutters were open here and the hot bright wind entered, fluttering the written pages, stirring the dust, lifting the pages of open books, glittering on the edges of furniture. The large dying face of Martin Eaton was intent, and there was gray sweat on his parched forehead and fallen cheeks.

There was something to be said in favor of a man who was dying with dignity, thought Howard Best, a man who asked for no pity, no sentimentality, no false denial of the truth. Howard had not the slightest doubt that the agonizingly written document he was about to read would right an evil and save a man from complete ignominy and injustice.

Martin laid down the pen and stared at the final paragraphs he had written. He said, "I have made this out in the form of an affidavit. I had thought of you to act as the notary, or the witness." He looked at Howard now, raising his eyes with a conspicuous effort, and what life remained in him shone, for the last time, with indomitable life and determination. "This has not been easy for me to do. I know this will destroy others. But there comes an hour when a man must do as he must do, and there is nothing else." He nodded at the papers, spent, and Howard reached to the desk and took them. Martin lay back in his chairs and closed his eyes.

The writing was amazingly clear and careful, as if written so there could be no conjecture over a single word. It was small and sharp though sometimes wavering, but every period and comma were there, every large capital.

"I, Martin Joseph Eaton, of River Road, Hambledon, in the Commonwealth of Pennsylvania, make this statement, on this date, August 29th, 1901, of my own free will and desire, and in my own handwriting, which can be verified, in order that Jonathan Ferrier of this town will no longer be the subject of calumny, odium, disgrace and scandal and libel, as he has been since November 5th, 1900. It has been in my power, and in the power of someone else to be named, to have righted this wrong, but I have refrained for reasons I will now set forth.

"The dead are beyond our feeble hatred and our derision, and this I should have known long ago. To protect the name of the dead is not only futile and sentimental—when they have caused misery and despair—but they would not have it so and perhaps do not wish it so. If God is a God of love, He is also the God of Justice and even of wrath, and so I dare not die until I have written all that must be written on this day.

"My niece, Mavis Alicia Eaton, was not my niece. She was the daughter of my brother's wife, Hilda, Mrs. Jerome Eaton.

"In my youth and young manhood I loved Marjorie Farmington, now Mrs. Adrian Ferrier of this town. But she married Adrian Ferrier, and I believed that I would care for no other woman. Then my brother, two years my junior, Jerome, met a young lady of considerable family and fortune in Pittsburgh, where he was a teacher of history. Her name was Hilda Gorham, and she resembled Marjorie Ferrier in a most extraordinary way. I did not know her until she had married my brother, for I was in Heidelberg at the time for a year's supplementary study. When I returned and saw Hilda for the first time, it was as if my whole life had been renewed, and Hilda told me later that she had loved me instantly. However, she had no reason to divorce my brother, and she was fond of him, and we both decided he must not be hurt, as he was a man of singular innocence and kindness and trust.

"I have no excuse to offer for my love for Hilda and our subsequent actions. Love, I have heard, is its own reason for being. It is also its own terror and suffering. When Mavis was born, it was Jerome who held her proudly in his arms and claimed her as his daughter, and not I. He was an unworldly man and was never suspicious, as he ought to have been under the circumstances, on which I will not expound."

Howard felt greatly moved and full of a sympathetic suffering. He looked up from the pages, but Martin lay back in his chair as if asleep, his face peaceful and resigned.

"My brother and Hilda and Mavis remained in Pittsburgh and I saw them only occasionally. Therefore, I was able to maintain my equanimity and composure, and to sustain Hilda in her silence. I saw the child infrequently, also, but loved her with a passionate adoration which should be reserved for the Deity only. I would gladly have given my life for her. When her parents died suddenly, I knew I must take her into my house. I had, in the meantime, married my dear Flora, who will be the one to suffer excessively when this document is made public, as it must be. I needed her devotion and her affection, for I have always been a lonely man. I believe our marriage has been happy and I have given Flora no reason to mistrust me.

"She, too, loved Mavis, who was the most beautiful child I have ever seen, and she happily agreed that we should adopt her as our own, for Flora could bear no children. She treated Mavis with affection and care of a mother, in all respects. Sufficient.

"To me, at least, Mavis was perfection, not only in appearance but in character and grace. When I held her on my knee and fondled her, I could hardly endure my joy and delight and love. As she grew to girlhood and then to womanhood my pride in her became daily stronger, my care closer. All who had seen and known Mavis can testify to her beauty, her winsomeness, her happy laughter, her gaiety, her fascination. This is no mere driveling of a father, but the truth."

Again Howard looked at Martin Eaton, but he had not moved. Howard thought, My God, how this will shake this town! It was not a pleasant thought, and Howard hesitated before continuing to read.

"I have always loved young people, especially those of beauty and charm like Mavis, and those of dedication, intelligence and honor, such as Jonathan Ferrier. He was not only my loved Marjorie's son, but he had her character and uprightness, though not her humor and tolerance. From earliest childhood he was somewhat relentless and a stickler for pride, and what he called, as a child, 'justice.' These are admirable traits, but like all admirable traits they can be carried to excess. I often told him when he was very young that he could never expect absolute honor and truth and justice in this world, but I discovered that he did not believe me, and I know that he was very angered when he was forced to per-

ceive the reality of evil and malice and cruelty in our midst.
There is much that is intolerant in Jonathan, and this has
been his burden and aroused much hatred against him—
though I confess that he was intolerant against all mendac-
ity, double-dealing, lies, hypocrisy, injustice, hardheartedness, and sentimentality. I often told him that it was excellent
to be against these evils but that he should soften his expressions when he encountered them, for it is the curse of mankind that it must pretend not to condemn when condemnation—if this were a good world—is necessary. 'Truth crushed
to earth will rise again,' is a pretty aphorism, but it is not
valid, and if it does rise, then it is a miracle for the ages to
stand before, agape.''

Amen, thought Howard, with deep sadness.

"I saw from the beginning that Jonathan would make an
excellent physician and so guided him into the noblest profession any man can pursue with the exception of the clergy. He
was much intrigued, even as a child, when I told him that
once all physicians had been priests, and all priests physicians. The thought fascinated him, and he saw immediately
that there was the closest of all relationships in those professions, for a man does not deal with the body successfully unless he considers the soul, nor does he deal with a man's spiritual vices unless he also deals with the body which manifests
them.

"I was his mentor. His father did not highly approve of Jonathan's choice of a profession, but I will not comment upon
Adrian except to say that I wonder to this hour why Marjorie
Farmington had married him. Marjorie, however, believed
Jonathan would make a splendid physician. We had many
quiet discussions about the matter. But Marjorie was also of
the opinion that Jonathan must curb, to some extent, his
pride, his intolerance, his relentlessness, if he were to live
among men with any comfort. I am afraid that neither of us
has been very successful with Jonathan in this regard."

That is putting it very mildly, thought Howard, and for the
first time since beginning this sad history he smiled a little.

"I loved Jonathan Ferrier as my son. When he told me,
when Mavis was only fifteen, that he wished to marry her in
good time, I was filled with happiness. The two I loved most

dearly in the world would be my children through their marriage. The day of their wedding remains in my memory like a beautiful painting, perfect, without a flaw. I will carry the memory of that day with me into eternity, if there is indeed eternity for us.

"I do not wish those who read this to believe that I was totally insensible to Mavis' faults, as if I were a stupid and blinded man. I knew her to be selfish and even petulant at times, and demanding, but it gave me pleasure to satisfy all her desires far beyond her needs. I knew Jonathan would so treat her, or at least I believed he would. I gave her to him less than giving her in marriage to another man, than in putting her in the arms of a younger father who would protect and guard and love her when I was dead. It was a fatuous error, and I have no explanation for it, and no excuse, though I know it was ridiculous. A husband demands more of his wife than does her father, and he has a clearer eye for her faults and a duller eye for her virtues. But this I did not know until the day of her death.

"All seemed well with that most auspicious marriage for nearly a year, and then I observed that Jonathan appeared distrait at times, and unusually nervous and abstracted. But he was new in his practice and I believed that was the trouble. As for Mavis, she was herself as usual, deeply enjoying life, radiant in the mere act of living, full of laughter and brightness and luminous smiles. If sometimes I thought that she seemed still a little frivolous for a young matron, I remembered her youth and her inexperience. She told me how deeply she loved Jonathan, and I had no way of knowing that this was not the truth—then. Mavis, Mavis."

Again Howard was almost unbearably touched at those last words, written as if spoken to Martin's deepest self and not to anyone who would read this. The heat in the dusty study increased, the wind was more dazzling, the light sharper. Martin Eaton had not moved a finger. He had withdrawn to some great distance where no one could ever reach him again with pain or despair or longing.

"I am growing weary," the dying man had written. "I must be briefer for I may die before this is completed. As the few years of that marriage continued I saw that Jonathan was growing more absorbed in his work and less in his wife, but I judged that to be quite common among doctors, who do not make the most desirable husbands in the world. If they are truly dedicated men—and only dedicated men should practice the holy art of medicine—then they cannot give themselves entirely to their wives and their children. Much of them belongs to their patients, and this must never be denied. Sometimes I told Jonathan that he must not pursue even medicine with such single ardor but that he should give some thought to Mavis. Invariably he agreed, but I remember, now, that his face would darken and he would quickly change the subject.

"Then, two years before her death Mavis complained to me that Jonathan desired no children. This was on the occasion when I delicately suggested to her that a child, or two or three, would crown her married happiness. I was much disturbed at her answer—that Jonathan wished no family. I hinted about it once or twice to Jonathan himself, but he would put me off with a smile, one of his harsh jokes, or a shrug, or again with a change of subject.

"I know the truth now—and from Mavis' dying lips—that it was she and not Jonathan who was averse to children. I know that she wished to keep herself uniquely herself, the first-adored of all who knew her. She did not want competition, nor had she any maternal instincts.

"For the last three years of their marriage, Mavis and Jonathan lived apart, and had no conjugal intercourse with each other."

Howard could not help an exclamation of astonishment, and it was abrupt in that hot and sunny silence. But Martin did not stir. He merely sank lower in his chair and appeared to dwindle.

"All this I discovered later. In the meantime, and I must confess it, I was feeling the stress of my years and my practice, and I could not forget Hilda, the mother of my daughter. I resorted more and more to whiskey for release and comfort. This is well known in Hambledon. I give this as my excuse for not noticing the signs of disaster in Mavis' marriage until less than two years before her tragic death. Mavis appeared to have become more petulant, more absorbed in her own desires, more impatient, and on a number of occasions and before me. I do not, even now, fully know the reason for this raillery of hers, but Jonathan never rebuked her. He remained silent, and for a hasty and imperious man this was remarkable.

"Then, over a year before she died, Mavis told me that Jonathan, on several occasions, had threatened to kill her, and that once he had even taken her by the throat in rage. She exhibited actual terror of him to me, when she told me, and I knew when Mavis lied and knew when she spoke the truth. She really feared him. I said I would speak to him, for I was outraged and appalled, but she implored my silence."

The stilted, old-fashioned phrases did not jar on Howard's mind. Now he felt intense alarm and consternation, and he was afraid. He felt for his pipe and lit it. He puffed a moment or two and again read those damning words. Then he hurried on with his reading.

"I tried to question Mavis closely. I knew Jonathan's rash temper, his disregard for consequences when he was in a rage. But Mavis was evasive. She was not certain, she said, what it was that so displeased Jonathan, but she thought it was because she was so much younger than he was and much less serious, and that he expected too much of her. I was relieved, God help me. I agreed with her that this was probably the cause of his anger and that time would improve the situation. She assured me that I was probably right and would speak no more of it. However, I did notice that when she would look at Jonathan, it would be with sullenness, defiance, malice, and apprehension.

"Jonathan had made my Mavis unhappy, had brought out in her those traits which were less pleasing than others, had caused her to fear him and to hate him. She was a light golden bird and he was a hawk, dark and somber. I see now, as I did not see until Mavis' death, that the marriage had been disastrous not only for Mavis but for Jonathan, and had inevitably been leading to tragedy. But Jonathan was older and wiser, and he was a man. Therefore, I hold him guilty of Mavis' death, and he alone."

Howard read this over, and over, and his consternation grew.

"Yes, I hold him guilty, though he did not do the deed of which he is still accused. It was not his child which Mavis was carrying. It was his brother's, Harald Ferrier's."

Oh, my God! thought Howard, with repulsion and incredulousness. He put down the sheets of paper and went to the window and looked out and saw nothing of the beautiful gardens below, or of Flora among the zinnias, or of the shining blue floor of the river beyond. He had a single, wild impulse to take those papers and destroy them, and only the quick knowledge that they must remain intact for Jonathan's sake prevented him from acting. He went back to his chair. He lit his pipe again, for it had gone out. The scratch of the match on his sole was like a shot in the silent room, and he started at the sound. But Martin seemed asleep.

"On October 30th, 1900, Jonathan Ferrier was called to Pittsburgh for a consultation, for over the years he had acquired a broad and excellent reputation. He remained there until the afternoon of November 5th, and of this there is no doubt, for so it has been attested to, under oath, by the most eminent men.

"On November 3rd, 1900, Mavis came to me, desperately ill, hemorrhaging. She brought to me the curette of Jonathan, her husband, and told me that he had aborted her on October 29th, for again he had told her he would have no children of hers in his house. As she was obviously almost *in extremis*, I took her to the hospital. Otherwise, I should have hidden this crime, this infamy, in my house. I will not write here of my suffering and despair and hatred and rage. I only will write that Mavis told me that she had been aborted, in Jonathan's own examination room, and by him, on the eve of his departure to Pittsburgh, on October 29th.

"As I sat by her bed in St. Hilda's Hospital, with all the help about Mavis which she needed, I swore to her that I would avenge her. I knew that she was dying. She was badly infected. Worse, they detected signs of mutilation, deliberate wounding, as by a savage madman who hated her. Then it was brought to my attention by competent colleagues whose word could not be challenged that Mavis' condition plainly showed that she had been aborted no earlier than November 1st. They preferred to believe that it was even later, on November 2nd. The septicemia, while fulminating and spreading rapidly, was not so advanced as it would have been had the abortion taken place on October 29th. And so I knew that Mavis had lied to me. But in the extremity of the hours I did not admonish her. She was so gravely ill, bleeding slowly to death, and agonzied with pain and fever. Her uterus had been perforated in several places. The vagina was lacerated. The abortion, I was told, had been done by an amateur or a fiend.

"Then I knew that Mavis was dying, that it was a matter of less than an hour. She had remained conscious throughout her suffering. I sent strangers from her room. I took her burning hands in mine and said to her, 'Before God, Mavis, you must tell me the truth, for you are dying and will soon face your God, and you must not go to Him with a lie on your lips.'

"The child was fearfully frightened. She struggled with herself, and then she confessed.

"Jonathan, she said, had long ago rejected her and was not living with her as man and wife. He despised her, upbraided her constantly, called her a fool and mindless. She had wanted only to be happy in her life, to dress prettily, to be adored, to be pampered, to be treated as a lovable child who must not be denied. It was most piteous. Mavis was a woman, almost twenty-four, yet she spoke as one who is only five years old, and as simply. She had often wanted to return to her old home, she said, to the arms of her adopted parents, for she was lonely and unwanted and unneeded and unloved in her husband's house."

Liar, liar, thought Howard. She still could not refrain from lies even when she was terrified and knew she was dying. She must leave behind her the blameless and luminous memory she had created in her life. All Howard's pity was for the stricken father and the maligned husband of that craven young woman on her dying bed, who must preserve a lie, and would have died with lies, if her father had not so pressed her.

"I listened to Mavis' faint and dying voice, so unlike her exuberant own, and did not fully understand at first. She told me that she had sought love and admiration apart from Jonathan, who withheld them from her. I do not remember clearly! I know she spoke of at least four men, but their names have gone from my recall. I was stunned beyond grief, beyond speech. Mavis pleaded for herself, for her forlorn state, and I could only hold my child in my arms and weep over her, and try to listen to this most important confession.

"Her last lover, the father of her aborted child, was Harald Ferrier. When she discovered her condition, Harald decided that she must be aborted, and told her that though he was fond of her, he did not love her and had no intention of asking her to divorce her husband and marry him. Moreover, he said, he was committed to another. He had regarded the liaison with Mavis as 'midsummer madness,' to quote his own words, and had not believed Mavis was more serious than himself. Their mistake could be rectified. I will not expound on the morals and degeneracy and bestiality of this man's character, a man judged to be amiable, admirable, kind and tolerant in this town, for all his light follies, which are well known. I leave the judgment to God.

"He told Mavis that he had heard of an abortionist, a competent surgeon in high esteem in Hambledon, who obliged unfortunate ladies in Mavis' predicament. This conversation, Mavis told me, was held in the Ferrier house during Marjorie Ferrier's absence, and in the weekly absence of servants. Mavis had sent for him to consult with him. When it was agreed that Mavis must be aborted, Harald Ferrier then called the scoundrel, the murderer, in Mavis' presence. She was afraid but not heartbroken. She confessed she had been deeply attracted to Harald Ferrier but had not loved him. The abortionist agreed to the operation, and named the time on the next day or so. Mavis, in her dying state, was not certain which was the date. She only knew that Jonathan had not been in town for at least two days. Approaching death was already confusing her mind.

"Then the abortionist made one demand. He asked that Mavis bring with her Jonathan's own curette, which, he declared, he had once seen in Jonathan's own examination room when they had been friends some years before. (I believe they had some disagreement later, which had caused coldness and aversion between them.) I am of the opinion that the abortionist demanded Jonathan's curette in the event that should Mavis suffer some consequences, he would not be held responsible. I refuse to believe that he had asked for the instrument with the deliberate intention of injuring Mavis, or even killing her, in order to involve Jonathan in his wife's subsequent dangerous illness or perhaps her death. No, no man can be that vile."

No? thought Howard, and felt the deepest bitterness of his life. Much was being revealed to him now than ever he had dreamed of, than ever he had feared of his fellows.

"The name of the murderer must be written here. It was Claude Brinkerman."

No! thought Howard, and then he said aloud, "Oh, no." For his own wife, Beth, was now expecting her third child with happiness and so was almost consoled for the death of the little girl, Martha. She had been delivered of her little son by Jonathan, but since he was leaving Hambledon, she had chosen Brinkerman, who had the highest reputation for dexterity and skill in obstetrics. If quite a number of his patients appeared to die, it was generally accepted as unfortunate and not the fault of the physician, and besides, women always had mysterious "inward trouble," due, it was said, to their tight corsets and heavy long skirts.

It was some aghast moments before Howard could continue his reading.

"Mavis knew where Jonathan kept his office keys, which he had not taken with him on his journey to Pittsburgh. She was able to secure the curette, which had been described to her by Jonathan himself long before. She then relocked the cabinet and replaced the keys.

"How can I continue this dreadful narrative, recalling everything with so much vividness and torment? Mavis died. That is, perhaps, the only thing that matters to me.

"The hospital had already been aware of Mavis' story that Jonathan had aborted her. She had screamed it over and over, in the presence of attending physicians and nurses, and myself. There were some who knew it could not be true. But Jonathan has many enemies. These were only too eager to believe the awful lie, even though they had been told it was not possible. They spread it through the town. I had sent a telegram to Jonathan the evening before to return, that Mavis was gravely ill and it was feared she was dying. He returned only three hours after her death, on the first train available.

"Why have I not, before this, told Mavis' true story to others, and to Jonathan? Why did I let him be tried for murder of his wife and unborn child—though he knew the child had not been his, and he had not injured my daughter? Why did I shout, 'no, no!' when the verdict of not guilty was brought in by the jury?

"You who read this, have pity on a father who adored his daughter beyond reason, and even with blasphemy. I believed that Mavis had spoken truly when she said that Jonathan had rejected her, had made her desperately unhappy, had almost driven her from his house. I still believe he had threatened her life. He had made my child wretched, and that was unpardonable. In her unhappiness she had sought love illicitly, and if that was wrong, it can be pardoned and understood. But she was so joyous, so affectionate. Love was part of her existence. She could not live without it and the admiration it brought. She wanted only to dance and sing and live, and this was denied her by both her husband and the man who murdered her.

"There was her name to protect, above all else. I vowed to keep clear and untarnished the lovely name she had made for herself not only in Hambledon but in many other places. Her good name was precious to me. No malicious scandal must touch her. No jeering name must dirty her. As she had lived, so she must be in death, loved, admired, remembered for her beauty and her youth, her laughter and her gaiety. The truth, spoken by me, would have condemned her name to infamy forever. What father would bring that upon his daughter?

"Would I have spoken had Jonathan been convicted for murders he had not committed? Before God, I do not know. I think I should have done so, as I write this, for there was the thought of Marjorie Ferrier, the mother of Jonathan, and I frequently confuse her in any mind with Hilda, for I loved them both. I should not have let Marjorie Ferrier's son die— at least I think that now.

"I must repeat: Had Jonathan loved my daughter as I loved her, had he been a second father to her, indulging her with affection, as I did, then she would not have strayed, she would not have died. Again, therefore, I hold him not guiltless of her death.

"I have but two things to speak of now. One is for verification, in the event that anyone might challenge a dying man's confession of his guilt and his love. I have written that no one was in the Ferrier house on the day the abortion was arranged except Harald Ferrier and my daughter. There was one other: Marjorie Ferrier. She had intended to be absent that afternoon, and Mavis thought she was alone in the house. But Marjorie, who suffers from a serious heart affliction, had decided to rest. She, too, thought she was alone in the house, but then, hearing voices downstairs, she came down, also, and overheard the conversation between her son Harald and Mavis, and the arrangements they were making.

"Marjorie has told me this. She said she was afraid she

would collapse in the hall. But she made her way upstairs and then fainted on her bed. Later, a physician was called for her. She did not know what to do. To speak to Mavis would have precipitated fresh tragedy, for Mavis was distraught. She dared not think what a revelation to her husband would have brought about: disgrace. The ejection from Jonathan's house. Marjorie knew that Mavis and Jonathan were no longer husband and wife in the meaning of the word. What if Jonathan learned that his brother was the father of the unborn child? So Marjorie, though the thought of an abortion was unspeakable, decided to remain silent, to let the 'culprits,' as she called my child and her lover, find their own solution. 'For the sake of all,' Marjorie said to me after Mavis' death. 'I kept my silence. My son Harald is my son, also, and though I do not condone, but only condemn, his actions, I must think of what would happen to him if Jonathan ever knew. I must think, too, of Jonathan. But,' she said to me much later, 'if Jonathan had been condemned to death for crimes he did not commit, then I should have come to you and told you you must tell the truth.'

"Marjorie does not know all the truth. She came to me after Mavis' death and told me that Mavis had informed her that Jonathan had aborted her in his own examination rooms. Marjorie knew this for a lie. She did not want me to believe such a lie.

"In a strange way we became conspirators of silence after Jonathan was acquitted. We have thought that best, best for the Ferrier family, best for Mavis' name. But Marjorie is afraid that in some way Jonathan will find out the truth and that he might try to kill his brother, not just for betraying him but for the anguish he had caused him, and the silence he had kept in the face of his brother's arrest. Jonathan is a violent man, and this I believe with all my heart. He is an unforgiving one, and implacable. I believe in Marjorie's fears.

"This letter should not have been written but for one reason. It is true that sometimes evil will out but not very often. Senator Kenton Campion came to me recently and told me that he knew that I 'knew' the truth about Mavis' death, that Jonathan Ferrier had indeed murdered his wife and child. He demanded the 'truth.' He wishes to destroy Jonathan for various reasons, and so do others equally malevolent. When I refused to speak, he informed me that he was aware that Mavis was my daughter. To protect Mavis I gave Louis Hedler the curette which she had given to me, and let him believe what he willed. For Mavis is, to me, still the only creature of consequence in the world.

"However, I cannot let Jonathan continue to be condemned. I cannot let him become the victim of powerful malice. I do not know what my sentiments are toward him now. I have been so confused for so long a time. But it is possible I still love him. And I remember that he did not testify to the fact that Mavis' child had not been his. Was he protecting me or Mavis?

"Humanity is not to be understood, no, not even by mankind itself. We do abominable things in the name of love. We do disastrous things to protect ourselves and others. We permit evil to grow more powerful every day and make no attempt to halt it. We are afraid. We are cowards. We do not possess the manhood with which we were endowed at birth; we lost it, we always lose it, through compromise, through hope, through lies to ourselves, through commitment to false ideals, through fear, through womanish timidity, through exigency.

"We condemn, we lie, by silence, when we should speak. But for that cowardice we cannot be forgiven.

"I beg Marjorie Ferrier's forgiveness in breaking my silence. She will know at the last that I did it for her son Jonathan, and not out of weakness or present fear of death. But what the results will be I do not know. I no longer care, except for Flora, my wife, who has been my dear companion and friend for many years and who will have to endure living when I am dead. The time has come to exonerate Jonathan Ferrier and protect him from the plot gathering against him. As I forgive him may he forgive me, and may he remember, as I do now, the years when I regarded him as my son.

"(Signed) MARTIN JOSEPH EATON, M.D."

The stark and blazing silence and heat in the study had increased. Howard could hardly breathe for emotion and physical oppression. He gently laid down the papers, contemplated them for a moment, then said quietly, "Martin? I have finished."

The lightless eyes opened sluggishly and looked with a dazed expression upon the younger man. Then Martin groaned as if from deep in his flesh rather than from his throat, and he pulled himself up in his chair with all the effort of his body. "Yes," he said. His look, his manner, forbade Howard to remark on the dolorous saga he had read, and Howard thought, with increasing compassion, that Jonathan Ferrier was not the only one in this miserable affair who was proud.

"I wish it notarized," said Martin. "I have witnesses here, or you may have your own, for there must be witnesses."

"Yes," said Howard. "I will arrange it all tomorrow."

Martin shook his monolithic head and for the last time, Howard was to remember, he smiled. "You lawyers," he said again. "It is always 'tomorrow' to you. Tomorrow. But it must be today. Now. Why does tomorrow always fascinate you so much? 'The law's delay—' Call your office. Ask for your seal and your witnesses. At once."

He looked imperatively at Howard. "I may die tonight," he said, "then it will all be of no use."

Why, indeed, not today? Howard telephoned his office and then he sat with Martin and drank some of his whiskey, and neither said a word. The papers lay between them like something with a life of its own, palpitating. There were many things Howard wished to say to this dying father. He wished to tell him that he had still been unjust to Jonathan Ferrier in his remarks that Jonathan had been harsh to his young wife and had rejected her. He wished to tell Martin that quite a little clique had known Mavis' true character, and her love affairs, and that a few, if not more, knew her heartlessness, craft and malice and self-absorption. But that would bring no peace to Martin Eaton, but only distress.

Two clerks, one with the seal, arrived in fifteen minutes, sweating wih zeal and the heat. Howard did not permit them to read the papers; he merely had Martin initial each page, followed by the initials of the clerks. The clerks were eager to read, but Howard was deft. He needed but their acknowledgment that they had seen Martin sign each page, and then his signature at the end, repeating the one he had already written. Then he asked Martin to raise his right hand and swear that everything he had written in the affidavit had been true, that he had made the affidavit of his own will and desire and had written it in his own hand. This done, Howard put his notary's seal on each page, very carefully. It was not necessary, but he knew Jonathan's enemies.

Martin chuckled as he laid down his pen and nodded when Howard refilled his glass. "Campion," he said in his dry rustle of a voice. He looked into the glass, then raised it and stared at Howard directly. "To justice," he said, and laughed for the last time in his life.

When Howard arrived at his pleasant house on the street which Jonathan had derided—Rose Hill Road—he said to his pretty wife, Beth: "Don't ask me questions, dear, or for explanations. But you must never see Claude Brinkerman again. We must find someone else when you have the baby."

"Well, really, Howard, he is the best," Beth replied with surprise, and looked at him searchingly. "I have recommended so many of my friends to him."

"You must never do that again!" he said with such emphasis that she was quite astonished and stared at him.

"Why Howard! You look—distracted. So pale, so concerned, so very, very grave. Is something wrong, dearest?"

"Very wrong, Beth. But you must do as I wish, for I know things you do not know. I've had a terrible three hours. I can't tell you. Just do as I say."

She continued to stare at him with wifely conjecture. Then she said, "Very well, Howard, you must have your reasons. I wish I had had your advice before, though. Only last November I sent my little milliner to him—a very talented girl with ribbons and plumes, she made my Christmas hat, and we both liked it so much that I permitted her to display it in her little window for a few days. You liked it, too, remember? Fawn, felt, with yellow ribbons and orange plumes, quite becoming, and you said— What's the matter, Howard?"

"Beth!" He had jumped to his feet. "What is your milliner's name?"

"Why—why—how extraordinary you are, Howard, and how peculiar you look! And what does it matter? It's Mary Snowden."

Howard smacked his hands together hard and clenched his teeth visibly with triumph. "I thought I'd heard that name before, by God! Beth! Why did you send that girl to Claude Brinkerman last November?"

"For goodness' sake, Howard! What questions you ask! It won't mean anything to you, and it is a little indelicate. She had female trouble."

"What in hell's that?"

Beth dropped her pretty eyes. "Inwardly," she said with a prim purse of her lips.

"Well, for God's sake, Beth, what *is* it? 'Inwardly' covers a lot of territory, I can see for myself. Please, Beth, forget you're a lady for a moment. You don't know how deadly serious this is. Let's be frank. Was the girl pregnant?"

"Howard! How can you say such a dreadful thing about a

poor, talented, good hard-working girl! So nice—so—almost —a lady. Well-mannered. Clever. Of course she wasn't pregnant. She isn't married!"

"Darling Beth, I love you. You are a treasure, a true treasure. I wish I could tell you how much you've helped me." He kissed her. She pushed him gently away so she could examine his face.

"Howard, are you perfectly well?"

"Bully, as Teddy Roosevelt would say. Fine, as he'd also say. Last November, you say it was, when you sent Mary Snowden to Claude Brinkerman?" He paused. "You would not, by the most remote chance of course, know a Louise Wertner, seamstress, would you?"

"Indeed I do," said Beth. "She is a friend of Mary's. Not so talented or so original, so I give her only ordinary sewing, alterations on old clothes, mending linen, and such. Why, Howard, she often comes here to use our sewing room, especially in the spring and fall. You must have seen her yourself, once or twice, at the least, a very meek, quiet girl, always keeping her eyes down and moistening her lips, poor thing. Neither girl is exceptionally prosperous, though I do encourage Mary, who should be more appreciated—"

"Beth, you did say that these girls know each other? Well?"

"I believe so. Howard, what does it matter with that class? Why are the girls so important to you?"

"Beth, has Louise Wertner ever suffered from female trouble, too?"

"Now, Howard, don't be ridiculous! How is it possible for me to know? Mary only mentioned it to me last November, when I remarked that she looked a little ill." Beth hesitated. Howard, she thought to herself, had one thing in common with all other husbands: a certain thriftiness. But she had had something on her tender conscience for several months, and so she sighed. "Howard, I bought four hats from Mary, and the bill wasn't as large as I said. I had Mary 'pad' it, as we say. You see, she needed fifty dollars, and so I helped her out. I hope you aren't going to be cross? She did go to see Claude and that was his fee for a slight, a very slight—correction—in his office. Exorbitant, for the poor, but he does have a reputation. Are you cross?"

"I couldn't be more delighted," said Howard with fervor. So the girls did not know each other, did they? "Buy yourself a dozen hats, my darling, tomorrow. Or at least one."

That night Martin Eaton died peacefully in his sleep. There was no autopsy, but his condition was known, and it was his physician's opinion that he had suffered another stroke. Only Howard Best, of all in Hambledon, wondered a little, and with sorrow, and then with relief. All that was Martin Eaton had abandoned this world, which had brought him small comfort and had left him bereft in his final years.

It was not expected that Jonathan Ferrier be present at the funeral services nor be a pallbearer. Nor, indeed, was he there.

CHAPTER THIRTY—THREE

"*I am afraid to leave you, Jon,*" said Marjorie Ferrier. "I don't know what has gone wrong, but something most certainly has. Is it Jenny?"

"Sweet Jenny? No."

"I don't believe you. You have been a different, even a terrible person since the day you told me you were going to see Jenny and arrange—"

"Mama, I don't want to talk about it, if you please. I'm a grown man now, or hasn't it crossed your mind?"

Marjorie looked at him with deep worry as he sat opposite her at the breakfast table. For three days he had eaten almost nothing, but he was drinking again and with gloomier determination than ever before. He had spent his time on his farms, had put up two for sale, had not gone to the hospitals more than once, had seen Robert Morgan but twice and then only briefly in the offices. But at night she heard him walking up and down in his room. His bedroom furniture was laden with clothing and other things and there was a huge trunk in the hall upstairs which she had used on her honeymoon. His

wastebaskets were heaped each morning, filled with torn letters, old records, notebooks. Suitcases and bags stood around
the walls, half filled. There was a growing pile of cast-off
clothing in one corner. Marjorie had thought with dreariness,
if it weren't that it meant that Jon was definitely leaving, I'd
be glad to see all that rubbish cleaned out of drawers, wardrobes, closets and attic at last!

So, he was leaving, and very soon, and there was no more
talk of Jenny. Marjorie had written the girl just recently that
she was to be in Philadelphia for a week or more, and that, as
Harald was also leaving, it would be safer for Jenny to be in
the Ferrier house in Hambledon. So far, Jenny had not replied. A lovers' quarrel? It was absurd to think that of either
Jonathan, who was nearly thirty-six, or Jenny, whose natural
restraint prevented her from overt quarreling. Then, it must
be serious, and Marjorie felt faint and sick when thinking of
the matter. Were her hopes again to come to nothing? Was
this house always to be desolate? She saw it boarded up, shuttered, lost in snow and wind with dark windows, silent, abandoned. Even worse, she saw it inhabited by strangers.

It had been a strong but ugly house when she had come to
it as a bride. The ugliness had been in the furnishings, in the
small if high boxy rooms, in the lack of many windows in
the too-stringent pattern of the gardens. She had removed
walls and painted wooden paneling; she had deftly, over a
few years, rid the house of its ponderous furniture. She had
created windows in gloomy little pockets of hallways and in
many of the rooms. She had brought grace and style and
color and elegance to the house. But until these last few days
she had had no particular feeling with regard that years can
make their own pathways through the heart and through unsuspected places, and the thought of leaving this house
brought her astonishing pain. There had been all the months
since "the trouble," as it was daintily referred to by her
friends, and she had known—and welcomed—Jonathan's intention to leave Hambledon forever. But in a way which
seemed very strange to her these days, she had not truly believed that Jonathan would go and that she would be left
bereft in this house, which she had loved all the years
without once suspecting it. It was no longer a house to her but
a home, and the transition had come as silently as an evening
mist. Her earlier fears, and her conviction that Jonathan, for
his own sake, must leave Hambledon, were almost forgotten.

She could not remain here alone. For weeks she had been

studying the house with a secret joy and anticipation. There would be the new suite of rooms for Jenny and Jonathan, a new white marble fireplace in their bedroom. There were rooms she had looked at with delight, hearing them filled with the cries and laughter of young children. She had planned a nursery garden, sheltered and fenced, with swings and sandboxes and wooden rocking horses and dolls. Now it had vanished like all her foolish hopes, and the house seemed a mournful weight on her spirit and a reproach. To leave it shuttered, bolted and shrouded would be impossible, for it was a living thing with a personality of its own, serene, calm, soft yet steadfast. Yet, to know it known to strangers, in all its nooks and entries and passageways, and to think of strange eyes peering from the windows, was intolerable.

But even more intolerable was the change, physical and in personality, in her son. In an incredibly short time he had become even more gaunt than when he had been released from prison, more taciturn, shorter of temper and sardonic when forced to speak. He appeared very ill. In the worst years with Mavis he had not seemed so tense and distracted and his eye had not had so hard a glitter of incipient violence. That violence was there, even when he was answering the most commonplace question, or asking such a question. It was like something held in him but not held strongly enough. There were times when Marjorie stammered when speaking to him for fear of unloosing that tiptoed savagery.

She had spoken of her worry about him on the day she was to leave for Philadelphia, and he had returned to the old jeering "Mama." She did not speak of his drinking, which he had resumed with more recklessness than he had shown even during his marriage, and since the trial. It was a somber drinking and brought him no relief; rather, it appeared to increase that waiting violence in him. She dared not protest even in love. She was too afraid.

Marjorie left that afternoon after the first futile effort to reach him. She came down the stairs fastening her white kid gloves slowly, her pale traveling suit trim and slender, her broad hat veiled. The station hack was at the door. Jonathan was walking restlessly up and down in the hall, which was hot in spite of the quiet coloring and space. She said, "Jon, dear, seeing you are packing, I have put something in your room for you, to take with you, something very dear to me, which I want you to have."

"Don't be sentimental, dear," he said, but he bent and

kissed her briefly on the cheek she raised to him. That cheek was delicately scented with her French packet of *papier-poudre*, the only cosmetic permitted a lady. It recalled to him the days of his childhood when he had stood at a distance and loved her but was too proud to approach her as she sat in the garden or in the morning room with young Harald on her knee. When she would hold out her hand to him, he would think, She's forgotten me until now, and now I don't want her! He would run away with a black darting glance at her as he did so. There was always his loving and foolish father to run to, and Jon always did so run, but the clasp of those undemanding arms, the sound of that gentle, unreproachful voice, never quieted his thirst for his mother.

She was looking up now with her beautiful hazel eyes, which he had always admired, but now he hated them, for they reminded him of his brother. She was examining his face, and her pale lips tightened with worry and melancholy.

"I hope for happier news when I return," she said.

He gave her one of his dark contemptuous smiles. "News of what?" he said.

She sighed. "Very well, if you insist on misunderstanding me, Jon. Now, I must go. I wish you were going with me. You seem so—tired. Harald is already in Philadelphia, as I've told you, arranging for a new show near Christmas."

"Bully for Childe Harald," he said.

She hesitated. "Jon, I'm concerned about Jenny alone, with the servants. Would you please go over a few times while I'm gone and—"

"No, dear."

"Oh, for heaven's sake, Jon!" She went rapidly from the hall to the blazing yellow day outside, her head bent. As she climbed in the hack he saw, through the hall window, that she was dabbing at her eyes. He cursed aloud. He knew he ought to have taken her to the station; he knew that at the very least he should have helped her into the hack. But he was filled to the very brim with black hatred and seething violence. He went upstairs to his rooms, even hotter than on the ground floor, and there, laid enticingly on his bed, was a portrait of Jenny.

He approached the bed slowly and looked at the lonely and longing face of the young girl his brother had painted, and the lifted, halted hand, at the quiet and desolate eyes. She had run to a window as if to answer a beloved call, or to

see a beloved face, and then had found nothing but emptiness and cold bright chaos.

"Jenny," he said. He sat down near the portrait on the bed
and looked at it. He touched it gently with his hand. Then he
said, "Jenny, how could you have believed that of me? You
believed so fully, didn't you, after knowing me all those
years, since you were a child, a little girl? Yet, for no honest
reason at all, you were willing to believe the worst, to fancy
the worst, out of a sort of innate viciousness, or an insane
fantasy. You don't believe the worst of anyone unless you secretly detest them. Love, or even kindness, impels anyone,
though adverse evidence is there, to hope, to believe, the best,
or to give the benefit of the doubt."

He did not, even for a moment, while looking at the portrait, think of applying the same argument to himself. He did
not remember the lies he had believed of Jenny, the unspeakable calumnies. He did not remember the silence he had kept
in the midst of lewd laughter he had heard directed at her.
Not once had he defended her or given her "the benefit of
the doubt."

So he looked at the portrait at first in sadness and despair,
and then the violence boiled out in him. He grasped the portrait and smashed the canvas across his knee. It ripped, tearing the still and painted face. He stood up and threw the
ruined painting across the room and it struck the wall and
the frame shattered. He could hear himself breathing, fast
and noisily, like a satisfied animal. "I wish I could do that to
you in the flesh, Jenny," he said. He picked up the bottle of
whiskey on his chest of drawers and drank it deeply. He was
panting heavily, running with sweat, his heart roaring, moisture showering down from his forehead into his eyes. He
toasted the portrait lying destroyed on the floor. "Sweet
Jenny," he said. The violence was now out in him, the violence which had been rising for many years, ever since his
childhood. He had known it with Mavis, had often known it
with his brother, and even more often had known it with his
colleagues. But it had never been so mad as now.

Becoming drunk, he swayed on the bed. His mind began to
heave with disjointed thoughts of grief, hopelessness, discordant crashes of music, rage, murder, longing, fury. Lines of
poetry rushed through his thoughts, and he began to sing
them raucously, with ribald extrapolations. Then a poem he
recalled from his college years came clearly and sharply to
him, and he said, "Milton, damn it, yes, it was Milton!"

He began to declaim:

"When I consider how my light is spent
Ere half my days, in this dark world and wide,
And that one talent which is death to hide,
Lodged with me useless, though my soul more bent
To serve therewith my Maker, and present
My true account—"

He stopped, and said in a slow, hoarse voice, "My light is spent." He began to laugh loudly, slapping his knees, rolling on the bed in an ecstasy of terrible mirth, rioting in a kind of awful rapture of self-loathing and hate and foaming ridicule.

He found himself lying prone, his hands in his hair, his body shaking with his uncontrollable merriment. He gasped into the pillow, "All those wasted, stupid, God-damned—years! All those books, the hours, the weeks, the months, the years! A whole smirking procession of them. Gaggles of them, mincing, prancing, dancing. Oh, I'd do a lot, I would, against pain and disease! I would be dedicated, I would, like a priest, raising my holy hands on feverish flesh and calming it and curing it! What a—" He filled the room with shouts of obscenity until even the servants, resting in the noonday heat in their rooms, looked at each other in fright, hearing the shouts piercing up through wood and wall, and catching some of the riper expressions. The cook said to the young maid, "Cover your ears, do, dear, it isn't nice for a young girl to hear such talk, and if Doctor weren't almost out of his mind —and who can blame him?—he wouldn't believe he could yell so."

"He's drunk again," said Mary, wiping her damp face with a sheet. "He's always drunk now."

"He has his troubles," said the cook in a dark tone. "Worse than most. It's all broken out in him, all at once, after almost a year."

The black and soundless hiatus of drunkenness fell over Jonathan, sprawled, sweating, on his bed. He never remembered those hours of utter, obliterated despair. The sun fell over his body, and he did not feel it. It left his body and touched his feet, lighted the wall for a little, then moved away, its scorching yellow radiance blasting grass and tree as it fell in the west. Eventually a hot and purple dusk succeeded it, then a warm velvety darkness filled with restless stars. Jonathan was unaware of it all, for dreams had come to him, frightful, chaotic, churning, terrifying, vivid with fear and hopelessness. He dreamt once of Jenny. He saw her in a desolation of gray chalkiness, near the side of a slipping mountain the color of ashes, and she was running down a twisting path which lifted and fell like the coils of a snake. Her black hair blew behind her and her arms were outstretched and her mouth was open on agonized screams. He tried to run to her, to seize her, to hold her, to quiet her, but she always a pace or two ahead of him, and at last he fell into a pit without a bottom and without a gleam of light.

He heard a loud and imperative knocking, and someone was shouting, "Jon, Jon! I know you're in there! Wake up! Answer me!"

"Go away," he groaned. There was a light in his eyes, and it stung them unbearably, and he blinked at the moisture. His head was like a drum, and someone was pounding it with iron sticks. He lifted his hands and held it, afraid that it would burst, and there was a dry and burning sickness in his mouth and in his whole body.

"Jon! Let me in! It's important! Let me in!" Then the voice swore and said, "Damn it, he's bolted the door!" The door rattled. "Jon!"

Jonathan could see more clearly now, and what he saw in his dazed state stupefied him. He was in his lighted office, and not the house, and not in his bed. He could not remember coming here. Someone, something, had gone wild here, for books had been taken from his medical library and torn and thrown all over the floor. Files were open and emptied, the papers scattered. The patient's chair was overturned, and flung aside. His framed diplomas had been ripped from the wall and smashed. The etching his father had given him, a sentimental but moving thing called "The Doctor," had not only been wrenched from the wall, its glass shattered, but someone had shredded it. The soft green draperies which Marjorie had ordered had been pulled from the windows and lay in gleaming heaps in the light of the one lamp on the desk.

"For Christ's sake," Jonathan muttered, looking at this mad destruction, this hatefulness expressed in ruin and violence and vandalism. A sudden turbulence rose in him, and he knew who had done this thing in fury. It had been himself. He did not remember coming here; he did not remember the hours when he had gone berserk, and a terror struck him that he had gone insane in some darkness he could not recall, and he wondered what else he had done.

"Jon!" the voice shouted, and the door rattled more strenuously.

Jonathan pushed himself out his chair and immediately staggered helplessly. He came up with a crash against a wall and almost fell. He shook his head to recover. He began to pick his way slowly through the destruction on the floor, the shards of glass, the scattered books, the frames of pictures and diplomas, the overturned furniture, the confetti of paper. He reached the door, and was again stupefied that he had locked it beyond the waiting room, for though it had been there for years, he had never shot that bolt before.

It took all his strength to release it, and then the door was flung open and there was Robert Morgan on the threshold. Robert stared at him, and then said in a subdued voice, "For God's sake."

"What do you want?" Jon asked, barring the way. But Robert saw over his shoulder and his face became horrified, and his reddish-gold mustache bristled. Slowly then he turned to look at Jonathan again, and he said, "Did you do this?" It was a foolish question, he knew, for now he could smell the rank alcohol. Jonathan's gray and sweating face and disordered black hair and soaked shirt were evidence enough of what had happened in this room. He saw that one of Jonathan's hands had bled a little; the brownish crust was all over the back in wrinkles.

"My God," said Robert.

"Pretty, isn't it?" said Jonathan. "Now, what the hell do you want?"

Robert could not look at him in this state, so he looked down helplessly at his shoes. "You. Dr. Hedler wants to see you in his office. It's very important. At St. Hilda's. He must see you at once. He asked me to come for you. He didn't want to use the telephone. All those listening girls at Central. It's most important—Jon. He's waiting for you."

"Tell Louis to go to hell. You can all go to hell," said Jonathan. "What does anything matter to me any longer? Good-bye, Bob. You won't see me again."

Robert looked up at him quickly, and his blue eyes darkened. "Oh, yes, I will. If you don't come with me now. I've got my buggy outside. I'll see you, Jon, and very soon—in jail."

"What?" Jonathan rubbed his hands over his wet face, then

stared at his injured hand. "What are you talking about? Go home, Bob, like a good boy."

"Worse, prison," said Robert. "Can't you hear me? Prison. For a long, long time—unless you help us to help you. There's a warrant right now in the sheriff's office for your arrest, waiting to be signed right after Labor Day. He's holding it up at Louis' request."

"You must be out of your mind," said Jonathan with awe.

"No, you are, you crazy idiot!" said Robert. "Look what you've done here!"

"What's that got to do with— What the hell are you talking about?" shouted Jonathan. "Sheriff. Warrant! Are you out of your mind?"

"No, you are," Robert repeated. He was quite pale. "See here, they are waiting, your friends. There's something you have to know at once. I won't tell you, so stop glaring at me. You must hear for yourself. Can't you clean yourself up in a hurry?" Robert added in pure desperation. He took Jonathan by his arm and shook him. "Clean up, in the washroom! Now! You've got to come with me!"

Jonathan frowned. He rubbed his throbbing head. He swallowed dryly. He examined his hand again. What had the fool said? Prison. He stared at Robert, who had gone to the washroom adjoining and was already running water into the basin. "I'll mop you up, if you're too helpless to do it yourself," said Robert. He came from the washroom with a wet towel and threw it into Jonathan's face. "You ought to be ashamed," he said in a suddenly boyish and broken voice. "Ashamed."

It was that tone that finally reached Jonathan. He pressed the wet towel over his face and rubbed the blood from his hands, and he was smiling a little. Then he went into the washroom and closed the door, and Robert, wincing, heard him being sick. While he waited Robert took a closer survey of the room, shaking his head. A few months ago he would not have understood, but now he knew too much. He had always known that Jonathan Ferrier was violent by nature, but the violence had remained pressed down for a long time. What had caused it to erupt? Robert sighed. He had a very clear idea. But if it had not been that, it would have been something else. The pent rebellion, for nearly a year, had finally grown too powerful to keep locked up and leashed. A tiger can be kept at bay only so long, and then it must charge.

Jonathan came from the washroom, gray but quiet, combing his dampened hair. He looked very ill, but at least he was as composed as a man like him could be. "Where's my jacket?" he asked. "There it is. Look at it. I must have slept in it. And where's my collar and tie?"

"Here," said Robert, taking them from the desk. "I suppose you don't remember anything. That's a fine state of affairs, a man of your position getting mad drunk."

"You must try it sometime, Sunday-school boy," said Jonathan. "What did you say? Old Louis wants to see me in his office? At this hour? What time is it, anyway?"

"Nine o'clock. What's wrong with your watch?"

It was dangling by its chain, and the two men looked at it and saw that it was smashed also. "My grandfather's watch," said Jonathan, and he detached it from its chain and laid it down on his desk. "A repeater. Nine o'clock? What is Louis doing there in his office?"

"I told you, he's waiting for you, and that is all I am going to tell you. Have some gratitude, if you can. Come on." He watched Jonathan fumbling with his collar button, then went to his aid deftly. He saw Jonathan's eyes close to his, black and whitely polished, in spite of his state, and Jonathan smiled at him almost gently. "You're a good boy, Bob," he said. "I'm getting very fond of you. What's on Louis' mind? Someone done some more slaughtering in the operating room? If so, I don't intend to do anything about it."

"Come on!" said Robert, with a sudden access of impatience. "You look like a tramp, but it can't be helped."

As it was half-past nine St. Hilda's was quiet but glowing with lights here and there in the hot darkness of the night. In silence, Jonathan and Robert went to Louis Hedler's office, passing only one lone nurse and one intern, who stared after them curiously. Robert opened the door and said, "Here he is, at last. I found him dead drunk, and I had to pull him together."

"A canard," said Jonathan. He stopped. He saw in the room not only Louis Hedler at his desk, a fat and foppish frog, but Father McNulty and Howard Best, in leather chairs near the desk. "What is this?" asked Jonathan slowly.

"Come in, Jon," said Louis, staring at him with a formidable expression. "You look very dapper, I must admit. Did Robert pull you out of a trash barrel? Robert, my boy, would you please lock that door behind Jon? We don't want to be disturbed for a while, at least." He stared at Jonathan again. "Is whiskey always your fortress and strength, Jon? Is that how you answer living?"

"Tell me a better way," said Jonathan, but he was watching Robert Morgan locking the door. He raised his eyebrows when Robert put the key firmly in his pocket.

"Hello, Jon," said Howard Best, rising and coming to him and holding out his hand. They had met occasionally in the last months, but Jonathan had never been cordial and never engaged his friend in conversation any longer. So, his temper rising again, he looked pointedly at the hand and did not take it. Howard dropped it, and color came into his kind face. "All right, Jon," he said. "You never give up, do you?"

"Why should I? Now tell me what all—"

"No, you never give up," said Howard. "A damned proud, bellicose bastard—that's what you are, Jon. An unforgiving —well, I won't call you that name because it would reflect on your mother, whom I respect, which is more than I can say for you. What's the matter with you?" Howard had begun to shout. "You and your damned choleric pride, your self-righteousness! I admit I was rough with you, I admit it. But, curse it, weren't you ever rough with anybody? Hah! Didn't you ever accuse anybody of something which was false?"

"Yes, he did," said Robert Morgan, standing beside Louis' desk. "He's self-righteous, all right. He believed all the lies of the town about Miss Jenny Heger. He told me some of them and laughed, too. But that's all right for Jonathan Ferrier! What he believes is truth, no matter how much of a disgusting lie it is. He makes all the judgments; no one dares to challenge them." The young man's face was quiet and resolute, but he looked the astounded Jonathan in the eye.

"I talked with Jenny today," said Robert, and now he turned his head aside. "I wanted to marry her. She is the loveliest young lady I've ever known. She was—well, she was just distracted. It seems that she had thought something unpleasant about Jon, but she didn't tell me what it was. But she did tell me that he had believed vicious tales about her, and had never defended her, and had behaved abominably to her. If—if I were more of a man, I suppose, I'd punch his teeth out, talking and thinking those things about Jenny, as he did."

Jonathan's face had closed, the muscles rising and standing up on it in hard ridges. He was thinking. Then the sickness he had felt in his office was nothing compared with this.

He thought of Jenny, and he put his hand to his forehead. He said, "I think I must sit down, if you don't mind." He saw an empty chair and went to it, walking very carefully, and he sat down and he looked at the edge of Louis' desk and felt the accusing silence about him. He said, "Jenny told you all that?"

"Yes, she did. She's a very reticent girl, as you ought to know, and very innocent and restrained. A lovely girl." Robert's voice shook a little. "She wouldn't have told me if I hadn't asked her to marry me for about the tenth time. I saw she was in a very agitated state of mind. She couldn't help herself. She cried. And so she told me. I'd like to know what you did to her, Ferrier."

Jonathan considered, then he look up and he smiled faintly. "You can punch my teeth out if you want to, Bob."

Louis Hedler laughed, and so did the priest, who had as yet said nothing, and Jonathan held out his hand to Howard Best frankly and said, "I don't deserve having you shake hands with me, Howard, but do it anyway."

"It almost kills me," said Howard, "it really almost kills me." But he took the offered hand. "And I bet it just about kills you, too, to show a little common charity."

Father McNulty spoke. "I think Aristotle, in his *Poetics*, mentions that the hero of a tragedy must be a worthy man, and admirable. He must also have some grave fault of character which is the source of his tragedy. That is you, Jon."

"Very well, I confess I am a swine, that everything that has happened to me is my fault, my own fault, my most grievous fault, Father—if I remember the Confessional." Jonathan's face had begun to spark again and temper showed in his eyes. "I was accused of two murders I never committed, and so that is my fault. I spent months in prison and was tried, and that, too, was my fault. This town believed that I was guilty, and drove me out, and lied about me—and that is my fault. I never wanted anything but good for it—but that is my most grievous fault. For that, of course, for all of it, I can't ever be forgiven. Unpardonable sins."

"Now, Jon," said Louis Hedler.

But Father McNulty was regarding Jonathan with stern sadness. "You are that worthy and admirable man Aristotle spoke of, Jon. But you have a terrible defect of character and soul. You demand perfection of everybody. You have no pity for weak human nature. You despise it—"

"Oh, so I should forgive and kiss and sob over every dog

who's licked at my reputation for years, must I, and thank him for the smear? Frank, I never considered you overly intelligent, but I did think that you had some understanding."

"Thank you." The young priest's face had flushed and his golden eyes brightened with his own anger. "No, no one expects you to fawn on your detractors who've done you an awful mischief, and those who falsely accused you of crimes you did not commit. But you have raised up enemies—"

"And that's my fault, too, I suppose." Jonathan's harsh voice grew louder. "I only had no patience for lies, for incompetence, for hypocrisy, for pretense. But I should have 'charity' for them, I suppose? I should smile at liars, incompetents, hypocrites, pretenders, and tell them they are dear souls?"

"No." The priest sighed. "No decent man would expect that. But there is a way of correcting error. This is also another way: using a sledgehammer. That's your method, Jon."

"Final, too," said Jonathan, and he laughed shortly. No one laughed with him.

"One should walk softly in this world," said Louis Hedler. "Not stealthily, but softly. What was it Nietzsche's *Zarathustra* said: 'Walk among your enemies with a sleeping sword.' That isn't your way, Jon, and never was. You never learned discretion."

"Is this what I came to hear?" asked Jonathan, rising. "Then, I will go home, if you don't mind."

Louis went on as if he had not spoken. "No one expects you to connive at evils, Jon, or even suffer them in silence. But you don't have to accuse a man, before others, of being whatever you think he is, or whatever he really is. If only in self-defense you should have a little more—call it self-protectiveness, if you will."

"Thanks for the advice," said Jonathan. "Bob, open that door, if you please."

Robert Morgan ignored him.

Jonathan's expression became furiously irascible. "Didn't Christ whip the money-changers out of the Temple? If I remember correctly He also addressed some of the men of His day in ungentle terms, such as 'liars, hypocrites, sons of the Devil.'"

"You are hardly Christlike," said the priest.

"But you think I've earned a cross? Such as this running lecture? It seems I came here under false pretenses. I heard a rumor of sheriffs and prisons." He glared at Robert. "To be frank, I've been drunk all day, and your errand boy disturbed me, and that is something I will remember."

Louis said, "I will repeat what *Zarathustra* said: 'Walk among your enemies with a sleeping sword.' A sword, Jon, always ready to be used if necessary, but not used constantly on small and unworthy objects. Used with charity, if that is possible. All this is preliminary to what we must tell you. You've raised up deadly enemies. Some men make friends, others collect foes. It depends on your taste. You tried desperately to make an enemy of me, Jon. You worked at it very hard, very sedulously, with admirable persistence. You concentrated on it."

Jonathan could not help smiling. "I'm afraid you are right, Louis. Very well. I apolozige. Is that why I was wanted here? To confess my sins, be absolved, and sent lovingly on my way?"

"Not quite. Please let me continue. You worked just as hard to make other enemies, perhaps even harder. Most of them, I will admit, are detestable men. For that reason alone you should have avoided them, for your own sake. Or, if you could not avoid them, there were other ways of dealing with them instead of that sledgehammer Father mentioned. Other men have been falsely accused, then cleared, and everyone was happy. But not in your case, Jon. People were disappointed. Why? Perhaps because the majority of men are naturally evil and malicious and they can't bear honest men, and partly because they were antagonized needlessly. Never mind. This was not a meeting to discuss morals or theology. It concerns you, only."

He glanced at Robert, Howard Best and the priest. "We who are here are your best friends, Jon. You have no better in the world. There isn't one of us you haven't insulted and derided, either in your usual bad-tempered way or in pretended indulgence. But, we are more charitable than you. We disregard your nastiness and your inpetuousness and your endearing ways, and remember you for a good and dedicated man, suffering the defects of his own virtues and stumbling blindly through a cave of snakes, absolutely unarmed. For that's what you've always been, Jon. Absolutely unarmed. Helpless against cruelty and malice and calumny. Not even recognizing your enemies. Not even stepping warily about them and watching them. You have our sympathy. Now, if you will draw your chair closer to this desk, I will give you something to read. It makes very bad reading, Jon."

He gave Jonathan a sheaf of papers. "Affidavits from Jonas Witherby, Mrs. Holliday, Peter McHenry. And a few others like them. But after you have read those, you will find much more—interesting—affidavits toward the end. Take your time, my boy, take your time."

Jonathan looked at Howard Best and frowned. "Affidavits. I smell a lawyer."

"Now, Jon," said Louis Hedler.

"Devil's race," said Jonathan.

"Thanks for your usual barb," said Howard Best, but he smiled.

Jonathan's hands were still trembling from his debauch, his fine dark surgeon's hands. He glanced about him suspiciously, then began to read. They watched his tense face. He was reading casually, and the first affidavit was Jonas Witherby's. "Not only did he accuse me of attempting suicide, but he tried to blackmail me into giving him money for his alleged wing at St. Hilda's Hospital for tuberculosis—"

"Why, the old dog," said Jonathan, and shrugged. "Poppycock. He didn't try to commit suicide. He tried to make it appear that Prissy had poisoned him. What trash."

Louis Hedler lit a cigar, Howard lit his pipe, Robert lit his, and the priest lit a cigarette. It was quiet now in the big handsome office with the soft lamps burning, and the windows were open and a night wind stirred the draperies. Smoke curled toward the high white ceiling. Jonathan continued to read, muttering under his breath.

Lightning suddenly snaked over the tops of the black mountains, licking them with a forked tongue. The wind rose higher. Now they could hear the thudding of a night train and then its long dolorous wail as it wound through the valley. There were subdued noises in the hospital at this hour, the rolling of a cart, suddenly quickened footsteps, the rapid tap of heels, the opening and shutting of a door, an abrupt cry, a wail, a soothing voice. The priest heard them and Howard Best, but the three doctors were accustomed to these sounds and they did not reach their consciousness.

Jonathan, as he read, was becoming paler and paler and his face narrower and narrower as every muscle tightened in it and elongated. In comparison his black lashes and brows and thick black hair became sharp and vivid. They saw him examine the receipted bills given to Louise Wertner and Mary Snowden. He reread their affidavits. He reread Edna

Beamish's affidavit. He looked up, cleared his throat, and spoke in a very quiet voice.

"These are all lies," he said. "Every one is a lie. I merely gave the Beamish woman a preliminary examination, told her her condition, and then she—" He paused, and looked from one still face to another. "As for these other women, I don't remember them at all. I don't know why they were sent these bills. I—I never touched them. If I had made a compete examination of them, I'd have remembered. The bills—they are exorbitant. I never charge women of that class more than five or ten dollars for a complete examination."

"They claim abortions," said Louis Hedler. "Those are higher."

Jonathan now fixed all his attention on the other doctor. "I never performed an abortion in my life. I never used a curette on a woman unless it was absolutely necessary to remove the results of a spontaneous abortion, or to save a life, or for diagnostic purposes. Do you believe me?" He appeared in a state of shock, but now the black eyes were beginning to glint and the livid ridges were appearing about his mouth.

"We believe you," said Louis Hedler. "If we did not, you'd not be here now. But here is a statement, or affidavit, made to me by Martin Eaton, who died two days ago and was buried today. He made it in my presence, and in the presence of others."

Jonathan's hands were trembling more and more so that the paper rattled. He read Martin Eaton's first affidavit, then reread it, made a slight sound, and read it again. He put it down and contemplated Louis Hedler and the black spark in his eyes was ferocious.

"Eaton lied," he said. "Or, it may be that he believed Mavis, in spite of all the evidence. He was besotted by her. She was always a liar and a humbug and a fraud. She is dead now, and I wish she had died before I ever saw her." His voice was all the more forbidding because it was so quiet. "I never used a curette on her, mine or anyone else's. I wish now that I had really killed her."

Louis, without speaking, opened the drawer of his desk, removed a covering of linen and laid it down before Jonathan. He nodded at it. Jonathan took the cloth and opened it and his curette lay in his hand. He looked at it incredulously. Louis said, "Martin gave that to me after he made that affidavit. I must admit he gave it up reluctantly."

Jonathan held it in his hand. He said, "I explained some of

the instruments to her. She was always curious about every-thing but rarely retentive of anything. When I explained its purpose she made a round, imitation frightened mouth and stretched her eyes. Then she cuddled against me. She was al-ways cuddling against—everybody. That was at least two years before she died." His low voice was suddenly charged with cold violence and hatred. His mouth opened and he choked. "I need a drink," he said.

"Give Jon a drink please, Robert," said Louis. Robert went to a cabinet and poured a glass of water for Jonathan and brought it to him. He looked at it numbly, as if it were a hemlock cup, then put it on Louis' desk. "I didn't mean that kind," he said.

"I suspected not," said Louis.

Jonathan again examined every face in the room. At last he said, "Is there anyone here who thinks I am lying?"

"No," they said. "No, no, no."

Louis folded his hands on the sheets of paper. "Kenton Campion is behind most of this, and this I know. He is the one who insisted that I send for members of the State Medi-cal Board. They will be here Tuesday. They will issue an—order—for you to be present for examination. The sheriff will also be present—with a warrant for your arrest, Jon."

The ugliest smile stood on Jonathan's face. "I might have expected it," he said. "I have too many enemies, as you re-marked yourself, Louis." He thought. "Campion. The traitor, the seller-out of his country. It's quite in character for him. Well, it all comes back to Mavis, doesn't it? She was the starting point."

They felt the ghost of Mavis Eaton in the room, like a rau-cous and exultant presence, even Robert Morgan, who had never seen her and had only heard descriptions of her. Jona-than repeated, "I wish I had really killed her. At least I'd have that satisfaction now."

"Mavis wasn't the starting point," said Louis Hedler. "You were, when you were born. Campion, these women, Martin Eaton, all the others who made affidavits against you, would be guiltless of this perjury if they'd never known you. You were the precipitating element, Jon. Now, wait"—and Louis held up his hand. "I am trying to make something clear to you. I am not blaming you for anything. Campion is a scoun-drel and I've know it for years. But I've never known him to hate anyone as he hates you, and he is a very sound hater. In a way you should be complimented"—and for the first time Louis smiled.

Jonathan said, "So they'll have their wish. I'll be tried on the strength of these affidavits and the evidence of these whores, and that will be the end of me. I should have left months ago." They saw the sudden shine of his teeth between his parched lips.

Louis nodded to Howard Best, who began to take a thick sheaf of papers from his briefcase. Louis said carefully, "Oh, I don't agree with you, Jon. While you were busy making more enemies and antagonizing more people and generally making a nuisance of yourself, your friends, who believe in you, were very busy. Very busy, indeed."

Howard was smiling broadly. "I've given up a great deal of my time to you, Jon, and your predicament. Louis called me and Father McNulty in some time ago and showed us those affidavits, and I've been busier than a bee since. Now, read these, and then you may make obeisance to me and perhaps I'll forgive you for slighting me over the past months. Perhaps."

Jonathan saw their smiling faces. He was still in a state of shock. He took the thick sheaf of papers and began to read. Louis had prudently removed Martin Eaton's dying statement.

There was Peter McHenry's abject apology and new affidavit, which Jonathan hastily read then put aside with bitter contempt. Then he said, "That poor little kid Elinor." He read Amelia Forster's "affirmation" closely, and he began to smile, and then he smiled exultantly. "So, that explains the bills! Good old Amelia! I must give her a pension at once. No, we can't spare her. God bless our Amelia. And the affidavits of my other patients: I see that they thought they were 'protecting' me from a false claim of injury to the Beamish bitch. There are times when I begin to hope for human nature, that is, when humanity shows itself, which is very rare."

Then he read Howard Best's affidavit of his interview with William Simpson, chief of police of Scranton, and Jonathan swore in delight, and laughed out loud. "So, she was Campion's little bed-pillow, was she! I ought to have thought of that myself. I can see it all. He sent her to me to involve me, and then to someone else who actually did the abortion. It would be a miracle if we could find that murderer. He might be able to tell me something about Mavis, too."

"Go on," said Howard, pleased at the sudden color in Jonathan's pale face. "You've only finished the soup of the meal. Wait for the entrees."

Jonathan read on. Howard had made another affidavit, attesting to the following affidavits of Louise Wertner and Mary Snowden. He mentioned that he had "persuaded" the young ladies, in the name of justice, to abjure their previous affidavits—which they had made under duress, and to make others which were absolutely true. (Howard neglected to explain, in his own affidavit, that he had visited the girls separately, told them he was an officer of the court—which had sounded terrifying to the unsophisticated girls. He promised them immunity from prosecution, or at least amelioration of any punishment for their being parties to the crime of abortion, and seeking out an abortionist, if they would now swear fully and freely to the truth.)

They did not name the abortionist but explained that they had given the name to Mr. Howard Best, to be opened in a courtroom if necessary, for they feared reprisals.

They testified on separate dates in November 1900 that they had been aborted "of illegal offspring," and that they were unmarried. They had paid fifty and seventy-five dollars, respectively. They had thought that the end of it, though each had suffered "minor inconveniences" afterward, which were trifling. Then, on July 15th, 1901, the abortionist had called at their residences, had declared that he was "under investigation" by various unnamed parties for performing criminal operations, and that if he were arrested, he would not spare their part in seeking him out, imploring him to be a party to a crime and working on his sympathy. "I," he had told them, "am a rich man. I may be fined. But you will go to prison for years, and then released only to the streets, where you rightfully belong."

However, related the cowed and terrified girls, the abortionist had promised to use his influence with "unnamed parties" if they would make affidavits to the effect that Jonathan Ferrier, physician of River Road, Hambledon, Commonwealth of Pennsylvania, had performed "these criminal acts" upon them and had extorted enormous fees from them. They were to go to his offices, during his absence—of which they must make sure—and claim to his clerk that they owed those sums of money but had forgotten the bills. They were to ask the clerk to predate the bills—as of the time of the alleged abortions—and then to receipt them. The clerk had followed their instructions "in all innocence and in good faith, believing the stories told to her." The affidavits then followed. The girls admitted perjury, begged for mercy and for understanding of their plight and their "natural terror" before a man who was rich and certainly powerful and who could do them great injury. They also added that when they had delivered their affidavits to Dr. Louis Hedler of St. Hilda's Hospital, of Hambledon, they each received fifty dollars from the abortionist "in appreciation of their services."

A peculiar look had been gathering on Jonathan's face, which no one present had ever seen before and which they did not recognize. It was a look of compassion and not disgust and anger. It was a look of pity and even sadness. It was almost soft.

"The poor girls," he said, and stared at the affidavits, his head bent.

The others were naturally startled at this and looked at each other with amused raised eyebrows. Jonathan said, "What can be done about these young things? When the case comes to court—as it must—will the girls go to prison for their part? I don't want that. I refuse to have it."

Howard chuckled. "Who said anything about court?"

Then a new and angry light glittered in Jonathan's eyes. "I demand it! I want full exoneration! I want revenge!"

"You shall have it," said Louis. "But now, here is the *pièce de résistance*." He held Martin Eaton's dying statement in his hand now, or rather a copy, for he was afraid to trust the original to the unpredictable Jonathan Ferrier. Louis became very sober. "Jon, this is a fearful thing I have here—a copy of a very long affidavit. It is a pathetic thing. It is a tragic thing. In a way, it will affect you more than anything else has ever done in your life, I am afraid, even your arrest and trial. I want you to compose yourself. I want you to read this quietly. I want you to display, for this man, some of the pity you have displayed for Louise Wertner and Mary Snowden, who had less reason to injure you than he. At least, they were under duress, and in fear. This man was under no such. He wrote it in his own hand to right a wrong. He exposed his soul and the soul of someone he loved more than anything else on earth—to help you, and for no other purpose. He admits that he wronged you, and explains why. Now he has rectified it."

Jonathan had listened acutely, and his eyes almost disappeared under his frowning brows.

"Jon," said Louis, "there is something else in this affidavit which affects you very close to home, and I must ask you in advance to control yourself and not to go off into one of your wild, uncontrolled, violent rages before us, and to promise that you will keep your peace about the matter until everything else is resolved. If you cannot give me this promise, I shall not let you read this."

"I promise." Jonathan's tone was curt. He was clenching his hands on the arms of his chair.

Louis hesitated. He was very grave. A deep tension rose in the warm room. Lightning flickered at the windows. The hospital was as quiet as death about them.

Louis spoke. "I have endangered my position by showing you these affidavits, Jon. I have done it out of regard for you, in spite of our past—differences. We have all endangered ourselves, with, perhaps, the exception of Father McNulty, whom I consulted long ago when I first heard of the plot against you. For this is confidential. None of it should have been shown to you, to your lawyer, or anyone else until after the hearing before the State Medical Board. Now you understand the gravity of the situation. You understand how we have jeopardized ourselves. For you to do anything, to say anything, of what you have read, and what you will read, or to name any names, or seek a private revenge on anybody— before the time is ripe—then you will have destroyed us. Have I made this clear, desperately clear?"

"You have," said Jonathan. He was beginning to sweat again.

Louis looked at the others. "I have shown these things to Father McNulty and to your friend, Robert Morgan, your replacement. I have consulted them all and asked their advice, especially Howard's. They said in all fairness—though it is very dangerous—I should show the affidavits to you, for they know your character. They wished you to read what you have read, and now this, so that an interval can pass so you can calm and prepare yourself and think clearly. If you should appear before the State Medical Board members and your enemies in a state of passion—as you should if you had not known all this—and with your usual recklessness and fury, you would be exonerated of the alleged crimes, but you would make such a vile impression on the members of the Board that you would be in disgrace for the rest of your life. The State Medical Board does not like physicians who lose their heads, and threaten, and rage. Your reputation would be irretrievably lost. Is that clear, Jon?"

"Louis," said Jonathan, and he was visibly moved. "I will do nothing to hurt anyone here. No one will ever know, before Tuesday, or even afterward, that you have shown me these things beforehand." He suddenly grinned, for the tension was growing. "I kiss your hand, Louis."

"I don't know which is more distasteful, your rages, your sarcasms, or your humor, Jon, if you can call it humor." But Louis smiled, also, and shook his head.

"The best thing, of course," said Howard, "would be to gag him right here and tie him up and hide him in that closet until Tuesday, allowing him out, still gagged and tied, for only strictly sanitary purposes."

"Excruciatingly funny," said Jonathan. He was white again. "Now may I read?"

"With compassion," said Father McNulty. "The man was weak and tragically foolish."

Jonathan made an unpleasant grimace. "I never had compassion for such men, Frank," he said. "Except for my father. He cured me of sentimentality because he was the most sentimental of creatures. I see these papers are typewritten. I thought you said they were in the man's own handwriting."

"The original is," said Louis. "But we have a reason, which no doubt you will understand after you've read the affidavit, to keep the original from you as of now."

Jonathan frowned at him, but Louis only nodded at the papers, and Jonathan began to read. After a moment, when he saw that this was the last affidavit of Martin Eaton, he uttered a loud and contemptuous curse and then was still.

They all watched Jonathan, and now no man smoked but sat very stiff and rigidly in his chair. They were like men watching a powerful but unpredictable lion, waiting for a movement of its eyes, a bristling of the mane, a twitch of a muscle, to inform them in which direction he was about to leap. By a flick of his lashes, the tightening of his mouth, the raise of his brows, and by his color, they knew almost exactly the paragraph he was reading. Amazement, hatred, repulsion, scorn, disbelief, somber melancholy, fury, even surprise: they saw them all.

They knew when he came to the account of Mavis' death, for every muscle in his body straightened and his mouth became ugly and hard. When he uttered one foul expletive, they knew he had come upon his brother's name. It was then that he looked up at them, and yet did not see them. He was looking inward, not outward, and there was an ominous expression about his eyes and mouth. He was too quiet. They watched him tautly, leaning toward him. The silence in the room became unbearable. They wanted him to speak, to swear, even to rave. That would have been more normal than this quietude, this glittering reflectiveness, this pallid lack of emotion.

Then he laid the papers on his knee and lit a cigarette and he smoked a little, still staring blindly at each face, then at the walls, then at the ceiling and the floor. They knew he was not conscious of smoking, and that in himself something very dire was going on, something so profound and explosive that it could not reach the ear or any other sense. His emotions were beyond human expression, too turbulent for speech. His nostrils were flared as if he were lacking oxygen, and then his eyes narrowed and he picked up the papers again and resumed reading.

I asked for calm, thought Louis Hedler, but I'd prefer raving to this. I'd almost prefer that he'd lose his mind—temporarily, of course.

Then he had finished. Very slowly and carefully he put the papers on Louis' desk and crushed his cigarette in the tray. He watched the last smoke curl up as if it were of the most intense importance. He finally said. "You have the original, in his own writing?"

"I have," said Louis.

"Where is it?"

"In a very safe place." Then Louis knew he had been very discreet, indeed, in having copies made by a trusted clerk and not giving Martin Eaton's affidavit to Jonathan.

"It must be destroyed." Nothing could have been more indifferent than Jonathan's voice.

"I thought you'd think that," said Louis. "But no. I am not going to ask you for your reasons. I suspect them. Your pride. The pride that kept you silent in the courtroom. Jonathan, you are not the first man whose wife betrayed him, nor will you be the last. In a way, you may have saved your life by your silence, for then there was no motive for any alleged crime."

Jonathan said, "I was trying to protect that old bugger, Eaton—his dream of Mavis. I remembered how it was between us when I was a kid and how he helped me all the years of my— He knew all the time! He knew the truth. Yet, he never said a word except to scream 'No, no!' when the verdict came in."

"Remember," said Father McNulty, "he did, in his grief and pain, believe that you were in part guilty of your wife's death. It was insane and twisted thinking, but who has not been guilty of that? Not you, Jon?" The priest smiled sadly. "I know it will take much understanding on your part to feel pity for that distraught father."

But Jonathan had relapsed into his profound meditation again and was lost to them. Robert Morgan was somewhat relieved, being still young and uncomplicated, at Jonathan's apparent control of himself when he had expected madness and terrible rage. But Howard Best and the priest and Louis Hedler knew Jonathan much better, and now they were greatly alarmed and very uneasy and disturbed as they watched the silent man.

"No one else must see Eaton's letter," said Jonathan, after long minutes.

"Jon," said Louis Hedler, "I'm not interested as to your reasons for asking that. I know it is the one thing that can lift the libel and hostility and hate this town feels for you. You must be exonerated from even the suspicion that you injured, killed, Mavis.

"There is another matter," said Louis, and now the froggy eyes glistened with inner excitement. "Brinkerman must not only have his license revoked, but he must be prosecuted for the crime he committed against your wife and those two other girls. God knows how many others he has maimed, caused to die, or aborted. I know his wife is the apple of his eye, and she is wildly extravagant. This has probably been going on for a long time. He must be exposed and punished, and prevented from other crimes.

"There is also Senator Campion. I have not yet fully planned how to approach him and expose him for instigating this plot against you."

"His son, Francis, will arrive tomorrow," said the priest. "I have sent for him to help you. But, as it is, his help may not be needed except as a point against the Senator."

"By precipitating a crisis," said Howard Best with satisfaction, but still watching Jonathan uneasily, "Senator Campion has done you a wonderful turn. You could never have lived with the knowledge that Hambledon, and perhaps the whole state of Pennsylvania, and probably other cities, believed you guilty of your wife's murder. You've been acting, since the trial, like a man without a care in the world, but I know you better, Jonathan. I know that you don't want to leave Hambledon, where you were born——"

Jonathan stood up slowly, and then in a most casual tone he told them what they should do with Hambledon and everyone in it. He expounded on the matter with easy eloquence, as if he were amused. But they saw his eyes. He was only half aware of what he was saying. The inner black turbulence was gathering force in him.

Louis interrupted. "You have forgotten that there is a clergyman present, Jon."

"Oh, I've heard all the words before," said young Father McNulty, whose rosy face now had no color at all, and though he smiled he looked a little sick. Robert Morgan was tremendously embarrassed and he had flushed. Howard Best pretended not to have heard.

"I think," said Louis, "that as it is nearly midnight, that we should disband." He looked at Jonathan who had gone to an open window and was looking through it, his hands in his pockets.

"Jon?" said Louis Hedler, and struggled to keep the pity from his voice. "I want you to think of this: In a month you will recall this night only occasionally. In a year you will not think of it at all. In two years it will be like a bad dream, almost forgotten entirely. You are still young. Your whole life is before you now, cleared, clean, ready." He hesitated. "Jon, would you consider becoming chief of surgery here?"

Jonathan said, as if he had not heard at all, "I have things to consider." He turned. The sallow calm was fixed on his face. He looked at each man separately. "I suppose I should thank you. Howard, send me a bill."

"Go to hell," said Howard Best.

"And Louis," said Jonathan, "I haven't any words. I still don't believe it." He actually smiled.

But Louis, studying him closely, did not smile. "Jon," he said. "You have given us your solemn promise, and you were never a man to go back on your word, for good or evil. You must not do anything—rash—or violent. We have put our own safety in your hands, our own reputations. You have promised."

"I don't break my word," said Jonathan. Then it was as if an inner and fierce convulsion ran through him and he shivered, and clenched his fists at his sides, and closed his eyes for a moment. "I leave Brinkerman and Campion to you, at least for the first attack. I will meet with you here at St. Hilda's, in the conference room, at what time on Tuesday morning?"

Louis exchanged a glance with Howard Best and said smoothly, "I will let you know the exact time later."

He stood up. "I think you can have that drink you wanted now." He went to a cabinet and brought out a bottle of brandy and several glasses. "I think we all need this."

Jonathan said, "No."

"I will drive you home," said Robert Morgan.

But the priest said, "I'd prefer to do that, Dr. Morgan. I want to have a word with Jonathan, probably about Francis."

To the surprise of everyone Jonathan said nothing more. He had relapsed into his inner dream again. He did not even remember to shake hands with the men who had saved him, and they understood. They shook hands with each other, murmuring in low voices, as if there were a corpse in the room or something that must not be aroused to some towering and fatal detonation. Then the priest touched Jonathan's arm and they left together, and the others watched them go, thankful that Jonathan was leaving, yet more anxious than ever.

"I don't like it," said Howard to Louis Hedler.

"Disliking it is putting it very mildly," said the doctor. "I've seen Jonathan in some dangerous moods before but nothing like this."

The priest drove his buggy through the dark and silent city, very dim now and asleep. The heat lightning still snaked and forked over the black mountains. There was a dry and burning scent in the air of withered leaves and dust and heated stone.

Jonathan did not speak. He swayed in the buggy as loosely as if he were unconscious, and the priest drove slowly, praying for words. He knew that Jonathan was not aware of being in the buggy or even that it was night, and he was afraid. He said, "Francis came at once when I cabled him."

Jonathan did not reply. He fumbled for his cigarettes, lit one, stared at it and the priest could see the ghastliness of his face by the instant flare of the match. Then the night took it again, and the priest felt a hard pressure in his chest and new fear. He spoke slowly and quietly.

"Jon, we are only fallible men, and so it is that often we are very wrong. It is possible, perhaps probable, that we erred in talking to you as we did tonight, urging you to walk and speak more discreetly in the future, and even implying that much of the tragedy which has come to you lies in your own nature. How dared we be so smug and so sure and so superior?" He sighed. "I think it was concern for you that made us speak so, for none of us meant that you should sacrifice principle, employ some hypocrisy, and be smilingly discreet in most situations. That is the way of cowardice, and you were quite right to rebuke us. It is the discreet man who, by his silence, or his smiles, or his prudence, is the cause of much evil in the world, for he who does not actively oppose it gives at least a tacit assent."

Jonathan said in that disturbingly indifferent voice, "The opinion of others never concerned me very much. It concerns me less now."

The priest frowned, thinking. "Still," he said, "in cases where it is not very important, and nothing moral is involved, or anything serious, it is best to be tactful."

Again Jonathan was silent, and the priest knew that he could not reach him. He had tried, and it was hopeless, and there was nothing left but prayer. However, he tried once more. "Jonathan, if many in this town did not love and respect you, you would be in a frightful position tonight, and in the days to come. Remember those who care about you."

"Don't worry," said Jonathan. "I won't do anything rash. Yet."

"I remember a section of a very melodramatic poem," said Father McNulty.

   " 'In tragic life, God wot,
     No villain need be.
     Passion spins the plot.
     We are betrayed by what is false within.'

"Jon, I know you do not forgive easily, if ever. But when you think of those men who injured you, remember that they were weak as well as bad, and many were confused and uncertain and baffled by their own desires, their own defects of character, and perhaps their private tragedies. Dr. Eaton was a very tragic man. At the last he made a supreme effort to clear your name, and died the next day."

"I hope," said Jonathan, "that it wasn't an easy death."

The priest said nothing. They reached the dark and closed Ferrier house, and Jonathan got out of the buggy and without another word or a look he walked to the door, and was lost in the shadows of the deep porch. The priest drove on, the wheels of the buggy rattling on the cobblestones, the horse clumping steadily, and the dust of the trees sifting down.

Jonathan crossed the lawns to his offices. The light in his private office was still lit. He walked into the room and looked at the havoc he had done, and the wreckage. It was like seeing the results of a nightmare. He was in a worse nightmare now. He must think and think and think, and know what he must do. He took off his coat and hat and collar, and set to work, lifting shards of glass, paper and books. It took him a long time, and he worked deftly and almost soundlessly. He filled every wastebasket. He found a broom in a closet and he swept the rug as best he could. He put the furniture in order. He rehung the draperies, which he had pulled down.

He went to the house and up to his room in the darkness. He lit the gaslights in his room and they bloomed into soft yellow. Here, too, was wreckage. He found Jenny's portrait and he straightened out the canvas and looked at the young and desolate profile.

"Jenny," he said, "I should have been a disaster to you before. I should be total catastrophe to you now. Good-bye, my darling."

He could not sleep. He resumed his packing, then stopped. He went outside and walked the streets, his footsteps echoing under the lonely trees, until the gray morning light stood in the east and a hot breeze rose. Once again in his bedroom he took a heavy sedative and fell into a mute and dreamless sleep.

CHAPTER THIRTY-FOUR

The next morning quite early Dr. Louis Hedler and Howard Best drove up to "Pike's Peak," the Hambledon residence of Senator Kenton Campion. It was cooler as the doctor's carriage carried them higher into the mountains, and here at least there was some blessed greenness and glossy shade. But the sky was still that curious saffron color, though it was hardly nine o'clock. They saw the fine houses on their smooth lawns, heard the hissing of hoses, the subdued voices of gardeners, the playful barking of dogs, the ringing voices of children. But the road was white with dust, and occasional walls pounded with hurting light.

"He seemed quite unconcerned when I called him last night, before we saw Jon Ferrier," said Dr. Hedler. "I told him it was important, that I must see him this morning, and not in my office, and he couldn't have been more indifferent or less curious."

"He probably thinks you are coming to plead for Jon," said Howard. "He threatened you not so subtly, didn't he?"

"To be sure. Kent is a very unworthy man, and a mean one. It doesn't matter. I am now in full agreement with you, Howard, to handle the affair this way, without publicity, without the newspapers, without the State Medical Board, without witnesses. Say what you care to about Campion, and I will agree with you heartily, but we must also admit that he's very careful of himself and knows when to withdraw and when to attack. We don't want Jon to confront all those people—we agreed on that. He was just about out of his mind last night, and God only knows what he is thinking today and what he is planning. So, for his sake we must spare him and conclude things quietly. When Campion gets a sniff of the carrion we are preparing for Brinkerman, he'll withdraw so fast you won't see him except for a blink. No scandal for Kent."

"And he won't have to pay for that stinking plot against Jon! A nice thought."

"Isn't it? But sometimes to help the innocent, like Jon, one must let the scoundrel get off scot-free. I hope Jon will appreciate that someday, though I doubt he is in a temper calm enough to agree as of now. In his own way, our Jon can be very vengeful. He won't thank us for this morning's work—yet. Later, he may."

The town lay below them, already shimmering in heat waves, and the water of the river was brassy. Dr. Hedler felt uncomfortable in his formal brown suit, and as he was also stout, he began to suffer. He pushed his straw hat far back on his round skull and puffed at his cigar. "You will be able to cancel that warrant out for Jon, won't you, Howard?"

"It isn't signed yet. Something tells me, as I told you last night, that Campion will hurry to call the sheriff and ask for cancellation, and to assure him that everything is splendid now. Oh, he'll cover his fat tracks very ably and very dexterously, you can be sure of that!"

Louis sighed. "I hate to see such a rascal come out of this without a single wound. I hate, even more, to think of that man back in Washington, doing his mischief as usual, serene and unctuous and loved and admired. I may have a talk with the Governor in the near future, a very discreet talk, and show him a few documents. Perhaps the legislature won't confirm Campion again, or perhaps they'll recall him. But that will bring in the newspapers, and reporters are avidly curious, and Jon may be drawn in. I must think about it."

"We have to walk very tenderly about Jon," said Howard. "If he were a more reasonable man, we could discuss things with him and lay our own plans. I think, I am sure, that it was knowing about his brother—that damned dilettante—that really knocked him off his precarious perch. The other things —he could be induced to look at them fairly calmly, in proportion, eventually."

"I'm sorry for Marjorie Ferrier, with two such sons," said Louis. "Now, she disproves our neat theory that much that happens to one lies in his own nature. Marjorie was always a great lady, a magnificent woman, tolerant, kind, composed, full of fortitude and intelligence. She never interfered with anyone."

"Perhaps," said Howard, "that was the whole damned trouble. Tolerance, I am coming to think, can create as much disaster as intolerance."

"I wonder what Jon will do now," said Louis as they approached the Campion estate.

"Whatever it is," said Howard, with pessimism, "you can be sure it will be the very worst."

The slim maid at the door assured them that they were expected, and they went into the shining marble hall and then into the room with the Florentine windows looking out at the gardens and the hot purple and bronze mountains. They found young Francis Campion waiting for them, fatigued and strained but smiling, in his black, habitlike clothing. "I arrived a little earlier," he said to them, shyly shaking hands but looking anxiously into their faces. "How is Dr. Ferrier?"

"As bad as can be expected," said Howard. Francis made a distressed sound. He walked slowly up and down the room, a thin young man with a delicate profile.

"Father McNulty sent me a long cable," he said. "And there was a letter from him waiting for me here. I can hardly believe it. It's a frightful story." He looked at them. "And true, too?"

"Quite true. And much worse," said Louis Hedler. "I don't know how much Father could squeeze into a cable and a letter, but there have been many developments since then, and each one is a little worse than the one before." He paused. "As it concerns your father so intimately, perhaps you'd rather not hear our conversation with him, Francis."

"I am staying," said the young man with resolution. "I have some things to say to my father, too. If necessary, I will say them in front of you. I've been a coward. I don't want to injure him, but I must think of my country first. It is possible something can be arranged so my father's name won't be blasted in the newspapers. It is entirely his choice."

Howard and Louis looked at each other, then Howard smiled and sighed happily. "You give us pleasure, Francis," he said, and rubbed his hands together.

They heard measured footsteps approaching, calm, casual footsteps, and Senator Campion entered, beaming, chestnut-colored, flushed with sleep and food. He was like a large, middle-aged cherub, plump but stately, happy with life and, thought Howard Best, he has probably slept like a lamb and as snugly. Always the politician, he greeted his visitors with hearty amiabilty, shook hands with them fondly, smiled at them, and studied them with his keen politician's eyes, watchful, hard.

"I see you've already greeted Francis," he said, and put his hand on his son's thin shoulder. When Francis moved away, the Senator did not even glance at him. "Such a pleasant surprise. Quite unexpected, too. Francis, as this affair my friends have come to consult me about is very private, and needs to be managed discreetly, will you excuse us?"

"No," said Francis. "I think this concerns me, too."

The thick chestnut brows rose, and slowly the Senator turned on his heel and stared at his son. "You? How could it possibly concern you, my boy?"

"I know it is about Jon Ferrier, and anything about Jon Ferrier now concerns me." Francis' thin face firmed and his eyes were no longer shy but direct.

"How do you know it is about Ferrier?" asked the Senator, and he was not as flushed as before.

"We told him," said Howard quickly.

"Oh, you did." The Senator's regard swept to Howard and there was a threat in the narrowed look. "I think that was very imprudent of you, Howard. As this is a legal matter, you have behaved unethically, and I think the Bar Association—"

"I always behave unethically to protect the innocent," said Howard. "Don't you, Senator?"

"There is a slight question of the innocence of your client, Howard. Or, is he your client?"

"Yes."

"How did that happen? How did you, or he, know about this private matter, not a word of which has so far been allowed to go beyond closed doors?"

"Jon heard rumors," Howard said. "Just rumors. So, he came to me, on the strength of the rumors."

"Rumors." The Senator contemplated Louis for a long moment. "From an impeccable source, I trust, Howard?"

"Impeccable. Trustworthy. News does get out in a little town like this, Senator. For instance, frightened girls' talk. Indiscreet ladies whisper secrets to each other. A colleague catches a breath of scandal, of danger. Another colleague overhears a private conversation and reports it to the interested party. People make quiet affidavits, and clerks gossip. It arrives at Jon's doorstep, all of it. Nothing very tangible, of course, but enough. So, he comes to me to ask me to protect his interests. Is that sufficient?"

"I think you are lying," said the Senator, but he still contemplated Louis Hedler.

"Oh, it won't matter in the least in, say"—Howard looked at his watch—"another hour. Then you will be grateful, and not annoyed, that we consulted you. Before we moved."

"Before you moved," said the Senator.

"Exactly. We do have a warm spot in our hearts for you, Kent, we really do. So, instead of calling in the newspapers, and getting out warrants of arrest, immediately, and mentioning your involvement, we came to talk to you."

"I don't know what the hell you are talking about!" exclaimed the Senator, and his look at Louis had turned murderous.

"Well, I do," said Howard, smiling. "For instance, I was in Scranton recently, visiting friends, and I discovered that they were close friends of a certain Mrs. Edna Beamish, and—you know how people are, Senator—they mentioned that you were, yourself, a very close, a very dear, a very intimate friend of Edna's. Very intimate, indeed."

The Senator had turned a curious color. He glanced quickly at his son, who was listening alertly. "What of it?" asked Kenton Campion. "I knew her husband well."

Then Howard, watching him closely for signs of guilt and fear, said, "You and she also know Dr. Claude Brinkerman, don't you?" He had no proof of the involvement of Edna Beamish with the doctor, but he struck this blow deliberately, hoping.

The Senator's face had become the color and texture of wet lard. But he was not a politician for nothing. He said, "I know Claude Brinkerman. What of it?"

Howard shrugged. "I, too, know Brinkerman and all about him. News gets out. To support his wife in the manner to which she was never accustomed, he turned to performing abortions. Now, I have it on excellent authority that Mrs. Beamish had occasion to visit Brinkerman, and I also have it on authority that you two are very close to each other—in Washington—and people do talk, as I've reminded you before. I also have it on good authority that Mrs. Beamish recently had an abortion, and so there is the whole story."

The Senator said, and they saw the engorged arteries pulsing in his thick throat, "Ferrier aborted her in his office, and we have the proof and the affidavits."

Howard shook his head kindly. "No, you don't have any such proof, Senator. But we do have proof that Edna was your little friend, and little friends often get into difficulties, and so they have recourse to the Brinkermans. Er, do you wish me to proceed before your son?"

Francis had been listening closely, white with horror. He turned to his father and said, "Edna? Edna? That was Edna I saw in your house a year ago in Washington, Father, when I arrived unexpectedly! She was in your bedroom, Father." Francis' mouth twisted with pain and disgust. "Edna left very soon after my arrival, rather disheveled. But I knew all about you, Father, and it did not surprise me. I've known about your little friends since I was sixteen. I never knew the names of the others, but I heard you call her by her name that morning, very early, urging her to get out as fast as possible."

Howard smiled with glee at Louis Hedler, who had been having somewhat of a bad time for some minutes, and Louis smiled back.

"Filthy, mean, dirty little spy," said the Senator, with hatred bleak and open on his face as he looked at his son.

"Yes, I was. And I am glad, too. For I learned a great deal about you, Father. Enough to make me want to die very often."

"I wish you had, I wish you had," said the Senator. He turned to the others. "I think we should sit down and have a quiet talk, gentlemen."

"I think so, too," said Howard with alacrity. "After all, there is a lady involved, Mrs. Edna Beamish, or Mrs. Ernest Beamish, and she has been party to a crime, and she has also perjured herself freely in making out an affidavit against Jon. Oh, news does get around, and people do peek and read!" Howard smiled affably at the grim Senator. "Now, if and when little Edna is arrested, and knowing the nature of ladies, especially ladies like little Edna, I doubt if she will suffer in silence. But you know Edna best, don't you, Senator?" He was teeming with elation.

Again the Senator looked at his son, and the loathing he had concealed for years under a paternal amiability was stark on his large face. "Get out," he said.

"No," said Francis. "I stay. And if you take these gentlemen to your room and lock me out, they will tell me everything afterward. Won't you, gentlemen?"

"Indeed yes," said Howard. "I must do everything to protect my client, Jon Ferrier. Besides, it will all be in the newspapers shortly, the national newspapers—after all, Francis, your father is a very important man—and you can read it for yourself."

"Newspapers," said the Senator and sat down heavily. "Are you threatening me, Best?"

"I certainly am," said Howard. "Don't the newspapers love a juicy little romantic story! Sweet little Edna and Senator Kenton Campion—and an abortionist. Tut, tut. Americans are still very narrow-minded, still, Senator, as you doubtlessly know." He sat down and faced the Senator and gleamed happily upon him.

"Let's be finished with lies and start with the truth," said the Senator. "Louis, you are responsible for this. You betrayed a trust, a trust put in you by your own medical societies, not to mention betrayal of private matters to this shyster."

"In a few minues," said Howard without rancor, "you will be glad that someone put trust in me, and very grateful. Indeed, let us start with the truth. Senator, I have here, in my briefcase, numerous documents. I don't think you will enjoy reading them, but you will find them interesting."

"I thought you might like to know, Kent," said Louis, who had regained his confidence, "that a warrant will be issued for Claude Brinkerman this morning. Men like Brinkerman don't keep their mouths closed. I think he may talk when the facts are presented to him, and then decide to throw himself on the mercy of the court. I've heard he was a close friend of yours, Kent, and not just a casual acquaintance. That is why he induced two young and frightened girls to perjure themselves and accuse Jon Ferrier of performing criminal operations on them. But read for yourself."

It was already hot even in this immense "second drawing room," as Beatrice Offerton called it, and the white and black marble floor glittered in the morning sun, which poured through the windows in cataracts of light. Edges of radiance surrounded the little statuettes which stood on their soaring pedestals of white and black marble, and the same radiance glowed through rosy alabaster groups on tables and consoles. It brightened the velvet colors of sofa and gilt chair and enlivened the shadowy hues in the Aubusson rugs, and turned the fretted metallic edges of marble tables into vivid gold. The light was so intense everywhere, glancing and sparkling and blazing, that it was hurtful to the eye, and there was no escape from it on looking through the windows at the smoldering mountains.

Senator Campion took the papers extended to him by Howard who, with Louis, was perched on a settee of gilt and pink silk, but the Senator looked fixedly at the younger man. The ripe color of his rich lips had turned purplish at the mention of Claude Brinkerman's name again; his blue eyes had narrowed, so that the color was hardly visible; his jowls quivered for an instant, and a lock of his thick chestnut hair fell over his sweating forehead. Then he began to read, after putting his pince-nez on his large well-formed nose.

He read with the suspicious and scrupulous care of the politician, alert to verbal traps and cunningly placed phrases, and sometimes he went back to reread a section of a previous page. He was poised and controlled by nature, and he had learned to be more so since he had become a politician. The three men watched him, his son Francis standing near a window, but except for his color and the sweat on his face he showed no emotion. Somewhere a big clock was ticking, ticking, and a gardener had begun to cut the grass outside, and a fountain splashed, and the cicadas raised their raucous song against the burnished sky.

Then the Senator carefully took off his glasses, let them spring back on the chain, which was fastened to his buttonhole, and laid the papers on a nearby ormulu table. He folded his hands on his flowered waistcoat. He looked at Howard Best. "What has this to do with me?"

Howard was, for a moment, flabbergasted. Then he smiled. "Everything, Senator. Everything. You surely have not missed Martin Eaton's remarks about you! That alone is very —incriminating. You surely understand we know about little Edna, and the abortion you procured for her at the hands of Dr. Brinkerman. It makes a nice story that you induced Brinkerman to seek out two of his more vulnerable patients to perjure themselves against Jon Ferrier. Then, of course, you and Jonas Witherby were overheard browbeating Louis here, by several of the staff. Oh, there's a lot that has to do with you, Senator! And that is not all. We have much more, which we are keeping for the final event. It would be very silly of us, wouldn't it, for us to tell you what they are?"

Again the Senator's eyes narrowed reflectively on Howard, and Howard knew that he was conjecturing if the lawyer were lying or not. Then Francis spoke. "There is what I know, also, of what I heard my father saying to his colleagues in his house, when he thought I was asleep, absent for a time, or not in the city. I have already told Jon Ferrier some of it. It would make appalling reading to the American public, and I am ready to give it to them."

The Senator slowly turned his big chestnut head and looked at his son. There was no fear on his face, not even now, but his large nostrils flared and a most malignant expression passed over his face like the glare of an edge of a knife.

Francis said with sad bitterness, "I asked Jon, only a few months ago, if I should tell what I had heard and what I knew, and he said if it were his father, he would not do it. You owe that to Jon, Father. But now I am ready to tell everything to any newspaper, with names and dates—that you are in an international conspiracy involving munitions, and future wars, for profit and power."

Louis Hedler sucked in his breath, and Howard stared at the Senator with repulsion, but the Senator looked only at his son.

"You are a liar," said the Senator with loud, hard precision.

"The invariable reply of a liar to the truth," said Francis, and he turned away and again stared through the window.

The Senator said to Louis Hedler after a minute, "Then, you did indeed betray all that was confidential to this shyster?"

"Kent," said Louis, "you and I are of an age. I am a rich man, as you know. I am economically invulnerable. You cannot hurt me. Complain of me to the State Medical Board? Do you think I care any longer? Compared to what I have saved Jon Ferrier from, my retirement, forced or voluntary, is nothing."

"I thought you detested him," said the Senator.

Louis said, "I detested many of his personal characteristics and still do. But I know him for a puritanically righteous man, for all his deserved reputation with the ladies in this town. He is a good man, the best of physicians, an expert surgeon. He has done so much for Hambledon anonymously that if the people knew, they would rise up and call him blessed." He paused. "Just as they will rise up and call you an entirely different name when they know the facts we have about you."

The Senator's mouth twitched, but it was not with a smile. He was a redoubtable fighter. "I know he is hated here. I know I am regarded with, shall we say, admiration, and I am respected. I can fight this thing down, drive Ferrier out of town still, and come up triumphant. Do you doubt it?"

"You've forgotten what I know, Father," said Francis from the window.

The Senator laughed out loud. "You! A creature who tried to hang himself only last June! A nincompoop, a defected clerical student! A penniless whimperer! The newspapers wouldn't dare publish what you'd tell them."

"Now, that is interesting," said Louis Hedler. "You leave us no recourse, I, Howard and Francis, but to go to the Governor with this evidence we have shown you, and the more important evidence we have not shown you. I will send a telegram at once to the State Medical Board to delay sending members here until I have seen the Governor."

"I think," said Howard, "that the newspapers will be interested in what Louis and I and Francis, together, have to say, and the Governor's subsequent remarks. I have heard he is not very happy about you any longer, Senator, and you have powerful enemies in Washington. There are ambitious young State Senators with rich and influential families and friends who are itching to replace you, and I am sure that the State Legislature, which appointed you, would listen to them—after the Governor informed them of what we have against you, your lies, your suborning of perjury, your connection with a notorious abortionist, and much more."

The Senator's face became violent, not in any contortion of feature but more in contour of his cheeks and the swelling at his temples.

"We came to you," said Louis, "not for your sake, not to spare you, not to make or beg a bargain. We came for the sake of Jon Ferrier, and his mother, Marjorie, and the memory of Martin Eaton, and even for the sake of those two poor girls induced to put themselves in jeopardy to satisfy your hatred and malice. Perhaps, even, for Mrs. Edna Beamish, who will certainly be prosecuted for perjury, at the very least, and I understand that she is not only a rich lady in her own right, and able to procure good lawyers, but is a lady of spirit. When deserted by you, she will think of herself, and she will be indignant. There are many we'd like to spare, and above them all, Jon Ferrier, who has suffered too much as it is. We hope to persuade him not to prosecute his enemies, among them yourself. We can only do that with your cooperation, and I beg you to give it to save a scandal which will rock the whole Commonwealth."

"We are even willing to let you return to Washington in peace," said Howard, "though it goes against our patriotism. We are willing because of Jon."

"I never knew he had such friends," said the Senator with enormous contempt.

"It is unfortunate that you did not know," said Louis Hedler. "Had you known, you might not have been so sure and so rash."

The Senator sat in silence, twiddling his thumbs. He had never been thwarted nor opposed before. He kept swallowing, as if something vile repeatedly rose in his throat.

"You interest me," he said. "In the improbable event that I should submit to these falsehoods this blackmail how do you propose to handle the situation? I suppose Ferrier has already seen these concocted papers?"

"Not all," said Louis, and wondered how much longer he would have to pretend to even more dreadful knowledge than contained in the documents. "But enough so that last night I was afraid he might come up here and murder you. But he was spent, and he had given us his word that he would do nothing until I gave him permission or the matter was concluded. Otherwise," and Louis smiled "Jon might really have committed a murder last night. You know how savage he can be and what a temper he has."

"And you think you can control such a madman?"

"I think I can," said Louis, and wished it were true. "He has no evidence against anyone except what we hold. He is sensible enough to know that he cannot make accusations without evidence or at least I will impress that on him."

"And the evidence?"

"It will go to a very safe place, copies to me, copies to Howard, to be destroyed in the event of our deaths, or to be opened—if necessary. Jon will have no proof."

The Senator reflected. He looked from one face to the other carefully and they could not tell what he was thinking.

"You have forgotten those three women Edna and the two girls. Their last true affidavits are a matter of public record?"

"No. Louise Wertner's and Mary Snowden's were made before me, at my behest," said Howard. "If we can settle this thing like reasonable gentlemen, if we can agree—then you, Senator, need only inform Mrs. Beamish that she must withdraw the complaint, which is the only one of public record and in the sheriff's hands. I wish I had known," said Howard with an affectionate smile, "and I would have dissuaded Mrs. Beamish from the very beginning with the information I have against her."

"Then, on whose public complaint to the sheriff will Brinkerman be arrested?"

"On Mrs. Beamish's. She is responsible, not I. But then she was following orders, was she not? As for the girls' affidavits, they were given to Louis, both sets, I may remark, the ones they falsely made—under orders—and the second true ones, admitting perjury."

Again the Senator reflected, and he sucked his purplish lips in and out and began to tap the table with his pince-nez.

"You have only to call your good friend, the sheriff, who received his support from you, Senator, and ask him, in the kindest way possible, to squash Mrs. Beamish's complaint and to destroy the warrant he has for Jonathan's arrest."

"And Brinkerman—you say he will be arrested?"

Louis looked at him. "He will be, unless Mrs. Beamish's complaint is withdrawn, unless you ask the sheriff to overlook—with a laugh, of course—her indiscreet perjury. I shudder," said Louis, his face changing, "to let such a man get away from the punishment he deserves. Yet, for Jon Ferrier's sake I will not let the sheriff read Martin Eaton's last and true affidavit. What Jon will say to that I do not know. But again, he will have no evidence. I promise you that. We did not even permit him to keep a copy of Martin's affidavit."

"You have not been entirely frank with me," said the Senator. "You threatened and bullied me, implied you had already moved against me and Brinkerman, for effect. Is that fair or just?"

Howard could not help it. He burst out laughing with genuine mirth and threw back his head. He choked, "Senator, that remark of yours, about 'fair and just' tickles me almost to death, it honestly does!"

"Now, Howard," said Louis.

Francis came from the window, his fine face tense and tremulous. "You actually intend not to expose this man as he should be exposed?"

"My dear boy," said Louis, "sometimes one has to keep silence to protect others, even if it goes against the grain, even though it leaves bile in one's mouth. Isn't Jon more important to you than your father's ruin?"

"No, he isn't," said the Senator. "This white-faced whelp has been trying for years to ruin me, from his own admission."

With the faintest and most distressful of sounds Francis turned and went quickly from the room and Louis and Howard watched him go with sorrow and sympathy. Then Louis said, "If that were true, he could have done it before, and not almost died of what he knew about you Kent. I've known him from childhood, from babyhood. He adored you. What did you do to turn him against you, Kent, your only son?"

The Senator's chestnut brows drew over his eyes and his mouth twitched again. He made no reply.

"Well," said Howard, "the sheriff should be in his office. I believe you have a telephone in the hall below, Senator. May we accompany you, just to listen to your remarks, and have the assurance that no move will be made against Jon?"

"But there is something else," said Louis, "and the most important. Howard and I have discussed this thoroughly. Everyone knows that you were a close friend of Adrian Ferrier's and that you have a high regard for Marjorie and I believe there was a rumor that you steadfastly declared that Jon was not guilty of Mavis' death. How admirable it will seem to the good people of Hambledon—and the national newspapers—when you announce that you personally undertook an investigation of the case and that you are happy to announce that, indeed, Jon was not guilty!"

"No," said the Senator with firmness.

Louis sighed. "Then, we will, in spite of everything, have to give a copy of Martin Eaton's last affidavit, which implicates you and Brinkerman, to the press."

"God damn you," said the Senator, in a very soft voice. "Isn't it enough that I may—may, I remark—ask the sheriff what you have suggested I ask him?"

"No, it is not nearly enough," said Howard. "Don't force our hands into making everything public. At the very least," he continued with cunning, "you will be thwarting Jon's explosive demands that it all be made public, for you know he can be wild, and he has suffered a great deal. By saying what we have suggested you say to the press, you will be frustrating poor Jon, and it is really very unkind of us to think of it at all."

"And God damn him, too," said the Senator, and stood up. He surveyed them. "I've met scoundrels before in Philadelphia and Washington, but you two bumpkins are the most conscienceless."

Now Louis laughed as well as Howard. The Senator was not ashamed or embarrassed. After a few moments he laughed himself, briefly and grimly, and spread out his hands. "Let us go downstairs to the telephone." He added, "I think I will return to Washington almost immediately."

"A very wise thought," said Howard, as they went down the shining marble stairs together. "One never knows what Jon Ferrier will do."

"I suggest," said Louis Hedler, "that you warn Brinkerman to give up his extracurricular activities. As for myself, I will ask him to resign from the staff and will hint to him as much as possible of what I know. One never knows with a man like Brinkerman, but that is the very least I can do." He sighed. "It is a very bad predicament in which I find myself. Ferrier would not be so discreet as I, but then he is much younger and he has not had much experience with mankind."

CHAPTER THIRTY-FIVE

On Monday, Louis Hedler called Jonathan Ferrier at his house. He said with extreme smoothness, "Jon, there has been a delay. The members of the State Medical Board will not arrive for a week or more."

"Why not?"

"Jon, they did not tell me." Louis paused. "I hope you are giving this matter a great deal of careful and judicious thought."

"Louis," said Jonathan, "you are moderate to excess. I am giving it thought, all right."

"That is what I am afraid of," said the older doctor. "You have kept your own counsel, haven't you?"

"I have. If those men do not arrive soon, I will go myself to Philadelphia and consult with them."

"Bringing the mountain to Mohammed. I wouldn't advise that, Jonathan."

"I heard a rumor at Phil Harrington's wedding yesterday that Brinkerman has 'suddenly been called out of town and may settle elsewhere.' Now, Louis, you don't know anything about that, do you?"

"I do. But this is no conversation to be having on the telephone, Jon. You will know everything in good time."

"Somehow," said Jonathan, "I have the strangest feeling that little mice, or perhaps rats, are running around in the dark, and I am not supposed to hear them."

"I do like your analogies, dear boy, but—"

"I also heard that Campion has been 'recalled' to Washington, and that's odd, for President McKinley, I hear, is going to Buffalo to speak at the Pan-American Exposition. I verified Campion's absence by one single telephone call to his house. What do you know about that, Louis?"

"I am not exactly Campion's best friend, Jon. Why don't you go somewhere for a few days and rest or something?"

"And why don't you go to hell, Louis?" Jonathan slammed the receiver into its hook. Louis Hedler shook his head. Jonathan's voice had been reasonably normal and controlled, but that did not deceive Louis. He dreaded the day and the hour when he must sit down with this immoderate man and tell him that his plans for vengeance must be put aside, and mainly for his own sake. Louis called Howard Best at his house and told him discreetly of his conversation with Jon, without mentioning his name.

"It's a fine thing that our friend up on the hill had the discretion to leave," said Howard. "I'm afraid our other friend wanted to visit him in the name of mayhem, or worse. When does the Big Smile release the story to the newspapers?"

"Wednesday."

"I wonder what our little playmate is going to think of that?"

"The imagination boggles," said Louis. "I have a feeling that I must visit my sister-in-law in Scranton before the release."

"And Beth has relatives in Wilkes-Barre. They have been

begging us to visit them. See you when we both get back to Hambledon, Louis."

"Yes. By the way, the members of the Medical Board must have heard a little something soothing, probably from the Big Smile, for they were very understanding and agreeable when I suggested that it may not be necessary at all for them to come here. They were not in the least surprised when I sent them my telegram, apparently, for their own was most amiable in reply and even a little indifferent."

"Ah, well, it is for the best. Good-bye, Louis, have a happy holiday."

Jonathan was not drinking. He knew he must have a clear mind if he were to carry out his plans. In the meantime he was finishing his packing. He had prospective customers for two of his farms. He would not let himself think of anything too acutely, for he was afraid that he would lose all his reason. He occupied himself with external things. He visited the farm on which Thelma Harper and her children were living, and to his surprise he let himself be persuaded to remain two days. He rode over the early autumn acres, had long discussions with his tenants, and played with Thelma's children and was more surprised to discover that he could sleep without a drink or a sedative. He had heard from Thelma of Senator Campion's attempt to persuade her husband to swear to a false affidavit against Jonathan, and to the young widow's astonishment Jonathan only smiled as if it were a great joke. She knew Jonathan well. He seemed calm enough, and even joked with her a few times, but she saw his eyes and was disturbed. She cooked him excellent meals, and though he sat at the table with her and her children, and teased them all, he ate almost nothing. At night she could hear him walking for a considerable time before he went to bed.

All that Jonathan had learned over a period of three months—the tentative tolerance, the increasing charity, the attempts at understanding, the new pity and flexibility—had left him entirely. He was one abscess of cold but fulminating hatred. Upon his return to Hambledon he did not visit his offices, did not go to the hospitals. "I just want to be alone," he said to Robert on the telephone. "I have a number of things to do and arrangements to make." He did not mention some inquiries he had begun.

So, thought Robert, he is really leaving. I just hope he doesn't have a gun in the house. I didn't like the sound of his voice.

Jonathan rode his horse down the River Road every day, not once looking at the island in the water. He knew he dared not do that. He would find little pine groves, and lie down in the dusty autumn grass and look blindly at the sky, and try to think of nothing at all. There was a time for everything, he would think. This is not the time. Yet.

The heat and dryness over the land continued and seemed to become worse. Each day there were hopes and prayers for rain, for autumn coolness, for surcease. The river fell lower and lower, and in the country the wells sank and the little ponds and streams dried up. At night the profitless lightning and wind began, but there was no thunder, no showers, no storms, though occasionally there was a growling in the mountains.

Each morning, back in Hambledon, Jonathan continued his rigid and self-imposed discipline. He would get up, eat a small breakfast if any, read his newspaper, then go out for hard riding, a sleep perhaps in the grass, and then a return to his house where he wrote business letters or read them, and communicated with his banks and his brokers. This took most of his day. He would eat his lonely dinner, sometimes glancing at his mother's empty place. After dinner he would read in his father's study, and sometimes he would come to himself with a start, realizing that time had passed, a long time, and he had not turned a page. Then he would go to bed.

He was like a condemned man counting out his last days. His thoughts were purely abstract and on the surface. He would not let himself think of Jenny Heger. Afterward—he would go abroad, perhaps for a year or more. He had his letters of credit. Upon his return, he would go—where? He did not as yet know. That year lay before him. When he came back, it would be time to think of how he must spend the rest of his life, and it was only then that he felt a black premonition of agony to be endured in the future. His life was wasted, gone. A man without hope, without plans, without a real destination, was truly dead, he would say to himself.

Robert Morgan, miserable and apprehensive, came down to breakfast one morning and his mother said with satisfaction, "We have an invitation to dine with Mr. and Mrs. Kitchener, Robert."

"Good." He looked about the dark hot dining room, where the windows were shut as usual against even the slightest breeze or touch of sun. Not that he cared for the sun lately, for he had never experienced such prolonged heat and dryness for so long a time, and there seemed no end to it. Each day the sky became more yellow, as if it were jaundiced, and once or twice a day thick black clouds would gather and darken the earth, but it never rained, and soon the sun would be out again, as fierce as ever. Robert said, "What did you say, Mother?"

Jane Morgan's grim gray face was simpering. "I do wish you'd listen, Robert. I merely remarked that Maude Kitchener seems much taken with you."

Robert thought of Jenny Heger and he felt the usual sick spasm of love and longing and hopelessness. He had not seen her lately. He felt that she would not welcome him on the island at this time, or perhaps never again.

"You haven't touched your toast, Robert," said Jane. "I don't know what is wrong with you lately. You seem so—so concerned with something. I trust everything is going well for you in this little town?"

"It isn't so little, Mother. Yes, everything is going well for me. I have now taken over all of Jon's practice." He looked at his cup of cooling coffee but did not lift it. "I wish he were not going away."

"He is compelled to," said Jane Morgan with acid pleasure. Robert looked up quickly.

"What do you mean by that?"

"Robert, it is town talk, not that I gossip or listen to gossip. But I do know Mrs. Beatrice Offerton quite well now. A very pleasant and comely lady, and so democratic, but yet so appreciative of our better station in Philadelphia. She knows Philadelphia, and we discovered that we have mutual friends. It may surprise you, Robert, that Mrs. Offerton has a very low opinion of that detestable man."

Robert felt that at last he was going to hear something interesting if he did not press his mother. So he waited. Jane bridled and smirked. "Indeed," she said. "Remember, Robert, that I never liked him, never trusted him, and never believed that he was not guilty of that crime. Mrs. Offerton quite agrees with me. She told me, only a week or so ago, or rather, I should say, hinted, that new evidence has arisen proving that he did, indeed, murder his wife."

Robert smiled, and his mother thought that his smile was extremely odd.

"You don't agree, Robert?"

"Of course not. Doesn't she ever go to Washington with her brother?"

"No."

"He is there now." Robert picked up the newspaper by his plate, folded and neat and waiting. Jane had always so placed her father's morning newspaper, and she would never have dreamed, as she did not now, of reading it before "the gentleman of the house" had first glanced through it. Jane was annoyed that Robert treated her news so lightly and then had dismissed it. He was not looking well lately. He had lost weight. He seemed preoccupied. She often heard him calling the Ferrier number, but apparently "that man" never answered his calls, and Robert would leave a message with the maid, hopelessly. Had Robert and he had a quarrel? She hoped so. She wanted no stain from "that man's" association with her son to remain on him. She studied Robert as he listlessly unfolded the newspaper, and she thought his color was not so bright as it should be, and that there was a new melancholy on his face. Ah, well, responsibility came hard to the young. He would soon adjust to it. And there was that lovely girl, Maude Kitchener, who was definitely setting her cap for him. Jane started. Robert had suddenly uttered a loud and gleeful exclamation, and he was grinning joyously at the newspaper.

"Dear me, you quite startled me!" said Jane. But Robert was laughing uproariously, and he was handing her the newspaper over the plates, and his blue eyes were dancing.

"Do read, Mother!" he said. "You will notice that the front-page item of the *Hambledon Daily News*, in a very prominent place, has a Washington dateline. As of yesterday."

Jane opened her glass case, put on her glasses, looked at her son suspiciously, then looked at the item he had pointed out to her. It said, *SENATOR DECLARES DR. JONATHAN FERRIER OF HAMBLEDON, PENNSYLVANIA, CLEARED OF ALL SUSPICION OF HIS WIFE'S MURDER LAST NOVEMBER!*

"Oh!" said Jane incredulously. She looked at the masthead of the paper, as if suspecting a deception. She peered at the columns below the heading. Her lips, dried and stiff, pursed as if she were about to cry.

"Senator Kenton Campion, senior Senator from the Commonwealth of Pennsylvania, today called a conference of reporters in Washington to clear the name of one of his fellow townsman, Dr. Jonathan Ferrier, who was arrested last December for the alleged death of his wife, Mavis Eaton Ferrier, after a criminal operation. The case will be recalled as having attracted nationwide interest and publicity, due to the prominent position of Dr. Ferrier and his wife and the extraordinary brutality of the crime.

"Dr. Ferrier's lawyer in Hambledon, Mr. Howard Best, had moved for a change of venue because of the alleged ill-feeling and indignation against Dr. Ferrier in that town. Mr. Best said that he did not believe that Dr. Ferrier would have a fair trial under the circumstances. The trial was moved to Philadelphia, and Dr. Ferrier was subsequently acquitted. Messrs. Cranbury and Oldsman, of the law firm of Cranbury, Smythe, Jordan and Oldsman, were Dr. Ferrier's attorneys during a long, dramatic and surprising trial. The case remains a mystery to this day, as no other person has been accused of the crime, or arrested.

"Reporters from every important city in the nation were present during the trial, which occupied some four weeks of constant and repeated testimony for the defense and for the prosecution. No motive for the alleged crime was ever brought to light, and the jury brought in a verdict of not guilty after prolonged balloting. At one time Judge Henry Morrissey appeared to believe that the jury could come to no unanimous conclusion and that he would be compelled to dismiss the jury and call for a new trial. The prosecuting attorney was Mr. Nathan Campbell of Philadelphia, who expressed his disappointment eloquently after the verdict was brought in.

"Dr. Ferrier returned to Hambledon and his practice. Then he later decided to sell his practice and leave the town. This was due, it has been rumored, to the fact that the town of Hambledon did not wholly accept the verdict of the jury in Philadelphia, and there was some popular feeling against Dr. Ferrier.

"Because of this, Senator Campion stated today, he himself decided that a full investigation must be begun to clear the name of Dr. Ferrier. Senator Campion is an old friend of Dr. Ferrier and a friend of the family. 'Yet this,' Senator Campion declared to your reporter, 'had no weight in my decision to see justice done and the name of an honorable man and a famous and worthy citizen of my hometown, Hambledon, restored unblemished and honored once again. Therefore, some months ago I quietly instituted an investigation of my own in behalf of Dr. Ferrier, fearless of the truth, and determined only to bring the full facts to public light.

" 'The investigation was private and conducted through the most estimable citizens and investigators, professionals in their craft. No expense was spared. No. stone was left unturned. No possible clue was ignored. The wildest statements were tracked down and proved false or true. No one who had the slightest connection with the case was overlooked. The investigators were sleepless. Finally they admitted that not a single piece of evidence pointed to Dr. Ferrier's guilt.

" 'Among those consulted sedulously was Dr. Martin Eaton, uncle and adoptive father of the late Mrs. Jonathan Ferrier, who had been present during all the long weeks of the trial. Dr. Eaton had been in failing health since the death of his niece, and evidence has been brought to light that he was, during the final two weeks, in a state of confusion and distress. When the verdict of 'not guilty' was brought in it was reported that he cried out, 'No, no!' He then collapsed in the courtroom, suffering from a severe stroke.

" 'Dr. Eaton's physical condition prevented him from making his convictions known, he told one of my investigators only three weeks ago,' stated Senator Campion. 'Then I consulted him also, praying him to give me the truth. Dr. Eaton thereupon declared to me that he had never believed Dr. Ferrier to be guilty and had fully accepted the defense's contentions that Dr. Ferrier had been in Pittsburgh during the crucial time, and had not doubted the sworn testimony of prominent physicians who had been in the company of Dr. Ferrier for several days and had been present at two operations which he had performed on well-known citizens of Pittsburgh. The reason for his ambiguous cry of 'No, no!' when the verdict was brought in, said Dr. Eaton, was because in his bereft and confused state of mind and grief he had believed that the jury had brought in a verdict of guilty, and therefore collapsed. He had been an invalid immured in his house since that time, receiving almost no one, and therefore was unaware that Dr. Ferrier's name was still obscured by the suspicions of the people of Hambledon. When this was brought to his attention, by me and my investigators, he emphatically declared that at no time had he for a moment thought Dr. Ferrier guilty of the heinous crime.

" 'Dr. Eaton also vehemently stated that the married life of Dr. Ferrier and his wife had been most happy and without a cloud, and there was no other woman in the case. Dr. Eaton, I regret to say, was so disturbed at hearing that his fellow townsmen still believed Dr. Ferrier guilty that he had a relapse and died on September 1st. He leaves his wife, Mrs. Flora Eaton, and several cousins in Philadelphia, but no children.

" 'I am *delighted*,' said Senator Campion, using the word with an obvious bow to his close friend, Vice-President Theodore Roosevelt, 'by the felicitous conclusion of this sad matter, and the final and complete exoneration of Dr. Jonathan Ferrier. The true criminal has not yet been uncovered, but that is not in my hands. I only hope now that Dr. Ferrier will forgive and forget the unjust and unfair suspicions of his fellow citizens in Hambledon and consent to remain in the town and hold his position as a member of the staffs of the two hospitals in Hambledon, and that his unstinted gifts will be as freely given to all of us who live there as they were before his arrest and trial. His father, the late Adrian Ferrier, was a leading citizen of Hambledon, a descendant of one of the Founding Fathers of the great Commonwealth of Pennsylvania, and his mother was Miss Marjorie Farmington of the Philadelphia Farmingtons.'

"Senator Campion showed every indication of immense joy and satisfaction in the results of his selfless investigation, conducted at his own expense, and declared that he had done so not only to clear the name of a dear and valued young friend but to prove, once again, that justice is not dead in America but will rise in all her glory when her presence is demanded, and that in the Republic of the United States of America no innocent man can be unjustly condemned, unlike in certain other nations. Senator Campion was a most ardent supporter of the Spanish-American War, it will be remembered, and wished to join his friend, Colonel Theodore Roosevelt, as a member of the Rough Riders. However, his age prohibited his engagement."

Robert had been watching his mother with a most unfilial malice and enjoyment while she read. Again and again she would glance at the masthead, still hoping for a practical joke. An unbecoming color was staining her thin cheeks, and now she kept licking her lips, as if thinking some malevolent thoughts. Finally she looked up and met Robert's smiling eyes.

She said, "Oh, that saintly, that charitable, that noble man!"

"Jon, I assume?"

"Robert! I mean Senator Campion. To perjure himself so, to spend so much money, to demean himself, a Senator of his country, to open himself selflessly to gossip and conjecture!"

Robert tried to sort this out, and failed. He called for fresh coffee. He appeared rejuvenated. "I shouldn't suggest, if I were you, Mother, to Mrs. Offerton that her brother, the Senator, had 'perjured' himself. That's a grave crime. In this case it is a libel."

Jane was frightened. "I don't mean it exactly so, Robert! How you always confuse my words! Oh, dear. Now I suppose that frightful man will remain in Hambledon."

"The unblemished Senator has declared that Jon is blameless and not guilty. What better evidence would you want? A message from Gabriel, in person? I don't know why you call Jon 'frightful.' You have no reason to think so. You never had. The Senator says not, himself, and if you want to remain on amiable terms with Mrs. Offerton, you had better declare it abroad that you fully agree with her brother."

In better humor than he had been for some time, Robert went to the offices, where he was greeted by a joyfully tearful Miss Forster, waving her copy of the newspaper at him.

Jonathan, at that moment, was reading the newspaper himself. As he read, his eyes kept blurring, and there was an ominous hard pressure in his chest. Mechanically, he noted that his blood pressure was rising. He concluded the reading, and sat back in his chair in the breakfast room, and stared blindly at the opposite buffet. He could feel the bounding pulses in his neck; he felt the tightness of his skull. A burning pain shot through his left chest and then down his arm. He made himself breathe carefully and slowly, until the enraged spasm had passed. Now he was sweating.

He got up and went to his telephone in the hall. He called Louis Hedler at St. Hilda's. He received the information that Dr. Hedler had been called hurriedly to Scranton the day before, as a relative was ill. Jon smiled a curious smile. He then called Howard Best's house and his office. Mr. Best was in Wilkes-Barre on a short vacation with Mrs. Best. Jonathan hung up, unsurprised. As he did so the telephone began to ring. Mary, the maid, hurried into the hall. Jonathan said to her, "Mary, there will be many calls for me this morning. Tell everyone that I am not in town at present, will you?"

Mary answered the telephone and gave the ordered reply, puzzled. Jonathan looked at the instrument. He would call the *Hambledon Daily News* and report that Senator Campion had lied, that his story was false, and that he, Dr. Ferrier, would be only too happy to tell the truth if the paper would send out a reporter. He reached for the telephone, then stopped. Louis Hedler and Howard Best had betrayed him for some damnable reason or another. Whom were they protecting? Someone they feared? Campion? Then it came to Jonathan ruthlessly that they were protecting him. Again he reached for the telephone, his face flooding with blood again, and again he stopped. He had given his word to those incredible scoundrels that he would say nothing until they gave him permission.

He walked into his mother's beautiful drawing room, and sat down on one of the silken settees, and smoked one cigarette after another, thinking furiously, filled with hate, frustration, rage, humiliation. Oh, no doubt they thought they had accomplished something very deft and clever, the bastards! Something to smooth over matters, to make everything tidy and neat and serene. To hide scandal, to prevent upheaval, and, in the meantime, to leave unpunished both Campion and Brinkerman, and, at the last, to protect the names of Mavis and Martin Eaton. Jonathan wanted to kill.

They don't trust me, he thought, and acknowledged that they had reason not to trust him. He went into the dining room and filled a glass half full of whiskey. He stood and drank it, thinking. No, he would not let them frustrate him, keep him quiet, keep him from vengeance. They could not hide forever. They could not run from him forever. And when he got his hands on them? The explosion that would rock Hambledon would be heard from one end of the country to another, just as the ridiculous and contemptible tale had already rocked it. He would ruin Campion once and for all. He would destroy Brinkerman. Then, as the whiskey began to work in his empty stomach and the fumes rose to his head, he burst out laughing. He should thank Brinkerman! He had killed Mavis. "I should strike a medal for him," he said aloud.

He looked through the window and saw Robert Morgan crossing the lawns to the Ferrier house. He watched him come, the sanctimonious red-gold bear of a Boy Scout! He had known all about it; he had read the newspaper. Jonathan drank the rest of the whiskey in his glass and waited. In a few minutes Mary came in and said in a whisper, "Are you home, Doctor?"

"Yes, Mary," he said in the very gentlest voice. "I am always home to Dr. Morgan. Send him in here, please, and then close the door."

The girl looked at the glass in his hand, went to bring Robert. He came in, and Jonathan, who had begun to refill his glass, saw that the young man seemed both elated and apprehensive. "Come in, Bob," said Jonathan. "Join me?"

"At nine in the morning? No, thank you." Robert paused and glanced at the glass, and watched Jonathan take a long swallow. "I see that you've read the morning newspaper."

"Yes. Darling little story, wasn't it? Was that Hedler's confection?"

Robert said, "I know only what you know, what you read that night in Louis' office. I'd heard some rumors long before that, and I finally went to Louis with them, and he knew I was your friend, and he took me into his confidence. My mother knows Mrs. Offerton, and I was given tidbits of little news, and I thought, finally, that Louis ought to know. He already knew more."

"And Campion's box of chocolates, cherries in cream?"

"I don't know anything about it." Robert looked at him defiantly. "But, what of it? This is the best way. Very ingenious of Louis and Howard. What did you want? Campion stamped into the mud? I admit I'd like that, too. But what would it result in for you? More scandal, libel, hate, confusion, trouble, calamity. Have you forgotten your mother?"

"Not at all. I remember her very clearly. I will always remember Mama, for what she did to me." Jonathan's black eyes were bloodshot and frightening. "I remember my brother, too. But I will deal with them in my own good time. First, there is Campion, and Brinkerman."

"Louis removed Brinkerman from staff, and he has left Hambledon. Didn't you know?"

"Yes. And all his crimes will go unpunished. It is a nice thought to use as a lullaby."

"He left his wife behind, and his house. Everything. He will not be practicing medicine any longer."

"That should console me, I suppose, for everything he tried to do to me?"

"Yes, it should. He's a murderer and a mutilator, but he is

also a doctor. Think what this will mean to him. Louis had promised him that should he hear of him practicing anywhere, he will bring out the whole story."

"Louis won't have to wait for that, Bob. When Louis returns and I'm free from my promise, I am giving the full story to the national newspapers."

Robert sighed and sat down heavily on one of the chairs near the polished dining room table. "For what purpose?" he asked.

"Damn you, haven't you any intelligence at all, any guts, any manhood, that you should think I should be satisfied by a creaming over of the truth, and forgive and forget?"

"If it were only you," said Robert, "I would think it right that you expose those rascals. But there are others. Your mother, even your brother, the girls who made out affidavits to protect you, the memory of Martin Eaton. To name a few. Above all, yourself. What do you think you will accomplish by exposing yourself to new notoriety, and injuring Louis and Howard Best, your good friends? Do you think you are a little Samson?"

"Do you think I care for this town, for anybody in it?" Jonathan flung his glass across the room.

"No," said Robert very slowly, "I don't think you care about anybody or anything. Not even yourself." He watched the rolling crystal as it moved across the thick carpet back to Jonathan. When it reached him, Jonathan smashed his foot down on it, and Robert was sickened at this display of senseless violence.

"There's someone else, too," he said. "Francis Campion, who came thousands of miles to help you. I've heard he's tried to call you a dozen times, but you won't answer your telephone. Do you know that he denounced his father before Louis and Howard, for your sake, and that he threatened, for your sake, to expose his father?"

"A sensible boy," said Jonathan. "I must call and thank and encourage him."

Robert's mouth opened on a faint sound. "And after he does expose his father, how do you think he is going to feel?"

"Cleansed."

"You don't believe that, Jon. He isn't that kind of a boy. Think if it were your father. Well. If you do what you obviously intend to do, then you will smash not only that glass there but a whole town. Yourself, above all. That is what Louis is trying to prevent. He's willing to let Campion and

Brinkerman escape to protect you—from yourself. He knows what you are."

"As you know so much," said Jonathan, with an expression of black ugliness on his face, "perhaps you can tell me how they managed to get Campion to pour that bucket of swill on the press."

"Well, Howard did give me a hint. They threatened him. How else could they accomplish it? They wanted to clear you once and for all. Merely ruining Campion would not do that. People would still put their own interpretations on your story, and as they love Campion, and obviously don't love you, they would finally decide he was a martyr to your vindictiveness. So, to force him into that nice and artistic concoction of lies, they outlined to him, I suppose, just what you are capable of doing, but, more important, how eagerly people would accept his story without question—to your benefit They would love Campion for his generosity to his young friend; they would admire him more than ever. And again, you would benefit, for no one would doubt his word. They'd doubt yours, Jon."

"So Campion is going to get his halo polished again. Is that the plan?"

"That isn't the exact intention," said Robert, smiling slightly. "The plan is to restore your halo, which, I may remark, is badly dented and corroded."

"I love all this solicitude for me," said Jonathan. "I am awed by it. But none of you has taken into consideration my feelings in the matter, and what I want, and what I deserve, and what I should have."

"I think," said Robert, "that all that was taken into full consideration."

Jonathan looked at him closely. "That sounds a little ambiguous to me."

Robert stood up. "You are always looking for a subtler meaning than intended."

"When Louis and Howard return, I am going to inform the newspapers."

"Newspapers do love resounding stories like this, full of scandal, murder, abortions, perjury, suborning of perjury, adultery, tarnishing of a public figure. I admit that, Jon. But, though the newspapers will be eager for your story, they will want evidence to prove every word. Do you have that evidence?"

Jonathan stared at him, his eyes dilating and stretching. "Evidence?"

"Yes. Affidavits. Martin Eaton's dying affidavit, for one. The girls' affidavits. Mrs. Beamish's affidavit. Oh, I suppose you could get a court order to demand that Louis give them up. But what if Louis denies there were ever any such affidavits? Louis is quite a power in this town, you know, and his word will be taken before yours."

He smiled at Jonathan's suffused face winningly, though he was still badly frightened. "Every probability has been taken into consideration to protect only you from the possible results of your own sweet disposition and your immoderate impulses."

Jonathan stood up too and went for another glass and half filled that, and took a deep swallow. He looked dangerous.

Robert said, "Louis wants you to stay in Hambledon, where you were born and your people before you, Jon. He knows, even if you deny it, how you love this town and how your roots are embedded here. He knows what you've tried to do for Hambledon. He knows what it will mean to you if you leave here. He has done everything for you."

"Dear Louis," said Jonathan.

Robert hesitated. "There's someone else I haven't mentioned yet. Jenny Heger."

Jonathan took the glass from his mouth. "Never mind Jenny. There's no future for Jenny with me. I have enough presence of mind to know that, enough clarity of mind to understand how it would be for Jenny if I married her."

"Well, women are peculiar, Jon. I hate to see a girl like Jenny marry someone like you. In fact, I don't think I can stay in this town if you marry Jenny." Robert was speaking very quietly. "It would hurt too much. But it would be Jenny's choice, and she has a right to make it."

Jonathan smiled a little. "I leave Jenny in your hands, Bob."

"A normal man wouldn't say that, but you aren't normal. Besides, Jenny isn't a commodity to be bargained over and delivered into the proper hands. She's a human being, a woman, with her own mind and her own desires. She told me, the other day, that she would never forget you and would never marry anyone but you. Yes, indeed, women are peculiar."

He found it unbearable to stay now that he had spoken of Jenny, and he opened the door and went out and left the house. Jonathan could see him walking across the lawns to the offices, and the bright red-gold head was bent and Robert moved like one who was too grief-stricken to be anything but burdened and weary.

Jonathan could hear the telephone ringing, ringing, ringing, and Mary's harassed young voice, "No, Doctor is not at home. Is there any message?"

Jonathan took the bottle of whiskey and the glass upstairs, and shut the door.

CHAPTER THIRTY-SIX

Not only Pennsylvania had been stricken by what the people called "the yellow drought." Parts of Virginia and Maryland and New York State were also suffering. The newspapers had laid the cause to "pressure," which explained nothing, and now they were saying that the underlying cause was "turbulence" in the Caribbean and "incipient hurricanes." One hurricane had already struck the west coast of Florida and another, and a fiercer one, was "moving up the east coast of the Atlantic." There were high tides near Cape Hatteras and tides were rapidly rising as far north as Atlantic City. Communities in low-lying sections along the coast were warned of possible danger and asked to remain in readiness for evacuation. No one, of course, took this seriously. The promise of any storm, with rain and resulting coolness, was anticipated with hope.

Then even the anxiety of the farmers and the news of the approaching hurricane were forgotten entirely. President William McKinley had been shot by a would-be assassin in Buffalo, New York, at the Pan-American Exposition. Vice-President Theodore Roosevelt was on his way to Buffalo, where the stricken President lay wounded, and from which issued bulletins full of hope and assurance to the country that "all was well."

Even Jonathan Ferrier, in his self-absorbed state of hate and lust for vengeance, and plots and plans, forgot himself for a few hours on reading the news. God save us from Teddy, he thought, Teddy with his Progressivism and his ebullience over "America's Manifest Destiny." A good man, Teddy, but a little simple and too much corrupted by hope and dreams and his belief that it was possible to change the nature of man, the only thing which had not changed in thousands of uncountable years, the only thing which was immutable.

The man of Plato's day, of the earlier days of the Pharaohs, of the caves, of Rome and Greece and Byzantium, of Persia and Arabia, was the man of the present, also, with the same weaknesses and viciousness, the same desires and hatreds and longings, the same passion and the same apathy, the same nightmares and fantasies. The ancient philosophers had talked of the "changing nature of man," but it had never changed. Only religion had sometimes breached that stubborn fortress of cruelty and poetry, of war and of greed, of child-like belief in progress and thaumaturgy, of pacification of evil gods and visions of eternal peace and brotherhood. Religion, however, had always sunken back, defeated, to await another crisis in man's history to wash again that unchangeable battlement, to dash rainbowed foam against stony walls, to dampen the seething wrath and mindless fury that lay within.

But Teddy Roosevelt, adamantly believing that man could be changed by "just laws" and government, did not know that. Law had never had much or permanent impact on man, and it never would, for it did not touch the primal spiritual essence which only religion could reach. Fads and fancies, "new" ideas, "new" ways of observing phenomena and "new" ways of responding to them—all these were so ancient and so tried and found wanting that it made intelligent men smile when they encountered the Teddy Roosevelts and their piteous hope and emphatic belief "in the future."

For a few hours Jonathan forgot almost everything as he reflected on the man who might possibly become President of the United States of America if Mr. McKinley died of his serious wound. He even forgot to drink. At sunset he actually went out to look at the sky and for the first time he was made uneasy. The enormous sunset, incandescent orange, filled the whole west, and it was sullen and threatening. Even the mountains, dark and rounded, appeared insignificant below that sultry panorama, at once sulphurous and jaundiced, hinting of danger and tempest. The falling sun burned in it, a great red eye, blurred of edge but flaming. The air was pent, hot, still, and the earth was like scorched bread, crumbling and powdery. As Jonathan watched, a great phalanx of black clouds began to boil over the mountains into the vast sea of orange and scarlet, and from them shot blinding bolts of primordial light. Then came the long boom of thunder, followed almost immediately by a tremendous flow of wind, and the dry trees rattled with a crisp and tormented sound, and the bronzed grass bent, and a livid shadow ran hastily over the earth.

Jonathan was fascinated by the spectacle, which reflected his interior mind and thoughts. He walked into his mother's garden, which, as it was on higher land, gave a view of the river. The water was liquid brass and the island stood in it blackly under the sunset and the increasing shadows. Then the rain came, huge plump drops falling with rapid splashing sounds, and the lightning flickered over all the country and the thunder howled hoarsely from the mountains. Jonathan ran inside the house, feeling a primitive exultation, a longing for destruction.

The cook and the maid were already running about, closing windows, struggling with shutters, catching blowing draperies, and moment by moment the house darkened and the storm rushed upon them. Jonathan wanted to shout with exultation as he helped the two women. He saw their pale and frightened faces in the dimming light. "Only a storm," he said between detonations of thunder.

The wind came heavier and heavier and the rain poured down the windows and gutters and eaves overran, chuckling and gurgling, and the glass rattled in its frames and strong doors shivered. The noise was becoming deafening. It sounded as if dozens of rapid freight trains were roaring overhead. The three in the Ferrier house lighted gaslamps, and the yellow glow and the quiet within only intensified the gigantic tumult outside. It was hard to distinguish between the bellow of the wind and the crash of the thunder. Fiery glares lit up the premature twilight that had fallen on the countryside, immediately followed by explosions of incredible sound. Yet some of the mountains were still outlined against the ocherous light in the west.

Jonathan, standing near a window, could barely see the

trees on the lawn, which were bent almost double as if in agony, throwing their leafy arms upward and about them, contorting themselves in fresh blows of the gale. They twisted, reeled, turned, stretching this way and that, anguished and nebulous shapes in hell. Sometimes they appeared to stagger, shaken to their heart-roots. Then branches were detached with a raging screech and shriek, and saplings were torn up and thrown across the grass. Jonathan went into the lighted kitchen to find his two employees sitting side by side, grasping each other. "I see we have the hurricane that was promised," he said. His easy attitude, his lack of fear, reassured them, until another enormous crash of thunder shook the old sturdy house and a flying branch struck a wall like a titanic whip.

"Never saw anything like it," said the cook.

"It will pass," said Jonathan. A glare of lightning lit the kitchen, brighter than any artificial light, and the two women saw his face and shrank.

But it did not pass. As the hours went on the storm increased in madness, and the wind quickened and trees fell and the river filled and the sepia land was flooded and ran with water, for the earth could not absorb it. At midnight the storm was worse, if possible. Now, between explosions of thunder, could be heard the bells and the rumblings of fire engines, and the sky, in all that rain, turned murky-red here and there. The air did not cool. It became hotter, seemingly, at midnight, especially in the closed house. Jonathan prowled from room to room, listening, exulting, trying to peer through steaming windows. Then a chimney was struck and the two women, in their upper bedrooms, screamed as they heard the tumbling bricks on the slate roof, and smelled the suddenly pervasive odor of ozone. Jonathan raced up the stairs to the eastern end of the hall and saw the bricks rolling down as the lightning lit them, and he waited for indications of fire. But the house had seen storms before, and the brick walls were impervious. Jonathan called up to the women, "It's all right. Just a small chimney."

Another lightning bolt showed him that at least three old giant trees had fallen on the lawn, and the ground was littered with leaves and branches and twigs. The heat was stifling, so Jonathan opened a casement with caution and immediately could smell the sharp electricity in the teeming air. He inhaled it with pleasure, though water splashed on his face, and it recalled to him very clearly an earlier storm like this, when he had been a child. It had lasted two days, the farmlands had been flooded and thousands of stock had died in the fields and crops had been washed out and typhoid had struck the town of Hambledon. Two very tiny islands in the river had been completely drowned and had disintegrated, and the largest island, now called "Heart's Ease," had been almost entirely inundated and four squatter families had perished. In fact, the water did not recede from the island to its original level for several days, and it left behind it a residue of sticky mud and debris, which prevented it from being the local pleasure and picnic spot until almost two years had past.

Jonathan stood at the window and forgot the storm and thought of the island and Jenny alone there with one or two of the servants. It was the first time he had permitted himself to think clearly of Jenny since the day he had left her in the grotto. She had invaded his dreams, but he had known that if he was to "settle" things for himself in Hambledon, he must not let his mind wander to Jenny.

Now he could see the island as he had seen it as a child after such a storm as this, and for the first time since he had left Jenny the brutalized and rational part of his mind became dominant. He knew he could not see the island from the house now, after midnight and in the storm, but he went to the east hallway and looked through the window, straining toward the river. He waited for lightning to light up the water, but when it did, it only illuminated the rain and made of it a frightful and silvery cataract, like a living wall. There seemed hardly a pause between the blasts of thunder.

So intense was the storm that the lamps of the town had gone out for some reason or other, and Hambledon showed, in the valley, like a broken huddle of pottery in the black lap of the blazing and streaming mountains. The thuddings of the gale mingled with the thunder, so that the whole universe seemed to have been caught up in unbearable noise and confusion and doom. As Jonathan still stood in the east hallway a closed shutter on a large window broke loose with a scream, and the glass gave way and above the uproar there would be heard the thin and splintery shattering. Jonathan ran downstairs, looking for the wrecked window, and he saw that a faint bluish mist filled all the rooms, a result of the strike at the chimney. He found the window. It was one of the four of his mother's drawing room, and water was already pouring in like a miniature falls and the carpet was dark with moisture and the parquetry floor swam in it. Careful of the shards of glass remaining in the frame, Jonathan leaned out into the drenching night and caught the shutters and brought them back to the window, but only after an effort that almost tore his arms from their sockets. He locked the shutters again. The wind savaged them, gushing through the apertures, and they rattled and shook. But they held. Jonathan watched them, panting, wiping water from his face and hands. His head was ringing with the constant and infernal noise.

He stood in the quiet room, and it was lit only by lightning and seemed apart from the disaster outside, calm in its lovely furniture, its beveled Florentine mirrors, its glancing prisms, its pale and paneled walls. There was a faint perfume here of spice, and roses and lavender, and the lamplight gleamed on green brocade draperies and polished every piece of glass and silver. He looked about him and thought, "I shall never know this room again, but I'm afraid I will always remember it." For the first time an abysmal loneliness came to him, a desolation.

He did not know what to do. To attempt to work in the bursting noise, in this threatened house, in this most lonely house, was impossible. To try to read, to think, were equally impossible. He began to move through the house slowly, slowly, looking at objects, at vistas, at corners, at hallways, at stairs, as if he were a ghost revisiting a house still dearly beloved. He thought of this, and the mournful delusion was complete, for the light bluish mist was everywhere like a supernatural emanation. He went to his father's study and only here did the quietness of the house seem spurious, just as in Adrian's lifetime the "retreat" had been spurious. Jonathan surveyed the room, not frowning now, but with sadness. He thought for a moment that he could see the apparition of his father in that favorite chair, anxiously serene, determinedly contemplative, deliberately in repose. For the first time Jonathan did not smile at the apparition with indulgent if scornful affection. He closed the door gently behind him when he left the study, feeling the deepest of compassions for the affected and innocent man who had never studied here at all and had never known any depths of emotion except fear.

A sane area in his brain had cleared and he thought that now he could begin to think with some moderation and reason. He went to his crowded room, heaped with luggage and boxes, and he sat down in a big wing chair and listened to the storm, which seemed to be lessening. I will think, he said to himself. Instantly he was asleep, exhausted from the turmoil and hatred and anger and pain of the past days.

When he awoke, it was to wan, quiet and watery sunlight, and it was morning. He felt for his watch, then remembered that it was still at the jeweler's being repaired. He looked at his bedside table clock and saw that it was half-past nine. He had slept for seven hours. He was cramped and aching, nervously itching. He got up and went to the windows and saw the ruin outside, the dying branches and thick green carpet of tossed leaves, the shattered trees. His mother's gardens were devastated. Every late flower lay flat on the torn earth. The flower beds and much of the shrubbery, including the lilac bushes, were smashed. Here, too, trees had fallen, delicate mountain ash, young white birch, a tall blue spruce or two. But, in the quiet sunlight, so frail and uncertain, the birds were singing their last songs of the season, and the sky was a ragged blue. The eye of the storm was over this section of the state, and though the air was clean and washed, it held a certain premonition. And everywhere, in low places on the lawns and in the streets were deep puddles of sky-blue water.

Beyond the gardens, beyond the lawns and the buildings on the far side, Jonathan could see the river, a cobalt blue, cold, and rushing turbulently. It was only his imagination, of course, but it seemed to him that the island, whose western point he could see, had sunken in the water, which had risen very high in the past few hours. Jonathan told himself that it had only now reached its normal level. He wondered if the "castle" and its trees had been damaged to any extent.

And then, without warning, it seemed incredible that he must leave here without Jenny. He leaned his hands on the sill of the window and let the sense of incredulity wash over him. He knew that he must control himself. There was nothing for Jenny in his coming life, for that life was already dark and bleak and without hope, and he must suffer in it until the end of his life or until— He thought of killing himself. The impulse was so immediate and so urgent that he could not breathe easily for several moments. It came to him it was the only solution. A life without Jenny and his work was not a life at all. It was only a mass of fallen stones, and he could not live in them. He gazed at the island and said aloud, "Jenny, Jenny." But he knew himself. He loved Jenny too much to take her and bring her into the ruins with him. For never again would he practice medicine or lift his hand to help any sufferer. He had done with the self-delusion that any man was worth saving, even himself.

I called others puerile and childish, he thought, yet all the time I was those things myself, secretly believing that somewhere there existed decency and honor and selflessness, in spite of what I said to many others. I chastised other people for their sentimentality, yet all the time I was revoltingly sentimental about pain and misery, despair and wretchedness. I laughed at young Bob Morgan's ingenuousness, but all the time I was even more ingenuous than he, and isn't that contemptible? I don't think I intended to leave this town at all! I think I just wanted it to repent and come to me and ask my forgiveness—so I could go on serving it with some self-respect! I made the gestures of departure ostentatiously and waited. There was nothing to wait for. But while I was the only one waiting, like a cowlicked country bumpkin with his feet shyly crossed and his finger in his mouth, hoping, the town was plotting vengefully against me. Why? I don't think the town knows, itself, and God knows I don't know. Perhaps my disposition, as Louis Hedler has said, and others, is not very endearing, but I never wronged a man, never betrayed one, never maliciously injured him. I gave of myself, and it was rejected.

Did I expect too much? Was I one of those whom Aristotle wrote: "The angry denouncers of men are the true lovers of men?" I don't know. I only know that whatever it was that I expected had no reality. Can one come to terms with truth and go on living? If others can, I am afraid I cannot. I am afraid I am as weak as my father. "Courage is the price." I don't have it.

He went back to his room and looked at the bags and suitcases, and a wave of exhaustion took him, and a feeling of the most awful loneliness and loss. He put Jenny from his mind forcibly. He undressed, bathed, shaved, and dressed again, in a haze of unreality which he welcomed, for it stopped him from thinking. But the sickness of loss remained. He went downstairs for breakfast and found a tremulous Mary who told him she had been afraid that the storm last night "was the end of the world." Jonathan smiled at her kindly, and she thought how withered and blasted he appeared, and how very pale. "I am afraid, Mary," he said, "that the world isn't that lucky." Mary retreated to the kitchen and informed the cook that "Doctor seems so strange," and the cook replied, as she was always replying these days, "He has his worries."

There was no mail, for the trains had been delayed, and the newspaper was only two pages today and was filled with news of the storm and of reports that it had been extremely destructive over several states. President McKinley was reported to be recovering from his wound, though several Cabinet officers had gone to Buffalo under urgings from Vice-President Roosevelt.

What will I do with today? thought Jonathan. He went outside and was surprised to find that within an hour the air had turned sultry again and was still and pent. He was amazingly tired and sluggish. The gardener came and wailed at the wreck of his careful work and Marjorie's. "Mrs. Ferrier isn't going to like this," said the old man, looking reproachfully at Jonathan. "It's bad along here, Doctor, very bad. Lots of windows got blown in, and I hear there's twenty people missing in town, and the news coming from the farms is bad, very bad. Water's rising in the river, too. It's going to flood. Farms is already flooded, they say, and stock drowned." He looked at the blue sky, with its rack of hurrying clouds. "They say it's all over, but it ain't. I can tell. I lived a long time, and I know weather."

Jonathan walked about with him on the soaked earth, his hands in his trousers pockets. "Jim," he said, "what do you think about living, anyway?"

Jim turned slowly and studied him, and his browned and wrinkled face was solemn. "Well, sir, Doctor, I guess you just have to stand it, don't you?"

Jonathan was intrigued. "But why?"

Jim shrugged. "Why not?" he replied. "What else can a man do?"

What else can a man do? Was that a stupid answer or was it a very wise one?

Jonathan said, "Let me help you clean up. It's all a mess and a ruin, but we can put it together again, I suppose. We can even plant new trees where the old ones fell. We can plant the gardens again and pick up the dead branches."

The old man, who had bent to examine a precious and battered shrub, painfully straightened himself and he smiled at Jonathan. "Well, that's what I've just been saying, Doctor."

Robert Morgan, coming to the offices, paused on the steps and blinked, and could not believe it. Far across the long lawns he could see Jonathan Ferrier in his shirtsleeves, filling a wheelbarrow with debris and wielding a rake and tugging at dead branches, working near the old gardener. Then he was vigorously using a pitchfork for heavier debris. He stopped to light a cigarette and look at the sky. Well, well, thought Robert, and went into the offices smiling a little.

At noon the sky turned brazen again, and the heat was appalling, and puffs of heavy wind were beginning to swirl fallen twigs and leaves in the gutters. At two o'clock the sky was very dark and boiling, and lightning snaked and thunder muttered discontentedly in the mountains. At three the storm broke.

Just as the water began to fall in the semidarkness Marjorie Ferrier arrived home in a station hack, hurrying toward the house, the driver dashing behind her with her luggage.

Jonathan, after a very light lunch, had felt so weary and numb that he had gone to his room and had fallen across the bed in a state approaching stupefaction. So, he did not hear his mother return. He did not hear the preliminary cannonading of the thunder. He slept heavily until five o'clock, to find a shrieking twilight about him again, and an infernal roaring in the air, and a pressure in the atmosphere like pouring steam. Someone had closed his open window and pulled in the shutters. His face and all of his body was sweating and his mouth was dry and he felt weak and dazed. For a moment he did not know where he was, what was the time of the day, or how it had come about that he was here at all.

He sat up, stunned and blinking, wiping his face, staring about him, listening. Then, after a long time, he got to his feet, bathed in cold water, and sat down to smoke and think. Something had happened to him, but what it was he did not know. He only knew that a sort of quietus had come to him, an area of nonfeeling or -thinking.

The room steadily darkened as the storm increased, but Jonathan did not light his lamps for over an hour. He tried to read, but the storm distracted his very slight attention, and so he confined himself to listening. Abruptly, the rain stopped but the thunder and lightning and wind intensified. There was a knock on his door, then the door opened.

"Jon?" asked Marjorie.

She stood on the threshold, very pale and quiet, her dark hair fluffed about her cheeks as if she had been sleeping. Her mouth was without color, and her eyes were unusually large and bright in the lamplight, as if she were feverish. She had taken off her traveling suit and wore a calico wrapper printed in gray and blue, and bedroom slippers.

Jonathan sat in his chair and looked silently at his mother and did not move, but the hard muscles sprang out about his mouth and his hands tightened on the arms of his chair. Marjorie gazed at him and saw that his black brows had met above his eyes and that his eyes were shining like black fire.

"Jon?" she said again, and moistened her lips. "I came home, but you were sleeping, and I did not want to disturb you."

She advanced into the room and the feverish brightness in her eyes had widened, and she began to breathe a little faster, as if she were very frightened. She clasped her hands tightly together. She said in a very low voice, "I know, dear. I read the Philadelphia papers last night. It's all over, Jon, it's all over."

"Yes," he said, and stood up. "It's all over."

They stared at each other in a silence broken only by the boisterous uproar outside, and the lamps flickered and somewhere a loose shutter crashed against a wall.

"I must talk to you, Jon," said Marjorie.

"And what will you tell me, Mama? More lies? More sweet evasions? You and old Martin were very clever about the whole thing, weren't you? A giggling little conspiracy of silence."

A look of deep alarm and suffering ran over Marjorie's face. She sat down near the door as if her last strength had left her. "Jon," she whispered. He could see her lips move but could not hear her. He moved closer so that she would hear everything he said, and his look was so formidable, and totally unknown to her, that she cowered away from him as from a terrible stranger. She could not endure the look on his face and in his eyes.

"Did you believe that swill in the papers?" he asked.

She tried to speak, then coughed and put her trembling hand to her throat. "I—I felt there was something else," she said.

"Oh, indeed, Mama, there was a great deal more! But you know a lot of it, don't you? Sufficient to say now that before old Martin died, he made out a last affidavit and confession, and he finally told the truth he and you both knew. The truth, Mama."

She swallowed, and even in her terror her expression questioned him.

"And a lot you didn't know, if that is possible. I won't tell you about that. Perhaps Howard Best will be glad to enlighten you." His voice, normally harsh had a sound in it she had never heard before, and her fright rose.

"Where is darling Harald now?" he asked, and loomed over her so urgently that she thought he was about to strike her, and in that abysmal fear she said quickly, "He returned yesterday morning. Jon!"

"Oh, yesterday morning." He looked down at her and smiled. "So, he is there with Jenny. He has been alone there with Jenny for a long time, and you knew what he was from the very beginning. and you did not care in the least for Jenny—alone with him. a man like him—so long as you could continue to protect him."

"Oh, Jon. he would never harm Jenny!"

"No more than he harmed Mavis. Is that it?"

"Jon," she almost groaned, "if you know everything, as you say, then you must know what Mavis was!"

"She was my wife."

Marjorie put her hand to her thin cheek as if he had hit her in reality, but she looked up at him and her lips moved soundlessly.

"My wife," he said. "A fool, mindless, wanton. Yes, all that, and more. But she was still my wife when he took her, as if she had been a common whore. She was still my wife when she conceived a child by him. She was still my wife when she died of her abortion, and he would still have lived, in all those lies, if it hadn't been for Howard Best."

Marjorie was too stricken to speak. She could feel the painful lurching of her heart and could hear the thunderous explosions outside and could see, almost blinding her, the steady and fierce lightning.

"My wife," said Jonathan. "It was nothing to you that he had done this thing to me, his brother. It was nothing to any of you. It meant even less when I was arrested for a crime that I had never committed, which I could never have brought myself to commit. If I had been hanged for that crime, you would still have kept your pretty lips well closed."

"Oh. Jon!" she cried. "You cannot believe that! You don't believe that! If there had been any danger to you at all, if you had been convicted, we should have spoken, Martin and I!"

"That is another lie," said her son, and his hand lifted as if indeed he would strike her, but now she sat upright and looked him fully in the face. "It was nothing to you, was it, Mama, that I spent those months in prison, that I spent those weeks in a courtroom before grinning crowds and reporters and had to listen in silence to the prosecuting attorney accuse me of every stinking thing under the sun, such as murdering my wife and my unborn child? No, it was nothing to you. You let it all happen to me. And when I came back here, you still did not speak, either of you, not even to me! You let a whole town malign me and despise me, and drive me out, and call me murderer to my face. Why, Mama?"

Marjorie dropped her head a little. "We thought you were strong enough to bear it, Jon. We watched and waited and prayed. If there had been any danger— You forget. Harald is also my son, weaker than you, we thought. We thought he— we tried to protect him from you, Jon, and you from knowing. Can't you understand? Won't you try to understand? It was really for you that I kept silent." Her head bowed lower. "You are both my sons. By not speaking I thought—I thought I'd saved you both."

He laughed abruptly. "And you never dreamed that the truth would come out, did you? It still would not have come out if a very nice little plot hadn't been laid against me by Kent Campion and various others, including the man who aborted Mavis and killed her. In the event that plot would have succeeded—tell me, Mama, would you have spoken then?"

She could only stare at him speechlessly, growing paler and paler. She put her hand tightly against her breast.

"A plot to send me to prison, probably for life, for alleged abortions," said Jonathan. "That would have been comparatively easy, with my first trial still fresh in people's minds, and the conviction that I was guilty of killing Mavis. Mavis has been the precipitant in this whole vicious mess, from the very beginning, but you helped very efficiently, Mama, very efficiently, and I congratulate you. While I was in prison, no doubt you were very pleased with yourself."

She got to her feet, staggering a little. "Jon! You can't believe that! You don't believe it! I refuse to believe that you are taking yourself seriously."

He said, "There is just one thing I want to know, and tell me the truth this time." His rage was rising, and the terribleness in his face was more than Marjorie could stand. "Did you know that he had seduced Mavis before you heard them both arranging for Mavis to be aborted?"

"Yes," she said. "I knew. But I couldn't say anything to Harald or to Mavis. I was afraid that it would—it would cause something, and that you would know. Always I was trying to shield you, Jon, to protect you from knowing. I thought it would end and it had ended, and it would all be over and no one would be hurt."

He said very gently. "You were quite successful in a way. No one was hurt, except that Mavis died, and I was tried for murder, and my name blackened all over the country. Harald went his way, and everything was lovely, and he lived on Myrtle's money and tried to get Jenny to marry him, and— by God, now I know that all the time he was laughing in my face!"

"Jon, won't you try to believe that it was all done to protect you?"

"And to protect smiling, laughing Harald?"

"Yes! Harald too. He is also my son."

He looked about the room and his eye lit on something. "You can protect him no longer. I am going to find him and I am going to kill him." He walked across the room to one of his bags and he picked up his riding crop which he had thrown there the last time he had used it. Marjorie saw, and she cried out, and when he was near her again she grasped his arm and looked up into his face, that appalling stranger's face.

"Jon! You must be out of your mind!"

"I think I am," he said. "But that doesn't matter, does it? You can thank yourself for that, Mama."

He flung her off and she fell heavily to her knees. She put up her hands to him like one pleading for her life. "Jon, think of Jenny!"

"I am the only one who has been thinking of Jenny. Not you, not Harald. Just myself."

"Oh, Jon, you believed all those lies about her, you believed them all, and now you can talk about 'thinking' of her!"

He paused and looked down into her suddenly flooded eyes. "I've been doing a lot of thinking, Mama. Who began those lies about Jenny? I made a few inquiries since you were away. I traced at least two back to Harald. Ah, I see that you knew that, too."

Marjorie put her hands over her face as she knelt.

"And you let that go on, about Jenny and about me, and

you kept your serene silence and never said a word in defense of anybody!"

He made to step about her and she reached up and grasped the crop in his hand with both of hers. "Jon, you have a life to live, a future before you, you and Jenny, here or anywhere else. But one reckless thing— Jon, in the name of God, try to be reasonable, try to think!"

He laughed again and wrenched the crop from her hands. "I've been thinking, Mama. I've been thinking of thousands of things."

She tried, in her extremity, to grasp his ankle, his leg, but he was quicker than she, and then she saw his face, black and murderous in the flickering lightning, and she quietly lay down on the floor and closed her eyes.

Jonathan ran down the stairs in the thunderous dusk, and flung open the door and was immediately outside, buffeted by the gale, almost blinded by the lightning But no rain was falling. He ran through the dark and deserted streets, splashing through deep puddles sending spray all about him. No lamps were lit. The city lay cowering under the exploding illumination of the storm and Jonathan was all alone, racing like a madman through the streets bounding across flooded curbs, flying toward the river and the little dock. He never remembered that wild flight, for he was conscious of nothing but his savage hunger for vengeance.

The little dock, he found, had been washed away, but one boat was pulled up on the bank. He slid down the bank in a welter of wet and slimy mud and almost fell into the river. He scrambled back up and got into the boat, panting, drenched smeared. His feet sank into deep water and he had to turn the boat over on its side to empty it. He found the oars, slippery and cold, and then the rain began again brightened by lightning, torn by the wind. He pushed the boat into the river, and the river caught it and almost wrenched it from him, for the water was high and roaring and rushing and swirling. He finally struggled into the boat and sat down, and he did not notice that his hands were bleeding, for the boat spun out into the river and swung into circles and fled out into the night.

It was a long time before he could control it, and now he was sweating and shivering in the fresh rain, and the river flared into violence under the lightning and then became a silent and hidden thing in the dark, tumultuous as if alive and filled with fury. He fought both the river and the boat. Looking over his shoulder, he could see the dusky bulk of the island behind him, lighted swiftly and regularly, its trees tossing, and it was like a struggling ship about to founder. His foot felt for the crop he had thrown into the boat, and he clenched his teeth and fought to gain the island in all that wildness and bellowing storm and night.

He was a strong man, and he was still young, but if he had not been impelled by his rage and his new fear for Jenny, he would have been swept down the river, the boat would have been swamped, and he would have died in the water. But all the intensity of his nature was driving him toward the island, all the frustration and anger and despair and suffering of the past months, all the shame and the insults, the rejection and the jeers, the hopelessness. It seemed to him that Mavis was in the boat with him, laughing in the thunder, her golden hair flying in the wind, her face gleeful in the lightning. "You were a fool," he said to her, "a silly, thoughtless, soulless fool. But you didn't deserve that! No, you didn't deserve that. I wanted to kill you many times, but I wouldn't have killed you, Mavis. No, I wouldn't have killed you and let you die alone in all that pain. If I had known, I'd have stayed by your bed, comforting you. If I had arrived before you died, I'd have been there, Mavis, for I loved you for many years, and loved you in a way, I think, even after you were dead, Mavis, even when I hated you."

For the first time, even in the frenzy of his thoughts and the savagery of his purpose, he could feel sorrow for Mavis, dead in her youth, and pity, and regret.

The rain dashed into his face, and he gritted his teeth and bent body and oars against the foaming water, and the boat heaved up and down between waves and fought with the swift current. Strange thoughts ran over his mind like dreams, like convolutions of nightmares. Then the boat grated on stones, and he had reached the island.

He sat there, huddled and soaking, gasping and trying to get his breath, his bloody hands sliding on the oars. Then he could stand up, and jump to the slippery bank, and pull the boat up on it and throw the oars beside it. He reached for his crop, fumbling in the flaming dark, and he turned and climbed the flooded path, feeling for it when he could not see it. When he had reached the top, his clothing torn by the lashing bushes and trees, he had to halt to stop the laboring of his heart. Then he saw that the island was deep in the river, and the walls of it were hardly a curb above the swirling water. He stood and looked at it, as it appeared and disappeared in the lightning, and he thought, It will be almost covered by morning. He went on, falling, staggering, fighting, toward the faint light in the distance.

CHAPTER THIRTY-SEVEN

Harald Ferrier was sitting in his study reading, for no other room in the castle attracted him, nor could he stand any other room and especially not the one he had shared with his dead wife. He listened to the storm uneasily. Unlike Jonathan, he could not remember that the island had once been almost inundated, for he had been too young then, but he wondered how much more the water would rise and if the walls could keep it out from the higher land. During the lull in the late afternoon he had gone out to inspect the damage and had almost been flung headlong several times by the gale. The damage was very great. Some of the finest trees had been blown down and battered, and the gardens were completely destroyed. None of the windows of the castle had been broken because they were all mullioned and deep-set and narrow. But all the walks had disappeared and ran like brooks, and there was water at least a foot deep around the walls of the castle itself, where the earth could not absorb it.

There had been storms over the valley and the state before, but he could not recall one as bad as this. He congratulated himself that he had thought to return yesterday, before it broke, otherwise he would have had to stay in Hambledon, and possibly in his father's house. He winced at the thought. He had never liked that house, had never felt that he was welcome there but only endured, a stranger tolerated because he was harmless and bothered no one and never interfered, and because he had learned to smile when he was the most miserable and lonely and forgotten. Even though he visited his mother occasionally, he still felt like a guest and never believed that she had ever liked him in spite of her gentle ways and kindness. She had never cared for anyone but his brother, he thought, and his father had never cared for anyone but his older son. It was a beautiful house, but Harald had not found it beautiful and never had thought of it as home.

As he was not vengeful by nature, or reckless, or bitter, he had not felt resentful all those years. He had made his own life. By temperament he was easy and adaptable and tolerant. It would have made him happy to have been loved and not overlooked, but as that happiness had been denied him, he had eventually accepted the fact. Now all he desired was Jenny and peace and his painting, and travel and ease and laughter and good wine and dinners. The world was a brutal place and so he had gracefully and smilingly retreated from it, never questioning it, never arguing with it, never fighting it, as Jonathan had always done from earliest childhood. Harald accepted what the world permitted him to accept, and he had no quarrel with it, for life was as it was and only a fool "kicked against the pricks." If he reached for something and the world of men denied it to him, he would search for something else he could have without a struggle. He had reached for women, and for Mavis, but never had pressed them, never had urged them, never had seduced them. They saw his hand and they took it, laughing, and he laughed with them. He had desired only the prettiest women, for he hated flaws and mediocrity, and his affairs had been gay if not very passionate. He told himself that he was—happily—incapable of strong attachments and emotion.

With the exception of Jenny Heger. As no woman he had ever wanted had rejected him, he felt that eventually Jenny would be "sensible" and accept him, too, in marriage and in a carefree and joyous future. She had hardly spoken to him since that ridiculous encounter in the grotto, but she was not angry with him. She seemed to be suffering and brooding. What an intense young lady! In time, he would laugh her out of her shyness and her moods and they would take, together, what they would be permitted to·take. Once or twice it did occur to him that Jenny would never change, and then he would feel, as if it were a stronger echo of his gently neglected and painful childhood, a spasm of very real and intolerable pain. For a man who was not very resolute by nature, he felt a stiffening of resolution when it came to Jenny.

The studio was lighted by oil lamps, as all the rooms were so lighted, and they flickered as gusts of wind found their way even around the locked and secure windows. Harald listened to the storm and it seemed to him that it was getting much worse, and he saw the lightning through the windows and shrank involuntarily at some of the more boisterous of the thunderclaps. He tried to take his mind off the storm, and looked with satisfaction at some of his canvases standing against the walls, and his easel, with a fresh canvas waiting. He would do another portrait of Jenny. He would sell this one, as he could have sold the first many times over. He thought of Jenny and stood up and slowly strolled about the studio. Jenny was in the library downstairs, where she always "lurked," and he hesitated. He wondered if she was frightened now, and then he decided she was not. She had not been frightened yesterday or last night. He had tried to talk with her at meals, but though she had answered him, she gave him the impression that she was hardly aware of him. Only once had she spoken voluntarily to him and that was to ask him when he would take her to their lawyers and conclude their contract.

"Patience, Jenny," he had said. "Besides, it is my information that the lawyer most concerned is not in town just now."

Suddenly he wanted to see Jenny, and it was an aching desire in him. He had the excuse of the storm, and so he lightly ran downstairs—he did everything lightly—and went to the library and pushed open the carved wooden door. There was Jenny, crouched under a lamp and reading, and she looked up at him blankly when he entered.

"I thought perhaps you were afraid," he said with his genial smile.

"Of what?"

"Well, the storm. It does sound awful, doesn't it?"

She frowned and listened, then nodded. She gazed at him with her great blue eyes, in which the lamplight danced, waiting for him to leave, and she pushed aside some of her fallen black hair impatiently. She was dressed in one of her least becoming frocks, a dull lilac cotton with a little collar of coarse lace at the neck, and it made her white throat whiter and took away the color of her beautiful lips.

"You know there has been a lot of damage," said Harald, still standing.

"I know. But it can be planted again." Jenny paused. "My father's rose beds have gone."

"I'm sorry, Jenny."

She smiled briefly. "I am, too."

There was another pause, and then to their mutual amazement they heard a banging at the hall door, and a shout. They stared at each other, disbelieving. The servants had already retired to their rooms, and Harald said, "Who, in God's name, can that be?" He went to the hall and walked down its echoing marble floor, and pulled back the bolts on the doors. It swung in on him violently, and he cried out, and Jenny came into the hall also.

If they had been incredulous before they were stunned into speechlessness now, as a battered, drenched, torn and muddy figure staggered into the hall, pouring with water, creating instant puddles on the shining floor. It was heaving and panting, and its hands were bleeding, and it was grasping a crop. Its black eyes were quite mad and staring, and all its hair was spiked and upright like a drowned bush.

"For God's sake," said Harald, and stepped back. "Jon!"

Jenny stood behind him, frowning and staring, throwing back her hair, her mouth opening in amazement. The light of the tall and flickering lamps, shaped like torches, which decorated the medieval hall along the walls, bent before the wind that roared through the open door. Jonathan looked at his brother and saw no one else, and he reached behind him and closed the door, and then leaned against it, breathing stertorously. Harald looked at him, still incredulous, and then when he saw Jonathan's face more clearly, he stepped back more and his ruddy brows drew together over his eyes and much of his high color disappeared.

"What?" he murmured. He said, with a kind of desperate hurry, "Is there something wrong with Mother?"

Jonathan did not answer. He lifted the hand that held the crop and wiped his face with the back of it. He was a ghastly color, and his chest rose and sank with his convulsed breathing. He still leaned against the door, and dark streams ran from his clothing. He had begun to tremble. The thunder detonated against the stone walls of the castle with a hollow roaring.

Jenny stood, transfixed, looking at Jonathan, still hardly believing that it was he, still disbelieving. Then she too saw his face, and she gasped, and she saw the crop in his hand. She glanced swiftly at Harald, who was as paralyzed as herself.

Then Jonathan said in a hoarse and unrecognizable voice, "While you were away, I found out the truth." His dark face was contorted and twisted and his eyes reflected the uncontrolled wrath in him. "About you and Mavis."

Harald said something faintly, but dared not look away from his brother. He said to Jenny, "Jenny, go away, please."

"No," said Jenny. She had come closer to Harald and stood almost beside him.

Jonathan did not even see her. He was standing upright now, and he seemed to fill the hall with a dangerous presence, not human, but more like the storm outside.

"You let her die all alone," said Jonathan. "You helped her die. You arranged the abortion with Brinkerman. It was your child she was carrying. You killed her."

Jenny cried out and put her hands to her cheeks.

"Jon," said Harald. His eyes left Jonathan for an instant, searching for some weapon in the hall. He had an impulse to run and lock a door behind him, but he knew that Jonathan, even in his present state, would be faster than he and he feared a blow on the back of his head.

"Tell me," said Jonathan.

"I don't know what you're talking about," said Harald, and now he was utterly terrified and water rushed into his mouth and he had to swallow quickly.

"I'm talking about Mavis," said Jonathan. "My wife, Mavis. She died because of you. While she was still my wife. It must have been quite a joke to you, laughing all these months to my face and behind my back."

"No," said Harald, feeling the greatest terror of his life. He had to fight to keep his shaking knees from bending and throwing him to the floor. "You must be out of your mind."

Jonathan laughed, throwing back his head, and they saw the shine of his teeth in the wavering lamplight. "I am," he said. "You did that to me. You let me be accused of a crime, and you let me rot away in prison and you let me be tried— for something you did. When I was acquitted, that must have been the worst day of your cursed life!"

"I don't," Harald began, and had to swallow again and he vaguely thought that what he had swallowed tasted like blood.

"Don't lie," said Jonathan. "You've lied all your worthless, stupid, useless life, while you danced and sang and smeared canvases. Do you know why I'm here now? I've come to kill you."

"Jon," said Jenny, and she stepped between the brothers and faced Jonathan.

He reached out his dripping arm and swept her aside as if she were nothing, and she fell against the stone wall. But she recovered instantly and flew again between them.

"Jon!" she shouted. "I'm here, Jon!"

He looked at her. "Yes, Jenny, I see you. Jenny, did you know that he told those lies about you in town, the dirty lies that made you a byword?"

"I don't care!" she still shouted. "Nothing matters at all except you and me, Jon!"

"And nothing matters to me but what I came for," he said. He saw that Harald was backing softly away and he lunged upon him and slashed him across the face with his crop. Harald staggered back and fell on the stairway, and flung up his arms to protect himself. Jenny caught Jonathan's arm with all her young strength and clung to it, though he tried to throw her off. Her hair swung with her efforts. Her teeth were bared and her dress blew out.

"Help! Help!" Harald screamed from behind his protecting arms. "Help! Help!" He heard the struggle near him and dared not look. His cries echoed back from the depths of the dark staircase with a frenzied sound. He started to scramble up the stairs, backward, and then Jonathan was on him again and his left hand was at his throat and the crop, wrenched from Jenny, was raised over his head.

"Don't kill me!" Harald cried, and he flung up his hand and caught the murderous wrist above him and fought to throw off the hand that was clutching his throat. "My God, don't kill me! They'll really hang you this time!"

Jenny had again recovered herself. She managed to seize the hand with the crop once more, and now in her fear-magnified strength she brought it to her mouth and bit it. She was like a young and panting tiger, and now Jonathan saw her again, in crazed wonder.

"Let him alone, let him alone!" said Jenny. She tore at the hand that was strangling Harald, and Jonathan was so amazed that he released his brother and Harald scrambled up a few stairs. The crop had opened his left cheek and the deep cut was running with blood. He was weak with his terror. He had never encountered violence like this before and he knew that it was not sane and that he would surely die if someone did not help him.

Jonathan was trying to throw Jenny aside, but she clung to him, facing him, her arms about his neck. They fought soundlessly and Jenny was strong as she had never been strong before. She knew that she must not release Jonathan, or he would be gone from her forever. She groaned over and over, trying to reach him, "Jon, Jon, my darling, my darling. Don't, for my sake, Jon. Jon, come back, Jon, look at me."

He had caught a huge handful of her black hair and he pulled her face from his shoulder and her white throat stretched in the lamplight and her head arched back from him. She closed her eyes but still clung to his upper arms, and the lower part of her body was pressed strongly against his. She was crying hopelessly and repeating his name. She would not let him go, and now he could only look at that vulnerable throat and see her tears.

"Jenny," he said, and he released her hair and her head fell on his shoulder again and she was sobbing and trembling against him.

"For my sake," she said, and repeated, "for my sake."

He was spent. He felt as though he would fall and die right there at Jenny's feet. He looked at his quaking brother, bleeding freely, and crouched on the stairway in a huddle of absolute dread and horror, overpowered less by his fear of death than by the total violence he had seen and encountered.

"All right, Jenny," Jonathan was saying in an exhausted voice. "Don't cry like that, Jenny. It's all right, my love, all right."

"Oh, Jon," she said, and she raised her head and kissed him fiercely on the mouth, and he tasted her tears and the softness of her lips.

Harald had pulled himself to his feet with the banister and was wiping his face with his handkerchief. The sight of blood had always frightened him, and he looked at his own blood and leaned against the banister in a half faint. Jonathan stared up at him from behind Jenny's shoulder.

"You deserve to die," Jonathan said. "You deserve to die like the dog you are."

Harald's collapse had indeed been less from fear than from what he had seen in his brother's eyes. He had made his life as calm and as easy and as pleasant and as controlled as possible. He detested emotional and riotous people; he felt a loathing for them. A man who could not compel himself to be moderate and civilized at all times was not a man to him but a wild beast. So he looked at Jonathan and hatred flashed between the brothers as bare and deadly as a thrown knife.

"I may deserve to die, as you say," said Harald, in a shaking voice, "but you are not far from that condition yourself. You must be insane." He straightened a little on the staircase, not caring any longer for his blood. "Listen to me, Jon, and if you do, it will probably be the first time in your life that you ever listened to anyone.

"Mavis wasn't your wife. She told me that you had rejected her only a year or so after you were married, and put her out of your life and out of your bed. Mavis was Mavis. You knew her as well as I did, and perhaps better. She was silly and greedy and stupid, but she was a woman. You had no right to marry her." Harald paused, to let a fresh thunderbolt die away, and as they waited they again looked at each other with that hatred.

"You never cared about her," said Harald. He was very livid and all his handsomeness was gone. "You only had lust for her. If you'd loved her, you'd have been patient and kind. If she wasn't what you thought she was, whose fault was that? Not hers. She never tried to deceive you; she didn't have the brains for that, and if you hadn't been as stupid as she was, you'd have known it. The fault was all yours."

"Go on," said Jonathan.

Harald's face became grim for the first time in his life. "I didn't seek Mavis out. She sought me. I'd never have—touched—her if she had really been your wife. She told me about you, how you had threatened to kill her, the names you had called her, disgusting names. She was sincere then. There wasn't any real love between us. She never intended to divorce you and marry me, and I never wanted to marry her. It was a sort of—consolation—to Mavis." He wiped his face again and again sickened when he saw his blood. "I wasn't the only man."

"I know," said Jonathan. Now his arm was about Jenny.

"Then, what?" asked Harald, with a weary wave of his hand.

"You let me rot in prison. You let me be tried and defamed. You let me live the miserable life I've led for nearly a year. And all you had to do was to speak." Jonathan's voice was rough with his exhaustion and his passionage rage.

"My God," said Harald. "Do you honestly think I'd have

let you be executed? If you think so, then you must really be insane."

"Then, why didn't you speak in the beginning?"

Harald smiled drearily. "Because I felt the great Jonathan Ferrier was a stronger man than I was, a less weak man, a man of more resistance. I felt you could bear what you had to bear, and it would mean very little to you. I was sure you wouldn't be convicted, and you were not. So, I let it all go, thinking it was a nine-days' wonder, and would all be forgotten. I hoped you would go away. You hated the town so much, and there were large fields for you. So what did it matter if I didn't tell anyone the truth? Who was hurt so much? Who was ruined?"

"I was," said Jonathan.

Now Harald regarded him with astonishment. "You!" he exclaimed. "It all meant nothing to you, or very little."

Jonathan saw that he actually believed this.

"It meant my whole life," he said. "I was never much of a brotherly-lover, but the town was everything to me. I gave it everything I had to give."

"Then, you aren't the man I thought you were," said Harald. He leaned his head against the wall of the staircase and gulped for air. "You were always our parents' favorite. They lived only for you. I was nothing. So I came to believe that you were indeed superior to me, a stronger man than I was, a more able man, a more resolute and powerful man. But they were just as deceived as I was, and for the first time I'm sorry for them. You gave the town everything you had to give! That's the most maudlin thing I ever heard anyone say, and I'm glad our father is dead, for even he would have been ashamed to hear that."

He looked at Jonathan below him with even more astonishment. "Why, you haven't any courage at all! You are only brave, and even an animal can be brave. For the past year I've suspected as much, watching you, but I told myself it was only my imagination. There were times when you were gloomy and looked desperate. I thought it was because your pride had been hurt, for God's sake. And all the time the damned town had broken your heart!" Harald laughed with faint weariness. "A town like Hambledon, which doesn't deserve to have even a horse doctor!"

Jonathan was silent. He looked into Jenny's fearful eyes and he pressed her to him reassuringly. His exhaustion was growing. He felt utterly drained and broken.

"I wanted you to go away," said Harald. "You won't believe me, but I thought it would be best for you, for you should have left years ago. Mavis was right, there. And then I wanted you to leave because I was afraid you'd find out the truth someday and you'd do exactly what you tried to do tonight. One of us had to go. I couldn't. I was bound to this damned island."

Jenny spoke now. "But you can leave, as you said you would."

Harald looked down at her and smiled. "Jenny, Jenny," he said. "I will go. With you."

She widened her eyes at him like a child. "But I never said that. Jon is the only man for me, and he's the only one I've ever wanted."

Harald's face darkened with pain. "Jenny, you've seen what he's like. Tonight. Do you think, when he's in a rage, that he'd spare you and not hate you? Your life with him would be a hell, and not a refined one at that. Thwart him, defy him, deny him, and he'll be at your throat—as he was at mine."

"It doesn't matter," said Jenny. "I can't help it."

Harald said, "I won't let you go with him, Jenny, tonight or any other time. For your sake."

He had not been brave before, but he was brave for Jenny now. He said to his brother, "You know what you're like, even better than I do. If you have any feeling for Jenny, let her go."

Jonathan had been reluctantly listening. Into the murky but slowly quieting reaches of his mind new thoughts were intruding like fingers of light, the thoughts he had been thinking over the past months, still, clarified thoughts, unique, thoughts detached from his own nature as if they had been spoken to him by someone else. He had heard them, had weighed them, had considered them, had been amazed by them, for a long time. They had been like calm and judicious voices, penetrating his chronic misery, giving him hope, exhilaration, speaking with authority, reason and detachment.

He said to Jenny, "You have heard what he has said. What have you to say, Jenny?"

"You are impossible," said the girl, and laid her cheek against his shoulder. "You are the most terrible person I've ever known. If I marry you, I don't think you will ever forgive me."

Jonathan said, "Probably not. And then again, possibly yes."

Harald turned his face away and sat down heavily on the stairs. He folded his arms on his knees and dropped his ruddy head upon them in an attitude of complete surrender and prostration. Jonathan said to Jenny, "Now, find a cloak and a shawl, for I am taking you home to my mother tonight. The island is unsafe; the water's rising." He touched her cheek. "I think, after all, I really came for you."

"Yes. Of course," she said, and went to the stairway. She paused as she reached Harald, and hesitated. She spoke to the back of his head. "Come with us, Harald." Then she ran up the stairs and disappeared into the darkness, to prepare to leave and to advise the servants to leave also.

Jonathan spoke to his brother's bowed head. "We've both lived in a sort of stupid confusion. I always thought my mother preferred you and I hated both of you for it. I always knew what my father was. If you will remember, I warned you not to take him seriously."

"I remember," said Harald in a muffled voice.

"I don't think," said Jonathan, "that the Ferrier men have been overly intelligent."

" 'Speak for yourself, John,' " said Harald from the depths of his folded arms.

For the first time Jonathan smiled, and it was a sour smile. He looked at the crop in his hand, then threw it across the hall, where it clanged against a suit of armor, rocked it, then fell to the floor.

"I don't think I would have killed you," Jonathan said to his brother.

Harald raised his head and Jonathan saw that he looked ravaged and depleted. "Oh," said Harald, "I'm sure you would have if it hadn't been for Jenny." He touched his cheek and winced at the sight of the blood. "Or, would you prefer to call this a love pat?"

Jonathan sat down in an armorial chair, and now there was no sound in the hall but the roaring of wind and water and thunder as they waited for Jenny. They did not look or speak to each other again. When the lightning flashed in, it showed only their averted faces.

CHAPTER THIRTY-EIGHT

Robert Morgan came into Marjorie Ferrier's bedroom,
where she was being sedulously attended by two sprightly
young nurses from St. Hilda's. Marjorie's eyes, even while
she lay high on the pillows under her, watched only the door,
and when Robert came in, they questioned him alertly,
though she could not speak. He smiled at her, and the girls
looked at him adoringly. He said, taking the weak and almost
pulseless wrist, "The river rescue boat went to the island for
them, and I've just heard. They are landing on this side. I
told you. You had no need to worry, Mrs. Ferrier."

Her white lips formed one word, "Both?"

He nodded. "Three, and the two servants. The rescuers signaled five people, so I assume that is all."

Marjorie's eyes filled with tears, and Robert pressed her
wrist and watched her face.

He had been called by the maid, who had found Marjorie
unconscious on the floor of Jonathan's room. The girl had
heard the stormy altercation, then the crash of the front
door, and then the silence filled only with the sound of thunder. She had discreetly gone to investigate, and then had hysterically reported to the cook, who had immediately called
Robert at his house, for he had not gone to the office that
day and had been able to visit but one hospital. Robert saw
that Marjorie was too ill to be moved, that her ailing heart
had suffered an almost fatal shock, and that she would probably die of it very soon. It was Robert who had sent for Father McNulty and for the nurses, and the priest was now in

the morning room listening anxiously to the storm and waiting news of the people on the island.

It was to Robert that Marjorie had whispered of Jonathan's frenzied rush from the house and what he had threatened to do to his brother, and he saw that if she were not relieved very soon, her death could not be delayed. He had done all he could do. He had alerted, through the harbor police, the men who had been busy through twenty-four hours of storm rescuing people from low-lying sections along the river, and from two islands upstream. The police, though harried and sleepless, had agreed to call Robert when the riverboat signaled the rescue of those on Heart's Ease. They had also agreed to furnish the rescued with transportation through the flooding night to the Ferrier house, or any other destination.

"They will be here soon," said Robert, who was red-eyed from exhaustion. He had worked on the injured and battered for hours after last midnight, and it was now approaching midnight again.

Marjorie was too spent to speak. She could only thank Robert with her eyes. She let her lids drop and her head rolled weakly on the pillow. Robert kept his fingers lightly on her pulse, counting and frowning. If she died before her sons arrived, then it would be all Jonathan's fault, and it was all he deserved. Oh, of course the damned fool had his grievances, and they were all severe and grave and deserved retribution, and only a clod would deny the truth. But to have shocked his mother in this fashion and to have told her what he intended to do was unpardonable. For a moment Robert hoped that Harald Ferrier had been able to defend himself ably, so ably that he had perhaps inflicted some painful injuries on his brother. Violence must be met by violence, Robert thought, and force by force. The cheek-turning fantasy was out of place under some circumstances.

Marjorie appeared to sleep. Robert sighed and gently released her wrist. He looked about him at the large and charming bedroom with its French furniture, its pale blue walls and olive-green draperies, its light gold Oriental rug, its little white marble fireplace, its chairs of blue and yellow and olive-green silk, its polished painted tables, its crystal and silver, and its faint fragrance of spice and old roses. It was a gracious room, the room of a great lady of taste and delicacy and worldliness, and it came to Robert that his mother was the most unworldly of creatures and the most tasteless, and for that he should feel considerable compassion. He forgot to feel resentful that she had destroyed his beautiful house. After all, she was old and had none of the sophistication of Marjorie Ferrier. He admired the lovely French bed in which Marjorie lay, its fine linen sheets, its embroidered pillows, its delicate yellow blanket. A little clock chimed on the bedside table, a fairy chime.

They should be here soon. Robert went down to the morning room.

The young priest was as exhausted as he, for he, too, had been working sleeplessly, consoling the stricken, helping to search for the missing. He looked up as Robert entered, hopefully yet fearfully.

Robert said, "She's holding her own, but that is all I can say. I wish they'd arrive soon."

The priest sighed. "So do I. That Jonathan! I pity him very much. If his mother dies without him seeing her, then he will never forgive himself. He can be much harsher on himself than his worst enemy, as he has proved over and over this past year. If his mother dies—he will really be destructive of himself."

"I can almost wish he would," said Robert, thinking of the dying woman upstairs. The priest smiled at him sadly, his golden eyes bright in the lamplight.

"No, you don't, Doctor. If Jon is a merciless enemy, he is also a merciful friend, and he has been kind to you, as you've admitted yourself. I heard that because he liked you from the beginning, he sold you his practice at half of what he was offered by others. Only Jon would do a thing like that, and yet he has the reputation of being a very shrewd man with a dollar."

Robert raised his red-gold eyebrows in skepticism. His mustache seemed not so full and jaunty as usual. He sat down. Then he said, after some minutes of thought, "Perhaps you are right Father. I saw how he treated many of his patients. The children and the old loved him. He was harsh with malingerers and joked roughly with others. But the sick respected and trusted him, and I suppose that is most important."

"It is most important, Doctor. Jon knows how to treat the sick. He never learned how to treat the well. The helpless touch his heart. He is ruthless with his peers. I've often thought he is the true Renaissance man, romantic, poetic and passionate, out of place in this dull and utilitarian age, which is certain to become even more so in the near future. Industry and technology will make man much more comfortable than he was in ages past, but they'll dim his soul. We talked about that in Rome only a year ago. Well Jon will have to come to terms with his era, for it is certain that it won't come to terms with him!"

Robert made a wry face. "I can't imagine Jon coming to terms with anyone, least of all with himself."

They listened to the storm. "I think it is lessening," said Robert. He almost laughed. "Did I tell you, Father, of what I saw Jon doing this morning? He was helping the gardener repair the damage to the lawns and the bushes and hauling away tree branches quite in amiable company. Yet a few hours later he could go shouting off to kill his brother! What lack of self-control." He sighed. He wondered how Jonathan would have responded to his own situation: Loving a woman who did not want him and who rejected him for someone else. He would probably butcher the man and take the woman by force. I wouldn't, thought Robert, put it beyond him. He thought of Jenny and sagged wearily in his chair. If she married Jonathan her life was certain to be lively, at the very least, but hardly restful and full of peace and tranquility. But Jenny was a girl of character. She would learn, perhaps, how to outshout Jonathan and how to control him. Robert had his serious doubts, and his longing for Jenny made him feel weak and bereft.

"I came to Hambledon only a few months before Jon's wife died," said Father McNulty. "I never knew the younger Mrs. Ferrier but I saw her about the town in her carriage. She is what the older men and the poets call 'a dream of fair women.' I thought how suitable, in appearance at any rate, she seemed for Jon, gay and effervescent and beautiful and sparkling. One never knows. If anyone had seemed less threatened by tragedy, it was young Mrs. Ferrier."

"He is going to marry Jenny," said Robert in a flat tone.

The priest nodded. "So his mother informed me quite a few weeks ago, before he knew it himself." He looked keenly at Robert. "What pleasant people those Kitcheners are, to be sure. And a lovely young lady, Miss Kitchener."

"Isn't she?" said Robert with indifference. This was the night he and his mother were to dine with the Kitcheners, but the storm had intervened. He suddenly saw Maude's pretty eyes and auburn curls and heard her shy sweet voice. How unlike Jenny she was. Jenny was a storm of blue and black and white, for all her apparent diffidence and restraint. Jenny was strong, but Maude was not strong at all, and suddenly Robert's tender young heart felt gentle toward her. The strong could be formidable and frightening.

The priest cleared his throat. He said, "I heard tonight at St. Hilda's that old Mr. Witherby died in bed last night."

"So did I," said Robert. He smiled suddenly. "Jon will probably send the widow his felicitations with a basket of the most expensive flowers."

"Yes. That would be just like him. Jonas must have been a frightful old man, from what I have heard, and have known, myself, and from what he tried to do to Jon."

"Corrupt," said Robert. "He had the appearance of a saint."

"Whereas Jon looks like a romantic version of the Devil. Did I hear a door open?"

Robert and the priest stood up, went along the corridor to the pale gray hall, where the chandelier was softly lighted. Three people were already there, drenched and dripping, Jenny, Jonathan and Harald Ferrier, and all were drained and stunned in appearance, and Harald's face was oozing with blood from a very bad long wound on his cheek. They stared speechlessly at the priest and Robert, and Jenny took the shawl from her head and aimlessly shook it, and the men shook water from their hands and bare heads.

"What?" asked Jonathan, looking from one to the other.

"Mrs. Ferrier," said Robert. He could not help it, but with Jonathan's own sharp ruthlessness he said, "She is dying. She's had a bad heart attack."

He watched Jonathan's black eyes deepen and narrow, and Harald uttered an exclamation and Jenny gave a little cry.

"Something," said Robert, looking into Jonathan's face intently, "gave her a severe shock. She was found on the floor of a room upstairs by one of your servants, who called me, about three or more hours ago. I've done what I could for her, but I am afraid that she won't live until morning."

Jenny again gave a muffled cry and started toward the stairway, but Jonathan caught her by her wrist and held her. "Never mind, Jenny," he said in a peremptory voice. He turned to the priest. "This is true?"

"I am afraid so, Jon," said Father McNulty with pity.

"You did this to her!" said Harald to his brother, and his hazel eyes were on fire. "You killed her!" His wound had begun to bleed again, and a few drops fell down over his chin. His ruddy hair was soaked, and his handsome face was drawn and suffering.

"Shut up," said Jonathan, and he turned to Harald and his expression was so daunting that Harald flinched. Then he turned to Robert. "Quick! What have you done for her?"

Robert told him. Jonathan listened acutely. He said, "That is good. And now I will see her myself."

"I think," said Robert, "that she wants to see both her sons, and as soon as possible. She wants to be sure you are—safe. Both of you."

He met Jonathan's polished hard eye straightly. "I will take you to her. Perhaps it might be best, though, if you both looked less like derelicts. We don't want her to have another shock, as though you had been dredged up from the bottom of the river."

"Where, Doctor, we'd now all be if it weren't for you," said Harald, and he was almost his gallant self again. "The police told us, and the river men."

"We'll save our lovely expressions of gratitude for later," said Jonathan, and he dropped Jenny's wrist as abruptly as he had taken it and was now leaping up the stairway. Harald watched him go and his face was not pleasant to contemplate. "Very masterful, my brother, isn't he?" he murmured. "Full of all the amenities of civilized conduct."

Jenny sat down on the French velvet sofa against the wall, and put her hands over her face, and Robert wanted to go to her and console her. But Harald was looking at her with naked love and misery, and he said, "Jenny, dear. Let us have some hope, if we can. You're exhausted, and I think you should go to one of the guest rooms and lie down."

"We're having coffee and some refreshments in the morning room," said Robert, and thought to himself, So here is another one of us! "Mrs. Ferrier is resting. There isn't any immediate emergency, and perhaps you, Mr. Ferrier, and Miss Jenny, ought to change clothing and then join us."

"I'll have to put on one of his damned funereal suits," said Harald, and tried to make his voice light. He still looked at Jenny. "We saw that the water was rising too high on the island to delay to pack any luggage. Jenny? Perhaps one of the maids can find something for you to wear."

The girl was shivering. She dropped her hands and they saw her white and tearless face and her grief. "Jon will never forgive himself," she said.

"I hope not," said Harald. He said to Robert, "I won't go

near him even to ask for some clothing. Would you be kind enough, Doctor?"

Robert now understood the situation. He regarded Harald's wounded cheek. "That's a bad cut you have there, Mr. Ferrier. Let us find a bathroom where I can take care of it at once." He hesitated. "A fall, perhaps?"

Jenny stared at Harald with the cold chasteness of her blue eyes, but Harald said almost gaily, "No, indeed. A gentle reminder from my brother that hereafter I must keep hands off his property. It seems he resented my kindness to his dead wife."

Jenny said, in her strong clear voice, "How dare you say that! You know why he did it!"

Harald gave her a little bow. "But thanks to you, Jenny, he stopped just short of killing me." He winked at Robert. "Call it a small brotherly altercation, if you will."

Father McNulty, who had been listening with perturbation, said, "Mr. Ferrier, I know you are trying to make light of the situation, but Jon's conduct was hardly—hardly—"

"Civilized," said Harald.

"Oh!" exclaimed Jenny, and she colored vividly. "You are giving Dr. Morgan and Father McNulty the deliberately wrong impression, Harald! You know how unspeakable your own conduct has been!"

"Appalling, we Ferriers," said Harald, smiling down into her eyes. "I should like you to keep that in mind, Jenny."

"I certainly will," said Jenny, and set her beautiful mouth firmly, and arched her neck. Then she stood up and walked quickly to the stairway and went upstairs, leaving behind her a pool of dirty river water.

The three men were silent until they heard Jenny in the upper hall, then Harald said musingly, "If I weren't determined to leave this contemptible little town very soon, I'd enjoy the spectacle of the coming marriage between Jenny and my brother. Jenny is no Mavis. In many ways she is a good match for Jon, and I don't mean that pleasantly."

"He can be murderous," said Robert, full of apprehension. "And Miss Jenny is still a young girl, and he is much older. But let us find that bathroom. I have my bag in the morning room and if you will wait a moment, I will get it."

Harald was alone with the priest. He had begun to mop at his face with his wet handkerchief and the priest gave him his own. "Thank you, Father," said Harald, with his charming courtesy. "I'm sorry that you've seen the Ferriers at a disadvantage."

"I've been seeing them that way for some time," said the priest, with a faint smile. "But not at Mass. Or in the Confessional."

"Oh, we're beyond absolution, I assure you, Father. Quite beyond absolution."

"Only God knows that, not you."

Harald smiled at him brightly. Robert came into the hall but stood at the foot of the staircase, and Harald joined him. They went upstairs together, and, with a sigh, the priest went back into the morning room. The storm was definitely quieting. The last cannonading of the thunder was echoing from the mountains, and the rain was only a whisper now and the gale only occasionally shook the windows and doors.

They met outside Marjorie's shut door, Jonathan and Harald in dark silk dressing gowns, and Jenny wrapped in a cotton wrapper Mary had found for her. She looked like a tall strong child with her hair dropping down her back, still wet but gleaming, and the wrapper, a trifle too short, showed her fine ankles and part of her round legs. She was unconscious of her disheveled appearance and only looked in mute earnestness at Robert. He said to her gently, "I will take them in to see Mrs. Ferrier, Jenny, and perhaps a little later you can go in."

Jenny became mutinous, but Jonathan said, "She needs to be disturbed as little as possible, Jenny, so kindly go downstairs and wait for us."

Their eyes met and clashed. Then Jenny angrily bit her lip, tossed her damp hair and went downstairs with a very emphatic footfall. "A young lady of spirit, as I have said, Doctor," Harald murmured. "It is going to be very interesting." His cheek had been cleansed, treated with antiseptic, and the cut closed with court plaster.

Robert opened the door softly and they entered the quiet lamplit room. Marjorie was awake again, and she looked at her sons and her mouth trembled. "Cain and Abel, Mrs. Ferrier," said Robert, "but I don't know which is which."

Jonathan went at once to the bed and took his mother's wrist without looking into her eyes for a second. What he felt alarmed him and made a line of sweat come out below his black hair. He motioned to Robert imperatively, and Robert brought his bag to him and Jonathan took out the stethoscope with hands that were very steady. He bent over his mother and listened to her heart, and one of her long fine hands raised itself slowly and rested on his head. But she looked at Harald and smiled tenderly, though her lips winced when she saw the evidences of his wound.

"Adrenalin," said Jonathan, and Robert prepared the injection, and the nurses clustered at the foot of the bed. Then Jonathan did something Robert would not have dared to attempt. He drove the needle into his mother's breast, and she uttered the faintest of gasps, and her eyes shut spasmodically, and a gray shadow ran over her spent face.

Jonathan sat on the edge of the bed. He looked, for the first time, at his mother's face, and held her wrist, and once his eyes shut as if he prayed. (Robert doubted it.) Harald came to the other side of the bed and took his mother's other hand, and was shocked at the coldness and dampness of it and for the first time since he had been a child he wanted to weep. His own hand was warm. He held Marjorie's hand strongly and comfortingly. He thought that he imagined it, but when he felt a dim returning pressure again he knew he had not. Now tears did come into his eyes, and he slowly knelt beside the bed and then let his forehead rest against it.

"Morphine," said Jonathan, "15 mg." His voice was calm and dispassionate. He looked at no one but his mother.

"I gave her the same just hours ago," said Robert.

Jonathan repeated the order in the same tone and Robert, flushing at the affront, obeyed. Marjorie had begun to breathe rapidly, and again Jonathan listened to her heart, and his color became more and more deathly. He accepted the needle from Robert without a glance, and thrust it quickly into her limp arm. He said to the nurses, "Hot water bottles."

"Do you think?" Robert began.

"Doctors don't think. They act," said Jonathan.

The nurses scurried for the bottles. Robert was seething. Then he heard a murmurous and monotonous refrain: "Christ, have mercy, Lord, have mercy." He saw that it came from Harald, whose face was hidden against the side of the bed. But he saw something else which startled him. Jonathan had glanced at his brother and the look on his face was both bitter and full of threat, as if he had been mortally insulted. However, Harald kept up his prayer, in anguish, and Jonathan said nothing, and there was only that murmur in the room now and Marjorie's frantic breathing and the sound of the wind at the long windows.

The nurses returned with the hot bottles in towels, and Jonathan flung aside the blanket and Robert saw Marjorie's feet, marble white and cold. Jonathan put the bottles against them, then covered his mother's long and slender body again, and resumed his watching. Marjorie began to sigh, over and over, deeply, and move her head.

Then Jonathan spoke. "Mother? You are going to be all right. Do you hear me, dear? We are here with you. I won't leave you, Mother."

"Oh, Jon," she whispered, from the depths of her pain. "Oh, Harald."

She removed her wrist from Jonathan's grasp and took his hand, and her other fingers rested on Harald's bent head. Harald said in a muffled voice, "Forgive me, Mother."

"Oh, my dear," she said.

"I'm sorry," said Jonathan. "Believe me, dear, I'm sorry."

She smiled then, a beautiful and peaceful smile and opened her eyes and they were clear and tender.

"I'm very happy," she said. "I haven't been this happy for years."

There was the slightest tinge of color in her mouth now. She closed her eyes and slept.

Robert said, "You both don't deserve such a mother," and he turned and walked out of the room.

Then the eyes of the brothers met, tentative, cold, wary. Jonathan said, "I hope you have a scar for the rest of your life." But he smiled. It hardly lifted the corners of his mouth.

"And I hope that Jenny murders you," said Harald.

It was midnight when Jonathan went downstairs to the morning room. Harald and Robert Morgan and Jenny were with Marjorie. Jonathan said to Father McNulty, "I think there is some reason to hope. Her heart is stronger and she is asleep. I will know better in a few hours. If she rallies, as I think she may, she will have to be in bed for months."

He let himself drop in a chair and the priest poured a cup of hot coffee for him. Jonathan took it. He seemed to have grown much older and to be on the point of collapsing.

"But, it will be a miracle," he said, as if to himself.

"God frequently grants miracles," said the priest.

Jonathan's thick black eyebrows twitched.

"Such as saving all of you," the priest added. "And preventing a fratricidal murder."

"Which I still regret," said Jonathan.

"Have a doughnut," said the priest, and passed the plate. Jonathan automatically took one and munched it. He was still frowning.

"You and your brother are an admirable pair," said Father McNulty, chewing a cake. "I don't know which I admire the more. From what I've heard your father was a kind and gentle soul, and your mother is remarkable for many things. It's very strange that they should have had such sons."

"Spare me the homilies, Frank, and refill my cup."

The pretty room was warm and bright and the wind had dropped to a soft mutter.

"I suppose," said the priest, "that Hambledon will not lose your talents after all."

"I haven't thought about it."

"Of course you have. What will you do about Dr. Morgan?"

"When the time comes, I will consider it."

"May I offer you my congratulations on your coming marriage?"

Jonathan looked up quickly. "Jenny?"

"Who else?"

"Time enough for that."

"Certainly. I'm very sorry for the young lady."

Jonathan gave a slight laugh. "I think, perhaps, in about a week or so."

They ate and drank in a little silence. Then the priest said, "Don't regard what I have to say as a homily. I'm very tired, and I must go home. So, I will be brief. You have always maintained to me that the opinions of others are a matter of total indifference to you. But, on the contrary, you have been exaggeratedly sensitive to them. You did not have the fortitude to defy local opinion, at least in your mind. A man of courage would not have been so extremely disturbed by the hostility he met here, after the trial. He would have understood human nature. He would not have responded as violently as you have responded. He would not have planned to leave town. He would have presented a calm face to friend and enemy alike, treating both with reason, secure in himself and in his innocence. And finally the town would have come to its senses."

He waited. Jonathan said nothing. So the priest went on. "It is ridiculous to demand that others understand us and know the truth about us. How is that possible? We can only do the best we can, in steady patience, and with inner reserves, knowing that we don't understand others, either.

"Jon, you need to cultivate that serenity and detachment of mind that, while keeping you kindly in touch with your fellowman, will make you less vulnerable to him, and his opinion of you. You have entangled yourself with others entirely too much, both in love and in hate, and that is childish and immature. A sensible man is moderate in all things, and particularly in his dealings with those about him. That takes courage. And that will bring peace of mind."

Jonathan bent his head, and the priest was encouraged, for he knew that Jonathan was thinking. Then Jonathan said, "It isn't in my nature to be lukewarm."

"But you can practice outward restraint and balance and firmness."

"And get ulcers."

"And keep out of trouble. Mankind isn't very brave and strong, Jon. It is timid and is growing daily more timid. It is brave only when in a pack. Individually, man is lonely and lost and weak. He is frightened at demands that he have courage. It threatens what little security he possesses. And how insecure is man, God help him! He suspects that there are forces outside his little life which are tremendous and terrifying, so he establishes a ritual of magical cant to placate the terror, just as his earlier ancestors did. Yet, all the time, as our Lutheran brethren sang in their noblest hymn, 'A mighty Fortress is our God!'"

He stood up and looked down gravely at Jonathan. "A man who trusts in man, who believes man is all, who thinks that man is capable of pulling himself up by his own bootstraps and attaining virtue and perfection all by himself, is to be pitied. His ignorance, his pathetic vanity, must make the angels weep. Worse still, his fellowman will inevitably teach him many rude and painful lessons. So, he will abandon his fellowman, or he will grow to hate and despise him. Both are evil."

Jonathan said, "Somewhere in the nest of your homily, Frank, there may be an egg of truth. I will give it thought."

"Give it plenty of thought, Jon," said the priest.

Then Jonathan said, "I never told you. When I was seventeen, I had already decided to be a physician. Martin Eaton encouraged me. He began to take me through the hospitals and let me be in his office when he was attending patients. I was full then of God and raptures and everything else, in spite of a few jolts I had received when I was younger. I would be another St. Luke. Then, as I went with Martin on his rounds—I saw pain. Senseless, ugly, murderous, devastating, hopeless pain. Senseless. Now, don't talk to me about original sin! I saw the pain. I saw it especially in infants and little children, and in good old people who had never, I am sure, committed what you would call a mortal sin. I saw the helpless pain. And that's when I lost, when I decided—"

"That a God who permitted pain like that either did not exist, or He was worse than the wickedest man?"

"That's right, Frank."

"Jon, I will leave you with just one bit of advice. I'm sure there is a Bible in this house. Find it. And read the Book of Job."

CHAPTER THIRTY-NINE

In the next few days the Ferrier house was filled with flowers and gifts for Marjorie, and letters of happy congratulation to Jonathan because, as they said, "Our dear Senator, Kenton Campion, has proved, beyond the shadow of a doubt, that you were innocent, as the majority of us believed from the beginning. Don't desert us now. We need you. We've always needed you."

Only a week before Jonathan would have read those letters with rage and disgust and would have replied to the writers with stinging remarks and contempt. But now he laughed almost indulgently after his first angry reactions. "They believe Campion," he said to some friends, "Campion, who was always a liar and a mountebank, and they never believed me, though I don't lie. Somewhere there is some irony in the situ-

ation, but I never particularly liked the Hogarthian jokes of
man or God. Human or Olympian humor of this sort used to
make me ill. That is because, perhaps, I never appreciated
slapstick or burlesque."

"Now, Jon," said Louis Hedler. " 'All's well that ends
well.' "

"Nothing ends well," said Jonathan. "I'm a confirmed pessimist." He eyed Louis with hard and unforgiving cynicism.
"Let me congratulate you, Louis, on a broad comedy. I don't
enjoy the spectacle of clowns as advocates. Truth, to me,
should have a certain dignity, or am I being naïve again?"

"It depends on the point of view," said Louis Hedler. "By
the way, am I right in believing that you will accept the post
of chief of surgery at St. Hilda's?"

"Were you serious?"

"Of course, my boy. Though I am a little apprehensive
concerning how you will treat the other surgeons. With somewhat less brutality, I hope?"

"Not if they are in the wrong. The patient comes first."

"Commendable. The patient must always come first. But it
is not always necessary to make a Roman holiday of a surgeon's honest error, is it?"

"Not if he is usually a competent man. But I want no diploma-mill hacks on the staff, Louis."

Louis sighed. "You would be surprised how very competent those 'hacks' are sometimes, and how wrong the scientific fellas. But use your judgment, Jon, though I do hope
there will be no public burnings."

Hambledon emotionally forgave Jonathan for the crimes
he had never committed, and so forgave itself and was prepared to grasp him to its bosom. It took all Louis Hedler's
diplomacy to prevent Jonathan from explosive retorts at
times, and all Father McNulty's admonitions. "Humor,
humor, Jon," said the priest. "If a man lacks a sense of proportion and inner humor, he is a barbarian. He must always
have some pity, even if he is the wronged one. Look at young
Francis Campion, for instance. He has a lot to forgive his father, but now he is with him for a few days in Washington,
and they were photographed affectionately together. Francis
had to make his compromises, too. He will return to his seminary, and I think you should be proud of your own part in
it."

"Compromises!" said Jonathan.

"Life is not nearly as simple as you have always believed,

Jon," said the priest. "It requires a great deal of courage and fortitude."

Marjorie was now past the danger point. Then Jonathan's case became suddenly unimportant to the town, for President McKinley died of his wounds in Buffalo, and Vice-President Roosevelt became President. Jonathan said to the priest, "Now we have Teddy, and all his exuberant ideas and his radical philosophies." The light of battle had returned to his eyes. "The future has become ominous. I think I will take part in it, after all, for I will have children."

Harald had diplomatically removed himself from his father's house and had gone to the Quaker Hotel. He could not endure seeing Jenny with his brother. He could not return to the island, for even the lower floor of the "castle" had been filled with mud and water. His lawyers agreed that his absence from the island in this emergency could not be construed as violating the terms of his dead wife's will.

Jenny had told Jonathan of the contract planned between her and his brother. Jonathan had been pressing her for immediate marriage. Jenny had remarked firmly that "it was less than a year, and would not be decorous." Then Jonathan, smiling, had said, "Dear child, you are still a minor and won't be twenty-one until December. You can't sign any contract at all that would be valid. Didn't anyone tell you? But if you marry me soon, I will be appointed your legal guardian and can make contracts in your name for you."

Jenny had retorted, "It is you, Jon, who needs a guardian, not I."

"Well? What is your decision? Are we going to free Harald from Hambledon and send him on his merry way, or are we going to imprison him until December, when you will come of age? There is another thing. I find it somewhat arduous to be under the same roof with you, my love, and not in your bed. Or will you be kind enough to leave your door open some night soon?"

Jenny blushed. "Very well. I will marry you on September 30th." She hesitated. "What will people think?"

"The hell with what they think, Jenny. We have our own lives to live."

Jenny assisted the nurses in caring for Marjorie. Marjorie said, "Dear Jenny, now I will have a daughter soon. I have always felt that you were my daughter. I used to watch you when you were a child and I envied your mother. Do have daughters, Jenny. They are so satisfactory to a mother. While no man ever understood any woman, women do have glimpses of the interior workings of men, and mothers and daughters can laugh together at the unpredictable and irrational doings of husbands and sons and fathers. But we must never let our laughter be obvious. Men are such fragile and sensitive creatures."

"And so very dangerous," said Jenny. "Sometimes I think I shouldn't marry at all."

Her blue eyes were very wise and she looked so innocent in her wisdom that Marjorie wanted to cry. "Somebody has to marry them," said Marjorie. "Otherwise they'd revert fast enough to the cave."

Jenny had suggested to Jonathan that the island be a museum, as he had once proposed, with his brutal jesting, that it should be. "And it will be supported by the Heger money," said Jenny. "There are so many treasures there, and it will be a landmark for those people who can never hope to see an authentic castle in Europe. We will add to the treasures, and have guards and guides." The island no longer had significance for her, nor was it a harbor now as once it was, and she often wondered why that was so.

Jonathan prudently estimated the cost. "I think a large wing for tuberculosis at St. Hilda's and another wing for the study of cancer at the Friends' would be more practical."

"I have money enough for it all," said Jenny, with a large gesture.

"After what Harald takes?"

"Jon, don't be mercenary. We can do it all. What is money for but to be used?"

"Jenny, when you look at me with such innocence, you almost convince me."

"People need medicine for their souls as well as for their bodies, Jon."

He kissed her ardently. "Perhaps you will minister to my soul tonight, Jenny?"

"On September 30th," she said. "Not a day sooner. I think we should inform Father McNulty."

Jonathan had long consultations with Robert Morgan. "I will buy back my practice, Bob. You can then be my associate, if you can bear staying in Hambledon."

"I don't know," said young Robert. "I will sell the practice back to you, as you obviously intend to stay here." His kind face was wretched.

Jonathan said, "Bob, you are young, and, as I've quoted to

you often enough, 'Men have died and worms have eaten them—' "

" 'But not for love.' Yes, that's a favorite saying of yours, isn't it, and I don't believe you mean a word of it. You went thundering over to that island to kill your brother, I've heard, but if Jenny hadn't been there, you wouldn't have gone mad and practically swum over there in the hurricane. You'd have lain in wait for him someplace, and perhaps smeared him over the landscape—before a good audience. No doubt to teach others a lesson."

Jonathan chuckled. "Perhaps. Still, the story, spread by a few 'good' friends, hasn't done my reputation much harm. On the contrary."

"The populace does love a swashbuckler," said Robert. "You are out of date."

"Oh, I don't know about that," said Jonathan, thinking of the new President in the White House. "People are still romantic. When a nation stops being romantic it stops being a nation or a force in the world. By the way, I hear Maude Kitchener has set her cap for you."

"You hear too many things," said Robert, and thought of Jenny, and wondered how he could endure living in Hambledon knowing she was the wife of another man. If Jenny had married him, he would have contrived to send his mother back to Philadelphia and have rescued his house, his beautiful house. It was almost worth marrying for, to save its beauty.

"Women are very sinister," said Jonathan. "You might be wise to run."

Robert was annoyed. "I am not running," he said. "Nor are you—anymore, I hope. Well, I will stay and be your associate, if you will have me. I only hope we will not end up someday murdering each other."

It was a cool September evening and Father McNulty was in the Confessional at St. Leo's Church. He had been there for over two hours, listening with sad compassion to the endless repetition of human error and human sin and human fallibility and human arrogance. He was young, but he felt as old as death and life. He was also getting hungry and cramped.

Someone entered the Confessional and knelt down and the priest waited. The penitent was silent. Then Father McNulty saw a familiar long dark head through the grill, and then, with growing joy and astonishment, he heard a familiar voice.

"Bless me, Father, for I have sinned—"

The priest sighed. "And about time," he said, and prepared to listen. He was sure that the penitent thought he had a remarkable story to tell, but it was as old as man, as old as the very stars.

FAWCETT CREST BESTSELLERS